# The Snowtear Wars

## Book 3 ~ The Hollows of Candlewick

by

Scot R. Stone

Behler™
PUBLICATIONS
California
USA

**Behler Publications**
California

The Snowtear Wars
Book 3~The Hollows of Candlewick
A Behler Publications Book


Author photograph courtesy of Glamour Shots in Denver, Colorado
Cover art by Steve A. Roberts – www. fantasy-graphic.com
Cover design by Cathy Scott – www.mbcdesign.com



Library of Congress Cataloging-in-Publication Data

Stone, Scot R.
The hollows of Candlewick / by Scot R. Stone.
p. cm. -- (The snowtear wars ; bk. 3)
ISBN 1-933016-43-4 (pbk. : alk. paper)
I. Title.
PS3619.T6825H65 2007
813'.6--dc22
2006035303

FIRST PRINTING

ISBN 13: 978-1-933016-43-6
Published by Behler Publications, LLC
Lake Forest, California
www.behlerpublications.com

Manufactured in the United States of America

*To my grandparents,*
*Carl and Ruth Stone*
*& Robert and Elerine Bruneau,*
*stars in the sky that have guided me to safe shores.*

**The Snowtear Wars Series**

The Chimes of Yawrana
The Ice Shadows of Arna
The Hollows of Candlewick

## ~*Acknowledgments* ~

No author is perfect, no matter how much he or she wishes it to be true. Every person who steps into this field must give thanks to *someone* for the incredible amount of energy that goes into his or her book. Whether it is through inspiration, creation, writing, editing, marketing or agenting, there is always a contributor standing shyly in the shadows, or, in my case, many, that do not ask for recognition for their role. But it would be wrong to ignore them, and an insult to their devotion to the craft.

Therefore, I will start with the Behler team, who saw the immediate issues in this third installment of *The Snowtear Wars*. They were dead on with their assessments, and I wasted no time in correcting those redundancies and oversights. I don't expect everything I turn in to be glistening with sunshine. That is a dream world, not the reality of publishing, even though we are dealing with fantasy in this case. Thank you editors Kristan Ryan and Erin Stalcup for your intervention.

Second, I would like to thank my wife, Holly, for her continued support and understanding of the odd hours I write, during the day or night, to complete this saga. The simple task of just writing is not always as easy as it seems. We authors have just as many restraints on our time as anybody else, and sometimes finding just an hour to finish one page can be a challenge. But as long as there is progress, then there is someone to thank for it. Holly periodically wakes up to watch me trudge off to my desk at 3:00 a.m. for over six years now. As crazy as it sounds, we both hope that trend continues. There is a price to pay for success, and the more time your put into your work, the more you want it to succeed. And this is a line of work I love.

And, without a doubt, a thank you must go to my fans. Your interest and responses have been overwhelming. I enjoy every letter I receive and always write back. You are as much a part of this dream as I am. Without you, I couldn't still be doing this.

Ignore an author if you find him talking out loud to walls. It's all part of the creation process.
~Scot R. Stone

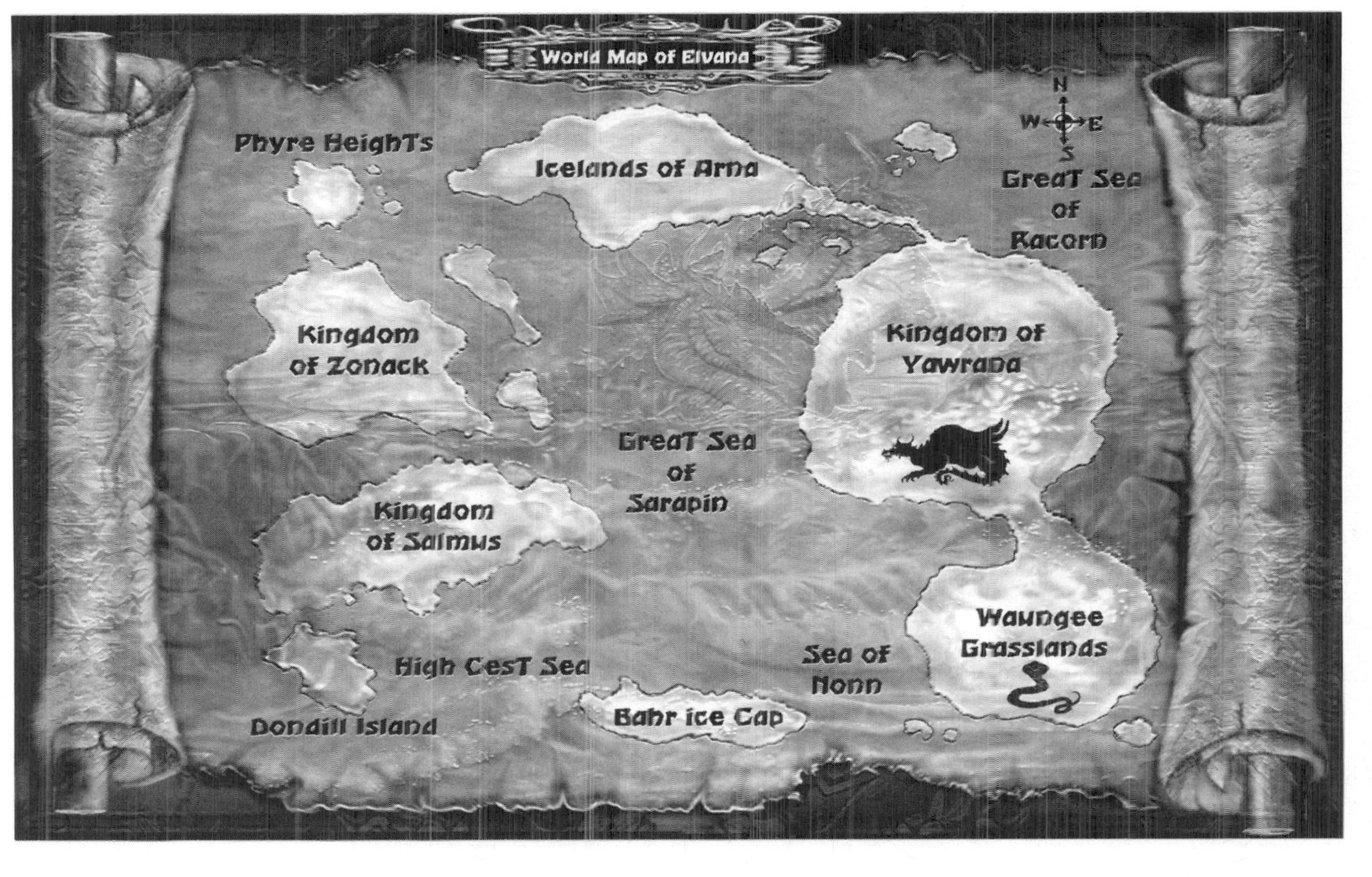
World Map of Elvana
N
W
E
S
Phyre HeighTs
Icelands of Arna
GreaT Sea of Racorn
Kingdom of Zonack
Kingdom of Yawrana
GreaT Sea of Sarapin
Kingdom of Salmus
Waungee Grasslands
Sea of Nonn
High CesT Sea
Bahr ice Cap
Dondill Island

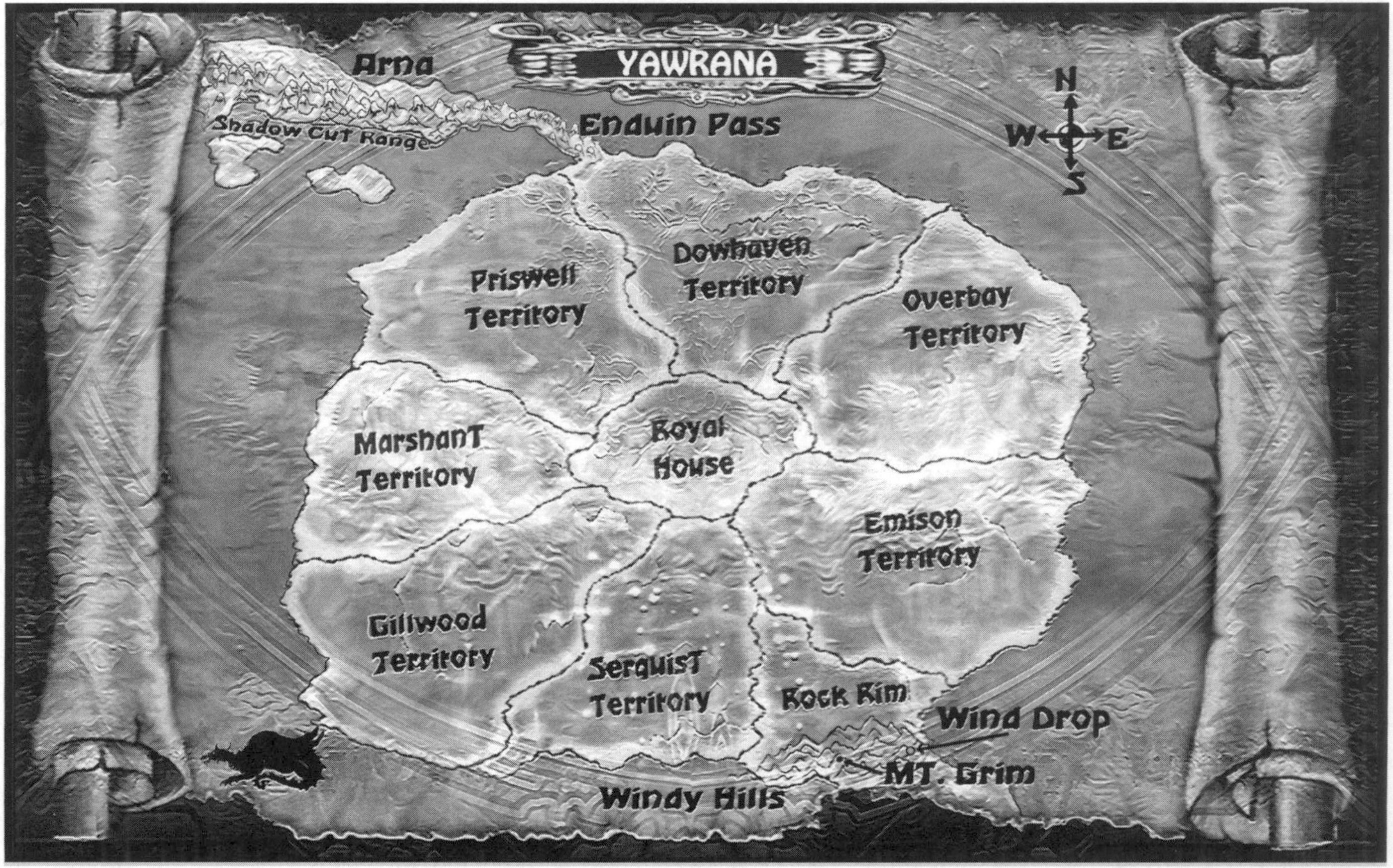

YAWRANA
Arna
Shadow Cut Range
Enduin Pass
N
W
E
S
Priswell Territory
Dowhaven Territory
Overbay Territory
Marshant Territory
Royal House
Emison Territory
Gillwood Territory
Serquist Territory
Rock Rim
Wind Drop
MT. Grim
Windy Hills

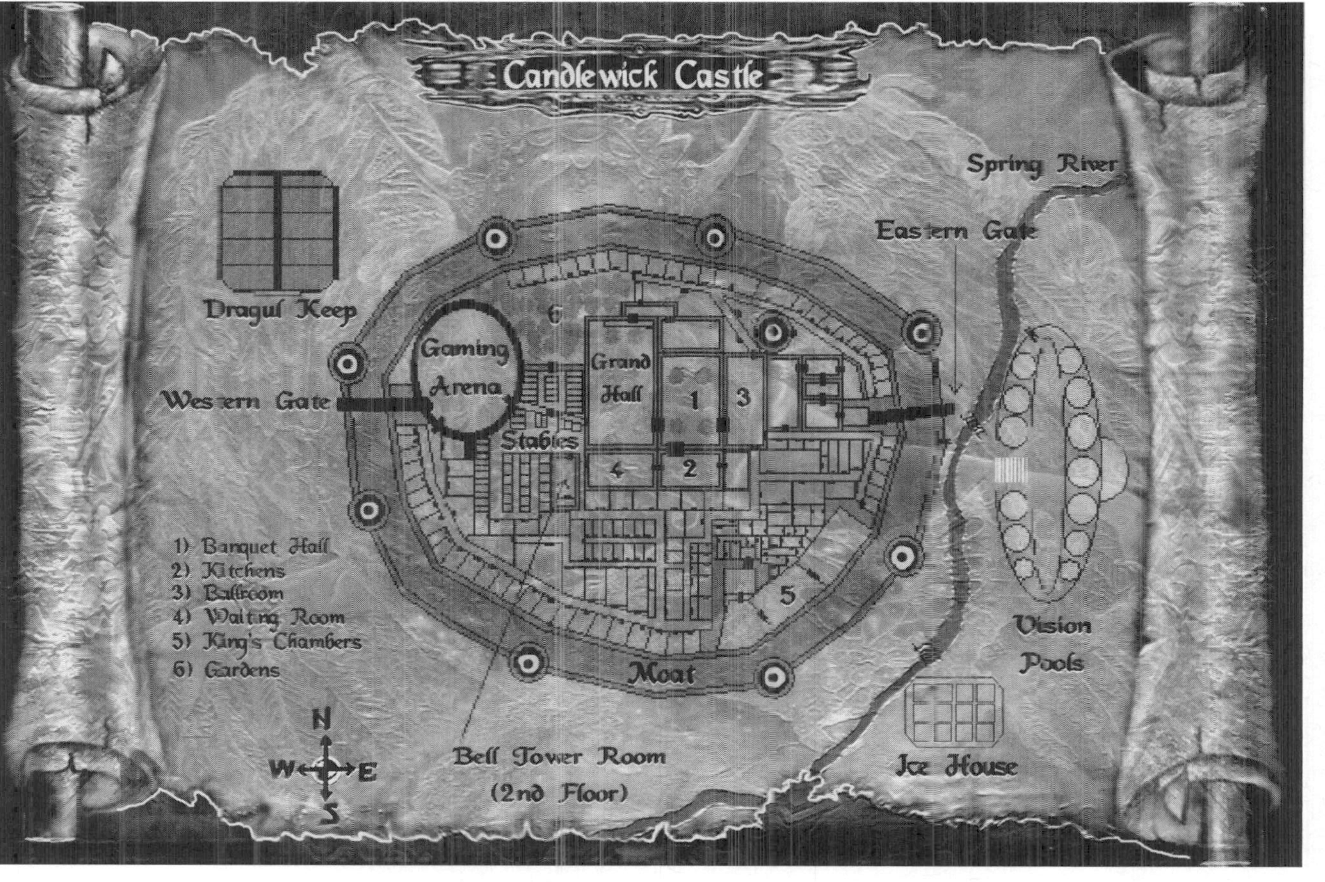

Candlewick Castle
Dragul Keep
Spring River
Eastern Gate
Gaming Arena
Western Gate
Grand Hall
1
3
Stables
4
2
6
5
1) Banquet Hall
2) Kitchens
3) Ballroom
4) Waiting Room
5) King's Chambers
6) Gardens
Moat
Vision Pools
N
W
E
S
Bell Tower Room
(2nd Floor)
Ice House

# PROLOGUE

## From the writings within the Royal House of Elders:

*The Chronicles of Yawrana*
*5441: Volume 1; Entry 1*
*Subject Notation: The Wandering Mangler Prophecy*
*Author, High Elder Elenoi Ironwood*

Ages have passed since my anointment to the indigo band after the celebration of my twentieth birthday seven hundred and ninety-nine years ago. Many prophecies have been foretold and have come to pass during the time span in which I have indebted my service to the Royal House of Elders. Key calculations in these visions, many from my own contributions, have been used to our advantage, and have changed negative forebodings to positive outcomes. Some today are still creating influencing ripples in the waters of time. Whether or not one understands the prophecies or how their effects can manipulate the natural progression of life's events is not important. It is only the people's belief in our practices that grants us the ability to provide them hope during dark times when all may seem lost. As long as the Elders continue to inspire and light the way for those who readily accept the challenges chaos sets before us, then Yawrana will always be adept at coursing its way through the most daunting waves to find its way into the tranquil harbors of peace.

And for the heroes and heroines who face adversity in its most predictable and unusual forms, I fear and pray for their continued safety as we offer our guidance when it will best suit the needs of the kingdom. The release of prophetic information at an inopportune time can lead to drastic, if not fatal, results. However, timely interventions can avoid precarious scenarios altogether. But it is more common than not for the Elders to withhold the details of a vision until they are ready to be revealed due to their great sensitivity.

With regret, my first prophecy as High Elder of the Order leaves me in such a circumstance. A creature born during sun's slumber will hunt the forests of the Royal House Territory and roam the outer grounds of Candlewick Castle. When one of the two moons hangs red in the sky, (which occurs once every thirty days for each moon, a regular phenomenon Yawranans believe is caused by those who died in battle and wish to be remembered for their sacrifices), this creature, which at first looks like a deformed watcher of Rock Rim Territory, but upon closer inspection resembles more of a maddon which has evolved into something much more mobile and dangerous, will emerge from the darkness to make itself known. Its hunger is unmatched during its feedings and it can't be killed with only a sword or dagger. Its full powers are as much of a mystery as its arrival. Having seen it, I shudder at its sight and find myself weeping for its mercy.

Beasts of this type have been reported before in Dowhaven and Gillwood Territory, but they seem to vanish as quickly as they come, causing no harm to any Yawranan during their wake. And no man or woman has been able to accurately describe them, nor is each description or encounter ever the same, leaving everyone to doubt which story is the valid one.

Perhaps it is the remote wilds of the unpopulated regions from where the sightings occur that raise no serious alarm, though I have heard the rumored death of a Trail Racer in one of these areas. Whether the creature itself was responsible was never proven. General Keys, leader of the Trail Racers, has attributed the messenger's death to a random wild animal attack, possibly a karrik or maddon. I was not convinced of his explanation, and since I had this vision I have ordered that the Racer's body be exhumed from the Catacombs of Emison. Never before has a hare of either General Hithel's Majestic Messengers or General Keys's Trail Racers been outrun and killed by any animal during a mail delivery assignment, including draguls. Dobbins are too agile and only the best are employed by each outfit to run the roughest trails and routes of the territories, knowing the lay of the land better than any other creature in Yawrana from their countless hours of map memorizations and travel. To further enhance my nagging suspicions, it is widely known that maddons rarely roam as far south as the castle.

In the end my intuition was proven correct. After completion of the autopsy on the Racer's body, I was informed the death was caused neither by karrik nor maddon. The body was only partially eaten and terribly mangled. A karrik would have devoured all edible portions of its kill, even if it were lucky enough to have captured a messenger. According to the Historical Record Keep's documents, no animal in the kingdom has ever been known to portray this bizarre eating behavior. The purpose of the mangling of the body can only mean that the creature enjoys torturing its victims before they die. Perhaps it is its way of revenge against nature for its own mangled appearance.

Eventually this beast, this mangler, will abandon food of the forests for easier prey grazing along the castle's farmlands. Cattle mutilations will coincide with the arrival of an important visitor in a white cloak at the castle's Western Gate. The identity of the visitor is not revealed by the vision. When the traveler makes his appearance, I must visit King Noran Deardrop and warn him of the mangler's enclosing presence. I fear telling him before the next red moon, for it could lead to the deaths of many close to him, including the Queen and his own two personal guards. The mangler watches with vengeful eyes, waiting to appear and strike the King when he least suspects it. Other men will die before he finds his fate, driving fear into those who are trying to protect him. As my vision breaks at its end, I see the King struggling in pain, entangled with it in a battle that he does not win. The mangler overpowers him as a beam of red moonlight crosses his path. The creature draws its strength from the rays, leaving Noran powerless to stop its relentless hunger. And during this conflict, a dark figure watches on in curiosity from the shadows, waiting in limbo for the inevitable to happen.

It is possible the dark shadow may be that of Herikech Illeon, Lazul king of the Waungee Grasslands and former brother of Herishen, first king of Yawrana, though I can't confirm it because of the blur that enveloped that portion of my vision. Herikech's wrath was made evident in the swamps of Serquist Territory and it is believed by the Yawranan Royal Court that he will not relinquish his fight with the Yawranans until he has conquered the territories. His plans are wicked and he may even call upon the creatures of the wild again to aid his cause. It is a distinct possibility the mangler may also be at his command to carry out his intentions and other Yawranans will be killed by it before Noran meets his fate.

The most critical missing detail of my vision, however, is the location of this battle between the King and wandering mangler. I have studied the details of the vision time and again, unable to determine where Noran may soon find his life's end. Without this information, he may be doomed to die. The window the moonlight shines upon during his struggle is the only clue given. Its frame is solid and gray. A horned beetle climbs the glass for its nightly mating, drawn to the red rays before Noran's encounter with the mangler takes place. The King must stay out of the beam's reach; it is the only chance he has for his own safety.

With these grave statements I end my first prophecy as the High Elder. I have consulted the Elders in the Order, and they, too, agree with my assessments. I, therefore, must carry out the most agonizing of all acts that any of us can bear while the future unfolds: wait helplessly while wringing my hands in anticipation.

# CHAPTER ONE
## The Sea in a King's Soul

Two stiff fingers in the ribcage was the most unwelcome awakening he could've received at two in the morning. It was not a light poke or tap, but a hard, direct jab that intended to wake a general who rarely slept soundly on any other given night. And not only did they intend to arouse him, their crude manner of intrusion into his dream state communicated an urgent message that something was wrong.

Rolling his eyes upward with fluttering lids, Rydor mumbled incoherently, "I already went to training . . . ."

"General Regoria, you must awaken," an anxious, deep voice responded.

A giant yawn escaped his mouth before he could cover it with the back of his right hand. Rydor choked on the cold air when he moved his hand across his lips. His fingers were cold as they brushed his cheek, having become that way from the draft of winter creeping through the etched, yellow window at the far end of the room. A set of drapes hanging around them was parted at the middle by only a few inches, allowing the wind enough room to wriggle through during the long stretch of darkness. He yawned once more, giving no indication he had fully awakened.

"General!" snapped the voice.

Rydor bolted upright in bed, his eyes forced to open as far as they could go. Cranking his head to his left, he could discern the dark outline of a large man standing several feet from the edge of the bed. The figure backed away only after the General lifted the heavy fur covers off of him and slipped his naked legs over the side so he could sit up. "What is it, Jime?" he grumbled, moistening his lips with the tip of tongue. They had dried terribly and were beginning to crack from the cold, dry air. "Has someone been disturbing the catacombs again?"

There was a brief pause before the guard contemplated his next sentence. Then it came as quickly as he could release the words. "No, General. This is much more important. A shore watchman has confirmed the sightings of three ships on Racorn's horizon. They will very soon be arriving in the bay—"

"Someone has taken the fishing vessels out after mandatory time—" Rydor couldn't finish his expected reaction before Jime cut him off.

"These are not *our* fishing vessels, General. They are drift ships."

Alarmed, Rydor stood up, revealing his entire nude form in front of his guard. Jime averted his eyes until the General could cover himself with his robe.

Once the belt was cinched at Rydor's waist, Jime spoke. "General Meel is asking for the Baron and you to join him at the beach as soon as possible."

Taking one quick, deep breath of fresh air, Rydor gathered his armor and began to hurriedly dress himself. "Don't worry about the Baron," he replied. "I will wake her."

Jime nodded and backed away, taking a brief glance over the General's shoulder. His eyes fell on the unmoving bulge lying in the bed sheets just beyond his superior. Trusting the General would do just as he promised, he turned away and shut the door behind him to wait in the hall outside. The click of the latch prompted Rydor to lean over and rustle the covers wrapped around the Baron's shoulders.

"Jada," he said in a raspy voice.

Her reaction was much more immediate than his had been. She answered, "What is it?"

"We have unexpected visitors in Drana Bay. You'd better get your things together. I'll meet you at the main beach."

The Baron snorted and shook her head in disbelief. "Why? What insane portal did we walk through this time? More treasure hunters from Zonack? Why didn't the Elders say anything about this?"

Rydor shrugged his shoulders as she looked up at him. Her golden hair was a tangled mess and her face bore the pressed lines of bed sheets along her cheek. Yet she was still extremely attractive to him, making him wonder how he had managed to convince her that he was worth taking a chance on. The General had only brief sprees of love in his adolescence, but since the day he took oath and accepted the responsibilities of the red band, he had neither the time nor desire to devote his thoughts to a serious relationship. In fact, he easily pictured himself going his entire life without having to deal with the cares that dragged many down into traps they wished they had never gotten themselves caught in. The probability of him finding someone to whom he could truly relate was as good as the chance of finding Herikech Illeon in the swamps of Serquist. But somehow he and Jada had found a way to connect and were continuing to make their growing love into something greater than he had ever imagined. It was this very feeling that constantly made him feel insecure—that she may be stripped away from him if he got too close.

"I thought you were leaving?" she said, yawning and stretching while letting her feet fall to cold stone.

"I'm on my way now." He finished pulling on his last boot, clasped his cape around his right shoulder and slid his helmet over his dark hair. He saluted to her by putting a fist to his chest and saying, "Baron," with a wink and a smile.

"General Regoria," Jime stated regally with a salute when Rydor stepped into the hall. Torches blazed brightly up and down the corridor with a dozen soldiers standing at attention. Jada's own guard, Rundle Kester, was also posted nearby. Rundle saluted Rydor and received a nod in return.

"The Baron will be out shortly," Rydor said to Jime.

Rundle was nearing sixty years of age, the oldest of all personal protectors currently assigned to a Yawranan Royal Court member. Two nights previous Rundle had informed Jada that he would be retiring by spring's end, ready to take his turn to walk down the Passage of Mirrors to retire his band and return it into the hands of the provisioners. The band would then be labeled with Rundle's name and placed into an honorary glass enclosure in the Vision Pools Center with the thousands of others already there. It was considered good fortune to honor the Elders and their prophetic gifts by giving back what they originally granted to others. And with Rundle's retired armband color, the final tribute would be paid to his years of service by blessing it with the waters from Spring River that fed the anointment pools.

As for the Passage of Mirrors for himself, Rydor could only guess what the Elders would see cast from his own life's reflections when he would one day complete the walk through the corridor. The Elders determined the images by studying the reflections formed by shadows and light during each ceremony, recording what they saw, good or bad, when the retired band member reached the end of the passage. Positive forms represented the enduring influences the candidates created from their sacrifices while negative shapes meant their tasks on Elvana had not yet been finished. If one was denied retirement after his or her walk, then he or she would not be allowed to return to the passage for five more years. It was a rare occasion that death preceded retirement. However, when it did occur, the band was then considered to never have reached its potential and would then be given to a newly anointed individual, who would continue carrying out its purpose. He had heard of one band being worn by three generations before it was finally laid to rest in the Shades Panel. Each of the three individuals' names who bore it was embroidered into the material.

As it was, Jada had become less stringent toward Rundle's duties. He rarely was at her side after she adopted the Lazul twins, Gailey and Haley, into her care. Although she would never outright admit it, her faith in Rundle's abilities had declined to a point where she only had him with her when it was absolutely necessary. Rydor rarely challenged the Baron on any of her principles, but he let it slip to the guard that Rydor would prefer Rundle to be more insistent at staying with her. Rundle took the hint and became glued to her side, fearing the General would notify the local sector board of his lax efforts. To Rydor, accepting an oath meant staying true to one's words, as long it was still within one's capabilities. He was convinced Rundle's steps were still agile enough to carry on with his duties.

Rydor and Jime both walked briskly down ten flights of stairs to reach ground level and then proceeded out the main double doors and into the yard. Jime never stopped asking questions the entire way.

"Do you think they are searching for Baron Oreus Blake and his crewmates?"

"Not likely," Rydor replied. "Only if Lanu and his men had been carrying Zonack wealth would the others have returned for *The Star Gazer*. The Baron's old acquaintances are more caring about the world's riches than of their own flesh and blood. If it were not for his poverty during his childhood, Oreus may have also been more like Lanar Lanu. Oreus was close to the point in his life where he could have easily started mimicking their backward ways. I thank the heavens Baron Blake reached us in time with his mind still open to influence, despite the suffering he endured while growing into manhood."

"I shall always remember how the Baron saved my life in Dowhaven," Jime said. "His soul is stronger than most in Yawrana." The guard rubbed the spot where an arrow pierced his chest from one of Johr Karagas's men. Jime was angrier with himself than Rydor had been when Jime carelessly allowed Princess Ola Yorokoh and Maker, now queen, Willow Deardrop to be captured and taken hostage into the frigid ice lands of Arna. If it were not for Oreus, death to him would have been acceptable for his critical failure. He told Rydor on several occasions that someday he vowed to repay the honorable deed to the Baron.

Rydor nodded to confirm. "Yes. I feel Oreus may have more to show of his true self yet. His emotions portray the characteristics of a lurking angel."

Jime laughed at the comment, unable to help himself. Rydor shot him a glare that silenced the guard immediately. "Sorry, General. I was not prepared for that to come from you."

Raising an eyebrow, Rydor asked sharply, "Why?"

"Well—you're so tight-lipped about anything to do with the higher planes of existence."

Rydor's face turned a light shade of red. "Just because I don't openly speak about life after death doesn't mean my faith isn't as strong as yours." He slid his index finger inside a pocket in his vest. His nail bumped against a flat metal container holding the very proof no one could deny, a feather from the wings of a spirit: Jada's deceased infant brother. After Rydor and Jada started their affair, she decided to let him keep it without any further protests.

Her words fell onto his thoughts like rain, *Do not be so smug with yourself, General. It would not have come back into your care if it were not meant to be. Just because you hold it in your possession, do not think for an instant it allows you to hold any additional weight over my decisions. However, when the day comes that you realize these foolish games you're playing are not getting you anywhere, it'll be too late. Viktoran would have turned it over the minute he was able to retrieve it.*

Her last statement was the one that bothered him most. She only said it to make him jealous and push him to do what she wanted. But he had no intention of making it that easy for her. As long as he held the feather, he felt she would not fall for Baron Viktoran Ilos's repeated advances. She courteously declined the Serquist baron's arrogant proposals, but it didn't stop Viktoran from trying any less. Rydor had become increasingly protective of where she spent her hours when she wasn't with him. Any advantage he held could only make their relationship grow stronger over time. It was as if their two identical feathers were not to be separated, drawing their hearts closer together.

And now that their love had recently escalated to a physical level, he felt assured that Viktoran's chances of winning her hand were lost. But did that mean he should surrender the feather to her since the circumstances had changed to his favor? His gut instinct told him that by doing so would only fade her interest in him over time. In his experience, it was sometimes better to be unpredictable to keep the thrill of love alive.

By the time Rydor and Jime had passed through the quartergate of the outer yard wall, a soldier greeted them, exclaiming out of breath, "General Regoria, the visitors . . . have just docked. General Meel . . . requests you to hurry!"

The three men sprinted beneath the twin crescent moons of Elvana and along the field paths of Emison Territory. Yellow horns stood silently in the distance, throwing their long, blocky shadows across the grass blades on which they feasted. The herd's leader growled, acknowledging the men's presence in their protected habitat. The three men delved into the forest to avoid being trampled by the roaming beasts.

"Could you tell how many men were aboard any of the ships?" Jime questioned between his gasps for breath.

"The shore watchman counted over a hundred heads on one vessel alone," said the soldier. "That was only what he could see on the upper deck, of course. What I want to know is, why did the Elders—"

"That is the least of our concerns right now," Rydor interrupted. "Let General Meel and me do the talking. Secure the perimeter of the shore with as many men as you can find."

"General Meel has already given the order, General Regoria," the soldier said.

"How many?" Rydor asked.

"So far twenty . . ."

"Twenty? That's hardly enough protection if they decide to swarm the shores . . ."

"More will come, General." Just as the obedient soldier had declared it, the tower's bells rang a warning sequence that gave precise directions.

Satisfied, Rydor let it be without another word. Orange lanterns with flickering candles inside them had been hung along the wooded trail to prevent the three men from going astray. The lanterns' guidance was adequate enough for the early hours of the morning and helped ward off any wild animals roaming the area. Glow bugs blackened their lights when the vibrations of Rydor's footsteps raced toward them. The large flying insects illuminated again once all three men were a dozen feet past them.

A storm had blown through the night before, downing several tree branches in a grove, which was normally open to ride horses through. Luckily, the opening was large enough to fit their bodies through. High winds were evident with a fair amount of rain intermixed. The ground was still wet in the deeper sections of the woods where the sun penetrated little.

Gradually the terrain began to slope, giving indication they were nearing Drana Bay. They could already hear the pounding of waves upon the rocks littering the shoreline. There were no breakers anywhere on the eastern coast, which made it rough for any ship trying to sail into the shallows. At times fishing vessels would be dragged by the pulling currents several miles down shore if they were not properly anchored

The trees thinned out as sand filled their shoes near the edge of a clearing. Rydor was the first to emerge onto the beach, and be greeted by a soldier holding an eye scope in one hand and a torch in the other. The man didn't say a word, but his face expressed many different emotions, including worry and confusion. He looked at the General and pointed to the three more-than-obvious forms floating fifty yards off shore. The stars were as clear as ever around them with the occasional dark cloud floating overhead. Panicky voices could be heard on the ships, followed by a chorus of cheers and applause. A rope ladder was flung over the side of the foremost ship and dragged across the surface of the water to the edge of a wet and porous rock. The last metal step smacked into the rock's largest crevice and went no further. The ladder wavered in the air gently at the middle until a figure set foot on the first ring and started to descend its length.

Rydor and Jime looked at each other, took a deep breath and walked calmly down to where General Rojer Meel was stationed, which was no more than ten feet from the scene of the first ship's overwhelming bow. It was carved in the image of a shark's head, the mouth open wide with bared teeth and a large hook through one side. The second and third ships hung back another hundred yards. Dozens of eyes watched from their decks. The blower engines hummed quietly on the wind beneath the lead ship. They kicked up spray that blew down shore, landing on a group of soldiers who had left the cover of the trees they had been hiding under. They backed up a few paces to dry off, showing their frustration. Golden sails adorned the masts of all three ships, but a different flag symbol was raised for each. A white shark on a black background decorated the front ship's flag, while a pair of squinting eyes and the likeness of an eel painted the flags of the other two.

"These ships are nearly twice the size of *The Star Gazer*," General Meel balked.

"It is not the ships I fear," Rydor said with a grimace.

Meel took a deep breath and watched as the tall man descending the ladder set foot on the wet rock. He nearly slipped, but caught himself at the last moment. Slowly, he straightened his posture and pulled on his coattails. With impressive grace and an uncanny smile he managed to work his way down the few natural steps he could find before he set foot on solid land. He dipped his hand and scraped up a chunk of wet sand, smelling and kissing it before moving toward Rydor and Meel. A dozen soldiers surrounded both generals with their swords and staffs ready in their sweating hands.

The man came to a stop only a stride from them, appearing to have no weapons from what they could tell. The only hair that covered his face was in the shape of a small, upside-down triangle on his chin. It was gray to match his hairpiece and was as choppy as the sea itself. His eyes were a brilliant green, like Oreus's, and his skin tanned and wrinkled. A dark purple vest overlaid a white shirt beneath his gray suit. His pants were soiled at the knees and below them were a pair of black boots pointed at the ends. General Meel stayed silent and waited patiently for the man to utter his predictable greeting.

"Ummm—er—hello?" he started pathetically, waving with half-curled fingers. When he realized wet sand still clung to them, he backed up, washed them off in the seawater and moved forward again.

The generals remained quiet with their arms crossed, gaining some pleasure from the man's shy awkwardness.

Unsure of what to make of the Yawranans, the man tried harder, "My name is Stewart Laney. I am pleased to see there are others like us inhabiting these lands—"

"What makes you so sure we are like *you*?" Meel snapped.

"Excuse me . . . you speak our language? I had no idea—"

"What is your purpose here?" Rydor asked, also losing his patience. "It is an early time of day to be milling about. Get to the point of your visit."

To further agitate their sleep deprivation, Laney pulled out a handkerchief and wiped the sweat from his brow. He turned several shades of red and white, embarrassed and nervous the encounter was not going well in any respect. "Forgive me . . . it has been very long since we have been on land and interacted with others outside of our own company. I forget my manners. We are from the lands of—"

"We know where you are from," Meel barked. What is your mission?"

"You know—you know of our lands? But that could only mean—"

Rydor added, "Yes. We have already met the people of Zonack. They have traveled here just as you have. But most of them have not made a favorable impression with us. So don't give us any of that nonsense about wanting to meet new cultures and learn their customs. If you are here for treasure like your predecessors, you can leave and find another culture who is not aware of your greed."

The man looked like a trapped sea rat aboard his own ship. He wiped his brow a second time and swallowed hard, not knowing what else to say. His feet began to shuffle backward as if he were afraid the generals would lash out at him like uncontrollable wild dogs. Meel couldn't help but smirk at Laney's cowardice.

"We are not from Zonack," Laney said softly.

Meel and Rydor exchanged confused glances, not having expected this answer. "Not from Zonack?" Meel said. "Then what unknown body of water have you ventured through to reach our shores?"

Looking baffled, Laney replied, "This one right here." He turned around and began pointing at the Racorn with sincerity.

Rydor shook his head, finding the man completely incompetent as an ambassador. "What the General means is, what country do you hail from?"

"Oh . . . sorry. I interpreted—"

"Where are you from?" Meel yelled.

"Salmus, Your Lord," Laney immediately replied. "We are from . . . Salmus."

"Where does Salmus lie?" Rydor inquired.

Talking as if the words were coming easier, Laney responded faster, "Directly south of the lands of Zonack. Our kingdom is guided by the fair hand of King Godwin Roule V. Forgive me for asking it . . . what is your name, sir? It is difficult to carry on conversation when one does not know to whom he is speaking."

Waving his hand in a circular gesture, Meel finally said, "I am General Rojer Meel. This is my peer, General Rydor Regoria. You have set foot in the Kingdom of Yawrana. I regret to inform you that none of your men may unboard at this time until we receive instructions from our king, His Majesty Noran Deardrop."

Miffed by what he should do next, Laney decided to say, "I shall consult this new information with my captain. He will be most interested in your decision. How soon shall we expect an answer?"

"Eight days at most."

"Eight days?" Laney gasped. "I don't know how the Captain will feel about that." He twiddled his fingers behind his back, struggling for a better solution. His eyes darted toward Rydor, pleading for a different voice on the matter.

Meel glanced at Rydor as well, who was already nodding. With a smile, Meel stated, "We shall have fresh food and drink brought down to you until we hear otherwise. Give our apologies to your captain for this inconvenience. Do not lose faith. King Deardrop has not the manners of a wild dragul. At the very least, there will be parting gifts for you to take when you leave."

"Parting gifts?" Laney said, surprised.

"Medicine, house ware supplies and more food and drink will be available if you require it."

"Ahhh. I see. That is a kind gesture," he said with a slight dip of his forehead. "And we do appreciate it. I shall inform the Captain immediately."

"If you need anything other than what I have mentioned," Meel continued, "we will take it under consideration." The generals watched Laney nod again and climb up the rock's slick, black surface. He almost fell again, luring Rydor a few feet closer to the water to help. The ambassador managed to catch hold of the ladder's lowest step with his long arms, putting the

General at ease.

Rydor sighed and receded up the bank with Meel at his side. They halted when they reached the edge of the forest.

Meel wasted no time relaying his thoughts. "I could see it in his eyes when I mentioned the parting gifts. They are definitely here for more than a mere handshake. I wouldn't part with a mellowin medallion for their entire fleet. Scavengers."

"Has word already been sent to the King?" Rydor asked.

"Yes. The moment they made waves in our waters I sent Captain Backfoot on his way. The Majestic Messengers will be speedy in their delivery on this matter. I gave Backfoot permission to use the Emison roller. I just hope he doesn't run anyone over in the process of getting the letter there. I can just imagine how the King will respond to this startling information." Meel sighed and cracked his knuckles in his right hand when he squeezed them around the hilt of his sword.

"The Elders will be more surprised than the King. Don't you think?" Rydor asked.

Gritting his teeth, Meel barely could make his next words audible out of bitterness. "We already rely too heavily on the prophecies to save us from our worst enemies. It makes us appear incompetent whenever they read a vision incorrectly or miss one altogether—-especially one as important as this. We scramble like fools in our own shock when we should always be prepared for the worst. It's because of the Elders that we have allowed ourselves to become vulnerable to the unexpected."

"A wiser statement has never been made," Rydor agreed, nodding.

"There you are," said a voice from behind them.

Looking over their shoulders, they knew the commanding pitch could only belong to Jada. She stepped into view wearing her full and silvery tight-fitting body armor, including an elegant dragul helmet and the prestigious green band encircling her right bicep. Rundle was behind her, having kept his word.

"Baron Annalee," Meel said with a bow.

Rydor also nodded and moved aside to let her into the clearing. The sheet lines on her face had been scrubbed away and her hair was pinned back in a ponytail with every last strand combed neatly into place. Her reaction was filled with calmness.

"So it's true. Three ships this time. How many more will it be the next? Have I already missed the negotiations?" Jada asked.

Meel said with a chalky air, "Sorry, Baron. The newcomers took it upon themselves to start sooner than we expected . . ."

"I see. Where do we stand?"

Both men paused before Rydor answered, "In the middle as usual. I don't think the new Captains are going to take our request very well."

Two flaming arrows suddenly shot out from the stern of the front ship. The pair of flying shafts split toward the second and third ships, landing in the railings of each. The fires on the arrowhead tips were doused before they spread and fed off the ships. A parchment rolled into a fireproof tube was untied from each of the shafts.

"Now that the remainder of our guests have been enlightened, I suggest two of us finish our sleep. What say you, Baron?" Rydor asked.

Rolling his eyes, Meel grumbled his obvious displeasure. "Both of you can be back here by sunrise."

Rydor began to smile when Jada spoiled his plans. "On the contrary, General Meel, I will take your place. Thank you for your patience and offer."

"That is not necessary, Baron . . . ."

"That is my final word, General Meel," she said sternly. "Save your energy for the upcoming days. I have a feeling it will be needed."

Meel turned toward Rydor, who was scowling. The two generals saluted each other before Meel disappeared into the dark forest. By the time Meel's footsteps had faded, Rydor was sitting against a tree trunk and shutting his burning eyes.

"Is my company no longer interesting now that it is not shared between the linens?" Jada glowered.

Cracking an eye half open, Rydor mumbled, "I'm confident the enticing Baron Jada Annalee can think of something to keep me amused."

She rolled her eyes and kicked a wave of sand across his waist. "You twit. I'm not here to entertain you like some court jester. You can either stay awake and think of something that's worth conversing about or take that swindling heart of yours back to Dowhaven where it can contemplate the missed sacrifices of love."

Brushing the sand from his waist and tipping his helmet up, the General replied sullenly, "You have my fullest and undivided attention."

Looking gratified from his wise assessment, she said, "Are you that convinced of the abilities of Dowhaven's new baron already? I remember how it was when I first entered the baronhood and it didn't garner me any more special attention because I was a female. The inexperience alone can be intimidating at first. Your guidance could be as much of a positive influence on Edin as it has been on Oreus."

"Getting his feet wet on his own for a few days is precisely what he needs to get started," Rydor said. "It will give him a good sense of what he is facing. So far I have seen little reason to intervene. His will is strong, which is exactly what Dowhaven needs to keep the rabble silent. The populace of that region has dealt with Johr for so long that they have come to expect the same from any who follow in his footsteps. I shall insert my opinion if and when I see it is fit."

The General pulled out a short, thin pipe and touched the glowing end of a stick from a campfire to light the leaf in the bowl. It ignited and set off a faint trail of smoke. He sat back down and nestled into the crook of a gnarled root, keeping a watchful eye on the ships hovering in the bay. When Jada was about to sit next to him, all three vessels quickly dropped into the waves to rest their blower engines for the long stay.

"Apparently everyone on board has finally settled to await the King's word," she said, relieved.

"Treasure hunters don't give in so easily."

"What if they are here for another purpose?"

"Such as?"

Shrugging her shoulders, she said, "How should I know? We have had no previous dealings with the residents of Salmus."

Rydor took a small puff on his pipe and blew a smoke ring into the wind. "One thing I have learned in all my years of dealing with individuals you know nothing about—expect the worst. Then you will not be disappointed when they let you down."

"That doesn't allow you to get to know the person if you constantly have your guard up."

Rydor chuckled. "Having been a guard, it is what I was trained to do. One can't trust anyone unfamiliar, under any circumstances, when he or she doesn't know what they are dealing with. And even then it sometimes isn't enough."

Jada stared into his peaceful eyes and sat down before asking, "What is your opinion on the disturbances that have been occurring in the catacombs the last few nights?"

"I am unmoved to make a judgment at this time on that particular topic." The General blew two long streams of wispy smoke out of his nostrils and then carried on. "As far as anyone can tell, nothing was taken."

"But some of the bodies were disturbed, moved out of position in their resting places."

Rydor nodded. "That is hardly anything to be excited about. Although it is suspicious as to why the guards were knocked unconscious each time the intruders came. It doesn't make sense why someone would go through the trouble of forcing an entry and then not steal anything."

"Do you think Herikech has anything to do with it?"

"I don't know. He's never been seen this far east and he's not surfaced since the last red moon. I can't imagine why he would have any interest in the dead. Whoever does, has been very careful about not leaving any evidence behind. The Elders also have had no visions regarding the disturbances since nothing was vandalized."

Jada tucked her head between her legs to stretch the cramped neck muscle between her shoulder blades. She rocked forward a few times before they loosened. Her expression changed from perplexed to angry as she tried to decide how the incidents could be solved.

"Rest your mind," Rydor said, rubbing her back. "One day it will be right in front of your nose, waiting to be discovered."

With nothing else to do, she decided to ponder it more anyway. "The catacombs are just not the type of place one expects problems to occur. Haley and Gailey have expressed interest in the burial of our dead on more than one occasion. It's very likely other Lazul children may have grown the same curiosities."

Rydor said, "I can clearly visualize how the Lazuls took care of their own when they passed on. The Uratan River is a good drainage system for such uses and there are creatures in those waters that are ravenous enough to dispose of carcasses. I imagine that feeding those monsters helps protect their underground city. I encountered one predator myself when I took an involuntary swim to save Oreus's life, coming within inches of being dragged under." Rydor shuddered at the thought of the large pair of glowing yellow eyes emerging toward him from the river bottom. Their sinister size penetrated him more deeply than the jabbing cold water that had seeped through his uniform.

"How did you escape?"

He shrugged. "It was bizarre. I've never been one to claim luck, but something happened I'm unable to explain. Part of the ceiling collapsed behind me and blocked its path. The collision deterred it long enough to permit Oreus and me to reach the shore." Blowing a few more smoke rings downwind caught the attention of the soldiers who inhaled them. They ducked and furrowed their brows out of disgust. Rydor smiled and pretended to pay them no attention, having done it on purpose to keep them awake.

Jada also looked at him with a raised eyebrow.

"What?" he asked innocently.

"I thought you were cutting back on the mince leaf?"

He coughed when he tried to respond. She smiled for having caught him at the worst time for a proper defense. With a hand, he covered his mouth to stop the brief air kickback. "I . . . buh-uh-uh . . . I best thought to do it at a slower pace." He controlled his breathing and continued, "It doesn't impede my training in the least." A minor cough escaped when he finished, but he stifled it enough so she wouldn't hear.

She frowned with an accusing look that read, *I don't believe you are taking this seriously*. Knowing how much he enjoyed his daily inhalations, she shook her head and decided to let it slide.

The night drifted along with the ships afloat in the bay. The waves became rough with the wind's increasing howls. The temperature also dropped, and she leaned her head against Rydor's shoulder for more warmth. The waves soothed her cares and the rocking ships lulled her mind to sleep. The General meditated until dawn while she dreamed.

Sunlight fell upon Rydor's gold-tinted armor the moment a cock crowed in the farmlands less than a mile north. Its repeated announcement of the new day shook Jada from her sleep. "Is it morning already?" she said, disappointed, as she yawned in his face.

"Good morning, Baron. Good morning, General," said a voice coming from the woods.

The bones cracked in Jada's neck when she looked sideways at General Meel. He was bathed, shaved, and gave her the promise of rest in a comfortable bed five miles away.

"Nothing out of the normal stirred from what I gather," Meel said. "I'm surprised they didn't try sailing up the coast for another opinion. Their patience so far has shown their words are not empty."

"Let's see how they feel when seven more suns have come and gone," Rydor replied, stretching his cramped limbs after he stood.

Rydor and Jada were about to return back to the tower when Haley and Gailey bumped into them on the way out. Gailey was thought by most in Emison Tower to be the more competent of the Lazul twin girls. She was able to keep up with Jada's timely and strict demands better than her sister. Haley's more reserved nature built up sporadic outbursts of retaliation against Gailey from the frustration of not being able to compete. Her resentment continued to grow over the last half year, but she held her tongue like always, letting Gailey get the bulk of the attention once more.

"Baron. General . . . ."

"You two have no reason to be down here," Jada said grumpily. "Turn yourselves around and march straight back to the tower. Only the army is allowed access to this area until further allowances are specified by the King."

Gailey instantly groveled as a persuasion tactic. "But, Baron, how will we ever learn to engage in foreign policies if we can't analyze them firsthand?"

"Your pleas will get you nowhere this morning, Gailey. Even though you have attended those training lessons at the academy, the use for foreign policy in Yawrana is extremely rare. It does not require your attention at this time," Jada said, which made Haley giggle with satisfaction. Gailey shot Haley a wicked look and tried a different approach for a better result.

"Can we at least help the provisioners ration the food and supplies to the voyagers?"

Jada gave the impression that she wouldn't allow it, but Rydor stepped in at the last second and said, "There's no harm in that, is there?"

Jada's face turned red briefly before she replied, "Very well." Haley's jaw dropped in disbelief before the Baron finished. "I want you back at the tower as soon as you are done."

"But that wo—"

"Not another word on it, Gailey. Take what you have been granted and argue no further. My patience is limited today."

Gailey saluted Jada with a fist to her chest and said, "Thank you, Baron."

Rydor hustled after Jada when they reentered the forest. She was walking at a rate that implied she was angry with him. Her arms swung with tension in them as she centered herself in the middle of the path so he couldn't walk beside her.

"You're angry? Why are you angry?" he asked when he saw her reaction.

She suddenly stopped and spun around with a finger pointed at his face. "Never contradict my decisions with the twins—*ever*. Haley has an inferiority complex when it comes to her more aggressive sister. Letting Gailey get her way only infuriates Haley."

"I didn't realize—"

"I do! I've been trying to stop them from fighting since I took them under my wing over two years ago. This will only further provoke Haley to do something more rash to compete. Do you know how hard I've had to work at steering them clear of the secret Lazul guilds those missing children have been forming throughout Yawrana? Already a third of the adopted boys and girls have not been seen since last season. Herikech is out there floating around in the forests of the territories, waiting to take advantage of them at every turn." Her face had become a bright red and her eyebrows were crinkled.

Understanding the situation completely now that it had been thoroughly explained to him, he uttered, "Forgive me, Jada. I was just trying to let them help . . . ."

Rubbing her temples, she replied in a lower tone, "I know. I know. But this is no game. They're in their rebellious age and I have been using every advantage I have to enforce discipline into their resistant four thousand-year-old natures. They respect my authority as long as it is not challenged by my equals."

He nodded and apologized again. "I am sorry. It was wrong of me to intervene. You know them better than anyone."

"And even that might not be enough for me to keep them out of trouble. Let's get some rest," she said, trying to massage away the dark circles under her eyes. "If I stay out in the sun too long, my body may find the urge to forget it altogether and go for a morning run."

While the eventless days dragged on for both parties in Emison, a dark mass of storm clouds began to spread across the territories of Yawrana from the west. The formations moved with an eerie swirl no one had ever before witnessed. Their slow unfurling revealed a menacing march of steady rain that lasted for four solid mornings and evenings. Many had to search far and wide for a patch of blue sky. The majority of the darkest thunderheads loomed over Candlewick Castle at the center of the kingdom's forest realm. Rivers had to be sandbagged to prevent overflow and the flooding of crops in nearby farmlands. Water was channeled from the castle's moats to decrease the water damage in the stables and Gaming Arena.

With the gates open to drain the run-off, the guards feared an attack of beasts serving Herikech Illeon's will. But there were no disruptions as normal shipments were hauled in and out of the protective fortress. However, the rain itself became so bothersome that solutions to get rid of the excess water were running thin. It began to pool and collect in areas that had never been wet before, causing a mild panic to stir among the servants. Out of desperation, dozens of additional empty wine barrels had to be brought in. Most were refilled with gutter water spilling over into the Yard while the remaining were filled from mopped up and wrung out leakage drenching the hallways.

When the heaviest downpours had passed, the clouds surprisingly stayed and continued to shield the castle from any light from above. A faint trickle was carried with the increasing wind, which pounded intermittently on anything that wasn't latched or secured down. Soon there was a rhythmless racket of noise that haunted every Yawranan's patience with each bang, thud and crash. Few could sleep well from the endless interference. They instead watched the blowing debris with bloodshot eyes as it danced across the fields and scraped against their windows.

Even Noran's private chambers held no refuge from an enemy they could not fight forever. When the message regarding the Salmus ships was delivered, it brought a smile to his face. He had been looking for the right opportunity to leave the castle since he returned from Arna half a year ago, and this was the perfect invitation. His wounded hands had healed faster than he had expected from his trials there. He could no longer stay indoors, forced to be a prisoner where there were no physical bars.

The generals all had agreed it was best for him to remain out of sight as much as possible until their enemies, Lazul King Herikech Illeon and his army, could be detained. Herikech had also resorted to bending the will of the animals of Yawrana to help wage his war by sending them to attack Serquist Tower, a mystery they had not resolved. Most of the animals that followed him were wild and couldn't be reasoned with. Noran only could suspect Herikech was using a brainwashing technique or drug to make them obedient. Thanks to the townspeople and farmers of Serquist, the tower was saved and Herikech and his men had fled back into the swamps.

He had complied willingly to stay within the castle, until now, because they believed the war for Yawrana and its resources was not yet over. The Lazuls' former home to the far south, the Waungee Grasslands, had been depleted of its resources and food. Herikech was ready to do the same with Yawrana, but had failed in each of his attempts.

Noran's only sanity during the stretch he had been confined to the castle was in his new bride, Willow, and his new son, Varen. Their presence was a breath of fresh air in his reduced role, but it did not provide the freedom for which he longed. Meeting the new voyagers could play a pivotal role in the kingdom's survival, as it had done once before. And since there was no prophecy he knew of that mentioned these new travelers, it would be essential for him to leave the castle and investigate the matter himself.

He would need to determine their intentions, good or evil, before handing over his trust, like his father had done once before with Lanar Lanu's mostly corrupted crew. It was a stern approach that would show he held no fear for the newcomers, but it also contained the element of risk. If something were to go wrong, his actions could be interpreted as rash, causing many more to become traitors like Hethro Trayson.

Hethro, a guard from the northern gates of Dowhaven Territory, said Noran's decision to bring the Lazul children of Maramis to live among the Yawranans was a mistake. In his heart, Noran couldn't let innocent children die from the flooding of the underground city of Maramis. There *was* a way out, to not let innocents die. There was another race that was prisoner to the Lazuls, the Shonitaurs, who could wipe away memories through a simple touch to one's head. He requested the Shonitaurs to use the method on the Lazul children, and it had been successful until Herikech resurfaced in Yawrana. It was more than likely he was informing the children of their past. It was said by the generals that some of the children started to form a secret Lazul guild to help Herikech wage war against the Yawranans. His failure left a bitter taste in his mouth.

Noran thought he could easily send a reply in a letter stating that the new voyagers were to be brought to the castle, or better yet, to leave Yawrana forever. But hiding behind words and guards like other kings was never his strong suit. Preferring his competence to be judged by his actions, he turned his elusive attention back toward General Hithel of the esteemed Majestic Messengers. The dobbin never relaxed as he waited for an answer from the King.

"General," Noran started.

"Yes, Your Majesty? Have you come to a decision?"

Chuckling, he said, "Yes, but no further deliveries to Emison are required at this time."

"No message?" Hithel asked, looking for a reason.

"I will be the message."

Hithel's whiskers twitched. Putting away his quill, inkbottle and parchment, he said, "You are going to Emison yourself? That is uncommon ground for a king to take the first step forward."

Noran nodded and finished dressing. "There is no cause for worry, General. There will be more than enough men there to ensure my safety."

"That is not what I'm worried about, Your Majesty. These voyagers may think your gesture is a sign of weakness." Noran looked at the dobbin with a grimace before Hithel added, "A reserved king is more powerful in stature when upon his throne."

Thinking up a logical response to appease Hithel's wise supposition, he said, "I will order that only their leaders be brought to me in Emison Tower. Separating the captains from their men should regain the advantage I lose by residing here. Many have never forgotten that Oreus Blake's former crew nearly was successful in emptying the royal vaults. The people of Yawrana will be highly suspicious of these adventurers' motives as well. By not letting them step foot inside the castle, I have removed the potential of it being stolen from the equation."

"That is very good thinking, Sire. Then the ancient wealth of Yawrana shall remain intact for now," Hithel said, and then smiled a toothy grin. "And what of the Elders? Should they also not be privy to this information?"

"Not yet. It will only upset them if they learn they had not envisioned this."

"What if they had and they're just not telling anyone?"

"That is likely, but I wish not to address them at this time. There is no need to create disruption when it's not called for, even if the Elders had no prior knowledge of the voyagers' advent. If after our discussions we decide to send the voyagers back to their homelands, then I will not have worried the Elders."

Hithel bowed and was about to leave when Noran stopped him. "I haven't dismissed your services yet, General Hithel."

The brown and gray hair on the General's neck stiffened from confusion. "I thought you stated a message was no longer needed at this time . . . ."

"To Emison and the Elders," he reiterated.

"I see," Hithel replied, pulling back out his parchment, ink bottle and quill to take down the script. "Ready when you are, Sire."

*Baron Oreus Blake,*

*Your presence is requested at Emison Tower immediately. Your participation in a private matter is crucial for consultation. This order also applies and has been related to the attention of Boris Groffen. I look forward to seeing you both there five days from your receipt of this information. Dragul transport will be provided to quicken your journeys. Once you reach Emison, you will be called upon when needed.*

*His Majesty,*
*The Sun of Yawrana,*
*King Noran Deardrop*
*Candlewick Castle*

Hithel lit a candle and sealed the letter with green wax. Once the dripped circle had almost hardened, he stamped a double M at the center. He dropped the scroll into a protective tube, recorded the time the message was taken and waited for final instructions.

"Please see to it this message is delivered by dragulback. Use Firewing."

"Firewing, Your Majesty?" Hithel asked.

Smirking, Noran explained, "Forgive me. That is what Baron Blake refers to her as. Immana. Take Immana. She favors the Baron."

"She has already been broken for riding? But all the other draguls took well over a year . . . ."

"Her tenth successful ride was completed just last eve. She has amazing speed and ability as a flier. A more intelligent dragul there has never been in our herd. The only negative side is she has all the males in a tizzy and vying for her attention."

Hithel's lengthy foot thumped against the floor, showing his anxiety about the topic. "Draguls have never been bred in captivity. It could present problems. They may become extremely protective of their young."

"It is not proper of us to deny their right to interact. More problems may arise if we don't allow them to."

"Then perhaps all that needs to be done is to divide them until those urges are no longer."

"That is a topic to be consulted with the Elders. Hopefully it is not another revelation that has escaped their visions."

The rain had not been as bad in Emison Territory as it had been throughout the Royal House Territory. The clouds permitted some sunrays to finger their way through now and then. Noran sat just out of reach of one of those rays with his head held high. He felt refreshed as ever while breathing the clean air. His mind and body were invigorated to be moving about again outside of the castle, even for this short period of time.

The dragul on which he was mounted, Hollinfil, landed smoothly on the PaCant platform only a few hundred yards from Emison Tower. Guards immediately greeted them.

"Your Majesty!" exclaimed a soldier with a bewildered expression. "You have come to see the voyagers?"

"Of course. Do you not greet a guest at your door when they come to visit?"

The man looked dumbfounded, as if he had never considered putting foreigners in the same category as a neighbor or friend. He nodded and said, "Yes . . . that is courteous, my Lord." After helping Noran dismount, the soldier led the dragul to a nearby holding house for rest and feeding. Bruneau

Palidon and Blaynor Garsek, Noran's two personal guards, walked with him to a group of soldiers stationed outside the gates of the platform.

"Your Majesty," a blond haired man in the squad began, "welcome to Emison. I am Sergeant Kale Milford. We weren't informed that you were coming. Is there anything we can do to make your stay more comfortable?"

"There is," Noran replied eagerly. "Please ask Baron Jada Annalee to have her banquet hall prepared for dining with the voyagers. I wish to speak with only the Salmus captains. Dinner will be at seven this evening. I think we have made them wait long enough. Ensure they are stripped of their weapons before they enter."

The sergeant bowed and sent a corporal on his way to deliver the order. "Anything else, Sire?"

After thinking a moment on it, he answered, "Take Boris and Oreus to Jada's private meeting hall. Let me know the moment they arrive."

The sergeant nodded and guided Noran to the tower's yard. Every soul the king came within range of quickly bowed to him before continuing on with their pressing chores. The sun finally faded as Noran and his men crossed the lush expanse of green, groomed grass within the perimeter walls. He remained optimistic the storm would eventually blow over and bring their spirits back up.

Jada rushed to the king's side as soon as he stepped foot inside the tower. She had just received the corporal's word about his precise instructions. She appeared ruffled. "My Lord. I had no idea— "

"All is well, Baron Annalee," he said, smiling and hugging her. His warm and calm demeanor additionally took her aback. "I take it you have been accommodating the needs of our new guests?" he asked.

She crossed her arms and said in a disgruntled tone, "Yes, Your Highness. And I have to say they have been nothing short of demanding. We have already gone through two hundred bags of long grain seed, fifty barrels of crimson wine, thirty barrels of rois, and two bushels of hop leaf to subside their complaining. Their supplies were exceedingly low after being lost during their endless travel at sea. The medicine makers also have been working night and day to resolve many of the minor sicknesses of their men. It was all we could do to prevent them from pulling anchor and sailing up the coast, which they threatened to do on multiple occasions by the third day."

Noran shook his head. "The sea can dishearten a man when it holds the upper hand. Even the best ships can find discourse among the Racorn's human defiance. Men were never meant to belong in its care." Still, Noran was unpleased with the voyagers' outcries. He decided to move the dinner up to five. This created a greater bustle throughout the tower for the chefs and servants. They now had two hours instead of four to be ready. Extra help was hired to beat the deadlines they faced.

The King was changed into his fresh royal green garments and sat at the head of the table for appropriate viewing. The dining hall was ten times more extravagant since he crossed Emison's Yard. The table was loaded with the most exotic food and drink available. The aroma from their simmering and cooled flavors was enthralling.

Emison Tower's lead House servant, Thom, rang a bell near the main entryway to announce the voyagers' forthcoming introductions. Noran straightened his elaborate, golden crown and sat up straight. The index and middle fingers on his right hand tapped his armchair.

Bruneau whispered in his ear, "Do not feel nervous, Your Majesty. Speak your heart and impose your courage. You are still the sea to them. They are at your mercy."

Noran nodded and turned his attention back toward the door. They swung inward and revealed a group of seven men and one towering woman waiting anxiously on the other side. The woman was dressed in furs and her brown hair was braided down her left shoulder. She was of barbarian heritage, like Boris.

The front three men were dressed in sharp black, brown and gray overcoats and pants. Their eyes darted back and forth around the room until they found Noran at the table. They appeared unimpressed and strolled toward the King with their heads held high.

The rest of the men surrounding the front three were taller by a few inches, with defined muscular frames. The largest man had no shirt, showing the ripples in his tanned stomach and the broadness of his shoulders. His legs and arms had impressive girth and his head was bald. An angler's hook pierced his upper lip like a fish that had been reeled in. He grinned with madness in his eyes, baring a set of yellow teeth.

The other three men in the group were normal as far as their sailing apparel was concerned. Their expressions were suspicious, as if they were waiting for something out of the ordinary to happen.

Thom broke out in a clear voice after they all came to a standstill at the opposite end of the dining table. "Voyagers from the kingdom of Salmus, you have rested your ships upon the shore of Emison Territory in the fertile land of Yawrana. Our beloved king, His Majesty Noran Deardrop, has granted you permission to dine with him this evening."

The entire party bowed out of respect, except for the barbarian woman. Thom quickly asked her to do the same. She frowned and did a quick nod before tugging on a strap slung over her shoulder. Attached to the strap was a horn as large as Thom's arm.

Thom finished by saying, "Please state your names and ranks for His Highness."

One of the three voyagers who looked suspicious gazed around him before stepping forward from the center of the group to speak. "Forgive our caution, Your Majesty," said the black-haired man. His eyebrows were bushy, his eyes blue and his smile contagious. "We asked our own guards to dress as the Captains for safety reasons." The three sharply dressed men in the front stepped to the side. "We became worried of your plans for us after keeping us at bay for over a week. We must be cautious when it comes to trade. You never quite know what the intentions are of a new culture."

"I can say the same may be said about you," Noran replied with a straight face. "Name yourself."

With a polite nod, the man announced, "For my gracious host, it would be a pleasure at last. Captain Ave Winslow of *The White Fin,* at your feet." Winslow called the other two captains forward, who were also disguised as crewman. He waved to the one who had curly, dirty blond hair pinned back in a ponytail. Green eyes stood out as this man's most vivid feature, but they held a note of arrogance. "This is Captain Sage Rollins of *The Wave Shocker,*" Winslow said. Rollins bowed again to prove it was not above him. "And this other fine gentleman," Winslow finished, referring to the lanky man with stork legs, shortly cropped brown hair and blue eyes, "is Captain Eason Soar of *The Misty Eyes*. We are all very proud to make your acquaintance and represent the royal word of King Godwin Roule V."

Captains Rollins and Soar each stepped aside to allow the King to lay his eyes upon the rest of their men. Captain Winslow introduced his own hooked-lip servant. "And to give due mention of these fine workers, this gentleman is simply known as Thorn. He has never revealed his true name to us, so we quit asking." A small chuckle erupted from Bruneau after the mention of Thorn's name, but he quickly covered his laughter when Thorn furrowed his brow and flared his large pair of nostrils at the guard.

Winslow didn't hear Bruneau's laugh and continued, "The three clean-cut men beside Captain Soar are—well—their names are quite long so let's just call them by their middle ones: Her, Gen and Trus. And the lovely lady in the back, standing eight feet exactly, is Windreed Sinker of the Lake Fog Clan of Phyre Heights."

Noran remained seated and quiet while judging each of their postures, expressions and sincerity. The voyagers looked at one another curiously as to why the King did not acknowledge any of them. The barbarian woman glared at Noran but his eyes were more assertive than hers. She looked away and blushed to end the exchange.

Thom was about to introduce Jada to the voyagers when Noran burst, asking, "Your purpose here is to gather riches for your own land, is it not?"

Winslow smirked at Rollins and Soar, seeing the charade was up. He fully admitted, "Yes, it was, Your Majesty. There is no denying it. We are opportunists to say the least. You have no need to worry, though. We would not unjustly take treasure that has already been claimed through the laborious efforts of your people. I understand that visitors of Zonack have arrived here first. Is this correct?"

Noran nodded.

"By any chance . . . was that expedition led by Captain Lanar Lanu of *The Star Gazer*?"

Jada's head snapped toward Noran, but he didn't look in the least surprised as he sipped from his wine goblet. Noran nodded again after he had completed wetting his throat.

Winslow sighed and said, "I can deduce from your expressions his time here has left a black mark. It is a great pity he arrived here first."

"And why is that a pity, Captain Winslow?" Noran questioned, not yet seeing how the two men weren't cut from the same cloth.

"Your Majesty, Captain Lanu and his men were only . . . thieves . . . more or less. Their manners were unenviable and do not mirror the morals of the people of Salmus. It would have been more of an advantage to Yawrana if you had the gratification of dealing with our practices before his."

"How did you become associated with Captain Lanu if you are both from different countries?" Noran asked.

Captain Winslow didn't appear bothered by the question and said, "He was a friend once. I met him at a docking port on the shores of the port city Grand Isle in Salmus. He was straightforward and we struck several agreements for supply trade over the course of the one summer season we did business together. Over that short period of time he left a bitter taste in my mouth and we decided to go our separate ways."

"What caused the bitter taste?" Noran pressed.

"To put it mildly, Your Majesty, he was *too good* of a negotiator."

Noran smiled, finding the comment humorous. He quit tapping his finger on the armrest of his chair and invited the voyagers to sit. "The meal is growing cold, Captains. Please fill your plates and stomachs. I am sure you could use the replenishments."

"Most kind, Your Majesty," Winslow replied. He ordered the rest of the crew to sit. Captain Rollins nodded while Captain Soar bowed courteously for the valued invitation. Rollins and Soar each took a different side of the table than Winslow, spreading out their power.

The remaining officers showed their allegiance to each of their captains by sitting near them, falling into Noran's trap. Noran felt more comfortable knowing the relationships the Salmus voyagers had with one another if he needed to interrogate them. It was better to isolate a dedicated servant from his master to find truth if there was cause for it. A servant was more likely to surrender hidden ambitions than those they served. The barbarian woman sat next to Rollins, and the fishhook man, Thorn, sat next to Winslow. The three regally dressed men, Gen, Her and Trus, all sat next to Soar, completing the display of compared equality of protection for each captain.

Once Noran took the first bite of food, the Captains and their followers ate with passion. The level of intensity in the room had lowered significantly by the end of the meal. The Captains thanked Noran for the food and waited for him to begin the conversations again. To everyone's astonishment, he stated, "I will be retiring to my chambers for the evening. Captains, you and your servants will stay in the tower until I have had ample enough time to contemplate what we will do with you."

"Your Majesty," Winslow said in a flustered tone, "we don't wish to be a burden to you . . . ."

"It's not about that, Captain Winslow," Noran said. "So far I have appreciated your honesty and patience, but in good conscience I simply can't allow you to enter my kingdom unless I feel it is necessary. I also can't allow you leave until I have determined whether any of your people will return here again under worse motives. I must consult with my counsel. They will be here two eves from now and their opinions may be more to your advantage if you are willing to comply. However, if you appeal this decision, then I shall order you to be taken to your ships to catch the next wind out of Drana Bay." All three captains were appalled at Noran's candor but were left speechless by his mandate.

A short time later and several corridors over in Jada's private meeting hall, Noran was explaining his thoughts on abandoning the discussions. "I've already deemed we will not get anywhere by using this approach. During dinner the voyagers hardly said a word. In most instances, those who have tight lips tend to be filled with foul air."

"Their resemblance to Lanu's crew is uncanny." Blaynor said. "Except this time there is no Oreus Blake in their company. Your instincts and prudence have played their part marvelously tonight, my Lord. Because one does not say anything does not mean he is any more innocent. Oreus and Boris will be here soon enough to verify the facts of their former crew's encounter with Winslow's. Perhaps Oreus can enlighten us as to the reason for that bitter taste Winslow spoke so fleetingly of."

Bruneau surmised, "Sounds as if Winslow met his match in Lanu, maybe even was bested by him."

"What are your true feelings, Your Majesty?" Jada asked, prying into the King's thoughts.

Rubbing his chin, he responded, "They have admitted they seek treasure. For that statement alone I am inclined to send them on their way. Our wisdom has taught us that we shouldn't endure a serpent's company if we don't want to be bitten."

"Then what tells you to allow them to stay for two more eves?" Jada asked.

The King paused a moment. He removed his crown, set it on the table in front of him and combed his blond hair with his fingers. "There is one item that prevents me from taking the safe but exceedingly offensive route. If they mean harm, would the Elders have not seen it in a vision? Perhaps the voyagers' visit does not contain falsehoods after all. We are basing our decisions on two different societies. Is it right of us to judge them if we take away their ability to prove us wrong? I want their behavior watched closely during the next two days here, Baron. Take them to the observation guest rooms. The wall paintings will allow us to hear or see anything unusual that we didn't witness tonight. Have a watcher roam with them in the halls and Yard when no others are around. At some point we should learn how valid our insecurities are."

# CHAPTER TWO
## A Gamble Worth Taking

Saddle sores after four days of flying nagged Oreus as he hobbled toward the front doors of Emison Tower. The rains had picked up again in Marshant Territory just before he had left, raising the dam water in the Cutler Highlands to a dangerous level. If it were to burst due to the insurmountable pressure that had built up, a flashflood would wipe out everything on its two-mile rampage to the valley floor. Evacuating the communities before he left was the only viable option. But knowing some of the locals, he knew they could not be dragged from their homes by an entire army. It was as if they wished to die, rather than face the prospect of losing everything they had worked so hard for.

"There's nothing else you could have done," Ola said, gently grasping his hand to pull him out of his fixation on the subject.

The Baron closed his palm around his love's left hand. "I fear we have offended Yawrana the Maker somehow," he said. "I have never heard of or seen such endless quantities of precipitation over a short period of time and across one specific belt. It's a shame some of its wrath couldn't have swung south to the Dunes of Pydora. I am curious to know what issue is so important here that it overrides the Highland's urgent situation. I'm not accustomed to just abandoning a perilous situation on a whim."

"Noran wouldn't have asked us to fly as far as we did for no good reason. Maybe the army has finally caught up with Herikech," she said, ascending the stairs to enter the tower. Oreus's personal guard, Quinn Rainsmoke, and two others, followed closely behind them. The foyer was pleasantly warm but the new oil lamp lighting was dim.

"Herikech caught? He's too slippery to be apprehended by force. The snowtears have given him a power we do not yet comprehend. The longer he's out there, the more dangerous he becomes."

A voice suddenly boomed from a corner before they handed their overcoats to the soldier stationed near the dining hall. "That skin an' bone sack wouldn't last a day in Phyre Heights." As Ola and Oreus peered through the darkness to their left, a large form emerged to hug them.

"Boris," Oreus said joyously. He had not seen the barbarian since the

King's winter solstice wedding.

"Greetings, blacksmith," Ola cried before one furry arm of his cloak smothered her. Oreus was pinned as well within Boris's other arm, finding it useless to resist against his immense strength. Boris let go so they could come up for air.

"What took ya two so long? Here I thought I'd be learnin' of the secret all by meself."

Oreus smiled and replied, "You know. Firewing—she's a got an appetite larger than any of the males. Had to stop at every slaughterhouse from here to Marshant." Oreus's own stomach growled, making Willow and Boris burst into laughter.

"It seems that she's not the only one who needs a bite to eat," Ola laughed.

"At least he's not the twig he used to be on *The Star Gazer*," Boris said, accrediting Oreus with his newly developed, muscular bulk. He was almost as strong as Rydor now and his stamina had increased threefold. Sergeant Eon Roundtree had stopped coaching Oreus full time when the Baron was finally able to achieve the highest grades in all endurance exercises. Roundtree handed those reins to Quinn to guarantee Oreus always stuck to his rigorous regimen. The sergeant now only concentrated on spending partial days with Oreus to teach him actual defense and attacking techniques in the art of the *Mellano*: fighting without the aid of a weapon.

The Baron smiled, taking the compliment well. "How is that artificial leg of yours holding up, Boris?"

Boris reached down and knocked on the hard wood several times. "Solid as ever. Been upgraded to a denser wood: pishel. It doesn't get nicked as easily as the other one did an' supports me weight better. Maker Yewi claims I can even run like a normal person with it. I 'aven't exactly had the chance to try it out though."

"I'm glad to hear it. Where are we to find Noran?"

"Follow me. I guess they've been sittin' up in Jada's personal meetin' room since early this marnin.' They've been all quiet until ya showed yar faces. I guess there's some guests that are causin' an uproar."

"Guests? From which territory?"

The barbarian shrugged. "Don' know, lad. Don' know. Quite odd that they need me to deal with it. Maybe some weapons need straightenin'."

"How's my ship coming along, by the way?" Oreus prodded.

Boris smiled and joked, "Your ship? I 'aven't even got the steerin' wheel attached and you're ready to take it out for a drive?"

"Do you at least have the sails attached to her?"

"Nah. But they're piled in heaps on the decks. Very soon, lad. Very soon. We just finished puttin' the last sideboards on and installin' the largest blower engine. I reckon' she'll be better than *The Star Gazer*. The metal in the engines is of a higher quality than the *Gazer's* and can push the ship up fifty feet higher from the ground."

Oreus' mouth dropped open. "Fifty! *The Star Gazer* could only maintain her weight at a thirty-foot height."

"Isn't it grand? Just imagine it," he said raising his hands, palms out. "You could float 'er above any mist that dares impede your journeys. And that's not all." The Baron almost felt faint after what Boris mentioned next. Ola had to hang onto his arm to prevent him from falling into her. Boris continued, saying, "I added a parasail off tha back if ya get an itchin' to do some flying yarself. There's also a secret room adjoinin' the Captain's quarters if ya need peace, and heaters along the upper deck in case the winds get a little too cold in icier regions. I've diverted some of the blower engine heat to come through stone stacks."

"You never cease to keep the surprises coming," Oreus said with a grin. "That's not even something the finest craftsman in Zonack would have conjured up."

Boris slapped the Baron hard on the back, almost knocking him from his solid stance. Oreus coughed and chuckled to catch his breath from the solid hit. If it were two years ago, he would have been on the floor.

Bruneau entered the room and greeted them, holding a straight face that they had become accustomed to seeing when there was a problem. "Welcome to Emison," he said, bowing quickly. "King Deardrop is awaiting your counsel."

"King Deardrop," Ola said, sighing. "I'm still getting used to Noran taking Willow's last name since their marriage bond. It's strange just hearing it announced out loud." She shook her head.

"I actually preferred Yorokoh," Bruneau added. "But, I may change my mind in a day or two. Guards are always adjusting their thinking to accept new challenges. A simple name change is not something that we should squander a second thought on. The shifting winds remind us that life is ever-changing."

Boris chuckled. "Deardrop is as good a name as any. Are you goin' to tell us what people we are to be meetin' or are ya just gonna stand there and keep the suspense up?"

Bruneau raised an eyebrow. "Follow me. The King will explain all shortly. Your timing is perfect as usual. We were just waiting for a report to be given before we proceeded any further." Bruneau rubbed the ends of his brown, wispy mustache with his index finger and thumb and let the others follow him through the winding corridors of Emison Tower. Many servants bowed to them as they passed, recognizing the power of the colored bands they wore. When they neared Jada's private meeting rooms, Oreus saw Rundle and a half dozen other guards lining the hallway. Rydor stood closest to the door with his arms crossed, grimacing.

"There you are," Rydor said, waving his hand in a circle. "*Onnaway*."

"*Onnaway*," Oreus, Ola and Boris said in response. Oreus saluted the General as well with a fist to his chest to show respect for his rank in the Yawranan army. The two men were nearly identical in size as they faced each other.

Rydor was brimming with satisfaction that the Baron's training had taken a new turn. "You look in pristine condition, Baron Blake," he said, smiling. "Sergeant Roundtree has informed me that you are one of the finest pupils he has ever had the pleasure to train." Before Oreus could thank him for his compliment, Rydor turned and opened the door to the private section of the tower.

The lights were dim when they entered, with only one pair of candles set directly at the center of a long dining table in the middle of the room. The air was heavy and dry, and the mood, sullen. Oreus glanced around the room at the others. Jada, Noran, General Meel and Blaynor were the easiest four to identify. There were also three others whom Oreus didn't recognize, and only one of the three carried a colored band. It was a blond male maker, wearing the standard solid blue band assigned to the medicine creators of the territories. The other two were women: one was a simple servant ready to give the King whatever he needed, and the second, a guard who had just finished whispering something into Noran's ear.

Oreus and Boris bowed while Ola curtsied in Noran's presence. They each found an empty seat. Oreus and Ola sat apart since there weren't two chairs unoccupied next to each other.

"Baron. Sister. Blacksmith." Noran nodded and smiled to each of them. "Thank you for coming. I won't keep you in the dark any longer now that you are in a secured location. Oreus and Boris, what do you know of the people of Salmus?"

An immediate look of surprise fell upon both of their faces. Oreus answered first before Boris could formulate a coherent sentence. "Salmus is an underdeveloped country, with roughly a third of the population Zonack has.

Mostly terrace farming exists there because flat land is not in great abundance. The wooded areas are littered with bandits and the coasts are made up of simple sea villages. However, the trading between Salmus and Zonack is constant enough to keep the kingdoms interested in each other. Zonack depends on Salmus for metallic resources." Oreus paused a moment, thinking of how Captain Lanu and his former crew had tried to steal a large quantity of precious metal from Yawrana's army supplies. "Salmus, in return, imports many varieties of ingredients for medicines that are common throughout its divisions."

Noran asked, "Are there any known tensions existing between Zonack and Salmus?"

"From time to time there are raids along the borders, but they are skirmishes provoked by random outlaws, and are not by the will of either monarchy."

Boris built on Oreus's statement in a more direct manner, saying, "Rogues lookin' for war. Many want the kingdoms to unite under one rule so they can build more trade routes to expand their profits."

"Thank you, barbarian," Noran replied. "And who builds the drift ships for Salmus and Zonack?"

"Neither," Oreus and Boris replied in unison.

"Neither?" Jada said, surprised.

Oreus repeated himself. "Yes, neither. Drift ships are built on Dondill Island, located southwest of Salmus. It is an independent region ruled by a dictator named Haverdash. He only allows minimal trading with Salmus and Zonack."

"More like a tyrant if ya ask me," Boris grumbled. "Knows he's got an advantage over both kingdoms because of the wood he supplies to make tha ships. There's nothin' stronger or more flexible when wet than mullin wood. Not even hyan fir." Boris tapped on Oreus's bow when he mentioned the hyan trees. The Baron had rested the elegant weapon on the table in front of him before he sat down. Boris finished, "The closest thing I've found in Yawrana that resembles mullin trees are juke spruce. It's a good thing they're in abundance, otherwise, tha Baron here wouldn't have himself a ship. Juke spruce just hasn't been tested over the long haul. We don't know if it'll hold together or not. Mullin's been known to take tha best beatin' a storm can throw at it."

"It has been tested already," Jada said.

"When?" Boris asked.

"Four thousand years ago, when a sailing ship set out with an Elder and many guards aboard to learn of the language and customs of Zonack. It should hold at least a hundred years."

Oreus acknowledged the statement, having just learned some of the details of Elder Harland Ghere's voyage to prepare for the prophecy that carried his name. "The Oreus Prophecy. Their ship was in the water the entire time on their journey. Juke spruce will hold up just fine, Boris."

"Then ya've got yarself a ship that's unsinkable," Boris laughed, slapping Oreus on the shoulder. Oreus felt as if his eyes almost popped out of their sockets.

"No ship is unsinkable," Noran scoffed. "There are more dangers than just storms that can bring one down."

Boris nodded. "Of carse, Yar Majesty. Now, why such interest in Salmus? Have the Elders seen somethin' in the waters that we need to prepare for?"

"Preparation was not on our side this time," Blaynor said, making his voice heard for the first time. "There are three Salmus ships docked in Drana Bay at this very moment."

Oreus and Boris immediately sat up straight and then leaned forward with anticipation to hear more. Swallowing hard, Oreus soaked in what Jada said to them. They looked at the golden-haired Baron as if she were the only one who existed in the room. Her lips seemed to move in slow motion until she finished everything that had happened up to then.

"We estimate there are at least a hundred men aboard each ship and a captain at the wheel of each: Soar, Winslow and Rollins. Do any of these names sound familiar to either of you?" Noran asked.

Boris pounded his fist on the table, rattling the few dishes present that contained fruit and wine. "Shut out the draft!"

"Excuse me?" Jada asked.

The barbarian chuckled. "Winslow? Hah! Now there's a man with a grudge."

"Explain, blacksmith," Noran prodded.

"Winslow lost *The Star Gazer* to Lanu over a game of high card draw."

Jada replied in shock, "One game of cards? A ship like that?"

Bruneau smiled, looking satisfied that his intuition about Winslow and Lanu's relationship had been proven correct.

Boris continued, "It was not even a game. One card was all it took. Lanu turned the table on 'im. Drew the only card possible that could have beat Winslow. I doubt it was luck. I had the feelin' Lanu had that extra king up his sleeve. Winslow is a gambler, through and through. When he's in a tight spot, he'll revert to his own games to get his way. Did it with Lanu twice before Lanu caught on and got his revenge. Winslow had never lost a hand up until that day. Was quite bitter when he was forced to watch one of his prized ships sail out of Grand Isle. I'll never ferget Lanu's face—could've erupted Mount Grim with that mocking smile. Hah!"

Oreus smirked, knowing Lanu was never one to be outdone in anything. The Captain would eventually get even with anyone who crossed him, one way or another. This was the first time he had heard of how *The Star Gazer* came into Lanu's possession. He originally assumed it was built by Queen Rimshaw's shipmakers, but now that was just another lie his mind had come to believe about the Captain and his made-up legends. Lanu was no more than a common man with an uncanny resourcefulness to create false impressions toward men who would willingly die for his own hidden indulgences.

Tapping his index finger on the table, Noran said, "There is one other item we should mention, Boris." The blacksmith ran his fingers through his thick, straight black beard and listened. "There is a barbarian with them as well, Windreed Sinker of the Lake Fog Clan. Ever hear of her?"

Boris's teeth slammed together so hard they rattled his entire jaw. Jada backed up a step when the barbarian crashed his fist down onto the table's surface, causing three long cracks to rupture from where his fist had impacted the thick wood. The loud crack could be heard from the hallway and the floor vibrated. "Sinker! That hag! She took me brother Boony for a fool."

"How so?" Rydor asked.

"Boony was set on marryin' her. He had to give up half 'is belongings just to appease the Chief of the Lake Fog Clan for her hand. When the vows were to be taken, she left him standin' to face the risin' sun alone. The Chief cursed Boony for scarin' off his daughter and bringin' the clan bad luck, and then banned him from Lake Fog Clan lands to keep all the possessions he had given up. But Boony didn't go without a fight. He managed to steal three of their warhorses and the clan's symbol of pride: a golden skull that was said to ward off spirits of tha dead—evil ones. It caused an all out war between the Shale Buck and Lake Fog Clans. I imagine the resentment still carries on to this day. But takin' those things still wasn't enough to replace what had been stolen from Boony—'is heart. He loved her like no other. Her betrayal caused him to pull stake and leave Phyre Heights forever. Me youngest brother Dale and meself went after him. Never did find where he ended up. After seven years of hunting, Dale and I decided it was best just not to go back to our lands. It woulda been shameful showin' up there without 'im."

Rydor questioned further, seeing the memory was eating Boris up inside. "Did you ever learn why Windreed left Boony?"

"Nah. Some of me family suspected she was carryin' another Lake Fog Clan member's child. She didn't have a little one with 'er, did she?"

Noran shook his head when Boris glanced his way.

"Bloody coward and a liar she is. Wait till I get a 'old of 'er!"

Rydor looked to Noran with a frown, understanding the dynamics of the situation had changed greatly with Boris's depth of knowledge about the new voyagers. Jada put a hand on Boris's shoulder and rubbed it gently to ease his agitation. His face remained red and the muscles in his back knotted even tighter, despite her effort.

"Have you reached a decision, Your Majesty?" Rydor asked, wanting to know the King's judgment. "You just said yourself that the watchers have reported they overheard Winslow and his men wondering if there was anything else here that could be of use to them besides treasure. Is that not enough to deny them camp here any longer?"

"What do you know of Winslow and his men, Oreus?" Noran asked.

"He knows nothin' of 'em," Boris responded for the Baron. "Oreus wasn't aroun' when the Captain won tha *Gazer*. There's nothin' of any use that lot can do for us 'ere. Winslow is jus' a little slippier than Lanu when it comes to negotiatin'."

Jada said, "Perhaps we should reconsider and consult the Elders, Your Majesty. Something doesn't seem right about all of this. No visions about their visits . . . ."

"No," Noran said, cutting her off. "I've heard enough. Boris's advice is sound. His judgment has saved us more than one time before. It's time I start listening to the wisdom of barbarians when it comes to determining who our enemies are." The King smiled at Boris. The blacksmith turned a deep shade of red from ear to ear. "If the Elders were meant to see their arrival, then they would be with us here, now."

Oreus shifted in his chair as if he wanted to say something, but decided to remain silent and nodded.

"Bring the Captains back into the main dining hall, Nonny," Jada ordered the female guard standing near Noran. "Have them there by sunset." The guard bowed and left in a hurry, accidentally slamming the door a little too hard on her way out. Oreus jumped at the loud bang as if an explosion went off in his mind.

"Are you feeling well?" Ola whispered.

Oreus shrugged and looked out the small, circular window to the outside world. A bird flew past in a flurry of wings, which reminded him of the increasing and fluttering tension in his stomach. What doom did these voyagers carry?

The hall was void of any servants this time and the dining table of any food. The voyagers were already waiting by the time Noran entered with his long and heavy, flowing green robe, outlined with white ruffles. His glorious crown sat on his head to enforce his commanding presence upon the unwanted visitors once again. Oreus, Ola and their guards sat along one wall while Rydor, Jime, Jada and a dozen other guards stood behind the Salmus group. The only men that appeared nervous among the voyagers were Captain Eason Soar and his three men, Her, Gen and Trus. Captain Ave Winslow, Captain Sage Rollins, Windreed Sinker and Thorn all remained calm, as if they could read Noran's decision before he even started speaking.

The court announcer, Thom, was only able to say a few words before Winslow broke in to spoil the verdict. "Salmus voyagers, His Majesty, King Noran Deardrop regret—"

"We know what the King wishes," Winslow blurted out.

Thom's tongue became tied, unsure of how to react to the Captain's outburst. He waited for Winslow to finish, but when no words came, Thom began repeating his last few words, "His Majesty, King Noran Deardrop regretfully must—"

Purposely cutting him off a second time to make Thom feel more uncomfortable, Winslow stated, "You still feel ill toward us because of the damage Lanu and his men have left, don't you, Your Majesty?"

Bruneau looked at Blaynor, who inched closer to Noran because of Winslow's unusual reaction. The guards weren't sure what to expect, but were ready for action, nonetheless.

"Captain Lanu once tried to take my people's wealth and now you desire the very same," Noran replied in an unwavering voice. "I don't take comfort in hosting thieves under my roof."

"You are correct, Your Majesty," Winslow stated, fully admitting his intentions. Captain Soar looked at Winslow confused, appearing not to know what his peer was talking about. "In fact, Your Highness, your caution deserves applause. I will not lie like that snake Lanu, or any of the company of rats he was associated with. If you don't mind me asking, where did Lanu and his men go after they left here?"

Oreus glanced at Boris. The barbarian was chuckling as a result of

Winslow's comment. The Baron felt his anger wash away quickly when he saw the barbarian wasn't taking the Captain seriously. However, Windreed Sinker, on the other hand, became stiff when Boris entered the room, noticing Boony's striking similarities in Boris's features. She never quit gritting her teeth the moment their eyes met. Boris didn't sit the entire time, supplying Noran's company with an impressive force of strength that couldn't be easily dismissed. Boris told Noran that he wasn't going to sit in the presence of Sinker at any given time. To do so would mean her actions were excused and forgiven by Boony's family and clan. It also would signify her clan's strength over Boris's in the midst of a political situation, something Boris wasn't about to let her achieve. His form was as solid as a rock in the corner where he stood.

Winslow was astounded when he first saw Boris enter, but then recovered his aplomb by forming his mouth into a straight line.

The King spoke loudly to make his words feel like knives jabbing into Winslow's confidence. "*The Star Gazer* and its former crew have been disbanded. Yawrana the Maker has filled a seat with Lanu's soul in the Underworld. Several of his other men are also deceased and others sit in dungeon cells to pay for their ill deeds."

"What of the barbarian with you?" Captain Rollins growled. "He is not of these lands. How has he won your favor?" Windreed's eyes narrowed into slits as she stared Boris down. Boris didn't budge, grimacing with hatred for Boony's sake.

"Boris Groffen proved his worth by saving my life," Noran replied. "He is an honorable man and saw Lanu's actions for what they were in the end: a mistake."

"And what of his ship—*The Star Gazer*?" Winslow asked with hope in his voice. "What have you done with it?"

Noran could see the lust for Winslow's lost ship return in the Captain's eyes. In a satisfied tone, he said, "It lives in the shallows along the Valiona Shores, broken like a toy in Gillwood Territory. The sea has claimed it for its own ravenous appetite, slowly devouring the wood planks one by one. It is no more than a decoration for my embittered people to admire. One should not ever forget the pain of the past."

Winslow shook his head, openly disappointed, and bit on his tongue until it started to bleed. "If we see something we like, we do not need to steal it, Your Majesty. That is where Lanu and I differ. You see, we forged a wager the last time we met."

Noran cut Winslow off this time and spoke directly to Boris, "Is this true?"

"The barbarian was not present at the time the wager was done," Winslow replied hastily. "This was a silent agreement that was made only between Lanu and me. Whoever was to find new land first and bring back proof in assets was to gain the right of prominent court presentation in both Salmus and Zonack."

"Prominent court presentation? Collecting on dues for notable services rendered?" Oreus asked out loud.

Winslow looked surprised that the new face he had not seen with the King earlier suddenly had an opinion. "Yes."

"Prominent presentation means only one thing in Zonack," Oreus said, "to acquire the land rights of poor villagers and farmers who can't afford to pay the courts' high taxes."

"Should I be aware of your name, sir?" Winslow snapped back uncharacteristically, having been called on the delicate point of a subject he was trying to avoid altogether.

"Oreus Blake. I was also part of Captain Lanar Lanu's crew at one time."

Winslow's eyes slid down to the green cloth tied around Oreus's arm and acknowledged, "I don't recall you being part of his crew, but I see you have achieved even higher recognition in Yawrana than your barbarian friend since you wear a band of the Yawranan Court. Your regional accent lends you to being of Zonack birth. What station have you ascended from there?"

"None. I was born on a farm near Beggar's Square. I come from a community in the flood plains of the Lowland Divisions—specifically, Uthan Mire."

"Uthan Mire?" Winslow replied, fighting back tears of laughter.

"Do you have something against Uthan Mire?" Oreus growled, hearing the dissension in the Captain's voice.

Winslow pretended to cough and cleared his throat. His voice portrayed a serious tone but Oreus knew otherwise. "Of course not, Mr. Blake. If one were to make a dramatic change in living styles, then Uthan Mire would be the ideal location to start from. Your persistence has apparently paid off . . . handsomely."

Oreus backed down, unable to think of a way to ignite an argument in defense of his poverty-stricken homelands. Ola kissed him on the cheek and glared at Winslow.

"Oh. I see," Winslow said, seeing Ola's peck. "That explains much."

Noran instantly became angry at the insinuation. "There is much you do not know about Baron Blake or the trials he has endured! You have no right—"

"Have you ever gambled, Your Majesty?" Winslow said before Noran was in a full rage.

"What?" Noran retorted, now angrier for being interrupted than for the subtle mockery of Oreus and Ola's loving relationship.

"Gambling. Have you ever played a hand?" Winslow started to pull a deck of cards from his ragged overcoat when Boris rolled his eyes toward Noran as a warning.

The King took the hint and decided enough was enough. "It's time you leave these lands and never step foot here again, Captain Winslow. Take your men and be gone."

Winslow acted shocked, but it was a poor performance. "But we have hardly had enough time for rest. My men are in no condition to take on the Sea of Racorn in their state. You know how rough the waters are, Your Majesty. The blower engines alone need cleaning. Improper maintenance can lead to their failure."

"It's no longer our concern, Captain. We have given you more than ample provisions for survival."

"Engines only take a day to clean," Boris intervened. "Your men should've had that taken care of by now."

Noran nodded at Boris for his valuable insight in a critical moment. Boris smiled and inflated with pride.

Winslow slowly grinned and looked at the other two captains. Rollins held firm and Soar was a nervous wreck, wanting to be on his way. Winslow continued, "You know there are more ships in existence, like the three you currently have floating in Drana Bay, Your Majesty. There are at least twenty new drift ships being made every year now. In time, they will all find their way here. It is inevitable. You can't stop progress and you surely can't hide from the rest of the world. Will you refuse everyone who sails here a stay in your kingdom?"

Not batting an eyelash, Noran said in a resounding tone, "Yes!"

"That's impossible, Your Majesty. Impossible . . . unless—"

"Don't play games with the King, Winslow. You're about to be thrown out," Rydor grumbled.

"And the hero speaks," Winslow said, glancing at Rydor. The Captain turned back toward Noran. "Your Majesty, a game is just what I had in mind, a simple one, nothing more. Are you familiar with High Card Draw?"

"Lanu was," Boris chuckled. "Too bad he isn't here to deal you another round."

Winslow ignored the comment and continued, "No? How about Kings and Jesters?"

"I will not entertain your card tricks," Noran stated flatly. "You have nothing that I don't already possess."

Winslow grinned again and replied, "There is one thing, Your Highness: peace of mind. Wouldn't you sleep more soundly at night knowing I was going to tell every ship merchant between Dondill Island and Phyre Heights that there is no habitable land beyond the known boundaries of the west? At the very least it would buy you more time to set up reasonable defenses along your shore that couldn't be as easily penetrated . . . as they are now."

"We could jus' toss ya in a cell and be done with ya, too," Boris yelled. "Then ya can't run yar trap at all."

"Imprisoning me will get you nowhere," Winslow said. "My men have been ordered to pull anchor and sail at midnight if we don't return to our ships by then. They'll bring reinforcements and put this kingdom on its knees in time. Your riches will be learned of, with or without me."

The room was dead silent after Winslow made his threat. Bruneau and Blaynor waited patiently for Noran to give his orders. The King glared across the long dining table at his adversary. He finally spoke, "How much time do you need?"

Boris's jaw dropped, unable to understand why the King was giving in to Winslow's demands. "Yar Majesty, ya don' need to cower to this pail of curdled puke—"

"Silence, blacksmith." Noran shouted, finding his description revolting and disruptive. Redirecting his attention back to Winslow, the King repeated, "How do I know you'll keep your word? I have no guarantee that you will do anything you say."

"I am honorable when it comes to betting, Your Majesty. If I wasn't, I would have never let Captain Lanu sail out of Grand Isle with the most coveted ship ever built in its time. *The Star Gazer* was a prize for which many would have risked their lives to steal. Understand, it was one of the first of its kind and meant prestige for the one who steered its wheel. Lanu rose to great acclaim and gained rapid favor from Queen Rimshaw because of it. His name was put on a pedestal the day Zonack's court learned of his ingenuity. In my position, it was very difficult to cope with, for it cost me many valuable missions. Lanu won the hand and the ship, and, therefore, the agreement was solid. If I wanted her again, I could have taken her back at any given time."

Boris growled and Oreus snorted, both finding the insinuation insulting.

Noran asked again, "How much time do you require, Captain Winslow?"

Winslow grinned and said, "Two weeks, or daysets as you call them here, Your Majesty. During that time I would like to request that my men be able to walk ashore and stretch their legs. Also, they will need three meals a day so they do not reduce the supplies we have just restored. In return for your generosity, this place will never exist on any map in Zonack, Dondill Island or Salmus . . . or anywhere else I roam. . . as long as I live."

Chewing his lower lip, Noran thought about the offer good and long before making his declaration. Oreus and Ola were getting worried that the King would explode at any given moment with the growing tension in the hall. Bruneau tapped his index finger on his staff and Blaynor tightened his grip around the handle of his. Rydor edged in closer behind Winslow. Thorn turned casually and raised the edge of his lip with the pierced hook through it, inviting the General to come closer. But Rydor stopped just out of range to prevent igniting a fight.

"Explain Kings and Jesters," Noran suddenly commanded, cracking the frozen air with his stern voice.

"As you wish, Your Majesty," Winslow said with a nod. After pulling out a short stack of blue cards no larger than his palm, he set them in a neat pile at the edge of the table and said, "It is similar to High Card Draw, in the respect that the King, the highest card in a Zonack deck, automatically wins if pulled. The jester, of course, is the doom mark. Cards are picked until one or the other surfaces. It's as simple as that."

Noran thought a moment and then ordered, "Bring your deck here, Captain."

Winslow rose slowly from the table. Before he proceeded forward, he put out a hand to prevent Thorn from following. Then, he pivoted and strode toward the King. He was stopped a few feet short of Noran when Blaynor interceded and took the cards from the Captain's hand. Blaynor scanned the backside of the top card quickly and saw a circle of fins swimming in an ocean on it. He then flipped the set over and fanned them out on the table with a wave of his fingers. Carefully inspecting each one, he noticed there were three Kings and one jester present in the flayed pile. Winslow reached down, plucked out two of the Kings and placed them back within his overcoat. Satisfied they all had been thoroughly examined, Blaynor restacked the deck into a neat pile.

"You may shuffle them if you desire it, Your Majesty," Winslow encouraged.

Noran, instead, waved to Blaynor to do it for him. The guard picked the stack back up and mixed them eight times before he was satisfied the king and jester were as randomly hidden as they could be. Blaynor set the deck on the table and fanned them out again.

Leaning toward the corner of the table and watching Winslow intently, Noran said, "You first, Captain."

"Ya should reconsider, Yar Majesty!" Boris exclaimed. "He may know where the king is right now."

Noran sighed and said, "Very well, blacksmith. Your judgment hasn't led me astray yet." Ola and Orcus approached the table and saw Noran go to the center of the arc and grab the corner of one that stood out a hair further than the rest. Exhaling, he turned it over to reveal a number nine emblazoned on the shield of a knight.

"Excellent pick, Your Majesty," Winslow said, amused.

"How is that excellent?" Noran asked.

"If you're not going to draw the king, then anything else is better than the jester."

Noran frowned and waited as Winslow reached down to pull the card furthest to the left. A loud scraping sound made everyone turn his or her head in the direction of Thorn. He had pulled a heavy chair from the table to sit down. The bare-chested guard cleared his throat and cracked his neck out of boredom. When everyone had returned their attention back to Winslow's pick, a great relief quickly swept over every Yawranan present. A pair of snakes was wrapped loosely around a number two in the center of the image.

The King reached for a card at the opposite end, but Blaynor cleared his throat just before the King touched it. Noran didn't know whether or not to interpret the noise as a disagreement from his guard or to believe Blaynor actually was hoarse.

"Perhaps you should get a glass of water," Winslow suggested to Blaynor, appearing disgruntled.

"It's just an itch at the back of the pipe," Blaynor replied, not wanting to leave the tableside for a moment.

Noran reached for it again anyway and turned it face up. A red seven with a castle in the background made Ola gasp. She could hardly deal with her own anxiety.

Winslow pulled a blue eight sitting in a golden tree next. The King followed with a sword that looked like the number one. The Captain and Noran started to turn cards faster and faster the more the king and jester eluded them. Noran was beginning to feel flustered and wanted the game to just end. But it continued on at a harrowing pace until there were only three cards left. No one could believe almost the entire deck had been gone through without either the king or jester being exposed

"Before I draw again, Your Majesty, may I double the offer?"

Winslow asked.

Noran didn't say anything, which Winslow took as an invitation to speak his mind.

"I assume when you allow my men to come to shore that they will not be able to leave the beach area, including those of us in this room after we finish this draw. Am I correct?"

Noran nodded and listened.

"I have no interest in letting any of the men back at the ships come any further into shore. However, the Captains and I, and our few close associates in this hall, would like to see more of Yawrana from an admiration standpoint."

"Ya don' 'ave any need to be gallavantin' about—"

"Boris!" Noran warned a second time. The barbarian blushed.

"And what for my people?" Noran asked.

Winslow smiled and waved forth Captain Rollins. After several exchanges of whispers, Rollins nodded and returned to the end of the table. "I shall give you the barbarian woman," Winslow proclaimed.

Windreed yelled, "Captain, what are you—"

"Say, 'Yes,' Yar Majesty," Boris begged, coming to the edge of the table.

Noran smiled at the blacksmith's comical and expected reaction.

Winslow finished, "I think we have both been enlightened as to the two barbarians' history with each other. You can do with her as you wish. She may even prove herself worthy once she shows proper forgiveness . . . ."

"No," Windreed whined, turning to Rollins with pleading eyes. Rollins didn't look at her, holding up the back of his hand to silence her protests.

"I accept," Noran said. Boris clapped his hands together and rubbed them excitedly. "Your turn, Captain." His tongue fell out of his mouth like a dog awaiting a well-deserved bone.

Winslow bent over and judged the three cards. He extended his hand for the one closest to Noran and flipped it up. A murmur ran through the room. Three sharks swam around the displayed number, which was half-submerged in the water. Three was considered good luck to whoever held it in any hand in Zonack. Oreus also was aware of this omen and clenched his fists.

"Two left, Your Majesty. I must say this has been intriguing, to say the least," Winslow said smugly. "I don't think anyone has ever played Kings and Jesters to its fullest that I am aware of. Our fates now lie in your choice."

Noran looked at Oreus, Ola, and Boris, and then at his guards, Bruneau and Blaynor, for help, but none of them had any idea which one he should choose. Winslow buttoned a sleeve on his coat that had come undone and waited patiently.

The King gazed up at the Captain with a disconcerting appearance, prying into his thoughts for what he might know about the two cards remaining. Winslow held the face of a statue, non-breathing. Closing his eyes and putting his fingers forward, Noran slid the card furthest from him across the table toward his body. Saying a silent prayer to the Maker, he ended the game and listened for a response. When there was none, he opened his eyes and saw a face with a green and gold bell hat, similar to the appearance of his father's ex-court jester Kuall, staring up at him.

Kuall had betrayed Noran's parents through a slow-acting poison. His father had perished because of it, but Noran and Oreus had found the elusive snowtear to save his mother. The rare and curative flower resided in the Waungee Grasslands, former home of the Lazul race. Kuall's reason for his betrayal was personal. He had eventually grown tired of his role as a court entertainer. He felt he had played the fool too long, and had become disgruntled toward his King and kingdom. No one ever expected Kuall to turn to murder, until they learned his role would change and he would be rewarded with riches beyond his imagination if he helped Baron Johr Karagas of Dowhaven Territory in his plot to overthrow the throne. Johr had also grown weary of the old ways of Yawrana and its laws, desiring to twist the land and its resources for what he considered better uses. But to ascend to the throne, Johr had to also kill Noran. As a result, Kuall was hung and Johr was banished and eventually killed in the frigid ice lands of Arna. But here was the jester again, in another form, to laugh at the King for being foolish enough to play the game.

"Damn it," Noran growled, pushing away the card. Everyone in the room was shocked and horrified, wondering what the King was thinking. The doom card looked malevolent as its hideous eyes bored into Noran. He picked it up and flung it away in anger. "Bah."

Windreed breathed a sigh of relief while Boris punched a fist into the palm of his other hand and cursed.

Blaynor bent over to look at the last card, the king, but Winslow had collected it and put it with the others before he had the chance. The Captain didn't look at the guard when he put the deck inside his coat. Blaynor glanced at Noran, who realized he should have looked at it as well.

Winslow turned to Captains Soar and Rollins and ordered, "Tell the men to drop anchor. We will be staying for an extended period of time. Two weeks precisely."

The Captains nodded and left with their own protectors. Only Thorn remained behind temporarily, curling his hooked lip in satisfaction so Rydor could see it.

"He knew I would pick the wrong card. He somehow knew it!" Noran shouted in Jada's private meeting room.

"He couldn't have known, Your Majesty," Jada rebutted. "All the other cards were gone. He made many incorrect choices himself . . . ."

Blaynor mentioned, "There was something peculiar about the way he played the game."

"What?" Noran asked, desperate to know.

The guard hesitated before saying, "It's almost as if he wanted the game to drag on, to make you feel confident in your chances of winning, Your Majesty—as if he was trying to not offend you."

"And yet he waited until the time was right and even left the final choice up to me," Noran said. "I drew the wrong card, not him."

"Which makes me feel all the more suspicious, my Lord," Blaynor added. "I couldn't find a trace of doubt anywhere in his expressions that he thought he was going to lose the match. He was not concerned that he wouldn't succeed."

Noran nodded in agreement. "Yes. I felt it too. He could have cheated, but I don't know how. You looked at the cards . . . ."

Rydor entered the room last, informing everyone, "Captain Winslow wishes to have a tour of Candlewick Castle, my Lord."

The King sat down and contemplated what he should do, but his word as a man was only as good as he proved it to be. "Baron Blake," Noran said, turning to Oreus, "I would very much like it if you would accompany our guests during their stay in Yawrana. You are most familiar with the people of Salmus and can give them the attention they require, while keeping a close eye on them. I have more important matters on my mind than dealing with them."

"Yes, Your Majesty," Oreus said with a nod.

"I can also help—" Boris started until the King interrupted.

"No, blacksmith. The conflict between you and Windreed is too great and may lead you both down a path I cringe thinking about. Please return to your forge and release your anger through hammer and anvil. Do not approach the voyagers during their stay here at any time."

Boris's face turned red, then purple. He looked as if he would pass out from lack of oxygen until Noran's comforting voice forced him to breathe, expanding his lungs like balloons in his chest.

"Please, blacksmith, understand. There will be another place and time for you to consult Windreed about her actions. Now is not it. If she has wronged your brother, then Yawrana the Maker will find a way to bring justice full circle."

The barbarian nodded, rose and left the room to cool off. Blaynor was about to go after him when Noran said, "Let him be. He will do as I have asked him to. Boris's allegiance is not something to worry about."

"I'm not so certain, Your Majesty," Oreus said. "A barbarian's lust for revenge can exceed any expectations you have of him. They never forget those who wrong them and will do almost anything for their clan's honor."

Noran sighed, looking hopeful that that wouldn't be what it would come to. "Baron Blake, have at least a dozen guards with you at all times in their presence. Give them rooms in the castle near the Gaming Arena stables. Perhaps the stench of manure will make them want to depart sooner." Everyone in the room laughed at the joke, even though it was truly an order and the stables did smell strongly.

"I believe several just became available," Oreus said, chuckling.

"Baron Annalee," Noran said, now looking at Jada. "Ensure the beaches remain secure at all times. Any man who steps on shore I want accounted for. I don't want any of them sneaking off into the forests and spying on us for information. The Shonitaurs would have been useful to me now. We could have had them wipe Winslow's and his men's memories and put them on course for Arna."

"I shall have the watchers roam the forests around Drana Bay as well, my Lord," she stated. "Any man caught trying to slip past the guards will be imprisoned immediately until Winslow and his sordid crew are ready to set sail."

"Your Majesty," Rydor said with a worried look on his face, "do you believe Winslow's admonition?"

"About other ships? Absolutely. One thing he was right about, we need to prepare for the arrival of the rest of the world on our front doorstep. When word spreads we exist and have untapped riches for the taking, maddons will be howling outside our door faster than you know. I don't believe we can maintain our current state of defenses and realistically survive against a more advanced age of weapons."

Jada crossed her arms, seeing where the King was leading. "You wish to abandon staffs and swords for more explosive and destructive armaments?

We would become more dangerous than the Lazuls, and our children—"

"It pains me as well, Jada. A warrior race is not what I want us to be, but we will have no children to keep safe if we do not take preventative measures. There will be a call to counsel on this subject the day after the voyagers return home. We must do what's necessary before it's too late."

Discussions about the voyagers went on for several more hours. Rydor gave his analysis of each of the voyagers and their fighting skills, intelligence and potential to cause problems. Winslow headed the list as the one to be most aware of, which Noran already suspected. The Captain had already proven himself as the most resourceful and clever of the bunch. Rydor considered Thorn the most dangerous because of his outstanding muscular physique, which he prominently showed by not wearing a shirt. Men who were willing to flaunt their strength tended to be unpredictable and deadly. Rollins and Windreed posed mild issues while Soar and his three men, Her, Gen and Trus, were not worthy enough of consideration to cause any great harm. Noran thanked Rydor for his thoughts, ending the meeting at last.

Oreus waited until everyone left the room, including Ola and Quinn, so he could confront the King alone. Bruneau and Blaynor remained at Noran's side as usual until Oreus requested them to leave as well.

"We can't do that, Baron Blake" Bruneau replied. "The King must have a guard with him at all times, by Yawranan law."

"Then can one of you leave?" he asked.

"What information do you have to tell me that is too sensitive for their ears?" Noran questioned.

"I'm . . . I'm afraid to say, my Lord."

"Afraid?" Noran said, surprised. "Am I still talking to the same fearless Oreus Blake who survived the crystal cavern, defeated the demon under the mountain and fought by his King's side time and again?"

Oreus nodded.

"Bruneau, please step outside." The guard frowned. Blaynor was a slightly better fighter than Bruneau and had one extra year of service under his belt.

"Yes, Your Majesty," Bruneau complied. He nudged Blaynor in the shoulder on the way out as a signal for Blaynor to tell him the rest later. Blaynor nodded and smirked.

Once the door clicked shut, Noran asked, "Speak freely, Baron. Your request for isolation worries me."

"And for good reason it should, my Lord," he stated bluntly. "I believe I'm the one responsible for the voyagers' arrival without previous warning."

# CHAPTER THREE
## The Water Glass

Being called to Candlewick in the middle of the night was not necessarily an unusual occurrence for Barons Windal Barrow and Viktoran Ilos. But the reason for which they were notified this time was. Never before were the Barons beckoned by the King to discuss the weather's implications on the territories. It was such a simple topic that neither of them thought it was worthy enough to take time out of their busy schedules to discuss it in great detail with Noran, although it did start to downpour again when they thought about complaining.

They were both puzzled to find Noran was not at the castle when they actually did arrive, missing him by only a few hours. They learned of his mysterious and unexpected trip to Emison through Troy Fields, General of The Royal House Territory. When Noran would return was unknown, leading to their impatience and desire to return to their own towers. The other barons had not yet arrived, making them wonder if they had come too quickly. But they knew their duties well and would drop anything at anytime at the King's request. Since the circumstances had changed, both men sat idly in the gardens near the Gaming Arena within the castle's walls, determining what excuses they could use so they could leave—that was, until a castle guard disrupted their thoughts with an urgent message.

"Baron Ilos. Baron Barrow. I'm glad you're both here."

"Where else would we be?" Viktoran said grumpily. "This is where we were called to meet with the King."

The guard brushed off the Baron's cold response and explained, "What I mean is, there is someone at the Western Gate requesting to see either of you."

"Who?" Windal and Viktoran replied in unison.

"I'm not sure. The individual is dressed in a white hooded robe. He initially requested to speak with the King, but since His Majesty is not present, the stranger requested to see any one of the Barons."

"Did you ask for him to shed his garments so he could be searched?" Viktoran asked to ensure the castle's guards were following standard entry procedures.

The guard slowed his speaking now that he had caught his breath. "He wouldn't let us, Baron Ilos. He kept muttering something about indecent formalities. We then asked him the purpose of his request. He wouldn't tell us that either, and said he didn't want to waste time with those who were of little importance."

Viktoran reminded the guard, "No man or woman may wander inside the castle's walls with the hood of their robe up, not even a priest. For all we know, it could be Herikech Illeon trying to pull some kind of trick to kill a member of the Royal Court. I hope you sent soldiers out to detain him."

"We were going to . . . but he threatened to leave if we did. The moment we started opening the gate, he disappeared into the forest. Several guards went out to search for him but had no luck in determining his location. When they came back empty-handed and unharmed, we grew suspicious. We were about to summon General Fields and inform him of the bizarre occurrence when the individual made a second appearance. He reiterated the same requests, this time in an upset manner, making it perfectly clear he would only speak to someone in a real position of power. He paced back and forth as if trying to decide what to do next. It was not Herikech, though, Baron Ilos. This wanderer was too short to be a Lazul."

Both barons looked at each other and then back at the guard, intrigued. "It could also be a follower of Herikech's," Windal said. "There are more than enough creatures obeying his commands these days."

"Get the first rank archers up on the walls right now," Viktoran ordered. "Both of us will go out to greet him. It will be safer having two against one. Whoever it is, I will not allow him to have control over the situation. We can't afford to have a raving lunatic roaming about the Western Yard. Any sign of trouble, shoot him immediately."

The guard saluted Viktoran with a fist to his chest and responded, "Yes, Baron." The man left in a hurry, ready to carry out his task.

"Any thoughts of which it might really be?" Windal said, whittling away at Viktoran's thoughts.

Viktoran pressed two fingers against his right temple and surmised, "Maybe this person is not an adult, but a Lazul child perhaps? They are the only ones foolish enough to dare demand the King or a Baron to come to them on even footing."

"What if he has a weapon and plans to kill us?"

Viktoran chuckled light-heartedly. "Then let him try. He will not succeed. However, I have a feeling this individual has concerns that his voice is not being heard, and therefore is taking extra measures to make certain that it will be. He might have information on Herikech's whereabouts and doesn't want any ears to overhear what he has to say. Whatever his reason for being here, it's time we learned it."

The Barons, each with their own guard at their side, left the castle gardens behind, and passed through the Gaming Arena. They walked at a steady pace down to the inner gate. After they were let out, they crossed the moat to reach the outer gate and waited until the archers were hidden and in position. The guard who had related his message waved to them to signal they were ready. Viktoran returned the gesture and signaled for the outer gate to be lifted. The chains rattled until they were pulled taught and wound through the gears. The heavy weight of the iron portcullis caused it to creak as it slowly cranked upward. Viktoran and Windal both unsheathed their swords the moment they saw the individual standing on the other side.

"You two stay here," Viktoran said, pointing at the two guards with them.

They both nodded and went to each side of the gate, drawing their swords but staying from sight so the stranger wouldn't see them.

"Stay where you are!" Viktoran yelled at the white hooded figure, which was taking his first step forward.

The stranger did not comply, walking directly beneath the gate itself, putting himself out of the archers' views.

Flustered he had not listened, Viktoran commanded, "Fall back outside the wall and lower your hood now, friend."

"I have not claimed to be your friend . . . yet," the stranger replied in a deep voice. "I will not put myself in a position to become an arrow pincushion!"

"Then I will slay you where you stand for not adhering to our safety concerns. Prepare for your death!"

Viktoran and Windal raised their swords as the Barons' two guards rushed from their hidden spots. The stranger suddenly yanked back his hood to stop both Barons and guards cold in their tracks. Windal's reaction was one of astonishment while Viktoran only raised an eyebrow in interest.

"Now that I have your undivided attention, I'm certain you wanti to know why a Nax has traveled such great distances and faced many dangers of the wild to visit the King of Yawrana," the stranger said.

"That would be a start," Windal replied, studying the albino figure from head to foot. His pink eyes were undeniably hypnotizing and the white, curly fur covering his head and body was as soft as a quilt. "The last Nax who came here was also an albino. He became a great leader among our people. However, his knowledge and friendship were recently lost."

"That can't be possible," the Nax stated in an unbelieving tone. "Mosia Mathis should have passed away ages ago."

"So you know of him," Windal said.

"Not only do I know of him, I am of the same blood."

Viktoran put away his weapon, wanting to dictate the questions from this point forward. "What is your relation?" Windal also dropped the tip of his sword to the ground and had no qualms with listening to the rest of the conversation.

"He was brother to a woman from whom I have descended, Pira. My name is Martell Fedrow and I have come to seek what Mosia found long ago."

"Which is what?" Viktoran asked.

"Deliverance," Martell shouted, raising both arms into the air, palms up.

"Deliverance?" Viktoran replied.

"Yes. I am an outcast of my people, just as Mosia once was. They fear me now as they feared him then. We are omens of evil. I am the next to appear since he left long ago."

Viktoran stated, "And what do *you* think you are?"

"That's what I came here to find out," Martell chortled. "The past holds the answers to the future, wouldn't you say? Eat the bread but don't toss out the crumbs."

"What?" Windal said.

Martell explained, "The crumbs—the leftovers—waste not what can still be useful. Even a crumb is a fit meal for a bird."

Finding wisdom in the phrase that Mosia would have appreciated, Viktoran offered, "What is it you wish to know about the High Elder?"

"Mosia was an Elder?"

Viktoran and Windal both nodded to confirm. "The head of the Elders' Order in fact," Viktoran said.

"Then he may have found the answers he sought. Rarely do humans risk the dangers of finding our dwellings in Overbay's chasm. The Elders and their powers have become known to us through the animals of the wood. Countless creatures have told us of their closeness to nature. Their wisdom is greatly revered in the Nax communities. But, I assure you, my people didn't know Mosia was one. Otherwise, they might have changed their opinions. Woodland creatures have no care for names. They only recognize features and the acts of humanoid forms. Funny they did not mention an Elder with white wings. Perhaps Mosia told them to never reveal his whereabouts and position to the people who banished him."

Windal finally asked, "Why do your people distrust albinos?"

"Would it not be best if we sit and discuss the rest inside? My legs are weary from the many roads I have traveled and the dangers I have overcome to be here."

"What about your wings?" Windal asked.

Martell scoffed, "I am not a bird! They are only good for short distances."

In agreement with Martell's request, Viktoran waved off the archers. After escorting the Nax safely indoors to the gardens, they sat on a circular bench to face one another in a triangle formation. A male servant approached them and inquired, "Does our new guest need food or drink, Barons?"

Martell removed his white cloak and let his white pair of wings flutter freely behind him. "Ahh. It does feel good to stretch them finally. I would gladly take bread and butter with a glass of water," he said, answering for Viktoran. The Nax's outfit was a deep brown underneath, trimmed in black at the cuffs and collar. A thick gold belt encircled his waist. From it hung a dagger and three pouches with unknown contents. A pair of boots caked with gobs of mud hugged his feet tightly and a sharp, black stone arrowhead hung from a chain around his neck. "The mention of bread earlier has made me rather hungry for a few slices." The servant nodded and was almost out of earshot when Martell said, "Make sure it's warm. Now, please tell me your names, Barons."

Viktoran smiled and said, "Viktoran Ilos, Baron of Serquist Territory. He is Baron Windal Barrow of the territory from which you have come. We are direct servants to His Majesty, Noran Deardrop."

Martell smiled at Windal and said, "So you are the new baron who controls everything within the boundaries of Overbay, including the Nax."

"No one can control the Nax because we can rarely find them," Windal said with a laugh.

"It is pleasant to see fruit that is unspoiled taking care of the ground under our feet—even if it is hard to reach."

"Unspoiled?"

Martell chuckled. "Yes. Sometimes age brings convolution. Do not take offense, Baron Ilos," Martell quickly added. "I can see your eyes do not yet hold it. They would be much more gray—clouded with delusions. Instead, with you, I see tints of green and red. You are in love, but jealous of another. Am I correct?"

Viktoran was astounded. Martell had identified his situation with Jada and Rydor exactly. "Ummm . . . even though you may see it, it does not mean it has a hold on me."

"That is good," Martell said, sighing. "Jealousy can be worse than delusions. It can blind men completely and lead to murder. Do not let it get that far."

Viktoran smiled. "You most definitely are of the High Elder's blood. You speak very much like him."

Unimpressed with the compliment, Martell replied, "I'm curious, Barons. How does one become an Elder?"

Windal responded to the question first, seeing the answer as one easy to explain, even though it was going to be rather lengthy. When he finished going as deep as the explanations for the colored bands of the Royal House and the anointments, Martell suddenly interrupted him.

"You are saying that he was given the title of an Elder because of a light reflection in a pool of water? That's ridiculous."

"Why?" Windal retaliated, acting as if he were being attacked.

"It's just too simple for something that seemed so complicated to achieve."

"It is the will of the land," Windal snapped, his voice becoming loud.

"It's ludicrous," Martell said, his voice now louder than Windal's. "You're talking about determining the fate of a person's life because of the way sunrays refract through water. How can you doom or idolize a person for something they have not achieved through their own hard work or lack of it? It's no worse than what my people have done to me. No wonder Mosia was so willing to accept your way of life."

Viktoran saw the servant coming with bread and water. He ordered them to turn around, leave the area, and not let anyone else in. Staring with a furrowed brow at Martell, he quibbled, "Do not judge our customs with a quick dismissal, Martell Fedrow. The Elder who administers the anointment has a special connection with the land's energy to be able to read the water's signs. It's not just about a simple ray of light at play here. The light that is cast emanates from within the individual's spiritual self. The color seen is drawn out when one is in the presence of an element, such as pure spring water. And since an Elder's soul is bound to a living organism, such as the sequeras, they can easily see the signs when they are revealed. The life force of all people tells of the abilities for which they were destined."

Martell flailed his hands about in frustration, unable to believe his ears. "Slow down. You're now saying that an Elder's soul is somehow tied to the soul of a tree?"

"Trees do not have souls, Martell, only spiritual energy. An Elder is connected to the tree's aura, or life force, giving the Elder the ability to live the lifespan of the tree. This explains why Mosia was able to live well beyond the normal years of a Nax."

Still unsatisfied, Martell took it a step further. "This process of binding sounds very confusing and has holes in it. You must fill them in for me, one by one if need be."

"It's not easy," Viktoran continued, "but I shall make it as clear as I can."

"Good. Now this is going to take some time so have that bread brought back." Martell's pink eyes pierced Viktoran like two swords as he waited.

Viktoran called for the servant at the door, happy Martell was now at least willing to listen. "As Windal was stating before, there are band colors representing each important faction of Yawranan society."

"Yes, yes, from the rainbow. What about white and black, or other colors such as brown, pink or tan?"

Frowning because he already had to back up a step, Viktoran said, "White bands represent commoners, while black symbolizes corruption. The other colors have never before been seen within the waters. Only the ones we have stated have been witnessed, which create the prismatic results of life's spectral, chosen colors."

"Chosen? I'm all too familiar with that term. I don't like it. And what's wrong with brown?" he asked, rubbing his hands up and down the front of his shirt and pants.

Ignoring his opinion, Viktoran moved on. "White represents the light from which the other colors are drawn, so it only makes sense that the large sum of individuals who are not chosen for a color wear it instead. Only the most worthy from the masses show their true inner selves during an anointment, and it is because of this ritual that Yawranans may be able to obtain a position of importance within the kingdom, no matter what their background may be. Even you may have the hidden power within you to be an Elder, Martell, if you so desired to be part of our society."

"I'm sure that's a role that is very demanding and requires extensive sacrifices."

"That's true," Windal said.

"It's too much of a responsibility for the few who carry the title," he snapped. "To never be able to marry and have children—what's the point of living?"

Viktoran gritted his teeth and Windal shook his head in frustration. Viktoran replied, "Any candidate who is presented a colored band may reject the responsibility, return to his or her own familiar life and do whatever he or she wishes."

Nodding, Martell said, "That is good. What about the bands? How do you know you have the right responsibility assigned to the right color? What if orange should really be for the army and blue should be for a Baron?"

"A fair question," Viktoran replied. "Each color's assignment was originally set when Yawrana was first founded. The rainbow was a symbol for the unification of the territories and our service to them. There were many tests created to verify the roles of the seven colors. They were difficult, wide-ranging, and well documented, ruling out any assumptions that were misconstrued. Our ancestors carefully determined how well any person anointed to a colored band would adapt to the different scenarios they encountered. Each situation was meant to draw out a unique ability that could only be natural to one specific color. If the hidden ability surfaced when it was intended to throughout the series of tests, which it did repeatedly according to historical records, it would confirm the individual possessed the same qualities as those assigned to the same color. These tests went on for nearly a decade before it was finally settled what each band was meant for. There were too many coincidences to be ignored. Green anointees behaved exactly the same as the others in their category during certain tests designed for their leadership talents. The same conclusions held true for the other colors as well, showing the relations between the colored bands and the people anointed to them were no fluke. Therefore, the stone foundations of our society were solidified for the future of our people."

Martell was quiet only for a few moments before he jumped on his next question, "And when Mosia, or any other Elder for that matter, was anointed to the indigo band, how then did he bind his soul to a sequera?"

"Another fair question, but a little harder to answer. The sequeras are the oldest trees in the land, living almost to fifteen hundred years of age. This makes them a logical choice for soul binding to extend the Elders' longevity. Their roots also go deep into the soil, and have a strong connection with the energy of the land." Viktoran paused and thought out his explanation before saying, "An Elder must sit with a sequera sapling and go through a starvation process that causes them to hallucinate until they can see the auras of everything around them. Human eyes alone aren't enough to perceive the auras on their own. The connection must be tapped into through the hidden recesses of the mind, paths that may only be opened to the living light when one's body is near extinction and the blood pounds for survival through one's veins. Vitality of life around us is no longer elusive when one is almost upon death. Everything is much more vivid and real."

"You talk almost as if you speak from experience," Martell said.

Viktoran nodded and finished. "As the Elder nears death, the sequera sapling is partially hollowed, which causes the tree to enter a weakened state. The proximity of the Elder and sequera's spirits causes them to reach out to each other for support, connecting in a bond of aid, nourishing each other's company until they grow together as one and are healthy again. The tree, unable to distinguish the Elder as another entity, willingly accepts the void within its trunk after it is hollowed, readily accepting the Elder as part of itself. After the binding is completed, the Elder's soul can feel the pain or sickness a tree would and vice versa. They are one and the Elder now has taken on many of the attributes they have never had. Each of their lives, in essence, has become dependant on the health state of the other. The closer they are in proximity, the more they act as one living, breathing being. The greater the distance they are separated, the weaker both become, feeling as if a part of their body is dying. The link between them becomes stretched too thin across space, making it difficult for either to properly function. And the longer they are apart, the quicker they can fall ill and succumb to death. It is not uncommon to see an Elder collapse, faint or get sick when they are outside of their tree for an extended period of time. When a sequera or Elder is killed or injured, the other will suffer the exact same fate, claiming them both."

"How did Mosia pass away?" Martell asked solemnly.

Windal jumped in. "He died from the hands of an arsonist who set flame to his dwelling. Mosia would have lived as long as the tree remained standing, if that were meant to be."

"Could the tree not have lived the age of Mosia instead, shortening its own lifespan through the binding process?" Martell challenged.

Windal shook his head. "No. It was the Elder who reached out and let himself be accepted as part of the sequera, so he chose to be part of its longevity. The most important attribute for any Elder is the ability to tap into the land's energy, giving each of them the ability to see visions of the future or past events that have already occurred. Since a sequera's survival always depends directly on the element of soil, it is in constant contact with every energy source touching it, which essentially is the entire world. If trees could speak, some of us would wish we were deaf. Luckily, the Elders have learned to not listen to many of the things they hear the sequeras say, taking their statements only for what they are—possibilities, not certainties."

Out of curiosity, Martell changed the subject to a more serious note. "Since the Elders are able to see these visions, and have a distinct closeness to nature, have any ever spoken with the dead . . . or even God?"

Viktoran almost laughed out loud, taken aback by the bold question. "One does not have to be an Elder to speak to the deceased. Spirits from past lives walk this plane all the time, communicating to us when they choose in many different ways, directly or indirectly. As for God—only in death is Yawrana revealed to us. The Maker cannot be witnessed on this plane of existence because of the limitations of our bodies. Only when our minds are free of flesh may we depend on and trust everything that we see beyond physical form."

Identifying a short silence in their conversation, a servant rushed in to bring the warm bread and butter Martell had been salivating heavily for. The Nax sunk his teeth into it, savoring the soft texture between his tongue and the top of his mouth. The butter was sweet and only made him want more. In no time at all he had eaten nearly half a loaf by himself. Windal and Viktoran only had one slice each, leaving the rest for the Martell to devour. Martell sucked the end of his fingertips to get the remnants of butter off before he asked, "When may I meet the King?"

Surprised he had no more questions about the Elders, Viktoran thought the Nax must have been satisfied with the answers he had been given. "His Majesty will be returning soon. I will inform him of your arrival. He would be interested in meeting a relative of the former High Elder. Is there anything else we may do for you until he arrives?"

Martell slurped from his glass of water in an annoying manner, as if he were doing it on purpose. There was an uneasy silence floating around them and Martell's eyes glazed over for only a moment before he wet his lips. Looking up, he announced in a gravelly voice, "It is time you take me to Mosia's grave."

With a single white candle to highlight his features and the objects within the short diameter of the study, Elder Garan shuffled through a stack of anointment papers containing the names of the morning's candidates. There had been many of late with the addition of the Lazul children to the territories, but the numbers were now beginning to fade with so many disappearing from their homes to unknown locations. None of the Elders knew where any of them were, making the seven remaining Elders desperate to have any kind of vision that would reveal their hidden schemes. They even increased their daily revelations from three times each day to five, hoping to catch a glimpse of something, anything.

The Elder suddenly felt an energy fluctuation rumbling along the floor of the study. It could only mean one thing—someone important was making an unannounced visit. He could sense it was urgent when the sounds of quick and heavy footfalls approached the door. A rap rang out as he expected it to, its noise demanding. He rose and crossed the floor. It was only a few steps before he was at the peephole. When he saw who it was, he immediately unlatched the three interior sliding locks to swing the door away from its frame. "Your Majesty," he cried.

Noran stepped in and hugged Garan, giving his old friend a warm smile. "Hello, Elder," he said, breaking away. "I'm happy to see you are still moving about like a hundred-year-old."

Elder Garan laughed and then his eyes lit up when he also saw Bruneau, Blaynor, Oreus, and Quinn standing out on the deck behind him. "You brought a party along with you."

"Yes. I have asked the guards to wait just outside so it will not make you feel too crowded. Blaynor will just be joining the Baron and me."

"Oh, for heaven's sake! They can come in, too," he said, smiling and pointing to Bruneau and Quinn.

"That's not *really* why I asked them to stay outside, Elder."

The Elder's face went drab when he replied, "Don't tell me you have had an assassination attempt on your life by Herikech—"

"Of course not, Elder. You would have heard about that before I even got here. The information is not that dire." Noran turned and shut the door. Bruneau and Quinn already looked like they were motioning toward it before he had it completely shut in their faces. Noran knew if he opened it now the two guards would come tumbling in onto the floor after having pressed their ears tightly against the wood. He knew the door was solid enough that they would only hear mumbled words from the outside. Blaynor stood with his back pressed against it, holding it shut. "However," Noran continued, "there is something else that troubles me. You have been the one, Elder, I have trusted more than any other during my years growing up, and I now call upon your honesty once more."

"The way you put it does make it sound dreadful," Garan replied.

Noran pressed a knob on the wall, which raised two wooden posts from the center of the eight-hundred tree rings spreading outward on the floor before Garan's desk. Noran and Oreus each sat on one while the Elder plunked down in his elaborate armchair, which was permanently attached to the innards of the tree.

Garan lit two more candles on his desk to brighten the room. "There. That is much better. Tell me what troubles a King so much that he needs privacy to discuss it."

With a chalky voice, he said, "Elder Garan, have any of the Elders recently had a vision of new voyagers coming to Yawrana?"

The Elder looked as if he were slapped, realizing Noran was not just asking a question, but informing him that it had already happened.

"By your expression I will take that as a 'no,'" Noran said, showing distress on his face.

"When did they arrive and how many are there?" Garan asked, surprised that an event so important had not been seen since Oreus's crew had landed upon the shores of Marshant.

"At least three hundred men among three ships. It has been ten days since."

"Ten days?" the Elder said, flustered. "Why did you not let us know sooner? We could've been consulting the waters to reveal their goals."

"We already know their goals," Oreus said. "They're no different than that of Lanu's."

Garan was breathing heavily and sweating. "I trust then they are no longer here? Surely you wouldn't let thieves walk in our kingdom freely, Your Majesty . . . ."

Noran sighed, cleared his throat, and said, "It wasn't by choice that I have allowed them to stay within the territories for two more daysets."

"*Two* daysets we have to endure their roving eyes?"

"Elder," Noran said, cutting him off. "I don't blame the prophets for missing the prophecy foretelling their arrival. In fact, there was a vision that presented itself to another. That man is sitting before you now."

Garan's eyes rotated left and planted firmly on Oreus's flushed features. The Baron grimaced, acting as if the Elder was peering into his soul for the answers. Oreus slid off his seat, stood and walked to the edge of Garan's desk and said, "I didn't know what I saw at the time was a vision."

Fumbling for words, the Elder could only muster, "How?"

Oreus reached across Garan's desk and pointed to a corner where there sat a glass filled with clear spring water.

The Elder began to hand him the glass, thinking the Baron was thirsty, when Oreus waved it away. "No, Elder Garan. My throat is not dry. That is how I saw the vision—in a water glass on a table next to my bed."

Rubbing his chin for a few moments while holding up his own glass before him, Garan stated, "Never before in the history of this kingdom has anyone other than an Elder seen a vision." Oreus was about to respond when the Elder added, "And, never before has anyone with a colored band possessed a second skill set intended for another. Tell me," Garan said, setting down the perspiring glass on the edge of an anointment paper, "what exactly did you witness?"

Oreus straightened himself, spun on his heel and lifted his chin toward the ceiling, closing his eyes to recall the image as best as he could. "When I was about to fall asleep—"

"No, Baron," Garan immediately interrupted. "I need you to start from the events that began your day—then proceed up to the point where you saw your vision. Please, take your time." Garan picked up a feather out of an inkbottle and pulled a clean parchment sheet from a drawer before him, ready to record every detail of Oreus's recount.

"Very well. My guard, Quinn Rainsmoke, awakened me at seven as the sun poked its head up over the western hills. I proceeded to dress—"

"Was there a water glass on your bed stand the night before as well?" Garan asked.

"Umm . . . no. I didn't have a glass the night before."

"Sorry for the interruption, Baron. Please, continue."

Sighing and opening his eyes, Oreus said, "After I dressed, I cleaned up and went for my run around the Marshant Tower's Yard. I didn't see or hear anything unusual during this run and completed three laps. From there, I went to the training arena and began my daily exercises in the *Urra Dur*. By nine I went to clean up in the bathhouses, and at ten went to the main hall to address issues occurring around the territory. After that, I ate lunch at one."

"What did you have?" Garan asked, not wanting to leave anything out.

"It included white grain rice over a bed of hop leaves—"

"Hop leaves?" Garan said. "You realize they are a mild hallucinogen, don't you, Baron?"

Blushing as if he were being scolded, Oreus said, "Yes, Elder. I didn't have enough of it to cause me any problems though . . . ."

"But you are taking it on a regular basis?"

Getting red around the ears, Oreus admitted, "Yes, Elder."

"Let the hop leaves be for now, Baron," Noran ordered so the Elder didn't have to.

"That is not what caused the vision," Oreus refuted.

"You don't know that for sure," Noran replied. "Hop leaves can remain in your system for more than a few hours. I know how much you love them so don't deny you have had more than your fair share."

Oreus took a deep breath and finished, "At three I went back to one of the local marketplaces to listen to the provisioners about the state of crops for the upcoming winter. The discussions were yawners to say the least and I really didn't pay them much attention, letting my mind drift most of the time."

"Hop leaves also can make one sleepy," Noran added.

"Once I left there," Oreus said, gritting his teeth and continuing, "I went to visit Ola in her guest quarters until I was ready to retire for the day." Before the Elder could ask, he explained what they talked about. "She wanted to know how I was feeling about having accepted the role as a Baron."

"How did you feel?" Caran interrupted again.

Being truthful, Oreus said, "I was confused, unsure if I had made the right decision."

"It is possible that the combination of hop leaves and your conflicting feelings over your homeland may have caused you to daydream—"

"That's not it," Oreus retorted. "I know what it is to daydream, as I have done plenty of it growing up in Beggar's Square in Uthan Mire. That's all one has when he is poverty stricken from birth."

"Excuse me, Baron," Caran apologized. "My words meant no wrong. It was only a supposition."

"I know what I saw! It was no dream. After shedding my garments and gear, I was wide awake when I climbed into bed. I was no longer tired at that point. The hop leaves could not have played a part in my vision."

The King crossed his arms and listened carefully.

"There was a white candle burning softly next to my pillow. I rolled over on to my side and gazed at it to force myself to get bored and go to sleep. Then what happened frightened me. The candle grew hot and sparks began to fly from the flame. Suddenly, the water in my glass nearby reacted to the candle's heat by bubbling against the sides. A tiny fireball leapt from the candle and landed in the center of the water in the glass. But the fire didn't extinguish as I expected it to. The red and orange ball sank like a marble just below the surface, disappearing."

"So it did go out," Noran said until Oreus shook his head.

Noran's eyes grew wide and the Elder could hardly breathe, unsure of what to make of Oreus's words. They both listened, clenching their fists to bridle their emotions for the ending.

"The fireball was no longer from candle flame. It rose from the surface of the water in the glass like a sun rising above the Racorn Sea at dawn. The glass brightened, sending out rays in all directions. Three specks emerged from the center of the intense golden source. They took the forms of drift ships and sailed toward me until they were large enough that the room around me became dark. The candle's flame faded to a trail of smoke and the edges around my sight turned to a white haze."

"Without a doubt, it was a vision," Garan said. "You speak as an Elder would when entering the State of Awareness. The mind becomes infatuated by the events unfolding before the third eye."

Oreus paused and asked the Elder to expound upon his comment.

"The third eye is the gateway to the future and past. It can see what the eyes of the living cannot. The white haze only occurs when the third eye is open to see what has been forgotten or what is yet to come."

"How do you know if it is a past or future event you are witnessing?" Noran asked.

"A wise question, my Lord. But the answer is rather simple. Study the details of the figures or scenes being depicted. If that doesn't tell you, then you must prepare for the event as if it were to come."

Following the logic, Noran said, "Then many of the visions that are recorded in the Historical Record Keep may be that of the past instead of the future?"

"Very few, my Lord. It is rare we are unable to determine a past vision from a future one. On average, only one out of every hundred can't be positioned along the line of time. For those we can't place, we can only guess and hope they have already come to pass - especially when the vision is a dark one. Yet we still must prepare for it as if it never happened."

When they turned their attention back to Oreus, he confirmed, "Winslow was aboard the lead ship. I remember his face vividly."

"You are absolutely certain?" Noran said.

"Without a doubt. Thorn was with him as well. I have never forgotten his hooked lip since I saw it in the water glass. Beyond their images, there is not much else to tell of. When the candle snuffed out, the image lost clarity and vanished."

"What was the date and time of this vision, Baron?" Garan asked.

"Around eight," Oreus said. "It was just getting dark outside. That is why I lit the candle."

"What date?" the Elder asked.

Oreus paused for a long moment before saying, "It was the first day of the week after I returned from Arna: Fore Day."

Garan twisted in his chair to look at the dozens of shelves behind him. He reached up to pull a thin green book off a lower one. The binding read *5440: Notable Historical Events*, the year Oreus first arrived in Yawrana aboard *The Star Gazer*. Going to a red ribbon hanging out at the center of the pages, the Elder flipped the book open and read quietly for a lengthy period of time.

"Aha!" the Elder finally shouted. "Baron Blake, there is a note here by me on that very same day, which is most peculiar. I was doing my nightly revelation at the exact time you saw your vision, at twilight. As you know, the Elders record everything we see in a vision."

Noran and Oreus both nodded, unblinking.

"Well, I began to have a vision, and according to this passage that I wrote down, it started the exact same way the Baron's did."

"And then what?" Noran asked, eager to know.

"And then the vision blanked out." Garan frowned. "The haze disappeared as if the energy supplying it were suddenly tapped into and harnessed for another purpose. I now believe it was the Baron who drained it from my sight."

Noran was stunned. The King swallowed, trying to believe that what the Elder was saying was related to Oreus's story.

"The notes I have written also say that the candle near my bowl of water behaved strangely, flickering wildly until it snuffed out entirely on its own. I was surprised, as you can imagine. The connection was lost and none of the Elders ever had anything remotely similar to the beginning of that vision since."

"How could I tap into your vision, Elder? I don't have any powers that would enable me to do that."

"We do not yet know the extent of your abilities, Baron. You are not of Yawranan blood and could possess far more traits than we, at first, believed. Your training and feelings for Princess Ola aside, have you felt any different from an emotional standpoint since you first set foot here?"

Oreus nodded and said, "Yes. My emotional connection to the land has intensified since we returned from Arna."

Noran smiled and said, "I am glad you said it first, Baron. I also have felt the same way. Arna holds many secrets that we were unaware of."

Garan looked at both men. "Did either of you bring anything back with you from Arna that I should be aware of?"

"Only a lot of wounds," Noran said amusingly.

Oreus began to turn green and then stated guiltily, "I did."

Noran's eyes turned dark as he said, "Baron, you . . . yet again surprise me. What have you claimed for your own from the ice wastes?"

Oreus's shoulders sank down a few inches before his right hand lifted to a pouch at his side. His left hand went over to meet it and together they untied it from his belt. The Baron loosened the drawstring and turned the pouch upside-down over Garan's desk. Out fell a long blue object that made Noran jump up from his post chair.

"You took a crystal from the cavern of evil spirits? Are you mad?"

Oreus defended himself. "No. It drew me to it, acting as if it wanted me to pick it up."

"It is an unholy relic," Noran spat, getting frantic. "Throw it away, Elder. Don't touch it. It was used for evil and may be trying to do the same to Oreus."

Remaining calm, Elder Garan asked, "Was this the only crystal in the cavern?"

"No, Elder. There were hundreds, no, thousands. They covered the entire ceiling of the cavern. I believe the spirits who tried to feed off our bodies for energy used them to divert energy and create the multitude of elemental plane traps we fell into."

Garan nodded. "Crystals can break up the power of the elements. But one crystal alone would not be enough to react on its own and cause your vision. Something had to induce it to interact with the element of water in your glass – that is, if the crystal was in proximity to the water when the vision happened."

"It was, Elder," Oreus confirmed.

"Was there anything else on your bed table that may have triggered a reaction to the crystal?"

Noran answered for Oreus, "Your Lazul dagger."

Oreus quickly unstrapped the case Ola had made for it from his belt and laid it down on the table a few feet from the crystal.

"What is special about this dagger?" the Elder asked, unsheathing it to reveal the full handle and blade for close inspection.

"I took this off a dead Lazul scout before the grassland war."

Garan continued to inspect each of the symbols on the handle.

Oreus continued, "There was a demon we encountered in Arna within the Shadow Cut Mountain Range. It tried to kill us and would have succeeded if I had not plummeted that blade into its heart—errr—where a heart should have been if the individual was still a living person."

"The demon wore the armor of a *Bethlen* warrior," Noran said, not forgetting the important detail.

"A *Bethlen* warrior?" Garan said, astounded. "Of the old Yawranan guard?"

Noran nodded.

"The warrior disappeared from the suit it inhabited after I killed it."

"Souls cannot be killed, Baron," Garan said quickly. "You must have driven it off, possibly hurting it somehow. It may have even returned back to the next plane of existence."

"I'll never forget its eyes." Oreus shuddered. "They were blue dancing flames of death."

"Blue, you say?"

"Yes. Why?"

"Blue is the color representation of water in spiritual form. Gray is wind. Red is fire or light. Black is soil. The demon must have used a water portal to reenter this world. And only one thing can drive away a spirit utilizing water for its existence on this plane."

"Fire," Noran answered.

Garan smiled. "That is correct, Your Majesty."

"This weapon was bound to the element of fire at some point when it was first created. Its interaction with the crystal and water was so intense it created the right conditions for the Baron to see the future without the intellectual depths and practices of an Elder."

"How do you know for sure?" Oreus asked.

Elder Garan looked at the crystal to his left lying near the edge of his desk. "We can test it. You know, Viktoran Ilos has a sword that he inherited that has been passed down for generations. It holds the same properties."

"Heaven's Light," Noran answered again. "But no one holds the knowledge of how to fuse an element with a weapon. The sword was the only one in existence of its kind—until now. Perhaps it came from the Lazuls like your dagger, Baron Blake. Since we were once slaves of the Lazuls, it is highly probable. It is time I start reading Herishen Illeon's Will and Testament again. It may hold clues to unlocking this mystery."

Oreus started, "If blue is water . . . ."

"Yes, Baron?" Noran prodded.

"The Mother of Life . . . was her soul not blue?"

"Yes," Noran said.

"How is it she used water to reach this plane when her presence was in the middle of a desert?"

The Elder smiled and said, "It may be that is why the Dunes of Pydora are what they are. From the King's statements, the entity was very powerful. She may have been so powerful that it sapped the land dry of moisture, bringing death to all plant and animal life around her. Be thankful she was there, for she may have saved the territories of Yawrana from being accessed by the Lazuls."

Noran took the theory one step further, saying, "What if the Mother of Life knew the ways of the Lazuls and how they were destructive to the creatures of the Waungee? Maybe, as a vendetta, she created the dunes from the next plane of existence to protect the lands we now use wisely. It would have happened long before the city of Maramis was formed. She may have even been a Lazul."

"And for the test?" Oreus reminded the Elder.

"Step over there, Baron," Garan said, placing the water glass within a few inches of the crystal. After looking at Noran and Oreus for only a moment, he moved them together until they touched. The water began to bubble in the glass but nothing else occurred. Next, he moved the dagger closer and closer until the blade erupted into flame, causing the Elder to fly back in his chair into a hypnotic trance.

Noran jumped to his feet and rushed toward the desk. A blinding flash caused the King to shield his eyes and fall. He bounced off the desk and fell to the floor, twisting his back awkwardly in the process. His crown slipped from his head and rolled across the floor, coming to a stop as it ran into a leg of a dining table. Neither the King nor Oreus could see for a few minutes as they tried to rub away the white light that had pierced their eyes.

The door to the outside burst inward. Quinn and Bruneau rushed in to assess the damage. Blaynor was already standing over the King, examining his state.

"Elder!" Noran called out, slowly getting up as the wrenched muscle in his back went into a spasm.

Blaynor helped him by the elbow, ordering, "Easy, Your Majesty. That was some fall. You scared the life out of me." Noran winced and walked slowly toward Elder Garan, who was laying face down on his desk. Oreus walked like a drunk over to the desk while Quinn tried to help him. He placed a hand on the Elder's shoulder. Shaking it several times awakened the Elder.

"W-what happened?" Garan stammered.

Looking at the desk, Noran saw the Lazul dagger sticking into a wall to his left and the crystal lying on the floor. The water glass had tipped over and spilled across the Elder's desk, making the anointment papers soak up the fluid until their ink had run and smeared across their pages.

"Did you see anything, Elder?" Noran asked when he saw Garan was uninjured.

The Elder searched for his spectacles that had flown off his nose. Oreus picked them out of a basket and handed the fragile set back to him.

"Ummm . . . thank you," he mumbled, sitting back and straightening his posture in his chair. "I saw . . . something strange."

"Tell us," Noran said, waiting for the Elder to straighten out his thoughts. Garan hesitated until Noran put a hand on the Elder's arm and said, "What is it?"

Garan looked at the King with a sorrowful expression and said, "Your Majesty, I believe I have just witnessed your death."

# CHAPTER FOUR
## Overhead, Under Hoof

The Grand Hall bustled with activities as the Royal House servants prepared morning feasts for the Court and discussions, which revolved around the endless rains sweeping across the territories. The latest downpour began three hours ago and was causing topsoil to run off into the rivers at an incredible rate. Crops were being destroyed so fast that no one was even sure how much food there would be left to occupy the space in the storage houses for the upcoming winter.

Farmers swarmed the hall's gigantic floor when the main doors were opened for those who wished to hear the resolutions being set forth to combat the floods. They were all getting used to being indoors, much like their animal herds, which were forced to stay in their barns in order to prevent them from becoming sick. Acres of lower pastures and fields filled in with water, forming instant natural lakes. Many of the farmers present lost at least half of the provisions they normally supplied to the marketplaces, drastically reducing their own income to purchase other supplies.

This, in turn, also prompted many food provisioners to come to the meeting as well. Their profits were lagging and they also would make their voices heard on the matter. Their violet robes hanging on their bodies were seen clustered along the hall's wall near the stained glass windows. The provisioners were bickering about ways they could regain their lost income. A few of them suggested replacing some of the farmer vendors with garment sellers while others went as far as wanting to hold auctions to sell off many of the valuable structures and decorations that made their marketplaces more attractive to the crowds.

Priests were also plentiful in the Grand Hall, giving blessings for the decisions that were about to be made, hoping it would bring good fortune against an enemy they were unsure of how to fight. Their brown robes brushed the ground a few feet behind them as they made their way toward the throne to stand near the Elders. The Elders were revered by all priests, gaining their full support in all facets of their lives: the anointment rituals, special sermons for burials, births and celebrations, replicating Historical Record Keep documentation, caring for the sequeras in which the Elders lived, and bringing supplies to the Elders on a daily basis so the Elders didn't constantly have to leave their homes and weaken their life energy. The Elders in several visions predicted the heavy rains. However, not even they expected the storms to be this problematic.

Noran sat on his tree throne and looked around impatiently. "Where is Baron Barrow?" he finally asked. All of the other barons and generals were present. "He holds our actions at bay with his absence."

Ballan stroked his gray, flowing beard, acting as if he hadn't heard the question. His white robe hung loose on him due to recent weight loss. But a newly carved and hooked staff gave him the support he needed. Ballan was nearly seventy-five, a common age for most House servants to retire. But the court announcer gave no intentions of leaving his station any time soon, despite his weak-looking state. Several minutes passed before he finally said, "Your Majesty, it has been reported there was an unexpected visitor at the Western Gate two days ago. It is said the traveler was a Nax, bearing albino qualities."

Noran became instantly attentive to Ballan's statement. The King contemplated what to say next. His eyes didn't want to blink as he stared down at the announcer.

"Your Majesty," Ballan said to wipe away the King's intense reaction, "Baron Barrow was halfway to Overbay before the Majestic Messengers had to chase him down and bring them back to the castle. He won't be here in time for the discussions. I think the meeting should begin without him."

Noran nodded to give approval. His mind flashed back to the sequera and the recent event that had taken place between Oreus, Elder Garan and himself. The Elder's words still clung to him like static, leaving worry wrinkles throughout his soul while he pondered what had occurred. The most nagging question that bothered him was when his life could find its end. He carried the thought with him since the dramatic light display they were dazzled by over the Elder's desk. The tremendous flash of white light was nothing they were prepared for and they expected a much less severe reaction between the crystal and dagger – similar to what happened during Oreus's vision.

Unfortunately, the Elder did not give him any more specifics than the one glaring sentence he uttered when he came out of his trance. Garan refused to speak any more on the topic until he discussed it further with High Elder Elenoi Ironwood. But Garan did say he would have the High Elder visit Noran soon when the time was "right" to disseminate important details. Obviously the Elders knew something he and the Court did not regarding his future—a horrific event that Noran knew he might not be able to avoid.

After the incident, Noran felt vulnerable no matter where he went. Looking over his shoulder was normally Bruneau and Blaynor's work but he now took extra precaution for the unpredictable. Guards were posted at every door. Only those wearing a red band around their bicep were allowed into the Grand Hall with any kind of weapon. Noran was no fool, though. He understood Herikech. The Lazul King's minions were not to be trusted and would get to him in time if they kept trying.

The other pressing question that revolved around Noran's brain like an annoying fly was about the other possible hidden powers the blue crystal could possess. In Arna it already proved to be strong enough to assist in opening portals into the next plane of existence. Before they left the crystal and Oreus's Lazul dagger with the Elders for further observation and study, Elder Garan explained the crystal was known as a "sheet" crystal. Some of the Elders believed sheet crystals could possibly be utilized to allow an individual to travel through a window into another dimension. Oreus had gone through one such window himself, a pool of water, a powerful doorway that was opened after enough spiritual energy from dozens of helpless warriors and animals fed its strength. The window was formed by three female, demon spirits lusting for vengeance from beyond, attempting to shift the balance of power in the world into the favor of evil for the end days when Heaven or the Underworld would clash with the physical plane of Elvana.

Elder Garan also mentioned that sheet crystals were rare and flat, as was the case with the crystal Oreus pocketed in Arna. The few that the Elder knew existed in Yawrana rested in the hands of local sector mine owners who were oblivious to the traits of the crystals. This made the crystals harmless in the owners' hands for the time being. Measures would have to be taken to collect every one of them through means of private purchases—a mission Noran had already put squarely on the shoulders of the Majestic Messengers. Other crystal types were used mostly for meditative or healing purposes. The medicine makers throughout the territories commonly employed crystal properties, experiencing mixed results from their use due to the wide range of patients being treated. Age, sex, weight, height, intelligence, and surrounding room conditions all played an important role during the all-natural healing processes. When there was no cure for difficult ailments, crystals were one of the last methods used to help a stricken patient.

The Elders decided they still needed to test the reactions of every other crystal formation against Oreus's dagger to record the effects they, too, portrayed. It would take time, but it was well worth the unique knowledge they would gain from the research. Under isolated conditions, the first test would be to group several sheet crystals together to see if the results would be the same or greater. Noran felt he knew the answer to that question but he would have to wait to hear the Elders' findings.

The King also wondered what item the three female demon spirits had exploited to cause the thousands of crystals in the Arna cavern's ceiling to react so strongly that they could open a portal and allow a physical being into a spiritual plane. Oreus's dagger was only one of many countless artifacts in the world that could cause such a reaction. It would remain a mystery forever since the cavern now laid buried beneath a ton of snow and ice to the far north. No man in his right mind would search the ice land's dangerous environment for such an object—no man of good heart, that is.

His back felt better, despite how badly he twisted it when he fell onto the sequera's floor. He had pulled a muscle in his lower back, but the pain had subsided by the time he reached Candlewick Castle, making him thankful he would not be restricted to rest like a lame dundel in the maker's medical wing. He had too many concerns that needed to be addressed.

As Noran sat waiting for order to assemble, he overheard a farmer discussing something odd. It was not the type of conversation he expected to hear with the floods occupying everyone's attention. He leaned forward and strained his ears as he focused in on the middle-aged man with the dirty white shirt, brown pants fraying at the ankles and short, curly brown hair. His complexion was lighter than most farmers. This man spoke as quietly as he could to High Elder Elenoi Ironwood, who did not notice the King was eavesdropping.

"The doors were locked," the farmer said, his face coursed with worry lines.

"Maddons do venture this far south at times," the Elder tried to say before the farmer cut her off.

"It was not maddons, High Elder. Part of the body was purposely disfigured—and little of its meat was eaten. It was disturbing. Maddons don't attack cattle like that . . . ."

The High Elder moved in a little closer to the farmer and put a hand on his shoulder, saying, "If the barn was locked, then how did the attacker get in and manage to kill your entire herd?" The High Elder's voice didn't sound as if she doubted the story, but was only trying to verify the details of the encounter so she could make a proper assessment before determining the next course of action.

"It came through a second floor window. There wasn't a ladder or object high enough for it to jump from to reach it. It must have clawed its way up the side of the outer wall . . . like an insect."

Goosebumps formed on Noran's arms and the hairs on the back of his neck stood out. He wondered if a creature that could climb flat wooden walls could also scale stone ones.

The High Elder was silent for a moment after hearing this explanation. The farmer grew anxious until she responded, "Have you told any of the other farmers about this?"

The man shook his head.

"Good. It's best you don't at this time. The rains have caused enough heartache for them. When this meeting is over, I wish you to show me the bodies. I need to see them for myself."

The man nodded. Noran looked away before they caught him listening. A servant came to his side, thinking he wanted something from him.

"Are you hungry, Your Majesty?" the servant asked, lifting a bowl of fruit up.

Noran waved the man away, not finding any of the selections desirable. The fruit smelled rotten, even though it appeared normal. He also thought it inappropriate to eat after what he had just learned. *An entire herd?* he thought to himself. The farmer's way of life had just been wiped out after one night of ill luck. It was hard for Noran to digest. He wondered how Herikech was involved.

Ballan disrupted the King's concentration as the announcer broke in with his introduction. "Attention! Attention all!" The Grand Hall quieted to a low murmur so everyone at the back could hear. "His Majesty, King Noran Deardrop, welcomes you to the Grand Hall to unite against the curse of rain that is drowning every farm and town throughout Yawrana. Your presence here only increases the importance of the dilemma you now face. You have good reason to be upset and wonder if the wrath you are fighting can be stopped. The eyes of Yawrana bear down upon you in disappointment."

Noran frowned, not liking where Ballan was leading the people's fears. He whispered in a low voice, "Ballan . . ."

The announcer carried on as if he did not hear the King's beckoning, heightening the rising tension within the room to where women cried and men's shoulders slumped in despondency. "The time to unite is at hand. Help each other or drown in the doubt of your own failures."

The King gestured to Blaynor to have him stop Ballan before he got any further. The guard strode forward and clasped Ballan's arm tightly to disrupt his next agonizing line.

Blaynor whispered, "The King wishes you to put an end to your ramblings. You are torturing these people. Can't you see that? They are already aware of how the gray days have blanketed their optimism."

Ballan yanked his arm away from Blaynor and cleared his throat loudly. He paused before responding softly with, "I think being realistic about the situation is just as important as trying to determine a solution."

"Get on with it," Blaynor growled.

Turning back toward the curious crowd, Ballan stated, "His Majesty wishes to first call forward the Barons of the territories, Viktoran Ilos of Serquist, Bal Grady of Priswell, Jada Annalee of Emison, Oreus Blake of Marshant and Edin DeHue of Dowhaven. The Court also calls upon General Merdel Ghosney of Gillwood and General Irvin Yeats of Rock Rim, who are overseeing each region until new barons are anointed and take their positions by Yawrana the Holy. And since Baron Windal Barrow was unable to be at this crucial analysis, the Royal Court will ask General Lyon Rammol III to speak for Overbay Territory."

Ballan bowed to the court's representatives and moved from the center of the floor to the side of the throne. He held his long hooked staff in front of him in silence until he was required to make the next set of introductions. Blaynor glared at him, happy his tongue finally found rest.

The King leaned forward in his chair, lifted his goblet from the small platform by his armrest and took a sip of crimson juice. When he set the goblet back down, he took a quick glance at the spot where the carved snakehead used to be when his father ruled the Court. Noran had the head sawed off and chiseled into a snowtear so he could not be easily reminded of the poison that was administered to Doran's drink by Kuall the Court Jester, leading to his father's rapid and painful death. Part of the snake's body had also wrapped around the queen's goblet platform, which Noran chiseled into a beautiful wreath of flowers.

Noran boldly stated his words so there was no mistake about his stance regarding the endless rains dousing the kingdom. "Barons and Generals, there is still hope in battling an enemy against which a majority of Yawranans feel we have no strategy. Where swords and shields play no part, vessels and pumps shall. I will turn the tide into our favor, giving our flame fighters the best combatant to aid their cause. I declare that stone silo storages shall be built for each waterhouse within the territories to hold the excess water. Construction on these silos has already commenced and will be completed nine sunsets from now. Masonry artists and rock cutters have been ordered to set all other labor aside until this task is finished. Not only will this give our orange fleet a faster refueling location for their water wagons, but it will also supply additional stored water for droughts during the hottest summers."

A round of cheers burst from every person within the hall. Everyone considered the idea brilliant and it took a long time before the applause died down. And to the surprise of the hall's occupants, the King was not yet finished with his declarations.

"Where fruits of the land perish, we shall resort to casting more nets to the seas to fill our plates. We will take back what is being denied us, equaling the balance of power between man and nature. For those of you whose homes cannot be reached by foot, you may find shelter within each of the territory tower's grounds and the halls of this castle until the land returns to what it once was. Bring your most treasured belongings. They will be stored safely in spare rooms. The sun cannot hide forever, as long as we always keep it in our hearts."

The hall erupted in cheer again, bringing a chorus of song among the people. Ballan was one of the few not singing and looked at the King while shaking his head. Noran nodded toward him as if he just gave him a lesson on giving hope to those who had none. The announcer nodded back, but then grimaced when the hall turned into a dance floor as people sang.

*Down by the river there's a place I know.*
*You bring your net and I'll bring my pole.*
*It'll be a secret we both can share.*
*Together we'll sit and see how we fare.*

*We'll cast our lines and sip some ale.*
*We'll bask in the sun as we create our tale.*
*If the fish won't bite, the larger it'll be.*
*But that's just between you and me.*

*And if our odds are ruined by showers or hail,*
*It'll only add to the story that'll entail . . .*

A sudden blasting gale force wind cut off the farmers' joyous song by blowing out the hall's seven stained-glass windows representing the bands of Yawrana. Women shrieked and men screamed as shards of glass flew inward from the western wall, cutting many across their exposed faces, arms and legs. Everyone in the hall scattered in a state of panic, shoving, pushing and trampling elderly women and several children who could not move to safety quickly enough. Guards went to aid the victims before the chaos cost them their lives.

Bruneau and Blaynor each seized the King by an arm and hurried him to safety in the private room behind the throne. Ballan went to the closest broken window to get a better look at the bleak sky outside. The Barons, Generals, Elders and priests all stumbled their way into the adjoining Banquet Hall. The glass windows above the main dining table also shattered above them, raining glass down in dangerous spikes. General Ghosney of Gillwood suffered a large cut down the length of his right arm while a large piece smashed over the top of General Yeats's metal helmet. The Elders and priests crawled beneath the table while the Barons and Generals lined up along the walls, watching the winds sweep in from the Grand Hall. A set of candles blew over onto the tablecloth of the dining table, catching it on fire. The Elders scampered from beneath after the wood caught flame and rapidly spread along its length.

As Elder PaCant crawled toward a wall, he was struck on the side of the face with a serving tray and knocked unconscious. Jada dragged him to safety before part of the frame from one of the windows over the hall came crashing down onto the stone where he had previously lain.

The smoke from the table's fire created a blinding haze, which added more confusion for others seeking protection in the large dining hall. Oreus worked his way over to a water station and filled a bucket by dunking it within the small, ceramic basin tub. Racing to the fire before it caught onto the chairs, he splashed down the center of the table, cutting off the flame's access to reach them. He took the wet tablecloth and flung it over the remaining fire, smothering it.

The wind continued to increase in strength, howling with the ferocity of a wounded dragul. Children cried as they huddled around their parents. Dogs barked at the variety of noises echoing throughout the castle. Wherever the winds penetrated, in or around the castle, anarchy was created. Pans clattered on the floors of the kitchen, loose hay and debris was picked up and strewn across the groomed Gaming Arena, gardens and Yards, and sturdy branches snapped like twigs from mature trees, which fell onto roads connecting the local towns to one another. Soldiers and guards barked orders to latch down shutters and close doors to restore a sense of normalcy where they could to slow the growing madness.

Lightning struck the high watchtower posts around Candlewick several times. A trio of guards ducked behind a windowsill of one when a bolt zapped a flagpole directly above them. The three-inch diameter of wood burst into flame from the intense charge. The fire crawled up to the flag and consumed the dragul emblem on its center. Another bolt streaked across the sky almost horizontally before it connected with an empty suit of armor standing in the window of a hallway. The metal figure tipped over and crashed into a table at its side. The head disconnected and rolled into a water pitcher, forcing the pitcher to tip and water to run everywhere.

The sky boomed with thunder angrily, causing the squeamish to wince in its reverberating range. Noran yelled in retaliation at the window at the other side of the room, "Why do you quarrel with us, Maker? Please let us be."

Bruneau and Blaynor thought his scornful words were hopeless. He glared at them for not feeling the same.

"It will pass, my Lord," Blaynor assured him. "Storms can't last forever."

"This one has," he grumbled, pulling his cloak over his shoulders as he sat in his chair, wincing as another strike hit a spire outside the Gaming Arena. He shook his head in disbelief. "The rains have lasted almost two daysets. Who says the winds won't as well? We'll never be able to finish the silos or think of venturing onto the rough seas with these insufferable hostilities forcing us to back down at every turn."

"It will pass," Blaynor said again, not giving in to the King's despair. "It has to."

"Why does it have to?" Noran asked. He scowled as he bit his lower lip. "We don't even know why it is behaving this way to begin with. Yawrana the Maker has decided we are no longer in his favor."

Ballan ran into the room. His terror-stricken face was illuminated by the lightning that flashed through a window in the hall. "Your Majesty, four dark funnels have extended from the northwest sky and crawl toward us like the fingers of doom!"

"We have to move to an underground location!" Blaynor yelled over a loud thunderclap.

"Where?" the King shouted back.

"Kuall's labyrinth below us has been sealed off."

Bruneau pulled the King by his arm and escorted him from the small room. "We won't reach the Secret Halls in time. Our only hope is to get everyone into the ice cooler below the kitchens."

The four men raced as fast as they could to the Banquet Hall. Blaynor screamed orders for everyone to follow. The Barons, Elders and Generals heeded and followed first, with the House servants, priests and farmers taking up the rear. They wound their way through the tables used by Carax Thume and the rest of the castle's chefs. Many of the pots and pans lay in a scattered mess on the floor. As they made their way to the cellar door, Noran almost tripped on the handle of a heavy skillet, but was caught by Bruneau before he could fall.

Blaynor twisted the heavy metal handle of the door that sealed the cold air inside and pulled it outward. Bruneau lifted a torch off the kitchen wall, led the large line of assorted Yawranans inside and down the old wooden steps to the deep levels below Candlewick. Each step creaked and groaned as they descended to the first room. A loud crash rang out somewhere above them, forcing them to make quicker decisions before anyone's life could be lost from the encroaching danger.

"The meat cooler is over there," Blaynor said, pointing to a large, thick door with an oval window near the top. "That may be the biggest area for all of us to fit in." Blaynor moved toward it, already smelling the potent aroma of raw steaks, stew meats, fish filets and fowl drumsticks hovering around the entrance. Sliding back the bolt, he entered. His torch illuminated dozens of hanging slabs of beef and rows of shelves with wrapped future meals waiting to be cooked and eaten.

Giant ice blocks sat in any remaining available spaces on palettes, dripping slowly into broad pans and troughs below. The troughs were exactly the same length as the blocks and at the end of the day would be returned to the icehouses outside the castle to be dispensed into the rivers.

Noran was still sweating in the much lower temperature, feeling as if he were coming down with a fever. He wiped his forehead with the back of his hand and looked for a place to sit. The smell of meat was almost too much for him, forcing him to once again reflect on the farmer's slaughtered and mangled herd in a nearby community. His nostrils flared to inhale as much air as he could before he held his breath to block it out of his mind. Blaynor led the King to a crate in the corner. Noran sat down and leaned his back against the wall, watching everyone else file in. The room was filled quickly and there were still farmers and priests standing in the hallway outside.

Suddenly, there were screams from a child echoing off in the distance overhead, causing a painful jolt to occur within Noran's heart. "Go find the girl," he commanded, not wanting to leave behind any soul in the mayhem of the raging twisters.

"What girl, Your Majesty?" Bruneau asked, unsure of whom the King was talking about.

"The girl that is screaming! Can you not hear her?" Noran's expression was as serious as it could be.

Bruneau listened closer and replied, "I do not hear a screaming girl, my Lord. Are you sure it is not the wind—"

"Go now and find her! She is in peril!"

Bruneau could only nod and pushed his way through the crowded space, bumping into elbows and knees along the way. He hurdled the last person who was sitting near the doorway. After climbing the stairs to reach the kitchens, the elite guard stopped and listened. To his surprise, there was a scream as the King had stated. He was astounded he had not picked up on her high shrill. It would only add to his growing list of concerns about his health. Was his hearing beginning to fail him as he entered the later years of his life?

He followed the shriek through the Banquet Hall and toward the Ball Room. Running the length of the dance floor to reach the only door exiting the hall, he found his way into a long hallway and headed north. The piercing screams grew louder as the thunderous roar of the winds whipped around the castle. He was now running west and out to the gardens. Clusters of trees with fallen branches filled his line of sight. Leaf parchments fluttered in the air with other lighter objects. The guard ducked when a large wood splinter came flying at his head like a dagger. It drove into the wooden doorframe behind him, embedding deeply in it.

As he combed the gardens with his eyes, they came to rest on a small form curled up in a ball beneath a bench at the far wall. A large figure lay motionless next to her, a woman with a streak of blood across the side of her face. A few feet from her, a large branch lay broken from the limb of a tree. The girl screamed as another unidentified object flew by her head in a blur.

Bruneau called, "Girl!"

She didn't respond and kept sobbing, her hands pressed against her eyes.

The roar of the wind was overbearing. Bruneau cupped his hands over his ears and ran toward them in a zigzag pattern as he fought the wind and dodged a volley of flying debris. The clouds were a grayish-green and the ground rocked beneath their feet. Chunks of stone broke off the turrets above them, smashing down only a few feet away. With no time to check for further injuries or a pulse, Bruneau slipped his arm under the blonde haired woman's neck and a left hand beneath her knees where the edge of her purple dress met.

The girl wiped her reddened eyes and shouted, "Are you taking my mother to the makers?"

"Not yet. First we must find safety."

The girl shrieked again and pointed to the sky. A tornado spun by the outer wall at the northern edge of the castle.

"Run for that door!" Bruneau screamed into the wind. He nodded toward it, seeing it was less than fifteen feet away. She was up and sprinting toward it before he even had the woman secure in a position he could carry her without inflicting more damage upon any unseen wounds. There was no more time to ponder it. The guard lunged forward and took the longest strides he had ever taken in his life. In five steps he was exiting the unprotected gardens and falling into a hallway adjoining the gandalay stables.

At the end of the hall, one of the doors entering the Gaming Arena had unlatched and was banging against the wall behind it. As the door opened and shut, the edge of a second tornado passed directly up and over them. The tunnel swirled like a vortex for only a few moments, lifting and throwing them toward the main entrance to the Grand Hall. They landed, rolled and were pinned against the gigantic doors, hardly able to move. A stone smashed against the door near Bruneau's head. He and the girl screamed as they felt the end was nearing. But as fast as the tornadoes had come, the wind was gone. And the rain, thunder and lightning accompanying the brutal wrath went with it, still moving in a southeasterly direction.

The young girl, no more than seven, cried as she laid her head on her mother's stomach. Tears drenched her face as she said, "Don't leave me, Mama. Don't leave me." To her joy, a heartbeat met the girl's ear and her mother's chest rose and fell more noticeably.

After witnessing the girl's reaction to her mother's survival, Bruneau raced toward the Gaming Arena and climbed up exactly one hundred seats encircling the stadium to reach the upper walkway. The aisle's outer wall had suffered extensive damage from its destroyer. He peered out a window beneath a large arch with a gargoyle poised at the top. Bruneau watched as the bizarre quartet of twisters slowed and dissipated back into the heavens once they reached the rim of the castle's Southern Yard. And to augment his amazement, the clouds covering the skies for miles around dispersed quickly as well, allowing the golden sun to shine down upon the vast destruction that littered the entire Royal House Territory.

Once again Noran was back on the throne in the Grand Hall. He awaited the tally of many things: the deaths and injuries of Yawranans and animals, the monetary estimates for the repairs that would be required to restore the castle and grounds, how many hours it would take to return the castle to functional order and how many men would be needed to secure the fallen fortifications that could be breached by Herikech and his diverse assortment of troops. There were other additional lists to consider, but the first four were the ones that weighed the most on his mind. It would take days to accumulate the numbers that he didn't necessarily want to hear, so he instead gave constant orders to keep everyone's attention where it should be—on their service to the kingdom.

The Elders all returned to their sequeran homes, knowing they had been remarkably unhurt during the ordeal. Not one of them displayed signs of sickness, broken bones or other injures that would indicate their soul mates were harmed. The barons and generals were all allowed to leave, with the exception of Viktoran Ilos of Serquist Territory. The Baron approached the King with a straight face, knowing precisely what Noran was going to ask him.

"You need not say anything, Your Majesty," Viktoran started as the King opened his mouth. Noran closed it when the Baron continued. "The Nax is an albino, as you have been told by Ballan."

The court announcer stood at the stair base near the throne, stroking his gray beard and nodding in agreement. His face held a condescending appearance that stated to any Yawranan farmer they had celebrated too early when the King made his declarations.

"What is this individual's name?" Noran asked.

"Martell Fedrow. He is a blood relation to the former High Elder, a descendant of his sister—supposedly."

"Why do you say 'supposedly', Baron?" Noran asked.

"I have never seen one who wears both wisdom and contempt on his sleeve at the same time. His words speak of a riddle where there is none, and his thirst for knowledge is reigned in by his impatience for it. Do you understand what I am saying, my Lord?"

Noran squinted his eyes. "He is volatile."

Viktoran nodded. "Of what he is truly after, we are uncertain. Deliverance was his original answer, but I believe there is more to him than he is telling. He wished to know of Mosia's role here and then demanded to see his grave once we told him."

Raising an eyebrow, Noran replied, "Did he say why?"

"When we questioned the purpose for it, he stated it was between

Mosia and him."

"For the sake of reconciliation," said a voice from the back of the Grand Hall. Everyone spun around to see Martell striding toward the King's chair. Windal was trailing him. Two guards intercepted Martell before he could get halfway across the floor.

"You can't barge in here!" Ballan yelled. "You must be properly introduced to the King before you can speak with him!"

Martell growled, "Remove your cursed hands, you vagabonds!" The Nax bit down on the hand of one guard. The guard screamed and curled his other hand into a fist to punch Martell when Noran ordered him not to harm the Nax.

"Bring him here," the King ordered.

The guard scowled, grumbled and then pushed Martell in the back to make him move.

"Sorry," Baron Windal Barrow mumbled, apologizing to the guard for the Nax's rude behavior.

The guard's eyes were flat with disapproval as he stepped aside to allow the Baron through.

"King Noran Deardrop," Martell announced, initiating a glare from Ballan, who was going to continue his complaints.

"Wait there," Ballan said, changing his lips to a thin white line. "You are not abiding—"

"It's all right, Ballan," Noran said, calming the Head of Royal House services. "Martell is welcome here out of respect for Mosia alone."

The Nax grinned and said, "You carry Doran's brevity in you."

"You have met my father?" Noran asked.

"Once—a long time ago. He had learned of the birth of a new albino Nax in Overbay. Your father was gracious enough to make my parents an offer for me to be raised by the Yawranans, knowing the ways of my people."

Noran felt relieved that his father had done so and granted what Doran couldn't now. "I, again, give you the option to live with us. And by staying here you may be anointed into our society and meet your destiny."

Martell paused and then laughed.

The King looked at Viktoran and Windal. The Barons were appalled Martell found the King's words a joke.

Ballan protested, "Silence your elation. His Majesty—"

"My destiny has already found me," Martell interrupted. "I didn't come here to be placed as a pawn on a gambling board for the kingdom's use."

Just as Martell said the word "gambling," a trumpet rang out at the end of the hall. When Ballan and Noran saw who entered, they rolled their eyes toward the ceiling.

Guards escorted the group of eight Salmus voyagers forward. Once they reached the area in front of the shattered windows, they halted and formed a line so Noran could clearly see them all. Martell stayed where he was while Viktoran and Windal tried shuffling off to the side to allow the King to greet the voyagers.

Ballan raised his voice, "Your Majesty, the voyagers of the Kingdom of Salmus. Captain Winslow, please come forward."

Noran turned his attention to the crowd and then leaned over to whisper something into Ballan's ear. The announcer nodded and added, "General Fields, please step forward."

The General did as he was instructed and said, "Your Majesty."

"General Fields, please have the Majestic Messengers fetch Baron Oreus Blake before he reaches the border of the Western Yard. I wish him to fulfill his task of entertaining the voyagers while I attend to the matters at hand."

The General bowed and plodded off to the Majestic Messenger post inside the Western Gate.

"Good afternoon, Your Majesty," Winslow said. "The weather in this country is rather frightful. It can only leave one to suspect that you have upset your god."

"Yawrana the Maker has never been ill toward us. The kingdom is entirely devoted to our creator—even its name," Noran stated proudly. "The storms are a fluke."

Winslow picked up a long wooden splinter, examining it as he said, "This is some fluke." Starting to point toward the broken windows, Winslow said, "Have you seen the extent of the—"

"I am quite aware of it," the King said to silence him. "I just lived through the hardships Candlewick has endured."

Ballan spoke, "If you wish it, Your Majesty, I will guide the voyagers to the gandalay stables. I will start the tour of the castle from there until Baron Blake arrives to relieve me of his duties."

Martell jumped in and said, "Yes! That is a splendid idea. Take them, Announcer."

Ballan glared at Martell to warn the Nax he was overstepping his boundaries.

Noran sighed, contemplating what he should do. After a few moments, he finally said, "Actually, Ballan, I have to agree with Martell. Your idea does sound appealing."

"Thank you, Your Maj—"

"I will join you," Noran quickly added.

"You . . . want to join us, Your Majesty?" Ballan said, surprised.

"Yes. I need some sun. I have missed the peace it brings. A good horse ride may do us some good. How about it, Captain Winslow? Are you up for a long trot in the countryside?"

Winslow smiled and replied, "I would love it, Your Highness."

"Good. Captain Soar and Rollins, I wish you to also come along. Your servants will be shown to their quarters until we return."

Winslow scoffed, "But, Your Majesty, we would feel more comfortable with our servants around us, just as you are with yours."

Noran nodded and said, "Very well, Captain."

Winslow smiled until Noran turned to Ballan and said, "Have General Fields and fifty men ready to ride with us at the Gaming Arena by five."

Ballan glanced toward Winslow and chuckled. He replied, "It shall be, Your Majesty."

"Show the voyagers to their quarters for now. Baron Blake should be here by the time we set out. Inform him as well of our plans," Noran added. Ballan nodded and walked to a stable hand to pass along the orders.

Winslow's face turned a slight shade of red before he bowed and left with his crew to get comfortable in their temporary surroundings. The smell of dung piles and the buzzing barn flies attracted to them, as they would soon find out, would be almost intolerable to cope with.

"They are up to no good," Martell said as soon as they left the hall.

"We know of their intentions," the King acknowledged.

Martell scoffed, "And they're still here?"

"It is complicated," Noran said, not wanting to explain his justifications. "Martell, what did you mean by 'reconciliation' when you went to see the High Elder's grave?"

"It is complicated," Martell replied, throwing Noran's own phrase back at him.

"You will answer the King," Ballan snapped.

"I don't answer to puppets," Martell retorted.

To prevent friction between the two, Noran asked Ballan, "My friend, please see to the voyagers for now."

"Your Majesty, I—"

"Now."

Ballan scowled in disgust at Martell, but withdrew his anger. He bustled off with his staff in one hand and picked up a pitcher of alcohol to hold in the other.

Martell looked suspiciously at Ballan out of the corner of his eye and said, "You smell like honey."

The announcer whirled and growled, acting unsure of how to take the comment. "What of it?"

"Only women wear honey-based perfume," Martell said, laughing.

Ballan raised his hand and curled his fingers to scratch at the Nax, but Noran warned, "Be gone, Ballan."

Two guards came to the announcer's side and helped pull him in the opposite direction. Ballan mumbled unflattering words under his breath while he made off to the guests' quarters.

"Do not taunt my servants ever again!" Noran yelled at Martell, his face a wrinkled and bruised mess of worry.

Martell shrugged, flapped his wings briefly and switched the subject back to where it had started. "To sprinkle this on his body." He held up a small vile of clear liquid between his index finger and thumb.

Noran was, at first, confused until he realized the Nax's method of communication was as sporadic as the storms ravaging the territories. "Is it some kind of blessing fluid?

"They are tears, Your Majesty. My tears, from the many days I cried as a child because of the abhorrent body chosen for my soul by God. I want to rid this pain that has welled up from inside me. Each drop has been collected from my years of anguish and mistreatment. I wish to dump it on the abomination that passed its torment to me and then burn it."

This time Viktoran exclaimed, "You shall not desecrate the body of the High Elder! Are you mad? That is not what you told us you were going to do. You only wished to pay your respects."

"I am far from mad and that is how I wish to pay them to Mosia," Martell retaliated. "Your lack of familiarity with our culture is your ignorance. Burning the body of all who were like me will rid the evidence of our existence. My shame is also soon to be vanquished. I cannot be responsible for all hope on Elvana."

"You do not wear shame in my kingdom," Noran said calmly, regaining his composure. "You will not take your own life and you will not be allowed near the High Elder's tomb. Tell me, Martell, why do your people shun the albinos? What makes them mistrust you?"

Unable to hold back his purpose any longer, he said, "We are the symbol that the end days of Elvana are growing near. All my life I have known that the god I have come to reconcile with is a merciless one for having made Mosia, me and the others before us what we are. Any living creature wouldn't want one walking amongst them who represents the world's fatal destiny. But," Martell said explaining the rest, "the Nax do not dare murder any who bear the mark, for it could help corruption triumph over the innocent. We are their reminding agony of what could come. The scriptures of the Nax Synod foretell that seven shall be chosen at birth during the history of the world, each an albino—one for each entry into a new age. The lastborn, the seventh, will signify the day of reconciliation is at hand. I . . . am the last of the seven," he said with a heavy heart, "which means the final age has already begun to take place—when good and evil will clash in a battle for supremacy, wreaking havoc upon Elvana until a victor stands over the enemy he has thrown down. Every intellectual race will play a part in the final days and no kingdom will go untouched. To disrupt the living lifespans of any in the chain of the marked seven will only bring the end days more quickly. I have found the first original five like me and, with fire, turned their bones to ash, and their flesh and hair to dust. If we do not physically exist, then perhaps the scriptures' pious finality can be postponed or avoided forever."

The King soaked in the message Martell relayed. His eyes penetrated the Nax's soul and felt Martell's long-standing fear within him. Ballan's honey scent still hung in the air around them. He, too, had noticed Ballan was probably trying to hide his age by using the cream. Noran finally smiled and said, "As long as your faith remains, the Maker will give us the chance to prove that the purity of our true inner strength will be our salvation. Together, we will be the strength the world relies upon to save it."

Martell only shook his head and said, "Your words are honorable, Your Highness, but it will happen as long as I am here."

"It will happen even if you do decide to take your life. You wish to abandon us before the future can properly unfold? You see, I do not agree that the world will end. It will only go through a transformation because our god is not merciless and does not desire to end everything he has created from his own glory. He, as I believe, will grant us the wisdom to end the pain and suffering which plagues us. And you will be one of the many who play a part in his design. That only leads me to the decision that I must assign you a guard at all times to prevent you from fulfilling the task you have set out to do."

Martell once again looked as if the chains of condemnation would not allow him to break free of the fate he was sent here for. He nodded to the King as Noran pointed at the first rank guard near the seventh broken, green window in the hall. Noran felt it was a sign to choose that guard because of where she was standing.

She was tall with black hair, and strode forward at Noran's request. "Your Majesty," she said, bowing.

"Your name?"

"Pelly Parkin, my Lord."

"How long have you held your position, Pelly?"

"I was just promoted yesterday, my Lord. Transferred from Serquist Tower."

Viktoran approved with a nod. "Pelly is a fine guard, Your Majesty. She is an excellent choice for the responsibility, having assisted us admirably in defending our medicine maker center against Herikech's horde of grime swimmers and treetop swingers."

Noran waved her to him so he could whisper in her ear, "Your role is critical in this matter, Pelly. The Nax may go where he wishes in the castle and Yards. However, he is not to leave the Royal House grounds without my permission. It will be arranged that he will stay in the northeast tower so he may look upon his homeland in Overbay Territory. His room is to remain locked at night and a handful of guards will be stationed outside his door and balcony window to give you temporary reprieve. Do not fail me, for it could have catastrophic effects on not only the kingdom, but the world as well. Use your judgment wisely."

Pelly's eyes widened when she gazed at Martell, realizing she had just been burdened with the most horrendous assignment imaginable.

The sun was pleasant as Noran stood still while Bruneau led his gandalay mount to him. A cool breeze flowed over his skin, trying to steal the satisfaction he had found from the sun's soothing, golden warmth. He changed into lighter apparel to allow his skin to breathe easier for the long ride. A white shirt beneath a cotton green vest covered his upper body and a pair of brown pants with black short boots dressed his legs.

Already at the Western Gate was General Fields, thirty soldiers and twenty guards at the General's disposal. They saluted the King with a fist to their chests when he exited the Gaming Arena to greet them.

"Your Majesty," General Fields called out, stopping Noran before he could reach his horse. "It has been reported by the Yard scouts that the trail to Rest End Waterfall is void of tree downfall. The rest of the territory is not worthy of consideration. It's as much a mess as the rest of the castle. It will take all season before we get the Yards groomed and the gardens replanted."

"What about the walls, General? Did any crumble during the storm? Herikech is waiting for the right opening to slink his way past our posts without being seen. This would have been the ample . . . ."

General Fields saw the dawning of an obvious realization upon the King's face. "My Lord, what is it?"

"Oh no. I think he may already be here."

"Herikech?" Fields asked with an uncertain tone. "What evidence proves it? The walls are still all intact, which is the answer to the question you were asking."

"He made the storms."

The General scoffed, "My Lord, no man can conjure up a storm—"

"He is no longer any mortal man, General!" Noran yelled, his muscles binding up in a row of knots down the middle of his neck and back. "Herikech walks both the plane of the living and dead! His powers are growing and we have just experienced it firsthand. He is beginning to control the elements. Wind and water are already at his fingertips. There is no telling how close he is to mastering fire and soil and what it will lead to if he does. When one controls an element portal, he is a force that needs to be reckoned with."

Bruneau backed Noran's words, saying, "I believe the King's estimations are correct. At the time Queen Willow and Princess Ola were taken hostage by Johr and his men into Arna, I witnessed a stormfront over Dowhaven that flew in with the wings of a demon. It would stand to reason that Herikech decided to test the extent of his new powers in a remote region first. And what region is more remote than Dowhaven?"

The General turned to a pair of guards near the gate, motioning to them. Both men approached. Fields was about to give an order when he noticed a long bruise on each side of one guard's neck. "Thatch, have you had the makers take a look at those wounds? They are deep."

The guard laughed and replied, "I got knocked around a couple of times by a few branches in the gardens. They'll heal up. I've had worse shiners from my brothers."

Fields frowned and said, "I want you two to inform Lieutenant Wrasp to assemble a sweep hunt and search every corner of this castle."

"Anything else we should tell him, General?" the second guard asked.

In a low voice he whispered, "Yes. We believe the enemy walks among us."

Thatch and the second guard nodded and marched off. General Fields turned back toward the King and said, "The voyagers are late. They continue to make unfavorable impressions with me."

"At least one voyager has finally arrived," Noran said, seeing Oreus on the other side after the outer gate was opened. He waved to the Baron, who quickly returned the gesture and rode up to the party.

"Noran," Oreus said with a salute, allowed to call the King by his first name.

"Oreus, I see the Majestic Messengers chased you down."

"No horse can outrun a dobbin," Oreus said, laughing. "Their legs are built for longer distances than old Lexa here," he said, rubbing the white gandalay mare along the right side of her neck. The horse whinnied, appreciating the consoling touch of the Baron's gentle hand. "Where are Winslow and the others?" he questioned, not seeing any of them in the vicinity.

Noran sighed. "Winslow is most likely getting even with me for putting his quarters next to the stables. I imagine he is deriving some form of pleasure by making me wait for him."

The sound of many hooves trotting along a stone hallway echoed toward them, ending their doubt that they might not show at all. Noran was ready to send a guard to fetch them when Winslow's prim face came within range, telling them he wasn't in the least upset with their sleeping arrangements.

"King Deardrop," Winslow said in a lighthearted voice. "I hope you have not been waiting too long for us."

"We were beginning to wonder if you had changed your mind," Noran replied.

Winslow laughed softly. "Let us not delay any further then. It feels refreshing to be riding saddleback again." Rollins, Soar and the rest of the Salmus voyagers brought up the rear, exchanging intimidating glances with many of the soldiers and guards under Fields's command.

Windreed sat upon a white thunder horse, the only breed large enough in the kingdom to carry her enormous frame. The barbarian's hair was no longer in a braid, but spilling down over the front of her chest. Oreus found her quite beautiful when some of the warrior image was stripped away. He knew, however, it wouldn't change Boris's mind in the slightest. He was positive that Boris would still try to kill her if they were both alone together.

The King waved for a guard to bring his horse over. The stallion began to resist as it drew close to Noran. The second the King placed his hand around the saddle horn and put his foot in the stirrup, the mount whinnied in a squealing pitch and tried to spin away from him. Noran managed to catch his foot over the top of the saddle and pull himself into an upright sitting position. But the stallion continued to protest and rear, knocking away the guard who was holding the reins until the King could get situated. The stallion shot forward unexpectedly while Noran hung on to the mane in fright.

"Your Majesty!" General Fields screamed, snapping his steed into action.

Noran attempted to reach out for the reins, which had bounced over the stallion's head and fallen below its neck. His opportunity was disrupted when the horse headed directly for a fallen tree branch and hurdled it, throwing the King. Unable to keep his grip, Noran suddenly felt himself thrust forward and flying over the head of the animal. His body hit the side of a muddy ravine, cracking a pair of ribs against a log on his right side. Turning over and clutching at the jabbing pain, a pair of hooves came at his head. He rolled just in time to avoid being killed by the brunt impact of metallic shoes. Noran's mind raced as to why the horse had not yet run off, but instead was now willingly trying to kill him. The gandalay brought a hoof down again, smacking against the side of his arm. He yelled while backing up on all fours, doing everything he could to save his own life. The stallion struck a second time, this time stomping down on his right leg. He screamed and grasped at the painful blow.

Blaynor lunged from his horse and threw up his arms to protect the King from the gandalay's unusual behavior. The gandalay finally backed down and ran to stand by the horse Bruneau was dismounting.

"What happened, my Lord?" Blaynor asked, seeing tears welled up in the King's eyes. Noran couldn't respond, using all of his energy to stave off the throbbing of his inflictions. His teeth were clamped together as tight as a vice.

"Get a cart and a maker!" Bruneau shouted when Blaynor signaled to him with a thumb pointed down.

Approximately a half hour later, the castle's maker, Fahlil Oyen, was riding in the front seat of the cart with a brown leather medical bag at his right side. The driver snapped the reins repeatedly until they reached the King. Noran was surrounded by the fifty-army anointees. Oyen jumped from the seat and shoved his way through the guards and soldiers to reach the King. To his surprise, Noran was sitting upright and laughing with Oreus. The

Baron had just finished an amusing joke.

"There you are, Master Oyen," Noran said, acting as if his pain was not as severe as the message said it was.

Out of breath, the middle-aged maker replied, "Your Majesty, you should be lying down. Blood is soaking through your pant leg."

"There is just some torn skin, Master. It will heal up with some stitches. It's actually quite numb at the moment."

The driver and Bruneau positioned a long stretcher next to Noran. They both helped lift the King carefully onto it. Noran grimaced when his ribs were jostled from the movement. After placing him in the cart, Bruneau and Blaynor took their seats next to him and latched the rear panel.

"Do not harm Shepherd. He is a noble horse," Noran ordered before the driver was back in his seat.

Fields stated, "My Lord, the stallion almost killed y—"

"Yes. But I don't know why. Have the animal makers perform a thorough examination on him, both physically and mentally, and keep him under close observation. Let me know what they learn. Maybe he is being controlled by Herikech somehow."

Fields saluted the King and glanced over at the horse. The stallion was whinnying innocently and eating grass as if nothing out of the ordinary had happened.

When the King was carried to the maker's wing, Willow was already waiting in the family room with a pale complexion, twisting her beautiful red braid in her hands. She stood the moment they entered and passed through the adjoining hall with her husband, talking softly to Oreus. The Baron went to her while they whisked Noran off to a back room where only Bruneau, Blaynor, the maker and his pupils would be allowed for the time being.

"Oreus, please tell me his condition," Willow said with a tear running down her left cheek. The Queen's green gown and crown of sparkling white gems made her appearance magnificent, even in the gloomy corridors of the windowless room.

The two guards with the Queen saluted Oreus. The Baron smiled, bowed to her and said calmly, "Noran will be well soon. His injuries are not severe enough to bring you concern. We are very fortunate he didn't suffer a worse fall, my Lady."

"The maker in me wishes to help Master Oyen so I can see his wounds for myself. But, I traded the blue band for the green and must respect his work. I have heard his gandalay, Shepherd, became spooked and tossed him. What could have led to this? His horse has never portrayed these symptoms before."

"To be truthful, my Lady, I worry for Shepherd. There may be an outside influence that forced him to react the way he did."

Knowing what Oreus was referring to, she said, "You mean Herikech. He somehow has forced Noran's own mount against him like he did with the animals in the swamps of Serquist?"

"It is a thought that has been considered," Oreus said openly. "How Herikech has turned docile creatures against Yawranans, has been troubling me. Even the great, ancient nefars wouldn't attack an army without provocation of some kind. Noran has also informed me he believes Herikech can control weather patterns, which would explain the heavy rains and twisters devastating the territories. How does one fight an enemy with powers only Yawrana the Holy should possess?"

"What if he turns the draguls against us as well?" Willow said, almost losing her voice from the mere thought of it.

Oreus's face went white from her comment. "I hadn't even considered that. I will discuss it with General Fields as soon as I leave here. There is one other thing, my Lady," he said with apprehensive eyes.

"Tell me, Baron."

"We must have you and Varen taken to a safe, hidden location. Herikech might be in the castle right now. The storms may have provided him the ability to penetrate the walls of Candlewick."

Oreus didn't need to say anything else to convince her. Willow turned green and sprinted from the room, heading straight for the private bedchambers of her infant son. Her guards gave chase and quickly caught up with her. Oreus hung his head and sat down, knowing she would be returning soon with many of her personal belongings and clothes packed for her new destination only he, Noran, the princesses, a host of guards, and General Fields would know of. It was a place of tranquility and was so well disguised that not even the best tracker in the land could find them there. Varen, the future heir to the throne, was once again threatened and had not even cut his first tooth. How would a helpless baby grow up under the conditions they were now facing? Oreus thought of how he could protect a child of his own under such circumstances.

It wasn't unrealistic to think he should wait to have any children of his own until Herikech was destroyed—if he ever could be. Ola's safety alone was enough to keep him awake at nights. The princesses had their protection tripled since the day the battle for Serquist ended. Ola had stated more than once how she hated crowds and preferred privacy at times. But the barons and generals all agreed the royal family was to be watched under close supervision until precautions were no longer required.

The King's surgery was fast after Master Oyen applied a numbing medication directly to the wounds on the King's leg and arm. A five-inch gash had been opened on his lower thigh. The master cleansed the openings well and kept the stitches small so the wound would heal nicely. Noran's arm was lacerated but only required half the thread his leg did. A potent cream was applied to the tender, sewn areas and then was covered by a large, white square bandage. It would stave off infections and help reduce the amount of bleeding while his body repaired itself. As for his ribs, his midsection was wrapped securely to help restrict his movements and keep his activities to a minimum. Bruneau and Blaynor were relieved when the maker had finished and started to give Noran directions.

"This is to prevent the onset of any fevers," Master Oyen said, handing the King a bottle of blue pills. "One each day should be enough. No more riding for now, Your Majesty. It is also in your best interest to not go running about every chance you get. Any physical exertion is out of the question and could pull apart the stitches. Keep them out of water until I remove them." The maker pointed at Bruneau and Blaynor and ordered, " I put you two in charge to ensure he takes my recommendations seriously."

Blaynor nodded while Bruneau smiled, knowing it was always a challenge to dissuade a King from doing what he wanted when he wanted. Noran's attention was known to wander easily when the King was in the Grand Hall. It wasn't uncommon lately and made the guards smile when he asked someone to repeat themselves multiple times during their presentation. Granted, some of the topics he was engaging could make any soul yawn out of boredom. However, the King's voice even in those particular matters was just as important as any others that were to be resolved by him alone.

"They will not need to remind me of your words, Master Oyen," Noran assured the medicine maker. The King looked at Bruneau. The guard raised a skeptical eyebrow, forcing Noran to say, "I have some reading to catch up on anyhow."

"I'll believe it when I see it," the master replied, unconvinced. "I have known you for too long, Your Majesty. Your energy is endless, just as it was with your father when he was your age."

There was a knock at the door when Noran sat up on the surgical table. Bruneau went and opened it, expecting to see the Queen or Oreus on the opposite side. To his surprise, it was neither.

"I need to speak with the King immediately," said a familiar female voice from the corridor outside.

"This is beginning to be a habit, High Elder," Bruneau replied. "Is your presence here for business or concern for the King's health?"

"Both," she answered.

"Hello, High Elder," Noran said, giving Bruneau the verification he needed to open the door and allow her to enter. The King smiled, but it vanished when he saw how bothered she was.

"Master Oyen," Noran said, "please take your assistants and leave. "Bruneau, guard the door and let no one in until we're done." After they had all left, he continued his greeting, "High Elder, your expression tells me you are here for purposes higher than my health. Does this meeting relate to the cattle mutilations occurring in the Royal House Territory?"

The High Elder was stunned the King had read her thoughts. "Has someone told you of the attacks?" she asked, still reeling from the revelation that he already knew.

Noran smiled. "Do not worry, High Elder. I overheard your discussion with the farmer in the Grand Hall before the tornadoes struck Candlewick."

She nodded, impressed his ears were able to pick up on their hushed conversation. "Yawrana the Holy has given you the hearing of a dragul."

"It's one of my few reliable traits," he replied modestly. "Maybe inherited from the Lazuls."

"Nonsense, Your Majesty. You have the blood of many talents in your veins, although they may not be enough to save you this time."

Blaynor went on edge, afraid what the High Elder was about to say and for good reason.

"It is time I inform you of a prophecy that was revealed to me when I first became High Elder. Elder Garan recently shed some new light on my original vision from your last meeting with him. He stated to you he witnessed your death."

Noran nodded when she waited for some kind of confirmation.

"The prophecy is related to the cattle mutilations, Your Majesty. I, too, saw your death. A shaggy creature that looks like a maddon, but walks on two legs like a watcher—a mangler I call it—wanders the territories of Yawrana and has now chosen the farms surrounding Candlewick as its next targets. Cattle, swine, yard fowl and even pets have been reported missing over the winter. Spring has only increased its feedings and torture on those it attacks until the weather began conducting itself in a manner not normal of itself. This predator rises when either of the two moons are red and relies on them, I believe, for its source of strength."

"Yes," Noran agreed. "We believe Herikech is behind the tornadoes and abundant rainstorms. He may also be controlling this beast you speak of. I'm almost certain of it. It's possible he is altering his forms of aggression to create mass hysteria."

The High Elder shook her head. "One detail I must allude to is that the attacks have extended back for more than two years. They have only just recently come to light because of its proximity to the castle and Herikech's involvement with the animals during the battle for Serquist Tower. Animal carcasses have been discovered from time to time in southern Dowhaven, but have never been reported, displaying the same vicious maulings of the latest attacks here. Every farmer along the forests north of us has now been questioned, leading to these findings. But, as far as we know, most of Herikech's army of beasts originated in Serquist. With that in mind, it's very possible this mangler is acting on its own instincts."

"But Herikech may have sent the creature from Serquist when he first entered the territories, most likely around the same time the attacks in Dowhaven first began to appear. He may have sent it solely to kill me."

"Yes. That is why I'm not ruling Herikech out. My Lord, the visions both Elder Garan and I saw show you fighting this beast. The odds do not bend in your favor if you confront it on its own ground—where red moonlight falls. Your fight with the mangler is to take place near a window when the second moon of Yawrana has changed and is shining through its drapeless opening. A hooded figure watches on with great interest. I'm positive it is Herikech because of the grin and sharp jaw-line I saw on the individual. He takes great delight in witnessing your struggle with the beast. If you can stay out of the moonlight, you may have a chance to survive. It may be your *only* chance."

"Where is the encounter to take place? Do you know why I am there?" Noran asked, feeling his life spiraling out of control.

The High Elder wiped a tear from her eye. "It's the one thing I can't determine. It could be any one of a thousand windows throughout the territories. You will know the attack is about to take place when a horned beetle climbs the window's pane. I fear for this day, Your Majesty, because . . . we may not be able to prevent it from happening." The High Elder couldn't stop her flood of tears any longer. She wept into the sleeves of her robe.

Noran went to her and hugged her. "Elenoi, there is always hope, even when times are darkest. We have overcome far too many obstacles together and this will just be the next."

"My bones tell me differently, Your Majesty," she said, collecting another few drops on her cuff. "The power in the moonlit room is too great for you to prevail. You are unable to stop what will happen and you will fall to the mangler."

Blaynor couldn't help but say, "Not while I'm around."

"You're unable to help the King because you're being attacked by someone else," Elenoi added, placing a doubt of fear into his mind. "I'm sorry, Blaynor."

"What about me?" Bruneau suddenly burst into the room from having obviously listened through the door as usual. "What about me? I will kill this beast before he can harm the King."

Noran, Blaynor and even the High Elder all laughed at Bruneau's comical entrance.

"What's so funny?" he snapped, blushing.

"Nothing at all, Bruneau. Your passion and persistence are plentiful as always," Noran said.

The guard growled, "I still don't see what's so funny about the King's death . . . ."

The High Elder said, "Bruneau's robust entrance reminded me of something I will share with you now, Your Majesty. It was about the night I gave you Herishen Illeon's will—on the eve of your wedding reception. I informed you to be in the ballroom before midnight so you would not miss the surprise."

"Yes, I recall you mentioning that," Noran said. "Willow gave me a carved wooden bead necklace. And on the carved chain hung three hoops, one from each of the three sequeras that were lost due to the arsonist's fire. It was a surprise I will never forget—"

"It was not why I had you leave your room at that time, Your Majesty, the mangler was about to attack you in your room that night, which is the main reason I was there. I had seen the vision in the water I was blessing you with from the Vision Pool's altar. It was truly a gift of matrimony from the Maker above. If you would have stayed and continued to read Herishen's will, the beast would have found you. At that point I instructed General Fields to not let you leave the ballroom until dawn."

It all suddenly came back to Noran as he sat with his mouth agape. "You purposely had my men get me so drunk that I couldn't be returned to my room? I do remember waking up in a servant's chamber with Willow the next morning."

The High Elder nodded. "You were brought there as soon as you had passed out."

"Does Willow know of this?"

The High Elder nodded again. "Yes, Your Majesty. It is also why any time there is a red moon you are deterred from reaching your bedchambers by any means necessary—out of fear that the mangler may someday return. One night, during a red moon, you fell asleep in Bruneau's room, and another, in Blaynor's. Willow also knew about the mangler and was moved to new quarters until the moon's color passed. Even though your son Varen sleeps in the Head of House's chamber during the evening, he stayed with Willow on those evenings. I'm sorry you had to learn it this way."

Noran started to say, "I would have gone willingly if—"

"You wouldn't have," the High Elder quickly cut in. "At least not on all accounts, Your Majesty. Eventually you would have grown resistant to the idea and returned to sleep in your own bed. A King's confidence can sometimes override his sensibilities. I don't mean to offend. All Yawranan Kings have the heart of a karrik. It is a greatness too hard to ignore."

Unsure whether to take the statement as a compliment or insult, Noran replied, "Enough men could have been posted—"

The Elder was already shaking her head. "All would have perished by the mangler's strength and speed. I couldn't tell you until now—using the guidance of the prophecy. A mysterious traveler had to appear first before I could say anything. Otherwise Bruneau, Blaynor, Willow, or even Varen could all be dead by now, which is why I had them help me in other ways before I could tell you."

"Martell Fedrow?" he asked. "He is the traveler?"

"I believe it is he who has set this prophecy into motion."

"Martell could even be associated with this mangler for all we know," Bruneau said suspiciously. "Why should we trust him so willingly just because he is an albino Nax like the former High Elder was? He has already shown us he can't be trusted. He wanted to go and set flame to Mosia's body for heaven's sake! Maybe he is the hooded figure you have seen in your vision, who watches the King fighting the mangler—not Herikech."

Noran found no reason to deny Bruneau's theory. With the latest attacks occurring so closely to Martell's arrival, it was a logical connection to make. "Bruneau, give a message to one of the maker's servants to send word to Pelly Parkin. I want her to consider Martell a possible threat to her safety. She must be extremely careful not to upset him if she can avoid it. If he does have some relation with the mangler, he could have it attack her. The Nax are close to many creatures of the wild. With Martell being an albino and the seventh of his type, he may have powers we have not yet learned of."

"I think she already feels that way, my Lord, but I will have it done." Bruneau saluted and left the room, shutting the door behind him.

"If the mangler has gotten into my room once before," Noran said, "then it can do it at any time. I must have my bedchamber moved immediately. There is only one area of the castle harder to get to than my quarters—the Secret Halls. I must make arrangements with the Head of House to move me to the largest room that is not being occupied."

"You are willing to wake up without the sun shining upon your face?" Blaynor asked.

Noran scoffed, "There has not been enough of it lately to even worry about with all the rain hitting my windows."

Blaynor laughed and said, "Your new quarters shall be ready for you by nightfall."

"High Elder, when is the next red moon?" Noran inquired, trying to remember when the last was.

"Four days from now the first moon, Radia, will be in crescent form with the blood of our forefathers on it, Your Majesty," she quickly said, having prepared the answer in advance. "I also must suggest that you do not go outside in the evening at any given time during that date. The creature will find you if it continues to try, especially now that Martell is here and Herikech is roaming the halls on his own free will."

"You know about that?" Noran asked in shock.

"Everyone in the castle does now. Fear has made its bed here. And, it will remain until they no longer feel their safety is threatened."

Blaynor offered a solution. "There is one thing we can turn to when the masses are restless, my Lord."

Noran turned his head slowly up to his guard and said, "Go on."

"We may have finally found a use for the Salmus voyagers."

Curious, Noran asked, "What is your proposal?"

Smiling, Blaynor said, "What gathers a crowd like nothing else in the territories?"

Blaynor's words lifted Noran's spirits. "The Arena games. That is a fantastic idea. The people could use a few good performances now more than ever."

"But what if the voyagers don't want to participate?"

"A bit of taunting never hurt anyone," Blaynor said and smirked. "The Captains' servants all look to be worthy of a fair fight in the challenges. Winslow is a betting man. I'm sure he would agree to it."

"What could we offer besides the castle's wealth?"

"How about the imprisoned Zonack voyagers for one of their prized drift ships?"

Noran looked confused. "Crag, Gunner and Stoffer? What could Winslow possibly want with them?"

"Winslow knows they are aware where the treasure vaults are since Lanu's crew raided them. Do you not think he would find that information useful?"

"If we lose, we might as well just hand the wealth over to them now," Noran exclaimed, not finding the idea alluring.

"Move the treasure, my Lord. You will be putting nothing on the line. We win either way—by gaining the new schematics for an improved flying vessel or by ridding ourselves of the Zonack voyagers forever."

The King couldn't help but smile. "Since when did you become so brilliant? I want the clandestine castle maps in my new quarters by this evening. Once the vaults have been moved, we will beat Winslow at his own tricks. For now, I must say goodbye to my wife before she disappears into hiding."

"There is one last part of the puzzle I have not yet mentioned about the mangler, my Lord," the High Elder said.

"More riddles?" Noran asked, tired from what he already knew.

"The death of a Trail Racer a time ago exhibited the same inflictions as the cattle mutilations I laid eyes upon earlier today."

"I thought that death was due to a maddon attack?"

Elenoi frowned and shook her head. "It was a lie by General Keys, Your Majesty. He was afraid to shut down one of his main routes through Dowhaven because of it. But, he was forced to anyway because no one else in any of his squads wanted to make the run, despite the money that was offered for several package deliveries. He then resorted to hiring a driver named Rhett, who saw the mangler but managed to escape unharmed. Rhett's testimony states he saw the creature feasting on the body of a deer in the same manner it did with the cattle it killed. The mangler is no rumor. It is indeed real."

"I will have to summon General Keys to the Grand Hall and confront him myself as to why he continued to endanger the lives of my people and the dobbins for the sake of business. I will shut down his delivery service faster than he can say 'carrus.'"

"What do we do about the mangler for now? Should we hunt it?" Blaynor asked, looking unafraid.

"No," Noran replied. "We shall let it come to us."

"And give it another chance to kill you?"

"No," Noran repeated. "Keep my bedchambers set up exactly as they have been for now. I want my smell and the appearance I am still sleeping there to remain. Supply new furnishings to my quarters in the Secret Halls. We shall set a trap in my old room and end the beast's life before it knows what happened. When the next red moon rises, we will be waiting."

"What do you want to use as bait?" Elenoi asked out of curiosity.

Grinning, Noran replied, "Me, of course."

# CHAPTER FIVE
## Bystol Biscuits

Once the candles were lit in his new, darkened quarters within the Secret Halls of Candlewick, Noran felt only a little more at ease. Not being able to view the sun or twin moons of Yawrana through an open bedchamber window made him feel claustrophobic, but he would have to adjust until the castle was safe again. Only a handful of items had been transferred from his original bedchamber to this one: a set of clothes for the new day ahead, his sword Arc Glimmer, an oil painting of Willow and him holding Varen, Herishen Illeon's Will and Testament, and the stinging bystol plant that normally rested just outside his room, waiting to attack anything that came remotely close to it.

The plant's multiple long tentacles were layered with tiny rows of teeth containing a white fluid that, when injected, temporarily put its victim to sleep. To prevent Noran from falling helpless to its ruthless, carnivorous appetite, the castle's chefs had taken normal, everyday dog biscuits and filled them with another type of sleeping drug that would cause the bystol to doze for half an hour while he bypassed it, unharmed, to reach his room. The plants were known only to exist in a drier climate at Emison Territory's southern edge where there were few farming communities to worry about their existence.

His leg and arm felt worse than ever now that his body had realized the damage it had sustained and repairs it needed to do. He was limping more than shuffling as he made his way to a desk that was obtained from an unused guest room on the north wing. Herishen's ancient writings sat in the center of the reading platform before him. The King pulled out the large, padded chair and sat down. A goblet and pitcher of wine stood on a table next to the desk. He poured himself some to relax his nerves for a good hour of reading. Noran's opportunities to read at all were few, to say the least. Normally he was entrenched in documents pertaining to the laws and customs of the kingdom. It was only now that he finally had the chance to read the next passage in Herishen's writings. It was the first time he had touched the book since the night of his wedding reception, which had made him frustrated for some time. It was always at the back of his mind, calling to him.

He slid a candle closer after he flipped back the heavy, gray cover to the desired page marked by a green ribbon. The parchment had been restored well enough to allow him to read the entire page.

*The tension between my brothers and me since father's death grows with each passing day. I must prepare for the danger that could result from this constant feud. If either Heritoch's or Herikech's intentions are what I expect – to conquer and reap the benefits of their siblings – then I must ready myself for my end days here. Heritoch is gullible enough to believe he will take the lands to the east and west of Maramis without great difficulty. Despite Herikech and me both being younger, we are stronger than he and can fend our lands from his initial surges for now. He will test our territory lines, determining which direction is the weakest to invade from. My scouts have started to send warnings of the first skirmishes near the high grass plains of the north. Therefore, I have ordered tunnels to Maramis to be blocked and roads through the plains to be disguised to throw off their advances. Many of my men will die needlessly to stave off war, but Herikech will, in time, send the main strength of his army to take what he believes is solely his by birthright. He cannot be reasoned with. He does not believe in the possibility that three identical brothers can equally rule this vast kingdom together. And it is by his hand he proves his faithless words.*

*I have consulted my prophet, Yarba Scraw, once again for guidance from signs in the waters. The four gods we have come to revere for our strength and pride have repeatedly shown favor for lust and greed rather than preservation and enlightenment. My faith in the old ways of the founding tribes is no more. Yarba says there is hope to prevail if we turn to a new, single entity to rule our hearts, rather than continuing to submit to the conflicting forces of the four gods. This new god must be just and unite the Lazul people under my leadership if we are to survive. The name of the One has come from a race that lives and thrives in the sun. We have recently encountered these new people trespassing in the Wailing Hills. Eighty men and women they number, claiming to have sailed from the lands of mist to the south. They bear a gift from their single god, who gives life instead of taking it. This precious plant, a flower they call a snowtear in their language, or a sunberrol in our own, has mended angry wounds and cured untreatable disease before my own eyes. The snowtears are a blessing, they say, from the one spirit that fulfills their souls with an everlasting peace like no other – Yawrana.*

*The voyagers refer to themselves as the Methulisians, after the homelands they left far behind. And though our languages differ, theirs is a simple one to learn. With them they have medicinal healers who teach it well as if explaining something as simple as a color.*

*Many names and faces there are to learn among them, but the few who I have come to know first are the main three within their circle of trust. Audra Xadu, the voice of the eighty in number, carries the Scroll of Truth. I do not yet understand the importance it contains, but my patience to learn the secrets it possesses will keep my patience plentiful. Kale Visher, the more elderly of the two males with Audra, is stern and untrusting toward me. I hear him whispering words of caution to Audra. The presence of our weapons intimidates him the most. His eyes portray a fear that says we will not let them leave once their purpose here is complete. The Lazul blood pumping through my heart has not warmed to disagree with that sentiment. Yarba has informed me the Methalisians may be far more important than I have envisioned and could aid in the brewing war. He advises to hold them here as a trade to Heritoch or Herikech if their victory is ever at hand. The last of the three Methalisians is the one my prophets fear, Hamner. Little does he speak, yet his few words and actions influence my decisions about their care more than Audra or Kale. His eyes have a power that penetrates my soul, perhaps seeing the promise in me the Methalisians are hoping for – another conduit to share with the world – the hope of a healed tomorrow.*

*To my delight, as a show of faith in the Lazuls, Audra has allowed the planting of a single snowtear in a solitary location within the Wailing Hills. The chosen place contains fertile soil that will allow the flower to reproduce through its roots. But it will take more than soil, water and sun for this flower to replicate over time. It is of a delicate nature and can only be recreated when the conditions are precise. The Methalisians will only show us these secrets if they can learn to trust us first. As the trust grows between our races, the flower will have the chance to as well. But Yarba believes they have many snowtears with them. How many is uncertain. Their ship remains hidden at this time somewhere along the western shores of the Waungee. My Bethlen guards have not discovered where it lays, but their skill is unequaled by any other warrior Maramis could produce. Nothing can elude their sight forever. Yarba has instructed them well in the arts of using the land's resources and creatures to their advantage. Their devotion to me can never be bartered for and those who tempt that path will only find death waiting to pounce. The Methalisian ship will be found, and any additional cargo it contains. Once that information is related to me, Yarba will decide the Methalisians' fate through the spring visionary pools in the western undergrounds.*

*For now Audra and her people must remain hidden in my care. If Heritoch or Herikech learn of their existence, suspicion will run through their camps like a fire out of control. My brothers would consider joining forces to overrun our barriers and blockades to have these new people for their own selfish uses. Mainly, slavery. Already they hunt another elusive race known as the Shonintaurs—they are black and hairless mud-bank dwellers, who thrive in the remote marshlands southwest of Verdant Forest. No map can mark the borders of the marshlands because they have never been fully explored and charted, so the forestlands remain as much a mystery as the Shonitaurs themselves. Herikech has become obsessed with their kind, cutting down trees and stripping the heavily wooded areas of brush. The forests are thinning at a rapid pace, but he doesn't seem to care. His lust for a challenging hunt only whets his appetite for a continued chase. He will not relent until he has caught his prey. Verdant Forest will be stripped and bare of its bark in time from his endless pursuit. He will cut every tree and limb, creating roads, bridges and rafts to fulfill his goal—to make his regions superior to that of Heritoch's and my own. My insides tell me he will be successful in time if he is not stopped. If one Shonitaur can be captured, all will fall under his rule. He will impose his will upon them through lies and deceit. By the time they taste his venom, their undoing will be complete.*

The thirty pages that followed only built upon the anxiety Herishen was beginning to feel for his own destiny. Many factors were tearing at his thoughts. The Methalisians only worsened his dilemma from the moment Herishen met them. He would not share with them the repetitive patterns of turmoil the Lazuls placed themselves in. The Methalisian voyagers would assuredly want to leave and take the snowtears with them to share with a worthier race. To help ease his tension, Herishen reverted to what he had been trained to do since birth, describing countless battle plans to defend the Wailing Hills from the growing forces amassing at his borders. No detail was absent from the Lazul King's thoughts, even the reactions of his prophets, army and close military advisors during the mounting eruption of swords and axes. Herishen stated that he could almost hear the cries of the wounded echoing in his skull. He wrote of the pain he still endured for the loss of his father, Ramseur. Tearstains speckled random words on one of the last pages of the passage like raindrops that fell from a clouded mind. Then, the Lazul King ended with: And so my wife Immana has once again saved me from venturing too deep into the dark corridors of my heart.

Noran stopped reading when he came to Herishen's thumbprint after the sentence ended. He sat back in his chair to contemplate the amount of historic significance the writings were playing on his own feelings. He recounted how Rydor and Oreus had saved Queen Immana from the dungeons of Maramis after four thousand years of repression. Her life had only been saved for that period of time because of the snowtears themselves. Little did she know how the sacred Methalisian treasure, brought to the Lazuls as a gift, would become the worst nightmare she could ever imagine. And here was Immana in Herishen's own words, influencing the future in her own way by driving off the conflicting demons tormenting the first King of Yawrana.

A heavy rap rattled the door only a few feet away, followed by a muffled voice. Noran placed the green ribbon where he stopped reading to mark his new page. When he opened the door he expected to see Bruneau or Blaynor. To his surprise, it was Master Oyen.

His tongue tripped over itself when he tried to say something, "Merker— Maker!"

Bruneau appeared in the hallway just behind the medicine healer with a red face. "Your Majesty, there has been an accident . . . ."

"Herikech's behind this," Oyen spat. "He is here."

Noran's face went white as a ghost. "What is it?"

"Blaynor's been injured, Your Majesty," Master Oyen continued. "He was attacked without warning by the stinging bystol while helping move it to your hallway door."

Noran was confused and asked, "But . . . didn't they try to feed it the sleeping biscuits first?"

"They did," Master Oyen said. "But the biscuits didn't work."

Bruneau snapped, "They always did before. There's no reason why they shouldn't have . . . unless they were tampered with."

Noran hung his head and said, "What is the extent of Blaynor's injuries?"

"He's been rendered unconscious. That much is to be expected," Oyen said, telling the easy part first. "His waist, neck and right forearm took most of the damage. The wounds are not severe enough for me to restrain him to a bed for too long. He has hundreds of holes in each wound area where the bystol injected its venom. His skin is peppered with a red rash as well, another side effect that will take time to go away. It will itch and he will scratch until it bleeds if we let him. I have put a thick coat of cooling cream on the areas to minimize the irritation. He should be up and walking around in a few days, but he will be unable to do very much in his condition. It will take time before his body rids itself of the sleeping toxin. He will feel as if he is walking through a cloud with objects appearing to him within a few feet of his range of vision. Over time it will thin to a haze and then finally disappear."

"Where's the bystol?" Noran asked.

Bruneau replied, "It has been chopped down and hauled away by the guards. You won't have to worry about it trying to kill anyone else."

"Take me to him," Noran demanded.

Oyen tried to protest, "It is best we let him rest now, my Lord. He is not— "

"I want to see him!" Noran yelled.

The maker could only nod. Bruneau smiled and followed the King and maker out of the Secret Halls and back up to the medical wing. Along the way, Noran stared at every plant in a corner suspiciously as if it would suddenly jump out and attack him.

"Has General Fields finished his sweep of the castle for Herikech?" Noran asked Bruneau.

"Yes, my Lord. No sign of him, or the mangler, anywhere. But it doesn't mean they haven't found a way to avoid our searches. Candlewick has many secret rooms that haven't been opened for hundreds of years. Some of them remain hidden for a reason and probably hold evil that we wish not to stumble upon."

"A guard's superstition can be his best ally," Master Oyen said.

Both of their comments made Noran feel worse. He remained silent, however, unable to disagree with the truth of either.

A soldier suddenly came sprinting from a southern stairwell, exclaiming, "Your Majesty, a fight has broken out in the Grand Hall!"

Noran and Bruneau raced after the soldier while Master Oyen returned to his medical wing to check on Blaynor's health.

"Who would be fighting at this time?" Noran asked. "It's nearly eight." Noran's leg throbbed, reminding him to slow down. The pain pulsed where the stallion had stomped him.

"My Lord, your leg."

"It will be fine, Bruneau. We just have to take shorter steps."

They crossed the Ballroom and entered the Banquet Hall. They could already hear the sounds of yells and the clatter of dishes before some were broken.

"How many are involved?" Noran yelled to the soldier ahead of them.

The soldier extended two fingers into the air before he reached the door to the Grand Hall. Noran's ears perked up before they reached the door as well, recognizing both voices belonging to none other than General Keys of the Trail Racers and General Hithel of the Majestic Messengers. Noran could only see a blur of hair and blue and red uniforms rolling on the ground when they entered. Several guards surrounded the two generals, trying to figure out a way to break apart the two long hares.

"Your squads are cutting in on my routes!" General Hithel cried.

"The trails are restricted from using carts, not trails!" General Keys retorted.

"They were only groomed for the Majestic Messengers," Hithel growled back.

"You can't hog an entire trail system for yourselves, you blithering idiot."

Noran got as close as he could, almost getting trampled in the process when General Keys bounded up and backwards with his lengthy and powerful feet. Hithel raised his fists and then dropped them when he saw Noran. Keys didn't see the King was standing behind him. The Trail Racers' general fell back to his paws, stretched his feet, ready to use them in a kickboxing match.

Hithel straightened his posture and then bowed to show his respect to the King.

"Ha! Found your limits?" Keys laughed. "You're a disgrace to your own runners."

"General Keys!" Noran shouted behind him.

The General jumped forward in fright and spun around. "Your . . . Your Majesty," he said in a quivering voice.

"That is *enough*."

General Keys bowed and backed several feet toward the throne to keep his distance from Hithel.

Noran glanced around the room, seeing Captains Winslow and Rollins with Thorn and Windreed Sinker standing in one corner, all smirking and whispering. They, in no doubt, found the bantering between the Generals amusing. Oreus was standing near the two Captains, trying to explain the situation as best as he could. Noran frowned in their direction and then turned his attention back toward the soldier who had fetched Bruneau and him.

"Tell me who started this," Noran asked.

"I'm not sure really," the soldier said, trying to remember.

"Anyone else here know how this fight started?" Noran said, looking at the other guards nearby.

General Keys tried defending himself, "Your Majesty, the Majest—"

"Quiet, General!" Noran yelled. "You will have your chance to speak in a moment." Keys swallowed and backed away another foot.

A guard named Vanus approached the King and bowed. With hesitation he said, "It was General Keys who taunted General Hithel to kick the first foot."

"What did he say to provoke him?"

"General Keys was bragging his squads could outrun General Hithel's any day on any mail route."

Not satisfied it was enough for General Hithel to act out of his normal, professional demeanor, Noran said, "And?"

Vanus replied, "General Hithel told General Keys the only mail in his bag was junk mail. Then Keys said he was starting up a special new squad for rush deliveries called 'Hare Mail.' Said they would 'wing' a package to their destinations on gliders with the propeller thrust designs they took from the drift ships."

Noran shot General Keys an angry look. "General, you know all new types of transportation must be approved through me. When were you planning on telling me about your new service?"

Keys bowed apologetically and said, "Just tonight I was going to bring it up. I was informed you needed to speak to me . . . so now seemed the opportune time to tell you." Keys grinned with his toothy overbite and blushed.

"You'll never get that contraption off the ground," General Hithel said. "You'll crash it into the first tree in your path. The propeller thrusts are too strong for gliders and you'll singe your tail hairs."

"General Hithel, please do not continue down this path or I will have you put in a cell over night to cool you off," Noran said as calmly as he could.

Captain Winslow suddenly stepped forward and intervened, "Your Majesty, if I may, I would like to offer a suggestion to resolve this dispute."

Noran raised an eyebrow out of surprise. "Why do you wish to be involved?"

Winslow smiled. "There is obviously a long running dispute between Generals Hithel and Keys about who provides the better mail service to the kingdom. Why not let them prove who is better in a set competition? Would that not end their fight?"

"On the contrary," Bruneau said, "knowing these two, it would only increase their hatred toward each other."

"Not if the stakes were high enough," Winslow replied. "Winner controls all routes."

General Hithel scoffed, "I will not even consider such an outlandish—"

"Perhaps you should let the King speak his thoughts, General," Winslow cut in politely. "At the very least, we could make it interesting in some other manner. Think of the money it would bring to the victor."

"I'm not afraid of even your best branch," General Keys said emphatically. "We'll do it!"

Noran spoke up before General Hithel's usually contained temper exploded. "Captain Winslow may be correct," Noran said. "I think the people have been waiting for a spectacle of this sort. I was originally going to offer a challenge at the Gaming Arena to get the peoples' minds off the storms' destruction, but a race as the opening event to the games could draw a larger crowd."

Winslow couldn't help but ask, "What kind of challenge at the Arena, Your Majesty?"

The King smiled at General Hithel and said to Winslow, "How do you feel about placing another bet, Captain Winslow? We could even double the offer."

Winslow smiled. "You do have a bit of gambling blood in you after all, Your Majesty. What are the stakes?"

"Your Majesty, my crew does not have to prove anything," Hithel said, beads of sweat forming on his nose. "You're not actually going to approve of Captain Winslow's idea, are you?"

"General Hithel, you know as well as I that the Trail Racers and the Majestic Messengers have been at odds now for the last two years. If two Generals are willing to fight in my Grand Hall, what will the runners resort to next? Sabotage of deliveries? I will not let it get that far and the people of Yawrana should not be the ones who suffer from your aggressive differences."

Hithel continued to protest, "But the Majestic Messengers were the first delivery system in the territories since this kingdom was founded. We own more than half the routes."

"Afraid, Hithel? Do you not have faith in your squads to beat us?" Keys said to anger Hithel more.

Noran said, "I have heard many complaints about slower deliveries lately, General Hithel. I know you wish to avoid discussing it. There is only one way to defend your pride and dignity. Systems can become outdated. It is time to prove if your standard methods from centuries past still hold up to the challenge. Generals, this is a chance for each of you to eliminate your opposition. The competition that has grown between you is no longer healthy. And so I declare that the winner of the race will hold ownership of all Yawranan mail routes for seven years. At the end of that period, the system will be reevaluated for improved solutions, and maybe even another race."

General Hithel moaned and shook his head in disappointment.

"Now all we need to decide is what routes should be used," Winslow said. "And the advantage should be on equal ground. Wouldn't you agree, Your Majesty?"

The King paused for a few moments and then nodded and said, "That would be the fair course of action. Half of the race will begin on the lower land trails, which the Majestic Messengers utilize. The other half will finish along the hillsides and ridgelines, owned by the Trail Racers. The race will begin at

Candlewick's Western Gate and encircle the entire Royal House Yard's boundaries, all of which are marked clearly. Each team will carry an empty scroll tube, of which only one will end up holding my proclamation for trail route ownership by the end of the race. As all of us here know, with the exception of the Salmus voyagers, the trails east and west of the castle comprise of flatter, groomed stretches, while the northern and southern ones are rockier and steeper, with dangerous cliffs and wild ravines where karriks and draguls are known to nest, among other dangerous creatures. A different dobbin will run each of the four directional legs of the race. Checkpoints will be located directly north, east, south and west of Candlewick. The empty scroll tube will act as a baton and be handed to the next runner at each of these land markers. The team that reenters the Western Gate first will be declared the winner. And to show there are no hard feelings to the . . . non-victorious, new work will be created throughout the territories to aid the runners for as long as they wish through the remainder of their lives. Their new work, of course, will not equal the pay scale each of them is making now, but none will be allowed to starve while looking for new employment."

General Keys greedily rubbed his paws before Noran added, "And a word of warning—scouts will be posted randomly along all chosen routes to ensure no shortcuts are taken. Generals, be selective and choose your most reliable runners. Speed is not necessarily always the best attribute in this type of wager. The race will commence at sunrise three days from now. Anything you wish to add, Captain Winslow?"

Winslow responded, "The dobbins know what they are up against, but what shall *we* put on the table for sacrifice, Your Majesty?"

"Once again I would like your silence about my territories when you return to Salmus," Noran said. "And since these are my lands, I will choose my team first. I choose the Majestic Messengers."

General Hithel grinned, happy the King hadn't lost faith in his business fully. General Keys, however, frowned and puffed out his chest to keep his air of pride from escaping his lungs.

Winslow smiled. "Very well. The Trail Racers are my kind of runners—gutsy and determined. Then my prize will be for the Zonack voyagers you have imprisoned here."

Noran's heart beat faster, but he remained calm, remembering he was going to use the Zonack voyagers only for the Arena Games wager. He thanked Blaynor in his mind a dozen times. "Roy Stoffer will be the first to babble about Yawrana if he returned to your lands. Why would I wish to offer him, Berringer or Gunner?"

"Yes, that could be a problem. If we win, I will force them to owe me their allegiance, Your Majesty. Or I will cut out their tongues. I have done it before." Winslow reached into his pocket and slowly pulled out a string of seven dried ones on a chain. "I am the voice of my crew. None other. Those who do not obey me face the appropriate penalties."

The site of the curled, dried forms dangling in front of him revolted Noran. He looked ill before he managed to respond, "What do they have they could possibly give you?"

"Sometimes, Your Majesty, the best way to get even with your enemies is to own everything they once had."

Noran found the statement clever, even though he already knew Winslow's true intentions for the Zonack voyagers. "I will agree to their freedom for the tournament instead, provided you supply your own men in the games against my best athletes."

Winslow tucked the tongues back within his pocket. "I respect your ambition, Your Majesty." The Captain looked to Windreed Sinker and Thorn, who both nodded to accept. "But If I must use my own protectors, may I suggest you use Baron Oreus Blake and Boris Groffen to oppose them?"

Oreus was stunned he was being dragged into a gamble as a bargaining tool.

"The Baron doesn't need to be involved," Noran said.

"Come now, Your Majesty. After all, they are only games," Winslow reasoned.

"I am not afraid, Your Majesty," Oreus shouted from the corner of the hall, hardly believing what he was saying. Noran knew Ola would slap him for his idiocy if she were here.

Noran said, "Baron, you don't have to—"

"It would be an honor to play for you and the kingdom," Oreus said, always having enjoyed the games from the stands and wondering what it was like to be in them.

"The man of Uthan Mire does not disappoint. I am sure your barbarian will also be happy to fight, knowing his history with Windreed." Winslow said.

It wasn't Boris's compliance Noran was worried about. He only could hope his fake leg wouldn't be a hindrance to his effectiveness.

"What of mine is worth three lives to you?" Winslow asked.

"Your drift ship," Noran said boldly.

"Ah! Taking a page out of Lanu's book, are we?"

Noran nodded and smiled.

"I accept."

"And what do you wish if the Trail Tracers win?" Noran asked.

"Contrary to popular belief, I am not against gambling for money," Winslow said, chuckling. His eyes rose up to the top of Noran's head. Thorn and Captain Rollins also laughed at Winslow's statement. "Your crown alone would make me rich for the rest of my days."

Noran said, "Captain Winslow, you set your sights too high. This crown was worn by the first King of Yawrana."

"Heirlooms are a precious thing, Your Majesty, and hold a great deal of sentimental value. But another can always be made. It is simply a well-crafted object made up of only metal and rock that has managed to survive the ages. Men like me covet rare antiquities of its type to make difficult trades more negotiable."

Noran could see the Captain was not going to back down. Caught up in the moment of the challenge and his faith unwavering in the Majestic Messengers' ability to win, he replied, "Done."

"I will see you in three days then," Winslow said, nodding to the King.

"My Lord," Bruneau whispered to Noran, "it seems illogical to send men or dobbins into the woods when Herikech is roaming about freely."

Noran whispered back, "The messenger race is only a front for us capturing Herikech. Every man and dobbin in the field will be equipped with a flare. I will have men ready with drugs to sedate Herikech if he is located. We will hunt him like a hound if he is sighted. This race could be our only chance to draw him out of hiding."

"You are very clever, Your Majesty," Bruneau said, smirking.

"Blaynor is rubbing off on me."

Captain Winslow stopped by Oreus on the way out and said, "I never forget a face. I now remember having seen yours before, on reward posters throughout Zonack. I can see why you have embraced the Yawranan culture. Challenging a knight to a duel?"

Oreus was shocked. He snapped, "Malcolm Hayward murdered my father in his drunkard state!"

"Hmmm. Interesting. You run from your troubles. Will you also run in the ring?" Winslow asked coldly.

Thorn followed the Captain, curled his fishhook lip at Oreus and whispered in a gravelly voice, "I never lose."

Oreus tried to respond with his own intimidating remark but Thorn had already left by the time he was ready to say it. He pounded his fist against the wall and gritted his teeth. "Snookery!"

After the Salmus voyagers departed, General Hithel soon followed, leaving behind his normal castle post to prepare his racers for the run of their lives. Noran asked General Keys to stay.

"General Keys," Noran began, "I asked you to come here to discuss the death of Captain Green Eyes."

Keys swallowed hard but remained silent.

Noran continued, "As you know, the Captain's death was very unusual. I know you're not aware of this, but his body has been exhumed by the Elders." Keys's nose began to twitch uncontrollably and his eyes watered. "General, we know this was no karrik, maddon or dragul attack. It was that of something much more dangerous. A creature called a mangler is now running about killing other animals. You purposely misfiled the Captain's death papers after he was killed to hide this evidence."

Keys gasped and said, "Your Majesty . . . no one was sure what had happened to the Captain on that route. Hundreds of packages were delivered on that trail before without a problem. The terrain was a little rough, but it gave me no reason to believe it wasn't safe enough for my squads."

"But no deliveries were made when a red moon was present . . . until Captain Green Eyes's. This mangler appears and draws its powers from any red moon, General. What bothers me is you never had his death, or the route, properly investigated for fear of losing your business. You have put your greed before the lives of your runners and cart drivers, a most dishonorable act. It is why I placed my bet on the Majestic Messengers and not the Trail Racers."

"Your Majesty, I care for my runners as much as Hithel does for his."

"General, your actions have not spoken for you, yet. If you come clean with me now, I will wipe the slate and you may go about your way. If you lie to me . . . you will find the cell chutes of Candlewick closing in on you faster than you could ever run."

The General's eyes watered for a moment but then ran dry after he cleared his throat. Straightening his collar and nodding, Keys said, "I will tell you all I know, Your Majesty. I will aid in bringing justice for the Captain's family."

"Good. Where was Captain Green Eyes delivering his package when he was killed?"

"Let's see," he said, trying to dredge up the painful memory, "it was a mansion . . . Maxhaw Mansion. That's it! Ean Maxhaw worked for the Shaba Sector board. It was he who was to receive the package."

"And what was in the package?" Noran asked, wanting every detail.

"Strangest thing, Your Majesty. It was nothing special really, for being a rush delivery. A dog's linked chain with a metal collar. However, I don't ever recall Ean ever having any dogs."

Noran's mind suddenly leapt to a thought about restraint. "This is exactly what I wanted to hear. I fear Herikech may be controlling the mangler for his own purposes. He has held a family hostage before for his own purposes in the swamps of Serquist. He may be doing it again in Dowhaven. Ean Maxhaw's life may be in danger." Noran waved forward a lieutenant, who had just entered after hearing about the dobbin's earlier fight.

"My Lord, good evening."

"Not quite, Lieutenant Ravel. Find General Fields. I need you both to immediately take a platoon of soldiers to Maxhaw Mansion in Shaba Sector of Dowhaven. General Keys will give you the address before you leave. We believe there is a dangerous animal . . . a type of wild, deformed dog running loose in that area. It needs to be killed and I want the body brought back here for the makers and Elders to examine. It is believed to have murdered a Trail Racer. Approach this task with extreme caution, Lieutenant. It is unlike any other creature you have ever seen."

The lieutenant bravely said, "Forty men will be more than enough to bring it down, my Lord. We will be there within two days to start our search." Ravel saluted the King and bowed at the same time.

Before the lieutenant left, Noran added, "Make sure your men search the mansion thoroughly, Lieutenant. Even if you do not find the beast, I want to ensure all is in order with Ean Maxhaw's estate."

The lieutenant nodded and set off.

"And General Keys, I don't want any more Trail Racers using the back road to Shaba until the mangler is captured or, better yet, killed."

"As you wish, Your Majesty."

"You will also pay Captain Green Eyes's wages to his family as if he were still running deliveries for you and they will get his retirement funds in full in advance as well. It is the least you can do for them."

The General nodded.

"Now, do you have the schematics for these new gliders you have spoken of?"

"Yes, Your Majesty," the General said, looking bewildered the King was going to give him the chance to use them.

"I will have my blacksmith, Boris Groffen, review them for approval. If he believes they are not a hazard, I will allow you to use them . . . for rush deliveries only."

"You're very gracious, my Lord," Keys said in a merry voice.

"However," Noran said like a cold rain that suddenly fell, "if you lose the race against the Majestic Messengers, the glider plans will be shelved until the seven year contract is up. Be on your way, General."

Keys saluted and bounded away in a hurry before the King changed his mind.

Noran left the Grand Hall with Bruneau now that the situation was under control. A short time later they were standing in Master Oyen's medical wing at Blaynor's bedside. The drapes were drawn over the windows to prevent little moonlight from entering. Noran could feel the thin shaft that was able to get through and warm his skin. It was comforting. The guard was unconscious and wrapped heavily where he had been injected. The King could see the hot rash that had spread along the guard's arms and legs.

Bruneau was teary-eyed and bit his tongue.

"My King," Master Oyen said, "it is as Bruneau has stated. The bystol biscuits have no trace of sleeping drug on them anywhere. We have talked to the Royal House chefs and discovered that the container that was supposed to have been delivered was switched out with this one." The maker held up a gold tin that was similar to the original, which was stored in an empty space beneath a stone in the floor outside the King's bedchamber. "This is not the container that is normally filled. It is a good replica. The difference between the original and this forgery is the material used in the lining. The original's interior was covered with a solid red, dyed cloth." The maker went to his bench and picked up a second container, the original. "This one has an orange tint and was found discarded in the kitchen's waste bin, still full." The maker shook the tin, hearing the unmistakable sound of dried biscuits shifting against each other inside. "This is the second time today someone has tried to murder you, my Lord. Only Blaynor was the victim in your place this time, and luckily lived."

Noran sat down, feeling his legs weaken from the reality setting in. "So it is true. Herikech is within the castle. The storms, my gandalay, the mangler mutilations and now this. What will be next?"

"You were wise to have the Queen and your son moved to an alternate location, Your Majesty," Bruneau said. "The princesses should be moved there as well. The entire royal family needs to be protected."

Nodding, Noran said, "Yes. Bruneau, please have a servant inform the Head of House to arrange it. Keep it quiet."

Bruneau saluted and left for a moment to give the order. When he returned, the guard said for the first time in his life, "I am no longer adequate protection for you either, my Lord, now that Blaynor is incapacitated for at least the next couple of days. You should have no less than five guards around you at any given time. Your father would do the same."

"You read my mind," Noran said. "He has entered my thoughts and tells me the same."

"Because of the type of assaults you have been experiencing, even five guards may not be enough to save you," Master Oyen said candidly.

Noran sighed as a tear escaped his eye. "Elder Garan may be right. My death may be unavoidable."

# CHAPTER SIX
## The Final Revenge

Noran sat quietly, eating his morning meal in the Banquet Hall with Bruneau and a handful of the castle's best guards. Blaynor was still recovering from the attacks he suffered from the previous day. The King missed the guard's trusted company in the short amount of time Blaynor had been absent from his post. To get his mind off of the double murder attempts on his life, he concentrated on other problems. The castle was beginning to return to a normal appearance now that the rains had decided to cease. All objects littering the Yard had been picked up and returned to their homes and any damaged outer walls had been repaired for protection. New windows were being cut for the Grand Hall and the fears of the people were subsiding—until Ballan entered the room to reopen the floodgate of emotions.

"Your Majesty," Ballan said, tapping his hooked cane on the floor to get the King's attention.

"What is it, Ballan?"

"A messenger has just arrived at the Western Gate with grave tidings."

Noran dropped his fork onto his plate, swallowed and wiped his mouth. "Send the dobbin in."

Ballan replied in a lower tone, "This messenger is not a hare, my Lord. It is a soldier from the Waungee."

The court announcer now had Noran's fullest attention. The King pushed aside his plate of food and asked, "Does he have information on the snowtears?"

"His tale is a lengthy one and I believe you should hear it for yourself so no detail is lost in the transfer."

Noran nodded and walked to his throne in the Grand Hall. The moment he sat down the man was brought forward. The soldier's feet dragged as he neared the throne, outwardly exhausted from the long journey from the grasslands.

"Your Majesty," the soldier said, bowing his head. The man was the lowest rank soldier one could be in the army, and he was soiled from head to foot. "My name is Glenn Mere. Thank you for seeing me at your earliest convenience."

"Where are the other men?" Noran asked outright. "Why are there no others with you?"

Mere's eyes watered at the mention of his lost comrades. "They are no more, my Lord. Captain Sundol and the entire platoon search party, except for myself, who was lucky enough to escape, have been defeated."

Noran's heart sank, knowing where the rest was leading. "By the Lazuls?"

The soldier nodded. "Yes, Your Highness. The remainder of our enemy from the underground city—Maramis."

"How many are there? Where are they now?"

"They now number around a thousand. I am certain they are heading for the southern forests of Emison, Your Majesty. They may be targeting the tower. Baron Annalee must know of their advancing position."

The King said, "Ballan."

"Yes, Your Majesty?" Ballan said, looking up.

"Have the Majestic Messengers send word to General Meel at Emison Tower immediately. A fortified defense must be in place to prevent a surprise raid. Send a battalion of the castle's soldier units and a company of archers to aid them. The Lazul army will fall before they reach Emison's Yard, and perhaps we will be rid of their oppressing influences forever. Finally, we have information that lightens my heart."

"Your Majesty," Bruneau interrupted. "Your men are needed here to protect the castle. With Herlkech wandering about, your safety is vital."

Noran nodded. "I'm getting to that. There is not enough time for help to reach Emison if we send orders to surrounding territories. Therefore, we must contribute to end the Lazuls' plans before they are carried out. Ballan, also have a message sent to Overbay and Dowhaven. We ask for their donation of a platoon each to aid us until the castle's full defense returns from Emison. Tell the Majestic Messengers I want regular updates as to the status of the battle."

Ballan bowed without argument, saying, "As you wish, Your Majesty. It will be done." The court announcer left the Grand Hall at once.

"What of the snowtears?" Noran asked, getting to the guts of the conversation. "Were your men trying to destroy them when they were killed?"

"Actually, no. We were trying save the Volars."

A confused expression appeared on Noran's face. "Did you say the Volars?" Noran's mind flashed to the thorny, one-foot-tall creatures in the Dunes of Pydora. The Volars had imprisoned Rydor, Oreus and him after they had crossed into their domain two years ago, after they retrieved the snowtears. The Volars were not the most pleasant of hosts, but freed them upon their leader's request."

"Yes, Your Majesty, the Volars."

"Did they ask for your help?"

"Their leader did. The one they call the Mother . . . ummm."

"The Mother of Life," Noran completed.

"Thank you. She came to Captain Sundol in a dream when we camped in the Wailing Hills. She called to him. King Herikech Illeon of the Lazuls was murdering the Volars."

"How did Herikech and his men find their dens? The Volars are a very powerful race."

The soldier grimaced. "Herikech's power was undoubtedly greater. The Mother of Life was thrown down in front of the Volars. Her energy was vanquished as easily as a candle and her spirit sent hurtling back into the next plane of existence."

"And the Volars—do any of them remain?"

The soldier shook his head. "Also wiped clean by the wrath of the Lazuls. They were merciless, my Lord. It was Herikech's final revenge. He accused the Mother of Life of barricading the doorway to the territories of Yawrana since the dunes were formed."

"An entire race murdered in cold blood. Herikech *is* mad," Bruneau said, unable to hold back his own feelings. "How did you manage to survive when everyone else was slaughtered?"

"Rain," the soldier answered.

"Rain? Explain," Noran said.

"During the clash between Herikech and the Mother of Life, rain fell heavily in the dunes, spurring a great flood that drowned the remainder of the platoon and Volars who didn't have the fortune of dying by sword or spear. The downpour was so heavy it was like trying to walk through a never-ending waterfall. Somehow I became separated from the rest of our men, and it wasn't until I stumbled far enough North that I could see the rest of my comrades perishing in its never-ending wake. It was as if the storms were withheld for dozens of centuries and it all decided to fall at once with a vengeful force to punish those who were responsible for its suppression. I waited in hiding upon the crumbled slopes of Mount Grim, hoping for survivors. After two full days and the emergence of only the Lazul enemy, I came to the undeniable conclusion there were none of us left."

"What happened to Herikech? Is he with the Lazuls in Emison?"

The soldier shook his head. "I didn't stay long enough to see, my Lord. I fled for my life to bring you this warning. His path could lead to unknown destinations."

"We are fairly certain where he is," Bruneau said with confidence.

"You feel he is not in Emison?" the soldier asked.

Noran nodded. "Herikech wanders the halls of Candlewick. In time he will be captured if he remains here long enough."

The soldier laughed and then covered his mouth to hide his unexpected reaction.

"You find my statement humorous?" Noran asked, feeling his blood pressure suddenly rising.

"Not at all, my Lord—only misplaced."

"Do not challenge the King's wisdom in his own hall!" Bruneau barked.

The soldier immediately apologized, "Forgive my doubt, Your Majesty, but the King of the Lazuls walks in a plane where the dead reside. He comes and goes as he wishes and is everywhere and nowhere all at once. The promise of finding the snowtears is, at most, idealistic."

"What prompts you to say such things to your King?" Bruneau asked.

"Do not take offense to my words, Bruneau Palidon, Protector of the King. I mean not to anger. But one has to console with the fact that we can't destroy what will never be found. Herikech now controls the lands just beyond Mount Grim. In time, he will control all of Yawrana as well."

Bruneau said, "Your allegiance has changed sides."

"No, I only tell the truth to those who wish not to hear it!"

Bruneau drew his sword, ready to cut Mere's tongue out. "You will not speak ill of the Royal Court's decisions."

"No, Bruneau, hold your anger," Noran commanded. "This soldier may have a point."

"He insults our abilities to defend ourselves."

"Herikech's army has already slipped through Rock Rim's guarded gates," Mere said. "Nothing will stop him until these lands are his. Nothing."

"Enough!" Noran's voice resounded through the entire hall. Every servant who heard his shout bowed his or her head in respect. "Herikech will not win this war. He can't hide the snowtears forever. Especially not in my lands."

The soldier bowed his head and waited for the King's instructions.

"It is not the will of Yawrana to surrender when the stars are not aligned in our favor. Our ancestors have faced many difficult obstacles as well and they resolved their issues over time. We shall do the same in their honor."

Ballan returned to the Grand Hall and announced, "Your Majesty, a hailstorm approaches Candlewick from Dowhaven!"

Noran jumped up from his seat and cried in fury with a raised fist to the ceiling, "Herikeeech!"

"Forced to sit inside again, Baron Blake? Perhaps we should have left for Salmus when we had a chance," Captain Winslow said. "Isn't it time you give us a tour of the castle? You've been careful to avoid it since we stepped foot here."

Oreus blew his nose to drown out the Captain's last few words, drawing a glare from Thorn. "I won't apologize for the inconveniences you have faced, Captain. As you have just stated, you had the option to leave. The King has ordered everyone inside due to a hailstorm. It will be here shortly. We can't control the weather."

"Yes, one can't expect the world from a race that devalues monetary gain," Captain Rollins said, shaking his head.

"Money does not rule the Yawranan world," Oreus said.

"Which is why a man of Uthan Mire is welcome here," Captain Winslow added.

Oreus's guard, Quinn, defended him. "The Baron has proven worth to the world far beyond what either of you have achieved. And he will prove it again in the Gaming Arena."

Winslow smiled and said, "What do you call one who serves a peasant, Captain Rollins?"

"Swine."

"Right you are, Captain." Both men laughed while Oreus restrained Quinn from jumping over the Banquet Hall table to get to them.

"You're nothing in my eyes," Quinn yelled.

"But the one who you serve is worth much in mine," Winslow said. "The bounty on his head is high. He should be rotting in the cell dungeons of Weatherwood Castle right now for challenging a noble to a duel. It is a high crime in Zonack."

Oreus felt his face go red. He could not reply out of embarrassment to Quinn and the House servants who were present.

"If one does not defend his actions, then the rumors must be true," Captain Winslow said.

"He doesn't need to explain himself to you, Captain," Quinn said, pulling his emotions in check.

Like a pest Oreus couldn't get rid of, Winslow said, "It would be appreciated if he did, though. How did Sir Hayward kill your father, Baron? Did he lose a card game?"

Oreus clarified, "He was actually trying to assist him after he fell."

"Is that so? Touching a royal subject without permission? Another punishable crime, one worthy of death."

"Hayward was drunk! My father was only helping when Hayward turned on him," Oreus said.

"No need to be defensive about it, Baron. I was only curious as to how he was gutted."

Oreus slammed his fist on the table. "You already knew how he died! You were baiting me."

"Yes." Winslow nodded. "I wanted to know what kind of a man you really are. How one responds to painful questions is an accurate indicator of his depth. It is no secret Captain Lanu boarded runaways and desperate men—neither of whom are respectable allies, in my opinion. You are the first of his crew that I have met who knows the true worth of his own resources, a type of man who would be of great use on my ship. You seem to be rather fond of your homeland with the way you defend it. It leaves me to believe you wish to return there. My ship could be your conduit if you are seeking passage. I wouldn't make this offer to just anyone."

"And you shouldn't be making it to me either," Oreus said. "I don't work for crooks."

Winslow laughed. "A crook? Is that what you think I am, Baron? I deal an honest trade. Some of my methods may be unconventional at times, but one has to take advantage of an opportunity when he sees it."

"What do you want from us, Captain? What are you waiting for?"

Winslow smiled. "The *right* opportunity."

"I wouldn't count on it falling into your lap," Oreus said.

"Nor do I expect it to, Baron. One must go after most deals in life. This situation is no different. Usually in the end I get what I'm after," he said with another broad smile to provoke Oreus into a yell.

Oreus remained calm to Winslow's surprise.

"Are you sure you won't reconsider my offer? If you join us, I may decide to pick up and leave here after my wagers with the King have come to a completion."

"I know what it is you wish to do. You would hand me over in an instant to the Zonack Royal Court and collect the bounty on my head once we set foot ashore. I'm not the fool you make me out to be. I know what you think of Uthan Mire and those who are born there. When I'm ready, I *will* return one day under my own free will and become their champion. They have suffered for centuries and out of it they will be victorious in the end."

The Captain sighed. "Ahh. I see. You fancy yourself their savior? Your parents would be proud to hear you make such a bold statement, if they were living."

Quinn replied, "You are vile."

Captains Winslow and Rollins laughed while Captain Soar blushed and shook his head. Winslow said in a voice filled with pity, "Dreams are for those who can't cope with reality, Baron. But make no mistake—most dreams are crushed before they come to fruition. They are unobtainable, which is why they are what they are. The world of Elvana is wrought with injustices. It will never change, so why not come to your senses now and save yourself all the worry?"

Hail suddenly pounded against the boards over their heads where windows used to be. The screams of men, women and children from the gardens and upper levels of the castle echoed around them.

"This conversation is at an impasse and you are only upsetting our host," Captain Soar said. "Baron Blake, since we are anchored to the indoors until this new storm moves on, may we request a tour of the castle to pass the time?"

"I second it!" Captain Rollins exclaimed. "How about it, Baron? A bit of walking may clear our heads for better thoughts."

Quinn whispered to Oreus, "Baron, they have seen all they need to—"

Oreus smiled deviously and cut Quinn off, saying, "A splendid proposal. I think it's time I did. Right this way, Captains. Right this way."

Noran could hear the hailstorm pelting countless objects, even from his new chambers two levels underground. It had lasted for half a day and showed no end. The beating of hailstones caused his head to pound harder as he struggled to find a center of stability within his soul. The compilation of recent events were overwhelming him: his gandalay's strange behavior, the arrival of Martell Fedrow, the wandering mangler, the Salmus voyagers and their wagers, the stinging bystol's attack on Blaynor, the secret guild of the Lazul children, the slaughter of the Volars and the Mother of Life, and now the latest storm in an endless string that had been ravaging the territories. He couldn't decide which to give most of his attention to.

Herishen Illeon's will sat in front of him, ready for its pages to be opened once more. He couldn't deny it now, not even with all the nagging problems

Yawrana faced. Deep inside he knew the will held the evasive answers to the snowtears that could aid him in defeating Herikech. His time was growing short and he wasn't confident he would be able to find them before his people suffered the same fate the Volars had. Drawing a circle around his heart and asking for guidance from the Maker, he said a silent prayer to sway the madness from overtaking him. After he opened his eyes, he pulled the will closer to him and went to the section his green ribbon marked.

*The Bethlen have located the Yawranan ship sooner than I anticipated, again surpassing my expectations. Their swift deliverance has brought me an unparalleled advantage. The contents aboard include other plant species also connected by root systems similar to the snowtears. It can be assumed many things from their world all have sprouted from one common source in an age long since. And from one root grew thousands of replicas. As proof of their find, the Bethlen have brought me a container with a dozens seeds from one of the plants discovered in the ship's bowels. It is labeled as a krek, a tree that gives life to a plump fruit used in the process of wine fermentation. It shall be also planted in the Wailing Hills for a future toast to our new, one god: Yawrana.*

*The remaining gifts aboard the Methalisian ship will be spared for now, kept safe from harm as battles continue to rage eastward. Heritoch's army has pressed my front lines back several miles. The sounds of their terror are growing closer. Messengers arrive daily from the clashes, many of them wounded and others soon to join death in its lair. Their updates have created alarm within my camp. Adhering to the advice of my generals, we have moved ten miles west and no longer have access to the underground tunnels. The intensity and blinding rays of the sun scorch our spirits and burn our pride. My men depend upon shield visors and mud cream during the day while they stand watch in the fields and on the hilltops.*

*I admit my ignorance in underestimating the strength of Heritoch's forces. His supplies from Maramis have kept his units refreshed and his weapons replenished.*

*Rumor has now surfaced that Herikech has surrendered his lands to join Heritoch's ranks in exchange for access to all resources within his region. The latest messenger who delivered this information stated the source responsible, for it was considered a reliable one. Something tells me Herikech has other plans tumbling in his mind if it is true. His bargain with Heritoch would only last the length of its purpose. For now, we shall hold our ground as long as the blood of Heritoch's army continues to stain the long grass of the Waungee.*

*Audra Xada, the leader of the Methalisians, requested a private meeting with me. Her intentions, at first, were unclear. Her divinely cut beauty captured my lust the moment she removed her cloak. She held a wanting in her eyes that I have only connected to once before in Immana's. If my wife knew of her presence in my tent at that time, alone and with another woman, she would hold the right to have Audra beheaded for attempting to soil the King's sheets with the impurity of her people. Immana, however, did not know of the meeting. Audra's purpose in my tent was for something much greater than unspoken love. Holding the Scroll of Truth in her hand, she stated it was a document that, if used to its full potential, could grant an army the power to save the world. With war at my borders, Audra learned of the turmoil to the east through my men's whispers.*

*Before she could entrust the wisdom of the scroll to me, I was to pass a test to prove my sincerity. She asked me to kneel before her, place my hand in a bowl of water and pledge my oath to use the knowledge of the scroll to protect those who provided a refuge for goodness in their hearts. When I pledged that I would, her response was cold and bitter. She could see there was a blackness in me that had its grasp on my soul since the day of my birth. It was bound to me through the blood in my veins and the atrocities my race inflicted upon the land and its inhabitants. She vowed she would share the knowledge of the scroll if I were willing to purge this demon from my life. But the demon was stronger than me and answered to protect itself, using my voice. The moment it surfaced, she placed her hand upon the back of my head and forced my face into the bowl of water. The demon struggled within me, flailing its arms within my own until a blindness overtook me.*

*An unknown amount of time went by before I regained consciousness. Audra was still there in the dim candlelight of my tent before me, smiling. She informed me how she had coaxed the demon out of its embedded den in my soul. My death was spared as it was released from my breath through the element of water and back into the next plane of existence. I felt naked, as if something I had depended upon was suddenly torn away from me. My vision was clear for the first time and I confessed how I had ordered the Bethlen to seize their ship for my own personal gains. It was then she knew I was free of the dark parasite that had plagued me since childhood. When I tried to give her the krek seeds in forgiveness, she said she would return the next night and begin teaching me the process of enlightenment.*

*When the morning arrived, everything living around me pulsed with the energy of a dozen lives. Yarba thought I had gone mad when I removed my visor in the bright light of day. I stared up into the face of the sun in front of the Methalisians and shouted blessings to their god. The golden rays warmed my bones and melted away my hardened shell. I squinted through tears at the once flaming and menacing glow and forced my real eyes to open for the first time in thirty-four years. The orb would no longer be my enemy and I would someday see the birth of my own children in its magnificence. I removed my wife's visor and kissed her passionately in front of my guards, an act never before portrayed by any Lazul male in an open setting. Immana cringed from the sun and reactions of the mesmerized warriors looking on, believing a demon had overtaken me. I could only laugh, knowing the exact opposite had transpired. She begged for me to lie down so the medicine makers could urgently attend to my needs. I pulled Yarba and her close and asked them to meet me in my tent that night to witness the dawning of a new Lazul era.*

*When Audra entered my tent, as promised, a shout of protest greeted her from Immana and Yarba. Yarba picked up a sword and went to kill her for entering a Lazul King's quarters, but I was able to stop him before he struck his fatal blow. I asked for both of their trust if they were to be by my side until my death. When they had given their promises, Audra exonerated their dark dwelling demons, as she had done with me. They, too, felt the veil lifted from their bondages. Audra asked us to sit before her so she could teach the transcendence of one's soul to the heavens by temporarily departing the physical body on Elvana.*

Noran's eyes started to slowly close as he fought to read the passage to its end, but it was not to be. His head dropped onto the center of the will and his hands fell limp onto the desk. Bruneau came in a short time later and found him snoring into the pages. They vibrated beneath the King's lips as he dreamed of his childhood days when life was far simpler.

The guard wrapped a heavy wool blanket around Noran's huddled form and smiled. He blew out the candle on a nearby table and said, "Good night, my Lord. May the moons of Elvana shine through your troubles on this long and weary eve."

"He mocks us!" Captain Rollins yelled in their private quarters near the gandalay stables. "He showed us nothing but the most barren hallways and rooms the castle has to offer."

"Yes, Captain. Baron Blake does have wit. I didn't think he had any beneath all those layers of clay-ridden soil he was raised in," Winslow replied. "He is nothing more than a swell we can cut through with our bow."

Captain Soar said through gritted teeth, "This I never agreed to. These people are not to be trifled with. You dare bring war to Salmus by stealing from them? King Roule will have your head on the chopping blocks if he finds out you were behind it."

"Your threats are stepping on my coattails, Captain Soar. I think you should remove them before Thorn does."

The hooked-lip servant stepped forward and growled in his gravelly voice.

Captain Soar cringed and backed away a few feet to let his own three men surround him.

"The deal has already been made with the Lazul. We have no option to back out," Rollins reminded Soar. "The treasure will be ours if we do as he says."

"*He* is not even human," Soar replied. "And could be listening to us now—"

"It doesn't matter *what* he is," Winslow said. "And if he is eavesdropping, then it is you who should be worried. If we continue to do as he asks, I foresee no harm befalling us. The time until his victory is growing short. Be prepared for the worst and it won't seem as bad when it happens."

"What about Baron Blake and King Deardrop?" Rollins asked. "They trust us the least and could pose a problem during the rest of our stay here."

"King Deardrop is a minor concern. The Lazuls will dispose of him soon enough. And as for the Baron, Thorn and he have a date at the Gaming Arena. It would be a shame to miss its finale when the curtain falls," Winslow said with a wicked smile.

# CHAPTER SEVEN

## For King, Crown and Contract

A cold spell descended upon the castle after the hailstorms had passed over, leaving a numbing chill for two solid days. Hailstones coated the Yards like bubbles floating on the top of a freshly drawn bath. Shovels and rakes were used to clear a straight path from the Western Gate to Bramble Wood for the first five hundred yards of the race. It was easier to get a crowd into the action if it was immediate and competitive in the beginning. No one would be interested in watching a pair of dobbins slip and slide across fields to reach the western forest. Commoners and royalty gathered at the outer wall of the Western Gate's southern tower, waiting for the delivery bugle to initiate the start of the race.

The Trail Racers and Majestic Messengers groups kept their distance from each other as they formulated their strategies. General Hithel was at the center of his band of hares while General Keys was scolding his block starter for not having brought along his night vision goggles.

"You hair-brain!" he yelled loud enough that the Majestic Messengers overheard.

"Looks like we already got a foot up on the competition, General," Captain Backfoot said to Hithel. "Rip Run's forgotten his lightening lenses."

General Hithel shook his head and handed over a map to Backfoot. "That was the reason why I fired him from my outfit. He broke more rules than I could count. It just added up to be too many in the end. General Keys was desperate for someone who could try to match your speed. He's the closest that's ever come to your record, Captain."

"The rest of his lot will apply some good pressure on our runners. Cracked Tooth, Ramp and Clutch are a resourceful bunch that shouldn't be overlooked."

Hithel shook his head. "Don't worry about them. Their overall combined speed doesn't match ours. Keys gets the leftovers of those who don't measure up to Majestic Messenger standards. Every hare on his team has been rejected by our outfit at one point or another."

Two other dobbins named Ted and Stan, employed with the Majestic Messengers as warmers, stood alongside General Hithel and Captain

Backfoot, working feverishly to keep them both loose by fanning the heat of a campfire their way. Ted was short for Tedious and Stan for Stanch. They always triple-checked any runner's gear before a messenger was sent on a long haul. Stan went over all of Backfoot's provisions while Ted rifled though his equipment to ensure there would be no embarrassing blunders similar to Rip Run's.

"That's enough already," Backfoot said, getting nervous. "I'm not a specimen to be prodded." The Captain zipped up his midnight blue, moon and star covered jumper to the base of his neck. Only his feet and paws remained uncovered below his neckline. He bounced in place a few times to keep his blood moving and his joints from becoming stiff.

"Just doing our job, Captain," Ted replied with a scrunch of his nose.

"How much time do we have?" General Hithel asked.

Backfoot pulled out a round, golden pocket watch with a long, silver chain and replied, "Twenty spins."

"We should get to the starting line. I'm counting on your burst to give us a sizable distance on the first leg. It may be the narrow margin that allows us to win this competition."

"I'll run like it's my last race to guarantee it won't be, General."

"Eat light whatever you do. And one other thing I haven't told you yet, the army is instituting distractions along the way to throw both parties off course."

Backfoot stopped walking and said, "What in the blazes for?"

"For the sport of it. A few extra challenges will heighten the suspense and push each group to its limits. The King wants the best group to win—the one who knows the codes and how to handle themselves in the field. If you ask me, he's right. We haven't been up to snuff on our duties, taking too many liberties when we're supposed to be meeting deadlines. One too many missed has led us to the brink of ruin. Now it's up to us to set things right and show we're still the best service that's ever set foot on a groomed trail or muddy mountain grade."

A large group of red and brass moved toward them. Recognizing the King at the center of his guards, the messengers bowed and gave him their full attention.

"Your Majesty," General Hithel said, greeting Noran.

"General. Is your squad ready to win?"

"As ready as we can be. The weather won't slow us down. We've faced worse runs than this in our history. I promise you a victory."

Noran nodded and extended his hand to the Captain. "Best of luck to you, Captain Backfoot. General Keys wants this contract badly," he said, holding up the tube containing the precious parchment. "I would hate to see it fall into his hands."

"He won't lay a paw on it if I have anything to do with it," Backfoot exclaimed.

The King smiled and said, "And what about the other captains?"

"I debriefed Whitepaw, Top Steam and Quickspeed two days ago when they left for their stations," Hithel said. "They are all in the best shape of their lives."

"Whitepaw? You're using one of your majors to run?" Noran asked, surprised. "It's rare one of his rank is used for a custom delivery."

"Yes, my Lord. I took your advice. I have many faster dobbins under my command but none are more reliable than Whitepaw. His sound judgment has proven to me that he can be a valuable commodity to our team."

"I don't doubt your decision, General. In fact, I commend you for your choice. Chief Braiy Decker will be interested to know Whitepaw is racing. I shall pass along the information to him. As you know, aside from being a supporter of the Majestic Messengers, the Chief and Whitepaw have become close friends since the Black Fever struck the territories."

The General smiled his toothy, overbite grin and said, "Thank you for your confidence, my Lord."

"I also would like to give your squad one more piece of advice before the bugle sounds. The weather will be the least of your worries. I have been informed by the Elders there is a wild creature called a mangler roaming the territories at will, killing entire herds to satisfy its hunger. I fear it may be under the control of Herikech Illeon. It is said to appear only when the moon is red. However, I want your hares to be extremely cautious when darkness falls. If Herikech is aware of this race, he might try to attack your team with other creatures, or in person. I don't doubt his powers any longer, and neither should you. I will have as many soldiers and sentries posted along the routes as possible for your protection. We will capture him if there's trouble."

"That would put my second and fourth runners at risk," Hithel replied. "Captain Backfoot, please make sure you warn Captain Top Steam before you hand off the scroll case. I will dispatch a runner to Quickspeed's and Whitepaw's post to let them know as well."

"General Keys's team has also been informed," Noran added. "Everyone's safety must be taken care of until this race is over. And it can't be soon enough."

"My dobbins have flares they can spark if they find themselves in a rough spot," the General said. "They'll not hesitate to use them if they encounter a threat or fall to injury. General Keys's runners also carry them, if I'm correct."

"Excellent," Noran said. "I will be present at the finish line. I hope to see Major Whitepaw in the lead. Remember, my crown is at stake and has been worn by every King since Yawrana's birth. I would hate to lose it to a man like Captain Winslow. He would melt it down and sell the gems to the highest bidder in Salmus. More importantly, it will make me appear weak to the kingdom if I were to lose it. To many it would appear as an act of submission or the relinquishing of our power to an outsider. We can't afford that impression if the people are to keep faith in the Royal Court. I would not have made this wager if I had any doubt you would lose. May the Circle of Life make good of your sacrifices." Noran waved his hand in a circle.

General Hithel, Captain Backfoot, Ted and Stan saluted the King as he nodded and left them to their nerves.

"You heard the King," Hithel said, slapping Backfoot on the shoulder. "You're not only running for us, but for all of Yawrana. We need to have a good showing at the start. I want you to make Rip Run look like he's standing still at the sound of the bugle."

Backfoot nodded and said as they entered the lowered Western Gate, "I'm feeling the furrow beneath my feet already."

"Uhh, you're standing on wood right now," General Hithel said, amused.

"You know what I mean."

General Hithel laughed, "Yes, I do. Just trying to keep those limbs of yours loose so your muscles don't get all knotted up in a bunch."

Hundreds of soldiers surrounded the Western Gate's entrance to ensure Herikech wouldn't have a chance of getting through. All crowds were lined up behind ropes in designated areas to keep the people from interfering with the start of the race. Noran, Bruneau and his other guards wound their way up the stairs of the southern tower at the Western Gate to see the entire field stretching out before the racers all the way to Bramble Wood. He looked down and waved once more to General Hithel. The General pulled the midnight blue Majestic Messenger flag covered with stars and the twin moons out of its holder at the starting line and waved it back and forth. Many in the crowd cheered and clapped at the gesture as the threat of a new rain sprinkled on their heads.

Noran nodded to Ballan, who stood silently on a podium below. The court announcer didn't seem to take notice of him. The King sent a guard to get his attention. Ballan broke out of his trance when the guard tugged on his sleeve and said, "The King wishes you to hurry with your announcement. The sky worries him."

Ballan smiled and said, "Tell His Majesty I would be glad to carry out his orders. These starved people deserve a show fit for the circumstances."

Satisfied with Ballan's answer, the guard saluted and left.

General Keys was trying to top General Hithel's flag waving by stepping in front of him with his own red and gold striped flag, shouting, "The Trail Racers are the future of Yawrana!"

"Get out my way, you garden raider," General Hithel said furiously.

"My boys will be polishing their buttons by the time your major crosses the finish line. Majors don't run for a reason, Hithel. They're too old! I thought you knew that." General Keys said, laughing. Supporters of the Trail Racers joined in on the chuckle.

General Hithel started to retaliate when he was cut short by Ballan's announcement. "You—"

"Good morning, Yawrana!" The cold crowd burst into applause, happy the event was finally giving indications of kicking off. "The sun rises but it will not be our friend for long as the enemy looms above once more. The King is happy to see a full Yard, knowing it will help ease your minds from an enemy that continues to drown your spirits and squelch your hope. Today we have a historic event that will mark the dawn of a new era in Yawranan mail service. Two equally qualified outfits have been in competition for many years now, safely delivering your most prized possessions and intimate thoughts from one door to the next in their illustrious care. Now, the practices of one will come to an end when the other passes within these walls to reach the goal line, claiming the ultimate prize." Ballan held up the scroll container with the precious contract inside. "Ownership for seven years of every transportation route in the territories! Will it be the esteemed Majestic Messengers who have been in service to the kingdom for three thousand years?" Ballan pointed to General Hithel and Captain Backfoot.

A majority of the crowd cheered to show their enthusiasm when it was needed most. General Hithel and Captain Backfoot saluted as a thank you.

"Or will it be the back country crossers, the Trail Racers?" Ballan pointed in the opposite direction at Keys and Rip Run.

The remaining part of the crowd tossed up red and gold confetti as a way to gain more attention. One boy went as far as having brought his own horn on which he blew an annoying long note to upset those who were losing their patience. General Keys and Rip Run hooked elbows and twirled in a circle while waving their paws to exhibit their appreciation.

"Dobbins, take your marks," Ballan stated to silence all parties. The rain fell heavier, making the field ahead dark and hard to see.

"Don't let your wet whiskers bear you down," Rip Run shouted to Backfoot as they stepped up to the line.

"This will be the second time the Majestic Messengers put you out of work!" Backfoot snapped back.

"Hmph."

Backfoot snarled and set up to get a good push off, but found his foothold was not as solid as he wanted it to be with the bridge's wood being wet beneath it.

Ballan raised a green flag in his right hand and checked the guard near the starting line, who was ready to sound the bugle. "May Yawrana the Strong guide both of you on the legs of your journey." The second Ballan released the cloth from his hand, the gate guard blew several short, and then long, notes.

The moment the last note sounded, an enormous lightning bolt struck the Western Gate's southern tower. The crowd gasped when they saw stone shatter near the spot the King stood in the uppermost window. His form fell away as General Hithel and General Keys barked their orders for their messengers to get running.

"Don't worry about the King! He's in good hands!" General Hithel shouted to Backfoot as Rip Run leapt off the bridge and onto the sandy road leading away from the castle. They raced past the dragul keep a few moments later and toward the woods. Firewing and Illeon growled inside the keep, smelling the dobbins as they ran by.

Rip Run took the early lead by eighty yards, having caught Backfoot off-guard as he waited to determine if the King was harmed or not. Backfoot was able to salvage some of that lost distance by the time he reached the edge of the western woods. He could hear Rip Run's voice taunting him if he happened to lose the first quarter. Twenty miles was the maximum a dobbin could run in a day, taking short breaks now and then for refreshments. Each leg of the race only was fifteen miles, a drop in the bucket for Backfoot and Rip Run.

The further the dobbin Captains ran from the castle, the more the rain let up. The woods were still wet and sloppy. Many downed branches and leaves littered the forest floor, which forced the hares to one side of a path or another dozens of times. Their long feet helped each of them to do quick cuts in case they rounded a corner and met an obstacle.

Just as the King had promised, a guard was posted along the path ahead. He was waving to Backfoot as he approached. Backfoot started to wave back until he saw that the man looked like he was in trouble.

"Captain!" the soldier shouted out.

"Yes?" he replied, frustrated he had to slow down for anything. Rip Run was nowhere in sight, driving fear into him that the Trail Racers had already taken a commanding lead in the race.

"I need your help."

"I'm in the middle of a very important race, sir. I don't have much time—"

"This won't take long," the man interrupted, his blue eyes looking vacant. "I need to use your flare. An animal is hurt, a stray dundel, down this hill. Looks like it was bitten by a karrik."

"I only have one flare, sir. If I surrender it to you, I have no one to help me if I find myself in a spot of trouble."

The man nodded as if he were agreeing, but then said, "I know it is your only one and wouldn't ask you for it if it weren't important. This particular dundel is from the Royal Court pens, branded with a dragul emblem."

"Listen, you are just going to have to make some smoke signals from a fire or something. I really can't afford—"

"Please, sir. The flare is much quicker. This animal may die if I don't get her help in time."

Backfoot grumbled, "What type of injury does she bear, did you say?"

"Some sort of bite to the neck." The soldier took his index, ring and middle fingers to show the place where the three puncture holes were made in the animal's jugular.

Backfoot swallowed hard and rubbed his own neck. When he tried to back away, he suddenly bumped into something behind him. He spun around to see Rip Run smiling.

"What in the blazes are you doing here? I thought you would be a few miles from here by now." Backfoot could see slight bruising around Rip Run's mouth, as if he was punched.

"I took a slight detour. The animal—hurt in the woods. It's a shame you weren't willing to help. We'll just have to do this the hard way . . . ."

"We?" Backfoot stammered, feeling uneasy about the situation. The skin below the hairs on the back of his neck began to crawl in warning. "What do you mean?"

Rip Run stepped aside to let Backfoot witness a dark shadow rise from the edge of the path. It slowly grew to a height of about seven feet and then floated toward him. It was a figure dressed in a tattered and burnt gray robe.

"Herikech?" Backfoot gasped. "What—what's going on here?" he said, backing away. The soldier was suddenly behind him. He ripped off Backfoot's backsack and hooked the dobbin's arms behind his back.

A cackle emanated from Herikech's mouth as his shadow fell over Backfoot's body. "Dobbins—passive creatures until they get a sense danger is near," Herikech said in a disappointed voice.

"What are you doing helping him? He is the enemy, you fool!" Backfoot screamed at Rip Run, trying to break the soldier's hold. Herikech held his left hand in his pocket and reached his right out to touch Backfoot's face.

Backfoot cringed. "No—"

"Do not worry, young hare. Your legs can be of service to me."

"I only will bow to one king," Backfoot sneered, "and he does not carry the name Illeon."

Rip Run remained silent as a stone, watching Herikech as the Lazul King ran his fingers in pity across Backfoot's cheek.

"King Deardrop's time is about to pass, as are all creatures bowing to his will. The others have recognized this importance, why should you not?" he said, smiling wickedly again.

"Because I don't serve murderers."

"Ah, yes. Those who do not see my vision make me out to be as much. The sacrifices of war are steep." Herikech suddenly grabbed Backfoot's throat and hissed, "I want to know where the King's heir and the royal family is hiding." His damaged and burnt face was in full view, causing a chill to run up Backfoot's spine.

"Hah! I would never tell you that even if I did know," Backfoot managed to say through the squeezing, bony fingers depriving him of full breaths of air.

Herikech let go, withdrew a few feet and said, "Hmmm. Interesting. The fabled Majestic Messengers do not know of their whereabouts as well." He looked at Rip Run and then returned his gaze to Backfoot. "Deardrop was wise to move his family before I found them. Who does know?"

Backfoot wiggled in the soldier's arms, but the man only tightened his grip.

"If you're not willing to help and you have no information, then you are not of any use to me as you are."

Panicking as Herikech drew near with his bony, blackened hand out, Backfoot bounced up and kicked hard into Herikech's chest. The King flew backward off the path, taken by surprise. Backfoot dropped his head forward and rolled with the guard to throw him off his back. The soldier collided with

Rip Run's body after the soldier sailed over Backfoot's head. Rip Run and the soldier were sent sprawling.

Herikech screamed angrily as Backfoot tried to sprint toward the castle. Raising his hands in the air, Herikech called up lightning from the clouds and sent them striking the path ahead of Backfoot. The dobbin shielded his eyes from the intense light and spun, running through the flying debris where the bolts struck. In a blur, he was past his enemies and heading the other way. Herikech sent more lightning bolts at him, but amazingly, they missed each time.

Herikech looked at Rip Run. The Trail Racer immediately bounded after Backfoot. When he had surpassed Herikech's line of vision, the lightning stopped and the rain fell. Captain Blackfoot glanced over his shoulder to see Rip Run coming his way with a grin and a heavy stick in his right paw. Herikech and the soldier's sinister cackles echoed somewhere in the woods behind the shaking dobbin.

"Back again, Your Majesty?" Master Oyen said sarcastically, attending to the dozens of large bruises and cuts along Noran's right side. Several House servants spread various creams and ointments on his nude form to heal his wounds more quickly. "Your leg is already almost healed from your gandalay attack. That is well ahead of schedule. I better take those stitches out. I don't think I've ever seen wounds heal so fast. It's good to see your blood is a good ally."

Noran moaned and continued to rub his eyes. "I'm still seeing spots from that bright flash. Herikech was behind this. He has been relentless in trying to get rid of me. That was a little too close for my taste. It appears I will have to be careful whenever I'm outside from now on. I'm once again chained to the interiors of these walls like a criminal in his own cell."

"It is for the best. Yawrana cannot lose their new king so soon into his reign. May I suggest you not attend the Tournament of Champions?"

Noran shook his head. "No, you may not. I must be there to show my strength and let the people know I am strong. I will not cower when I can be in plain view of thousands of people. My throne is protected beneath stone enclosures. His bolts will not reach me there."

"Good day, my Lord," a familiar voice said on a table next to him.

Noran turned his head and saw Blaynor was awake and smiling. "My friend. It is good to see you are doing well."

"Well enough now to protect the King," he said, sitting up and inspecting his fading sting marks from the bystol plant. "I've had as much lying here as one can tolerate."

"I must approve your release first," Master Oyen said. "Lay back down. If you are fit, you may be allowed to leave with the King."

Blaynor frowned and did as the maker asked. "The King needs me and I no longer become nauseous when I'm awake. The bystol's toxins won't keep me down."

Bruneau said mockingly, "In the halls of Candlewick, no soul rests less than Blaynor Garsek. His penetrating eyes watch the King like a gargoyle from the watch towers."

"Even though flattery is needed now and then, your words do not hold their water," Blaynor replied. "I know you would rather have me lay here so you can reap the benefits of His Majesty's company all for yourself."

Noran laughed. "I see a few days of separation has not dulled either of your tongues. I think he is ready to be at my side, Master Oyen."

The maker nodded and said, "Yes, I can see he will harass my servants and understudies if I leave him here any longer. But it's his body, not his mind, that needs to be checked before I set him loose."

The maker walked over to Blaynor and bent his joints to see their range of motion. "Your right leg does not have its full flexibility yet. It could hamper you in flight or fight."

"Flight? The noble Blaynor Garsek does not flee from danger," Blaynor said before Bruneau could set up a challenge.

"The rest of you appears to be in order. I believe one more day in the wing wouldn't hurt you any."

Noran overrode the decision by saying, "If he can match the strength of my own leg stride for stride, then he is meant to be with me."

"Thank you, my Lord," Blaynor said, immediately getting dressed with the help of a servant.

Master Oyen bowed and said, "The word of Yawrana shall make it be. However, do not aggravate your injuries, Blaynor, for they may become your enemies. The effects of the bystol's stings can cause seizures and muscle spasms several daysets after an attack. Something as simple as the increase of your heartbeat may cause you to be ineffective during a strenuous situation."

"The death of the King without my aid is a far greater concern of mine," Blaynor said.

"The death of your king because of your hampered aid, could be greater," Master Oyen said with a raised eyebrow.

"That's where the other guards and I come in," Bruneau said in Blaynor's defense. "One man will not be responsible for a king's fall."

Backfoot hurdled a crying tree that had fallen. It was still half alive and trying to right itself back into its original root hole. It struck out at him, feeling the thuds of his approaching footsteps. It missed by a foot as Backfoot jumped higher than its free branch could reach and shook its leaves at him in anger

Rip Run was clipped in the paw by a smaller branch, forcing him to drop his weapon onto its body. He grabbed the branch that struck him and snapped it off for a new club. The tree retaliated by lashing out at him in all directions. Rip Run cried and ducked as a lightning bolt struck the trunk next to him and caught fire, forcing it to let go. In a few steps Rip Run was free and ducked into the woods to find another suitable club. He took off his sack and dropped it to the ground. Inside, his paw touched the most desirable of aids: tracking goggles.

The path to the first post hand-off would be ending shortly before it crossed into rough terrain. It was five miles before the end of his run and Backfoot wasn't sure he would reach it. His jumper outfit was soaked with sweat and his legs were fatigued. He also had no more flares after the soldier who had tried to detain him raided his backsack. He was running out of luck. But the one thing he still managed to hang onto was his empty scroll case, which would hopefully soon hold the contract. Instead of returning it to the inside of his backsack, he attached it to his side. He decided it felt more comfortable to have it hanging there.

What a stroke of luck! With their scroll case in the hands of Herikech, the Trail Racers' messengers would be disqualified from the race and lose all of their business to the Majestic Messengers. But business was growing further and further from his mind at the moment.

Staying on the original path would leave him in the open to be targeted by another of Herikech's creatures. The Captain was worried other Yawranan soldiers along the route would also be under Herikech's control. There was only one choice before him now: to venture into the woods and take his chances off the transportation paths the Majestic Messenger's had become so dependant upon for their own safety.

"To the long shadows that keep the creatures of the night quietly in slumber while I tread through these woods," Backfoot said out of superstition. He made a Circle of Life sign around his heart and stepped into the forest before Rip Run could find him. The density of the plants on the ground was not as bad as he expected it to be, giving him hope there would be no low-lying beasts to take him out at the knees.

Backfoot hummed a tune in his head so he wouldn't draw attention to himself as he kept to the open areas. After two more miles of hiking, he came to an enormous boulder with moss covering every square inch of it. "This is highly peculiar," he said, examining one side of it as he walked by. Exactly in the center of the boulder was a long, thin object protruding from it like a broom handle. It didn't have any moss and appeared as if it was sticking out of a hole. Not one to touch a strange object with his bare paw, he picked up a rock and tapped the end of it a few times. It suddenly withdrew into the boulder and emitted a high-pitched whistle, forcing him to clamp his paws over his ears and back away in fear it would draw Rip Run in his direction.

"Oh dear. What have I done?" he said, picking up his feet and bounding away before he could be located. Looking back, he could see nothing stirring near the boulder. When he turned around he was suddenly face-to-face with a giant man standing seven feet tall and dressed completely in furs from head to toe. He slid to a halt before he collided with him. A scar ran down between the man's eyes and to the end of his nose. A tall staff was in his right hand, carved with the head of an owl on the top.

"Umm, hi," the Captain whimpered, stepping away in fright. The man walked to the boulder and inserted the bottom end of his staff into the hole. Twisting it slightly caused the pole rock to force his staff back out as it returned to its normal position. The blaring noise ceased, bringing Backfoot great relief to his long and sensitive ears. "Allow me to tip an ear to you for taking care of that," he said, bending his right one forward with a quick flap. "If you don't mind me asking, what exactly *is* that thing?"

"It calls all woodsmen to meet for an important purpose."

"Oh. I thought it was some sort of warning device."

"It is."

"I mean—to scare away intruders."

"It is," he said, walking toward Backfoot.

"Oh, I see. I really have to be going," Backfoot said, not wanting to be a bother to the man any longer.

The stranger grabbed Backfoot by the back of his collar. "You have entered my woods without permission."

"I'm sorry, but I have no time to talk about it," Backfoot said as he turned around after the man let him go. "I'm running a race and I have a wicked leader and his followers chasing me at the moment."

"The skeleton in black?"

"Yeees—Herikech Illeon. An ugly fellow with tremendous powers. A Lazul—if you know what they are."

"There are many roaming the forests these days," the man said in a gruff voice.

"Really? That's not what I expected to hear. Is the King aware of this?"

The man shook his head and said, "The rangers are gathering information, but many children are beginning to disappear from their sectors. The skeleton knows of our plans and has set a mangler loose to whittle our kind from standing in his way. I am one of the few remaining."

"A ranger you say? After all my years of running, you are the first I have ever met. Which one are you?"

"Skin Tracker."

Backfoot's mouth dropped open. "Skin Tracker? The legend that walked through a wall of fire to save three flame fighters from a burning waterhouse?"

The ranger nodded and said, "I hear the footsteps of another. Who have you brought here?"

"I have brought no one. It is another dobbin like me—under the power of the skeleton—as you call him. Herikech has convinced the messenger to join his forces."

The ranger grabbed Backfoot by an ear and dragged him behind a tree.

"Hey! Ow!"

"Silence," Skin Tracker said while pressing his hand over Backfoot's mouth. Instead of Rip Run, it was the soldier who had attacked Backfoot. The ranger pulled out a single stone from a pouch at his side and waited for the man to come closer.

"Is he with the skeleton?" he asked Backfoot. The Captain nodded and watched as the ranger whipped the stone with great velocity at the soldier's temple. The man clutched the area for a moment and then looked up with an evil stare.

Skin Tracker leapt forward to attack the man. Before the soldier could draw his sword, the ranger punched him and pulled out the soldier's blade for him. In one clean stroke he removed the man's head from his body.

Backfoot exclaimed in awe, "I've never seen anyone disarmed and killed with his own weapon before."

"It is unusual he did not fall from my rock. I rarely miss a kill with a stone," Skin Tracker said.

"Well, he's dead now," Backfoot said, kicking the soldier's lifeless body.

"We must hurry from here," Skin Tracker said. "It's not safe. I will guide you to your destination. I strongly recommend you warn the others not to continue this adventure you have agreed to."

"That's impossible. It would cost us our entire service, and the King his crown, well, I mean, not his royalty, his actual crown." Backfoot pointed to the top of his head to explain better. "The race must continue. This is no ordinary delivery I am on. The King has placed his own wager on the outcome of this challenge. If the Trail Racers win—and if they're all under Herikech's influence—it could mean tragic things for the kingdom. Spies would intercept mail at every turn and gain the secrets of where the King's family is being kept."

The ranger was silent for a long period. Only the sounds of birds chirping around them filled the woods. Skin Tracker finally said, "Then it is important we equip you and your friends better for the remainder of the race."

"You will accompany all of us until the finish line?"

"No." The ranger picked a pouch off of his side and handed it to Backfoot. "This contains five powder bursts. They are used to put prey into a doze. The powder must be directly inhaled for the target to be affected. Strike here for the best results," Skin Tracker said, slapping Backfoot on the chest with the back of his hand. "Or the face, if you can get that close without being killed."

Backfoot took the pouch and put it safely within a pouch inside his jumper suit. "Grateful I am for that."

"Also, pass this along to your second runner," he said, handing him a short wooden tube. "The forest he travels through is home to the mangler. The beast detests the instrument's song and it may save his life if he encounters the creature."

"Captain Top Steam will also be grateful, although the King has said the mangler makes its appearance only when the moon is blood red."

"The King is correct. But every precaution must be taken. As each night passes and Radia draws closer to turning her color, the mangler grows stronger and could attack someone to satisfy its lust." The ranger grabbed the Captain by the arm and pulled him away from the boulder. "We must move. I hear the rush of another's footfalls."

"I don't think a dobbin has ever set foot in the regions we just walked through," Backfoot said, disgruntled. "Those wild animals—"

". . . Were not a concern, Captain," Skin Tracker replied calmly. "Many creatures carry the look of evil but are as harmless as you or I if left alone. The nefars are a good example of this."

Backfoot nodded. "I guess that's true, but it still doesn't mean I want to go roaming about by their nests. How close are we?"

"Our journey is near its end. The stand of trees before us is our last obstacle before we reach the next Royal House Territory outpost."

"Thank heavens! I'm starving."

The ranger and dobbin walked through the trees and soon could see the blaze of a bonfire ahead in the distance. The light grew as they walked their steady pace toward it. The outline of a dozen silhouetted figures standing around the fire came into view. They walked up a steep embankment and came into the circle of soldiers standing around it to gather its warmth.

"Captain Backfoot!" Top Steam exclaimed, bounding toward them from the exchange line twenty feet away. "Quickly! Give me the baton!"

"First, let me give you these," Backfoot said, pulling out the powder bursts and whistle to hand them over. Top Steam tried to take the items but a sergeant grasped Backfoot's arm and twisted it behind his back.

"What are you doing?" Backfoot asked as he was spun around to get his wrists lashed together.

"You are under arrest for the attempted murder of a Trail Racer," the sergeant said. The sergeant then turned and gave the powder bursts and whistle to a soldier, saying, "These may be the weapons he used to wound the Trail Racer. Put them in safe-keeping for evidence." The soldier nodded and took the items with him.

"Those are for Captain Top Steam's protection," Skin Tracker said.

The sergeant looked at Skin Tracker and replied, "Rangers need to stay in the wild where they belong. Leave here before we arrest you as well."

"I have done nothing!" Backfoot screamed. "Captain Rip Run was the one who tried to kill *me*."

Top Steam untied the scroll case from Backfoot's belt and said, "I must go. We have already fallen behind by several miles. Captain Rip Run stumbled and died at the finish line earlier, Backky. He claimed you were responsible before life left him. I'm sorry it has come to this. I truly hope you were not the one who's behind his death. No dobbin's life is worth a contract." Captain Top Steam put on his night vision goggles and bounded away into the darkness, unprotected.

"Don't worry," Skin Tracker said, "I will help him." The ranger ran into the night after Top Steam, disappearing into the woods in only a matter of seconds.

"Listen to me," Backfoot tried explaining to the sergeant, "Rip Run was working for—"

The sergeant brought down the hilt of his sword on the side of Backfoot's head before he could finish his sentence. The messenger collapsed to the ground with a stream of blood running down his face. The strong smell of honey filled his nostrils before his vision blurred and faded.

"Place him in the holding wagon for later questioning," the sergeant ordered. The soldiers picked him up and laid him inside as Top Steam and Skin Tracker headed south and east toward the next checkpoint.

"Hold!" Skin Tracker yelled at Top Steam, but the dobbin continued, waving him off. "Your life depends upon it!"

Finally, Top Steam halted and turned. "You're going to cost me more time."

"Captain Backfoot is innocent. His words are true."

"Fine! I will be happy to talk to you about it later. I have a race to finish."

"Not yet. You need my help."

"What for? I've been traveling these woods for years—"

"This Trail Racers' road intersects with another that was banned due to the death of one of their runners two years ago. A mangler wanders this area. It has killed dozens of rangers and may be under the influence of the skeleton in black."

"Herikech? Hah! I've heard rumors from soldiers he is wandering around in the castle."

Skin Tracker shook his head. "Not at the moment. He is the one responsible for Rip Run's death."

"How do you know? Were you there when it happened?"

"I have seen the black skeleton in the woods myself. He controls many creatures, including the mangler that travels in the direction you are headed."

Top Steam shuddered and said, "How do we fight it or Herikech? They are both more powerful than you or me."

"We stray from the paths and travel the woods. The other Trail Racers may also be under Herikech's influence. We can trust no one at this point."

Top Steam replied, "Then why should I trust you?"

"Because I would have killed you by now if I were lying."

Top Steam looked the giant ranger up and down and then nodded.

"That's logical."

"Where's the next checkpoint?" Skin Tracker asked.

"Five miles from here," Top Steam said. His face scrunched to figure out the number. "At the water mill crossing."

Skin Tracker grimaced. "Precisely the area where the mangler killed the Trail Racer two years ago. The moon has almost risen. The beast may return to its old hunting grounds before we reach the checkpoint. We must hurry!"

"Where is the King?" Ballan demanded to know. "Why is he not in his bedchamber?"

"He has moved to a new location due to Herikech's presence," a soldier said at the private entrance to the King's old quarters. "Only those closest to him are allowed to know where he currently sleeps."

"And I don't count among those numbers?" Ballan retorted. "I'm just as concerned about the King's health as anyone else."

"I've been informed the King is not to be disturbed for the rest of the evening. He is not feeling well since the recent lightning strike that almost claimed his life."

Ballan frowned and looked at the other two soldiers in the vicinity. Their eyes followed the announcer as he paced back and forth searching for an answer. "How long will he be staying in his new quarters?"

"It is unknown. Possibly until the threat of Herikech has passed."

"So he hides like a worm in a hole in his own castle? He has plenty of protection—"

"Do not refer to the King in those words. I must ask you to leave if you don't have a valid purpose for being here," the soldier cut in. "These halls are not meant to be occupied for long by visitors."

Ballan banged the foot of his hooked staff on the floor and replied, "The voyagers are requesting to dine with him this evening. That is my *valid purpose* for being here."

The soldier shrugged. "Speak with General Fields. He may advise the King."

"Ah. General Fields. Yes. Why didn't I think of that?"

"But General Fields is away on errand."

"Then who is taking his place?"

"General Regoria of Dowhaven."

"Goodbye," Ballan sneered. His white robe swished behind him as he walked quickly out of the hall and to the army's headquarters in the castle. He was met with the same resistance when he approached the guard at Rydor's door.

"State your purpose for your arrival, Ballan" the guard said.

"I need to have a private conversation with the General about the King, if you don't mind."

"The General is not seeing anyone at the moment," the guard said. "He is busy preparing for the security for tomorrow night's tournament."

"Yes, I have to speak with him about that subject, too."

"I'm sorry, Ballan, but he specifically ordered not to be interrupted for the remainder of the evening."

"Oh, it will just be for a moment. Come now. This is getting ridiculous."

The guard raised his sword to Ballan's chest and stated, "Do not tempt me, old man. I have never cared for your ramblings as it is."

Ballan's face became flushed "I'm appalled at your behavior," he said. "I demand to speak with the General now. I will not be an outsider of the Royal Court during these times."

The door suddenly flew open behind the guard. Rydor came into the hall and barked, "What's going on? Who is shouting?"

The guard pointed to Ballan with his sword. "The court announcer wishes to speak with you. He would not leave when I asked him to."

"What is it, Ballan?"

"Could we talk about this in private?" Ballan asked.

"Talk about what?"

"I don't want to say here."

"Then come in," Rydor said.

Ballan tried waving him down the next corridor. When Rydor didn't follow, he said, "Let us walk. There are too many ears about."

"Does this have something to do with the King's safety?" Rydor asked.

Ballan nodded. "In a way you might say that."

Rydor closed the door behind him, stood next to the guard and said, "Make it quick."

"Are we not to walk?"

"No. Tell me here and now."

"But does this guard have to be here?"

"Since when do the guards of Candlewick pose a threat to your words?"

Ballan sighed and said, "Forget I was here. I will just have to talk to someone else."

Rydor shook his head and followed Ballan. "Stop. Go in there," he said, pointing to a small room ahead of them.

After they both entered, Ballan checked to ensure no one was around before saying, "It's the voyagers. They are requesting dinner with the King."

"That is what you need to tell me in private?" Rydor snapped.

"Not just that. They wish to have their quarters moved from the stables."

Rydor shook his head. "It's the King's wish they stay there."

"Which is why the King needs to speak with them over dinner about it," Ballan insisted. The announcer's eyes pierced Rydor to influence the General's decision.

Rydor replied with a straight face, "I'm sorry. There's no reason to move them at this time. They will have to endure what they have been given if they wish to stay. They already know they are unwelcome here."

"They fear Herikech may be after them."

"Good."

"You will let innocent men die at the hands of that madman?" Ballan said, waving his hands about. His frustration was becoming a concern to Rydor until Ballan straightened his posture and said, "Can you not at least move them further into the castle for their own safety?"

"No. We owe them nothing more than what was promised. Good night, Ballan." Rydor walked out and slammed the door behind him, leaving Ballan with his mouth agape and on the edge of his next sentence.

Skin Tracker peered out of the brush at the stony bridge that spanned the Willock River a hundred feet away. Both moons reflected in the slow flowing waters beneath, one in crescent shape, Lumly, and the other, Radia, red and nearly full. The outlines of trees on the other side towered over the road leading to the bridge. Their swaying and creaking made any onlooker's spine feel as if a ghost's fingers were tapping up and down its length. Captain Top Steam was no exception as he cringed behind Skin Tracker in fright.

"We may be too late," the ranger said, watching for any sign of movement anywhere near the bridge or banks.

"See something?" Captain Top Steam whispered.

"Not yet, but it's not an indication there's no danger present. The night is cool and everything is uneasily quiet. Insects do not sing their lullabies this eve. Something is here, waiting for you to make an appearance."

The Captain stuck his head into the small opening to take a look for himself. "We have to cross the river. I would prefer not to swim it."

"The mangler was reported to have been seen near the banks half a year ago by a driver delivering packages for the Trail Racers. He was the last to witness the creature and survive the experience. Crossing the bridge is our only hope to get to the woods on the other side quickly."

"Then the sooner, the better."

"I'll go first," Skin Tracker said, raising his chin. He turned to look at the messenger and put a hand on Top Steam's right shoulder. "If battle should come to me, then take to the river and don't look back. The Trail Racers must not win this race or the black skeleton's spies will control all trade routes within the territories."

Top Steam rolled his eyes and replied, "No pressure."

The messenger watched as Skin Tracker stepped cautiously out into the pasture before the bridge. After a few minutes had gone by, the ranger walked slowly toward its beautifully carved rails and tight-fitted stones. Each footstep that drew him closer lifted the lump in Top Steam's throat higher. Skin Tracker froze when a droplet of rain landed on the scar on his nose. More hit his face a few seconds later, causing him to turn his head skyward. A black cloud was moving in from the west. The ranger continued to move and stepped onto the bridge, walking to its center. Without warning, a hooded figure rose from the water beneath the bridge and hovered out of sight beneath Skin Tracker.

"Herikech," Top Steam whispered. The ranger was open to attack as he watched the Lazul king raise his arms to call upon the weather. The dobbin stuck two fingers in his mouth and whistled a call familiar to a jay's warning.

Skin Tracker spun toward the woods and then ran from the bridge to the other side of the pasture. A heavy fog suddenly filled the area from the woods, blocking Top Steam's view of anything more than five feet in front of him. "Black Skeleton, come and face me!" Top Steam heard Skin Tracker call.

Top Steam ran toward the river, avoiding the bridge altogether. He crossed the pasture and slid down the bank to set one paw in the water, feeling its cool silk pass through his fur. After taking one look up and down the bank for the mangler, he saw nothing. He was soon in up to his waist and swimming across the short distance that separated him from the opposite bank. A sudden cry rang out, prompting him to swim faster. He scrambled up the grass slope and slipped over the edge, feeling out in front of his body in the thickening fog. When he stood he found himself face-to-face with Captain Cracked Tooth of the Trail Racers.

When Top Steam tried to scream, Cracked Tooth slapped a paw over Top Steam's mouth and said, "Shhh. This way."

"Are you siding with Herikech, too?" he asked when Cracked Tooth took his hand off Top Steam's mouth.

"No. Come on."

A gurgled scream filled the fog in the area. "What about the ranger? He may be in trouble . . . ."

"Come now or die like him," Cracked Tooth said. Top Steam looked backed to the fog and shook his head before he followed. The fog started to recede from them as they entered the woods. They came to a hollowed tree and found shelter in its base.

"I don't bow to the Lazul king," Cracked Tooth said, licking his split bucktooth on the top ridge of mouth. "I wasn't more than five yards into my run when he showed up. The moment I recognized who he was, I cut into the woods for safety. Luckily for me, an unwitting karrik broke off his pursuit and allowed me to get away. I reached the bridge just before he did and knew he was going to kill you if I didn't do something."

Top Steam frowned and said, "I'm sorry about Rip Run. He was a good furrow friend. Herikech will pay for his death."

"I don't know, Toppy," Cracked Tooth said glumly. "No one may get to see revenge done. This Lazul is not like the others. You see what he's doin' with the weather. What's to stop him from zapping us all to death?"

"We'll find a way. Don't you worry. Now, how do we get to the next checkpoint without getting caught? He's bound to have his spies watching the trails the rest of the way."

Cracked Tooth rubbed his chin and then said, "I didn't want to tell you this, but the Trail Racers had an emergency plan."

"A what?" Top Steam asked, twitching his whiskers suspiciously.

"To put it plainly, we were gonna cheat."

"What?" Top Steam gasped. "How could you?"

"It was all Keys's idea. I would just be following orders."

"Of all the nerve."

"Keep it down, Toppy. Remember old gray face is still out there."

Top Steam shook his head and said, "How?"

"The General said if we were behind the Majestic Messengers at the end of any run, then we were to use the propeller thrust gliders to catch up. He gave us each a map with a marked location of where one would be hidden. For me, there's one not far from here in Waterhouse One's woodshed. Since the shed's not in use right now, it's the ideal place to store one."

Thinking a moment of the location, Top Steam said, "That's two miles. We may not make it."

"It's our only chance. If we reach the waterhouse, we both can use the glider to reach the second hand-off."

Top Steam let out a sigh. "Since I don't have anything better, I will take you up on it. Maybe we should just call the race off altogether."

"You and I both know the Generals would have our hides for even suggesting that option."

Top Steam glowered and said, "We should win by default anyway now that I know you were going to cheat."

"You're still going to tell the King about the gliders?"

"Shouldn't I?"

"I honestly wasn't going to use mine. I can find work elsewhere if this race doesn't go our way. I'm not as devious as General Keys. Just a little slower in the noggin' I guess," he said, rapping his knuckles against the side of his head. "I like things simple. Keeps trouble out of my head. I don't want to be thrown in a cell for something that wasn't my idea."

Satisfied, Top Steam said, "As long as none of the Trail Racers resort to using one to win, I don't see the harm in it. However, I'm glad we have it available to us to save our necks. Ready?"

"As ever."

Top Steam peeked out of the hollowed tree base and saw the fog spreading into the woods. He ducked back inside and said, "All right. On three, I'll race you to the woodshed and we'll see who's truly faster. Got your runnin' legs on?"

Cracked Tooth wiggled his toes and stretched his legs. "Righty and lefty." The dobbins readied themselves, bracing against the innards of the tree trunk they were hiding in to get a good push-off.

"One . . . two . . . three!"

The second they left the trunk a set of sharp fingernails raked at the material on the back of Cracked Tooth's suit. Several strips of red material tore away as he looked back to see Herikech's hooded figure floating after them. "He's found us, Toppy! Run your heart out!"

The two hares took the longest bounds their legs would allow. Herikech rained hail, threw lightning bolts, and summoned windstorms and rainstorms to slow them down, but they pressed on through all obstacles, their bodies aching and their courage waning. Herikech screamed curses at them and even called upon creatures to attack the runners. Top Steam avoided being bitten by a log snake while Cracked Tooth kicked away a large mane bat that attempted to pick him up and bite him.

"Get off me, ya bugger!" he cried. The bat came at him several more times until Top Steam grabbed a broken tree limb and whacked it out of the air. It flew into a tree and dropped to the ground. Top Steam dropped the heavy branch onto one of its wings so it couldn't fly toward him.

"Stay down before I stake ya to the ground!" Top Steam hollered.

"Come on," Cracked Tooth yelled. "He's comin'!"

In a final attempt, Herikech surrounded the messengers in a blinding fog. Top Steam pulled out a compass to direct them to the woodshed. Cracked Tooth walked into it unexpectedly when they thought they were getting close.

"I think you found it!" Top Steam exclaimed as Cracked Tooth rubbed his head.

"Undoubtedly."

They made their way around to the front and unlatched the wood handle. Inside the glider sat with its wings folded up. They ran behind it and pushed it out the door, putting all their strength into their legs. It cleared only by an inch on each side of the frame. Cracked Tooth pulled down each wing and locked them into place.

"Hurry! He could be here any moment!" Top Steam cried.

"I know. Crank that lever!"

Top Steam did as he was asked and saw the carriers of the glider stretch out to accommodate up to two individuals.

"Strap yourself in while I start up the thrusters."

"Are you sure this thing's going to work?" Top Steam asked.

"I've never personally flown one, but I took a crash instruction course last evening."

"Wonderful."

"Have a little faith in your old pal." Cracked Tooth checked a few more levers and secured several joints to validate everything was ready for take-off. "Keep your head and ears low until we're in the air. It'll help cut down on the resistance."

A cackle sounded behind them as the Herikech's form came floating toward them with outstretched hands. "You fools!" he shouted.

"Fire it up!" Top Steam screamed.

"Hang on!" Cracked Tooth yelled. He pulled on a rope and listened to the engine roar into life. The Trail Racer then slammed his paw down on the wheels' lock releases. The glider lunged forward just before Herikech could grab hold of a wing. They sped toward a crumbling woodpile. Cracked Tooth twisted a knob, which caused the glider to swerve sharply to the right. The left wing knocked a cut log off the top of the pile, ripping a piece of the water-resistant material.

"Got to patch that up when we land."

"He disappeared," Top Steam shouted into the whipping wind. "My night goggles aren't picking up any heat traces from his body."

"He's there. Don't kid yourself. He can mask himself like a bug in bark."

The glider lifted from the ground as they approached the waterhouse. They both screamed as it barely avoided clipping the rotating waterwheel at its side.

"The engine's hot! I feel like my fanny's on fire!" Top Steam complained, checking to make sure it wasn't.

"Sorry. Mine is, too. Bend your feet down a little. It helps."

A bolt of lightning illuminated the sky before them. They shielded their faces as Cracked Tooth turned the knob in a complete circle. The glider flipped upside-down and shot across the tops of the trees.

"We're going to crash!" Top Steam cried.

Cracked Tooth turned the accelerator knob up to gain momentum. Turning a small to his right wheel, the glider righted. "Here we go! I'm turning it up to full speed."

"My tail can't take the heat!"

"It's a lot milder than those lightning bolts! We'll be close to the second checkpoint before you know it."

Both dobbins screamed as they frantically wove through an obstacle course of more lightning strikes for the next three miles. Once the bolts faded to a series of bright flashes behind them, they sang in victory, neither caring how terrible they sounded with the rumbling thunder rolling in their ears. They set down in a golden pasture of wheat and coasted to a stop. Cracked Tooth turned off the engine before it set the entire field on fire.

"Quick! Douse those flames with your canteen water!" Top Steam shouted as he poured his own rations on a few shoots that were starting to spread.

"Got it," Cracked Tooth said. He ran out of water after he dumped out his container, having to use one of his feet to stomp out the rest. "Whew!"

"We need to complete the hand-offs before Herikech catches up to us. It'll give us enough time to inform Captain Quickspeed and Ramp of the dangers they could face."

The hares sped off as a farmer came out of his house to inspect the noise in his field. He shouted vulgar names at the dobbins as they ran to the edge of his field and ducked into the forest.

They took everyone by surprise when they showed up together at the checkpoint a short time later, three hours ahead of when they were expected to arrive. They crossed the hand-off line at the same time and handed over their scroll tubes.

"How in the world—" Captain Ramp started to ask.

"Didn't think we could do it in that amount of time?" Top Steam said. "You'd be surprised how fast ya can run with Herikech on your tail."

"Herikech? The Lazul king?" Ramp replied, not trusting anything a Majestic Messenger said.

"You heard 'em right," Cracked Tooth scolded. "He chased us the whole way here. You two are gonna have to stay off the regular trails and take to the woods if you want to save yourselves."

"What's going on here?" a soldier asked as he came toward them.

"Get going. Both of ya. Yawranan soldiers are under Herikech's command as well. NOW!"

Cracked Tooth pushed Ramp into the woods. Quickspeed followed, bounding out of sight in one long hop.

"Where are they going?" the soldier asked.

"They're racing. Where do you think they're going?"

"The path is over there. You two watch your tongues," the soldier retorted, "or I'll have you imprisoned."

"I'm sure that's what your superior would want you to achieve. Let's go and have a drink, Toppy," Cracked Tooth said with a smirk.

"Splendid idea," Top Steam said, slapping Cracked Tooth on the back.

The soldier watched the dobbins as they went into a tent and shut the flap so he couldn't see what they were up to. Laughter rang out and then whispers. The soldier grunted and kicked dirt on a fire nearby. A few seconds later he looked around and slipped unnoticed into the woods where Quickspeed and Ramp had entered.

Quickspeed and Ramp were faster runners than Top Steam and Cracked Tooth. However, neither could match the speed of the Yawranan soldier that trailed them as they ran through the trees a hundred feet off the delivery trail. The soldier didn't seem to tire no matter how fast they went, and not just any human could keep to the pace they set.

The moons hung silently overhead, shining rays of light through the canopy to light their way as the trained sniffer, also known as a tracker, increased his pace to catch them. Both knew something was terribly wrong and that this man had somehow been convinced to join Herikech's army—by force, bribery or some other demented means.

"What are we going to do about this crackpot that's following us?" Quickspeed asked Ramp as they matched each other's swiftness.

"You mean, what are *you* going to do about him while I finish this race."

"Just as I should have expected from a Trail Racer," Quickspeed scoffed.

Ramp replied, "Just as you should have expected from your competition. My family's life is supported by this business. If I lose, they lose. I don't have time to worry about Herikech. That's the King's business."

"Herikech is controlling animals, brainwashing Lazul children and is now infiltrating emissaries in the Yawranan army. What is not to be concerned about?" Quickspeed said. "Your little ones will be next."

Captain Ramp shoved Quickspeed away and bounded back towards the trail.

"Where are you going?"

"To the quickest path! See you at the finish line!"

"You maniac! You'll get yourself killed if you stay on the open trail!" Quickspeed shouted.

"If you ask me, it's more dangerous to stay down there. May the Circle of Life eat you!"

Quickspeed growled and jumped into the direction of the path, refusing to let Ramp's idiocy get him killed. The soldier picked up their change in direction several minutes later and smiled as he ran to follow.

To calm his anxiety, Quickspeed sang a delivery song to keep his nerves from exhausting needed energy.

*Moss and mist won't collect on me.*
*No they can't slow the fast and supreme,*
*Runners conquering the valleys and hills,*
*Marshes and fires,*
*Blisters and chills,*
*Mountains and mires.*

*In the dawn of the day,*
*Through the thrills of the night,*
*By the edge of the sea,*
*To the mountain in sight,*
*The path will remain,*
*Until we reach our goal,*
*Through the snow and rain,*
*To home and hole.*

*We are the Majestic Messengers,*
*The army of word and package.*

*We're here to assist you,*
*We're your advantage!*

*The moons are high and the storms are comin',*
*But that won't stop me from boundin' and runnin',*
*From the dwellings I've been,*
*To the posts I'm goin' –*

"Will you shut up already," Ramp complained. "Go back to the woods!"

Quickspeed changed his song to a hum and stayed on Ramp's heels for the next five miles, annoying him every possible chance he could get. "He's getting closer. I can feel it in my bones."

"Maybe he'll do me a favor and kill you first." Ramp suddenly halted. Quickspeed bypassed him only a few feet before he did the same.

"What's this all about?" Ramp asked.

"Lazul children." Ten stood in their way, half of them with black cloaks, but all brandishing swords and staffs. "One of the secret guilds!"

"Announce yourselves," Ramp requested.

"Dobbins have no right to challenge us," a boy said with his blade raised in front of him.

"May I remind you that you are on *our* path," Quickspeed said while taking a step back.

"The master wishes you to join him," said another older boy with a hooded cloak that darkened his features.

"You have no idea what you have gotten yourselves into, young man. But I assure you, Herikech is not the proper role model for you to take advice from," Quickspeed answered.

"One way or another, you'll see his way can't be denied," said the largest boy of the group, who was nearly two hundred pounds for his five-foot stature.

"Stay back or I shall strike you with these feet! They got more power in 'em than a club!" Ramp said, bounding in place.

The head boy laughed and lowered his hood.

Recognizing the boy, Quickspeed said, "You're wanted by the army for assisting in the plotting of the murders of three Elders, Brassus Beel."

"Yes. And so are Throy and Grutt," Brassus said, waving the two larger boys forward. They also lowered their hoods to show their features. "They can easily cut those feet from your legs, hare."

Ramp backed up to stand beside Quickspeed. They heard footsteps come to a slow pace behind them. When they glanced over their shoulders, the Yawranan soldier approached with an evil grin.

"Eleven to two. Hmm. Care to return to the woods now?" Quickspeed asked.

"Never. We can be at the next checkpoint by sunup if we race hard."

"How do we get by them then?"

"You don't," Brassus said, taking a swipe at Quickspeed with his sword. The dobbin did a back flip to miss being sliced in two.

"Make a decision!" Quickspeed hollered.

"The trees!" Ramp said, jumping on Grutt's shoulders to reach a branch above him. The dobbin swung three times in a circle around the limb and launched himself into the upper sections.

Quickspeed jumped onto Grutt's back as he started to get up and followed the same pattern of acrobatics to join Ramp. The hares bounded from one tree limb to the next, making it difficult for any of the children or soldier to see them. The soldier ran further down trail and began ascending a tree to impede their progress.

"We're going to do this all night? I can barely see with all these leaves in my face," Quickspeed cried. "Ouch!" he screamed as a branch thwapped him in the face as he dove for the next tree. He nearly fell until Ramp caught his arm and used Quickspeed's falling momentum to throw him to a different branch instead.

"It's the only chance we've got," Ramp scorned. "Keep moving!"

"Hares aren't meant to swing in trees."

"Then take to the ground and see how you fare."

It was no use in arguing any further. Quickspeed used his agility to land safely in each new tree. An arrow sliced his right ear. "Yow!" he screeched.

Ramp looked back and saw blood running away from the wound. "Don't stop or the next one'll be in your head!"

The solider suddenly appeared from behind a tree and thrust his sword out of the dark at Ramp, impaling him in the middle of the chest.

"Noooo!" Quickspeed screamed. The soldier yanked the blade back out of Ramp's torso and kicked the dobbin from the tree. Ramp's body lost life before he hit the ground. Quickspeed slid down the tree trunk and ran to Ramp while the soldier jumped down to interfere. In one move, Quickspeed kicked the soldier in the face and turned Ramp over. Seeing his friend was dead, he snagged the backsack from Ramp's body to take with him. The Captain bounded back onto the path with the Lazul children bearing down on him with their torches, swords and clubs.

The sun slowly rose as Quickspeed ran to daylight and the next checkpoint before he was caught. The Lazul children and soldier disappeared before he got within a hundred yards of the territory's outpost. Collapsing on the ground and out of breath, he managed to say, "Ramp dead. Here's his . . . scroll . . . tube."

"D-dead?" Major Whitepaw stammered. "Was it Herikech?"

Quickspeed nodded and grabbed his side in pain. "Notify King Deardrop that one of the secret Lazul guilds are taking sanctuary in the forests of Aydor Sector. They are heeding to the call of their old Lazul king. King Deardrop must also be warned that members of the Yawranan army are aberrantly falling prey to Herikech's vices. The King must be careful whom he keeps in his company. Trust no one until you reach the gates of Candlewick."

Whitepaw turned to the last Trail Racer, Clutch, and said, "Then you and I are in for the run of our lives. We'll finish this race together or we'll die apart." Whitepaw handed Ramp's scroll tube out to the Trail Racer. "Carry it in his honor."

Clutch took it and added, "When the castle is in sight, it's every dobbin for himself."

"May the best outfit be blessed to serve the territories," Whitepaw said with a nod.

They both raised their empty scroll tube cases and rapped them against each other as a spontaneous racing salute. Bounding side-by-side, Clutch and Whitepaw left before any suspect soldiers could interfere with their mission.

"How wonderful," Whitepaw said with a scowl. "A mudslide. Look at how far it stretches! I can hardly see where it ends. I should have expected something like this."

"This is what the other messengers were talking about?" Clutch asked. "I suppose it's to deter us from taking this route and force us into Herikech's clutches by straying from the path."

Whitepaw nodded. "Brilliant. That rat has more tricks in him than any Royal House jester. I wouldn't be surprised if he's hiding behind that black tree over there at this very moment, waiting for us to step one foot out of line."

"Yes. That would seem a very clever place for one to make his grand appearance before two frightened hares out in the middle of nowhere. He's probably laughing back there right now, pleased with his own deluded scheme he's come up with."

"Frightened? Are you suggesting I should be shaking in my jumper suit over a little mud?"

"Of course not. That's exactly what he would want us to think, eh?" Clutch said, elbowing Whitepaw in the ribs.

"He'll get no such fear from me."

"Or me," Clutch seconded.

A thunderous growl suddenly erupted from the woods behind them. Both of the messengers jumped from the noise and hopped toward the mudslide.

"I hope that was your stomach, Major."

"I wish I could say it was, but I didn't feel my tummy rumble. It could be a random wild animal movin' about."

"Then it's time we be on our way. Ever participate in the fall festival's Wet Slip and Dip?"

Whitepaw smiled. "No, but I've heard there's specific techniques that must be used to catch the weasel."

"It's all about keeping your traction. That may seem impossible in a field full of mud, but it can be done."

The growl erupted again, this time coming from their right, near the dead tree they had been eyeing all along.

"Ahem, Captain. I think you'd better start doing more demonstratin' and less explainin'."

"Just a quick drink first. It helps if the insides are as wet as the outsides are going to become." Clutch tipped back his wineskin and let the red fluid pour into his mouth. After a few good gulps, a large gust of wind blew up, spraying a long stream across his face.

Whitepaw laughed, finding the Captain's shocked reaction amusing. "That teaches ya right for sippin' crimson juice during a race. Don't you know about stickin' to good ol' fashion spring water for long distances? That stuff'll give you cramps."

Clutch squirted a shot of the juice into Whitepaw's face.

The major quickly tried rubbing away the terrible staining beverage with his white paw. "Now look at what ya done, you dolt!"

"Ha, Ha! Think ya know everything? Try to get that out of your fur. This will give me the burst I need to leave ya watchin' my rear at the end."

Whitepaw kicked out with his right foot, sending Clutch flying backward into the mud. He flailed helplessly for a moment and found himself sliding downhill. "Heeeelp!" he screamed.

A fierce, closer growl made Whitepaw also jump forward into the mud.

As his body slid downward after Clutch, he glanced up to see the largest karrik he had ever laid eyes upon run from the dead tree and jump in after them. The creature went headfirst while Clutch and Whitepaw slid away from the path on their backs, feet down and arms out.

Whitepaw yelled, "How do we stop?"

"We can't now until we reach the bottom," Clutch shouted. "You blew the technique I was going to show you. A hare isn't supposed to get his arms dirty!"

The major's foot struck a log and spun him upside-down. "Yaaah!" The karrik was almost upon Whitepaw, sliding forward on its stomach. It swiped its humungous black paw out to rake him. Whitepaw lowered his head to avoid being cut by its razor-sharp claws.

"River ahead!" Clutch yelled.

Whitepaw sucked in his arms to make his body slide with less resistance into its flowing salvation. The major landed with a large splash directly beside Clutch. They both let the current carry them south before the karrik hit the surface a few feet behind them. It growled and swiped at Clutch's arm.

"I can hardly lift my arms against these currents," Whitepaw complained.

Clutch reached out and grasped Whitepaw by the ear and then fumbled for a tree root at the edge of the bank. His hand grabbed hold but then slid down its length and slipped off. "The river's too strong."

"Let go of me!" Whitepaw snarled, batting away his paw. "You're hurting my ear!"

The karrik growled and was nearly on top of them. It swung its paw at the major a second time when they both bounced off a rock in the river's middle, cutting off a row of Whitepaw's whiskers on the left side of his face.

"Die on your own then. I know this river," Clutch said. "There's a waterfall ahead, just around that bend!"

"Good morning, Your Majesty. I was going to inform you of last evening's simple request by the voyagers, but General Regoria decided it was best I leave you alone," Ballan said to Noran, who was sipping a cold glass of ice water in the Grand Hall. Its soothing effect felt good on his lips and against his dry throat.

"I miss my family and there appears to be no end to Herikech's unyielding aggression," Noran said.

"It is understandable you would feel that way, Your Majesty, however, Herikech's powers are impressive even if one is not able to admire them. They will one day show their full strength."

"General Regoria was correct in his orders. He told me of their complaints. Herikech would impress me more by doing me a favor by disposing of the voyagers for me."

Ballan laughed and then said, "I have other information that should also raise your interest. It has done so to mine. We were just informed by the south tower the messengers have passed the last checkpoint before they reach the Western Gate. They will be here by sundown, a record time for both teams over the distances they have traveled. If you wish it, we may start the Tournament of Champions this evening."

Noran scanned the few faces in the hall before he said, "The tournament shall be at the time and date that was stated to the kingdom. Ready my armor."

Ballan bowed and said, "My Lord?"

"Ready my armor. I wish not to go anywhere without it until Herikech is gone from the territories. I will be at war wherever and whenever I walk outside these walls. My body cannot take much more abuse. It is time I wear a shell to protect it."

Ballan paused as if he were to object and then said, "As you wish."

"Who is leading the race?"

"They are dead even," Ballan said with a smile.

"A possible tie? No one is prepared for that."

"But the masses need not worry, Your Majesty. I'm confident the Trail Racers will win."

Noran looked at the announcer with a concerned expression. "Why?"

"Because, Your Majesty, Major Whitepaw is no threat against Clutch in the final hundred yards of a race. His burst of speed is unequaled by even the gandalays over that short of a distance."

The finish line was packed elbow to elbow, with the King, his guards and voyagers standing over the crowd. Ballan stood behind a telescope on a lower platform. He pointed the lens at the edge of the western woods to watch for either dobbin's appearance.

"Here they come!" Ballan announced to the crowd through a large shell echoer. He gazed back at the King and added, "And they're covered in mud and blood!"

"Blood?" Noran repeated.

"Yes, Your Majesty," Ballan said after taking a second look. "It has soaked their faces."

The crowd applauded and cheered for their favorite messengers the moment they appeared as specks on the horizon.

"What is the purpose of the messengers claiming the ranks of your army as their own?" Captain Winslow asked Noran.

"Bearing the weight of a letter is equal to that of any sword or axe carried by a soldier in my kingdom," Noran explained. "The dobbins are an ancient race that have survived more dangers in their day on a single run than any of my men or women have protecting Yawrana's kings in the castle over a lifetime. They have earned those titles."

Ballan called out, "The Trail Racers have taken the lead."

Part of the crowd cheered wildly while the other half booed. Noran put his hands together and mumbled a prayer on Major Whitepaw's behalf.

"The Majestic Messenger has fallen!" Ballan shouted.

"What?" Noran asked, hoping he hadn't heard him correctly, leaning over the railing surrounding the platform to get a better look.

"The Major has fallen," Ballan repeated. "He's getting back up, but appears to be moving slowly."

Noran pounded his fist on the railing and squinted out at the field. The enlarging bodies of the messengers were sending the crowd into a frenzied state. "Don't fail me now, Major," Noran muttered.

Captains Winslow, Soar and Rollins all looked at one other with a grin when they heard the King, then looked back to the field.

The crowd gasped again. A few moments later, Clutch crossed the bridge and raised his paws triumphantly. Every Trail Racer mobbed their greatest hero and lifted him into the air, pouring celebratory wine over his extremities.

Noran shook his head and descended from the platform.

Whitepaw crossed the line and collapsed in exhaustion. General Hithel patted him on the back and said, "You did your best, Major. Don't think twice on it."

"Captain Clutch, please bring forth your scroll tube," Noran announced as the crowd hushed to hear the King follow through with his promise.

Reaching down to the belt at his side, the Captain pulled out a short, thick object and held it out to Noran. It was covered in mud.

"Clean it off for the King," General Keys said, snatching it before Noran could take it. "Where are your manners?"

Clutch started, "But, General—"

"You don't want to soil His Majesty's hand." Keys rubbed away the thick layers of mud. His eyes suddenly grew large. "What's this? Where's the scroll tube?" he screamed, waving a broken tree branch in Clutch's face.

"I lost it in a river," Clutch said, lowering his ears and head. The Trail Racers who had just been praising him, were stunned by his misfortune and put him down. Clutch could only shake his head and bury his face in a paw.

Noran smiled and turned to Whitepaw. "Major, do you have your scroll tube?"

Whitepaw and General Hithel hugged each other in jubilation. Stepping forward, the major proudly handed his over. The crowd exploded into applause as Noran handed General Hithel the contract.

"Congratulations, General. Your team has performed admirably under the circumstances." Every Majestic Messenger in the vicinity tackled Hithel and Whitepaw out of joy.

"Be careful," Hithel said. "The Major's been injured."

"I'm not hurt," Whitepaw replied, holding his white paw up while licking it. "It's only crimson juice." Hithel and Whitepaw laughed, which became contagious to everyone celebrating around them.

Noran stepped back and looked to Captains Soar, Winslow and Rollins with a smirk.

"They only won because of a technicality, Your Majesty," Winslow said bitterly. "Something that won't happen in the Tournament of Champions."

# CHAPTER EIGHT
## The Tournament of Champions

The candlelight was invigorating to Noran this evening, a gift dramatically delivered by the Majestic Messengers as a result of their win over the Trail Racers. He was happy they managed to keep their dedicated and entrusted service alive throughout the territories. But after learning of the price that was paid to achieve that victory, his smile vanished in the candlelight's soothing glow. Two Trail Racers had died as a result of their sacrifices and their team didn't have a contract to claim for their efforts. General Keys nearly fainted when he learned of Rip Run's and Ramp's deaths, his nose running from sniffles and his eyes watering from the tears he was holding back.

Captain Clutch and Lieutenant Whitepaw also almost lost their lives during the last leg of the race. They each gave similar views of their entanglement. Both watched the karrik fall to its death as it went over a waterfall. Whitepaw escaped the river by hooking his backsack on a tree branch to climb out while Clutch scrambled from one rock to the next, jumping his way to safety. Noran was glad both long hares had survived, but the death of the others would always haunt him. The best he could do was promise General Keys and his dobbins they would be taken care of until all Trail Racers' runners, sorters, processing clerks, distribution handlers, cart drivers and mappers could find other work elsewhere.

Noran also ordered the release of Captain Backfoot from the army's dungeons once he learned of the dobbin's imprisonment. Backfoot came to the castle to personally thank him for his kindness, talking of Herikech's involvement and his near death experience by the Lazul king's own hand.

But what weighed heavier on Noran's mind more than the deaths of the two Trail Racers was the betrayal of two army soldiers and a sniffer. He thought he would never see the day when those who gave oath through blood and pledge to king and kingdom would turn to help the greatest evil the land had ever known. One soldier had been killed by a ranger while the other and the sniffer escaped into the woods with a secret Lazul guild, which left Noran no way to discover the reason behind their disloyalty. He could only hope there were few others in the ranks waiting to kill him. Noran ordered all lieutenants to keep a close eye on any strange behavior under their command and report it immediately for investigation.

And as for the secret Lazul guild and the mangler, General Fields was now leading the best sniffer and well-trained squad in the castle to follow the trails of both. The sniffer chosen was a man named Argil Meridot. He was accompanied by the White Light Squad, which was chosen by Fields for the task. Noran gave strict orders for Fields to send reports to the castle every sundown with daily confirmations as to their findings.

Martell Fedrow offered to accompany Argil and use his abilities to have birds deliver messages by way of air so the messengers' lives would not be put in harm's way. Noran thanked Martell for his offer, but declined, not wanting the Nax to die. It was a greater fear to Noran to lose the one believed to be a catalyst that would prevent the end of the world. Instead, Noran requested the use of one of General Keys's engine-propelled gliders to complete the delivery of the messages. And it would be General Keys's hares journeying with Argil and the White Light Squad into the forest depths of Dowhaven Territory. Captains Cracked Tooth and Clutch would be the vital link between the castle and Argil. Both dobbins felt it was a privilege and a way to achieve revenge for the losses of Rip Run and Ramp. They agreed to the bestowment and set about preparing a glider to be pulled on the ground until it was needed for flight.

The bedchamber was cold tonight. The walls felt oddly close around him, almost as if they were stifling his every breath. No warm moons to lay his eyes upon and the fear of the mangler's possible appearance the next day carved out solid concerns in his mind. His old bedchamber had been set up to give the appearance he was still sleeping there, in hopes of catching or killing the mangler if it had not returned to its home in Dowhaven. He had to take extra precautions in the event it stayed close to the castle to do more harm to farmers' flocks or change its appetite to feed upon the unarmed people of Yawrana. He rubbed his eyes with his fingers, wanting to wipe away the horrified faces of children that would tremble before the mangler if it wasn't captured. Their images were sharp and real as if it had actually happened. What if it was his own son that eventually became a victim of the beast? Noran shook his head at the thought and switched his attention to tomorrow.

The Tournament of Champions was originally scheduled to begin at sundown, but since the messenger race had completed a day sooner than expected, it was moved to midday while the sun would be at its highest peak in the sky. Noran asked Oreus if he still wanted to compete in the challenge, but the Baron said it was best for the kingdom to know their leaders weren't afraid of the new visitors. The King had no need to ask Boris if he was ready to do battle with Windreed Sinker. To avenge his brother's honor was incentive enough for the barbarian to enter the gaming rings and humiliate Windreed in front of thousands of witnesses. Noran mustered a smile for Boris. The King's curled lips reflected in his golden crown on the shelf in front of him as he sat at his desk.

Noran was thankful Major Whitepaw's dependency was accurately judged by General Hithel's standards. Whitepaw's ability to follow procedure when carrying mail through flooded regions not only won the Majestic Messengers their continued service, but also another promotion for the Major as well. After the race, Hithel filed the proper paperwork to have Whitepaw's rank raised a couple of notches to Colonel before the sun set.

Noran's eyes looked down to Herishen Illeon's Will and Testament once more. The large bound volume sat before him, patiently waiting to take him back to a battle that reached its boiling point long ago. His hands touched the yellowed pages between the covers, creating a simmer in his mind of what could only come next—betrayal of a king to his own kind. Herishen's heart was not that of any normal Lazul. He cared more for peace than lust for blood of a feuding race that never learned from its past mistakes. Herishen wanted it to end and Noran would be the first since his ancestor's day to know why.

He parted the covers and went to his marked place at the center of the book. The first symbol he stared upon was one of hope. A sun and its enlightening rays met his eyes, as it had once done for a lost king awakening from a long, dark dream.

*It has begun. I have seen more life in the last three days than I have during my entire lifetime. I no longer am forced to travel beneath the surface with the sun casting its penetrating arms to burn my skin. It is now the ally I have always longed for and has given my men and me the advantage we need to press back Heritoch's lines. One by one, Audra is freeing each of the demons within my men, winning them into my favor. We have regained our stronghold in our tunnels and reduced the numbers of my brother's army in a surprise bloodbath while they lay sleeping. I have not allowed Audra to learn of this, for fear she would curse my men and me for using our newly discovered freedom for ill. But it is a necessity that must be completed if we are to change the future the way my father had intended, but never achieved.*

*Yarba has read the waters again. He sees my strength growing and favors our new path since his mind has been freed. The visions he now yields are through clear springs instead of the clouded mud pools of the underground tunnels. Water and sunlight are better companions for the gift of sight than a river by fire in the night.*

*Audra has shown Yarba how to see what is important, what is needed, rather than what is wanted. He now senses the life force of every living creature around him while in his trances. Their energy glows the beauty that is life. He feels their pain, their joy and their need for self-preservation. It is a communication one must learn for himself.*

*Like Yarba, I have also started learning the first phase from the Scroll of Truth. Audra has taught me the First Truth, Inner Being, which is to find the worth within. I sit for entire evenings, listening to the sounds of nature moving around me. I can hear what has eluded me all these years. The simple sound of wind whistling through grass blades tells of treachery and deceit by those who spoil water and soil. These creatures of the night, my people, are wounding the land, destroying what has taken millions of age cycles to create. The land can only suffer under our careless rule. It is unable to repair itself fast enough and keep balance and harmony for the living plants and animals here. It cries for my help to stop these atrocities. With every stroke of a blade or arrow piercing a hide, it grieves and its state weakens until what has been lost is replaced. But to defend it would mean the traditions the entire Lazul race has embraced must end. Our spirits would have to submit to its mercy, something no warrior race would ever be willing to do.*

*Yet, a victory can be ours if we continue to free the souls of all my men through the enlightenment process. Every warrior converted could lead us to heal the land in time. But there are a few who are skeptical of these new rituals, clinging to the darkness in their hearts because of the fears they have always relied upon. Two of the strongest that resist the path I now walk have always been close to me. One is a Bethlen, Gerrith Dragul, a warrior who has been at my side since my birth and the only Lazul who has refused to drink from the sacred cup of baskal blood when anointed as a member of the Bethlen guard. It was I who spared his life for his defiance, an act deemed unworthy when accepting the oath of high allegiance to the King. It pains me he has not the courage to believe in my decision and give back the trust he nearly lost. He only stands and silently watches Audra as she frees the others' souls, possibly believing those who are converted are succumbing to illusions that will betray them in the end. I dare not make him do what he resists—joining either of my brothers' armies. No one in my army can defeat him in combat. He is strong, cunning and fluid in spirit. He is valuable, and in time may be convinced to set all his fears aside. Perhaps, at this time, it is good that one of my men remains as is, to protect me from the creeping terrors the Lazul mind is capable of.*

*The second man who doubts the Methalisian practices is a general of my southern forces, Cullen Murka. He has a tough heart, one that could not be made tender if all the salt of Elvana was poured into its valves. War and he are one. The thought of peace is a temporary reprieve until his next battle. He has been at the center of chaos for so long he cannot recognize life without it. His lust for blood boils hotter the longer I keep him from the front lines. His men are the heart of my army and if he falls, so shall the rest of us. Twice he has sent messengers requesting permission to flank the enemy. But his impatience could cost us everything. It is why I have asked him to come tonight to let the light open his mind. I will have to trick him before he understands what will take place. If he can be turned, the others who still doubt my rebirth may change their stance. Murka is the key.*

The room was becoming increasingly hot to Noran as he read on. He poured over more details of Herishen's connections to the land and the creatures depending upon it. Herishen had drawn many detailed diagrams of the rich and vibrant colors surrounding everything and everyone. Noran was beginning to understand what the Elders were accustomed to experiencing every time they opened their eyes to a new day. How glorious it would be, he thought, to share in their respect for the land and bow humbly to the world he thought he knew.

Yawranans learned to trust the land to help Candlewick rise to greatness. And now, once again, the harmony and balance within the land was being threatened. The walls they had come to depend upon were slowly being torn down, stone by stone, by Herikech's madness. Noran could only wonder why this had come to be. Why would the land create creatures like the Lazuls that could potentially harm it? Did the land intend for itself to be destroyed so it could be reborn for another time and other races? Was this what the Circle of Life truly was—to find new life through death? And what would happen if the cycle was one day broken, if life and death were no longer divided?

Noran focused on the candle in his room until his eyes closed. His breathing slowed as he listened to the sounds of the night and what the winds whispered.

A spider crawled along a top corner of the tent's door. Oreus watched the bulbous insect as it moved toward its prey, which was caught in a web only a few inches away. He thought of himself as the helpless fly caught at the web's edge, struggling to find life in the mess in which it had become entangled. A part of him felt as if he should lose the tournament, to free his old imprisoned crewmates from *The Star Gazer*. Roy Stoffer, Nale Gunner and Berringer Crag all were considered respectable men at one time. But it wasn't because of their history that he wanted them freed. He still longed to return to Uthan Mire and free his people. To accomplish that, he would need the old crew to survive the Sarapin Sea to reach Zonack's shores.

"Now what are you thinking about?" Ola asked, watching him from a bench as a squire fitted a metal chestplate on Oreus.

"My homeland," he replied. "I miss it."

"Why do your thoughts always reside there when you have so much here? You told me you had nothing left in Zonack," she said.

He shook his head. "My brother is there. I never mentioned him before because I didn't want you to worry about it."

"But if you worry about him, so should I. What was he like?"

"Nothing at all like me. More rational. Not as reckless. The last I knew, he was working as a kitchen servant in Weatherwood Castle. Then I met Captain Lanu, and now, I'm here."

"I know this is a painful subject, Oreus, but what happened to your father? You rarely talk of him. I know there is pain there. I can see it in your soul."

Oreus's tears welled up. He looked to his squire, who just handed him his sword. "Please leave us for a moment."

The man nodded and exited. The spider in the corner of the tent was now spinning a web around the fly. Oreus's face turned red, feeling it was unavoidable to hide anything from Ola. "My father was murdered by a knight named Malcolm Hayward. A coward who kills those who get in his way, even innocent men." Oreus covered his eyes with his hand and lowered his head.

Ola stood, walked to Oreus and sat down beside him. She kissed him on the cheek and said, "I will bear this pain with you if you allow me to. Tell me more. You can trust me with your heart."

He looked up and smiled at her. "I know. The sorrow strikes me as if it only happened yesterday. My father and I were passing a tavern one evening when a knight of Zonack's Royal Court, Hayward, came stumbling out. My father tried to help the knight up out of kindness. Sir Hayward was embarrassed to be assisted by a lowly peasant. Most knew Hayward couldn't hold his drinks and had a temper when having too many. And in his extreme drunkard state, the knight shoved my father away and accused him of interfering with a royal subject and his private affairs. My father, of course, was flabbergasted and wouldn't take such a foul accusation in front of his son and friends, even from one in such high standing. He called Sir Hayward for what he was truly known to be, 'A disgrace to Zonack's Royal Court.'

"You can imagine what happened next. Hayward drew his sword and my father found his destiny from its point. Out of blinding anger and tears, I picked up my father's longbow and fitted an arrow to it for the first time. I never used a bow before and shot wide right, missing Hayward completely. If only I was as good of a shot then as I am now. Before I could take a second aim, local peacekeepers arrested me and threw me in jail to cool me off.

"I don't recall how long I was in that cell, but I came to a decision that one day would lead me here. My brother and I took care of my mother until she passed away. After that, it was time for both of us to make something of ourselves. While Derrick went to work at the castle, I worked on a neighboring farm, taking archery lessons from the man who hired me. He was a friend of my father's. There was nothing more that I wanted than to see Hayward getting his own punishment: death. I trained with my father's bow for nearly three years."

"Then what?" Ola asked, seeing Oreus was starting to struggle at the end of his last sentence.

"One day the urge finally took me. I plotted out my plan. There was word that Hayward was traveling to Bhime Barren, another poor division made up mostly of farming villages. Queen Rimshaw III was sending him there to collect the deeds of many landowners. Those who could not pay their annual dues to the kingdom lost their property rights and were forced to sell their homes. The properties then were divided among the nobles of the court to reap the lands for their own uses.

"On his way there, I set up a roadblock to challenge him to a duel. Hayward wouldn't allow me the honor of one, even after I accused him outright that he had unjustly killed my father. He simply scoffed at the remark and ordered his men to slay me where I stood for delaying a representative on a mission for Her Majesty. Knights were only allowed to accept challenges from other nobles, which is something I didn't know at the time. Otherwise, I would have shot him with an arrow from the forest and ended it that day. My father wouldn't have approved of the method. He would have seen no honor in it. So I tried it my father's way instead, and ended up running for my dear life . . . all the way to the port of *The Star Gazer.*

"There I met Captain Lanar Lanu, who agreed to take me on board after I hastily explained to him of my predicament. Without a second thought, he ordered me below deck and protected me from the division authorities while they conducted their routine questioning. 'I suggest you look elsewhere for the boy,' the Captain said in his usual stern voice. Lanu was a respected man in the Queen's royal fleet. Most men wouldn't dare tangle with the legendary sea captain out of fear of what he could say about them to the Queen. After several moments of bickering, they finally gave up. Eventually the incident was forgotten by most and I became a permanent member of his crew.

"I once asked the Captain why he didn't hand me over to the authorities that day. He said, 'You remind me of your father. He was an honorable man.' The Captain always did appreciate honest workers. It, of course, allowed him to play it to his advantage so he could always get the most out of his crew, apparently for his own underhanded purposes. But it turns out my father had supplied Lanu's crew with grain for many of their missions. Irony at its best."

Oreus and Ola looked toward the door when the horns of the tournament blared throughout the Gaming Arena. "You better go," she said, kissing him again. "Thank you for sharing your past with me."

Oreus kissed her on the lips and bowed to her. "My Lady." He exited the tent when he saw her smile.

The arena was packed. The stands were overflowing into areas not meant for standing room. Cheers erupted when Oreus walked toward the King's chair. His nerves tightened after he sheathed his sword. The Salmus voyagers were sitting near Noran, giving their last instructions to Windreed Sinker and Thorn. When they saw Oreus coming toward them, Windreed and Thorn entered the arena to stand before the Royal Court. Boris came striding from another corner of the arena, dressed in battle gear from head to foot. Oreus felt relieved he wasn't competing against Boris. The barbarian could crush him with one swing of the mace he carried at his side.

"Baron Blake," Boris said as he nodded and stood next to Oreus. Boris glanced at Windreed and saw that she, too, was adorned in heavy armor and brandishing a battleaxe. "Hmph. Look at her," he said, elbowing Oreus in the side. "Thinks she can wield that weapon like a chief. My mace will break 'er and send 'er runnin' for the hills."

Oreus looked at Thorn. "Why is he not dressed in armor?" Thorn snarled at Oreus and rubbed the fishhook in his lip. His appearance had not changed at all since he met him at Emison Tower. "Doesn't he know the rules?"

Boris chuckled. "If he wants ta be bludgeoned to death, then let 'im 'ave his wish!"

"Somehow, I don't think he's worried about it," Oreus said, tearing his stare away to focus on Ballan.

"On your feet, Yawrana!" Ballan shouted into a large shell echoer. The stands clapped and cheered. "We haven't had a competition of this magnitude since the Tournament of Wills!" The stands roared again. Many threw objects onto the arena grass and stomped their feet. Ballan waved his hands to settle everyone down. He stroked his beard until they made him satisfied. "On behalf of King Noran Deardrop, we welcome the voyagers from the distant lands of Salmus."

The voyagers bowed to the crowd and to Noran to show their respect.

Few applauded the new voyagers, unsure of their purpose in the lands. Many wondered if their arrival was in relation to a prophecy seen by the Elders.

Ballan went on. "Tonight's event, as you all know, will feature four new participants. I am proud to announce that Baron Oreus Blake has agreed to show his strength and courage for Yawrana." Screams and cries echoed for Oreus. Ola joined Noran and applauded the longest. "And," Ballan continued, "the head Royal House blacksmith, Boris Groffen, will be at his side." Boris bowed and waved to a specific section that loudly supported him, including many of the men who worked in his shop.

Thorn leaned over and whispered to Oreus, "Boys should not pretend to be men."

Oreus looked into the man's gray eyes, ground his teeth and replied, "Only worms find themselves on hooks."

The pupils of Thorn's eyes dilated, taking Oreus by surprise. He stepped closer to Boris as his mouth partially fell open.

"What is it?" Boris asked.

Oreus shook his head and said, "I'll tell you later." When he looked back, Thorn's eyes had returned to normal. The voyager turned his attention back to Ballan.

"And also joining the tournament will be two of the new voyagers, Windreed Sinker and Thorn," Ballan yelled. The crowd applauded and waited for the rest of Ballan's speech, which he was all too eager to deliver. "There will be four events this evening in honor of the four new contestants: The Obstacles, The Lines, Disruption and The Knuckles Duel."

The crowd went wild, chanting, "Baron Blake! Baron Blake! Baron Blake!"

Having heard of all of the events, Oreus felt his stomach sink. They were the newest grueling challenges created in the last decade. He looked at Boris and raised an eyebrow. The barbarian winked at him and slapped him on the back. Oreus felt the wind escape his lungs. He coughed until he was able to get it back.

"The top winners of the first two rounds will compete in The Knuckles Duel," Ballan continued. The court announcer pointed to a guard, who nodded and unlatched a gate. "To make the competition tougher, the arena's most famous athletes will also be competing against our guests. Give applause to Callous, Nastor, Slam, and Breakeeerrr!" There wasn't a soul sitting by the time Ballan said the last name.

The noise of the crowd was deafening. Most of the applause was for Breaker, the Gaming Arena's most popular figure. He wore a black mask that covered his eyes and had a yellow band around his right bicep. The rest of his body was covered by burgundy, ripped garments that fluttered away in strips from his body like a torn flag. Nastor, Callous and Slam also held the yellow bands of entertainers and each held an imposing presence. Nastor was tall with toned muscles, wearing a simple silver chest plate like Oreus, only his had a Circle of Life instead of a dragul on it. Callous wore all black, carried an azzel staff and was the biggest of the four gamers. Slam was the opposite, half the height of Callous. His frame was wide and low to the ground as he crouched, as if ready to spring at any given moment. Spikes were wrapped above each elbow, below each knee and around his wrists and ankles. Green and gray material covered the rest of his body, fitting tightly against his stocky form.

"Prepare yourselves for The Tournament of Champions, players," Ballan shouted. The crowd screamed and cried again, waving their flags for those they supported.

Oreus and the others made their way to a large constructed contraption at the center of the arena. Soldiers were prepping instruments used to throw a runner off his balance as he made his way across a narrow beam to a large ring door at the end.

Ola, taking away Oreus's breath, sang *The Tribute to Yawrana*. He had no idea she could sing so beautifully. He saluted her and watched Breaker ascend the steps to the stage. Ballan announced the rules of the event. "Any competitor that falls from the beam is automatically eliminated from the tournament. The more rings one collects from the stage, the more points he or she will be awarded. Each ring represents ten points and there are ten in all." Ballan held one of the small gold circles up, which was a foot in diameter. "May the best survive."

Oreus didn't like Ballan's use of the word 'survive.' Games were known to be dangerous at times and this was no exception. However, there were always medicine makers present in the event of a serious injury. He looked to Noran, who nodded and saluted. He returned the gesture and said to Boris, "Will your leg hinder you on the beam?"

"Nah!" Boris said. "I just'll 'ave to move a bit slower than the rest of ya."

"Doesn't seem fair they included this event because of your disability."

"What disability?" Boris snapped.

Seeing the barbarian getting upset, Oreus said, "Forget what I said," and kept his mouth shut.

"Don' feel sorry for me," Boris said, putting a hand on Oreus's shoulder and looking him square in the eye. "I can 'old me own. Me new leg is just as good as me old one."

Oreus nodded and took his place, last in the line, following the instructions of a soldier in charge of the stage. He was certain Captain Winslow was the one who insisted on using this particular event, having somehow heard of Boris's handicap. It would give all the other gamers a supreme advantage in beating the barbarian.

"What were ya goin' to tell me, lad?" Boris asked, his temper calming.

Thorn looked back at Oreus and then at Boris. "Nothing," Oreus said, not wanting Thorn to overhear his explanation.

"Make up yer mind," Boris said, handing his mace to a soldier.

"Oreus turned to look at Quinn. His guard was standing near the base of one wall and saluted him and smiled. Oreus turned back toward the stage and pretended he wasn't paying attention to Thorn. The voyager curled his lip and pivoted toward the stage when a bell rang for Breaker to start his run.

A door opened before Breaker as he sprinted forward onto the foot-wide beam. Flaming torches came hurling his way. He ducked and spun to miss all four. At the end he collected a ring attached to the side of the beam. A few seconds later, he was up and running again. A cage of mane bats was opened below the beam just before he reached the area. The creatures squealed and flew upward in a spiral around him. Two of the bats had rings attached to their body. He snatched one out of the air but was unable to get his hand on the other. Another bat became caught in his pant leg. He freed it and wobbled. The crowd gasped when he nearly lost his footing. Soldiers at the side of the beam used spears to force him forward. He jumped over a series of six poles at knee level, collecting three more rings along the way between each set. The beam suddenly ended at one point. He jumped five feet over a sand pit where it picked up again. A ring was on the end. Breaker snatched it before a barrel of water dumped on his head from a beam overhead.

A slick of oil coated the next section of the beam. He flipped in mid-air and avoided it altogether, landing on the center of the beam on the other side. One ring was on the side of the beam and another partially hidden beneath it, which he missed. The last golden ring hung from a hook in the circular doorway at the end of the beam. When Breaker reached for it, his hand couldn't grasp it. "A painting!" He punched his fist through it and into a box. Feeling around inside, he found the real ring. The door opened and he walked through, raising his arm. The seven rings fell to his shoulder. A guard counted them and recorded his points.

Windreed Sinker was in line next, faring poorly by collecting only four rings. Three of those four came between the three sets of poles. She punched the beam as she walked by it, cracking it down the center. Several guards guided her back to her tent. Captain Winslow gave her a disapproving glare from the stands. She caught a glimpse of it and cracked her knuckles.

Callous was only slightly better than Windreed, picking up five rings and a series of scratches along one side of his face from a bat. He killed it out of revenge and tossed it into the crowd. A girl shrieked and fainted when it landed in her lap.

Nastor shocked many by falling in the sand pit when he took his running jump. Oil residue on his boot prevented him from making a solid landing. His foot slid forward and off the beam. His head cracked loudly against the wood when he fell onto his back. A medicine maker rushed over to him. Nastor was slowly helped to his feet, having suffered a mild concussion from the blow. He staggered from the arena with the help of several soldiers. Ballan announced his disqualification, drawing many boos from the crowd.

Slam beat Breaker's performance. He obtained all ten rings. Not a single bat touched him and his leaps and bounds were amazing to watch. Breaker nodded to Slam for a well-accomplished feat. Oreus tried seeing what the actual obstacles were, but the position in which they were placed prevented him from getting a good view of what was to be expected. He only could watch Slam walk by him and the other competitors, who were eagerly waiting their turns. Slam made sure they could see him carrying all ten rings around his arm.

Thorn was also brilliant, gathering nine rings. The only one he missed was the final behind the painting. He tried going back through the door to find it, but the door locked once he had passed through. He pounded his fist against it, breaking it off its hinges. The judges deducted one ring from his total as a penalty. It took some time until the soldiers were able to repair the door so it worked for the other contestants.

Boris tried his best in the event but was unable to do well. He picked up five rings, which made him satisfied he was ahead of Windreed. Noran stood and applauded Boris for his efforts. The barbarian blushed and tried walking over to Oreus to give him some tips but soldiers had to turn him away so he didn't give the Baron an advantage.

A soldier asked Oreus to ascend the steps for his turn. He looked to Noran and took a deep breath as the door before him sprang open. He ran forward and saw the torches being flung his way. He ducked and fell onto his chest. The side of his face slammed against the hard wood of the beam. Women in the crowd cried for him to get up. Oreus crawled forward and collected the first ring as another torch bounced off his back and sent a shower of sparks over his body. Just as he got up and went forward, a new cage of bats was released. His arms pinwheeled backward. Oreus fell, bringing the crowd to their feet. At the last moment his hand caught the edge of the beam. His feet nearly brushed the ground as he dangled eight feet below the beam. His fingertips hung on until he could put his other hand on the edge and work his way back up. His arms shook and sweat dripped from his brow.

"Concentrate!" Quinn hollered from the crowd.

Oreus jumped all three poles and picked up the easiest rings. The next two obstacles were easier than he thought they'd be. He made a perfect leap across the sand pit to collect his fifth ring. The beam was regreased with oil and the slick was longer than it had been for the others. Oreus was able to land on his left foot and right knee, sliding only a few inches forward. Noran and Ola hugged each other as Oreus collected the main ring and partially hidden one to bring his total to seven. When he came to the painting, he was confused as to what he was to do. Finally, not understanding he was supposed to punch through it, he opened the door and walked through.

"Go back!" Quinn shouted.

By the time he turned around it was too late. The door clicked shut and locked as he thrust his shoulder into the wood panel. A guard counted his rings and held up a scorecard with a seven for everyone to see. Most were satisfied with the marks, giving Oreus a healthy applause that made him hope the upcoming challenges were not much harder.

Oreus and the others returned to their tents while the court jester, Marian the Minstrel, sang a song written for the tournament, which was to be recorded in the volumes of the Historical Record Keep.

*On this historical day a challenge awakes,*
*And we witness how legends are born.*
*Heroes Sinker, Slam, Breaker and Thorn,*
*Battle Groffen, Nastor, Callous and Blake,*
*In the sun's bake and wind's scorn.*

*Watch their courage,*
*Embrace their hearts,*
*Live their moments,*
*Whenever one starts!*

*Ask yourselves what it is you wish.*
*Appease your appetites at fury's dish.*
*Feast your eyes on the clashes and thrills,*
*Until you are satisfied and find your fill.*

*A champion of champions will rise.*
*There can be only one.*
*The winner will claim the prize,*
*When the struggles are done.*

*When all is past, the rain will fall once more,*
*No matter which victor rises from this fight,*
*To bring his honor and pride home tonight.*
*The words of today will find their store,*
*On the shelves of the Keep, behind yesteryear's door.*

Captain Winslow approached Noran and said, "The Baron has more skill than I expected, Your Majesty."

Bruneau stayed close to the King with his hand on the hilt of his sword.

"Where one is born does not determine their worth," Noran replied. "Oreus will prove his to you, as he has done to so many from your lands before."

"You are referring to Captain Lanu? Well, you can't blame an experienced sea officer for being careful of whom he brings on board. Baron Blake, after all, is a wanted man in Zonack."

Noran, Bruneau and Blaynor all looked at Winslow in curiosity. "What do you mean, Captain?" Noran said with an edge to his voice.

"Come now, Your Majesty. He didn't tell you?"

"Tell me what?" Noran snapped.

"The Zonack Royal Court is seeking his arrest for challenging a noble to a duel. It is a high crime that deserves trial."

"What are you suggesting, Captain?"

"Your Majesty, to put it plainly, Queen Penelope Rimshaw III would expect a royal member of Zonack or even Salmus to apprehend a criminal when identified."

Noran stood and walked to the Captain, his face turning red. Bruneau and Blaynor took a stance on each side of the King to make his presence stronger. Captain Rollins stood next to Winslow to give him his support. "Do not trifle with my people," Noran said.

"Trifle, Your Majesty? I merely am stating what has already transpired and the proper course of action that needs to be taken."

"You could care less what crime Baron Blake has done. You would only use him as a bargaining chip to fill your pockets with more coins from Zonack's court. Don't even think you are going to get him from me."

Winslow nodded to Noran and said, "If that is your decision, it will be considered, Your Majesty. But you should ask yourself, is one man worth causing a war between three kingdoms?"

Noran was about to reply when the horns of the tournament blared again to signal the start of the next event. He returned to his chair instead of replying to Winslow. The two Captains also took their seats with a smile on each of their faces.

"Do not give him a second thought," Blaynor said, making the King feel more confident about his response.

"Why did Oreus not tell me this?" he replied.

"Perhaps he wishes to leave his past where it belongs," Blaynor said. "Something tells me he had a true purpose in challenging the knight, which Winslow didn't explain. Or, Winslow is full of more foul air than we originally guessed."

"What was that all about?" Ola asked Noran, coming to his side.

"Nothing," Noran said, not looking at her. "The next competition is about to start."

Ola stared at him for a few moments but Noran didn't give in to her glaring intimidations. She finally shook her head and looked toward the playing field.

Oreus exited his tent and went to three long, parallel lines drawn in the sand at the north edge of the arena. Boris and the other gamers were already there with a short staff in each hand. A soldier handed a pair to Oreus as well when he took his place behind Boris.

"What do we have to do now?" Oreus asked Boris.

"Fight." He pointed to five guards taking their place at precise intervals along the middle line. "If one of 'em knocks you outside the two outer lines, you're disqualified. Get the guard's ring as you get past each of 'em. This is where ya start showin' yar true fightin' skills."

Oreus noticed the patch stripes on their arms. "Each guard is more skilled as you get toward the end?"

Boris nodded. "Yep. Never thought about fightin' someone like Rydor before, have you?"

"Yes, I actually have. But never wanted to."

"Wise, lad. Guards like 'im are not easy foes. In fact, yer chances of beating a first ranker is slim ta none."

"Thanks for the encouragement," Oreus said, shaking his head.

"Tap that reserve," Boris said, pointing at Oreus's chest, where his heart beat beneath.

Oreus nodded and watched Thorn go to work with his half-staves. He hooked the first guard's staff with his right staff and spun when the man tried to strike. Thorn raised his arm to let the ring fall to his elbow and moved on, leaving the first guard flustered he was so easily bypassed. Thorn did a flip in mid-air and kicked out at the second rank guard's chest, sending the man flying onto his back. He jumped on the guard's chest while the man was down and disarmed him. When he placed a stave against the guard's temple, the man obediently handed over his ring. Thorn jumped off the man with another flip and moved forward. The third rank guard struck at Thorn with his stave and snapped Thorn's left shorter stave in two. Thorn tossed it aside and tackled the third guard. He immediately head-butted him and put him into a daze. After claiming the ring, he moved on to the fourth. In place of the half-stave he lost, he held one ring in his left hand. The guard whipped his staff in an arc above his head and struck Thorn in the shoulder. The voyager fell to the side and clutched the wound in pain. His eyes suddenly dilated. The guard gazed at him, confused at what he had just seen.

Thorn growled and charged. The guard thrust out his staff but Thorn used the ring in his left hand to catch the end of the pole. He slid the ring up the staff's length to prevent the guard from withdrawing it. With his right leg, he did a backward flip and kicked upward, catching the guard underneath the chin to knock him out cold. Thorn tossed aside the half-stave and took the full length one instead. Moving on, the fifth rank guard was ready. He struck Thorn three times before Thorn could even throw a punch or strike with a stave. He fell back and reassessed his new opponent.

The guard took a new stance and smiled at Thorn to make him angry. Thorn curled his hooked lip and ran forward. Midway through his run he jumped and spun in midair, kicking the guard across the side of his face, knocking him outside an outer line. The guard got to his feet and realized where he was. He hung his head and handed over the fifth ring to the voyager. Thorn placed the ring over his arm and raised it to let all five fall to his shoulder. Many in the crowd booed, but all three Salmus Captains stood, applauded and looked at Noran.

The King paid them no attention and watched Windreed Sinker take her turn. With her immense size, she had no trouble with the first three new guards. They fell like card houses. She threw the fourth guard into the fifth and took both their rings simultaneously, finishing the competition quicker than anyone else would.

Slam couldn't get past the third guard. When he tried a running and tumbling move, the guard kicked out and knocked him off-balance, and Slam's right hand landed just beyond the right line, disqualifying him. The crowd gave mixed reactions, some complaining and others using vulgarity to express their displeasure. Slam only bowed and waved his hand to the Royal Court. He exited the arena to watch the remainder of the tournament from the stands.

Boris used many of the same tactics as Windreed had but didn't find as much success. When he reached the third guard, the fourth joined to help the third. Boris swung left and right, but both men ducked and cut his legs out from underneath him. Boris fell onto his back and rolled to get up. The fourth guard kicked him in the back and sent him sprawling. Boris's face landed just before the outer left line. He pushed himself up and used his fists to bash his way through the two. He hurled himself at he last. The fifth guard didn't expect this and couldn't raise his staff in time before Boris landed on top of him. The crushing weight of the barbarian forced the guard to surrender the ring quickly. Boris raised the three rings and grumbled as he waited and watched his friend go next.

Oreus used his training in the *Urra Dur* to disarm and defeat the first two guards. His skill had grown tremendously over the last two years, bringing pride to his instructors and members of the Royal Court. The third guard and he were evenly matched, countering each other's moves perfectly, as they were trained to do. Oreus held up well, but he was punched in the gut and smacked across the back by the guard's staff. He fell to his knees and tried to catch his breath. The guard backed off and looked to the King, afraid to harm the Baron any further.

Captains Winslow and Rollins looked at Noran and waited. Noran gave the guard a thumb up. The Captains sat back in their chairs and frowned.

The guard raised his staff to strike Oreus when he got to his feet, but the Baron jumped up and caught the man's swing. He threw a hard fist and pushed the guard outside the lines. Oreus collected his third ring and received a salute and smile from the guard when he recovered. Oreus fought harder against the fourth guard. Knowing his skill was not as advanced, he worked the man toward an outer line and did a leg sweep. The guard's head fell just outside the line, ending the match. The fifth and final guard attacked him right after he picked up his fourth ring. Oreus raised the ring to deflect the blow. The metal slapped against his knuckles, forcing him to drop it. The guard kicked the ring beyond his reach, outside a line.

The crowd booed and threw objects onto the field. Some jumped out of the stands and raced toward the guard to take revenge, but soldiers apprehended the individuals and dragged them outside of the arena. "How can you let the voyagers win?" cried a woman. "You traitor!"

The guard ignored the woman and battered Oreus left and right. But Oreus wouldn't allow himself to be beaten in front of his followers. He grabbed the guard by the wrist and swung him around in a circle. The man teetered at the edge of a line. The crowd rose to their feet and prayed. With one kick, Oreus sent him flying past the line and into the dirt. The noise in the arena was deafening. Noran and Ola were on their feet and cheering like they were excited children at a birthday party. The guard got up, handed over his ring and the ring he had kicked outside the lines to Oreus. The Baron hugged the guard. People were jumping up and down as all five rings were counted for his hard work.

Callous was already halfway through his duels before the crowd finally quieted for Oreus. Brute strength wasn't enough, however, to defeat the third-ranked guard. The guard forced Callous's hand toward an outside line after he wrapped an arm around Callous's neck. His lips turning blue, Callous gave in and let his fingertips stretch out as a trade for oxygen. The guard helped him up and backed off when Callous shoved him away. Callous stormed from the arena to head to the Sunrise Barrel House for a drink.

The first guard in line took Breaker by surprise by throwing one end of his staff in the dirt and spinning his weight around it to catch the entertainer across his face. Breaker fell backward with blood flowing freely. He licked his upper lip to clean some of it away and made a run almost as impressive as Windreed's. Within twenty seconds he had collected three rings and in ten more he snuck by the third and fourth guards with precise maneuvers, stealing their rings and putting their high training to shame. Oreus had heard Breaker was trained by Kuall, the former Court Jester, in some aspects of his gaming to improve his talents and give him an edge during the regular games. There was no doubt of this in Oreus's mind after he saw Breaker's last two moves to claim all five rings. The crowd became almost as loud for Breaker's brilliance as it had for Oreus's. The trumpets blared to signal the end of the event.

Marian the Minstrel reappeared to sing two more songs and then was followed by a marvelous display of acrobatics by the Loop Troop. As Noran watched the scenes unfold, he suddenly felt queasy. He put his head in his hand. His head pounded and his stomach felt like it was in knots.

"Are you ill, my Lord?" Bruneau asked, seeing the painful look on the King's face.

Noran's thoughts revisited his father's death, when Doran was poisoned by Kuall.

"My Lord," Bruneau repeated, putting a hand on Noran's shoulder.

"I'm fine!" Noran snapped to cover up the bizarre feeling. He sat back in his chair and took a deep breath of air. The pain slowly ebbed away. He felt his forehead—it was surprisingly hot, even though he no longer felt sick.

"Sorry, my Lord," Bruneau replied. The guard looked around and saw Captains Winslow and Rollins looking their way. He spun his index finger in a circle as a suggestion for them to turn around and mind their own business. Winslow smirked and did as Bruneau asked.

"It's not you," Noran said to Bruneau, looking up.

With unnatural speed, a gray cloud moved in over the tournament and opened up a flood of rain upon the crowd. Thunder crashed, making many children cry and women scream.

"Get down!" Bruneau screamed. He grabbed Noran by the front of his robes and threw the King to the floor. A bolt struck his chair only a moment later, catching the seat on fire. Blaynor grabbed a bucket of drinking water and splashed it down to put out the flames. Another lightning bolt struck the wall that Noran was behind. Stone flew outward in all directions. People screamed and ran from the arena, causing a widespread panic to occur. Men and women were trampled, some falling to their death during the chaos.

"We must get you underground," Bruneau said into Noran's ear.

"No!" Noran yelled. "Get off me!"

"I must not . . . for your own protection," Bruneau said, resisting with all of his strength.

Noran overpowered him and threw him aside. "I will not go into hiding." The King turned toward the sky and looked up into the driving rain. "Do you hear me, Herikech? *I will not hide!*" Baron Viktoran Ilos ran to the King's front to protect him and held up his sword, Heaven's Light. A lightning bolt zapped the sword and set it aflame. Viktoran managed to hang onto it and keep himself in front of Noran. As if a river had been dammed, the rain suddenly stopped and the cloud moved on.

"Guards!" Noran shouted. "Search the arena for Herikech!"

Any man bearing a red band went into action, with the exception of Bruneau and Blaynor.

"Why did it leave?" Blaynor asked.

"Herikech is behind these acts, Your Majesty," Viktoran said. "He fears my sword. I once wounded him with it. He fled before, and he still does now."

"Unsheath it," Noran ordered.

Viktoran did as the King asked and handed him his blade.

"I know of your sword and its powers, but do you know how it was originally created?" Noran asked.

"No," Viktoran replied. "It has been passed down through the generations of my family since Yawrana was first founded. It was never explained how it was forged."

"How does fire come from it?"

"From my confidence. My soul," Viktoran explained.

Noran looked toward the sky and raised the blade. "Come fight me," he shouted. Nothing happened. He tried again, giving his soul his full confidence that he could defeat an entire army by himself. "*Fight me!*"

Viktoran frowned when only a brief glow appeared at the blade's tip. Noran turned back toward the Baron and handed it back to him. "Make it work."

The Baron held the blade up and it instantly caught fire and glowed. "It took me a long time to find its power," Viktoran started to say.

Noran shook his head, looked at Blaynor and Bruneau briefly, and then turned back toward the Baron. "Viktoran, from this day forward you shall be my third personal protector. General Corsay will be handling your territory duties for now. I need Heaven's Light to ensure my safety."

Viktoran nodded. "Yes, my Lord."

"Bruneau, send word to the Majestic Messengers and have it done."

The guard nodded and walked at a brisk pace to complete the command. The crowd slowly returned to the arena when they saw the danger had passed.

Ballan came over to Noran and said, "A little rain and half the stadium empties."

"A little rain? Did you not see the lightning strikes?" Noran asked.

"Yes," Ballan said. "It was fortunate you had a wall and the guards to shield you. Herikech is getting closer. He may now have to wait for the prime opportunity with Baron Ilos around. If I were you, I would watch your sword at all times, Baron."

Viktoran nodded and raised an eyebrow as Ballan walked toward the shell echoer and announced, "My friends, you have nothing else to fear. The storm has moved on. The tournament will continue."

"Wait!" Viktoran said. "What about the King's safety? What if that cloud comes back?"

"I doubt it," Ballan said.

"All is well, Viktoran," Noran said. "With you at my side, I no longer fear the weather. Ballan, call everyone back."

"How can you be so sure, my Lord? Even my sword may not be enough to save you," Viktoran argued.

"That's true," Ballan said as he stroked his beard. "What is it you wish me to do, Your Majesty?"

Noran sat in his wet and burned chair and demanded, "On with it!"

Ballan turned and waved to the trumpeters. They raised their horns and played to signal the start of the next event. The remaining five competitors raced from their tents to the southern section of the arena. Oreus was, again, the last to arrive at the next challenge: Disruption.

"Yer not tellin' me somethin'," Boris said to Oreus, squinting one eye at him. "It's 'bout Thorn, isn't it?" he whispered so the Salmus voyager wouldn't hear. "I saw the moves he was doin'. They ain't natural."

Oreus pulled Boris a few more feet away from the large pit and said, "Yes. His eyes—they're not human."

"Huh?" Boris replied, glancing at the voyager again. "If he's not human, then what is he?"

"Ever hear of nightwalkers?"

Boris looked at Thorn and then back at Oreus. "Nah! That's impossible. They eat the dead and hate the light. We've seen 'im dinin' at the King's table."

"Who's to say they can't eat regular food, too? And what if they have adapted so they *can* walk in daylight. My brother said he once saw one traveling through Uthan Mire, near the graveyards. The eyes of the one he saw dilated just like Thorn's did when I looked at him."

"Do you know what you're sayin', lad? They're not easy ta kill."

"I know. If Winslow decides to make him attack us, then we're in trouble."

"What's holdin' Winslow back if that's true?"

"Maybe he's testing our strengths."

Boris shook his head and said, "Look, why would a nightwalker be travelin' with humans? And how could Winslow keep one under his control?"

"You forget that nightwalkers once were human. I've heard they are transformed when they denounce death through some type of ritual. And, yes, eating the dead is involved somehow when it takes place. Maybe by eating the dead it brings them everlasting life. My brother asked the local farmers about the one he saw. They told him what he was and to avoid him at all costs or it would be eating him next. For all we know, Thorn could be thousands of years old."

"If that's true, then how da ya kill somethin' that can't be killed?"

"I don't know," Oreus said. "We seem to be having way too much of that problem lately."

Breaker took the lead, showing he had no fear of losing. When a large wooden platform was slid into place over the pit, he walked twenty yards out to the center ring and stopped. He looked back at Oreus and listened for the mase to blow. Two soldiers stood twenty paces from the pit and lobbed wooden balls at the platform. Breaker dove and caught one and then raced back to catch the second before either touched the platform. The pace was slow at first but began to pick up when Breaker was catching everything thrown his way. Finally, one slipped past his hand and hit the platform. As soon as it touched it, a large circle opened up in the pit from the impact. Breaker jumped over the circle to continue catching other balls. A few moments later a second and third hit opposite edges of the platform. He was unable to reach them both in time, causing another dark opening to swell above the pit. Out of the holes climbed treetop swingers, human-like creatures with long arms and shaggy brown fur covering their entire bodies. They immediately ran after Breaker. He jumped to the side to catch another ball but missed. An opening occurred and sent the swinger falling back into the pit. The mase blew again, ending his playing time. He collected nine balls in all for ninety points.

Boris went second. He was not as fast as Breaker but had long reaches to catch each of the balls thrown his way. Many treetop swingers clung to his legs by the time his round ended. He only managed to pick up six. He growled and threw the swingers back into the pit before the platform was reset.

Windreed Sinker followed. She also was doing well until a ball landed on her foot and then rolled onto the platform. A hole opened up beneath her, sending her plummeting into the pit. Boris cried and shook a fist.

"Why are you mad?" Oreus asked. "You did it. You beat her."

"If only I could have beat her with me fists in the Knuckles Duel. How can I do that if she's disqualified?" Boris said.

The platform was removed from the pit to allow Windreed out. She was shrieking as a swinger pulled on her hair as she tried to get it away. A soldier knocked it off, sending it back into the pit. The platform was slid back into place and reset. One swinger got away, however, and raced around the arena, frightening children as it tried to find a way out. A guard tranquilized it and trapped it near a gate.

Oreus went next, leaping and tumbling across the platform. His movements were swift and exact, allowing him to catch every single ball thrown his way. When the mase whistled at the end of his round, not a single spectator was sitting. Ola threw a flower toward him and blew a kiss his way. He had taken the lead, having caught fifteen balls.

Thorn finished out the event and missed only two balls at the end when they hit the edge of the platform. He couldn't get to them in time and caused half the platform to disappear before him. He almost fell in but caught the grassy edge of the pit just in time. A swinger grabbed onto his leg to pull him down. He turned and looked at it with a growl. The creature whimpered when it looked into his eyes and let go. Thorn pulled himself back up onto the platform to prevent being eliminated.

The arena trumpets sounded again to end the event. As the four men who were left returned to their tents to rest for The Knuckles Duel, Ballan spoke. "The final event is almost upon us, Yawrana." The crowd cheered as the stands refilled with new people to see the longest running event since the games were first founded. "The points have been tallied. The man with the highest number of points will fight the one with the fewest. Second and third place finishers will battle each other. The matches will be as follows: Baron Oreus Blake versus Boris Groffen and Thorn versus Breaker. The two remaining standing at the end of these two bouts will face off against each other for the ultimate prize: to claim the golden cup of champions!"

Not long after Oreus returned to his tent, a soldier entered. "His Majesty wishes to see you."

Oreus was about to get up when Noran, Viktoran, Bruneau and Blaynor entered. "Well done, Oreus. You are truly a champion of my court."

"Thank you," Oreus said, saluting the King with a fist to his chest. "But how am I supposed to fight Boris? He's three times my size."

"Has your *Urra Dur* training already slipped your mind?"

And then, it hit him. "Pressure points?"

"Yes."

"But that could cause him injury. I don't want to hurt him."

"And he doesn't want to hurt you either. If you both would have met in the last bout I could have ended the tournament altogether. The last thing I need is two of my own men trying to maim each other. But as long as Thorn remains a participant, the tournament must finish. I have instructed Ballan that Thorn and Breaker will fight first. If Breaker manages to win, I will make it so you two don't have to fight."

"That would be a relief," Oreus said.

"Don't worry, I'll make sure Boris doesn't squash you."

Oreus chuckled. "And that he would. The Knuckles Duel favors him the most. I'm proud of him that he's made it this far."

Noran rubbed sweat from his brow and smiled.

"You are looking pale, Your Majesty. Are you not feeling well?" Quinn asked.

Noran didn't answer.

"Maybe we should take you to see Master Oyen," Bruneau suggested.

"Has he not seen enough of me already in the past few days?" Noran said.

"Once more wouldn't hurt," Blaynor replied. "You have pushed yourself too far."

"You two don't have to tell me what is best for me," Noran growled.

Both of the guards went silent. Oreus also was at a loss for words, rarely seeing this side of Noran's temper flare.

"Forgive me," Noran said. "Herikech is making me lose my patience. I will see Master Oyen later if it will make you two happy. Now, let's leave Baron Blake be so he may prepare for his final matches. May the Circle of Life bring good of your sacrifices, Baron."

Oreus softly replied, "And to you, my Lord."

"Oh, and one more thing," Noran said, turning back. "Ola asked me to give you this." He handed Oreus a green silk handkerchief.

He smiled and tucked it beneath his green armband. "Tell her she is victorious over the champion of champions."

Noran nodded and left with Viktoran, Bruneau and Blaynor.

Quinn, who was sitting in the corner, said, "Boris tends to shift his weight onto his good leg. He is vulnerable and will be off-balance if you force him to his bad one."

"I will not take advantage of his handicap."

"But it could mean the difference between you winning or losing your match with him."

"Then I will lose if I must. I will fight him fairly. If my skills are not enough, then he will best me. He is just as capable of beating Thorn as I am."

"I don't think so," Quinn said, standing up. "His moves are crude and he is too slow. He cannot defeat Thorn, who will undoubtedly take advantage of his weakness. Boris would much rather have you beat him than Thorn. His pride will be crushed if he loses, which he will. It's your decision, though."

Oreus finished removing his armor and asked, "You don't think Breaker can win?"

Quinn shook his head. "Not in this lifetime."

The trumpets blared outside, grabbing their attention.

"My only problem with fighting Boris is his reach. How can I punch someone when my fist can't connect with his face?"

"I think you need to worry more about not getting hit," Quinn said. "You better go."

Oreus nodded as his guard saluted him. The Baron went to a ring located in front of the Royal Court's section. Ola waved to him. He smiled and bowed to her.

"If ya want me to withdraw, Baron, I will," said a familiar rumbling voice behind him.

When he turned around he saw Boris with his padded cross cattle gloves already on.

"Don't be foolish, my friend. You deserve the right to be a champion as much as me."

"How would it look if I were ta beat a baron?" he said as he shrugged his shoulders. "People would expect me ta lie down."

"If you do, I'll never forgive you," Oreus said with a smile. "Pretend I'm Windreed."

"Nah! If I did that I would 'ave ta kill ya."

Oreus laughed and said, "Then someone else you are not very fond of."

"On your feet, Yawrana!" Ballan shouted into a shell echoer above them. They ran outside to see the action as the crowd rose to listen. "The final event is upon us: The Knuckles Duel. Breaker and Thorn, please take your positions in the ring before His Majesty."

Both men entered and had their feet chained to a pole at the center. They each slipped on their gloves and raised their fists. Breaker bowed to Noran and Thorn bowed only to Captain Winslow.

"The one still standing moves onto the final duel," Ballan said.

The crowd chanted, "Start the fight! Start the fight!" until a soldier made his mase whistle.

Breaker threw a fast punch but Thorn ducked, rebounded with a direct punch to Breaker's nose and followed with a left uppercut. Breaker was driven off his feet and into the pole. The crowd was stunned when Breaker didn't move.

"Get up!" Slam and Nastor cried from the stands.

But Breaker collapsed to his left and crumpled onto the ground. Thorn turned and stood at the edge of the ring while a soldier came to inspect Breaker. He tried shaking him, but the entertainer didn't stir. The soldier waved to a medicine maker. Blood covered Breaker's nose and upper lip. His eyes were closed. A strong wind suddenly blew through the ring and then died down. When the maker arrived, he checked Breaker's vitals. He then stood and stared at Thorn, who waited for the words.

"You killed him," the maker accused.

Noran stood from his chair when an older woman, Breaker's mother, shrieked and ran to the ring's side. She kissed her son's face as tears flowed down her own. "Noooo!" she repeated over and over. Two soldiers immediately brought a stretcher out and lifted Breaker onto it. They exited the arena with his body while the mother dropped to her knees with her hands over her face.

Noran called Captain Winslow over to him.

"Yes, Your Majesty?" Winslow said, not acting surprised by the outcome.

"Your thug has killed an innocent man!"

"Not by my orders, Your Majesty. I'm sure it wasn't intentional." The crowd was screaming for justice from every section of the arena. Many wanted Thorn's head. Soldiers had to keep commoners from jumping the walls and going after him. Thorn stood silently as a soldier disconnected the chain from the voyager's ankle. Thorn stepped out of the ring and walked toward Winslow and the King.

"Why did you kill him?" Noran yelled.

Thorn remained still and didn't respond.

"Answer me!" Noran shouted. The crowd became quiet and listened.

Thorn smiled and said, "His nose was weak."

Breaker's mother came running at Thorn with her fingers curled to rake out his eyes. Two guards apprehended her before she could touch him. "Noooo! I want his death!" she screamed at Noran. "He has murdered my son!"

Noran raised his hands to calm the crowd. He looked down to the guards restraining the woman and said, "Take her to my private meeting chambers. I will talk to her there after the tournament."

The woman shrieked and tried to break the guards' grips, but was unsuccessful. "No, Your Majesty, you can't let the tournament go on. Respect my son's death!"

Noran waited until they were out of the arena and then turned back to Winslow. "Your man will be imprisoned when this tournament is over."

Winslow replied, "That would not be wise, Your Majesty. He would take it to heart."

Noran growled, "Take your seat, Captain."

Winslow raised an eyebrow and said, "Hmmm. He will be yours to deal with then. May your god have mercy on you." The Captain turned and walked back to his seat.

Noran asked Ballan to wait before making his next announcement. He left the stands to speak with Oreus and Boris. "Baron Blake," he said as he approached Oreus. "I must ask you for a favor."

Oreus stepped toward Noran and said, "Anything."

"Withdraw from the tournament."

"What? After he killed Breaker? Not a chance."

"I command you to withdraw," Noran yelled. "I will not put one of my baron's lives in danger needlessly. I already have the blood of two dobbins on my hands to deal with."

Oreus looked around. The crowd was silent. Boris walked over to them and said, "I can beat him, lad. Let me do it. All I need is one punch."

"Don't underestimate him, blacksmith," Noran said. "It will take more than one hit to defeat him."

"Boris hasn't had training in the *Urra Dur—*" Oreus tried to say before Noran cut him off.

"My decision is unchangeable, Baron. You will obey me and withdraw. I do this for Ola, not you. My sister will not grieve your death for the rest of her days over a tournament match."

Oreus sighed and bowed. "Yes, Your Majesty." He turned and walked to the soldier holding the mase and informed him of his decision.

Noran returned to the stands and told Ballan what was transpiring. Ballan tried to protest but Noran silenced him by shouting, "Do it now!"

Ballan's face wrinkled in frustration. He turned to the shell echoer and made the announcement to the crowd. "It pains me to inform you Baron Oreus Blake has chosen to decline further participation in the tournament." The crowd wanted answers but Ballan finished, saying, "The final duel will be between Boris Groffen of Yawrana and Thorn of Salmus. Please give applause to Marian the Minstrel and the Loop Troop as they perform their final act and pay their respect to Breaker."

Oreus walked with Boris to his tent and went inside. Quinn and two other guards joined them.

"What in tha bloody hell was that all about?" Boris asked. "Can't ya make yer own decisions anymore? Tha King is makin' ya appear weak."

"His intentions are valid," Quinn said when Oreus didn't speak. "He must protect the Royal Court's members at all costs. For all we know, Thorn may be planning to kill Oreus. It was no mistake how he eliminated Breaker. It takes a precise hit to kill a man that way. Be glad it wasn't you, Baron."

"I'll get even for Breaker," Boris said. He flexed his arms and back and then rotated his neck until it cracked.

"Keep your stance high and it will make it hard for him to punch you in the nose. Your height will be an advantage," Oreus said. "Keep your weight on your right leg or he will be able to attack you easier."

"Is that what you were plannin' ta do against me?" Boris asked.

Oreus looked at Quinn. The guard nodded.

"Watch your knees is what I'm saying," Oreus covered. "He will chop you down like a tree if he has to. Boris—"

"Don' say it, lad. We will 'ave more adventures together. No doubt in me mind." Boris winked at Oreus and left the tent with them trailing behind. Oreus and Quinn joined Noran in the Royal Court's section and watched as Boris entered the ring to be linked to the post. Thorn was already there waiting, curling his hooked lip upward.

"Yer gonna be the next ta die," Boris sneered.

Thorn smiled with satisfaction that he had gotten to the blacksmith already. "Barbarians are just bigger prey."

Boris removed his shirt to show his massive muscular form. Many in the crowd started placing bets he would win after seeing his intimidating size. "Get him, Boris!" Ola yelled. She covered her mouth when her three sisters looked at her in surprise. "Sorry," she said. But Roma, Anyiar and Dea also started screaming their support for the barbarian, finding it was appropriate. Their contagious yells caught on with the crowd and spread around the arena.

A soldier stepped up to the edge of the ring and blew a mase when Boris and Thorn raised their fists. Boris took two steps and threw a hard right. Thorn ducked but was unable to perform the same move against Boris as he had against Breaker. The barbarian followed with a second swing to force him around the post. Thorn jumped onto the post and climbed it. He grabbed a ring dangling from a chain at the top and swung a foot out to connect with Boris's jaw. Boris kept his stance, quickly shook it off and slammed his right fist into the base of the post, snapping it in half. Thorn jumped from it as it fell toward the soldier judge, who jumped out of the way before he was struck by its heavy form. The wooden edge of the ring splintered when the post crashed on top of it, causing fragments to fly in all directions.

Thorn jumped onto Boris's back and wrapped his chain around the barbarian's neck. He pulled it tight, but Boris managed to push his fingers underneath it to give him some breathing room. With his right hand he grabbed Thorn's leg and tossed him into the side of the ring. Boris removed the chain while Thorn was dazed. He picked up the smashed post to wield it like a club. He went to crush Thorn but the voyager rolled just before he was destroyed. The crowd clapped, encouraging Boris to take another swing. He was happy to oblige, throwing the entire post at his foe. Thorn jumped over it and kicked Boris across the face a second time. The barbarian fell into the dirt. The crowd booed and cursed Thorn.

Winslow stood from his seat and shook his head when Thorn looked at the Captain. Thorn nodded and flipped in a forward arc, landing with his knee in the middle of Boris's back. The barbarian cried and fell to the ground, clutching at the pain.

Ola and her sisters shrieked.

"Watch out!" Oreus screamed.

Thorn picked up his chain again and wrapped it around Boris's neck a second time. When Boris attempted to get up, Thorn pulled the chain harder and whispered in Boris's ear, "Stay down and save your miserable life."

Boris's face grew red as he grabbed the chain in two places. Slowly, he started to pull the links apart. A weak one started to bend at the center between his fists. Thorn pulled again but Boris had given himself a chance to breathe. The link suddenly broke and freed him. Boris jumped to his feet and punched Thorn in the chest. What would have crushed the lungs of any normal man only knocked the wind out of the voyager as he was sent flying backward. The crowd erupted in applause and chanted for the barbarian's victory.

Thorn stood up and his eyes dilated. He curled his hooked lip and smiled. Boris glanced at Oreus and then back at the nightwalker, believing the Baron's story.

"I know what ya be," Boris said.

"Then you know it was a mistake to step into the ring with me," Thorn replied, running toward Boris. The barbarian crossed his arms to shield his face but Thorn's foot slid between them and connected with his chin. The barbarian flew backward, pulling the post still connected to his leg along with him. He fell and tripped over the ring's wall, landing outside.

"Disqualified!" Ballan announced into the shell echoer.

"Damn," Noran said, slamming his fist on the arm of his chair. He glanced toward Winslow, Rollins and Soar, who were already leaving.

The crowd rushed from the stands in anger. The soldiers surrounding the arena walls couldn't hold the mob back as people poured onto the field to fight Thorn. The moment the soldier unlocked Thorn's ankle chain, the nightwalker raced from the playing field, jumped out of the ring and climbed the wall toward the entrance Winslow went through. He disappeared into the protective blackness of the Royal Court's private arena chambers before he was struck by a mass of flying objects.

"Arrest him!" Noran shouted, sending a handful of guards in pursuit.

# CHAPTER NINE

## Maxhaw Mansion

"Which one is he in?" Noran asked as he entered Candlewick's deepest dungeon hall. He removed his crown to wipe away the sweat that had accumulated beneath it.

A soldier at the end of the hall saluted and pointed to a door to his left. "This one, Your Majesty. He hasn't talked since we threw him in there. Captain Winslow said a few words to him before we had a chance to do our questioning."

Noran peered through the bars of the chute cell's window. Thorn's unmoving outline stood in the back of the tubular room with his back facing the door. "Let me in," Noran said.

"He is dangerous, my Lord. Perhaps—"

"You heard me," Noran yelled at the soldier. "Bruneau and Blaynor will be at my side."

The soldier blushed and nodded. "Right away, Your Majesty." He unlocked the door and swung its heavy form away from the frame. The hinges creaked until it stopped against the exterior wall outside the cell.

Noran strode inside and came to a rest a few feet from Thorn, who still had his back facing them. "Turn around," Noran ordered.

The muscles in Thorn's back rippled.

"The King gave you an order," Blaynor snapped. "Obey!"

They waited but still he stood as silently as the walls that surrounded him. Noran glanced at Blaynor and nodded.

The guard stepped forward and prodded the nightwalker with the end of his staff in a battle ready position. "Face the King!"

With one quick move Thorn grasped the end of Blaynor's staff and yanked it from his hands. He snapped it over his knee into two pieces and then tossed it aside so he could return back to his position.

"You killed an innocent man!" Noran yelled. "You owe his family an answer as to why."

A few moments passed in silence. Noran was about to give up when Thorn finally said, "He was not the hero many idolized him to be."

"He was a good man," Bruneau retorted.

"'Was' is the correct word."

"Whip him. Twenty lashes. No less," Noran said with a straight face.

"Bring in the flogger!" Blaynor shouted to the soldier at the door.

Thorn turned around and glared at the King. Noran felt a magnifying glass was placed on him. "A decision that will lead you to your downfall," he said.

"Fine. Have it your way. Whip him until he's ready to speak in a more civilized manner," Noran replied. "Chain him to the wall."

"If they touch me you will die before you leave this cell," Thorn said, his muscles tensing all over his body.

"You are in *my* kingdom!" Noran screamed at him. "You dare threaten me here?"

Thorn grinned, the annoying, out-of-place fishhook rising on his face with it. Noran wanted to reach out and rip it off right then, but his instincts told him to hold back longer.

"Chain him," he said to Bruneau and Blaynor again.

"We will need more men," Blaynor said. "He could be too dangerous."

Noran barked, "He's not better than both of you. You are well-trained guards. Do what your King commands."

When the flogger entered the cell, Blaynor turned to Noran and said, "Please leave, my Lord."

"I want to see him in pain," Noran said with a hunger in his eyes.

Instead of arguing, Blaynor said to the soldier at the door, "Lock it."

The moment the man started to close it, Thorn jumped upward and kicked Blaynor in the neck. He flew to the side and into the flogger. Thorn spun once more and kicked Bruneau across the face to send him to the ground. He claimed Bruneau's staff and beat him repeatedly across the back and head until he was unconscious. His helmet rolled toward the King.

Noran turned and ran for the door. He shoved his arm through before the soldier had a chance to completely close it. "Wait!"

Thorn ran after the King and kicked him squarely in the back, which sent Noran flying through the door and into the soldier on the other side. The nightwalker turned and tried to kick Blaynor again but the guard blocked with his metal wrist cuff and punched Thorn in the groin. The voyager didn't seem to be affected and punched Blaynor across the face. The guard fell backward, his head hitting the wall on the way down.

The flogger whipped Thorn across the chest, splitting the nightwalker's skin wide open. No blood drained from the wound. Thorn snatched the whip and snapped it against both sides of the flogger's neck. The flogger screamed in agony as he fell to his knees, clutching both sides as blood poured between his fingers. Thorn then pulled the stunned flogger toward him by his shirt and broke the man's neck. The entry soldier tried shutting the door behind Thorn again, the hinges squeaking as it was closing. Thorn did a back flip and hit it with his heel, sending it flying outward again.

Thorn exited to see Noran running down the hall shouting for help. Before he reached the end, Thorn killed the soldier at the door and gave chase. Noran sprinted up the steps and ducked behind a dozen soldiers who had come to his call.

Seeing he had no chance to get near the King, Thorn dodged down a side tunnel and jumped into a hole in the wall.

"He's gone into a waste chute," shouted a soldier.

"Where does it lead?" Noran asked.

"Into Spring River," the soldier replied. "But it's barred at the cap. If he manages to get through somehow, he'll be gone before we can catch him. It's a direct feed to the outside."

"Get the hunt hounds out now. I want him caught."

"Yes, my Lord."

Blaynor entered the room and frowned, hearing Thorn had escaped. "I advise against letting your men out of the castle, Your Majesty. Herikech is in the woods. He will kill every man you send into the wild, just as he did with the rangers."

"Stop!" Noran said before the soldier could get out of earshot. The soldier halted and turned to wait for more directions. "Give me advice I can't ignore," Noran said to Blaynor.

"Place spies throughout the castle. I have a feeling he may not stray from Candlewick. He will wait for the right time to reunite with Winslow."

Noran nodded. "Yes. Your wisdom is usually correct. If he is caught, have him killed."

"That's what worries me, my Lord," Blaynor said, wiping blood from his lip. "I don't know if he can be. He doesn't bleed."

The shadows of the trees slipped into darkness one by one as the sun's rays receded from the forests of Dowhaven Territory. General Fields sat on his gandalay mount, Mercer, staring at the strange footprints embedded along the trail. He shielded his eyes with his hand from the bright light and bent over to take a better look.

"Definitely not a man's footprints. Also doesn't appear to be any creature

I have seen before. It has some resemblances to a wolf's print," said Argil Meridot. The sniffer rubbed his fingertips along the edge of a toe line and picked up a long brown hair. He lifted it up to eye-level and examined it. "Feels like a maddon's hair, too, but the coloring has a strange reddish tint. I think this is what we've been searching for."

"Maxhaw Mansion is just ahead," Sergeant Crane of the White Light Squad said. "King Deardrop was suspicious the mangler may be living up this way."

"How are you going to capture it?" Ramp asked. The Trail Racer's nose twitched as he munched on a beekok leaf.

"That's not our intention, Captain Ramp," Crane said.

"You want to kill it?" asked Captain Cracked Tooth. Both dobbins backed up a step when the Sergeant stepped toward them.

Crane smiled and said, "Surely you don't want this creature alive?"

"No. Not at all." Ramp said. "But I heard the Elders say it has killed dozens of cattle in the surrounding farms. I just think we should be cautious."

"Yes," Cracked Tooth added. "Being cautious is always good. We have run these trails more than anyone. Anytime we see a print like this we immediately head for shelter before the sun sets. Look! There's one of the moon's heads now."

All the men turned to see Radia start to rise the moment the sun disappeared from view. Its warm rays fell upon their company as they gazed up at its crescent red form.

"Let's get moving," General Fields ordered. "I want to reach the mansion before it has completely risen."

"We agree," Ramp said as he and Cracked Tooth each walked alongside Fields's mount. Ramp and Cracked Tooth pulled the glider on a cart behind him. It bounced and shuddered as it rolled along the rocky path. It almost tipped over at one point, but a soldier caught it before it could topple and damage a wing.

The company walked as fast as they could until they approached a barred black gate at the end of the trail. Ivy wrapped many of the bars, preventing their entrance. Spikes extended at the top of each bar and a pair of gargoyles sat on posts on each side of the gate, their appearances menacing. One licked its lips and the other bared its fangs, warning them to keep out.

"Will ya look at those beasties," Cracked Tooth cried. "They're not the friendliest of hosts!"

"Ugly bugs!" Ramp said, building on their heightened fear. "My mother would whip our hides for being out here."

"They're just used to create superstition in trespassers. Candlewick Castle has far worse ones in its deeper hallways," Fields said, dismounting Mercer and tying the stallion to a bar on the gate. He pulled on one of the doors. It opened a few inches before it stopped. A chain at the center became visible when a few leaves and cobwebs broke away from their resting spot to reveal it. "Locked. Someone doesn't want anyone on their land."

"Don't be surprised if it's Herikech," Ramp said, shivering. "Probably s-slinkin' around in the woods right now, r-ready to pounce on us at any—"

"Keep your voice down," Fields said sternly. "You're going to draw attention to us."

"Who do you have to fear, General?" Cracked Tooth asked. "You're the King's right hand enforcer. You *are* the law. Who would want to trifle with you?"

"I have no fear of Herikech or any other living creature, that's true. But those without fear are foolish."

"Then what do you fear, General?" Ramp asked.

"Not seeing my children again."

"Oh. I guess that's pretty important," Ramp replied. "I'll shut up now."

Fields nodded in appreciation and waved for Argil and Lieutenant Ravel to follow him. "Everyone else . . . wait here."

"Glad to, General," Cracked Tooth said, sitting down next to a gray brick post.

Radia was almost up when Fields and Argil appeared on the other side of the gates.

"You're through!" Cracked Tooth exclaimed.

"And by no easy means," Argil said. "This property stretches on for dozens of miles and there's few entrances that reveal themselves for the brave of heart who are willing to go for a midnight stroll."

With his right hand, Fields reached into a black hole in one of the gargoyle posts. A few moments later, he pulled out a long and thin, rusty key. "An easy place to remember." He unlocked the padlock at the center of the gates and let the thick chain fall to the ground with a thud. Each link that slid across the bottom bar made a racket. Fields pressed his foot against the chain to stop it before it awoke any animals that could be guarding the grounds. He picked up one end and dragged it to a section of the wall nearby.

Argil opened one of the doors to let the squad and dobbins through. He then walked around almost in a full circle before he came to a wheelbarrow. An intense odor drifted up from a giant pot resting in its center. "General Fields, you should see this," he said, covering his mouth and nose with a palm.

The moment Fields saw what Argil had called him over for, he ordered, "Stay in a tight group. Dobbins at the center. Leave the glider here." He drew his sword and kicked the wheelbarrow over. The pot tipped and flipped upside-down. Fields broke it with his sword. The ancient ceramic holder fell apart. Shards, dirt and rocks spilled down over a round form. Nudging it with the tip of his boot, he rolled it over.

"Is that a head?" Cracked Tooth asked, getting in the middle of the soldiers as he was ordered to.

Fields nodded. "I knew this man. Jon Buce. He was on Shaba's local sector board for twenty years. He was their eldest member . . . with many unmoving opinions. Many board members wanted him ousted and he was reported missing not long ago. It seems his latest disagreement got out of hand. Someone will be coming back with us in shackles."

"What if it was the mangler that killed him?" Ramp asked.

"Then we need to know if it did it on its own behalf or another's." Fields turned to look at the moon, which moved the last of its body into sight. The second moon, Lumly, also began to show itself further down the horizon.

"What has Ean Maxhaw gotten himself involved in?" Sergeant Crane asked.

"Let's hope he's not dead, too," Lieutenant Ravel replied.

"The mangler's prints pick up over here," Argil said. "They lead in that direction, toward the stone walkway of the mansion. Should we just walk up to the front door?"

"No," Fields said. "Let's take a walk in the woods and circle around to the back. You would be surprised what you will find people doing when they receive surprise company."

Following Fields and Crane through a section of brush parted by a thin path that led away from the stone walkway was a challenge. They filed in one at a time, staying as close together as they could while trying not to make too much noise. Branches would bend, crack or snap on the ground or along the path if they didn't watch where they stepped. Fields lit the only torch and carried it low so the light couldn't easily be seen throughout the forest. They walked until midnight, when the chirping crickets around them strangely went quiet.

"There's the mansion," Fields said, putting out his torch. He guided the men toward a collapsing fence at the edge of a pasture and stopped to look upon the building standing no more than a hundred yards away.

"It's a wreck. Someone hasn't been keeping up with their house duties," Argil said. Every section of the yard was in disarray. Dead cattle were covering the pasture between the mansion and them. A shed had an enormous hole punched through the side with fowl feathers lying below the opening. Claw marks ran along the side of it and ended at a corner. A woodpile was tipped over with an axe handle sticking up out of its center. Arrows were sticking out of the side of the building and a small tree was bent at an awkward angle with part of its root system torn up at its base. A wooden swing still dangled from one of its branches with one of its two ropes cut.

"But someone's still up," Fields said, pointing to the soft glow on the third floor. "There's a light on in the attic window."

Crane put a pinch of ground leaf between his cheek and gum and said, "Maybe they're having trouble sleeping."

"If I had heads in pots on my property, I would have trouble sleeping, too," Ravel replied. He wedged his body between two of the fence's crossbeams.

Fields climbed and jumped over instead, his armor too wide to fit through. The rest of the men and two dobbins slipped through like Ravel and continued their straight line to the rear of the building. Before they reached the woodpile, the light in the window went out.

"I think we may have been seen," Argil said when he saw the curtain covering the window pull back and then fall to a close. The brief image of a chin and nose came into the light before it receded into blackness.

Fields hurried and motioned his hand to make everyone run toward the back of the building. He waited a few moments and listened. When there was no sound coming from the house, he whispered, "Surround the servants' door." It was ajar. A breeze made it sway back and forth, lightly rapping it against the frame.

Everyone froze when they heard a growl come from somewhere deep within the mansion.

"That's no karrik," Argil said, gripping his short sword tighter. "And it's too low a pitch for a maddon."

"Sergeant," Fields said, waving him and the White Light Squad toward the door. "Secure the first room the moment we enter. Don't make any noise if you can avoid it. This thing may try to attack us, despite our numbers."

Crane saluted, lit a torch and entered. He pressed the swaying door open and threw himself against the inner wall. Each of the men in his squad did the same until they all were inside. They spread out and covered two more doors leading into other hallways of the mansion. Pots, broken glass and linens were scattered everywhere along the floor. Tables were on their sides and two bodies were motionless near a stove. Their white aprons were smattered with blood and shredded.

"Cooking must not have been that good," one soldier said to Crane.

The Sergeant shook his head and tossed a broken ceramic shard out the door.

Fields entered last, leaving Argil and the two dobbins outside. The General put up a hand for them to hold the position for a few moments. When the mansion remained silent, he waved them to the larger door at the far end of the kitchen. Crane nodded and made his way to it with sweat beading on his face. He passed a beam of red moonlight that shone through a window and fell across the floor. When his foot stepped into it, another growl sounded closer. His heart was racing when he pushed the door open an inch to scan the next room. It was dark, except for a thin patch of red light reflecting off a pair of candlesticks on top of a fireplace mantle. He looked back at the General, who gave him a thumb up.

Crane pushed the door open and held it for the other men. They all moved and took new positions around the room while Crane held his torch up to illuminate the study. A dead man sat in a chair with his throat ripped out. Fields had to shake his head and look away for a moment, at a carpet that was stuffed into the chimney. It was burned at the edges, as if it was thrown over the logs to smother the fire.

Crane walked over and saw that the dead man was a younger gentleman dressed in a smoking jacket. The stench of his rotting flesh was overwhelming. Terror was still in his eyes from his last moment of life. His fingernails had raked back the cloth on each of the chair's arms. His clothes were in perfect condition, except for the blood that had drained from his neck wound onto the collar of his eggshell colored nightshirt. A spilled bottle of ink was lying on the floor next to the chair with a quill beside it. A blood-splattered piece of paper was sitting on the man's lap, folded in two. Crane picked it up and read.

*Sister,*

*I can no longer stay here. By the time you have read this letter, I will have left in the morning. The cries are too much to bear. They haunt this house and wake me in the night. I can no longer look beyond the beast and see the man we once knew.*

*There is nothing either of us can do. The entire fortune has run dry to find a cure, and we still have no answer. Save yourself and return to the Historical Record*

*Keep to continue your duties under Princess Roma's direction. Don't waste yourself here because of the tragedy that has fallen over this home. Perhaps in the record logs of the Keep you may find a way to help him. I have not the heart to end it myself or I would have already spared his pain.*

*I will meet you in the*

The sentence ended in a smear of ink, cut off in a moment of violence and horror.

"Who is it?" Fields asked, startling Crane when the General whispered in the Sergeant's ear.

"Do you not recognize his features?" Crane asked.

Fields stared at the figure a few moments longer and said, "Ean Maxhaw's son, Tomas. I didn't realize it at first because of the mustache."

Footsteps began to walk along the floor above them. They both looked up toward them, their eyes following to where they were leading.

"Whatever it is, it's moving in that direction," Crane said, nodding at the broad staircase that rose up to the second floor. "Its footsteps are too close together for it to be a creature that travels on two legs." As if proving the Sergeant was correct, a growl came from the top of the stairs where torchlight met darkness.

"Where is he hiding?" Noran asked with ten men guarding him.

Winslow approached the King and bowed his head. "Thank you for taking the time to visit me in my quarters, Your Majesty. I could have come at your request to the glory of your throne—"

"Enough of your split tongue," Noran said. "Where is Thorn?"

"I don't know what you're talking about. Your men took him to the dungeons—"

Noran responded stiffly and pointed to a soldier. The man put a spearhead in Winslow's face. "You instructed him to escape," Noran said.

"Your Majesty," Captain Rollins said, intervening, "there is no need for you to do that. Captain Winslow has no more control over Thorn than you or I do. He is his own man and walks his own road. He surveys the world as we do. . . ."

"I didn't ask for your opinion, Captain Rollins. Now sit down!" Noran turned back toward Winslow and said, "I'm only going to ask you this once more, Captain Winslow, *where is Thorn?*"

Winslow chuckled at Noran's rage, unable to help himself.

"Why do you laugh?" Bruneau asked, grabbing Winslow by the shoulder and forcing him to one knee. "Answer the King!"

"Do you want me to make up a lie?" Winslow said, his nostrils flaring at the guard. Bruneau's strong grip caused a numbing sensation to spread down the Captain's arm. "Why do you think I had anything to do with him killing your entertainer? Thorn doesn't feel remorse for his actions. He does as is required to survive in the situation he has been placed."

"He is no more than an animal then?" Noran said. "Someone who only acts on raw emotions without thought?"

Winslow nodded.

"Well, if your dog doesn't return to his cell by dawn, you shall take his place. Do you understand me? If he is truly an animal, then he needs to be kept on a leash."

"You are mad," Winslow said. "He will not bow to you and if harm comes to me, you put your own life in danger."

Bruneau punched Winslow, knocking him to the ground. Blood spilled from Winslow's nose. He shook his head and pulled out a black handkerchief to wipe it away. He stood and straightened himself out. "You may as well take me now then," Winslow said, putting his arms out in front of him.

"Don't do this," Rollins said, trying to block Bruneau from tying Winslow's wrists.

"Do not fear for me," Winslow replied. "Thorn will do what is necessary when the time is right."

"What is that supposed to imply?" Blaynor barked. The guard looked around the room, his gaze coming to a rest upon a vent in the ceiling. A pair of white eyes glowed through the wooden slatted cover. Blaynor grabbed a soldier's spear and hurled it at the rectangular lid. The spear split it down the middle and clattered against stone on the other side. An echoing pair of feet and hands scurried away until they faded.

"You knew he was here all along!" Noran screamed.

Winslow shrugged his shoulders and said, "How much do you wish to wager I didn't?"

Bruneau punched Winslow in the gut to take the wind out of him. "You scum! You'll be lucky if we don't hang you by dawn."

"Take him to Thorn's cell. And give him the lashes his pet wouldn't take," Noran said.

The guards entered the room and lashed Winslow's limbs together so tightly that the twine cut into his skin and caused him to bleed. He screamed and called out for help as he was dragged to a fate he could not avoid.

"If you catch Thorn, inform me immediately," Noran said to a guard at the door.

Captain Rollins approached Noran and said, "Your Majesty, there still is one item we have not yet finished."

Noran scowled at Rollins.

"The Zonack voyagers? You promised if we won the Tournament of Champions you would release Stoffer, Crag and Gunner into our care. I hope you are a man of honor and would uphold—"

"I can't see how it would hurt any. I have had to tolerate more from them than I can stand," Noran said, taking Rollins by surprise. "They will join you here soon and will be your complete responsibility until you leave Yawrana. If they step out of line, you will be punished for their actions."

Rollins nodded and went to a corner to speak privately with Windreed.

Captain Soar and his three guards bowed to Noran and approached the King. "Even though Winslow doesn't represent the entire collective mind of the people of Salmus, I don't agree with your decision to imprison him, Your Majesty."

"Captain Soar, your opinion really doesn't matter," Noran said, looking away.

Soar persisted, not deterred by the King's stubbornness. "Thorn is a dangerous man and may resort to killing more of your men until Winslow is back on his ship. I will do everything I can to prevent that from happening. If you need me or my men's help, all you have to do is ask for it." Soar glanced at Rollins, who was whispering something into Windreed's ear. Soar grimaced, knowing Rollins was displeased with his offer to the King.

Noran smiled, also having seen Rollins's reaction. "Captain Soar, you remind me of someone else close to me, who at one time also did not share in the opinions of his former crewmates. I can only hope your intentions are as noble as his were." Noran spun toward the door and left the room, gagging from the smell of the gandalay stables penetrating their quarters. After Blaynor closed the door, he said to a guard assigned to the room, "Don't let these men out of your sight. They are no longer our guests. They will remain here until their required visitation days have ended. Their rooms are now their cells. If they try to escape, kill them."

Fields waved for the men to position themselves around the bottom of the stairs. The footsteps paused when they reached the top of the staircase. Fields strode to the base of the stairs and held his sword in front of him, daring the creature to attack him. Another growl came from the darkness at the top step, but the creature remained cloaked in the safety of its black protection. The General set his foot on the first step and said, "Come men. If the beast won't come to us, then we shall go to it."

When Fields reached the middle of the staircase, the creature growled once more and then unexpectedly barked.

"Down, Ket!" said a young woman's voice.

The creature whined and then came into the light.

"It's a only dog," Crane said, letting out a sigh of relief.

The large animal moved aside to let the woman come into the light of Fields's torch. Its hundred-pound, shaggy black form was shaking, as if it was anxious about the new visitors in its home.

"Why are you here?" the mousy woman said, putting on her thin-rimmed spectacles. A flowing white nightgown extended behind her as she descended a few steps. Her eyes were dark and her hair uncombed. She repeated herself to get a quicker answer.

"We have come for the mangler," Fields said. "The dead man in the chair down there obviously knew of it."

"You must leave. It isn't safe here."

"The King has asked for the mangler's head," Crane said. "We're going nowhere."

The woman stepped back and paused before she said, "It's not here."

"Why have the men down there been left to decay where they died?" Fields asked. When he held the torch closer to her, he could see tears streaming down her face. "Are you all right? Have you been hurt?"

"You will fail, just like the others before you," she said.

"Others?" Fields asked. "What others? You mean there have been men here before to take the mangler?"

She nodded. "They were members of the local sector council. They came for him."

"Who?" Crane asked for her to clarify. "What is your name?"

She turned and ran down the hall.

"Wait!" Fields yelled. "We want to protect you!"

"Protect yourselves by leaving," she replied.

Fields went to the top of the staircase and was met by the dog's teeth. It lunged at his arm and clung on. The Sergeant grabbed it by the collar, dragged it into the nearest room and threw it in. After he shut the door, Fields waved the men up the stairs and checked his arm, which bled lightly. "Let's go. I want every room of this house searched."

Crane and the soldiers went up to the second floor and did an intensive sweep of the bedrooms and washrooms. The woman was nowhere to be seen. Fields looked for a door to the attic, but there was none that he could see. "Has anyone found her?" he yelled down the hall.

After a few moments of exchanged conversations, Crane yelled, "Not yet. Have you found access to the attic?"

Fields walked back toward the staircase. "It must be a secret entrance. She is using it to hide from the mangler, but for some reason wants to protect it as well."

"Why?" Crane asked. "You think she has some kind of relationship with it? The creature is savage—"

"Yes. Something tells me she has reason to stay here, even with an obvious danger present."

"General!" shouted Ramp from the bottom of the staircase.

Fields asked, "What in the hell are they doing in here? I thought I told them to stay outside."

The White Light Squad came back to the top of the stairs behind the General, Lieutenant and Sergeant to see Argil and the two dobbins being held with knives pressed against their necks. A dozen armed and cloaked figures filled the study below. Argil had been stripped of his sword and his arm was bleeding.

"Release them or it will be your deaths," Fields commanded.

"We do not bow to your king, General," said the voice of a young man holding a knife to Ramp's throat.

"Lazuls!" Fields retorted. "You are part of the secret guild."

"Leave now or we'll slit his throat," the Lazul replied.

"If you harm him—"

The man pressed the blade tightly against Ramp's throat and hissed.

"Stop!" Fields said. "You don't have to obey Herikech. His heart is black and you are only puppets to him."

The man sliced Ramp down his arm. The dobbin clutched the wound and screeched. Fields jumped down the staircase and kicked out at the Lazul. The man went flying backward. The White Light Squad went into action and slid down the banisters to come to the General's aid. Cracked Tooth managed to break free and bounded into the kitchen and back outside. A Lazul ran after him with a raised dagger.

Argil was stabbed twice beneath his shoulder blade and fell forward. He crawled away into the next room and leaned up against a wide door. Blood dripped from his punctures onto the door, down to the floor and rolled underneath. Over the clashing of blades and screams of death, Argil heard what sounded like a creature sniffing the ground behind the door he was resting against. He stood up and leaned against the wall, trying desperately to keep his vision from blurring by focusing on the door's handle. A loud growl echoed behind it before it exploded off of its hinges and flew at him. The force of the impact knocked him backward and out cold. Argil slumped to the floor, not seeing the giant flash of red tinted fur run by him and into the study.

Noran sat in his private quarters, his stomach feeling ill since the tournament ended. The thought of any food made him sick. Bruneau was about to leave him when the King said, "Send word to Master Oyen that I will be visiting him shortly. I might need medication of some kind to help rid this nausea I'm having a difficult time with. I don't think I'm going to sleep a wink tonight if I don't have it checked."

Bruneau bowed. "A wise decision, my Lord. I will make sure Master Oyen clears his schedule for the remainder of the day. I suggest you lie down until you are ready. A little isolation and quiet can't hurt any."

"Do you think I was too harsh with Winslow?"

"I'm surprised you didn't imprison him sooner, my Lord."

Noran smiled and watched Bruneau leave. Three candles lit his room, the tallest sitting near Herishen's Will and Testament. He almost didn't have the energy to read, but he found himself walking toward it and flipping through the pages to a new section before he could say, "Not tonight." A nagging feeling told him he was running out of time to finish learning about his heritage. Compelled by guilt to continue, he read on.

*When I informed Audra that not all of my men would be easily convinced of the purpose behind our transition to enlightenment, she asked for me to arrange a special meeting and have only those who resisted attend. General Murka, Gerrith and seven other high-ranking officers within my army gathered around a table at the center of my tent, questioning the goals of the Methalisians. Murka has been the most vocal, demanding us to do away with them and return our attention to the war. I listened intently outside, testing their patience until they decided to leave.*

*I entered and told them to return to the table for the beginning of the process. They grumbled but kept their minds open for me.*

*Audra came in when I called for her. Two other Methalisians also entered, one carrying a metal bowl and the other, a long metal box. They set the two containers on the table and promptly left. Audra thanked them and purposely stood between Murka and Gerrith.*

*The priestess asked General Murka for his sword and Gerrith for his dagger. Both men were hesitant to relinquish their weapons, not knowing why. She explained in order to show them how the power of the land could help them rid the world of enemies they had to trust her. Gerrith unsheathed his blade and gave it to her, but I was disappointed when I was forced to order Murka to place his sword in the metal box. He warned Audra that he would cut her head off if she failed to convince him how to win the lands back from my brothers.*

*Taking Gerrith's dagger, she held onto the handle and tipped the blade into the bowl. One of the Methalisian's returned to the tent, hauling a bag of small sticks over his shoulder. He dumped a small portion of the bag into the bowl and the rest into the metal box, leaving only the handles of Murka's sword and Gerrith's dagger visible. Audra created a fire in both containers by clacking two fire rocks together. The moment the wood fire caught in both, she placed one hand on the bowl's edge and the other on the metal box.*

*The men whispered to one another, wondering what witchery she was enacting, thinking she would burn herself as the metal box and bowl heated. They had never seen Yarbu or any of the other prophets perform such a ritual. The fire in each of the containers erupted and arced. Several of the men backed away, stunned by the reaction of the flames. The fire brightened the tent, but didn't throw any additional heat into the air. Frightened, Murka asked for her to stop, but Audra couldn't. She insisted on finishing the process or she would be burned to death during her access to a place called the Enclave. What this meant, she had not the time to explain.*

*The fire consumed each container, bringing the metal to a red-hot glow. They scorched the table beneath, causing the wood to smolder and almost catch fire. At the last moment the flames died and cooled to the point of room temperature. She lifted her hands from the metal. Where she had touched it, her skin was blistered, but her injuries were not severe enough that her hands wouldn't heal.*

*The wood within the bowl and box had been reduced to cinders. Murka reclaimed his sword and slapped the blade's edge against the table to clean it off. Audra handed him a damp towel so he could wipe the rest of the ash away. Gerrith also took his dagger, did the same and asked what had happened.*

*Audra explained about the four elements that reside within the Enclave, the givers and takers of life. Each of the four elements has the power to create havoc or heaven when reached. Murka, his patience limited, interrupted and asked to know how this is accomplished. Audra knew he would not accept the answer she would give, but still told him the truth. She was not one to let lies destroy her efforts in building trust. "The mind," she said. Murka glanced at the other men and then stormed out of the tent, feeling he was being mocked.*

*I went after him. He argued that he had no time for demonic behavior when we were about to lose everything we had. I agreed with him to calm his anger, but asked him to do me one favor before he left. I remember his words as clear as a cloudless night, "It is Heritoch I should be siding with." I promised him if he did this one favor for me he could join my brother if he wished. Finally, he asked what the favor was.*

*When I was certain no one was near, I asked him to draw his sword and hold it before him. That wasn't the difficult part of my request, however. He balked when I told him to find courage and bravery within him and let it rule his emotions. He thought I was mad now and turned away. I grasped his arm and begged him. He raised it to strike me. The blade became engulfed in fire before he finished his swing. The General dropped it into the sand out of fear and backed away, checking himself for burns.*

*I picked up the sword for him when the fire faded. He walked back over to me and bowed, asking for forgiveness. After handing his sword back to him, I gave him the forgiveness he sought and asked him to rejoin me in the tent.*

*Back inside, Gerrith was holding his dagger up before him, bright and full of flame. The men around him were in awe, asking for their weapons to be transitioned next.*

*But in the moment I felt I had convinced my men we would be victorious, the drums of war sounded in the distance. A messenger entered the tent and informed me Heritoch's and Herikech's entire armies had combined and spearheaded an effort to drive back our weakest defense in the north. My brothers' fiercest warriors were already swarming our camp. I took Audra and the Methalisians with me into a new underground tunnel that was being dug for a last defense if such an emergency were to occur. Audra and her people requested their release so they could return to their ships, but I knew they would not reach the shores of the Sarapin without sacrificing a large share of my men to guide them there. My officers, guards, prophets and wife fled with me into the Wailing Hills, hoping General Murka and the rest of my army could reclaim our positions or drive back the lines long enough to give us time to form a new battle plan.*

Noran closed the book and thought about Viktoran's sword, Heaven's Light, and the dagger Oreus claimed from a dead Lazul scout in Rock Rim Territory. He believed they were the same weapons Gerrith Dragul and General Murka once possessed. It made sense and could be no mistake. Viktoran ruled over Serquist, his sword handed down to him since his ancestors founded many of the sectors within the territory. Murka, the main swamp in Serquist Territory, was, without a doubt, named after the leader of Herishen Illeon's army. It wasn't impossible to believe Baron Viktoran Ilos was a descendant of Murka. In fact, it was very likely.

And what would become of Gerrith's dagger he would have to learn after he visited Master Oyen for his new examination. He only knew that it had the power to destroy the demon *Bethlen* they had faced in Arna. Noran stood and blew out the other candles, leaving only the one next to the will burning bright.

General Fields fought three Lazul guild members at once. They pressed him back toward the fireplace. He was not able to hold them off for long and thought he would be killed when a mass of flying fur jumped onto the Lazul nearest him, raking the man to death in a few bats of an eyelash. The Lazul's hood fell away to reveal the nameless face of the young individual. The two remaining Lazuls Fields was fighting stopped and raised their weapons to prevent the mangler from killing them, too. The creature turned and jumped on a Yawranan soldier whose back was turned toward it instead. The man screamed and crawled a few feet until he was mauled to death.

"Get up, Throy," said one of the two Lazuls to the dead boy on the floor. When Throy didn't respond, the individual backed away from Fields with the other Lazul. The Lazul who spoke tried kicking his comrade one last time, but it was futile.

"Identify yourself!" Fields yelled at the two Lazuls. They both looked at each other and ran out of the room into an adjoining sunroom. Fields pursued and threw the door open. The two Lazuls threw anything they could get their hands on at him. The General raised his left arm to deflect each object as they sprinted through an open door at the opposite end of the room and out into a garden.

"Surrender!" Fields shouted as he gave chase.

"Lord Herikech will get the mangler in time and he will send it for you," said the faster of the two Lazuls. They crossed the field before he could catch them, climbed the fence and raced for the forest.

Fields repeated their exact movements and soon found himself in the dark shelter of the trees. Limbs creaked around him when he stopped to listen. Screams echoed from Maxhaw Mansion in Yawranan and Lazul tongue. It was eerie hearing their cries of confusion amid the echoes of growls.

A branch snapped to his left. Two dark figures ran into a patch of red moonlight. He pushed his way through the brush and kept his eyes on the shifting forms. A tree limb slapped him across the face, bruising his cheek and making his eye water. He grunted and blocked the pain from entering his mind. The two Lazul men spoke to each other and then split up. He kept on the trail of the thinner one he thought to be the leader.

The Lazul led him several miles through the forest before it gave way to a cemetery. He scanned the headstones made up of life circles, animals, angels and poems. Nothing moved in his line of vision. Fields got down on his hands and knees to crawl through the dewy, groomed grass. He crept slowly, not letting the Lazul see or hear him. A flat headstone with only one word on it provided a good place for him to rest his back against. What the word meant summed up his current situation: *Misplaced.* Why someone would want to put that particular word on a loved one's tombstone didn't matter. He could only sit and wait. Perhaps the individual was another victim of the mangler.

Something moved but he could not determine which direction it came from. He peered over the edge of the tombstone. His eyes rolled from left to right and froze when he saw a shadow moving near a tree at the cemetery's border. He dropped back to the ground and wove his way between more stones and across graves. Saying a continual prayer under his breath would have to suffice and excuse his motives for disturbing sacred ground. The shadow moved to his right and slipped behind a tree. Fields moved faster, fearing he was going to lose his target. A fog was settling in over the graves, impeding his view. He wouldn't have much longer before his pursuit would be cut short. The Lazul reappeared only for an instant and then vanished when the fog pulled away from Fields. It formed into a thick column for the Lazul to walk into, and then rolled and spread out on the other side of the cemetery's fence. The figure he was chasing appeared once more, running back into the woods.

Fields jumped up and ran after him, but the fog formed a wall in front of him to prevent him from reaching the fence. Another figure floated toward him out of the wall with outstretched hands. Fields ducked and rolled in another direction. His mind panicked, realizing this was Herikech and the Lazul boy had lured him out into the forests where no one could help him.

"There's no use running, General," Herikech said as Fields climbed the fence and threw himself over. The General immediately got up and dashed for the closest tree lining the edge of the woods. He found shelter once again and could see the Lazul man in the distance up ahead when he entered a moonlight patch. He glanced over his shoulder and saw the fog crawling through the woods after him. Herikech's form had disappeared but he could hear his cackle echoing around him.

Fields ran faster until rain fell in sheets wherever he went. Branches fell from trees, some coming close to hitting him. Before he knew it, he had lost the Lazul and his sense of direction. He continued to run forward to keep Herikech from finding him until the rain ceased. His weight suddenly was claimed by a heavier gravity. His armor dragged on him, throwing him into a roll down a steep hill. The next thing he could remember was tumbling end over end and crashing into a wheel of a wagon. A horse whinnied from the collision.

A man sitting in the cart looked down at him and said, "General Fields?"

When he could right himself and stand, he saw it was Chief Cyon, a flame fighter from the northern sector of the Royal House Territory.

"What are you doing out here? I thought you weren't going to leave the castle until Herikech was caught," Cyon said.

"Chief? Almost the opposite just happened," Fields said, shaking his head. "Where am I?" When he looked beyond the cart, he could see a bustling town filled with people and stores.

"In Dixon. Did you just say Herikech almost caught you?"

The Chief nodded. "Did you see a man in a black cloak run this way?"

"Yes. I didn't think anything of it until you just mentioned it. He headed into town. I'm not sure if you'll find him now. He blended right in with the night life the moment he hit the main road."

The soft glow of lanterns swung from posts along the street, giving him little light to see which way the Lazul may have traveled. The General cursed and pulled off his helmet to let his head breathe. "Chief, I need you to give me a lift. My men are in danger. I need to head back over to Maxhaw Mansion as fast as you can get me there."

"Maxhaw? Fan's place?"

Fields nodded and climbed up into the seat next to him. "I also need your wagon to haul some of my men to a maker center. I'm sorry to inconvenience you at this late hour."

The Chief snapped the whips and said, "Say no more. My men won't come stumblin' out of the Lakeside Tavern for who knows how long. Celebratin' Loel's marriage tomorrow. You can help keep me awake by tellin' me the rest of your story on the way."

As the cart began to roll, Fields looked over his shoulder at the top of the hill. Any clouds that had drenched him were gone and not a trace of the fog was left. The moon Lumly was now showing its entire white crescent shape in the sky as they sped through town and cut onto a back road, a little more than two miles from the mansion.

Not a single noise could be heard when Chief Cyon pulled on the reins to stop the cart in front of the servants' door. The light in the attic window was not lit this time and none of his men were waiting for Fields, as he hoped they would be.

"If you hear any commotion, leave immediately," Fields said. "There is a dangerous creature roaming the property resembling a maddon. It manages to walk on its hind legs, though, when it needs to."

Fields took a torch from the Chief's wagon and drew his sword.

"Sure you don't want me to watch your back?" the Chief asked. "I've faced far worse life-threatening situations than ravenous animals."

"I appreciate your bravery, but it will only get you killed in this circumstance."

"That's what they told me before I rescued a newborn child from the nursery of a burning building. By the way, I was only a trainee then."

"Be ready," Fields said, acting unimpressed so the Chief wouldn't change his mind.

The Chief gave a non-committal response by shrugging his shoulders and rubbing his blond beard. He watched the General walk into the mansion with the torch above his head to cast a broad circle of light around him.

Moonlight brightened the kitchen as if it were day. Fields stepped around the cooks and two mangled soldiers of the White Light Squad. He drew a circle around his heart and said a short prayer for them. As cautiously as he could, he pushed the door to the study open and slipped inside. He passed the torch across his body to see the full extent of the bloodbath on display. Not a single soldier or Lazul in the room was left alive. All had either killed each other or were ripped apart by the mangler. There were few men missing at least one limb among the carnage. Fields circled the main pile of cadavers and approached a black doorway. He had not seen this many dead men in one place since the Waungee Grasslands War. He listened for noises that could be interpreted as someone struggling for help. But even the dog in the room at the top of the staircase was silent.

Fields went back into the sunroom and inspected the area for more bodies. When he entered, he found more than he bargained for. A large form sat on the ground, huddled in a ball. The fur on its back slowly rose and fell with its breathing. Realizing what it was, his heart froze with fear. It began to shift. His brain told his feet to back up, knowing he was in jeopardy of never seeing his children again. The form started to stand and stretch its lanky legs and arms. They looked disproportioned, but they were fluid in motion. The red moonlight entering the sunroom was rejuvenating the creature. It grew several inches when it moved into a ray and lifted its head to emit a spine-chilling howl.

Fields's heels bumped against the step entering the sunroom. He lifted each foot up, praying the wood wouldn't creak when his full weight bore down. Everything was going to be all right after he ascended back up the first two steps, or so he thought. As if his destiny was written to fight this creature, the sheath of his sword scraped along the edge of the doorframe. The mangler's ears perked up. It sniffed the air while turning its head in the General's direction.

Fields felt a knot rise in his throat. He stopped and held his breath. If he stayed as still as possible, maybe, just maybe it would not detect him. This was not to be his lucky night, though. Its elongated snout turned all the way toward him before its body followed suit. A pair of golden eyes recognized his unmoving body as an intruder that had not yet been taken care of.

He could no longer hold his stance and sprinted for the staircase. The mangler growled and leaped through the door. It sprang a second time in the study, bowling him over before he could reach the kitchen. It rolled forward and spun to attack again but the General was already halfway up the staircase, his only option for survival. The mangler growled and leaped toward Fields, but was met in mid-air by the black, shaggy dog that attacked him earlier. The two creatures fell down the staircase, biting and clawing at each other as they rolled end over end.

"Come with me! Quickly!" said a figure at the top of the stairs.

Fields looked up to see the mousy woman who ran from them earlier had returned.

"Now!" she yelled.

He pushed himself up and finished climbing to meet her. They took a glance down to see the dog was being bitten on a leg. She pulled on his arm to make him follow. They sprinted down the long hallway and into the last room on the right. She shut the door quietly behind them and locked it. There was a closet on the other side of the washroom that she pointed to.

"In there," she said.

A squealing cry rang out. A few moments later the heavy footsteps of the mangler came thudding down the hallway toward the washroom. The woman slid the closet door shut and pulled on a rope above them. A set of stairs unfolded and touched the ground. She pushed Fields up and climbed after him just as the mangler started pounding on the washroom's door. He could hear it sniffing and snarling between each bang. She grasped the rope and pulled the stairs back up after them. Once they aligned with the attic's floor, she slid a bolt into place to lock it and yanked the rope she had used to pull the stairs down to the second level, back up to align them with the attic's floor.

Fields sat down and wiped the sweat from his face as he watched the woman lock the hidden door into place. They listened to the door of the washroom break off its hinges and crash into a ceramic tub near a window. The creature growled and paced back and forth within the room, trying to pick up their scent again. The closet door slid open below them. The woman put an index finger to her lips to warn the General. Fields kept a firm grip on his sword.

The beast could be heard rummaging through a pile of boxes in one corner of the closet. When it couldn't find them, it punched several holes in the wall and howled again. After a few moments, its footsteps left the closet and then the washroom. They listened to them fade down the hallway and into the lower levels of the mansion.

When Fields looked around the rest of the attic, he saw two familiar faces sitting on the floor in a corner. They waved to him, afraid to say anything. He walked over to them and knelt down.

"How's he doing?" Fields asked Crane, who was sewing up Argil's back.

Crane whispered, "Not as bad as it looks. Now that I've gotten the bleeding to stop and the wound cleansed, the rest will be easy to do. The other men weren't as fortunate. Lieutenant Ravel was the last to go."

"I saw the mess," Fields said, staring back at the woman. She walked over to the window and looked out onto the grounds.

Fields just realized that the Chief could still be waiting outside. When he stood to join her, she said, "He left not long after you entered the building. I hope he is not bringing help back here. There will only be more death."

"Who are you?" Fields asked again. "Are you a Maxhaw?"

She nodded and said, "Etna."

"Then that was your brother in the chair."

She nodded again, looking like a ghost standing in the white moonlight of Lumly as it shone through the window. Her pale skin and white gown glowed where the light touched it.

"You would not be here if you were not helping the mangler. Tell us why."

Appearing reluctant to answer the question, she turned back toward the window.

"Why would you serve a creature that hunts for blood?" he pressed.

"He is my father."

"Father?" Crane asked. "It is an animal."

"Only when one of the twin moons is red," she snapped, wiping a tear from her eye.

"How did he become what he is?" Fields asked, feeling the conversation was growing extremely awkward.

She sat on a rug spread across the floor and stretched her legs. A heavy, blue wool blanket was draped on a stool nearby that she pulled on to wrap around her shoulders. "He was bitten two seasons ago. He and two friends had traveled to the northern gates of Dowhaven to hunt for pelts. To their astonishment, they learned they were the ones who had become the hunted. The creature that infected my father was traveling with maddons when it was in their form. As night begins to give way to day, the beast becomes more the mangler than man before it changes back into a human."

"I read in your brother's letter you were working on a cure. How have you been testing it?"

"I slip it into my father's morning drink when he first awakens from the nightmare. He remembers nothing after each transformation, not even the mangler. We once told him what he was. He begged for us to leave until he could heal himself. We couldn't bring ourselves to just abandon him. Every red moon that passes . . . he becomes stronger. One day I fear he will not change back into his old self. His human blood is weakening. I have seen it through his blood tests. His cells are not the same as yours or mine any longer. They have been distorted."

"Why did you not ask for help? The makers—"

"Wanted to kill him," she snapped. "Most men have no compassion for things they don't understand. They turned on us and informed the sector council. My father worked for them his entire life. But he could not tell the difference between friend and foe when they arrived here with their swords and nets."

Crane finished patching up Argil and told him to sleep only on his side so the stitches could heal more quickly. Argil grimaced from the intense pain, pulled his shirt back on and fitted his chestplate into place.

"I'm sorry," Fields said. "But they are right. He can't be allowed to live. He has killed too many already, which now include men in the army."

She nodded and wiped away her tears. "I didn't have the heart to put his soul to rest, even when he has asked me to. His memory of what he once was is fading. It is becoming harder to reason with him. I see the light in his eyes giving way to the darkness of a demon. My brother and I hoped he would only feed off the woodland creatures, but after he murdered Mr. Tomas and those men, my sorrow for him was gone. It was time to kill the beast that had taken him. I have been living up here until I could find the courage to do it. Tomorrow was going to be the day I said goodbye and leave him here to find death, somehow."

Fields nodded and said, "What of the hooded men in black? Was it the first time they have come here?"

"No," she said. "A skeletal man was the first to make his appearance in our pastures. He has been watching the mansion since his arrival two sunsets ago, but he never comes close enough for me to see who he is. His skin tone is similar to the children of Marmais."

"He is Lazul, as were the men in the black robes," Fields said. "He goes by the name of Herikech and is the leader of the secret rebellions taking place throughout the territories. He has been killing rangers and whoever else gets in his way. Your father is a prized possession because of his sickness. Herikech wants the mangler for his war."

"What would he use him for?" she asked.

"To kill the King and claim the castle, which is why we are here. I'm afraid Herikech was planning to capture your father tonight before you had your chance to say your farewell."

She stood to look out the window when the mangler howled. "He's here."

"Herikech?"

She nodded. "He's coming now. What should we do?"

Fields ran to the window and peered through the curtains to look out onto the yard. Herikech floated toward the mansion with his arms outstretched. The mangler was crawling along the ground toward Herikech, growling and snarling. It crouched to prepare itself for an attack.

"Your father will not win this battle, not even in his current form," Fields said. "Herikech's power is too great."

They both watched helplessly as the two figures drew closer to each other, waiting for the precise moment to make a move.

Herikech's form stopped and rose higher in the air, a swirl of fog rotating beneath him. The mangler jumped onto a fencepost and lunged for him. A lightning bolt shot from the sky and hit the mangler in the back. The creature dropped and groaned in pain. Etna covered her eyes and buried her face in Fields's chest. He wrapped his arm around her and held her close. She wept and asked for Yawrana the Holy to forgive her father's sins.

Crane and Argil joined them at the window to watch. Argil hunched over on the windowsill to prop himself up. His face was pale from the loss of blood.

The mangler recovered and stood up on its hind legs as Herikech commanded it to obey him. It snarled, picked up a piece of wood and hurled it at him. Herikech ducked and threw multiple lightning bolts at the creature. A wave of electricity coursed through its body. It fell into a ball as Herikech settled onto the pasture and approached it. Herikech put his hand outward. A ball of lightning appeared in his palm. When the mangler whimpered, Herikech lowered his arm, spoke to the beast and then backed away. Remarkably, it was moving again, appearing to have only been stunned by the lightning. Herikech yelled commands at it again. This time, it did obey.

The mangler turned and stared up at the window of the mansion they were looking out. Its eyes had a vengeance in them that it intended to carry out for its new master. Herikech cackled and disappeared into the woods to leave the mangler to do his bidding.

"It knows where we are," Fields said, pushing them away from the window.

The building suddenly shuddered. Fields looked back out and exclaimed, "It's climbing the ivy on the wall!" He lifted a heavy trunk and pushed it out the window. The mangler was struck in the shoulder and fell fifteen feet, crashing onto the steps below. It threw the trunk off its body and growled.

"It didn't even slow it," Crane said, his eyes wide in disbelief.

"Help me with this," Fields said. He was pushing a heavy sage armoire from a wall toward the window.

Crane pushed beside him and moved it into place just as the mangler's head appeared in the window. They pushed against a side to hold it in place. The armoire shook several times. A furry fist punched through the back of the armoire and through one of the doors on the front. Crane slid down so he wouldn't be clawed.

Etna couldn't watch. She dropped the attic stairs back into the closet and went down to the second floor.

"Where's she going? Get her!" Fields yelled. Argil went after her, clutching his shoulder. With a swing of his sword, Fields chopped the mangler's hand from its arm.

The creature quickly withdrew and fell from the window in shock.

"Down the stairs!" Fields barked, picking his torch back up. He and Crane climbed down and ran through the washroom, calling out for Etna and Argil.

Her scream echoed up from the first floor.

"She's in the study," Fields cried. They ran down the hall and toward the staircase.

After they descended the stairs, the mangler knocked Argil off his feet with one swing when he put himself between Etna and the creature. He flew into several spindles on the staircase, breaking them.

"Stay down," Crane ordered as he put a hand on Argil's shoulder.

"Get out of here!" Fields shouted at Etna.

Instead, she picked up a sword from one of the dead soldiers and held it in front of her. The mangler growled and knocked it out of her hands with one downward slap. It stepped into a beam of red moonlight shining through a window and raised its stump where its hand used to be. The bone suddenly grew fingers. Muscles and skin stretched to cover them to make its arm whole once again. Fields and Crane looked at each other in disbelief.

"The beast can regrow lost limbs," Etna cried. "Men have tried killing it before."

Fields and Crane moved in front of Etna to keep it away from her. "How were you planning to kill it?" Fields asked her.

"Poison. But it hasn't been tested yet."

"You have worked in the Keep and done research on these creatures. Is there is no other way you know of?"

The mangler curled its fingers to test them, howled and turned its attention to them. It growled, picked up a chair and hurled it. The three of them dove out of the way. It crashed into the mantle behind them and knocked off the candlesticks that were sitting on the shelf.

The creature jumped over several dead Lazuls and through a gap between Fields and Crane. It landed at Etna's feet. She stabbed it in the leg with another sword but the creature yanked it out as she let go. The creature threw the sword at Crane. The blade caught the Sergeant by the shoulder and pinned him against a wall. He screamed and tried to pull it out as blood poured down his chest. The mangler's leg immediately healed over where she had stabbed it.

Etna picked up a candlestick and smacked it across the face, creating a gash across its cheek. It clutched at the wound and yelped. It backed away and gauged her with its golden eyes.

She looked at the mangler and softly said, "I know you're in there father. Harm no one else, and they'll let you escape."

Fearing for Etna's life, Fields intervened and swung. The mangler ducked and knocked the sword from the General's hand, sending it flying across the room, well out of reach. With a second punch to Fields's chest, the mangler sent him crashing into the wall, knocking a large oval mirror with a white frame from its hook. He and the mirror both crashed to the floor. Fields looked down at his chest in pain. A large dent was visible where the beast had struck him, its knuckles clearly outlined in rows. It growled, jumped forward and landed within striking distance. Without his sword, he was vulnerable. The only item he could use as a weapon lay in pieces around him. Desperate, Fields picked up a large shard from the broken mirror and held it up to stab his enemy.

Unexpectedly, the mangler recoiled when a ray of red moonlight reflected off the raised shard in Fields's hand and shined on its shoulder. It yowled and backed away, stunned when its fur began to smoke.

Fields was baffled as to what just happened, but saw where the sear mark had injured the creature. He held the shard up into the moonlight again, reflecting the ray back toward it. He aimed the beam directly for its face. The mangler stumbled backward, yowling as it took the full blast of the reflected light. Like a spruce tree, its hair fell from its entire body like needles. Fields was mesmerized as he watched the creature wilt before him. Its face was badly burned and the man within resurfaced in a short span of time. Ean Maxhaw fell short of them and landed face down on the floor. When he tried to lift himself up, his naked arms quivered. He collapsed and fell onto his side. The rest of his form changed back to normal. Etna cried and went to him. She rolled him over as he finished transforming. His face was only a shadow of its former self.

"No! Father!" Tears were running down her cheeks as she held his hand.

He grimaced and whispered, "Tomas is here to take me," he mumbled as he looked past her. His eyes were glazed as he looked toward the red moonlight. He touched her face and then exhaled for the last time. His hand fell onto her lap.

Etna sobbed and put her head on her father's stomach. She hugged him a long time to say a farewell she realized she was not ready for.

Fields helped release Crane from the wall and attended to his wound. Argil also woke from his blow and sat on the steps to soak in what had happened in the short time he was knocked unconscious.

Another creature opened the door to the study and peered in. They all looked up at the movement, afraid Herikech had returned. Fields breathed a sigh of relief and said, "Come in, Captain Cracked Tooth."

The dobbin entered and gasped at the death laid out before him. Cracked Tooth stared at the impaled, naked man lying next to Etna. "Ean Maxhaw?" he asked, coming to the correct conclusion.

Fields nodded. "We have succeeded in killing the beast but have failed to save the man."

~~~

Chief Cyon and the flame fighters returned by the time Fields finished covering up the bodies of the soldiers and the young Lazul men. He moved all the deceased into the study, lining them along one wall. Every man was accounted for, including the victims who once served in the mansion. The Chief gave Etna, the General and his men a ride back to Dixon to seek medical attention and rest. It would take the local army seven days to clean everything up and find the bodies the sector council had sent to kill the mangler. Their remains were scattered for miles over the grounds. And when the local sector board did their final evaluation of the tragedy, they ordered the mansion to be demolished before autumn's end. Etna returned to the Historical Record Keep, determined to one day find answers to the curse that destroyed her family.

Master Oyen pulled off the last of Noran's leg bandages and saw his wound was healing well. "Your gandalay would be happy to know you're almost back to normal."

"I don't know if I can ever be normal under this duress," Noran said.

The sun was nearly down when he looked out the lone window of the maker's small lab. Oyen's assistants left the room to inform Bruneau and Blaynor he was almost done.

"Am I wrong in suggesting you should see your family? Maybe it would be good for you to spend some time with the Queen and your son."

Noran smiled. "There hasn't been a day that my thoughts haven't been with them. I will not endanger them, even for a visit. Eyes watch me everywhere I go. I will not be the one who leads Herikech to them."

"But how long can you wait? Eventually the heart gets lonely."

"My heart has nothing to do with their safety. It will still beat, even if it aches."

Oyen went to a cabinet and put away the cleaning lotions and tools he had used to examine Noran. Bottles clanked as he shifted a few around to make room for more he was planning to mix.

"Did you hear that?" Noran asked.

"Hear what?" Oyen asked, turning around. "The thunder?" The maker went to the window and looked out at the approaching mass of gray clouds on the northern horizon. Heavy sheets of rain fell from their bulky, bunched mass.

"No. It was something else," Noran said. "I could have sworn I
~~~

heard a maddon howling."

"A maddon, Your Majesty? I did not hear it. They rarely come this close to the castle. They prefer the cold northern—"

"I know, but I just heard it again." Noran cupped his ears.

Oyen went to him. "What's wrong?"

Noran sat up and swung his legs over the side of the table. He stood from the table and listened by leaning forward.

The sun finally gave way to the moon's rise. Radia was a red sliver in the sky, while Lumly just began peeking its head up. A small red ray landed on the windowsill, warming it.

"Something's wrong," Noran said, pulling his hands away from his ears. He stood and went to the window. "Shadows are falling around us. I fear someone is going to die soon." That thought made his stomach tighten and caused him to think of his young son. "We must leave here and have the army do extra rounds. My instincts are going mad."

"Why do you think this?" Oyen asked. He watched in curiosity as the King crossed the room.

The bright red moonbeam that occupied Noran's attention widened as he neared the window. "I can sense it. I don't know how," he said. When he looked out, his muscles tightened and he cowered in fear when he gazed upon a new enemy in the sky.

A startling loud crash came from within Master Oyen's lab. Bruneau, Blaynor and Oyen's servants all looked at one another.

"The King!" Blaynor exclaimed, pushing on the door. Something was preventing it from opening. He threw his shoulder into it. "Something's blocking the door!"

Master Oyen and Noran's voices were both screaming inside. Oyen was crying for help and then his voice became gargled.

A creature howled within the room, sending a chill up Bruneau's spine. "The mangler is in there! It must have come in through the window." Bruneau also threw his weight against the door to help Blaynor break it down. It finally fell inward and took a cabinet with it. The glass on the front panels shattered inward as it impacted with the floor. The guards fell forward and quickly got up to inspect the room.

Master Oyen's body was on the floor in a pool of blood. His throat had been torn out. His servants cried hysterically when they entered. One ran for help while the other tried to repair the wound. But it was far too late.

"Where's the King?" Blaynor asked, his head whipping back and forth as if he had been slapped both ways. He and Bruneau went to the window and looked out onto the Yard below. They could see no sign of the mangler or Noran, but could follow the trail of screams along one wall running west. The wall prevented them from seeing if the King was being harmed. Soldiers in a tower a hundred yards away pointed to a section in the Yard below. One of the men fired a flaming arrow across a wall top to alert a group of guards standing near a crenel. The guards went into action after they determined the situation, running through the closest door.

"It's taken him!" Bruneau cried, ripping a drape off the wall in frustration. "It's a fifty foot drop to the walkway below. Herikech must have helped the beast reach the window. The man is using the wind to fly. He controls tornadoes as if they were toys." He sprinted from Oyen's lab and to the bell tower room. He instructed the bell guard to ring the sequence to notify the rest of the army stationed throughout the castle that the King's life was in danger. Bruneau ran as fast as he could to the Western Gate, shouting orders along the way. A dozen gandalays were saddled by the time he reached the stables.

Blaynor remained a few moments longer at the window in Oyen's lab, hoping to see where the beast was taking Noran. But the creature was clever enough to stay out of sight. His gut wrenched when he looked down and picked up several long, dark brown strands of hair clinging to the windowsill.

# CHAPTER TEN
## Red Moon Malady

Blaynor jumped onto the top of a water barrel, and then into the saddle of a gandalay as Bruneau held the reins of his friend's horse when the guards rode by.

"What have the tower and wall guards reported?" Bruneau asked him.

"Only one tower guard caught the glimpse of a shadow moving along the southern wall. He couldn't tell if it was an animal or man. It was only visible briefly."

"What way are we heading?"

"According to Rip Run, he saw Herikech in the western woods during the messenger race. If the mangler is doing his work, then it most likely will take the King there."

The group of two-dozen guards, led by Viktoran, exited the castle at full speed with torches in hand to light their way. Viktoran was waiting for Noran to return to his bedchamber in the Secret Halls when he learned of the King's kidnapping. He was angry that Noran had asked him to stay there and protect his sleeping quarters instead of joining him in the maker's wing. Blaynor and Bruneau assured him that his presence would not have staved off the mangler's mission. Viktoran argued and vowed he would not rest until Noran was found, even if they had to ride for fifty days on end. The Baron drew Heaven's Light and held it up. The blade blazed a bright red and guided them deep into the forests to begin their hunt.

A scout rode a mile ahead of the main group with three long leashes in his hand. They were connected to three hunt hounds following the fresh trail they had picked up. The dogs stopped at one point when a strong breeze blew through the trees. They went left before they decided to go back right where the scent was stronger. Viktoran's group slowed their pace when they saw they were gaining on the scout.

A loud whirring noise approached the group from behind. When Blaynor turned around, he saw Colonel Whitepaw and General Hithel sitting inside the Royal House roller. A light dangled from the center of the spiked three-wheel contraption as it hummed along, tearing up soil wherever it traveled.

"Whose idea was it for the dobbins to join us?" Blaynor asked.

"Viktoran's," Bruneau said. "If the King is severely injured, we'll need the fastest means possible to transport him back to the medicine maker center. A dragul would have trouble following us under this thick canopy. That left only one other option that was swifter than a gandalay."

A sudden cry echoed above them. A giant shadow flew over the riders.

"Dragul!" Bruneau shouted. Two figures waved torches from the back of the beast. It coasted low enough that Blaynor could see the golden scales on the belly of the creature.

"You must have lost our invitation," shouted a male voice from the front saddle.

"It's Baron Blake and Quinn Rainsmoke," Blaynor said, waving at the two. "I think he has proven you wrong, Bruneau." Firewing screeched and lifted further up into the sky. The twin moons outlined their shapes. "Never hurts to use all your resources."

"I think we're going to wake every farmhouse from here to the Sarapin," Bruneau grumbled, shaking his head.

"We can't allow the mangler to reach Herikech before we find them. It's all or nothing at this point," Blaynor replied, kicking his boot heels in to increase their speed. "The King may be dead by dawn!"

The hunt was grueling and tiresome as they rode on. They were a great distance from the castle now and losing hope by the mile of ever capturing the mangler or retrieving Noran. The horses needed rest, which Viktoran wasn't, at first, willing to give. Other men riding with the Baron finally convinced him it would be best to take a small interruption before going any further. The party had gone fifteen miles over both flat and rough terrain. One thing was for certain: the mangler was incredibly fast on foot.

The sounds of thunder echoed in the distance—another of Herikech's storms on the move toward Candlewick. Bruneau and Blaynor hoped it didn't mean Noran had perished and the Lazul king was moving in to destroy the castle for once and for all. But they kept their spirits up by drinking and singing in the short amount of time they sat near Viktoran.

The roller hummed at a slow speed a dozen yards away. Colonel Whitepaw and General Hithel were squabbling about when their next meal might be coming. Neither dobbin let up until Hithel ordered Whitepaw to bite his tongue before he demoted him. The conversation ended at that point, with Whitepaw munching on his latest snack stored in the overhead supply holders.

When Viktoran started to order everyone to remount, there was a sudden crunch and growl in the woods less than twenty yards from their camp. The men all drew their swords and quieted their voices to hear it again and locate its origin. The mangler suddenly howled and then followed with an eerie moan, putting everyone on edge.

"Is it going to attack?" one soldier asked.

"It could be waiting for the right opening," Viktoran said. "Stay near the group or you may get grabbed."

"It's staying out of our torches' range," Blaynor said. "As long as we have light, it may leave us alone."

A tree branch snapped above them, making them all look upward. Bruneau thought he saw a dark form jump where the noise was made, but it wasn't of an adequate size to be the beast. The men clumped themselves together in a tight circle to protect their numbers. Oreus and Firewing flew over them occasionally, checking on their progress. The dragul cried and drowned out the sound of another branch cracking near them. Viktoran cursed. He was at a loss as to where the mangler was.

The dobbins shrieked as a form jumped onto the seats in the roller between them. It growled and knocked away their light before any of the three archers near Viktoran could fire a shot to kill it. Hithel fell backward against the control panel, his body bumping against several levers. The men ran toward the roller, but the wheels bolted forward before they could reach it. They dove out of the way to avoid being run over. Whitepaw jumped from the rear seat, escaping the claws and teeth of the beast. The creature howled and bounded into the seat where he had just been.

"General!" Whitepaw cried, fearing Hithel's life was about to end.

Viktoran screamed, "Get to your horses! After them!"

The men scrambled to untie their gandalays and shaya. Only a handful of them could mount fast enough and pick up the speed needed to catch the roller. It crashed through the underbrush, waking every forest animal in a five-mile radius.

"Get off!" Hithel yelled, defending himself with a dining fork. The General stabbed at the mangler and then glanced at the control panel, seeing the shifting lever had broken off. "You bloody bully, how dare you mess with Majestic Messenger property!" The General's voice was snooty but frightened.

"Take that side. We'll go on the right," Viktoran commanded, pointing the men behind him to spread out in the opposite direction around the roller.

The mangler raked at Hithel but came up with only a handful of fur from the General's paw.

"That'll take a season to grow back," Hithel complained when he checked the spot where he had been shaved. He continued to jab his fork along with the broken steering level at the mangler's arm, only striking air with each swing.

"Jump, General!" Viktoran shouted once he was close enough to be heard. The Baron suddenly had to veer off before he was crushed between the roller's right wheel and a thick tree. He rode around it and lost some ground.

"I'll get trampled!" Hithel shouted back.

With one swipe, the mangler slashed the chair Hithel had just been sitting in. The dobbin jumped onto the control panel in front of him. The roller hit a large log and caused Hithel to lose his grip on the panel. He slipped down behind it and grabbed a bar underneath. His tail rubbed dangerously close to the spokes of the center wheel spinning behind him. "Yaaaah! Baron Iloooos!"

The mangler leapt onto the control panel with ease and growled as it peered over the edge at Hithel's struggling form with its yellow, hungry eyes. It raised its paw in the air. Five razor-sharp claws extended from each digit for the kill. An arrow shot from one of the soldier's bows and sliced the beast's raised arm. The creature howled and dropped his claws to his side. The soldier fitted another arrow to his bow and took aim. In a blur, the mangler dove from the roller and raked the archer from his saddle. When the other men looked back, they heard the archer scream for a few moments before the creature ripped his guts out. Viktoran ordered the men to stay with Hithel and help him while he challenged the beast.

Heaven's Light blazed in Viktoran's hand as he raced toward the creature, spurring his gandalay to pick up speed. "Give us back our king," he yelled with the blade out to the side and ready to swing. The creature jumped behind a tree to force Viktoran to stop his gandalay a few yards from the trunk it was hiding behind.

The moment he slowed his stallion, the beast picked up the soldier's body and flung it up in the tree above them. The man's limp body draped over a branch so the mangler could reclaim it for a feast, if it survived.

"Give him back or die!" Viktoran yelled.

In a quick move, the mangler jumped up into a branch above him and spun in a circle around the limb, knocking Viktoran from his mount before he could strike the creature. Heaven's Light flew into a patch of brush before his body hit the ground. The mangler swiped at the gandalay and snarled. The royal mount reared to protect Viktoran while the Baron lay on the ground helpless in his stunned state. Viktoran shook off the blow and got to his feet. He glanced to his left and right, seeing the sword wasn't in sight. He held out his hands in both directions and felt the anger grow within him. The mangler was about to attack him after the gandalay backed away to expose him, but then the beast saw the rage in Viktoran's eyes. Beads of light swirled around the Baron before an explosion of light erupted in the woods to his left. He wasted no time and ran toward the blaze.

The mangler chased him on all fours, bounding in giant strides to catch up. Viktoran rolled forward into the brush and shot out his hand to claim the handle of Heaven's Light. His fingers curled around it just before he was able to stand and take a swing. The mangler ducked. Viktoran's sword sank into a tree, setting it afire. The beast grabbed the bright blade, unaffected by the hot metal. It howled and yanked. Viktoran kicked the creature in the knee and pulled Heaven's Light free when he saw the flames spark and spread up the trunk. The flames multiplied and spread to other trees interconnecting in the canopy above.

A loud crash echoed through the woods a few miles away. Viktoran could only imagine the wreck the roller had just created when it found its end.

He and the mangler danced in a circle, waiting for the other to make a mistake that would leave him vulnerable. A loud flapping noise came directly over them. Firewing set down behind the beast and made the ground tremble. The mangler spun and cried as the dragul's mouth emitted a long screech that would scare any creature that heard her call.

"Attack!" Oreus commanded, prodding Firewing with his boot heels. The mangler rolled behind a tree when the dragul's large claw swung at it. The tree broke like a toothpick and exposed the mangler's cowering form. Viktoran came at it from behind with his sword raised. With one kick, the mangler sent him flying backward. Five steps later, it was disappearing from sight into the burning and smoke-filled wilderness around them.

A large tree branch above Viktoran caught fire and snapped off. Firewing shot her claw out to catch the falling object before he was struck. The fire had no effect on the dragul's scales while she held it. She dropped it a good distance from him and pulled Viktoran out of the area before a tree collapsed.

"We must go after the beast," Viktoran cried, pointing the way with his right hand.

Firewing lowered her head to allow Viktoran to take a seat on her back between Oreus and Quinn. The moment he was in, Oreus shouted, "After the mangler, Firewing."

The dragul took off like an arrow, breaking and smashing trees that were in her way. Deer, birds and every other gentle or carnivorous woodland creature in their path scurried away to find new shelter from her and the flames spreading through the forest.

"The flame fighters will be coming here the moment they see the smoke getting kicked up," Oreus said. "They could be in danger if the mangler circles back to hunt them!"

"We can't worry about them," Viktoran said. "They carry weapons with them for any blaze they battle. There are too many creatures, besides the mangler, that can kill them for a meal. Don't worry, they're well prepared."
"And what about Herikech?" Oreus replied.

"Let's hope he's not in this region."

Firewing trampled miles of trees as she followed the strong scent of the mangler. When she came to an enormous rock face, she looked as if she had lost the trail. The dragul sat back and let Viktoran, Oreus and Quinn make their way down from the saddles to look for tracks. After several sweeps they came back and formed a triangle.

"Nothing," Viktoran grumbled.

"Not a trace for us either," Quinn said. "The beast is clever, fast and cunning. Excellent attributes for a servant in Herikech's army. If the King dies— "

"He won't," Oreus retorted. "Not while there is a breath still in me."

"Then where do we look next?" Quinn asked, lowering his voice.

The three men stood and stared at one another, and then looked into the woods when they were unable to come up with an answer. They all began to look up into the tree branches until Firewing sniffed the ground near the rock face and whined.

"What is it?" Oreus asked, approaching her.

She growled and clawed at the ground. Sticks and leaves caved inward to reveal an oval hole. Viktoran and Quinn both came over.

"You think the mangler could squeeze down there?" Oreus asked.

"You would squeeze down there if you were being chased by a dragul," Viktoran replied with a smile. "The question is, can we?"

"Don't even think of it," Oreus said, planting his feet firmly on a rock a few feet away. "I don't like tight spaces. My brother once locked me in a closet. I broke the door off its hinges to get out. Took half the frame with the broken lock. I say we remain here and wait for it to emerge again."

Viktoran didn't let him off so easily. "We can't afford to sit still while this beast is holding the King's life at stake. What if Noran's down there with it right now and it's deciding to kill him before we can get to him?"

Oreus bit his lower lip and thought about it.

"I agree with Baron Ilos," Quinn said. "We have no choice, Baron Blake. It has to be caught now."

Flustered, Oreus replied, "You're going in first then." He pushed Viktoran toward the small opening. "You have the sword of flame. You can light the way for us."

Viktoran nodded and stuck the lit sword and his head in first. Taking a look inside, he could only see several feet in. He pulled himself back out. "It widens as it goes deeper. You may not have to worry about getting stuck."

"Then what are you waiting for?" Oreus said. "Get in there before we lose any more time."

Viktoran smiled and shoved himself into the hole on his elbows and knees, inching his way forward until he disappeared.

"You next, Baron," Quinn said, tipping his head toward the hole for Oreus to go. "You'll be safest in the middle."

"I'm not afraid to fight it," Oreus said, getting down on all fours. "I just don't like tight spaces."

"Yes, you've already made your point clear on that," Quinn said, watching him disappear next. The guard took one look around. Firewing was watching them curiously a dozen yards away. She sat on her hind legs and waited while Quinn wedged himself inside.

Oreus felt as if the air in his lungs was slowly being squeezed out of him as he moved forward. He could feel the moist soil soaking his cape at the edges. A large spider crawled in front of his face and then vanished into a tiny indentation to his left. He decided to keep his eyes fixed on Viktoran's boots so he wouldn't have to worry about any other insects that could be crawling across or beneath his body. The light ahead was faint and the air was foul.

"Something must have died down here," Quinn grumbled behind Oreus.

"Probably was killed before it was dragged inside. Let's not think about anything being dead in here at the moment," Oreus said.

"Here we go," Viktoran said just before his body fell downward. A shaft of light from his sword shone upward for Oreus and Quinn to crawl to.

Oreus felt himself fall for a brief second. He looked up and cleaned away some dirt that had collected on his lips from his landing. Putting his legs beneath him, he found he could stand almost upright. His head was tilted at a slight angle. He decided it was far more comfortable than being on his hands and knees.

Quinn dropped down and pushed himself up to inspect the tunnel ahead. "Doesn't look any prettier from this view either."

"Keep your voice low for now," Viktoran said. "I don't want this thing to know we found where it went."

"But we don't know if it came this way," Oreus said.

"You should trust the nose of a dragul, Baron," Viktoran replied. "They're usually not wrong." Viktoran turned around and walked some more. Worms wriggled themselves away from the light as Heaven's Light flashed by. A black and brown diamond patterned snake slithered between Oreus's feet and then around Quinn, making the guard jump. It didn't hiss or bite, preferring the company of the dark they left behind.

The tunnel went on for nearly a mile before it ended at a wall. Viktoran raised his sword above him and saw a hatch above his head. "Interesting. Where have you gone, mangler?"

"What do you see?" Oreus asked.

"There's a wooden door. Listen for a moment."

The three men stood in silence and slowed their breathing enough so it would not interfere with any noise coming from above. But there were no sounds. Not even from a cricket or rockhopper.

Viktoran took the tip of Heaven's Light and put it at the center of the door. He pushed upward, hard. The blade scorched the wood where it touched before the Baron's strength was enough to open it. Dirt and dust fell down on him as it gave way and flipped up. "Easy enough," he said. He jumped up and threw his elbows over the edge of the hatch's frame. Oreus helped push him up. "Thanks," Viktoran said when he got his knees under him. After a few moments he lent a hand to Oreus, who grabbed it and found himself being lifted with ease. Viktoran was stronger than he had estimated. They both then put a hand down for Quinn and helped the guard through.

Standing up, Oreus looked around and saw they were in a small cabin. To his shock, an elderly man was sitting in a chair at a table, eating soup from a shallow bowl. The man looked at them as if they weren't a bother and dipped a piece of bread into the broth. He swirled it slowly to mix the ingredients until Viktoran could form a question that would make sense.

"Tongue failing you, Baron?" the old man asked Viktoran.

"Who are you?" he asked.

"That wasn't so hard, was it?" the man said. "Henry the Hanger."

Viktoran started repeating the man's words before he was cut off. "Henry—"

"The Hanger. Yes. You heard me right."

"You used to be an executioner for Candlewick's dungeons."

"Indeed."

"You retired."

"A miracle," Henry said and then took another bite.

"You don't seem surprised to see us here in your dwelling." Oreus said. He couldn't stand it for a moment longer that the man was as casual as he was about their appearance from his floor.

"Why should I be surprised? You're obviously looking for something important or you wouldn't be here, would you?" Henry took another long sip of soup from his spoon and another bite of bread. He continued, "I've seen enough strange things in these parts lately that nothing surprises me anymore."

"Do you know anything about a mangler in this area?" Viktoran asked.

Henry took a drink and said, "Yes. Ugly creature. Looks like a walking dog that has a bad case of fleas."

Viktoran became excited and asked, "Do you know where it is?"

"No. No. But shows up around here once in awhile. I just make sure the doors and windows are locked up tight before it can get in. It's not strong enough to break through hand-carved sequera. I once caught it scouring the cellar for my meat that you just came out of. Had to move it after that."

"You're sure it didn't come through the entrance we just did?" Viktoran asked.

"I saw you three, didn't I?"

Viktoran nodded. "If I were you, I would lock this door now." He pointed at the hatch in the floor.

"I lock it only when I'm sleepin'. I need it in the event I need to escape enemies who break into my home."

"Does that happen often? What enemies do you have out here?" Oreus asked.

"It's bound to happen sooner or later with those Lazuls walkin' about."

"There are Lazuls here? Does one wear a cloak and resemble more a skeleton than a man?" Quinn interrupted.

"Haven't seen him yet. But I imagine he'll show up sooner or later. I've been resourceful enough to fight off the others for now. They try to steal the supplies from my shed. But a few of 'em found more than they bargained for. I had some traps set. I've cleaned more fingers out of it than you can imagine."

Quinn glanced at Oreus and smiled. Oreus returned his own and said, "Do you know if the mangler travels in the same direction as the Lazuls?"

"Not sure. It only started showin' up recently. Seems more interested in the cattle east of here than the Lazuls. They've never been witnessed together, if that's what you're hintin' at."

Viktoran looked toward a window and saw the red, crescent moon rising higher in the sky. It cast a beam across the table the man was sitting at. Henry sipped some more soup and set his spoon down. He then wiped his face with his napkin and stood up. "How do you reach the closest farm from here?" Viktoran asked.

"Use the path at the back of the cabin. That's the one the beast's been running on. Seems like it can sniff a good meal a mile away. The last herd attacks came from the Morishar Farm. Maybe it's looking for a second helping."

Viktoran nodded and the three of them headed to the back door. "Thank you, Henry. If you see the grinning skeleton, inform the guards at the castle. He's the one the King wants."

"And, I suspect, he's the one who wants the King," Henry replied, taking another sip of water while giving them a wink. "When you're looking for someone who wants something badly enough, you don't have to look far from the object of desire."

Viktoran thought about the comment and then nodded. "It seems that there's more than one suitor in the King's case."

"There always is. It's the price of power."

After Viktoran shut the door behind them, he stepped onto the thin dirt path leading away from the cabin. Oreus handed him a torn piece of white cloth.

"A shred of the King's shirt," Viktoran said after he held it up in the moonlight. "There still may be time."

The mangler's footprints were easy to follow. The impressions they had made in the soil were deep, five inches across and fifteen inches long. Marks from the nails also were visible, separated from one another by almost an inch each, indicating the creature was heavier than it looked. The beast was a solid mass of muscle that would be hard to overpower and bring down if one were to wrestle it.

"What makes Heaven's Light shine like a torch?" Oreus asked Viktoran as they followed the path set before them.

"My courage," Viktoran said without any hesitation.

"It can sense it?"

"It's not a living being like you or me, and doesn't have the senses we possess. It reacts to my courage as if it's a catalyst that sets it to flame."

"As one would start a fire?"

Viktoran nodded. "Yes. It feeds off my emotions as if it was kindling. But I also have to be comfortable with the blade as if it were a part of me. Not just anyone can pick it up and call on its power."

"How long have you had it?"

"Since I've been a Baron. High Elder Mosia gave it to me many years ago. He taught me how to use it. I'm the first baron to inherit it. He said it's been in my family for ages, possibly since the first days of Yawrana. Who its original owner was and how they gave it its power is unknown to me. I heard you also hold a valuable weapon as well."

Oreus nodded and pulled the Lazul dagger out of its sheath. It suddenly lit with flame when he held it near Viktoran's sword for him to see. He dropped it onto the ground in fear of getting burned. The three men halted and looked at one another in amazement.

Viktoran picked it up for Oreus and held the dagger closer to Heaven's Light. "These blades are brothers."

"But I retrieved that dagger from a dead Lazul," Oreus said. "How could it be so?"

"Maybe my sword is from their culture as well. Yawranans were once slaves to the Lazuls. It could have been stolen from them. That would be a shame since I have believed it to be an honorable heirloom for all these years." A flame connected between the blades and made them both burn even brighter. Viktoran broke the connection and handed the dagger back to Oreus.

"Thank you," he said. He backed up a few feet and let the flame diminish to a dull red glow. "The Elders just gave this back to me. They were studying it, along with this crystal that seemed to have a reaction to it when water was near." Oreus pulled out the crystal for Viktoran to examine. He handed it back to Oreus when he was through and shook his head, not knowing what to make of it.

"I'm sure the Elders will want to know what your dagger can do now," Viktoran said.

"Gather your courage, Baron Blake," Quinn said, testing Oreus to see if he could get it to blaze.

Oreus looked at Viktoran, who nodded his encouragement. Oreus grimaced and concentrated as he held the dagger before him. He stared at it intently, but it remained a dull red.

"From within," Viktoran said. "Your heart is the source for its energy, not your mind. Pretend you are one with it." Quinn watched on, his eyes burning for Oreus to succeed.

Oreus tried again. His chest expanded as he took a deep breath and felt a wave of blood rush through his chest. The dagger suddenly lit and shined brighter than Viktoran's sword. Quinn shielded his eyes with his hand as Viktoran squinted from the bright light.

"You have a tremendous source of inner-confidence," Viktoran said, impressed. "You are the prefect warrior to wield it. One has to say more than just words of courage to command it. This dagger killed a demon, did it not?"

Lowering the blade, Oreus nodded. "Yes. On Enduin Pass in Arna."

"Then perhaps Heaven's Light has the same power. Let's hope your dagger has the same effect against the mangler." A howl sounded in the distance. They all froze and listened as its cry became fainter. "It's on the move! Let's go!"

The men ran hard and stayed to the path. Oreus worked up a sweat but was able to match Quinn and Viktoran's pace. A year ago he would never have been able to keep to it, but due to his rigorous training he had become more conditioned than he could have ever imagined. Quinn actually was the one breathing and sweating the heaviest after they covered a good distance.

They soon arrived at a large clearing in the forest. Rolling pastures lay out before them in the shimmering moonlight. The grain waved back and forth from a cool breeze that swept over the land. It felt good as it caressed their skin.

"Do you see it?" Viktoran asked.

Oreus and Quinn shook their heads.

Their eyes fell on a barn near a huge lodge at the opposite end of the property.

"Look," Oreus said. He stepped close to a patch of grain that had been trampled. More had been parted further in, turning into a trail that cut directly across the fields toward the homestead. A scream filled the night as a figure in a blue gown near the main building was running from a large shadow along the front porch.

The men didn't hesitate and sprinted through the high crops to reach the stone steps leading up to the front door. The stairs were lopsided, having partially collapsed from many years of overuse. Viktoran almost slipped off the edge of one as he planted his foot on the edge of a slick pool of blood. "I think it's injured the owner." He wiped his foot on a mat near the front door, which was shredded.

Oreus pulled his bow from his back and fit an arrow to the string. The boards beneath their feet creaked as they walked inside the building. Another scream came from the top of the stairs. Viktoran raced up them and held his sword outward for defense. A shadow lowered behind him from the second floor. Oreus took a quick shot at it and hit the beast in the shoulder before it could lunge at Viktoran. The mangler fell onto the stairs between them and pulled out the shaft with a cry. Its yellow eyes turned onto Oreus as a deep growl filled the air.

Not having enough time to reload another arrow, Oreus pulled out his dagger and let it shine. The mangler leaped upward and grabbed the edge of the ceiling that surrounded the staircase entrance and kicked outward, connecting with Oreus's chest. The Baron was sent flying backward and tumbling down the stairs. Quinn caught him before he fell all the way to the bottom.

The mangler pounced on Quinn's shoulder's to avoid Viktoran's swinging blade from behind and sprung back out the door. Quinn was knocked backward by the move and hit a mirror on the wall behind him, cracking it. He turned around to look at his fractured image reflecting back at him. "Bad luck," he said.

"Get that thing!" a woman screamed from the top of the stairs. All three of them looked up to see her bleeding from a gouge in her leg.

"You need medicine," Viktoran said, taking a look at the wound.

She knocked his hand away and scolded him. "If you don't mind, I'm in my nightgown. I used to be a maker. I can sew myself up. Get the intruder!" she said, pointing at the front door.

Oreus and Quinn ran onto the porch. Viktoran followed only after he argued a few more moments with the woman. Finally, he gave up so he could finish his task. To his surprise, she followed him out the door with a pitchfork in her hand.

"Leave the beast to us," Viktoran ordered.

"Not until that *thing* is off my property," she retorted.

"This is no time to be stubborn. That thing can kill all of us!"

"Not if I have anything to do with it," she snapped. She ran by him and out the door, seeing Oreus and Quinn moving to the north along a tree line. She slipped on a pair of boots and ran after Viktoran when he bypassed her.

The mangler was faster, increasing the distance between itself and Oreus. Three times Oreus stopped to take a shot, connecting with each one. The arrows seemed to have no effect whatsoever in slowing it down. It simply pulled each arrow out when they struck its leg, hip and back and continued on.

Once the mangler reached a tree carved in the shape of a messenger, the lodge owner stopped giving chase and checked her leg wound. She saw it was bleeding worse than ever, soaking much of her lower garment. Viktoran noticed her turn back toward her home, drop her pitchfork and limp away.

All three of the men began to tire but pressed on anyway. Oreus thought the mangler would have to tire soon, too, but the longer they ran, the more he doubted it.

"Where's it hiding the King? Do you think Herikech already has him and the creature is jut leading us further away from him?" Quinn asked.

"Maybe Noran was left at the farm," Oreus said.

Viktoran caught up to them and shouted, "Do you need rest, Baron?"

"No! Someone needs to go back and check the farm for the King. It would be hard to believe the mangler dragged him away this far and then returned to kill us off when we entered the forests. It must have been left him behind somewhere, hopefully not dead. Quinn and I will keep on the beast." They both turned and picked up their pace, no matter how much their legs and lungs burned.

Viktoran returned to the farm a short time later and rested to catch his breath.

"What are you doing back here?" the woman farmer sneered from her front porch as she sewed up her thigh.

"The King may have been hidden on your land by the beast. I must do a search to see if he is here—"

"The King? You let him out of your sight long enough for that *thing* to capture him? What incompetent—"

"I'm not looking for your opinion on the matter, my lady, just a quick search through—"

"I would've killed it for you if you wouldn't have barged in. Now that *thing* is still on the loose."

Viktoran was growing impatient and replied as calmly as he could, "I don't have time to argue when His Majesty could be bleeding to death . . . ."

The woman opened her mouth to argue but then shut it when she realized Viktoran had said something different than she was expecting. "Do it and be on your way."

He frowned and went to the barn first. While entering through a side door, he lit Heaven's Light. Four goats came to the edge of their pen and watched him pass as he went to the back of the barn. All the remaining pens were empty, having once housed the woman's cattle. Traces of blood were still present in many of the stalls where the heifers once stood. He carefully searched every corner, trough and barrel. There was no sign of

Noran anywhere. "Where could he be?" he asked himself out loud. "My Lord?" he called out.

A wooden ladder hung against one wall. He went to it and climbed. When he pulled himself up onto the second level, a maze of hay bales filled the floor in front of him, stacked four feet high. He wove his way in and out of them, calling Noran's name over and over. A cat jumped up onto the top of one, scaring the life out of him. He pulled his arm back at the last second to prevent himself from slicing the innocent animal in two. The cat moved on when he did. The last set of bales provided no new clues as to where Noran would be. Viktoran kicked one over and looked out through a window onto the property. The woman was now cleansing her wound near a well. She glanced up at him and furrowed her brow.

He moved away from the window and said, "Probably killed her husband with those stares."

Viktoran finished searching the main home, the icehouse, the outhouse and the storage cellars. He then walked around the edge of the property and several dozen yards into the woods on the north, south and east boundaries. If he couldn't find Noran, then maybe at least he could find a clue as to where he might have been taken. Finishing his search, he painstakingly went through the field rows one at a time. His search took so long that by the time he was done a rooster crowed from the entry plank of the henhouse. Its call carried across the countryside and signaled for exhaustion to take over in Viktoran's arms, legs and mind. He couldn't think anymore. He tried fighting the urge to rest, but he could no longer hold his stance. As the sun's rays greeted his eyes, his heart passed on any hope he had left for Oreus and Quinn capturing the mangler. His legs crumbled beneath him as he landed on a soft patch of wheat to let his cares slip away. The woman farmer watched him fall and ran to his aid.

Rydor sat in the Grand Hall at a table that was brought out near the throne. He had never dealt with so many pressing issues before, feeling sympathy for the King. There were more territorial disputes between farmers than he could count, a growing number of missing Lazul children from their homes (mostly boys), and another heavy rainstorm moving toward the castle from the west. The cloud was dark and massive, but there were no funnels in sight and no hail being reported from the messengers.

Martell Fedrow and his assigned guardian, Pelly, stood nearby, watching all the cases brought before Rydor and how he handled them.

Martell looked grumpy and impatient, his arms crossed and a scowl spread across his face. He validated his mood by saying, "Nothing like sitting around and waiting for the end of the world to sneak up on you, eh, General?" Rydor frowned at him and then went through the new stack of paperwork that was delivered to him by Ballan. A strong scent of honey drifted with the court announcer as he came in and out of the room.

"Looking a bit pale today," Martell hollered after Ballan.

Ballan shook his head and left the room, keeping his voice low enough so that the Nax could not hear his displeasure with the comment.

"He's a good man, Martell," said Rydor. "He takes his position very seriously."

"Yes. But there's a difference in him than in others who have similar work. He thinks he's more important than he actually is. Believes his opinions are above most. That isn't necessarily a good fit for the Court."

"Since when have you become an expert on customs of the Royal Court, Martell?"

"One can learn much very fast if he sits and pays attention, which is all I've done since I've arrived here."

Raindrops splattered against the repaired stained windows of the Grand Hall. They all looked up at them with dour expressions.

"Excellent. I feel like a walk in the rain to wash me clean," Martell said, getting up and strolling toward the door.

"Stop him!" Rydor shouted to Vance, the guard nearest the entrance.

The guard intervened and put a hand on Martell's shoulder. "Sorry, Martell. It's for your own good."

"How can being stuck inside these rock walls day and night be good?" he yelled. "Get out of my way!"

Vance stepped in front of him again and drew his sword.

"There's no need for that. Put your weapon away," Pelly said, putting a hand on Vance's arm.

Vance looked toward Rydor and waited.

"Go with him," Rydor ordered as he picked up the top sheet from the stack Ballan had left. The General shook his head and muttered something to himself.

Vance lowered his sword and nodded for Martell to go around him.

"Shame on you," Pelly said to Vance as she walked by him. "Everyone can use a little fresh air now and then."

Vance rolled his eyes and followed them. On his way out, General Keys of the Trail Racers entered the hall.

Rydor stood to stretch his legs to meet him. "General Keys, what brings you here at the this early hour?"

"I just beat the storm and it's a drencher." Keys shook his body to rid it of hundred of water droplets. A few splattered on a parchment Rydor was trying to read.

"Thank you for that report. What else do you bring me? I hope it's something interesting. I can only take staring at overdue property payments for so long." He smiled and put out his hand to accept a scroll Keys handed to him. "What's this?"

"Word from Dowhaven. General Fields has completed his mission."

Rydor broke the wax seal and unrolled the parchment.

*King Deardrop and Royal Court members,*

*The mangler has been killed and identified. It only takes the shape of a deformed maddon when not in its original human form. Your instincts were correct, Your Majesty. Maxhaw Mansion was the location where the beast lived. Ean Maxhaw was the beast, transforming into the creature during the red moon. This explains why it only made its appearance during these times. The beast was killed when a mirror shard was used to reflect moonlight, which burned and destroyed the creature.*

*Several members of the Shaba Local Sector Board were killed by it. The entire White Light Squad has also perished as well, with the exception of the Sergeant. The mangler killed some, while others were slain by a secret Lazul guild that turned up at the same time we encountered the creature. Argil Meridot is still alive as well, but has sustained injuries from the fight.*

*I will be spending time in Redstone to track two members of the Lazul guild who disappeared into hiding there. I hope to find where their headquarters are located and arrest any members we encounter. I will return within three sunsets if nothing is found.*

*General Troy Fields*
*Dixon, Dowhaven Territory*

"That's one more of Herikech's minions mashed. Ean Maxhaw. Another good man lost because of the snowtears," Rydor said, setting the parchment down on the table. He picked up his pipe that was resting in a bowl at the left-hand side of the table and was about to inhale when a guard burst into the Grand Hall.

"General Regoria, there's been—an intruder!"

Rydor set down his pipe, drew his sword and replied, "Where? Who?"

"The King's bedchamber!"

"The old or the new?"

"Both!"

Rydor sent General Keys on his way and ordered a handful of guards to accompany him to Noran's old bedchamber first. When they arrived there, a grotesque scene was laid out.

"They're *all* dead?"

"Yes, General," said the guard who had informed him. "Murdered. All assigned to catch the mangler here. I was nearly among their numbers. When I entered the room I saw the creature for myself at the window. It . . . it was horrible looking, as if it were an outcast of nature. Its face was twisted as if it was in agony, and looked weak. There is some blood on the sill over there. It leaped out the window before I could slay it."

Rydor's eyes went wide. "This is troubling. Many of these creatures are running around when we initially believed there to be only one." Rydor inspected the bloody print on the windowsill. It was in the shape of a paw but with, what appeared to be, fingers extending from the claw tips. "It must have been transforming when you saw it. The red moon is down."

"Transforming?" the guard asked. "It changes shapes?"

"The beast is a man when there is no red moon." Rydor walked between the bodies of the dead men throughout the room. A man containing many of the facial features of Noran, the King's closest look-alike, was ripped in half at the end of the bed. His face was in shock from the traumatic event. Rydor took a corner of a sheet and folded it over him. "One of these manglers believes it has killed the King. This may be to our advantage. We can keep King Deardrop in hiding and draw Herikech out of the western woods. He may come out into the open if he thinks the King is dead."

"General," the guard said, as Rydor was forming his plan.

Rydor looked up and asked, "What?"

"The new bedchamber . . . would you like to see it as well?"

Rydor looked around once more at the bodies and then nodded at the guard. "What are we going to see there?"

"I'm not sure how to explain it," the guard said. "You need to see it for yourself."

They made their way down into the Secret Halls and twisting passageways to reach Noran's new bedchamber. When they entered, Rydor's heart dropped into his gut. He quickly shut the door so the others with him could not see the display. "How did the intruder gain access to this chamber?"

Rydor snapped. He stared at a string of dead rats dangling across the room from Noran's desk chair to the bed's closest foot post. Their bodies had dripped blood from where they hung and collected on the stones below. A message was written across the floor, the blood used as ink.

*There is no corner you can hide in.*

"Herikech, General?" the guard asked.

Rydor didn't answer. He crossed the room, stepped over the message and went to the wall on the other side of the bed. He looked at it from top to bottom. A spider ran by his boot from behind a large vase filled with a bush four feet high. One fragrant orange night rose bloomed at its center.

"What is it, General?" the guard asked, seeing a comprehension come to Rydor.

"Help me move this," Rydor said.

The guard walked to the plant and helped the General roll it away from the wall. They both looked at each other, appalled.

"Curses!" Rydor yelled.

A stone no wider than two feet was missing at the base of the wall. Rydor pushed the other stones around it but they didn't budge. "No door here. Whoever gained access is walking between the walls of the castle and can go anywhere he pleases. Thorn. Get the mason cutters in here right away."

The guard bowed and left the room.

Rydor picked a candle off of Noran's desk and put it through the hole. He stuck his head and arm inside, holding the candle up to lay his eyes on a long, narrow tunnel filled with thousands of cobwebs. Moss grew along the walls and a thick layer of dust covered the floor with a trail of footprints left behind that could have been made by Thorn. A distant *drip, drip* echoed from somewhere inside the secret, ancient corridor. Rydor held his candle up and shouted, "I'm coming for you!" into the darkness. His voice echoed for a long distance before it left him to act upon the only available option there was.

General Hithel and Colonel Whitepaw stood outside the farmhouse where Viktoran was reviving, watching Firewing as he ate a rooster from the henhouse in one swallow. They both scolded the dragul and pushed it away into the wheat field to keep it from attacking any more of the owner's remaining animals. But it was too late. The woman who owned them saw the beast devour it from her front porch. Viktoran sat next to her, shaking his head as she walked over to Hithel.

"Get that *thing* off my property."

"It's a dragul, miss—" General Hithel tried to explain. "They have a hard time controlling their eating habits."

"I know very well about their habits. That's an unpredictable creature and it doesn't need to be *here*."

"Please understand," Hithel said. "We need it here for the Baron."

"That's not my concern. He has two feet to walk with. Make it fly away."

"We can't do that," Whitepaw exclaimed. "Firewing is a Royal House mount!"

"I don't care! Get it out of here," she demanded, raising a fist in each of their faces. "I am tired and I don't need to deal with it. It's crushing my crops!"

"There will be no need for that," said a voice behind them. The woman turned and saw Oreus and Quinn approaching. "It's my dragul," Oreus said. "I will take her from here shortly. We will pay for any damage she has done. How's the roller, General?"

Hithel straightened his glasses and shook his head. "Destroyed. Ran into a thick stand of trees. Didn't stand a chance at the speed it was going. The entire center wheel is punched inward and the right support rolled off and disappeared. Who knows where it stopped. Hopefully it didn't run anyone over."

Whitepaw couldn't help but laugh. He stopped himself when Hithel gave him a sharp look.

"Sorry to hear that, General," Oreus said.

"Not as sorry as I am," Hithel croaked. "Second roller ruined within one year." Hithel glared at Whitepaw, who turned away and pretended it wasn't mentioned. Whitepaw cleared his throat and waited for Oreus to speak again.

Oreus obliged, knowing Whitepaw still felt guilty about the one he and Chief Decker demolished near the Hillhouse Tavern in Wilholm Sector. Whitepaw took the roller without the General's permission, which didn't sit well with Hithel. "Where's Baron Ilos, miss?" Oreus asked.

"Over there," the woman said. She pointed to a bench under a window. Viktoran was washing his face with water from a bucket next to him. "Quit calling me 'Miss.' My name is Cyndi."

"Sorry for troubling you, Cyndi."

"You should be. Did you kill the beast?"

Oreus shook his head.

"Why am I not surprised?" she said, throwing both her hands up into the air. "Your hunting team can't even stay together, much less manage to kill something."

When Viktoran saw Oreus, he came over and joined them from the porch. Cyndi left and said, "Excuse me while you sort out your affairs. I want you all gone before I come back out, which is by the time I finish eating breakfast."

After she went inside, Quinn said, "Strong woman."

"She runs the place herself," Viktoran said. "Her husband was killed by the mangler. She buried him herself without reporting it to the Local Sector Board."

"Isn't that a violation of law?" Oreus said.

"Do you want to inform her of that?" Viktoran asked.

"Not really."

"Explains why she is so mad at us," Viktoran said. "She was ready to take her revenge when we entered her home. Trouble is, she doesn't understand she wasn't going to win that fight. Did you tell her that you didn't kill it?"

Oreus nodded.

"Did you injure it?"

Oreus shook his head. "I hit it three times but my arrows seemed to have no effect."

Viktoran let out a long sigh. "Then it is still on the loose."

"Quinn and I believe it could be circling back to the castle, maybe to look for the King where it left him. If we take Firewing, we can easily beat it back and have traps set before it gets there."

Quinn asked dryly, "Has anyone considered that maybe the King got away during the kidnapping?" Nobody responded, including Oreus, who had more faith in Noran than anyone standing in their circle.

Viktoran rubbed his chin and looked at Firewing. He then looked above her to the sky, pointed and cried, "Another dragul!"

The group looked up and saw a large form gliding over the treetops toward them. A few moments later, Illeon landed with Baron Windal Barrow on his back.

"Baron," Viktoran greeted as Windal stepped down.

Windal waved, came over and cried, "The King has been found."

Illeon and Firewing raced each other as they flew back to the castle. Firewing won by a claw when she touched down first on the Royal

House PaCant Platform.

Viktoran jumped off Firewing's back and ran to Candlewick's Western Gate. He recited the passwords to let them all in. The doors were quickly closed behind them after they entered. The three Barons and their guards never slowed a step as they passed through the Gaming Arena, by the gandalay stables and into the Grand Hall. They took a shortcut by using a flight of steps adjoining the hall to reach the bell tower level. Viktoran led them down three more corridors and past a large statue of an owl. They turned right at the statue and went three doors down to Master Oyen's previous wing. Viktoran knocked the secret code. The door flew open. Bruneau and another guard from the hunt were already there.

"How did you beat us here?" Oreus asked the two.

"Hollinfil found us before Illeon found you," Bruneau said.

"Where's Blaynor?" Quinn asked.

"In with the King. Noran's being examined by Master Hurran right now. Hurran doesn't want anyone else in there until he has finished. The King has sustained many injuries."

"How many?" Viktoran asked, glancing at Quinn out of the corner of his eye.

"There were too many for me to count before the maker kicked me out," Bruneau said, appearing to hold a grudge. "The King's a mess. He didn't stand much of a chance without Arc Glimmer at his side."

"Where was he found?" Oreus asked.

Bruneau finally relaxed the tension that had built up in his shoulders. "In the bell tower. The man who found him is being held for questioning. Didn't give many details. Just said he found the King shivering in a ball with a drape over him, as if he were waiting to die. The mangler must have given up on him before he even got out of the castle. Knowing Noran, he put up one hell of a fight before it finally let go of him."

"Why wasn't he found by the bell tower guard sooner?" Quinn asked, finding the scenario unusual. "They are required to inspect the room every evening and morning."

"That's the problem. The tower guard was also killed. He was decapitated. The corridor guard, Ken Murcy, says the King was in a spot not easy to notice. Said it looked as if the King had crawled in there to hide. The tower guard may have fended off the beast long enough for Noran to protect himself."

"Where exactly *was* the King found?" Viktoran said, growing angry.

"Inside a gear box of all things. It may have been what saved him.

They're not easy to get into without getting pinched or crushed. With the injuries he sustained, he probably became incapable of fighting and did the only thing he could to survive. We're fortunate he didn't bleed to death before he was found."

"Where's Murcy being held?" Viktoran asked. " I would like to have a few words with him myself."

"Cell chute thirty-eight."

Viktoran left. The moment after he exited the waiting room, the door to Master Hurran's lab opened. They all rushed toward the servant who was coming out. She cringed, afraid she was going to be trampled.

"Give her some space," Bruneau said, seeing her reaction.

"Thank you, Bruneau," she said, appreciating his request. "The King is awake but most of his body has been bandaged. His wounds have been closed and his color is slowly returning. He has asked to see you, Baron Barrow."

Windal looked at the others, surprised Noran was even conscious. He looked back toward the woman and nodded. After he entered, the servant closed the door quietly behind them. The lab was dark with the drapes drawn shut at the window. Blaynor stood near the King with heavy wrinkles around his eyes. He looked away from Windal to hide his shame.

Noran's head was propped up with a pillow. The rest of his body was covered with a heavy blanket to stop the chills running through his body.

"Your Majesty," Windal said, bowing before he came near.

"Windal," he mumbled, using the remainder of the strength he had left to talk as his body fought off infections. "Windal, are you there?"

"I'm right here, Your Majesty. Right next to you."

Noran's eyes were open but they were glazed over. "I see you now. I need you to give my farewells to my family."

"You will pull through this, Your Majesty—"

"My body feels as if it is beyond repair. I need you to tell them that I love them—"

"No, my Lord. You *will* survive. You are strong."

"Do it!" Noran said, tears rolling from his eyes. They landed on the pillow next to his ears and absorbed into the soft material. "Please."

"Yes, my Lord," Windal said, lowering his head. "Do you remember anything when you were taken? Anything that could help us catch the mangler?"

"Screaming . . . there was only screaming. The High Elder was right. My death is upon me." Noran's head fell to one side as he passed out.

Windal put his ear to the King's chest and could hear a heartbeat as his chest slightly rose and lowered.

"He fights for every breath," Blaynor said, his voice chalky.

"You are not to blame," Windal said.

"The hell I'm not! We're all to blame!" Blaynor yelled. "It shouldn't have come to this. Herikech has played his last hand. If the King dies, there will be nothing to stop me from finding him. Herikech can't be as strong as he is without the snowtears being somewhere nearby. It is time we find them and burn them."

# CHAPTER ELEVEN
## The Jewel of the Vault

On his way with two guards to meet Ken Murcy in his cell, Viktoran was pulled aside by a soldier passing through the Grand Hall. The man appeared nervous and upset at the same time. His blond hair hung over his eyebrows as he stood eye to eye with Viktoran. "Baron Ilos, I hear the King is back in the castle. Is he allowing visitors?"

"Not at this time," Viktoran said. "What is it?"

"The dragul keep. Something went wrong last night while you and the others were searching for the King in the western forests."

"What?" Viktoran replied.

Getting straight to the point, knowing Viktoran's impatience, the soldier said, "It's Garagor. He trampled two of the keep's guards just before dawn."

"Garagor is the most mild tempered of all the draguls. Are you sure it was him?"

The soldier nodded.

"And?"

"The guards heard a disturbance inside the keep. When they entered, they saw Garagor screeching in his stall. The other draguls started screeching as well when the guards went over to him. They thought maybe Garagor was hungry . . . until the mount lashed out at them. It took off the head of one the guards and stomped another to death. The remaining guard fled and ran for help. He was uninjured."

Viktoran was appalled and remained silent as he thought about what had happened. The thought of the battle for Serquist Tower came back to him. "Is Garagor still in his stall?"

"Yes, Baron. No one has gone in there since the bodies of the guards were retrieved. Will you take a look at the dragul?"

Feeling there was much more to be explained, Viktoran said, "Yes."

Once they arrived at the keep outside the castle's walls, a pair of soldiers opened the giant doors to let Viktoran in. The sunlight shone inside and woke the sleeping red giants. Illeon was the first to arise. He squawked when he saw the Baron enter and approach. The dragul kicked a bale of hay it was using to rest its head on at one of the soldiers with him. The guard put up his arm but the force of the blow knocked him over.

"Illeon, you scoundrel!" Viktoran scolded.

One of the soldiers helped him to his feet just as the doors of the keep suddenly shut behind them. All the draguls began screeching and trying to break the chains that held them in their stalls. None were successful. The soldier who had led them there unsheathed his sword and unexpectedly struck down the two guards escorting Viktoran. The Baron jumped backward to avoid losing his own head.

"What the hell are you doing?" Viktoran yelled.

The soldier grinned and was soon joined by three others entering through a small door at the opposite end of the keep. Viktoran leapt for the main doors and pounded his fist against them, screaming to be let out. But the soldiers who opened the doors to let them in, drowned out his cries by banging on a drum and singing an army song outside.

Viktoran spun around and ducked in time as a sword sparked against an iron ring on the door. "Why are you attacking me?" he asked, drawing Heaven's Light.

"Because you betray your King," said the soldier as he looked for his next opening.

Viktoran stalled to get more answers by flinging a water bucket at the soldier. "I have always been loyal to the King."

"Noran Deardrop is no longer the King. Haven't you realized that by now? Has there not been enough destruction to Candlewick as proof that you are losing the fight?"

"You serve Herikech?"

The soldier only smiled again and took another swing at Viktoran's head. The Baron blocked with Heaven's Light and unarmed the man with a spin of his sword. The soldier backed away to let the other three soldiers surround Viktoran. The draguls screeched when they saw the Baron become cornered.

"Kill him!" said the unarmed soldier.

"Wait! What power does he hold over you? Is he holding your families captive?" Viktoran asked.

"Kill him now!" the first soldier ordered again.

The other three rushed Viktoran all at once and swung in unison as if they were part of a trained act. Viktoran jumped over all three swords and kicked outward. Two of the soldiers were sent flying backward. The remaining soldier swung high. Viktoran fell backward and watched the blade pass over his chest and face, missing him by inches. He rolled right twice to avoid two more swings and spun along the ground to cut both of the man's feet off. The soldier fell forward onto his leg stumps, leaving his boots standing where they were behind him. The sword flew out of the man's hand as he fell onto his face. Viktoran drove Heaven's Light through the man's upper back and prepared himself as the two soldiers he had kicked advanced again.

"Surrender and your life will be spared," said the first soldier. The man found his sword that Viktoran had knocked away. The man waited and watched to see how the other two fared in the battle against the Baron.

"A baron never surrenders to a traitor. His life is forfeit first." Viktoran's blade burned brilliantly as he cut the air left and right multiple times, driving back his two opponents. One backed up within range of Plunav. The dragul turned in his stable and lashed out with his tail to knock the soldier into a wall. Before the soldier could get up, Plunav curled his tail around the soldier's body, leaving only the man's head exposed, and then squeezed him to death like a boa constrictor would. His head popped off like a flower's from a stem.

Viktoran pressed back the other soldier against another wall between the stalls of Illeon and Firewing. The two draguls growled as they peered through the high bars of the windows to look at the man. A moment later, Firewing smashed a claw through the thick wood. She grasped the soldier's head and a moment later Illeon followed her example and got a hold of the man's feet. Each dragul pulled the part of the soldier they were holding toward each stable. The soldier was stretched between them until he was ripped in half. His upper and lower halves were dragged away and became a tasty meal.

Smiling, Viktoran turned and rested his eyes on the last soldier, who realized he was in trouble. Heaven's Light burned brightly in the Baron's hand as he held it up and asked, "Where is Herikech?"

"Surrender!" the soldier yelled.

"You can't be serious?" Viktoran replied. "Why are you siding with the enemy?"

"I don't owe you an explanation."

"Where *is* he?" Viktoran moved toward the man and raised his sword. It flashed fire and blinded the soldier for a moment.

The soldier bumped into a trough as he stumbled backward. He slid his way along the length of it and grabbed a torch off the wall when he regained his sight. "Stay away from me or I'll burn the keep and all the draguls with it!"

Viktoran lowered his sword and walked toward Firewing's stable.

"Hah! You care for the beasts more than I thought," the soldier said, chuckling. "You treat the creatures of the land as if they were equals. You are all fools."

Viktoran looked at Hollinfil, Jallad and Plunav and said, "What do you boys think? Should we invite him to the roast?" The three draguls turned their snouts toward the soldier. Before the man could raise the torch again, his screams echoed through the keep when a toxic cloud of green death shot from the three draguls' lungs. His entire body fused into a glob of organs, bones and flesh where he stood.

"Guess you were the main guest of honor," Viktoran said. He waited for a long while for the cloud to settle to ensure he would not inhale any of the deadly fumes. Once he was certain it was safe, he walked toward a ring containing the eight keys of the stables' chains to unlock all the draguls.

The two soldiers outside were still beating a steady rhythm on their drum, expecting the soldiers they were covering for to come out of the keep at any moment—victorious. In the span of five seconds, they instead found themselves crushed underneath the five-hundred-pound doors of the keep when they burst open off their giant rusted hinges and landed on them. The seven ten-ton draguls walked over the doors to reach the fresh air outside. Viktoran mounted Firewing and spurred her into the air. She glanced back at the other draguls, screeched a call and then took flight over the castle wall. All six males followed eagerly. They circled the Gaming Arena's upper seats to stretch their wings and then touched down a short time later to rest on the groomed grass of the southern playing field.

Viktoran dismounted and walked toward the nearest group of guards who saw them land.

"Baron Ilos," said Vance. "Why have you brought the draguls to the arena?"

"Herikech will be after them next. They are to stay here until he is apprehended. Let the army know. I will inform the King of the situation."

"I thought Garagor killed two men at the keep last night—"

"He did it only in defense. The soldiers guarding the keep changed their allegiance to the enemy and tried to murder me."

The guard was shocked. "Why?"

"I don't know. I only can tell you that there may be others throughout the castle who are spies."

Confused, Vance asked, "Then how do we know who we can trust?"

"I don't have that answer. I'm giving you the responsibility to keep an eye on the draguls and to take no orders from anyone except the King, Barons or Generals for now. If anyone has a problem with that, they can come to me. Perhaps it will flush a few more traitors out."

Vance nodded and saluted. "Very wise, Baron."

"I need men I can count on, of which there seem to be too few. Our time is running out."

The dungeons of Candlewick were normally filled with moans, groans and screams at any given time, night or day. But they had been eerily quiet since Thorn had escaped. Soldiers opened doors at times to find men dead or whimpering in their cells over the man with the hooked lip who had come to visit them. Most had surrendered their meals as a trade for their life. One prisoner missed five meals in a row to spare his life. He had bruises over his entire body after each new visit.

Ken Murcy was no exception. The moment the door shut on him, Thorn made his presence known to him as well. Viktoran was bothered to find Murcy cowering in a corner under a bench when he entered his cell. He had a hard time coaxing him to come out, and assured him it was safe.

"You don't understand," Murcy cried. "He could be listening to us right now. Please let me out of here. I'm innocent!"

"Let's talk and see if I come to that conclusion," Viktoran said, bending over to gaze under the bench at Murcy's frightened face.

"I have already told Blaynor Garsek everything."

"Maybe he didn't ask you the right questions."

There was a pause before Murcy replied. "I've said everything."

"Then let me hear your words for myself. I will let you out if I feel you are telling the truth."

Murcy's left hand and part of his face came into view. He looked up at Viktoran. "You give your word? I hope you keep it."

"My word has always been true."

He crawled out of his hole like some wild animal that was checking his surroundings for signs of danger before he completely emerged. When he hoisted himself up onto the bench, Viktoran saw a line of dirt along the length of his right side that showed evidence of how he'd been sleeping. Viktoran crossed his arms and waited for him to make eye contact. Murcy's eyes kept darting back and forth between the Baron and a vent in the wall on the right side of the cell. Viktoran turned to look at the shaft's cover and saw only darkness behind the bars.

"How is Thorn accessing this cell—through that panel? It's impossible to penetrate."

Murcy looked at the vent again and whispered, "He only watches us from the ventilation shafts. He enters this room through a stone in the floor."

"Which stone?"

As if he were afraid to say it out loud, Murcy stood and walked to the stone, standing on top of it long enough that Viktoran would understand it was the one. Murcy turned and went back to his bench and sat down.

"Give me a moment," Viktoran said. "Guard," he called through the door's barred window.

The door unlocked and opened. "Yes, Baron?"

Viktoran hesitated and then said, "Have an anvil brought down here."

"Baron?"

"An anvil. Bring one down immediately."

The guard bowed and left to send the message along to another soldier so he could remain at the door.

"Ask your questions," Murcy said.

Viktoran crossed his arms and paced back and forth as he did. "What does Thorn want with the prisoners?"

Murcy looked at the vent once more before he answered. "He's trying to convince us to join the Lazul king. If we don't, he's going to kill us all."

"Were you alone when you found the King?" Viktoran asked, not dwelling any more on Thorn, knowing Murcy was telling the truth so far.

"Yes."

"And you found him in a gear box in the bell tower room?"

"Yes."

"At what time did you find him?"

"Not long after sunrise this morning."

Viktoran nodded. "You can relax a little. But those were the easy questions. Let's get to the ones you weren't expecting."

Murcy appeared to tense up more. His shoulders were hugged inward and he put his hands together in prayer form.

"Was the King conscious when you found him?"

Murcy shook his head.

"Was he dragged through the door or through one of the windows?"

Thinking a moment, Murcy said, "A window."

"What gives you that belief?"

"The door to the bell tower room is normally locked. There was no forced entry. And since the bell tower guard is stationed in the hallway, why was his body found inside the room? It only makes sense he heard screams inside and went in to investigate."

Viktoran nodded. "Why do you think the mangler would want to bring the King into the bell tower room? There must be a reason for it."

"I don't know. I doubt it. Maybe it had to drop the King somewhere after His Majesty wounded it. Why don't you ask the mangler?" Murcy said sarcastically.

The Baron gritted his teeth and said, "That response will not get you released any sooner."

"Sorry, Baron. It has been a long night." Murcy hung his head and rubbed his eyes. He raised his eyes and looked at the ventilation shaft once more. Only darkness was present.

"Was the door to the bell tower room closed when you arrived?"

"Yes."

"Now that is peculiar. Why would it be closed and who would have closed it if the guard was killed inside?"

"With all the windows in that room, the wind probably blew it shut. Or, the mangler may have shut it to prevent the guard from sounding an alarm."

Both thoughts were reasonable and were enough to let the questioning about it end there. Viktoran moved on.

"You still haven't asked me the one question the others haven't," Murcy said.

And then Viktoran did. "Why did the King have a drape over him?"

Murcy didn't answer at first. He looked at the Baron with wide eyes and then the light went on. "That is bizarre. I know when I'm exhausted I get cold. Maybe after his battle against the beast the same happened with him. The windows in the tower room are always open to let in the air. The closest thing he could have covered himself with would have been a drape."

"I think it's time we let you out of here."

"Bless you, Baron. I knew you would see I was telling the truth."

"I want you to go to the bell tower with me."

Murcy reeled. "What? Why?"

"I want you to retrace your steps for me."

Panicking, the soldier replied, "So you're going to throw me back in here after you are done with me? I haven't done anything wrong."

"No. You haven't. And there's no evidence that I can see to keep you here. You will be free after we're done in the bell room."

"The anvil is here, Baron," the guard said as Viktoran exited through the door.

"Excellent." Viktoran picked up a stone from the floor and moved it to the spot where Murcy had shown him. "Place it right here."

"Yes, Baron," the guard said, waving to Boris Groffen, who was wheeling it along on a cart in the hallway outside. Viktoran nodded at the barbarian when he stopped whistling.

Viktoran returned his gaze to the guard and ordered, "After you have it in place, search the other floor stones in every cell in Candlewick. If any are loose, do the same with them."

"Has someone escaped from a cell?" the guard asked.

"Not recently."

Murcy kissed the Baron's hand and said, "Thank you." He looked at the ventilation shaft one more time before they left the room. The anvil was slid into place before they were out of the dungeons. The moment the door closed behind the guard and Boris, a pair of glowing eyes appeared behind the ventilation shaft's center bar.

"Did you bring it?" Noran asked, propping his head up on two pillows in the medicine maker's wing.

"Yes, my Lord. It was in the lowest drawer of your desk in your old bedchamber. Herikech could have found it if you had left it where you normally do." Bruneau handed Noran Herishen's Will and Testament with both hands due to it being so heavy and thick.

"I didn't put it in the drawer," Noran said, perplexed.

Bruneau was silent, trying to understand how it had gotten there. "Maybe Thorn took it there."

Noran looked at the cover and saw four long bloodstains along the cover. He turned it over and saw a short, thick one on the other side. "The mangler has handled this."

"The mangler?" Bruneau came over and looked at the volume again. "You mean those stains are new?"

"Yes. Look. These fingerprints appear to have claws."

"Your windowsill had the same marks. General Regoria showed us. It never crossed my mind that it could've broken in to do more than just murder you. Herikech must know about the will. Maybe he is searching for information about the snowtears."

"Why would he do that?" Noran asked.

"Maybe he is trying to find more of them."

"Hmmm. I believe you're right. The more he has, the more

powerful he becomes."

"Have you read anything in the will that would indicate where others could be?"

"Herishen has spoken only of the original mound that we found in the Waungee. But it's possible he may have planted more elsewhere to hide them from his brothers to guarantee their existence would continue. But the snowtears are fragile since they are connected by one large root system. To tear them apart could put damage them."

Blaynor relinquished his spot at the window and let Bruneau replace him.

"Get some rest," Bruneau said, shutting the door behind him.

"Don't let him out of your sight."

Bruneau nodded. "I think we've learned our lesson."

Noran opened the will and shut everything else from his mind, including the pain that was throbbing in every part of his body. The medication numbed it some, but the wounds he had suffered were deep and would take a long time to completely heal.

The King scanned through many sections written by Herishen that held little concern for him: the defense fortifications set up by General Murka and his men, the Methalisian negotiations as to when they could be released to return to their island homeland, and what other weapons they could bless with fire or other elemental power. He finally came to a crudely drawn picture of a skull with carrion birds circling above it—signaling the winds had changed in who had control over the western grasslands.

*We have been stripped of all weapons and find ourselves imprisoned by the fate that we have chosen, undeniably connected to the Methalisians. Three eves ago Heritoch's lines broke Murka's defenses, leaving most of my men to waste and to feed the carnivores of the Waungee. We reached the new tunnels for protection, but couldn't hold back the numbers that combed the long blades looking for us. Capture was inevitable, as is our trial in the city of Maramis.*

*Tonight, at moonrise, the Council of the Elders will congregate with King Heritoch and deliver their decision. Even though Heritoch will deliver the final judgment, he will first consult with the Council to be certain our deaths will not trigger a chain of events that could lead to his downfall. The last thing Heritoch or Herikech can afford is another rebellion within either of their armies to divide the lands as it was in the days of old. At this point, however, the Elders' announcement is a formality blocking the door to our doom.*

*The three Elders on the Council do not have the extent of knowledge that my own prophet, Yarba Scraw, has. Yarba has not yet seen our deaths in the waters, nor has he seen us achieving a victory of any kind. He has been watching the ripples continuously since we were imprisoned. Everyone has contributed a small portion of his or her drinking water to supply Yarba enough to tap into its energy. Even though the water is not entirely pure, he has enough experience to see beyond the mud and find the resolution we desperately need. If we are able to establish our new kingdom, Yarba will train other men to read the elements, as he has learned to do.*

*Audra has deep respect for Yarba, but says he has only tapped into a small amount of energy the land is capable of providing. But she feels we are not yet ready to gain that wisdom. The time will come, she assures us, when her people will take us to a level that seems to be more dream than reality. It is the Enclave, a place where one can feel invincible and humble in the same moment. It is a portal between time and space, born when the stars, sun and moons were first created. My skepticism would have prevented me from believing such nonsense had I not witnessed Murka's sword and Dragul's dagger bond with the ancient, everlasting fire.*

*As I sit and wonder where my heart has been and why I feel conflicted over my betrayal to my own kind, I revisit this journal to reaffirm the faith I have now embraced. Its comfort relieves me of the burden of reliving the same worries that haunt me every night. The journal is one of the few belongings we have managed to keep hidden from my brothers. I intend it to be passed on to the future generations of the new kingdom, where it and all other valuable knowledge will one day reside. They will be stored in a grand keep for all to learn from and build upon. Our vision will be realized, our sacrifices honored, and our founding laws preserved. The ink that fills these pages is the testimony of our desire for the new order that will one day rule not only my good people, but also the land in which we live. It is my duty that this book be completed and will serve as a reminder of what we can never allow ourselves to become again – a parasite that feeds off the blood of the land. The new order must maintain the balance and harmony of all life forms for them to coexist.*

*My personal guard, Gerrith Dragul, is devising a method to free us. Less than three hundred of us are left, but it is a large number to account for when planning an escape, which, if we were to choose traditional passages, would be impossible. Sentries will be posted every five hundred feet, some with hunt hounds and others with baskal mounts, neither of which will be easy to defeat without losing more lives. Obtaining weapons will be a critical part of the plan, as well as gathering food and medical supplies to treat any wounded – if we reach the surface.*

*There is one tunnel that may provide the best hope, and it is flooded with water as a drain overflow from the Uratan River. It runs on for one hundred miles to its destination at the western shores of the Sarapin. Boats and rafts are useless due to its depth and absence of current. We will be in darkness through much of our travels in its bowels. Trudging through its muddy bed will be tiring and raise many complaints.*

*Will this untraveled road be the one that permits us to meet our aspirations? Or will it become the home to a mass grave that we cannot escape, a destiny unyielding to any other outcome? Either way, the risk for life is better than the wait for death. Torches will need to be spared and utilized every ten miles to reassess our numbers and supplies as we take rest. Murka's sword or Gerrith's dagger will not provide enough light for all to see. Audru has instructed them that their courage must be at its fullest for the blades to burn the brightest. But courage is hard to find when the hanger's noose is waiting to stretch our necks. I fear most for the elderly clan members. The probability of them surviving the journey in the drain tunnel is poor and they will slow us considerably, slimming our chances of finding freedom.*

*Our only opportunity to set our plan into motion will be at the conclusion of the trial. As we are escorted to the dungeons, we will unleash our revolt. There is a short, darkened tunnel between the bathhouses and archery range, near an off-shooting branch to the weapon-shaping rooms. The door to the rooms is locked but is accessible if one holds a crown of the Waungee – one such as myself. A point of my crown may be removed and used as a key to gain entrance to all areas within the city, with the exception of unlocking any prison door – a twist of bad luck since we currently reside in one. The secret of the key was taught to us by our father when my brothers and I were very young, to use as a resource if there ever should happen to be an uprising against us. I may be the only son who has remembered its value. With any luck, it is a detail my brothers have overlooked. Herikech and Heritoch never have had the need to use the crowns in this particular manner. Guards have always opened any door for them.*

*Once we have secured the weapon-shaping rooms, we will be able to gather provisions and medical supplies used by Heritoch's army. The storage chests for these items are in an adjoining room near the water-cleansing room. The room is also locked, but again, is an issue that is not a concern to us.*

*There are two items that do worry me, though, that will be awkward obstacles to bypass. The first, a rumor has been whispered by the guards outside our cell door that they have caught a handful of the black creatures known as the Shonitaurs, living south of Verdant Forest. They have caused Heritoch many disruptions since their capture. The guards have said they can cause confusion and terror with a single touch to their skin. Heritoch has ordered all guards who are in their proximity to wear protective clothing. As for the men who were touched, they have been telling every detail of their life stories to anyone who will listen. They have been sent to an evaluation wing for study, many thinking they have gone mad. Heritoch will put the Shonitaurs to work. He will bend them to his will and make them pay for the suffering they have caused to his men. If we encounter these creatures in the water-cleansing rooms, they could impede our escape and use it to gain Heritoch's favor. A creature would do almost anything to protect or save its family, including turning against others who suffer the same plight.*

*The second, and by far the bigger problem of the two, is funneling all of my men into the weapon-shaping room without any sign of disturbance. Heritoch's guards will most likely split my army into three waves as we are herded like cattle to our slaughter. If alarm is raised while the first wave is securing the weapon-shaping rooms, the entrance to the bathhouses will be sealed off, trapping the remaining two waves underground. The first wave must execute their part without a single flaw. It would take only one of Heritoch's men to end our hopes. I have instructed Gerrith to be in the first wave. I have more faith in his abilities than any other, including General Murka, who will stay with me in the third wave. Gerrith has asked me to also go in the first wave, but by me staying with the third will only further push him to not fail in his efforts to get all of my people to safety. I refuse to put my life ahead of them when it will be they who will build the future kingdom with their backs, sweat and pride.*

*I must note one other factor that is a concern of mine. Sentencing my men and me to our deaths does not include the Methalisians. Heritoch became intrigued when he learned of their presence in my camp. He questioned me about their purpose, but I have lied like the serpent Heritoch has become. Revealing any information about them has cost me more than I could have imagined, however. His men have found the Methalisian ships at the shores of the Sarapin and set fire to them. I have not had the heart to tell Audra that her people's method to return home has been stolen from them. She could reconsider sharing information that would help the new kingdom thrive and flourish. Heritoch may put Audra and her people to labor alongside the Shonitaurs, or he may have a darker purpose in mind for them that I can't even comprehend.*

*The Methalisians are the other reason I will remain in the third wave. When the second wave has entered the weapon-shaping rooms, General Murka will lead a sweep skirmish to encircle and guide them to join the others. A dozen of my men and I will divert Heritoch's guards' attentions while the Methalisians are led onward. I will be the bait that lures the fish away from its weed bed. The guards will be more inclined to detain me than follow my men if I stay behind. My guards and I will enter the hundred-mile tunnel through the bathhouses to draw Heritoch's forces after us. All water is drained from the houses once every season, emptied into our escape tunnel through a drain cap ten feet under the King's pool at the center of the steam room. Heritoch or Herikech will never suspect where we have gone and will believe we have fled back into the city. It will take them several nights to learn they are hunting the streets and searching the buildings in vain. When they realize what has happened, it will provide enough distance between my men and my brothers' armies, allowing us to reach the edge of the Dunes of Pydora before their baskals and hounds run us down.*

*This may be the last time this precious volume of text is expanded with a new entry. Therefore, I have done what every man or woman who owns property must, declare beneficiaries for what he or she owns. If no will is left behind, the few belongings I had remaining at our camp would've been forfeited to my oldest blood relations – my brothers. In accordance with the Lazul Laws of War, created when the tribes first united, no objects for inheritance belonging to any Lazul may be claimed through pillaging. If documents are found containing instructions for the passing of ownership for any particular object, the law applies.*

*My greatest possessions no longer apply to the Lazul Laws of War, and have not been documented in the camp that we were forced to leave. The instructions for these items have, instead, been left with my prophet, Yarba Scraw, to be carried to the new kingdom. My crown and throne to the new kingdom will be inherited by default to the oldest male child born of my blood. If no male is birthed, then my oldest daughter shall inherit the status of Queen through marriage by an eligible baron in service to me. If no eligible baron is unwed, then marriage to her will become available to any officer of the army ranking no lower than lieutenant. If there is more than one baron or officer unwed, they will be allowed to compete for her hand, the strongest of which will emerge and honor my place.*

*As for the objects that do apply to the Laws of War, instructions were left behind in clear view for my brothers to find. No warrior would be foolish enough to take any object from a king's tent without consulting a superior officer first. He would be beheaded for such a direct violation of the laws. The officer would then notify my brothers of the will. They, of course, would question the validity of the documents and consult the Council of Elders, where it would be confirmed through the trial. With witnesses present and the laws clearly stated, my belongings would be awarded to the designated recipients. However, the laws also state that no object of inheritance may be given to a Lazul prisoner. I have, therefore, chosen individuals under Herikech and Heritoch's command who are known to be rebellious in nature and could cause an uprising if the occasion presented itself. Once the recipient inherits the object, it cannot be given to any other until his or her own death. It is in the best interest of the recipient to immediately create his or her own will to protect the object if it is of great value. Knowing their life may be put in danger because of it and the feelings of animosity the object generates from their peers or superiors, the recipient will have no choice but to go into hiding to protect him or herself. Herikech and Heritoch will desire these objects (especially since the items were once owned by their own flesh and blood) and will do what they can to persuade the individuals to leave the objects to them in their will through death threats. My brothers will be outraged I have not left the items to them and their jealousy will run deep. The only way to overcome envy or threats is to rise to a position of power – a result I am counting on.*

*It is with this purpose in mind that I award three items of importance:*

*The first item is the most sought after, the land itself that I have inherited. Heritoch will stop at nothing to have it. And, after carefully having thought who should own it, I have given the deed to Fex Meadols, a General under Heritoch who holds many of the same traits as Murka. He is a man who could be pushed for a new order if he had certain key figures aiding him. His temper is short and he has support from more men in the army than Heritoch. But Lazuls are not as willing to betray a king if the bloodshed is expected to be widespread.*

*The second item is more personal in nature and one that many would consider an omen to even own: a band that fits over the left or right bicep of one who has died, depending on which arm he used to wield a weapon. Most bands hold no value for trade and are more a symbol to ward off demons than invite them, to protect the body of a warrior while the spirit lives in the plane beyond. They are woven by shamans from the reeds that grow in the burial lands to the south of Maramis, at the outer edge of the city. The tiny burial region is unfit for living and is where all dead are brought to rest. There is not enough soil to cover their bodies. They are, instead, slid into the bogs to keep the baskals and mane bats company. To own another's band before their death is considered to be an invitation for it. However, some feel that the bands that once belonged to Kings and Generals possess the power of their spirit, thus giving the new wearer the strength to rule the land. My band will be given to a squire, a man who is of little consequence in Heritoch's army. The gift will instantly change others' views of him, raising their opinions enough to promote him to a more prominent role in the army.*

*His life will be in the greatest danger since he will be the least knowledgeable in dealing with the political affairs of Heriotch and his court. Heritoch will want to rid the man from the army's ranks, and the band with it. The ones who value the band would think it unwise to do so, and believe the power of the band could call upon the dead to invade the city and destroy it. They would do anything to prevent that from occurring, including guiding the individual to the throne someday. The individual must be strong, despite his standing, and he must be one who could be clever enough to avoid danger long enough to gain wealth and prestige. The best man for this position is Jamze Detas, squire to Ronan Beel, Herikech's only son.*

*The last of the items I relinquish is an amulet worn by the most powerful tribe leaders since the world was born. It is an object of great respect, a single, white round gem called a Starlight, believed to have been carved from a star that fell into the Wailing Hills. Its inner glow is said to contain the spirits of the four gods of the Lazuls. The one who releases the spirits will have them at their command. Heritoch has been eyeing the amulet since the tribes of the East were conquered and it came into my possession. This is the only object of the three I will give to a person already in a position of power. It will belong to Arretis Wade, one of three Elders sitting on the Council.*

*Heriotch will be hard pressed to contrive a way to get it from the Elder without raising suspicion. The Elder is in perfect health and the youngest of the three, which makes his death as unlikely as my escape from the Waungee. An Elder has never been murdered, and if one ever were, it would surely cause a split of loyalty within the city. Their abilities are well respected. The Lazuls are too superstitious. Only a fool would dare cross an Elder and bring a curse upon the city, but Heritoch is enough of one to try. The amulet will also give the Elders incentive to make the death sentence of my people and me less painful – which leads us to the hanger's nooses near the bathhouses. Hanging is one of the quickest forms of death an Elder can grant a prisoner. The torture chambers are the slowest and what I believe Heritoch has in mind for us. The chambers are in the opposite direction of the bathhouses, another problem that could cause our plan to fail.*

*And as for the snowtears, they will be vital for the journey across the dunes. After we reach the Sarapin, we will not be far from where they were planted in the Wailing Hills. It will be detrimental to our separation from the hunt to bring them with us, but they are important to harden our skin against the baking sun. My brothers will follow us into the dunes. Though, they will soon realize it will cause them suffering and great losses. Their determination and lust for blood will be their failure, as it has always been.*

In light of this new evidence, Noran was struck by several sentences that enlightened him. During Oreus's anointment to become a baron, there was a Lazul to be anointed as well. The boy's name was Beel. Brassus Beel. Thinking hard, he remembered he was one of the Lazul children who were currently missing from their homes within Yawrana. Brassus was reported to be the one individual responsible for starting the secret Lazul guild, and led a fight against Haley and Gailey Annalee in the Sunrise Barrel House with his two friends, Throy and Grutt. He wondered if Brassus was a direct descendant of Ronan, which would make him a direct descendant of Herikech. If that was true, then there was no doubt in Noran's mind Herikech was using Brassus to help carry out his plans to overthrow Yawrana.

What was almost as insightful was how Herishen had carefully laid his plans to bring about the downfall of Maramis even before he went to trial. This made Noran appreciate Herishen's skills more as a leader. How he could have formulated not one, but three different tactics to get revenge was nothing short of brilliant.

His eyes growing weary again from the medication fighting off the pain in his body, Noran handed the book back to Bruneau, and slipped into a dream state filled with horrid images of his people's suffering.

~~~
~~~

Viktoran inspected the length of both corridors leading to the bell tower room. The walls, windowsills and floors were all spotless. Sunlight spilled down each, giving the feeling everything was as it should be and had always been. Murcy stood near one window, watching Viktoran do his investigation. The soldier eventually got bored and looked out onto the gardens below. They were absent of any playful children, something that no Yawranan was used to seeing.

"How is the King?" Murcy asked, breaking the silence between them.

"I don't know. But he still lives, which is more important than anything." Viktoran ran his hand down the front of the door to the room. When he turned it over, he saw only a thin layer of dust crossing the middle of his four fingers. He rubbed it away and asked the new bell tower guard to unlock the door.

The man nodded and quickly opened it.

Murcy moved away from the window and followed Viktoran inside.

The guard shut the door behind them to give the Baron and Murcy privacy. "Just knock if you need me to reopen it," he said before it closed.

Viktoran asked Murcy, "Which gear box was it?"

Murcy led Viktoran around a bend in the room to a large stack of stones four feet wide by four feet tall. As for the length, it lay ten feet from end to end. Viktoran bent over and grabbed the wrought iron handle of the wooden door near the base of the floor. He pulled it upward toward himself. The hinges at the top of the door allowed it to rotate toward his chin. He continued to lift it until it locked at the highest point it could go. A few moments later, Heaven's Light burned brightly in his hand. He pointed the sword into the darkness and illuminated an interlocking jigsaw of wheels spanning the stretch of the box.

"You see what I mean?" Murcy said. "I still am amazed how the King worked his way in there. The gears had to be locked for the maker to squeeze in to study him."

The gears were still locked, which Viktoran was thankful for. He stood and pulled off his armor.

"Why are you going in? What do you expect to find?"

"I don't know. Maybe nothing. Hold this," Viktoran said, handing Murcy his sword. The flame immediately extinguished when the soldier gripped the handle. He jumped when a few sparks landed on his face. "Ouch."

"Hold it still."

Murcy held it further away from his body so it would stop emitting a shower of red. "How do you make it stop?"

"Be at peace."

The moment Murcy relaxed the muscles in his arm and shoulder, the blade's color returned to silver.

Viktoran pulled off his chest plate and took the blade back. It ignited again as he crouched and entered. He went left around a large wheel wider than his body. Only a two-by-two foot opening allowed him to get any further. He crawled through it, and dragged his feet through when he was around another wheel. Next, he pulled himself over the top of an axel and dropped down on the floor to reach the compartment Noran had hidden himself inside.

To his surprise, the drape that had covered his body was rolled into a ball in the corner. He picked it up and let it fall open. The smell of blood on it met his nostrils. The garment was still damp, as if the King had been sweating heavily with it wrapped tightly around his body. The box was hot now that Viktoran was sitting still enough to realize it. A bead of sweat ran down from his temple to the edge of his upper lip. He licked it away and turned the drape over. A tiny protrusion scraped against his hand. He set down Heaven's Light to pull it out. Picking his sword back up, he found it to be a pointed, blood-covered nail that had been ripped away from the finger it was attached to.

Viktoran tucked the nail in a pouch at his side and bundled the drape beneath his arm. His eyes wandered along the rest of the box and wheels enclosing the cramped space. As far as he could tell, the only trace of evidence from Noran's encounter was now with him. The space was so tight he had just enough room to turn around.

"Find anything?" Murcy asked when Viktoran's head emerged through the two-by-two foot space beneath the wheel parallel to the door.

"Not really anything important," Viktoran said, feeling no need to share the information with Murcy.

"Then I'm glad it was you who crawled in there and not me."

Viktoran finished worming his way out with the drape beneath his arm, stood and walked to the window for a breath of fresh air. A cool wind was blowing in. He leaned into it and closed his eyes for a moment. When he opened them, he turned and scanned the remainder of the room. A bloodstain was on the floor where the bell tower guard had fallen and died. It was positioned five feet from the box Noran had crawled into. Viktoran shook his head, disappointed there wasn't more evidence than what he had found.

"Give up?" Murcy asked, sounding hopeful.

"I have one more visit to make, but I prefer to go alone."

"Who are you going to see?"

Viktoran didn't respond. He put his armor back on, strode to the door and knocked as the guard had requested to be let out. "Get yourself cleaned up," he said to Murcy. "I want you looking your best when you report to Army Headquarters."

"Army Headquarters? Why am I going there?"

"That's where you'll be safest."

"Safe—from whom?"

"Herikech."

"Herikech? Why would he come after me?"

"Because you are a loose end. Thorn isn't the only one listening in on our conversations. He has spies everywhere."

"I didn't do anything—"

"You have told me everything you know about what happened here. Herikech may be afraid we will track the mangler with the information we have gathered and kill it before it gets to the King again. That would ruin his appetite."

"What information? You said you found nothing."

Shaking his head, Viktoran said, "Ken, you have learned too much already. Just report there as soon as you can."

"But what about you? Won't Herikech come after you as well? You seem to know more than I do . . . ."

"Don't worry. I have protection that is better than any guard," Viktoran said with a smile.

Murcy's eyes fixed onto Viktoran's sword. "You mean Heaven's Light."

"Ken—"

"I'm going. I'm going."

After Viktoran and Murcy parted and disappeared out of sight, the guard at the bell tower room walked to a ventilation shaft on the other side of the hall and said, "Ilos is heading toward the maker's wing. He has evidence about the mangler with him. Now is the time, when he is alone. Retrieve the drape and the sword before he gets there."

"That was rather unpleasant," Jime said, studying the gross rat droppings he had stuck his hand in while climbing into the inner walls of the castle.

Rydor entered next and then was followed by five more guards through the hole behind the vase in Noran's new bedchamber. All the men were handpicked by Rydor and brought to the castle from various parts of the Royal House Territory. The men questioned why they'd been chosen for the assignment. Rydor was truthful and wanted to see how they reacted. Each of them was confused, which made him more comfortable about his selections. He explained to Jime why he chose the men he did before he sent for them. It was important that he had men around him he could trust, and by trust he meant not having sided with Herikech.

Three of the guards held torches and all were heavily armed with swords, daggers and throwing spikes.

"Other than rats, what type of creature is willing to live in these conditions?" a man named Hobbs asked. The man was as physically fit as any of the others he was with in the three-foot wide hallway.

"Skeletons that go bump in the night," Rydor said, turning to face them at the front of the group. "Your torches will be your best weapons. Use them against Herikech if you see him. If you see anything unusual, alert the group immediately. Stay together in a tight line. Do not wander off and do not tarry. It may cost you your life."

The men all nodded.

"Good. Kill Herikech on sight. He has a habit of floating in midair." Rydor looked at the man behind Jime and said, "Samuel, fire your night arrows if he tries to go over us."

"Yes, General," Samuel replied, taking one out of his quiver to get it ready.

"Warner, did you bring a bag of white pebbles like I asked?"

The guard held up the bag. "I know what to do, General. Basic training fundamentals." He dropped one stone near the entrance to the King's chamber and another three feet from the first. Warner tied the bag back onto his belt and scooped a handful more out to drop as they went.

"Hobbs, Gizer, Phelps, you three must be prepared to move in either direction in an instant if we run into some trouble. If I yell back or forward, I mean it. I don't want any of us getting pinned or trampled if things go awry."

"What if we become surrounded?" Gizer asked, pessimism echoing in his voice.

"Then we fight our way back to the King's chamber—unless we win. Any other questions before we continue?"

The men shook their heads.

"If any of you wishes not to do this mission, you may back out now."

"Where else would we be better off than with the finest officer in the castle?" Warner said to build the men's confidence.

The other men saluted Rydor, honored to be assisting the General in aid to the King on a special assignment. The firelight of the torches flickered across their faces, showing pride and courage emanating from them. Jime was the only one who had grown accustomed to Rydor's intimidating but stoic stature.

"Let's make this a night we can celebrate," Rydor said, returning the salute.

The first wall they came to was partially blocked off by a section of stone that had crumbled from the wear of weather over the centuries. Black lines from rain seepage ran down the stones around them. A pool of water had collected in the passage from the endless rains that had been bombarding the castle. It was almost two feet deep, soaking their boots and garments tucked in around their legs. Rydor moved ahead as fast as he could to a higher passage on their right so they could get out of it.

"Will you look at that," Gizer said, staring at the countless symbols carved into the black stone slabs leaning against a wall in the tunnel. There were four stones total, each no shorter than seven feet in height. "What are they?"

"I think they're referred to as anchor stones," Rydor explained. "Placed here as a blessing to keep the castle standing strong and tall against any enemy it faces." Rydor stopped and pointed at one of the smallest and said, "The language is ancient that few know how to speak. It is even more infrequently used than the language of Baron Oreus Blake's homeland. It is similar to the markings on Methalis, the monition stone in Dowhaven—only these stones give no warnings."

"They should now for the enemies using these tunnels," Gizer said.

Warner dropped a white pebble near the smallest as they moved on. The tunnel continued to rise. They walked at an angle upward for fifty yards. It became so steep at one point the men were having trouble preventing themselves from sliding backward. Hobbs wedged his fingers between stone blocks on the floor to pull himself forward. Gizer almost slipped and sent Phelps rocking back into Warner. Phelps shot out his hand and planted it against the wall to catch himself.

"It's leveling out," Rydor said. "We must be on the second floor."

"Listen," Jime said, putting a hand on Rydor's shoulder. The men were still scrambling up the slope while they were trying to hear the noise again.

"What did it sound like?" Hobbs asked.

"I thought I heard someone yelling for help on the other side of this wall."

"There's no way we can reach them from here," Gizer said, stating the obvious.

"It sounded as if someone was in pain," Jime said. "There are ventilation shafts running throughout the castle. Maybe we can find one and determine what happened."

"They don't exist on the eastern or northern walls of the corridors," Warner said. "We are on the wrong side."

Jime placed his ear against the stone. His eyebrows rose when a ray of light no thicker than a staff shot out of a hole in front of his eyes. It vanished and reappeared a few moments later before if disappeared altogether. They all went to the wall and listened, but nothing else penetrated the giant, polished stones.

"It's gone," Jime said. "I think it went that way," he said, pointing toward the sloping tunnel. "Why is it we always seem to be in the wrong place at the wrong time?"

"You believe that to be a coincidence?" Rydor asked.

"Not any more," Jime said.

The next passage was clean and straight as an arrow. But when they reached the end, there was no way to turn left or right. A square opening in the floor led to a shaft that went straight down. Rydor put his torch inside and breathed a sigh of relief. "There's a ladder. It looks solid. All metal steps."

"Here," Warner said, handing him a pebble.

Rydor took it and let it fall into the darkness. Three seconds later is struck something and echoed up towards them. "This will be a short descent."

He entered the shaft and went down. Jime, Hobbs, Gizer, Phelps and Warner all went in one after the other like ants entering their hill in uniform fashion. When Warner reached the bottom, he saw Phelps walking down a set of stairs. A railing was attached to a wall for him to rest one hand on. The steps were thin and at a steep angle. Twenty feet later they were standing in a giant oval room with a table at the center. Ten tall-backed sequeran chairs were pushed in neatly around it with a dinner setting in front of each. The plates were filled with bones containing fowl meat and shriveled fruit. Jime picked up a golden goblet and saw the bottom of it caked with krek wine.

"The meals were never touched," Rydor said. "Looks as though something prevented them from eating their dinner."

"Why did they never clean it up?" Phelps asked.

"This used to be a room that could be accessed from a main tunnel in the castle," Rydor said. "That door has been walled up. It looks like they didn't have a chance to enjoy any of it." He pointed to a tall door with an elaborate archway at the top. Stones were packed from floor to ceiling within it. Three tapestries hung on the wall opposite the door. Their scenes were faded by the amount of dust that had collected on their fibers. Only the most vibrant colors were still visible through the layer. A suit of armor stood in each corner, overlooking the scene at the center of the room. Overhead hung an elegant, but simple, black wrought iron chandelier. The candles on it had melted down to the point where they had overflowed onto the dishes at the center of the table below. A finely woven carpet covered most of the floor, but was badly water-stained in most areas.

"Forward," Rydor said, pushing open a door at the end of the room. It fell inward and crashed on the floor. The hinges and their bolts showed rusting and were ready to give way at any moment. Rydor stepped onto the door and entered the new room. His torch highlighted dozens of glistening gems in every stone on the walls. "A stunning display. Vagon gems mined from Dowhaven. They were never removed from the blocks so they could be used as decorations for this room." Another enormous table filled the room. A series of bowls ran down its center from each end, going from smaller to larger toward the middle. The chairs were all pushed in here as well, showing no sign of having been sat in before the room was closed off. A fishing net stretched across the ceiling, held up by the corners with thin-linked chains. Lures, paddles, poles, fish strings and even a giant fish skeleton were tied to the net across its length for decoration.

"A king's meeting chamber," Jime said. "One of my history lessons at the Greenleaf Academy spoke of these. I think these rooms were some of the first in Candlewick. We must be standing in the original castle. Over the years they built around it to make it into the symbol of dominance it is today. These rooms were perfectly preserved for a reason—to honor the ancestors. The meal left behind was no accident and is also part of that tribute. It is a place where the spirits can return to dine whenever they wish to visit."

"I hope they will protect us if we run into any trouble," Hobbs said, looking at a chest sitting against a wall. He opened the heavy lid and saw it stuffed with piles of paperwork. He picked up a sheet from the top of the closest stack and read the title. He set it back down and shut the lid. "Records of their gatherings."

They entered the next room and saw it returned to another tunnel that ran on for dozens of yards. "Back to the boring," Rydor said, waiting for all the men to join him. Warner brought up the rear again and shut the door. He nodded when he saw the General was looking at him.

"It's like taking a tour of Candlewick's history," Jime said, hearing water slowly dripping up ahead. They came to another door that held a warning carved above its arch. "Children not permitted," Rydor said, reading the words aloud to the rest of the group. "This sounds like fun."

When they stepped inside the rectangular room, every torturing device imaginable filled the walls and floor. "Ah, now I see why," Jime said. The door suddenly slammed behind them and locked. The men whirled and saw the man they had been hunting grinning in the presence of their torchlight.

"Herikech!" Rydor yelled, introducing him to the rest of the men.

"General Regoria," Herikech replied with a cackle. "Once again we meet under circumstances that again are not to your advantage. This is one of my favorite rooms in the castle. Do you like it?" He stretched a body hand across his body to cover them all.

"Samuel," Rydor said.

The guard loaded an arrow, lit the tip on Rydor's torch and fired it at Herikech.

In one fluid motion, Herikech grabbed the shaft out of the air and held it up in rage. "Is that how you greet an old friend?"

"Samuel, two," Rydor whispered

The guard loaded a pair of arrows on his string, lit them both and fired again. Herikech caught one with his free hand but was struck by the second in the middle of his chest. The fire caught onto his robe and spread quickly.

"Noooo!" Herikech screamed, putting a hand to his chest. An ice patch formed and spread beneath his palm, putting out the fire with a sizzling sound. Herikech flew toward Warner before he could swing and seized him by the throat. He lifted the guard into the air, hissing. Feeling the air being denied to his lungs, Warner dropped his sword to pry away the bony fingers crushing his throat. His lips turned blue as he stared in horror at the charred human before him.

Samuel loaded another flaming arrow as Herikech spun Warner between Rydor's group and him.

"No!" Rydor said before the guard let the shot off. "You'll hit Warner."

The doors at each of end of the room let in a flood of Lazuls. Samuel turned his arrow onto the closest hooded figure and released. The arrow struck the man in the head.

Herikech clenched Warner's throat tighter until he could feel the guard's windpipe collapse. A gurgled noise escaped Warner's mouth as Herikech let the guard's shaking form fall to the floor. Herikech's body lowered to the ground as a mist swirled around him. "Spare the General," he ordered.

The guards backed into a corner to let the fight come to them. Gizer fell after he took a hit to the shoulder. Rydor yanked him back up and killed the warrior by shoving the entire length of his sword through the foe's torso. He kicked his leg out to pull it back out. The warrior fell backward into another who was trying to replace him.

Jime strapped a man down on a stretching table and punched the lever to set it spinning. The warrior shrieked as his arms and legs were gruesomely pulled from their sockets.

Gizer checked his wound and decided he could still fight. He picked a spear out of a tubular container and hurled it at another wave of warriors entering the room. The front man ducked to let his comrade behind him take the blow of the weapon. With a handful of throwing spikes, Gizer picked the Lazuls off one by one, striking each in an eye.

Herikech watched from his shroud of mist in an upper corner of the room. It became so dense that only his blue eyes were visible from the creeping cloud around him. Another hooded Lazul stood still near him and said, "Your time will be here soon, Master."

Samuel fired a flaming arrow at the Lazul talking to Herikech. A tendril of water shot from Herikech's cloud column and knocked it away. The tendril then snaked its way toward Samuel along the ground and wound itself around the guard's leg, moving upward. Samuel tried to push it off but his hand only became wet as it passed through the mist. The water tendril entered his mouth and forced its way into his lungs. Samuel found himself being lifted toward Herikech, his eyes watering from the excruciating pain tearing up his insides.

"You see, Brassus? They are weak," Herikech said. "The only way they know how to defend themselves is with barbaric weapons. They don't understand the true power of the elements." Samuel's legs dangled ten feet above the ground. They kicked less and less until they no longer could.

Brassus laughed when Samuel's body hit the floor in death. "Mortals, my Lord. They are all mortals. They all deserve to die."

"Back!" Rydor shouted, seeing their chances of winning were being nullified as more Lazuls entered the room.

Phelps moved to his left, cutting down two more warriors in the process. The warriors bounced back up as if they weren't hit at all. Gizer shuffled behind him with Hobbs and Rydor now bringing up the rear. They reached the door but an arm of water shot out from Herikech's column and forced it back shut.

Rydor took his torch and thrust it into the watery arm. Herikech screamed. The arm broke into thousands of separate water droplets and fell upon the Lazuls and Yawranans below with a splash. Rydor's torch hissed as it went out. He used it to club a warrior across the face and then threw it in the direction of another. It struck the Lazul in the chest, knocking him down. Rydor slammed the door behind them and sprinted across the meeting chamber with the others, except his own personal guard Jime.

Jime killed two more warriors who threw open the door and entered the room. They fell aside but then got back to their feet after Jime turned his back. The warriors raced after Regoria and the others while he went back to the door. After he saw the horde of Lazuls advancing, he slammed it shut and held it while the others ran around the dining table and climbed into the shaft. Phelps decapitated the two warriors chasing them as a sword tip burst through the center of the door, giving Jime a scare. He looked back over his shoulder to see Phelps's boots entering the shaft after the others. He looked to his left and tipped over a suit of armor to barricade the door. The first few Lazuls coming into the room tripped over it, causing a pile-up. Jime raced for the shaft to join the others.

Herikech called his commands from the meeting room as Rydor led the way for his group by frantically working his way up the shaft, hand over hand. He was almost to the light at the top when something entered it and jumped onto his back. He felt himself start to be dragged down. The creature growled in his ear. The first thought that entered his mind was that the mangler had attacked him. But the creature was significantly smaller than what the beast was reported to have been. Hobbs reached up to grab the creature and pull it off the General, but only came up with a handful of fur.

"Keep going!" Phelps shouted from below as he dropped his extinguished torch. It thudded as it hit the face of a warrior who had just grasped Jime's boot. The Lazul shrieked and lost his grip, falling onto two more men who entered below.

The creature grasped Rydor by the chin and pulled backward.

"Ahhhh!" Rydor yelled, as he ascended two more steps. "Let go, you fiend!" He elbowed it twice in the gut and sent it hurtling onto the pile of bodies below. Screams echoed out in confusion. He had no idea if any of his own men were knocked off in the process. The General exited the shaft and helped Hobbs out.

Rydor shoved Hobbs out of the way. "Move it! Now!"

Spinning on his right heel, the guard changed direction and ran toward the sloping tunnel. He got down on his butt and slid all the way down to the bottom. He realized Rydor was not with him when he looked back over his shoulder.

"General?" he yelled back up the sloping passageway.

Gizer came next," The General orders you to keep moving!"

The sounds of blades clashing met the two guards' ears, and then two Lazul warriors came sliding down the tunnel. When they hit the bottom, Gizer and Hobbs killed them. They turned their backs on the Lazuls they had killed to look toward the tunnel that would take them to their safety, but it was a mistake that cost Hobbs his life. A dagger plunged into his back. He cried and fell. The two warriors they thought they had killed were attacking them again. Gizer caught the hand of the second warrior and twisted the Lazul's arm until he was forced to drop to one knee. Phelps came sliding down the slope and beheaded the first warrior for his comrade before he could attack Gizer. Hobbs let go of the other and let him run toward Phelps as he appeared in the corridor. The guard sliced the warrior apart limb by limb, not letting his injury prevent him from finishing his maneuvers. Gizer collapsed and held his wound, breathing heavily for reprieve. Phelps went to him to help him back up.

Rydor came rolling down the sloping tunnel, embroiled in battle with a large ball of fangs and fur. The beast that had attacked the General on the shaft ladder was biting him again. Jime slid down last and tried whacking it off as he slid after them.

"Get this thing off me!" Rydor cried, trying to rip it from his back.

Jime could see it clearly for what it was in the light of Hobb's torch that lay on the ground. It looked at him with its snarling face and then knocked Rydor's helmet from his head. Jime grabbed the grime swimmer by one of its ears and yanked hard. It yelped and fell to the floor. Jime stuck it with his blade several times before it finally quit struggling.

Rydor said. "A grime swimmer. A leftover from the battle in the swamps of Serquist."

Phelps's and Gizer's voices came screaming back down the tunnel toward them. Rydor saw the floor covered by bannels, a deadly animal that dwells underground with multiple white rings around its body. Stingers extended from their shells as they scurried ahead of the two guards and converged at a point to stop their retreat. Phelps and Gizer halted and backed into each other to hack at them with their swords. Gizer was unable to hang onto his torch and swing at the same time with so many to fight off. It fell into the white horde of bodies as they buzzed and clattered to sting and swell their bodies to five times their normal size. Every part of Gizer's and Phelps's bodies became covered with bannels. Gizer took two steps before he fell, screaming from the prick of fifty stings along his back and legs, before he finally went numb. Gizer could only kill a handful before they swarmed and brought him to his knees. His last cry was muffled as he died.

Rydor and Jime stood frozen as a dozen warriors came out of the sloping tunnel behind them. Jime dodged the first man that jumped at him. The warrior's body tumbled toward the rushing mass of bannels. The bannels split and went around the warrior, not inflicting him with a single sting.

A stream of mist appeared above Rydor and Jime that took the shape of Herikech's face. The bannels stopped in a straight line before they reached the two Yawranans. The warriors also ceased fighting Rydor to give Herikech their full attention.

"You will now serve my army," Herikech said, his voice booming inside the small corridor.

"Maybe you haven't been paying attention," Rydor said. "We're the good guys."

A lightning bolt struck out from the mist and electrocuted Jime. The guard was in shock as he fell onto his side and went into convulsions with a glassy-eyed look.

"Noooo!" Rydor said, stepping over his body and holding his sword up to protect him.

Herikech cackled and said, "That one was not lethal enough to kill him, but the next one can be—"

"I will not betray my king and country. You will have to kill us both. We'll die honorably together."

"I am your king."

"Hail Deardrop!" Rydor retorted, raising his sword above his head.

The warriors to his left raised their swords and the bannels came several feet closer on his right, maintaining their straight line.

"I admire your loyalty, General, but you're more valuable alive to me than dead right now. I have a better purpose for you in mind."

"Finish it now! I will not be your slave!" Rydor shouted.

"You're right, you won't be. For now, General, you'll be the jewel of my vault."

Rydor awoke a long time later, his head pounding and flashes of light burning in his vision. He stumbled when he tried to get to his feet. His ankle twisted as he fell forward and crashed into a golden pitcher that tipped over and spilled out dozens of maka medallions. He grimaced from the pain and felt four different lumps on the back of his head. His memory was fuzzy from what had happened in the last few moments before Jime and he were mobbed. Herikech's misty form blasted him backward before he could comprehend the fight that played out.

He held his index finger up in front of him to allow his eyes to focus on its form. When he was satisfied the room was no longer spinning, he took a deep breath and gazed at the only source of light near him. A single candle was lit a few feet away, Jime's body lying next to it.

"Ahhhh!" Rydor cried, attempting to stand on his sore ankle. The pain was severe enough to deter him from putting any weight on it. He limped toward Jime and checked the guard's pulse. The General dropped his head onto Jime's chest. After thanking Yawrana the Merciful a dozen times for his friend's steady heartbeat, he glanced in every direction for a door or window. There were none. He realized that Herikech had already found the new locations of the castle's treasure since it had been moved from the old vaults.

"Herikeeech!" he screamed, hopeful his voice would be heard by someone.

When only his voice echoed back, he looked around them and saw thousands of glittering coins, gems, weapons and other rare treasures the land had produced. Rydor scraped up a handful of the coins, meaningless to him at the moment, and flung them in an arc as he cursed.

# CHAPTER TWELVE
## The Secret Lazul Guild

The solitary sound of Viktoran echoing footsteps made him nervous. There had been few times since he had been anointed into baronhood he was without protection. His own guard was waiting in the King's new bedchamber for his return. Murcy's words kept repeating over and over in his thoughts. The more they nagged him, the faster he walked to reach the maker's wing.

The nail in his pouch was as important a find as any other clue he could have discovered. Somehow, he hoped the makers would find a way to use it and locate the mangler or learn its weaknesses. Viktoran had fought a great range of creatures during his lifetime, many fast and strong, but the mangler was different. It not only held the intellect of a man, but the instincts and senses of an animal. It could even be more dangerous than Herikech himself. But Herikech was somehow controlling it, driving fear into a creature that was only used to instilling it in its own prey.

Viktoran stopped in the middle of the hallway for a moment. He looked behind and ahead of him, thinking he had heard the sound of another's footsteps walking almost in unison with his own. He started again, but at a slower pace, listening for the sounds to return. When they did, he bristled in mid-step, hearing one that was not his own fall against stone. He waited to see if they would continue on their own, but the hallway was still. His mind raced to make the footsteps into something else—the echo of a guard's footfalls while he or she patrolled several hallways over, the wind banging a shutter against an outer wall, or a servant chopping wood in the Yard. His imagination even went so far as to think a ghost had decided to visit him and thought it was being humorous by playing off his fears.

Knowing as soon as he took the next step it could return, he gave in. Five steps later the hall only echoed back his own, relieving his paranoia. And at the moment he felt most comfortable that they were not of any consequence and could have been activated by his own lack of sleep, a flash of fists and feet pummeled him from above. Considering he was blind-sided, Viktoran took the blows without losing his balance when he glanced up. A streak of flesh had fallen from a vent in the ceiling, rotated in midair, and twisted to land on two feet in front of him. He saw the drape was no longer in his grasp. Thorn held it between his elbow and waist before him.

"I was wondering when you were going to make a mistake, like challenging me," Viktoran said, drawing Heaven's Light. Flame spread along the blade as he held it up in defense.

"Challenging you is no mistake, Baron Ilos. It's been intended."

Thorn turned and ran toward a wall, then up the side of it. Viktoran swung but missed as the nightwalker did a back flip over the Baron's blade. Setting himself squarely, Viktoran's sharp eyes watched the position of Thorn's feet to predict which way he would go next.

Thorn was forced to keep his distance when Viktoran adjusted. "You are a seasoned warrior, Baron. There are few like you who would not be dead by now. Do you not wish to call for help?"

"I was going to ask you the same question."

"I need no help to dispose of you."

Viktoran jabbed outward. Thorn bent backward, letting the sword slice the air above him. With his right hand, Thorn grabbed the flaming blade. His flesh burned, but by the look on his face he appeared unaffected. He hung on until Viktoran pulled with both arms to free it.

Thorn grinned and held up his palm to show the Baron where a long black line had been left. It slowly dissolved into his hand as his body repaired the wound. "You see. I cannot be harmed."

"You know of the snowtears?" Viktoran asked.

"I do not need snowtears. I have made a pact with death. You can't kill me. My life belongs to someone else and only he can take it."

Viktoran lowered his sword and backed away as Thorn walked toward him. "You serve Herikech?"

Thorn shook his head. "I'm only helping him for the time being until he can free the Captains. You've been thinking all along we wanted to stay, haven't you? As you must know, every voyage has debts that need to be paid. And it will be the Yawranans who will do the funding."

"So you *are* here for the treasure."

"Are you disappointed, Baron Ilos?"

Viktoran backed up to the edge of a set of stairs and had to stop before his foot slipped off the top edge. "You were meeting the standards I expected all along. History tends to repeat itself."

"Ahhh. Yes." Thorn stood three feet from Viktoran, giving the Baron no room to break past him. "Captain Lanu's crew. It's too bad they spoiled our surprise. At least your people removed our competition."

Viktoran screamed for help and raised his sword. The full power of Heaven's Light grew quickly and then shone a white-hot fire, shooting out an immense blinding orb that covered the floor, ceilings and walls in every direction within ten feet. Thorn's entire body was immersed in it. The nightwalker rolled forward and kicked up to send the sword from Viktoran's grip and clattering down the stairs.

When Viktoran's vision had cleared, he saw that the nightwalker's clothes were smoking and his skin was seared in patches, but he still moved as if he were unharmed. With a right uppercut, he sent Viktoran flying down the stairs after his blade. The Baron's armor protected him as his body was battered and thrown around like a rag doll during the fall against each step. His head cracked against the last near the bottom, giving him a concussion.

Viktoran struggled to push himself up with one hand, while his other held the lump along his front hairline. Blood trickled down into one of his eyes. He tried putting his second hand down but then found them both going flat, dropping him onto his stomach. His body began slide away from the sword.

Two guards entered the hallway and saw Thorn standing over Viktoran with a sinister grin. They halted and looked down at Viktoran.

Viktoran saw them approach and begged, "Arrest him."

Thorn shook his head. "Still think everyone is on your side, Baron?"

The guards laughed at Thorn's joke, turned and walked away.

"What have you done to our men?" he muttered, turning his head just enough so he could see Thorn sit down on the last step.

"Your castle is no longer in your control. Your King just isn't aware of it yet."

"I will not be a dog in Herikech's army," Viktoran snapped.

"Funny you mention that. We now control them, too."

"You scum!"

Thorn laughed. "Scum. Vagabond. Traitor. Yes, any of those will do."

Viktoran pulled his elbows underneath him and raised his head.

"It really would be better if you just stay down until Herikech comes for you. I wouldn't want to kill you in your vulnerable state. He might become angry with me."

Viktoran spit on Thorn's shoe. "Rot in the Underworld."

"There is no rotting there, only burning. Ask me how I know."

"You're a demon."

"Not quite, but I like the comparison. You should talk to Baron Blake and the barbarian. They know what I am . . . but not what I'm capable of."

Viktoran scowled and got to his knees. His blurred vision portrayed a double image of Thorn. He tried to throw a fist but Thorn deflected it and kicked him back to the floor. Thorn picked up Heaven's Light, anticipating Viktoran would try reclaiming it. Thorn was correct when Viktoran's hand slid forward just as Thorn took away Viktoran's hope. Trying to push himself up again only prompted Thorn to kick Viktoran hard across the face.

Only a short time had lapsed while Viktoran's head went for a swim. He felt the presence of water, which made him think he was in an ocean without a raft. It crept over his face and hands where his skin was exposed. He could hardly breathe and shook his head back and forth to resist the sensation that he was about to drown. His lungs felt constricted, but then they were able to expand when his back suddenly hit the ground with full force.

A cackle echoed around him before a voice said, "A match meant to spend the ages together."

"Viktoran!" said a familiar voice as a hand tightened around his arm. "Viktoran!"

"What?" he replied dully, putting a hand to the side of his face. His cheeks were sore and deeply bruised, and the throbbing sensation returned in his forehead.

"Here," said the voice. Viktoran found himself being lifted to his feet by both his arms. His eyes cracked open and saw a dragul staring at him. He was startled until he realized it was only a statue, painted with exacting detail to match the beast's fearsome glare. He turned his head and saw Rydor on his left and then right when Jime released his arm.

"Why is he stashing us down here?" Viktoran said grumpily.

"Vanquishing us is not part of his strategy," Rydor said.

"What strategy? I haven't figured out what the hell is going on around here yet." Viktoran stood on his own, ripping his arms away from Jime and the General. His hair had fallen out of the neat ponytail it was once in and hung past his shoulders. He brushed a few strands that were distracting him away from his eyes.

"Neither have we, and what is more vexing is there is only one way in and out of here," Jime said.

"And it is undoubtedly guarded by our own men who have been convinced to support Herikech, thus giving the appearance that nothing is out of order," Viktoran replied, feeling better with each passing moment.

"You know of others who have switched sides?" Rydor asked.

"Four soldiers attacked me in the dragul keep and two others watched as Thorn had his way with me."

"So he is working with Herikech," Rydor said.

"They both have a common goal, to plunder Yawrana's wealth and resources. The shadows of Herikech's clouds are smothering the land. If we don't find a way out of here, his army will grow until it sweeps the territories and controls the towers. The army will be put back on its heels. His control over the weather alone is destroying crops and bringing panic to the masses. They will succumb to his tyranny if the food supplies are cut off."

Jime slapped Viktoran on the back and said, "When the odds are the greatest against us is when we can hold the advantage."

Rydor and Viktoran looked at Jime as if he were out of his mind.

Jime half smiled and said, "Now that Herikech believes we are stuck down here, he won't pay us any more attention."

"You're saying we turn the table on him and become the ghosts," Rydor replied.

"Where can I get one like him?" Viktoran said waving a thumb at Jime while winking at Rydor.

"Not sure. We don't even know who we can trust anymore," Rydor said.

"There are some, General." Jime said. "Noran. Oreus. Windal. Jada. The Elders and Ballan. If even one of them starts searching for us, then we stand a good chance of being freed."

"How do we know they aren't in the same danger right now as we are?" Viktoran asked.

"When are you going to put that thing down and give your eyes a rest?" Bruneau asked, his boredom taking over. Blaynor normally kept his attention occupied, but since his friend was not present and resting in his quarters, Bruneau attempted to draw Noran into a rare conversation about something other than the castle's problems. "You have a guard here that enjoys conversation."

Noran looked up from Herishen's will. He smiled, closed the cover and set it on a table next to the bed. "Bruneau Palidon, have I ignored you for too long today?"

"The King must put his interest where it is required, but that does mean coming up for air now and then."

"Very well. What is it you wish to talk about?" Noran studied the guard's features, trying to decipher what he really wanted.

"Your father always had his nose stuck in a book, too. I regret that we never talked more outside of the Grand Hall."

Noran nodded. "I was in the same predicament with you in that matter, and I was his son. So don't feel cheated. The complexity of the perilous positions we have been finding ourselves in lately is occupying my thoughts and keeping them from being where they should be. Somehow, I think my father enjoyed isolation whenever he could get it. And I can understand. A king has no time for his own worries when the sum of so many others takes its place."

Bruneau left his corner near the window and came to Noran's bedside. "But rarely does a king have the type of worries you are experiencing, my Lord. You and Herishen Illeon share the same fate—having dealt with Heritoch, and now Herikech, which explains why you're having a hard time putting down his journal."

"Besides his own family and race, Herishen also helped the plight of the Methalisians. Only the strongest soul could have done that. He could have just worried for his own people and left the Methalisians to his brothers. I don't think we're as similar as you believe us to be. I'm not sure if I would've been able to do what he accomplished."

Bruneau shook his head in disagreement.

Noran continued, "There were few he could depend on, which *is* the situation we are in right now. How many of my men have turned against me and are helping Herikech rise to power?"

Bruneau shrugged his shoulders. "A question that will be resolved in time. We can only trust our instincts until we have more information. While you were taking rest, I learned General Fields has killed a mangler at Maxhaw Mansion. The beast was a man who transformed into the creature."

"It morphs? Incredible. Who was it?"

"Ean Maxhaw, which is why it hung around that particular area. It hunted close to home."

"Your words have cut me like a blade."

"They have also cut me, Your Majesty."

"So where is the mangler that attacked me?" Noran asked. "It didn't occur to me there could be more than one enslaved to Herikech."

"Nor I. All I knew of was the one that killed the Trail Racer. I hadn't heard any reports of others prowling through the territories. I guess we assumed the two were one."

"I would like to talk to General Fields about his encounter with the creature."

"He hasn't returned from Dowhaven yet. A message was sent to General Regoria about the incident. He's in Dixon hunting members of the secret

Lazul guild. Apparently some of them showed up at the mansion. The White Light Squad was almost entirely wiped out from the mangler and the Guild."

"I sent them to their deaths," Noran said, shaking his head.

"My Lord, you had no other choice. Men will be in danger during times of war and will sacrifice their lives if it will save others. It is the honor of being in the army. It is unrealistic to expect everyone to live through these trials."

Noran grumbled, "I'm starting to believe none of us will live through this."

"Hope is all we have. Don't let that be taken from your heart, too."

A knock came at the door, making them both turn their heads toward the disruption. Bruneau patted Noran on the shoulder and walked across the room to open it. Noran could see one of Master Hurran's assistants standing outside. Bruneau stepped out into the corridor to speak to her. A few moments later he put his head through the doorway to announce, "You have two visitors waiting to see you. They didn't come here together, though."

"Who's here?" Noran asked, now looking forward to being social again. His pain was starting to subside from the drugs in his system, giving him the strength to talk for longer periods.

"Chief Braiy Decker and Baron Jada Annalee."

"Good. Send them both in."

"Jada has word on the Lazul army and Emison Tower. Do you want the Chief to wait outside until she is done giving her report?"

"No. The Chief can hear whatever she has to say. He's one of the few I can still trust."

Bruneau nodded and opened the door, waving them both inside. Jada entered first, the Chief letting her in ahead of him. Jada saluted Noran while the Chief took a bow. Bruneau shut the door and returned to his post at the window.

"Jada, Chief, thank you for coming. Baron, you have some information to share?"

"Yes, my Lord," Jada said, taking a seat on a chair at the King's bedside. The Chief stood behind her. His black beard had grown out more with some gray streaks, giving him an older appearance. Jada's silver armor was polished as usual, reflecting everything that was around her. She removed her helmet to let her silky blonde hair spill onto her shoulders and down her back.

"Your presence here tells me the Lazul army has decided not to attack the tower," Noran said.

"Yes, my Lord. The army hasn't done anything we were expecting. In fact, they have completely disappeared. The scouts can't locate them. They didn't leave a trace as to where they may have gone."

"How is that possible? How can an entire army just vanish?"

"I don't know. But my sniffers are doing what they can to find them. It's almost as if they knew we found out they were going to attack the tower and decided to change plans. Maybe they are heading for Overbay now instead. I have sent a message to General Rammel that the Lazul army may be coming his way and to be prepared."

"You have done well, Jada."

"Have you seen Rydor? I was expecting him to be in the Grand Hall . . . but he wasn't there."

Bruneau replied for Noran. The King's face was beginning to look pale again. "General Regoria is doing an investigation in the King's bedchamber at the moment."

"If you see him before I do, tell him I will be in the Banquet Hall."

"Don't leave just yet, Jada," the Chief said, putting an arm out to block her from reaching the door. "I think it's time we had a word with the King about your involvement."

"Now is not that time," she said, trying to dodge around his arm.

"Yes it is," he said, stepping in front of her. "There couldn't be a better time and we may be able to use them to our advantage."

"So you did follow me here to rat me out!" she said, punching him in the arm.

The Chief acted as if her hit had no effect on him. "Yes, I did come here to inform the King of your affairs, but it is in the kingdom's best interest. I saw you crossing the Eastern Yard and, given the current dilemmas we are drowning in, I decided someone had to let the King know."

"Let me know what?" Noran asked, his face turning from white to red. He was becoming agitated that they were talking about him as if he wasn't in the room.

"Don't tell him," Jada said. She pushed the Chief in the chest to make him move, but he was as solid as a sequera, standing tall and strong.

"She has contacts with the Silhouettes."

"Arrrhhh!" she screamed. She threw her helmet across the room. Bruneau watched it bounce and roll to a stop next to a cabinet.

"The Silhouettes?" Noran gasped. "Jada—"

"It's not what you think, my Lord. Don't listen to him—"

"You must tell me," Noran said, sitting up on the edge of his bed.

Jada whirled on the Chief and gave him a look that said she wanted to kill him for exposing her. "I don't want to put your life in danger, my Lord," she said. "They will kill whoever learns their identities, even a king."

"They are outlaws who should be arrested," Bruneau said, intervening. "They are involved in many unlawful activities."

"That's not true," Jada said in their defense. "They are not the mercenaries people make them out to be. But they must protect their ring to ensure their work is completed."

"What work? Why are you involved with them?" Noran asked.

The Chief spun Jada around by the arm and grabbed the golden chain around her neck.

"No!" she said, clamping down on his wrist so he would not pull up.

The Chief's strength was twice hers. He slowly lifted the necklace from beneath her breastplate and revealed a pendant containing a crescent moon with an arrow piercing its center.

After three Elders were murdered by fire, he enlisted the help of the Silhouettes to find the arsonist behind the attacks. The Silhouettes requested a steep upfront fee for their services and if he was late to the designated location, they would charge three times as much. The trouble was, the location they chose was almost impossible to reach by the time the meeting would start. Luckily, Whitepaw got him access to one the Messenger's rollers that had been decommissioned for safety reasons. The rollers could travel great distances in a short amount of time. The Silhouettes were not happy he had beaten the deadline. But they managed to trick him through hypnosis and stole all the money he had with him anyway. And to make matters worse, they demanded more money and for him to meet them at a new location. Their games were endless and he would have gone poor before they would have surrendered any information on the arsonist, had it not been for the help of a castle watcher that had been at the new location. Using his own persuasive methods, he overpowered the Silhouette and got the information he sought. The Silhouette, ironically, was a relative of High Elder Elenoi's, Dami Ironwood. That knowledge had the Silhouettes chasing him since, for fear he would expose their ring.

"This is the symbol of the Silhouettes," the Chief said, letting it go now that he had kept it out long enough for Bruneau and the King to see.

"I thought that was given to you by your mother," Noran said.

"It was," Jada said, letting go of the Chief and backing away from him a few feet so she could regain her composure. She slipped the pendant back into hiding. "She passed it on to me before she died."

"How did it come into her possession and what does it represent?" Noran asked.

"My mother was a Silhouette," she said and then bit her lower lip.

"Ellen?"

Jada nodded and sat back down. "She was responsible for obtaining materials for their headquarters. The pendant is a symbol of their protection. No other Silhouette can harm an individual who bears it—unless their identity is revealed by that individual."

"Which is why Dami Ironwood was murdered," the Chief said.

"And why your life is still in danger, Chief," Bruneau said.

"Yes," the Chief admitted. "They think I know more than I do. They have made several attempts on my life, but have failed."

"No place is safe from the Silhouettes," Jada replied. "They are everywhere, just as the Lazuls are now. Only the Lazuls don't know about them yet—as far as I know."

"Then that will help us," Bruneau said.

"The Silhouettes don't help anyone . . . at least not for free," Jada said.

"They helped me," the Chief said. "But I had to force it out of them. I think they were going to take my money and run."

"No," Jada said. "But they would have kept you giving more until you were broke. Only then they would have surrendered the information you were after. Forcing yourself on Dami was not wise."

"She was not going to give me the information," the Chief said hotly.

"She would have. But the timing was not right with another Silhouette observing your situation. You should have let her go."

"The watcher was the one who attacked her."

"I know," Jada said, shaking her head. "I was informed. I have even been asked to kill you."

The three men were stunned by Jada's words. They remained silent so she could finish.

"I wasn't going to comply, of course. I don't want your blood on my hands."

"It could've been the other way around if you would have tried," the Chief said, crossing his arms.

Jada shook her head. "You really don't know how deep you're in, do you?"

The Chief didn't respond.

"You're a marked man. That's something you will not easily shed."

"Tell me more about your mother," Noran said, turning the discussion away from the Chief.

Jada frowned and replied, "She was invited to join them through an acquaintance. The woman was someone she hardly ever conversed with, but when they did, it usually was about important subjects. The woman was curious about my mother's beliefs, the Royal Court, the founding laws and her interests. When my mother told them she was excellent with a sword, their interest in her deepened. She had no idea the woman was a Silhouette, and didn't know what she had become involved with until she had already accepted a role in their society. She was called to a secret meeting between her and one of the leaders. When the offer was put on the table, she couldn't resist the amount they would pay her."

"Your mother bore the white band," Noran said.

"Yes. We were poor until she accepted. My father died of a stroke when I was twelve. It made it difficult for my mother to care for the house and land on her own without some kind of help. She decided not to remarry, her heart still belonging to my father. The Silhouettes found her dilemmas to be fitting to what they were looking for in a candidate."

Noran shook his head. "It sounds as if they took advantage of your mother because of your situation."

"Yes. They did. That's what they do. They make everything to their advantage. Otherwise, there's no deal."

"Then you also received protection of the Silhouettes through your mother's agreement?" Bruneau asked.

"No. I just took her place when she died. They believed I would be the perfect replacement since I no longer had any family and there would be a high possibility I would want to do as my mother did. You can imagine how surprised they were when I was anointed a green band and became a baron."

"That certainly puts you in a difficult position," the Chief said.

Jada nodded. "There is no backing out once you are in. It's either loyalty or death."

"You know all of their members?" Bruneau asked.

"Not all of them. Only the two leaders know every member. There are always two, in the event one dies. Of the two, I know one, as well as four other associates. I did know of Dami's involvement, which made it that much harder to accept that I could never leave the ring."

"We will not ask you to break your trust with them," Noran said.

"Why not, Your Majesty?" the Chief said. "We can imprison them all so I don't have to look over my shoulder for the rest of my life."

Noran replied, "I'm sorry, Chief. You knew the Silhouettes were a dangerous group and you made the decision to get yourself involved with them—"

"To find out who murdered the Elders!" he retorted. "Your father would have agreed with me."

The Chief's words silenced Noran. Even though the Chief was right, he couldn't put the life of one of his Barons in danger. Jada was too valuable to the kingdom to lose. But he also knew she was too valuable to the Silhouettes as well, having access to private information within the Royal Court that the Silhouettes, otherwise, couldn't get. That's when these two ideas met to form another they could take advantage of.

"Jada," Noran said, rubbing his chin, "I need you to meet with them."

"Why?" she said, looking afraid of what the King was about to ask.

"I want to know what they know about the Lazuls. I need to find where Herikech and his men could be hiding and how they are turning my own men against me."

"That is very dangerous information, Your Majesty. Information that could lead Herikech to their ring and break it."

"That would be a shame," the Chief said sarcastically.

Jada growled, "As it would if they killed you."

"Enough," Noran said. "Chief, you have already dealt with them. Perhaps you should go with Jada."

"What? And walk into the kat's den?" he said. "Why would I want to do that?"

"Maybe you can reason with them."

"You can't reason with them," Jada said. "And they certainly wouldn't let him join. There are few men in their care, for skill reasons. You would offer them nothing."

"You must try, Jada. Whatever price they name, I will provide the money," Noran pushed when he saw the Chief about to explode.

"My Lord, if they knew what I'm telling you now—"

Noran smiled. "They don't have to. But that doesn't mean I can't support your efforts. I want the Chief's life off the hook, or I will be forced to send the army after them. I will also imprison you if you disobey my command."

Jada was shocked by Noran's words.

The Chief smiled. "Well said, my Lord."

"It's your choice, Jada," Noran said. "We need to know what information they have on Herikech. It could make the difference in who wins this war."

"They may not accept payment for the Chief's life," she said, glancing at Decker. "No amount of money may be great enough to convince them to back off. Their first rule of the code is to protect the ring, no matter what the cost.

They may even kill me for bringing him to their headquarters."

"We're running out of time, Jada," Noran said. "The Silhouettes would be wise to listen to you. Their ring will fall if Herikech prevails. It is in their best interest to help the kingdom any way they can, or there will be nowhere for them to hide."

The Chief looked just as nervous about the thought of meeting them as Jada did. The Baron stood and walked to the cabinet where her helmet lay. She picked it up and put it back on.

"I guess I don't have much of a choice," she spat. "I will do what I can, but I'm making no promises that they'll help us, or that we'll even live through this ordeal."

"I could have archers accompany you—"

"No, Your Majesty. We must go alone or they will kill us before we get close to the front door."

Noran nodded and lay back down on the bed. "Then I pray for your safe return."

"Just don't tell General Regoria about this," she said. "I would rather inform him myself."

"I don't see the need for this information to leave this room," Noran said. The King looked at Bruneau, who bowed.

"Not a word, my Lord," Bruneau said.

"That includes Blaynor," Noran added.

"Yes, my Lord."

Jada saluted Noran and left the room. The Chief approached the King and said, "If I don't see you again, then I will give my best to your father for you."

Noran reached up and pulled the Chief to him for a hug. When the two men let each other go, they found they were out of words. The Chief left to catch up with Jada while Noran pondered what he had just asked them to do.

The hum of Captain Cracked Tooth's voice soothed General Fields's growing irritation. The General stared out the window on the second floor of the inn they had chosen to stay in and watched for suspicious figures lurking about on Dixon's main road running through the center of town. He had been sitting as still as he could for half a day, waiting for the one moment he would catch the glimpse of a black-cloaked figure entering any of the taverns, supply stores, clothing stockrooms or other inns lining the road. With the rain drizzling down and the sun starting its descent for another evening, his eyelids twitched as they weakened from concentrating too long on one individual dressed in a green robe. The man had fallen asleep in a chair in an alley at the side of Ginny's Brewhouse. He appeared from the back of the alley before deciding to take rest in the chair. The man's head bobbed occasionally until it finally tipped back against the chair and fell to the side on his shoulder. The General had to smirk, wishing he could do the same.

"Hope the letter got to General Regoria in good time," Cracked Tooth said, eating a piece of stale bread that housekeeping had missed from the previous occupants of the room. Cracked Tooth didn't mind—as long as the person who had sliced it hadn't bitten into it. It was the only one of three he found in an ice bucket that wasn't.

"I'm sure it did," the General replied in a monotone voice.

"We're lucky. We just set up that Trail Racer post at the end of the road last fall. Took me most of the morning to teach the runner how to use the glider, though. That tested my patience a bit. It's not too difficult once you get one into the air. The tricky part is landing. I'm sure he figured it out before he got there."

"You didn't have to stay and help me," Fields said again for the third time.

"You can use the help since you're out of men."

"I can get men from the local station here at any time."

"Yes, but why bother them when you don't even know if you're going to apprehend any of the Guild members?"

"That's why they're still there and I'm here with you." Fields's breath was fogging up the window. He backed away a few inches and wiped away the patch with a handkerchief in his uniform.

"Sure you don't want to lie down and get some rest while I take watch?" Cracked Tooth asked, his ears standing straight up as he waited for a positive response.

"You don't have the trained eyes of a guard, friend. Otherwise, I would have been more than happy to accommodate your request."

Cracked Tooth sniggered. "You think these old peepers can't hold their own any more? Do you know how many times I had to decode handwriting in the sorting rooms 'cause people can't spell their own names? How's that for a trained set?"

Not wanting to upset the dobbin, Fields said, "I can tell you were passionate about your work."

"Were?"

Fields winced, having fallen into the trap anyway.

"I'll have you know I'm *still* just as enthusiastic about my profession as you are about yours, General. Why, I can spot a moth on the back of a shaya at a greater distance than you could out that window."

The Captain went on and on until Fields finally put his hands up and said, "All right, Captain. All right. You've made your point. My eyes are burning, and I'm too tired to argue. You can help me if you wish."

"My granda always said I had the best—what—I can?" Cracked Tooth said, sounding choked up the General had changed his mind.

"I really can use the shut-eye. If you see *anything* out of the ordinary, don't hesitate to wake me. I mean *anything*."

Cracked Tooth bounded toward the window and picked up a chair along the way. He planted it next to the General's and took a seat, sitting on it backwards with the back against his chest. "Take as long as you want. Get something to eat, too."

"Pay close attention to the man in the green robe over there," Fields said, letting a loud yawn escape.

Cracked Tooth's gaze fell upon the man, who was still fast asleep. "He doesn't look like he'd cause much trouble. Just takin' a napper. There's a dozen more men down there that are more interesting—"

"Watch him."

"Not gettin' anywhere with me spyin' on 'im."

The General shook his head, crossed the room and threw himself on the bed in the next room. He was snoring noisily before he had a chance to pull off his boots.

Cracked Tooth laughed and peered back out the window. "Don't know their own limitations . . . ."

The weather turned dismal, from a light drizzle to a steady downpour, soaking the road and forcing everyone inside, except for the man in the green robe. The rain didn't seem to bother him, which Cracked Tooth found interesting. He wondered if he might have died and no one knew it. The dobbin pulled out a monocle and placed it over his right eye to get a closer look. When the rain began to let up, the man's right hand rustled at his side and then fell off his stomach to hang motionless.

"That's a man who knows how to sleep."

The Captain's stomach growled, indicating the bread he had eaten had already been digested and was waiting for something new. "Not now!" he said, tightening his stomach muscles to make the complaining stop. But it growled louder and made his muscles quiver. "No, sah! I'm gonna keep these peepers glued to the dirt road. Food is not the priority here." Cracked Tooth continued to look up and down the road, seeing no man, woman or child coming out of the stores or homes within view. "Well, maybe just a bite," he said. He left the window and crept past the General's bed to reach his backsack on a table near a potbelly stove. The fire in it crackled, giving the room a toasty feel with the smell of smoky, pine wood. "Just like home," he said, lifting the sack to take it with him back to the window.

Activity along the road was still dead, but the man in the green robe had disappeared. "What in the blazes?" he asked, trying to locate where he'd gone. "The General's gonna kill me. Where are you, you bugger?" Cracked Tooth slipped his monocle back on and strained his eye at the chair the man was sitting in. Muddy footprints led away from the chair, up the stairs and across the front porch of the tavern, where they vanished inside. "Ah hah! Gone in for a drinky."

Cracked Tooth turned his attention from the window once more to his sack. He untied the leather strings and rummaged around inside with his paw. Something hard came into his grasp. "Thanks for packin' a roi, mum." He pulled out the red fruit and took a bite. As he did, the man in the green robe exited the tavern with two others in black ones. He tried to swallow but found himself choking on the juice.

"Fields—ber her, her, her—Generaaal!"

Fields was snoring heavier and did not hear Cracked Tooth's cry. The dobbin watched the three men as they passed objects in sealed envelopes back and forth before they crossed the road and came toward the inn. The front door below his window could be heard slamming open, and then shut.

"Fry a gizzard!" he exclaimed, bounding up and over his chair with the roi still clutched in his paw. "General! General Fields!" he hollered until Fields woke with a startle.

"What—what is it?" the General said, jumping up from the covers and clearing his throat. One of his legs became tangled in a blanket and wouldn't let go. He had to stop and rip it away as Cracked Tooth spit out his roi to speak.

"Two men in black robes are downstairs right now. Joined the one in the green. They exchanged some items before they came over."

"Good, Captain. Stay here. I'm going down there to see what they're up to."

"You're going to leave me here? Don't you need my help?"

"I want you to keep watching the road. These men might not be part of the Guild. Wearing a black robe doesn't make them guilty of crimes. I'm going to see if I can catch wind of their conversation."

The dobbin nodded. "I'll keep the door cracked open, just in case. Give a whistle if you need my help."

"I don't think it will come to that, Captain. My job is to keep civilians safe, including messengers."

"Yes, General. Leave the door open anyway. Need a bit of fresh air in here. Can still smell honey perfume from the last occupants of the room. She musta been caked in it."

Fields raised an eyebrow and watched the Captain sit himself back at the window before he left.

Cracked Tooth turned his attention back to the window, longing to have gone with him instead of being stuck in a chair on watch duty. The sun was radiating a red glow over the hills it was descending towards, drawing onlookers out from the buildings to enjoy its beauty. It wasn't long before the road was flooded with bodies again, people rushing in every direction to make up for lost time to fulfill their obligations for the day. Cracked Tooth became infatuated with a cart of sweet melons that pulled up in front of a general store. He licked his mouth and munched his roi until it was only a core. With a flick of his paw, he tossed it over his shoulder and into a garbage bucket without looking.

He tipped an ear toward the door as he kept his eyes peeled for something exciting to unfold outside his window. Cracked Tooth waited longer than most dobbins would have, doing everything he could to hold his position. But in the end, his bottled energy won. He stood and stretched his legs, took a few bounds to the door and extended an ear out into the hallway through the crack. He shut his eyes to listen to everything that it picked up, which was ten times as sensitive as any human ear. A man with a deep voice was talking in boisterous tone. Cracked Tooth slid his ear down the wall and to the floor to pick up the inflections better.

"I don't have any of that either," the man said, grunting at the end of his sentence. "Just ran out."

"You're lying, Peter," said a second voice, much harder to hear. Cracked Tooth filled in any missing words he couldn't understand for it to make sense.

"I don't do business with your kind," the innkeeper named Peter said.

"You fear us? You have only standings to gain if you assist. Those who do not will find themselves in . . . adverse situations."

"You will not come in here and tell me what to do in my own establishment!" Peter said, his pitch heightening. "I never liked you the moment you stepped foot in Yawrana. Far as I'm concerned, you can head back to that hole you crawled out of."

"Is there a problem here, Peter?" asked a third voice.

"Fields!" Cracked Tooth said, recognizing it as the General's.

"I don't need the army in here either," Peter said. "You'll scare away my customers if they think something's wrong." Cracked Tooth assumed Peter only said that to make himself look better to the dangerous Lazuls in the Guild.

"What is it you're looking for?" Fields asked. Cracked Tooth guessed the General had turned and talked to the stranger, whom he surmised to be a Lazul.

No one responded and then the front door to the inn slammed again.

"Get out!" Peter shouted. "This is not a meeting hall."

Cracked Tooth's eyes widened. He forced himself back up and raced to the window. Three more black robed figures were entering the building after who knows how many others just did. "The General! He's in trouble!"

The dobbin bounded out the door and down the hall. In three giant leaps he was at the top of the stairs. He stopped himself and listened to the much clearer conversation now taking place one floor below him.

"Back for more?" a scratchy voice said.

"Get out of here!" Peter yelled.

"Or what? You'll call the army?" said another new voice. You have the top man right here. Who else are you going to inform?"

"Identify yourselves," Fields said. The sound of a blade being drawn from its sheath put Cracked Tooth on edge.

"You've been a nuisance, General, and are getting involved in something you'll come to regret."

"Lower your hood, by the order of the King's army," Fields barked.

Cracked Tooth counted the sound of at least five more blades being drawn.

"Not in here!" Peter screamed. The sound of several doors on the first floor clicked shut and locked.

Cracked Tooth picked himself up off the floor when the sound of the first two blades clashed. He slid down the railing to the first floor to see the General being disarmed and his faced pushed into the floor. Six Lazuls had surrounded him and twisted his arm behind his back. "You are slow and overconfident, General," said the one holding his wrist.

Another put a sword to the innkeeper's throat and said, "Back away, Peter, if you know what's good for you."

Peter stiffened and did as the Lazul ordered, slipping down behind his counter and out of sight.

The General put his lips together to whistle but found a blade cutting into his throat. "What do you think? Should we cut his tongue or eyes out first?" the man with the sword asked the others.

Cracked Tooth couldn't wait any longer as he hid behind a banister post. The General would be dead in a few moments. A cartwheel across the floor and three bounds later, the Captain was kicking the Lazul restraining the General. Cracked Tooth's foot struck the enemy's face, knocking him backward. The other Lazul Guild members backed away as the hare spun upward with a leg out to create space. Fields jumped to his feet and picked up the sword that would have killed him. He thrust it into two of the enemy as they drew their weapons. The Lazul who had lost his sword threw a fist at Cracked Tooth, but missed. The Captain dropped backward onto his paws as the fist passed over him, then rebounded and shot out his two large feet onto the Lazul's shoulders. Their long ends closed and curled around the Lazul's neck, closing off his air passage. With all the strength in his arms, back and legs, Cracked Tooth rolled backward and took the Lazul with him, launching him into the air at the end of his maneuver. The Lazul went flying upside-down into the banister post Cracked Tooth had hid behind and smashed it.

Fields was fighting two other men at the same time while the last went after Cracked Tooth. The Lazul clipped one of the Captain's ears as the Captain threw himself out of the way of the blade's flurry of movements. The pain was tolerable as the wound bled. Cracked Tooth felt it as he backed his way up the stairs and over the body of the Lazul he had thrown. He stepped on the downed man's head when it started to rise, grinding the Lazul's face into the wooden stair. The man moaned.

Cracked Tooth tripped on a step, his back landing hard against four others on the staircase. The Lazul's sword came down at his face. The Captain ducked right and let the silver flash embed itself in the step where his head had been. By the time the Lazul loosened it, Cracked Tooth kicked out and connected with the man's chest. The Lazul flew backward and landed with a loud thud against the wall at the bottom of the stairs. Not giving him the chance to get back up, Cracked Tooth jumped from the step he was on and kicked out with both legs to send his opponent through the wall. The dobbin looked to his left and saw Fields diagonally slash a man across his stomach, spilling his insides onto the floor. The last Lazul changed his mind and ran from the building.

Fields waved to Cracked Tooth and shouted, "Come on."

The dobbin ran toward the door and stooped to pick up a sword along the way. A scream filled the town when a horse-drawn carriage swerved to miss the Lazul as he ran from the inn. The Lazul threw up his arms in fright and fell to the side, but it was too late. The right two wheels of the carriage cut across his back, crushing organs and bones. Fields watched the whole event up close. He turned his head and cringed when the second wheel hit and ended the Lazul's life. The General walked over to the dead man and flipped him over. Grabbing the edge of his enemy's hood, he pulled it away to see the face of anguish. Not knowing the Lazul youth, he quickly pulled the hood back up so others gathering around wouldn't see.

"Get back to your own business," the General said, a low rumbling in his voice.

One of the townsfolk said, "Good riddance. Damn Lazul."

"Bite your tongue, man," Fields snapped. "He didn't know what he was doing."

The man said over his shoulder, "Can't keep making excuses for 'em, General. It was wrong to bring them here."

"To save one life is a noble deed," Fields retorted.

The man continued on, waved it off and walked back into the tavern.

Fields spun and walked past Cracked Tooth, who went to the driver of the carriage. He and his passengers were standing near the back of the carriage in shock.

"It wasn't your fault, sah," Cracked Tooth said to the driver. "This man was fleeing from the army. Probably would have found his death another way if it weren't by this one. You're free to go."

The driver tipped his hat and asked his passengers, two men and one woman, to get back into their seats. They nodded and quickly shut the door. With a snap of the reigns the horses sped them from the scene.

Two soldiers from the army's local post came striding toward the dead Lazul. They exposed the man, as Fields had done, and then covered him with a blanket. One of the two turned and looked at Cracked Tooth to say, "Were you a witness to this man's death?"

Cracked Tooth nodded and saw Fields coming back out of the inn, dragging the only Lazul left alive by his boots. The messenger recognized it was the man he had thrown into the banister. The Lazul had his arms spread wide and was yelling curses at Fields. When the General reached the two soldiers, he let go of the Lazul and punched him in the gut to take his wind away.

"General Fields," said the two soldiers, saluting Fields with a fist to their chest.

Fields responded, "Names?"

"Lieutenant Laudner," the first soldier said.

"Allen, General," the other said with another salute.

Fields nodded and said, "Lock this man up. I'll be by shortly to question him."

"Yes, General." The two soldiers pulled the man to his feet by his arms and worked his wrists behind his back to bind them. Fields didn't budge until they had the Lazul under control and led him away.

"Not likely he's goin' to say anything to us, General," Cracked Tooth said.

"Exactly," Fields replied, "which is why our interrogation will be that much more efficient."

Confused, Cracked Tooth twitched his whiskers. "I don't quite follow—"

Fields had already walked away, heading back inside the inn. Cracked Tooth followed and looked back over his shoulder at the dead Lazul. The rocks lining the town's main road were brighter than ever after the rain, having been washed clean from the heavy downpour. The black blanket covering the body vividly stood out against the red landscape, drawing all eyes toward it, evil or good.

Peter was straightening the papers on his counter when the General stepped back inside. "Get your men to clean up this mess, General. My customers are scared to come out of their rooms with all these bodies lying about."

"They will be gone soon enough. What did they want?"

"Nothing. They stay here from time to time."

"You don't have to lie, Peter."

"Who said I was?"

Fields drew his sword and slapped the flat edge of the blade down on the counter. He slid the point in the direction of Peter. The innkeeper backed up several feet before his back was against the wall. Fields stopped his extension and said, "I no longer have time for games with the kingdom at stake. The next lie I hear will cost you your life. You will be burned as a traitor."

Peter swallowed and said, "Y-yes, General."

"Wise. Indulge me."

Peter couldn't talk faster to get the words out of him. "The Lazul who've been abandoning their foster homes have been renting out many of my rooms."

"How many others are there?"

"They come and go in groups. They don't like to stay in one place too long, for fear the army may find out where they're hiding."

"Any more checked in right now that I haven't killed?"

Peter shook his head. He slunk around the General's blade and reached down to pick something up. Fields raised the point back to Peter's throat. "Don't try anything that could cost you your life—"

"Just getting the room list," he said, putting it up on the counter. "You can take a look at it yourself. All the dead men here are accounted for. They've been staying up on the third floor—"

"One of them was asking you for something. What did he want?"

"They'll burn this building to the ground if they find out I have been telling you anything," Peter said, shaking his head.

"It'll only get worse if you don't tell me."

Peter paused and then finally caved. "It was a strange request. Didn't make any sense. Said he was looking for natron and any cooking oils I might have."

Fields lowered his blade.

"Tell you the truth, General, I don't even know what natron is."

"It's a mineral."

"A what?" Peter asked, dumbfounded. "That an army term?"

Fields shook his head. "Basically, it's salt, and can be found in dried up lakebeds."

"Well, there aren't any of those around here."

Fields nodded to agree. "But there are many to the east and south in Rock Rim and Emison Territories."

"So what would they want with those items?"

"Well, they're not making popcorn," Fields said, rubbing his chin. The General turned to Cracked Tooth and asked, "Do you have any money?"

"Look at him, will ya? Sitting there like a mushroom," Laudner said, hanging up the keys to the four cell chutes at the army's jail in Redstone.

"Maybe now they know what it feels like to be on the other side of those bars," Allen said with a laugh.

The Lazul said nothing in response and sat as cold as stone on the bed in his cell. He stared at the two soldiers without blinking, legs crossed and arms folded over each other.

"What do you suspect he's doing?" Allen asked.

Laudner took another glance and guessed, "Looks like some kind of meditation. Won't do him any good to try to concentrate in here, though.

Once old Longcoat wakes up, he'll start making a fuss there's a Lazul in the same room with him." Laudner and Allen turned their heads in the direction of the cell directly opposite of the Lazul's. A bundle of wrinkled brown material lay beneath the bed next to the wall.

"Why does he sleep like that? Looks uncomfortable," Allen said, tapping a dagger on the edge of a table.

Laudner lifted and placed his feet on the same table. He reached behind him and grabbed a jar of jerky and pulled out a long piece. When he saw Allen licking his lips, he coddled the jar in his right arm as if holding a newborn.

"When are you going to share some of that with me?"

The door to the room suddenly flew open. Allen and Laudner jumped from the noise. A tall figure in a black cloak entered the room.

"Lazul!" cried Laudner, dropping his jar of jerky. It smashed onto the floor as he drew his sword.

The Lazul in the cell broke out of his trance and stood up. He ran to the bars and chuckled, watching in delight.

Allen charged with his sword out in front of him. The hooded figure parried and pulled out a dagger, driving it into the back of Allen. The soldier buckled and fell. The figure caught Laudner's wrist and ran him through the stomach with the same dagger. The jerky Laudner had left in his mouth, spewed from it. With one quick punch, the Lazul flattened Laudner out across the table. The Lieutenant's arms fell limp at his sides. The Lazul flipped the table over, spinning Launder to the floor with it.

"Get me out of here before any more of them come," the Lazul in the cell yelled.

The hooded Lazul turned toward the cell, his face buried within the darkness of his robes. Taking a gloved hand, he reached through the bars and grasped the prisoner's shirt. The hooded figured yanked hard, slamming the confined Lazul's face against the cold metal of the chute's door.

'Ahhh! What are you doing?" he cried.

"Why have you allowed yourself to be caught, you fool?"

"Who are you, brother? I haven't—"

"Shut up! Do you not know your own king?"

The Lazul prisoner suddenly trembled in the hooded figure's hold. "L-Lord Herikech?"

The figure cackled and let go of the prisoner.

"B-but I thought—"

"What have you told them?" Herikech asked.

"N-nothing, my Lord," the Lazul said, bowing. "I obey the rules you have declared. Any Lazul imprisoned would take his own life before speaking."

Herikech nodded in approval. "But how do you know your friends didn't?"

"They're all dead—"

"Fool. You're too young to know a dead warrior when you see one."

"One of them lived? I thought they were all slain by the General—"

"General Fields is a better fighter than you give him credit for. You have failed to kill him and now he is gathering local enforcement to hunt the rest of us down. Do you know what this could do to my plans?"

The Lazul searched for an answer but couldn't find one. Instead, he said, "They have learned nothing, my Lord. They know nothing about the shipments."

Herikech hesitated and then snapped, "The location needs to be changed. Where are they being delivered now?"

"Where you specified, my Lord."

"Remind me!"

"The lone house at the top of Crest Ridge. The A-frame."

Herikech was silent for a moment. When the prisoner started to look nervous that he had done something wrong, Herikech asked, "When does the next shipment arrive?"

"At dusk, my Lord."

Herikech turned and walked toward the door.

"Wait! Are you not going to release me, my Lord? What about the new location? I have been loyal—"

Herikech turned and walked back toward the cell. He raised his gloved hand and curled it into a fist. A look of bewilderment fell upon the prisoner's face for a moment before Herikech's fist shot through the bars. The side of the prisoner's face was slammed by the blow, knocking him unconscious.

"Lazul!" cried a voice behind Herikech. Longcoat had awakened from his sleep, his eyes wild as they stared at Herikech. "They've come for me! They're goin' to kill me!" Longcoat screamed as Herikech walked from the room and shut the door behind him. "He's here! He's here!" Longcoat shouted over and over until his voice finally became hoarse.

Outside the jail, Herikech's form came to standstill. Cracked Tooth bounded toward him and asked, "Did he fall for it?"

With his right hand, Herikech pulled back his hood to reveal he wasn't Herikech at all. "Perfectly," Fields said with a grin. A few moments later,

Laudner and Allen exited the jail and joined them. Fields handed them each a green piece of parchment. "Congratulations, you both have received a raise. It was a performance that could have fooled a court jester."

"That's one heck of a right hook you have, General," Laudner said, rubbing his jaw.

"Sorry, had to make it look real," Fields said with a smile. "There's only one way to do that."

"Well, it worked," Laudner said, shaking his head and smiling.

Fields pulled the imitation dagger out of his cloak and pushed the palm of his hand against the tip. The blade disappeared inside the handle from the pressure he applied. "This collapsing blade was what really did the trick, though."

"I would like one myself," Allen said.

Fields tossed it to the soldier. "It's yours. The entertainment stores have licenses to carry them for the local actors. Don't let anyone see you walking around with that or you'll be in a cell next."

"Yes, General," Allen said, stashing it in his vest. The two soldiers thanked Fields for their raises and returned inside to revel in their accomplishment.

"So, General, what did the Lazul have to say?" Cracked Tooth asked, anxious to hear the results.

"Secret shipments are being delivered to an A-frame house at the top of Crest Ridge. We'll need to put the house under surveillance and confiscate all packages when they arrive. Being the messenger that you are, I assume that I don't need to ask you how to get there."

Cracked Tooth looked as if someone had sucked the joy out of his improved mood. He had to sit down on a bench to take a deep breath.

"What is it, Captain?" Fields asked, shedding the cloak and gloves he had worn for his disguise.

"General, are you sure that was the location he said?"

"Positive," Fields replied. "Why?"

Cracked Tooth's nose turned pink, which meant the dobbin was either embarrassed or sick. The General was unsure of which it was until the Captain's eyes watered and he said, "That building is the head office for the Trail Racers."

"My butt's itchin'," Cracked Tooth complained, scratching the irritated area through his thick, red jumper suit. "The bark on this spruce is not the best cushion."

"Keep your voice down," Fields whispered. "We don't have any other choice. They could approach the building from any direction."

"Where are your men? I can't see any of them."

"Just down the hill in that ravine," Fields said, pointing at a thin, dark crevice a hundred yards away.

Cracked Tooth shook his head. "They may not get up here in time if we get in a rough spot."

"There is no 'we', Captain, remember? You are only to identify members of your outfit after we have secured the building. When you hear the whistle of my mase—"

"Yes, I remember. You don't have to explain everything again."

A light turned on at the back porch. "That must be the signal," Fields said, pulling out his eyeglass enhancer. He placed the device to his eye and peered through to get a close-up view of the house. Turning it to his right, he found the back porch. Three figures cloaked in black were abandoning the cover of the woods and walking toward the steps, each with a package under an arm. A fourth figure opened the rear door to greet them. Out of precaution, the individual looked around before hurrying them inside, as if the Lazul sensed something was not right. One of the Lazuls appeared in the only open window on the first floor and shut the shade. The silhouettes of all four Lazuls appeared on the shade briefly as they crossed the room.

"Time to make a special delivery," Fields said, letting himself down off the branch he was perched on. It cracked before he straightened his fingers to let his body drop to the ground. He landed behind a bush and stayed put to make sure no one in the house had heard him. When no silhouettes appeared at the window, he crawled into the yard and hid behind a large milk can. He stayed still until he talked himself into dashing across the rest of the yard. When he was nearly at the window, a silhouette appeared in its rectangular form. Fields ducked and rolled, his body coming to a stop as it met the stone foundation. Pain shot through his knee when it cracked against a sharp rock. Grinding his teeth helped force it from his mind.

Cracked Tooth watched from the tree and held his breath. The figure in the house lifted the shade and took a glance out. Satisfied there was nothing interesting to see, the Lazul closed it and left the window.

Pulling his eyeglass enhancer back out, Fields scanned the trees with it and saw Cracked Tooth's eyes between two boughs. The dobbin's paw appeared and was motioning to him that the silhouette had moved. Fields let out a sigh of relief and relaxed his hurt leg. The pain subsided when he rubbed it out. The General stood and went to stand next to the front porch.

With a finger in the air, he waved it in a circle.

Twenty men from the local army post bolted from the ravine and crept to the closest trees around the house, surrounding it. Cracked Tooth watched a man take position next to the tree below him. The soldier looked up at the dobbin and smiled. Cracked Tooth saluted him and shook his head when the soldier turned away. "Don't know what he's so happy about," he mumbled.

As soon as his men were where they needed to be, Fields stepped up onto the porch and went to the front door. He raised his fist, paused and then banged on the door. The mumble of voices from within silenced. The light coming through the shade of the porch's window went out. Fields stepped to the front door's side and put his back against the wall. He drew his sword and raised his elbow up high enough where he could chop off a head if he had to. He could hear the door handle turn, but couldn't see anything from where he was standing.

A foot finally came into view, causing the porch board beneath it to creak. Fields heard what sounded like knuckles cracking. He swung his sword out just in time to catch the blade of a Lazul trying to strike him.

The sound echoed into the woods, sending the army into action. The men ran toward the house as the three other cloaked Lazul figures sprinted out the back door. Seven soldiers closed in and tackled them. One of the Lazuls got to his feet and kicked out to give him enough of a chance to run. Two soldiers chased the Lazul into the shelter of the trees. The other two detained Lazuls went unconscious when Lieutenant Laudner pulled out a pouch and poured sleeping powder into their mouths.

Fields forced the Lazul back inside, realizing he was fighting a woman. His swings kept her at a disadvantage. She deflected them with all the strength she had, which was barely enough to keep her alive. She tried kicking the door shut on him, but he wedged a foot inside to prevent it from closing. It bounced back open, allowing the General entrance. The woman turned and ran into an end table, knocking over a lantern sitting on it. The table crashed and broke apart. She came up from the awkward landing clutching her side and put her sword up to bat away another of Fields's swings.

"Drop your weapon," Fields commanded.

She hissed and backed into Laudner, who had come in through the back door. He grabbed her wrist and twisted it until she cried and let go of her sword.

Fields picked up the blade and asked, "Where are the packages?"

The woman kneed the lieutenant in the groin and punched him in the neck with her free hand. He collapsed in pain but was able to turn over and watch her get run through with a sword by a Yawranan soldier.

"No!" Fields screamed. "I wanted answers."

The soldier who had killed her, pulled his blade out of her torso and apologized.

Laudner raised his hand and pointed to a shelf built into a wall behind Fields. Pulling himself together, the Lieutenant got up and inhaled deeply. The remaining soldiers went upstairs to search the rest of the house for other fugitives. Cracked Tooth came in through the front door and saw everything was under control.

The General went to the packages sitting in a row on the lowest shelf. He sheathed his sword and tore at the red paper wrapping marked with the Trail Racers' symbol.

"That would be considered a violation of law. Only the recipient—" Cracked Tooth started until Fields gave him an impatient look. "Sorry, General. Go ahead."

The rest of the paper fell away to show a white box underneath. Using his index finger, Fields forced the lid away from the side of the box. It popped open once he managed to get it all the way in to break the wax seal. A pile of straw lined the top. Putting his hand inside, he flung it out until the tops of six corked bottles appeared.

"What is it, General?" Laudner asked.

Fields lifted one out and asked for a torch to be lit. The soldier who killed the female Lazul went to work immediately on the task. Once it was lit, the soldier handed it to Fields. The General saw the label had a name on it. "Baron Oreus Blake?" he said, his voice hardly able to say it.

"Did you say Baron Blake?" Laudner asked.

Fields nodded and pulled out a third. "Baron Edin Dehue." He read the names of four others, which included Baron Windal Barrow, General Irvin Yeats, Baron Jada Annalee and his own. "Why is my name on one of these?" Fields asked when he pulled out another. "What the hell is going on around here?" He used his teeth to pull the cork out of the bottle with his own name on it and smelled the contents. "Honey? It's just honey. What significance could it have?" The General went to the other two boxes and found the same in each of them, with most of the names of high-ranking officers in the army labeled on the glass. The only two missing were General Rydor Regoria and Baron Viktoran Ilos, from what he could remember.

"Probably not just honey," Cracked Tooth said. "Not if a Lazul had it. Must be something mixed in with it. You should have the makers take a look at its ingredients."

Fields agreed. "It's time we return to the castle. Bring these two prisoners and the one at the jail. They have some explaining to do."

"Yes, General," Laudner said.

Footsteps came down the stairs from the second floor of the house. Fields and Cracked Tooth looked up at the soldiers descending the stairs. "General," one of the men said, "our worst fears are realized."

"Oh, please don't tell me—" Cracked Tooth said, his voice breaking off.

"It's not what you think, Captain," the soldier said.

"It's not?" Cracked Tooth said. "You mean none of them are dead?"

"No. It's worse."

"What is worse than death?" he asked.

"There are letters—many with the signatures of your fellow runners on them. They are assisting the enemy. They have become traitors—"

"They must've been forced into it. Blades were pressed against their backs. Their families had to have been threatened," Cracked Tooth sputtered. "I know these hares! General Keys would not have let his messengers—"

The soldier shook his head and frowned. "I'm sorry, Captain. This one," he said, holding a yellow parchment up, "states, 'my faithful ones will rejoice the day King Deardrop's head is on a platter.' It is stamped with a delivery time of seven yesterday morning and was signed by General Keys himself, who is freely walking about Candlewick Castle at this very moment."

# CHAPTER THIRTEEN
## Martell's Anointment

"Are you sure you want to go through with this, Martell?" Pelly asked. "We really shouldn't even be here right now. The King would have a fit—"

"The King is the one who offered to let me do this in the first place. The only reason why I'm agreeing to it is because I'm bored to death. Cobwebs are growing beneath my armpits."

Pelly laughed and straightened the collar on the Nax's white bathrobe as they waited. A ray of sunlight was shining through one of the vision pool chamber's small, octagonal windows. It moved slowly across the floor and into the crystal clear waterfall at the center of the room. A guard near a door rang a bell, setting others into a sequence throughout the building.

Martell pressed his hands over his ears. "Do they really have to do that? I'll go deaf!"

"Yes," Pelly said, laughing. "It's part of the ritual. The sound stimulates those to be anointed so their energy level is at its highest when they are in the water."

"They could have fed us. That would have helped." The ringing stopped, but he continued yelling unitl everyone in the room looked at him with a curious expression. "Stop staring!" he said to make them avert their eyes. Most did, with the exception of a blonde girl with brilliant green eyes. The girl smiled at him and then turned her attention toward the guard at the back door. Martell felt a smile form on his mouth for her. He then turned and watched the guard pull open the door to let an old, distinguished gentleman into the room. His long, flowing white beard, thin-rimmed spectacles and indigo band on his right bicep gave him the distinction of one who was respected in the kingdom.

"Who is that?"

"An Elder, Martell. The prophet who is to anoint you," Pelly said.

"Him? He looks like he can hardly stand up. How can he even see where he's going?"

"It's true the Elders are very old, but they are as healthy as you and me . . . and can hear every word you're saying."

The Elder looked in the direction of Martell and furrowed his brow.

Martell hid his face behind his hand. "Why didn't you tell me that to begin with?" he whispered. "Is he still looking at me?"

"No," she said. "He's about to make his announcement. You can uncover your face now."

When Martell looked up, the guard allowed a servant to enter the room. The middle-aged woman carried a silver tray before her and stood by the pool's steps. On it Martell could see a wide range of colored bands.

"Are those what they tie on our arms?" he asked.

Pelly nodded and put an index finger to her lips.

"Welcome, everyone, to the Vision Pools," the Elder said in a chipper voice. "I am Elder Dillon PaCant of the Royal Sequera House. Thank you, all of you, for being here on time. I see many promising young faces before me, which gives me great hope for our future. All parents must remain seated along the walls during each anointment until everyone's calling has been announced. The four to be anointed today, please step forward."

Martell looked at Pelly as if he were having second thoughts. "You know, maybe this wasn't a good idea—"

Pelly pushed Martell toward the Elder. He almost fell into the pool but caught himself on the top step. He grumbled, made his way over to Elder PaCant and stood next to the three children, who were ready to take their first steps into the real world. The children placed their hands upon the Elder. Martell did the same, resting his fingers on the Elder's left arm.

PaCant stated, "Do you swear by the laws declared by the Kings of Yawrana that you accept the station you are about to receive in good manner and will devote yourself willingly to for the rest of your lives?"

"I promise," replied each of the five, Martell muttering last.

"May Yawrana the Holy be with you," Pa Cant said. "Please be seated with your families. When I call your name, enter the pool and turn your back into the waterfall. Once I proclaim your station, the House servant will tie the color of your band to your arm. You must wear it wherever you go to signify your rank in Yawrana. When you leave, High Elder Ironwood will inform you of your future permanent residence, unless you are of the white band. A celebration will be held for all anointees in the Eastern Yard after the ceremony, if you wish to attend. Best fortunes be with you, and serve Yawrana well."

Martell shuffled back over to Pelly and sat down. "This is insufferable. He will probably try to drown me after what he heard me say."

"The Elders are not vindictive. You have nothing to worry about," Pelly said, trying to keep him calm.

"Tonjia May, please come forward," the Elder announced once he was waist deep in the pool.

The blonde girl that had smiled at him walked to the pool's steps and looked at Martell before she went in. The water came up to her chest. She turned around and let the water cascade down her back to soak the rest of her gown. She shivered, feeling its coolness along her spine.

"They could warm it," Martell grumbled. "She's going to get sick."

"Please remain silent during the anointments," the guard at the door said, speaking loud enough for everyone to hear, even though his words were meant for Martell alone.

Martell crossed his arms and stared at the Elder to get on with it.

"We are blessed!" the Elder said gleefully. "Indigo band!"

Everyone in the room stood and applauded, except for Martell. Pelly was louder than anyone else, impressed with the young lady who would become one of the most revered women in the kingdom before the start of autumn. PaCant hugged Tonjia as her parents came running over to embrace her. They didn't care she was drenched and had a hard time letting her go. PaCant patiently waited and smiled, knowing this was a rare occasion. It wasn't every day a Yawranan was anointed to be an Elder. Prophets were few and far between. Tonjia had the gift of sight, a rare treasure, whether or not she knew it yet.

Pelly suddenly stopped clapping and looked at Martell. "I was actually expecting you would become an Elder."

"She can have it," he said. "Why would I want to be imprisoned within a tree for the bulk of fifteen lifetimes?"

Martell found Tonjia staring at him. She had been standing in front of him during his rambling. "Why do you feel this way?" she asked.

"What?" Martell replied, acting as if he didn't hear her.

"Why do you feel conflict for something you have had no experience with?"

"Oh, ummm. I don't feel conflict, my dear. It's just my observation," he said, backpedaling.

Pelly watched Martell squirm, covering her smile with her hand and looking away and back several times.

"Your judgment is shallow, yet you still manage to drown yourself in your own bathwater."

Pelly burst into laughter. Martell shot her a frown and said, "What are you laughing at? The girl is confused."

"I am not!" Tonjia said, raising her voice so all in the room were looking in their direction.

"You're disrupting the others," Martell said, dropping his voice back to a whisper. "Lower your voice, girl."

"I owe you no such favor," she said. "I can see there is much to be resolved within you and it does you no good to talk about others behind their backs the way you have been. We," she said, waving at the others in the room, "on the other hand, would be thankful if Elder PaCant called your station so you could go back to bothering someone else after you leave. Perhaps then we will get some peace. I expected better of a Nax." Her parents only nodded, finding no reason to disagree with her now that she was going to be considered one of the wisest people in all of Yawrana. She walked off with her head held high and sat down to wait for the outcome of the next candidate's future.

Martell was shaking his head. "That's the problem with Yawranans. You all believe I'm the second coming of Mosia. I would gladly wish him to rise from his catacomb so you all would quit thinking I am going to solve your problems."

"I think they've already moved past that, Martell," Pelly said, seeing the others in the room looking at him with the loathing of killing an insect they had just discovered was crawling in their beds.

Elder PaCant looked toward the guard at the door and nodded. The guard skipped a name on his scroll and announced, "Martell Fedrow!" Martell saw the exchange and rolled his eyes, feeling flustered he was now the center of attention.

"Think positive," Pelly said as Martell rose.

"This doesn't require any thinking at all," he replied, shedding his robe. The cool water didn't affect him as it did to Tonjia. The thick white fur covering his body kept him warmer. His wings fluttered behind him when they became soaked by the waterfall. They stretched stiffly and he held them upward until PaCant finished his reading, parting the waterfall away from his head. The Elder took Martell's hands and held them tightly while studying the ripples around the Nax's body.

"How long can this take?" Martell asked.

"Your impatience will not make it go any quicker," PaCant said while he kept his eyes focused on the colors swirling in the water around Martell, playing off his energy for the Elder to choose one.

Martell's fur was cleaner than most humans' skin, showing its brightness clearly through the bubbles produced by the waterfall. He looked at Pelly. She sat with a smile on her face. He didn't understand what she had to be so smug about.

"You are complex, Martell," PaCant said. "It's as if the colors cannot decide on which band you should belong to. I continually see a rainbow surrounding you. The water has never reacted this way before at any anointment, not even at former High Elder Mosia's."

"Complex. Yes, that's the label my race has decided to brand me with," Martell growled.

"I don't have the same ill feelings toward albinos as your people do, Martell. This could be a sign of hope for Yawrana." PaCant stared a while longer.

"Has a color come forth?" Martell finally asked, losing his faith in the process.

"No. The rainbow has only increased in its solidity. This is your fate. You do not represent only one band of Yawrana. You are a symbol for all."

"What does that mean?" Martell asked, becoming grouchy. "Which one do I wear? I can't just be running around with seven bands on my arm."

Pelly and the others couldn't hear the conversation between Martell and the Elder due to the waterfall, but they leaned in anyway, trying to pick up on any bit they could.

"No, that would be too much of a burden," the Elder said. "We'll have to create an entirely new band containing the whole range, fine strips sewn together to display your importance to the territories."

PaCant left the water and announced to everyone, "The rainbow!"

Everyone gasped. Pelly applauded and shot to her feet to help Martell. He stood on the top step, his feet still submerged in the water. She handed him a towel and his robe so he could dry himself. "Well done, Martell," she said excitedly.

"For what? I didn't do anything. I just stood there with my mouth open."

"What does it portend, Elder?" Tonjia asked.

"A difficult question to answer, my pupil. Never before has an entire rainbow presented itself to an anointee. This is a historic occasion the kingdom must not take lightly. Since Martell represents all bands, it is only fitting he be a counsel to the King in all matters. He is now a member of the Royal Court. His rank will be higher than that of any baron or general, having only to heed to the instructions of His Majesty." The Elder bowed to Martell. Tonjia did the same, despite her previous words, respecting Elder PaCant's wisdom. Soon, every person in the chamber was bowing to Martell, including Pelly.

"Please! Please! You don't need to bow to me," Martell said. "I—"

Martell trailed off as a ripple that swirled in the water at his feet suddenly stole his attention.

Elder PaCant crouched near the pool, looked at the area Martell was examining and saw nothing. Pelly started to say something but PaCant silenced her by putting up his hand. She abruptly stopped and saw Martell was engrossed in other matters.

PaCant waited until Martell's gaze was broken from the pool before he addressed him. "Martell?"

But the Nax was deep in thought about what he had just witnessed. He stood like a stone that wasn't going to be shifted.

"Martell?" PaCant tried again.

"Martell," Pelly said, taking her turn.

"The King is in danger!" he shouted, running out of the pool. The Nax snatched his robe from Pelly and dashed from the chamber, yelling, "Come, Pelly! We must hurry!" PaCant and the others were too stunned to say anything about the dramatic reaction.

Blaynor was at full strength when he returned to the maker's wing. "My Lord, I understand there is much to worry about, but you rest little as it is and now is not the time to deny yourself it."

"My friend, I almost feel like my old self again," he said, walking easily about the room. "It's incredible. Whatever the maker has done for me is unexplainable. Master Hurran will be promoted to my new personal maker."

Bruneau asked, "Will you be attending the services for Master Oyen's departure this evening?"

Noran paused to consider that he shouldn't be so excited about replacing the deceased maker. "Yes. His accomplishments will not be forgotten. He was gifted and won't be overlooked, regardless of the misfortunes beating down our door. His family will be cared for as long as they need our guidance."

A knock came at the door. Bruneau pointed for the King to take a seat in a chair in case it was Master Hurran checking up on him, whispering his name. The maker would be outraged to find the King pushing his limits by strutting around the wing so soon after the attacks. When Noran was ready, Bruneau said, "Come!"

"Your Majesty," a House servant said, entering as if gliding on wings with her white flowing gown, "there is an urgent message that just arrived from Martell Fedrow."

"Martell?" he said, standing up. Bruneau waved at Noran to take a seat.

Noran did after the guard reminded him.

"Yes, Your Majesty, I informed him Master Hurran is not allowing you any visitors during this time. But he is very adamant about telling you his message himself."

"Send him in," Noran said.

"But, Your Majesty, the Master will not approve," she replied with prudence in her tone.

Noran knew the Master had grown angry with him for letting Jada and the Chief in earlier and demanded he not see anyone else until his recovery was full. Even though Noran was royalty, the maker had an undeniable knack for making him feel guilty enough to listen to sound advice. But this time it wasn't Noran who wasn't listening. Martell brushed by the servant girl and walked toward the King, his bathrobe clinging to his damp body.

The servant began scolding him, shaking her finger at him. "I told you to wait outside. You can't come in here without permission—" Pelly also walked by her, and cut her off in mid-sentence by shutting the door in her face.

"Master Hurran will not approve of this intrusion," she said as she reopened it before Pelly could lock it. The servant then shook her head and shut it.

Noran started, "Martell, you need to—"

"You are in danger, Your Majesty! The castle is no longer your haven!" Martell interrupted.

Bruneau and Blaynor ran to the King's side, ready to pick the chair up he sat in to carry him to safety.

"From whom? Herikech or the mangler?" he asked.

"Neither, Your Majesty. Ballan."

Noran, Bruneau and Blaynor all said in surprised unison, "Ballan?"

Martell caught his breath and nodded. "I had a vision that he is to betray you."

"Where? When?" Noran asked sitting upright in his chair.

"The Vision Pools, not long ago."

"What were you doing outside of the castle? I strictly ordered—"

"I was there for my anointment."

Noran sat back, astonished the Nax had changed his mind. "I thought you were firmly against it."

"I decided to make the right choice, as Nax often do." Martell grimaced and quickly explained himself. "While I was in the water, I saw him leading you into a trap. You were surrounded by many of your own men who now serve the Lazuls."

"What did he say?"

"There were no voices and I'm not talented enough to read lips. But the court announcer raised a sword to your chest and plunged it into your heart."

"We must have him arrested," Blaynor said, striding toward the door.

"Wait, Blaynor!" Noran ordered. The King turned his attention back to Martell when the guard halted and smiled at Martell. "You have the gift of sight. You were anointed an Elder like Mosia—"

Martell shook his head. "No, Your Majesty. I will not be an Elder."

Noran's shoulders and mouth sagged.

Martell struggled to explain the rest, looking to Pelly for help.

She smiled and said, "Your Majesty, Elder PaCant envisioned every band surrounding Martell. He is now your right hand counsel and only answers to you."

Noran looked at Bruneau. "Every band? That is unprecedented." The guard didn't understand either, his jaw hanging open like a buffoon.

"Yes, what she said," Martell said. "I'm just as baffled as you are, Your Majesty. I think the Elder needs some new spectacles."

"No," Noran replied. "The Elder is correct. This should be no surprise to any of us considering the prophecy of your people, Martell. You, most of all, should see the truth in it. You are not only everything to us, but to the world as well—every band, every tree, every creature and flower. If Herikech discovers this, he will either kill you or force you to serve him." Noran turned to Blaynor and said, "Have a servant send word to the Vision Pools and inform the Elder of my orders. Anyone who was present in the room at the time of Martell's anointment must be restricted from speaking about it. He will only be a guest in the kingdom's eyes . . . for now."

Blaynor nodded and left, returning only moments later.

Martell frowned, knowing the King was right. He flew up to Noran's bed table and sat on the edge. "This is crazy! How can I alone be responsible for saving the world? Why is it me?"

"You are not alone, Martell. We will make this journey with you and see it through to its end. I will not allow harm to come to you. Yawrana the Maker has bound our fates together." Noran thought about what he just said and then turned to Bruneau and asked, "Where is Viktoran? Shouldn't he have returned from his investigation by now?"

Blaynor left the room again, needing no further verbal nudges to send another servant along to relay the message.

"You can't leave this wing, Your Majesty," Martell said.

"We can just have Ballan arrested and be done with it," Bruneau said.

"No. That will not be enough." Noran ran his fingers through his hair to help him think. "We will need to catch everyone who is working with him as well. Were you able to see any of their faces?" he asked Martell.

"There were so many that my attention would not drift from Ballan."

"Ballan's betrayal does hurt me," Noran said. "He has been loyal for so many years to the Court that it's hard to think that he would've chosen this path."

"Kuall was loyal, too," Blaynor said. "Look what he did."

"But Kuall wasn't as close to my father and me as Ballan has been. He is involved in everything the Court says and does."

Blaynor leaned against the closed door and rubbed his forehead. The guard let out a sigh of disbelief. "Which means he's been telling Herikech all our strategies. It's no wonder he has so easily avoided us, or led us into traps. And with his help and many of our own soldiers, Herikech can slip in and out of corridors with no one confessing he was there."

"But how is he converting my people?" Noran suddenly yelled in anger. It was rare when Noran lost his composure to the point where it made him feel ashamed. "I don't even know if my family is safe. I can't allow anyone near them for fear of Herikech holding them hostage. And Willow and Ola have had their fair share of that already."

"Martell, the Elders recount details in their visions to help them prepare for what is to come. Did your vision give any indication where the King was to be slain?" Blaynor asked. "Er—sorry, Your Majesty."

Noran didn't say anything, waiting for Martell's reply.

Martell fell quiet as he tried to recall the scene. His eyes squinted as if he were looking at it on floor of the room. Pelly couldn't help but glance down to see if there was anything forming on the stone surface. Only a spider scurried from a crack where two fitted together. "I've seen many halls like it in the castle," Martell admitted. "But I'm convinced it is the one in front of your new bedchamber. As Blaynor has stated, details are important and there is one that was so obvious that I overlooked it."

"General Regoria," Blaynor said, standing straight. "He's down there right now. He could be in trouble." The guard left the room for the third time.

Noran's face wrinkled with doubt. "You don't even have access to the Secret Halls. How do you know that's where it will happen?"

"Does your sleeping attire have green buttons down the front of a gown with a silk rope of gold at the waist that closely resembles your Banquet Hall garments?"

The King tensed up, turned to Bruneau and said, "Fetch my night robe."

Tears were few for Master Oyen outside of the King's company, a tragedy in itself for a man who had given so much to receive so little in return. Noran's eyes counted each soldier near Ballan that was without emotion, seventeen in all. He found it insulting the soldiers and guards that stood callous and cold near the court announcer would not instead stand by their king. Noran's mind went over each of Ballan's reactions to the recent events since his downfall. They were small but noticeable changes in his demeanor that were only distinguishable if one had known the old Ballan for as long as Noran did. And even he didn't pick up on them with everything else that had been happening.

Martell also took notice of the increased men around Ballan. He whispered, "Look how bold he is. He flaunts his growing power in your presence, Your Majesty. Those men flocked to him just before the ceremony began."

"Resources can be found in many places, Martell. Men alone will not win this war."

"But they are a big part of it. If we have no one to support us, it makes our chances bleak."

"You have already reversed my fortune with your vision," Noran replied, smiling at Martell. "If you had not chosen to be accountable and complete your anointment, I would have been dead before dawn. And that is only one of the advantages I'm referring to."

"It was only because I was bored that I went in the first place."

"The reason why you went does not matter, but the fact that you accepted your destiny does. Inspiration doesn't have to be derived from courage or faith for it to be influential. In the quiet times, when we are alone, is when we find our worth. If you discard blame and failure, the answer will be there for you to find."

Martell chuckled. "That's a speech I shall not forget."

"Good. Then I'm glad it didn't sound too contrived." Noran smiled again as High Elder Elenoi finished the service with one of her own songs. The words touched Oyen's family deeply, helping bring them one step nearer to closure. Oyen's wife also sang a song and said a long farewell to her husband for their children, who were still not familiar with the concept of death.

When the last candle was blown out in Candlewick's wake chamber, everyone went out into the gardens to enjoy the fresh air. New flowers were planted in one area of the garden to replace those that the storms had washed away. It was one of the many gestures to bring life where it would otherwise be barren. It was a tribute fitting to the deceased maker's outlook on life.

Ballan had not said a word to Noran until this evening. Bruneau and Blaynor both commented how it was not like the announcer to shy away from any member of the Court, especially the King, when they were at hand. Noran normally had trouble evading Ballan when he had no patience or use for his endless advice. He only merited Ballan's attention when he was ready to leave the gardens to return to the maker's wing.

"You are looking splendid tonight, Your Majesty."

"Thank you, Ballan," Noran replied, sensing the hatred in Bruneau and Blaynor for the announcer's charade.

"The missing block behind the vase in your bedchamber has been replaced and sealed shut. The room has been closed off. When you are ready to retire for the evening, I would like to escort you to your new room and talk of the future."

"Very well. Where is General Regoria? I would like to speak to him about his findings."

Ballan cleared his throat and said, "Ummm . . . the General . . . yes. I'm sure he's completing his report at this moment. He must be tired after his search. I will talk to him first thing in the morning and—"

"It's not like him to withhold information when it is important to the kingdom's security. Sleep is a luxury for the General when others are in need." Noran watched Ballan's eyes shift to the floor as the announcer stumbled over his next answer.

"Well, ummm . . . yes, of course, Your Majesty. I'll have one of the men look into it immediately." Ballan thrummed his fingers against his hooked, wooden cane for a moment before he waved to a soldier and gave him the order. The man walked away at a leisurely pace, glancing over his shoulder every few feet as if he were interested in their conversation. Ballan continued, "Would you like to go to your new bedchamber?"

"Master Hurran has not yet cleared me to leave the medical wing," Noran said, testing his old friend.

"Let me take care of it, my Lord. It is a longer walk to the maker's wing than your new bed. I will have a few soldiers escort you there."

"Why don't you take me and send one of the soldiers to tell Hurran? We haven't talked for some time. I want you to give me the full details of what has been troubling you lately." Noran started strolling from the room.

Ballan smiled and stepped in front of the King to take the lead. "A pleasure for me, Your Majesty." Another soldier came walking over to them when Ballan waved his hand again. But this soldier didn't seem to be interested in their conversation when he left them.

"Where have you been hiding these days?" Noran asked, inhaling the strong scent of honey that wafted from Ballan's robes.

Martell found himself gagging behind the King, hardly able to stand the overpowering odor.

Bruneau saw the Nax was not feeling well and offered him a piece of mint from a pouch at his side. "Here." Martell gladly took it and ground it between his molars to make the nausea go away. His face looked better after just a few yards of walking.

"Hiding, Your Majesty?" Ballan asked, stroking his beard. "Only the Lazuls do that."

Noran laughed, mockingly. "Very true. Very true. Then what has been occupying your time that you haven't been able to visit your king while he was ill?"

"I thought no one was allowed to see you until your recovery," Ballan quickly said, as if that were the answer Noran was looking for

"You have always tended to me when I have been sick. I was disappointed that you didn't take time from your House duties to at least see how my health was." They left the main floor of the castle and descended through a private door that led down to the lower halls of the castle.

Ballan was quiet until they reached them. "I will make up for my absence tonight, if you want. Once we get to your bedchamber we can plan a few activities together."

"What do you have in mind?" Noran asked.

"Let me make it a surprise for you, Your Majesty. Not knowing is half the excitement." Ballan smirked and distanced himself a few feet in front of the King. Noran shot a look of warning toward Bruneau, who nodded, satisfied with Ballan's dubious behavior. The guard pulled out a dog whistle and blew into it. They walked for a while longer, deeper into the castle's narrowing and isolated innards. When they entered a corridor that ended at a door, Ballan stepped aside.

Bruneau, Blaynor and Martell also stopped several feet shy of the King's door. They heard the sound of dozens of footsteps before Noran could say another word.

"I think I shall save you the trouble, Deardrop," Ballan said, grinning wickedly.

Noran looked confused and asked, "Clarify your statement, Ballan. Your tone does not sit well with me."

Every single one of the men that Noran had counted in Ballan's presence at Oyen's funeral entered the corridor, including the two Ballan had sent away on errands. Their bodies crowded the small passage to the point there was no chance for escape. Bruneau and Blaynor drew their swords while Martell ducked behind them.

"You are no longer the master of this castle," Ballan declared. "It is time you witness the power a true king should have."

Blaynor turned to test the door handle of the new bedchamber, but he found it wouldn't turn. "He's locked it. As you expected, he's tricked us, Your Majesty. They've joined Herikech. Get behind us. We will protect you, my Lord."

Ballan cackled. "Four of you will not defeat seventeen well-trained soldiers. Drop your weapons and get on your knees." Ballan took a sword from a soldier next to him and held it up, pointing it in the direction of Noran's chest.

Noran started to laugh, drawing a look of ire from Ballan.

"What is so amusing?" Ballan sneered.

"I never thought I would see the day when one of my most trusted servants would turn on me. I don't know what Herikech has offered you—"

Ballan spat, "It no longer matters. You'll learn soon enough what you're up against. Get on your knees and worship me!"

"Where are Baron Ilos and General Regoria?" Noran demanded.

"In safe-keeping, just as you will be."

"Where are they?" Noran screamed. "Tell your king or face death!"

Now it was Ballan who found Noran's reaction amusing. He cackled again, saying, "Arrest them!"

The soldiers advanced toward the King, but then suddenly stopped.

"Something the matter, old friend?" Noran asked with a smile on his face.

Forms began to solidify out of thin air around Noran and his small band, increasing their number from four to fifteen. "I hope you don't mind," Noran said, "but I thought I would invite the watchers to be witness to your words."

Kap-al-Crey, the leader of Candlewick's invisible forces, warbled an eerie cry, sending a shudder through Ballan and the soldiers serving him.

Noran smiled in his moment of triumph. The watchers occasionally wandered the castle's grounds on their own free will, and were one arm of the King's defenses that had escaped Herikech's attention. They rarely made themselves visible, preferring to keep to isolation in exchange for valuable food that was not in great quantities in their homeland of Rock Rim Territory. They were difficult to contact at times, but Noran relied once again upon the Majestic Messengers to deliver his plea for their help. He never expected himself to feel reliant upon anyone's army but his own, until now. His father, Doran, had once told him not to become accustomed to using the watchers. They were wanderers of the wild and never liked to sit in one place for too long.

Ballan fled through the soldiers and shouted, "You will all die!"

Noran fell to the back, near the door, and attempted to break it down. He thrust his shoulder into the wood, but it wouldn't budge.

The two groups clashed in the small corridor, the watchers immediately gaining the upper advantage with the first strike when their front line disappeared. The soldiers found themselves swinging at thin air and were surrounded before one got a lucky hit and wounded a watcher.

Noran continued to pound his shoulder into the door, feeling the lock beginning to give way. Martell helped him, throwing his small frame into the wood as well.

Another wave of soldiers fell, reducing their number to half of its original size. The watchers bludgeoned each of their opponents until they no longer moved. The bodies were thrown aside to make room for the watchers in the rear ranks to advance.

The door finally flew open to let Noran inside. The King ran to a chest at the end of the bed and lifted the lid. He pulled out his night robe and laid it on the bed. When he unfolded the material, Arc Glimmer's exquisite beauty glistened before him. He unsheathed the sword and ran into the corridor with Martell trailing behind. He raised his sword and yelled a battle cry, but then was forced to stop.

"Sorry, Your Majesty," Blaynor said with a guilty smile.

"You didn't leave me one to fight?"

All of the soldiers were laid out in piles lining the corridor, not a single man left alive.

"There's still one," Bruneau said, listening to the tapping of a wooden cane against floor stones echoing away in the distance.

The Grand Hall was unnervingly quiet as General Fields crossed its length to approach Baron Windal Barrow. The Baron sat idly at a table near the throne that was previously occupied by General Regoria. Dawn's light was at full strength, shining brightly through the seven stained-glass windows on the western wall. Windal looked peaceful and was devouring his morning meal of pepper potatoes, cheese eggs and bacon strips—until he looked up.

"General Fields," Windal said, standing and saluting Fields. The two men shook hands as well, showing they were more than just casual acquaintances. Cracked Tooth appeared from behind the General and grinned his toothy overbite. "Captain," Windal added, acknowledging the dobbin.

"I need to speak with General Regoria, if he is available," Fields said impatiently.

"That could be a problem. General Regoria hasn't been seen since he investigated an issue in the King's bedchamber. Apparently there was a hole in the wall, one that Thorn had used to access the King's quarters. He took a handful of men through it and as far as everyone knows they returned, but no one has seen them and the wall has been sealed."

Fields asked, "Is everyone sure they were out before it was sealed?"

Windal nodded. There were several witnesses, but now those men are being called into question and a search has begun for Regoria, his guard Jime Drace and Baron Ilos."

"What happened to Viktoran?"

"Ken Murcy, the bell tower guard, was the last one to see him. He said the Baron was on his way to the maker's wing when he left him. Somewhere between the bell tower and wing he vanished."

Fields shook his head. "Men like Ilos do not simply vanish. He must have been attacked, which brings me to my next order of business. Have you seen General Keys?"

Windal nodded. "Yes. He was here just a moment ago. He's on his way to see the King. Says he had a package for him from Dowhaven."

"What package? Did you clear him?"

"Don't know what it was. It was a small box, about five inches wide and fifteen long. Said it was a gift from the new Baron of Dowhaven. I checked the signature on the form and verified that it matched Baron DeHue's."

"Do you know of its contents?"

"No. He was in a hurry. Said it was paid to be a Rush Run."

Fields ran from the Grand Hall with Cracked Tooth and Windal chasing him. The trio took the shortest route possible to the maker's wing, using the last of their breath to prevent a tragedy.

"Walking about the castle without first consulting with me? I come back to an empty bed without a note." Master Hurran said, waving his hands in the air. "When has the opinion of a master maker not been taken into consideration? I may as well return to the center in the Southern Yard where my talents can be put to better use."

"I had justification for doing what I did, Master," Noran explained. "There was some cleaning up that needed to be taken care of."

"So now you're doing House servant work—"

"Not exactly," Noran said, shaking his head. "I'm not at liberty to tell you what happened this time, Master."

Hurran sighed. "Your Majesty, my main concern is for your health. Because you are able to walk and swing a sword doesn't mean you are fully recovered."

"I didn't really get a chance to swing a sword," he said, glancing at Blaynor. "I do feel I should start getting some exercise again. I have become lethargic from sitting in the wing one too many times."

Hurran let out a long sigh and said, "Keep it to a minimum if you can. If you feel a spell or faint, take rest for the remainder of the day. I'm putting you in charge, Blaynor. Make sure he takes me more seriously than he has been."

Noran looked at Blaynor again, who was bowing with a smile. "The King is a hard man to contain, but we shall put forth our best efforts."

Sounding unconvinced, Hurran frowned. "Just keep it to a minimum," he repeated. "Now get out of my wing before I change my mind." "Thank you for your diligence, Master," Noran said with a smile. The three men quickly exited before Hurran regretted his decision, which he was known to do often. They strode to their next destination with one goal before them, to uncover the truth as to why Ballan had become a traitor. But before they could exit the wing, a House servant intercepted them. She bowed to Noran and moved aside to let Rydor, Jime and Viktoran by.

"Where have you three been?" Noran asked, sounding relieved when he asked the question.

"Counting coins," Viktoran responded first. "Herikech imprisoned us in the Royal Treasure Vaults. Said he had plans for us. Not sure what that entails but it didn't sound like a hot steam bath and massage. We banged on the door long enough until a roaming watcher let us free. Kap-al-Crey killed three of our own men to reach us. They wouldn't explain to her why they were keeping us locked prisoner in the vaults, and then attacked her. She said she helped you out of a scrape, too."

Noran nodded. "Yes. Ballan has betrayed us. He also has sided with

Herikech, for unknown reasons."

Viktoran shook his head and added, "I'm afraid that's not the end of the troubles on our list, Your Majesty. I no longer have Heaven's Light in my possession. He had Thorn take it from me. It's no longer the excuse preventing him from murdering you outright. I'm afraid the guards will be as effective as I am now. No offense," Viktoran said, looking at Bruneau and Blaynor.

They both smiled, seeing no harm in it.

"Unless," Viktoran added, "you have Oreus Blake let me borrow his dagger. We believe it is a brother to my sword."

Noran nodded. "More than you know, Baron." Before Viktoran asked for an explanation, Noran said, "Well it's good to see you again and I'm thankful Herikech spared your lives." He put a firm hand on Viktoran's shoulder. "I also had an interesting evening yesterday. Ballan has decided to join the enemy."

"Ballan?" Rydor said. "He was one of your most loyal subjects."

"So I thought. But he and seventeen other men attacked Bruneau, Blaynor, Martell and me. Trouble was, they didn't know we had company. Thanks to Martell's anointment, we were able to turn the tide." Martell looked away and blushed, muttering to himself.

"I see no band on your arm," Viktoran pointed out, "what is your station?"

"It's too long to go into," Martell said, acting embarrassed. "Not for corridor conversation."

"Nonsense," Noran said. "It's important they know the value of your calling."

While the men became engaged in the discussion about Martell's new responsibilities, they didn't see the approach of General Keys from the passage behind them. The hare pulled at a ribbon that tied a box together he carried, and removed its lid to reveal a red-jeweled dagger with a wavy blade inside. Keys took it out and hid it behind his back as he walked softly from the shadows of the corridor toward the King. His paw clamped the handle when he came within a few yards. Martell saw the shadows of two long ears fall across his boot, which were cast from a torch behind Keys. The dobbin raised the dagger in the air, poised to strike Noran in the back. Martell lunged, throwing himself at the King's waist. Noran's body bent in half as the dagger cut through the air and sliced Martell's forearm. The Nax clutched his arm and screamed in a whistling pitch that pierced everyone's ears. Keys raised the dagger again but Viktoran punched over Noran's body, his fist slamming into the General's chest. The dobbin flipped backward, turned and picked up speed as he bounded away.

Viktoran only heard ringing from Martell's scream after failing to cover his ears during its duration. He stuck an index finger in each canal and wiggled them to make it stop. Rydor, Jime and Blaynor sprinted after Keys.

Martell fell down from shock as blood gushed down his arm. Noran and Bruneau picked Martell up and hurried him off to the maker's wing. Master Hurran was just about to lock up the wing when they raced toward him with the Nax's blood spilling everywhere.

General Keys rounded the corner and ran into Fields, knocking him down. Keys jumped up and off Fields's chest and somersaulted in the air over Windal and Cracked Tooth.

Cracked Tooth turned and bounded after him, calling, "General Keys!"

Jime helped up Fields while Rydor and Blaynor ran past them on the heels of Windal. Cracked Tooth had already gained a considerable distance ahead of them, starting to catch the older and less fit Keys.

"Give us a chance to hear you out," Cracked Tooth tried saying before an ill-timed chorus of rooster crows in the Southern Yard drowned his words. "Shut up you pile of feathers!" Cracked Tooth yelled out the open windows as he passed by them. "I never wanted to hear you anyway!"

Keys kicked out and knocked down two more soldiers coming up a set of stairs at the end of the bridge walkway that extended over the gandalay stables. The General bounded away to the door of the closest watchtower. Flinging it open, he disappeared into the winding dark staircase spiraling up two hundred feet.

Cracked Tooth came to the door a few moments later, finding it bolted from the inside. "Confounded!"

The two soldiers Keys had kicked down the stairs started to arrest Cracked Tooth, thinking he was attacking Keys with a sword he held in his paw. "You're arresting the wrong hare!" Cracked Tooth yelled. "Ouch! You're cutting off my circulation! Ouch!" The soldiers shoved his face into the door to take the fight out of him. They pulled him back to do it again but Cracked Tooth shot his feet out in front of him and climbed up the door while the soldiers pushed against his back. He did a backward flip over them to break free. Cracked Tooth saw Rydor, Windal and Blaynor running in his direction. He jumped out of the soldiers' grasp before they could retie his wrists and let the others come to his defense.

"Out of the way and leave that dobbin alone," Blaynor ordered. "He's not the one we're after."

The soldiers backed away and looked apologetically at Cracked Tooth.

"Our error," one of them said with a grimace.

Not giving them a chance to grovel further, Cracked Tooth bound through the door into the tower after Blaynor broke it open with two spinning kicks.

"Two hundred stairs. One hundred and ninety-nine. One hundred and ninety-eight," Cracked Tooth said, counting each one as he went.

"Count to yourself, Captain," Windal scolded, knowing full well how many they had to climb.

"Sorry, Baron," he replied, lowering his voice to a whisper. "One hundred and ninety-five . . . ."

The climb was exhausting and each of them had to stop several times before they reached the top. Blaynor was the first to reach the watcher's door. He caught his breath and then used his spinning kicks again. This time, however, the door held and his foot bruised from the impact with the heavy sequeran wood.

"You'll never break that one down with a buckle kick," Rydor said. "The watchtower doors are meant to hold up against great pressure."

"I already found that out," Blaynor replied, limping on his swelling foot. Windal and Cracked Tooth joined them on the platform.

"Zero," Cracked Tooth said, gasping for air when he joined them.

"Perhaps we should just try knocking," Windal suggested. No one was in the mood for his joke. "Or not," he said to lose their intolerant gazes.

Cracked Tooth looked behind them and said, "That'll get us through."

"Right," Rydor said, walking by the Captain and drawing his sword. "Hold the top end, Blaynor." The guard nodded and did as the General asked. Rydor hacked the bottom end of the last beam in the staircase railing to loosen it from its block post. The wood cracked beneath the heavy blows he was unleashing on the aged wood. After eleven strikes, it splintered and fell onto the step on which he was standing.

"Got it?" Rydor asked.

"Yes," Blaynor replied, taking a secure hold of the rail's other end. Rydor pulled his end toward his body to slide the other out of its stone compartment. Blaynor's body tensed when the cumbersome wood weighted down his arms. The two men lifted it up the stairs and set it down on the platform. When they were ready, all four of them picked it up together and aimed Blaynor's end at the center of the door.

"Go!' Rydor shouted, sending them forward. The end of the rail battered into the door, shaking it in its frame.

"The wood is old and breaking! Again!" Blaynor called after they had backed up to the edge of the staircase. The four warriors ran forward, sweat beading on every inch of their faces. The end collided with the door and cracked it down the center.

"One more should do it!" Windal exclaimed.

On the final charge the door suddenly opened. All four of them went flying through and crashed to the floor, landing on top of the beam in the process. Cracked Tooth's paw became trapped underneath, breaking his radius bone. The hare screeched and yanked his arm free, making him cry a second higher note.

A sword flashed at Rydor's head. He threw up his wrist at the last moment and deflected the blade with his metal wrist cuff. Sparks shot off it as another came down. The General rolled to let Keys's sword hit the floor.

Windal, Blaynor and Cracked Tooth picked themselves up and drew their weapons. A dead soldier lay near the window, brutally cut down from behind. Seeing his chances of winning the fight were slim, Keys dropped his sword and bounded toward the window.

"No!" Rydor cried, stretching his hand out in the direction of the General's flying form. The dobbin leaped over the sill and into the open air beyond.

Blaynor and Rydor ran toward the window while Windal stood frozen from shock at the turn of events. Everything felt as if it was moving in slow motion as Rydor watched the helpless form of the hare fall to his death, missing the moat by five feet as he landed on the stone walkway running along it.

"Noooo!" Cracked Tooth whimpered on the floor. "General, why? Why!" The dobbin sobbed into his jumper suit uniform, his ears twitching and his body shaking repeatedly over the General's final rash choice.

Rydor hung his head on the windowsill and said, "How did Herikech convince Keys to try and murder the King?"

"However it was done," Windal said, "included him being willing to commit suicide to protect that information."

# CHAPTER FOURTEEN
## Jada's Trade

"Are you sure you're going the right way?" The Chief slung his axe over his right shoulder after their short rest in the deep northwestern woods of Marshant Territory. He removed his orange armband, which signified him as a flame fighter and put it into his pocket so it wouldn't attract the eyes of unknown creatures or outlaws, including the Silhouettes. His black soot-stained outfit was dark enough to make him not stand out like a yellow horn on the plains of Emison.

Jada also changed into a pair of green pants and a shirt embroidered with golden leaves and vines spreading along each arm and leg. A brown cape hung down her back and her sword was at her side in a darkly tanned sheath. On her head sat a leather hunter-green cavalier hat, her golden hair tucked up inside it to keep it from falling in her face, giving her a more rugged appearance. The band on the hat once contained a bright white feather. She had plucked it so it would give the hat a more subservient look in the presence of the Silhouettes. The last thing she wanted was to appear arrogant if they were expecting to walk out of these woods alive.

"I've only been this way once and it was a long time ago, when I was only a child," Jada whispered. "It was my induction—the darkest day of my life. Youth makes us impulsive and at the mercy of money. It was a deal I wouldn't have accepted had I known what trouble lurked behind the door."

"How could your mother not have warned you?" the Chief asked.

"My mother's health was never ideal. She didn't believe I could achieve the kind of wealth anywhere else that I could with the Women of Shadow. She never knew everything I have come to know, only a bat blinded by the sun."

"I mean no disrespect to her," the Chief replied as they walked underneath a thick row of branches that had been purposely cleared for a human to walk upright. It was a tunnel running through the heart of a dense tangle of thorns. They could hear twigs snap and branches break around them, but were unable to do anything about it due to the forest's thickness. Jada clutched a torch at her side, her arm growing tired from holding it in the same position for such a long time after they entered the never-ending gloom of the swaying black-barked trees. But her stubbornness would prevail. She would not allow the Chief to see her growing tired or needing rest.

"I know you will not forgive me for telling the King the truth," the Chief admitted, "but we can no longer let our fears hold us back if we are to—"

"Hold your lecture, Chief," Jada sneered. "You and I could be doing the same as we are now without the King's knowledge."

The Chief grabbed her by arm and stopped. "Do you think I like looking over my shoulder every day and night, wondering where the next assassination attempt is going to come from, Baron? I want this to end, and if by sticking my neck out to tempt the blade is the way it needs to be done, then that's what I'll do."

She wiggled her arm out of his grasp and snapped, "Welcome to the life of a Baron. Do you believe any member of the Royal Court doesn't always have to do the same? You should be used to facing death with as many fires as you brave, Chief. I don't see how this is any different."

The Chief was about to argue when Jada asked him to keep his voice down after walking past a tree with a section of its bark stripped away. "We don't have many miles to go. This shaving is familiar."

"Karriks are known to feed on bark in the winter when their food supplies are low."

"A karrik would not eat such a small patch," Jada said. "They require much more to sustain them through the lean season. This mark was made where a ray of light penetrated the forest's roof. It is a superstitious practice to thwart light from penetrating their world."

"And an unusual punishment to a tree," the Chief said.

"Your dry humor will not sit well with them once they find out we've trespassed onto their lands. If I were you, I would restrain myself from making those types of comments while we are negotiating."

"Another reason not to like them."

The tunnel widened and opened up into a ring of trees. Their branches stretched over the fifteen-foot circular area so that light could not shine through the canopy. An oval stone slab lay flat on the ground at the center of the ring. It was marked with a crescent moon, its center pierced by an arrow, matching Jada's pendant.

"Guess that proves you're right," the Chief said. They walked around it and entered another tunnel, this one half the size of the first, forcing them to walk single file. The ground slanted at a slight angle downwards. "We are walking into a snake pit," the Chief said, the forest closing in around them. Branches scraped against their shoulders, as if wanting to hold them back.

One caught the Chief by the elbow and snagged on his shirt. It took him several moments to unhook its life-like hand.

Jada whispered, "It's time to be silent. Sentries will be ahead now that we have voluntarily crossed their icon. Most who come this far don't return to see the light of day. Watch where you walk and don't step on any sticks." The random ones Jada spoke of littered the lush grass path every few feet. "They are nature's alarms if broken, craftily strewn by the Silhouettes to arouse their guards."

The Chief could hardly see the smaller ones in Jada's torchlight. Instead, he did his best to step where she did so he would not sound an alarm. The forest became warmer the further in they went, producing a sufficient amount of heat to keep the Women of Shadow warm through the hard winters. He was sweating when they came upon a stump in the center of the path.

"Only a few hundred yards now before the first gate is upon us. It will look as if the tunnel has ended and there is nothing beyond. Only one method can be used to unlock the hidden door." Jada went to the stump they came upon and crouched down, bringing her torch near. She put her hand into a section where two roots split into the ground, slid her fingers between them and pulled out a wooden key with three teeth on one end, and the crescent moon with the arrow on the other. She held it up for the Chief to see and winked.

Just as she had proclaimed, a wall of trees greeted them around the next bend in the path. She went to the center trunk and examined it, finding a line running down its center. A small hole was present at chest level. She inserted the key into it and rotated it to the left. A branch on the tree suddenly struck out at her and knocked her from her feet.

"Ahhh!"

"Jada, are you all right?' the Chief asked, running over to help her up.

She rubbed her sore arm and said, "My memory has just been jogged. I was supposed to turn it to the right." She went back with the key and was successful on the second attempt. The tree groaned and fell toward them as if was going to crush them. "Hold still," Jada said, keeping the Chief from stepping to either side of the path, which was precisely where the two sections of trunk flared out and landed. "Another trick to do away with unwelcome guests," she said.

Where the trunk had been, there was now a tall, thin door, capped by a crown of broad leaves. They cautiously entered and watched the tree pick itself back up into position to close the gate. Its leaves rustled as it fell back into place.

"Now that was a wonder," the Chief whispered.

Jada put a finger to her lips again and snuffed out her torch by dropping a handful of dirt onto it. "No light allowed in here." The walls of the new tunnel were no longer lined with trees. Huge trapezoidal stone blocks with crawling ivy guided them, inviting members to a small lodge at the end of the row.

"Sentry point," Jada said, pulling the Chief next to a bush of over-grown ivy on the wall to hide them.

"How do we get around it?"

"Don't know if we can. If we are caught, our chance of meeting with the leader is highly doubtful. I wouldn't be surprised if we have been seen already." Jada froze when she heard a door open.

A cloaked figure exited the building and strode in their direction. "The tree gate must have sent warning to them," the Chief whispered, trying to suck in his potbelly stomach.

"They may have changed some things since I was girl," Jada said.

The figure stopped a dozen yards from them and looked toward the tree gate with a pair of night goggles over her eyes. Jada peered between two leaves and held her breath. When the Silhouette saw it was standing as it should be, she turned around and went back inside.

"Must have thought they heard it open," the Chief said.

Jada nodded. "That was close."

The Chief studied the tunnel. "These walls are too tall to climb and spaced too far apart at the top to walk across. There appears to be no other choice but to walk up to the front door and knock."

Jada looked at the Chief and then smirked.

"What?" he asked.

With two fast punches she struck him across each side of the face. The Chief was dazed and in shock. She took her torch and whacked him over the back of the head, knocking him out cold. "That makes us even," she said. Jada worked her way under his heavy body and draped him over her shoulders. Staggering toward the front door as if she were drunk, she dropped his heavy form onto the doorstep just as three cloaked figures exited the building. They looked at Jada and then at the Chief's unconscious form.

"Baron Annalee," the shortest of the three said, "who have you brought to us and why are you here?"

"I need to speak with Asial about the Lazuls."

"What about him?" the figure asked, pointing at the Chief. "He looks familiar—"

"This is not Chief Decker," Jada cut in. "His name's Marc Moore, a flame fighter often mistaken for the Chief because of their similarity in appearance. Many people think they are twins. I stumbled onto him nosing around the outer tunnel. He was clearing some brush with this." Jada handed the figure the Chief's axe. "Tie him up and drug him. I will take him out of here when I'm done talking to Asial. He won't remember a thing."

"Wait here a moment," the short Silhouette said.

The three figures entered back into the building and shut the door. The one Jada had been talking to came back out by herself and said, "Leave him out here. Strangers are not allowed inside the point of entrance. I will take you to Asial, but I can't guarantee she will see you. She has had her hands full with the army lately. Several soldiers showed up here a few days ago asking about the Silhouettes. When we were evasive, they tried to kill us. I wish I could say we left them alive . . . but you know our code."

Jada nodded. She followed the Silhouette into the building. There was a narrow hallway with three doors down each side, giving no hint to what they accessed. Only one lantern hung overhead, throwing just enough light for them to see. They walked past all six doors and out a seventh at the end of the hall. Jada's guide knocked three times and then paused before rapping a fourth. The door opened and quickly shut and locked behind them. Jada looked at the hooded individual who had let them in and then at an amazing town that had sprouted up around the few central buildings she remembered from her childhood. The town was illuminated by cauldrons filled with fire, each sitting upon identical stone columns at the ends and middle of every street. Small sequera trees no older than two hundred years were planted down the center of each street since there was no need for carts here. They provided a thick blanket of leaves above the town to shut out any rays of sun trying to reach the refuge.

"You really are strict about staying in the shadows, aren't you?" Jada said.

"Any rider flying over on a dragul could expose our world. The trees are our shields."

They turned left past one of the original structures at the end of the closest row. Jada could hear the sounds of sawing and pounding coming from inside. One Silhouette stood on the porch and watched them walk by. The figure's head turned slowly to watch them until they were out of sight.

"I see you're doing some renovations to the place," Jada said.

"There are many buildings needing work. Things are constantly in a state of flux here, adjusting to our interests. We finally decided to have most of the operations moved to one central location. I have to inform you, Baron Annalee, that Asial has not been pleased with your participation lately."

"My duties to the King must come first, or else he may suspect something."

"I'm not speaking in general, Baron. Asial wants Chief Decker dead."

"All things will work themselves out in time. The army heavily guards the Chief. I can't risk my position. I would be hanged."

"You'll be lucky if Asial doesn't do it first." The woman led Jada past a shipment of fish and a giant glass tank with a brown-spotted eel inside. The creature hissed at Jada when they walked past, showing its powerful jaws that could break any bone in two.

"You keep interesting company."

"If you only knew the rest."

Jada expected them to enter one of the buildings along the street they were walking, but the guide turned and went down a set of stairs at the base of a sequera. A sign with a thick oval burned into it hung on a post near the stairs. "I don't have to relieve myself," Jada said.

"Not all is as it seems." The guide entered through the door and into a tiled room with wash buckets and sinks. Three enclosed stalls sat at the back of the room. They came to a door that read *Supplies*. When the woman unlocked it, the Baron saw the storage space was filled with toiletries, towels, mops, brooms and soaps, all items one would expect to be available near a refresher room.

"Come in," the Silhouette said, and then asked Jada to close the door behind her. "Stand still and hang onto that shelf." The Baron did as ordered. The Silhouette pulled on the mop handle until there was a click. The entire room spun one hundred and eighty degrees. Jada heard a whirring before it stopped, opening to another set of stairs that led downward. They descended them and came to a wall with five doors. The Silhouette went to the fourth one from the right and knocked.

A large shadow with a pair of glowing eyes filled the doorway when it opened, sending a chill up Jada's spine. If she was right, the shape before her was of a morusk, a creature with a human-like form but containing no hair or skin. Their habitats were underwater caves along the Racorn Sea. The creatures were known to be only fish-eaters. Once in a blue moon a fisherman would see one basking in the moonlight on a rock, but the occasions were rare since morusks rarely left the water to clean themselves. Glimmering green scales covered its chest and a hard white shell the rest. Its teeth included only fangs and four blunt teeth on the bottom of its mouth. A long, pointed and white tongue licked the inside of its mouth when its luminous eyes looked down on Jada. The only place she had seen them was in drawings in the Historical Record Keep. She now wished it had remained that way.

The Silhouette guide pulled out a mase and blew into it to make the creature back down. It lowered its body, fell to all fours and withdrew on its four-fingered hands; the middle fingers that once contained lethal poison-filled nails were missing. Jada entered and noted that they had been cut off.

The guide announced, "Jada Annalee to see you, Asial." The back of a hide-covered chair was facing them. When no reply came from it, the Silhouette nodded and shut the door, saying, "Keep your sentences short and you will be heard out."

Jada nodded and turned her attention back to the chair. The morusk disappeared into a cage in the corner with only its glowing eyes remaining visible and blinking at her.

"May I speak?" she asked.

"You may explain," a woman's voice said.

Fear in her throat, Jada asked, "Explain?"

"If you have come hear requesting a favor, Baron, King Deardrop will soon be asking 'Whatever happened to the great Jada Annalee?' Since I know that is not the situation, you must be giving an explanation for your avoidance in executing Chief Braiy Decker."

"The Lazuls."

The chair turned slowly toward her, the woman in it coming into full view behind a lantern beam shining through the ceiling. It fell onto her features and highlighted her brown eyes, sloped nose and double chin. A head of black hair dusted by gray was cut short in the front but left long in the back. White garments covered her upper body and the pendant of the Silhouettes rested firmly against her bosom. "Hardly the topic I expected you to bring up, Baron."

"Lady Asial, do you know of Herikech Illeon?"

"The Lazul king of the underground city of Maramis. He has been giving Deardrop his share of headaches recently. But Deardrop brought it upon himself by stealing the Lazul children to begin with."

"Herikech is starting to gain control of King Deardrop's army. No one can be trusted anymore."

"I know the feeling," Asial said.

"We don't know how Herikech's converting the men and have nowhere else to turn. The King needs help or we all will suffer under Herikech's oppression."

Asial laughed. "His rule will not reach here—"

"I'm sorry . . . but it will. He has powers you are not aware of. The relentless storms are his doing."

Asial was silent for a moment. She cleared her throat and said, "What you are suggesting is impossible."

"I wish you were right."

She stared at Jada for a few more moments to consider the Baron's words. "Three of the King's soldiers were trying to get past the entrance point guards . . . ."

Jada was already nodding. "Not by the King's hand. Those men are no longer under Deardrop's command. Do not be so bold as to think that Herikech hasn't found you. Now that he knows, he will stop at nothing to take control of this town."

"What do you need from me?" Asial asked, her voice becoming sharp.

Jada relaxed a little, relieved the conversation had reached its purpose. "Herikech not only is converting men, but animals into his army as well. There is a mangler, a maddon-like creature, on the loose and terrorizing the castle."

"Yes. I have heard about the King's kidnapping."

"I believe if we can find the beast, we can entrap Herikech."

"The mangler is not easily tracked. The Silhouettes do not know where it sleeps. Only the best trackers in the land will be able to find it."

"The army's sniffers—"

"I am not referring to the sniffers, Baron. They are not as skilled as the men I have relations with."

Jada thought about Asial's response. "The rangers?"

Asial nodded. "There is one that would be especially useful. He knows all the forests surrounding the Royal House Territory better than any other. I wouldn't doubt if he already knows where the beast is."

"Who?"

"Nothing comes without a price, Baron."

"It's in your interest to help us!" she replied angrily. Her face turned red, taking Asial by surprise. The morusk came out of its cage and growled. Jada turned and recoiled.

Asial picked a mase off her desk and blew one note. The creature crawled back into its nest.

"One more whistle and I shall have it kill you, Baron. What will it be?"

"Name your price," Jada said, knowing the entire sum of Candelwick's treasure vault was at her disposal to spend.

"Five hundred maka medallions."

"Five hundred? No piece of information—"

Asial lifted the mase to her lips again. "Even without its poison stingers the morusk can gut a human before they hit the ground."

Jada could smell the light odor of rotting fish coming from the creature's cage, a stench that made vomit creep up to the back of her tongue. "Fine! Fine!" she said, swallowing hard and taking another step away from it.

"I will be sending two shadows to Emison Tower to collect it in twenty days. If you fail to deliver, they will be bringing your body back instead."

Replying through gritted teeth, Jada vowed, "By my oath it will be there."

"Outstanding. You still occasionally impress me, Baron. Ten miles south of here is Bane Sector. A trail is there we refer to as Snake's Weave. It follows the edge of Guts Gorge, which eventually leads to Soul Lake. At the end of the gorge there is a fork. One branch goes to the lake and the other onto private land, which is incidentally wrought with traps to keep rovers out. Guess which you have to take?"

Jada was discouraged and then glanced at the morusk's cage to make certain the creature was not creeping up on her. She looked back when she realized her nerves were getting the best of her.

"If you manage to get past the traps, there will be a cabin at the trail's end. It belongs to a ranger named Relic. He should be able to tell you what you need to know."

Searching for the courage within her, Jada stood as she bit her tongue. She knew Lady Asial had been more than generous, circumstances being what they were. The morusk sensed her fear. It clacked its teeth and scraped at the side of the cage, hoping Asial would give it the order to feast.

"Why are you standing here when the bargain has been completed?" Asial asked, perturbed Jada had another request.

"It's about Chief Decker. He's a good man—"

"What he has done in his lifetime is not my concern, Baron," Asial coldly said. "He has gained valuable information from Dami Ironwood and that alone has put us at risk. You should have taken care of him the moment we notified you."

Jada had to defend the Chief, as much as she regretted doing so after the Chief told the King about her relations with the Silhouettes. She fought off the urge to just let him deal with the Silhouettes himself, but then said, "He doesn't know anything beyond Dami's involvement. He just wants to live a normal life and be left alone."

"That is your presumption, not a fact. Chief Decker is a good friend to King Deardrop. That makes him expendable."

"I'll pay you whatever you want to let him be," she replied bluntly.

"No price could be set high enough—"

"Please, he's my friend."

"I wouldn't care if he was your brother!" Asial yelled, leaning forward in her chair and slamming a fist on her desk.

Jada ripped the pendant from around her neck and slapped it down on a pile of papers in front of Asial. "This symbol was not meant to represent murder and greed. My mother would spit on your boots for what this place has become."

Asial's hand went for her mase, but then she stopped herself at the last moment and said, "You do not dictate what I can and cannot do. Your oath is a bond that is unbreakable. It is a fine line you are walking, Baron. If I were you, I would take what you came here for and not come back any time soon." The two women stared at each other across the desk, neither backing down. Jada's hand itched to go to her sword, but her eyes fell downward to a small portrait on the desk. It was Asial standing next to a young boy no older than twelve with dark hair and striking blue eyes that she had come to know very well. Asial's eyes followed the Baron's to the picture. Jada grabbed it before Asial could face it down on the desk.

"Give me that!" Asial screamed.

The morusk jumped from its cage, salivating at the mouth. Jada's sword was out in a flash. She stabbed the creature twice in the shoulder. It howled from the pain and scampered back into its dark hole. She could hear it licking at its two shallow wounds. With a flick of her wrist, the Baron then turned her sword on Asial, who tried to go for her own weapon, a short sword hidden conveniently within reach underneath her desk.

"Keep your hands where they'll be safe," Jada sneered. "I have also been known to swiftly filet a foe or two when it counts.'

Asial put them back on top of the desk and cried, "That picture is of no meaning to you!" But she knew Jada had recognized the boy standing with her.

"There is only one man in the world I know who has a grin that is this charming. He has your eyes and Baron Milet's nose and chin."

Asial couldn't respond. Her eyes were watering and her pride, deflating. She used a thumb to wipe away a tear that ran down her cheek.

"Your son could never forgive you if he learned you were alive, Lady Regoria."

"That was a long time ago. I no longer choose to go by that title." The tears were coming and Asial could do nothing to hold them back, except use the sleeve of her robe to staunch their flow.

"Did you not hear what I just said? Rydor believes you died!" she yelled, her own voice crackling with anger. "How could you have done this to him? You were his mother."

"I wanted him to live without my shame. I slept with a man who was already devoted to another woman. He was better off without that knowledge."

Jada's own tears were evident by her wet cheeks in the lantern light's glow. "At least his father was strong enough to tell him the truth."

"Not until it was too late!" Asial cried. "He threw us out! Baron Milet was no saint! A son of a Royal Court member did not deserve to live in rags. I had to do something to save us both. It is why I came here. It was the only thing I could do to protect us both. No one had seen Rydor since he was an infant. But someone would eventually have found me with him when he was a boy. There were some in the Western House who knew of our affair, and what better way to disgrace a Baron than have the proof of a bastard child? Milet's enemies hunted us for many years. A farmer finally agreed to take Rydor if I contributed monies to help save the farm's sinking debt. You have no idea what we went through—"

"You should have gone to the King and claimed sanctuary."

"Hah! He would have protected the Baron to save face for his court! I was a peasant girl, nothing to him. Do you not think that the King had lovers of his own?"

Jada slapped Asial and retorted, "I don't know what kind of a man you think Doran Yorokoh was, but you truly didn't know him."

Asial sat back in her chair, still reeling from the sting of the past coming back. Her face had gone white and her hands were shaking. She slid them up over her eyes as she wept. Jada turned toward the morusk's cage. The creature was still licking its wounds and moaning.

Asial suddenly looked up at Jada with jealous eyes. "You love him. That's how you recognized his features! The Silhouettes have kept this information from me. Cowards—"

The Baron nodded and said proudly, "Yes. They are afraid you might have a change of heart and return to him. And I will tell you this, Asial, I will never abandon Rydor when he needs me. Now, I will give you a choice. And this time I hope you make the right one."

Asial sat rigid, cleared her throat and said with the last amount of dignity she had salvaged, "I will spare you your breath, Baron. I ask you for only one thing in return when you leave here for the last time."

Jada nodded, seeing the pain had never left Asial. As if she could hear Rydor's voice in her heart, Jada replied, "Do not worry. I will take good care of him."

"I really am sorry." The campfire Jada had created followed army specifications so it wouldn't burn down the forest. The nights were beginning to cool and they gazed at the gold, orange, red and rust hanging from the trees around them. Their vibrant colors brought a fleeting peace within her that told her they didn't have much longer to enjoy such simple splendor.

"I don't care about the bruises," the Chief said, scowling as he threw more wood onto the growing fire. "They'll go away. And I accept your explanation for why you did it. But for the last nine miles you've been tongue-tied about how you were able to bargain for my freedom with the Silhouettes. You must really have something important on them to have pulled off that kind of stunt."

Jada stayed tight-lipped behind the heightening flames. Mentioning the fact that Asial was Rydor's lost mother to anyone would put her own life at risk, as well as the Chief's again. What troubled her more was how to confront Rydor about it, if she even should at all. It would instigate arguments and even form a rift between them, for she could not put his life in danger and tell him where his mother was. Rydor would not rest once he learned Asial was alive. He would try to find his way back to her to learn the truth for himself and close a chapter in his life he thought would never be opened again.

"Just trust me in knowing they will not be a hindrance to you any longer," she said, "nor the guards who were assigned to protect you. I will inform His Majesty they can quit eating out of your cupboards and sleeping on your floor."

The Chief stared into the flames that had become his enemy for so many years and studied its hypnotic dance. Sparks shot from the fire to find a way to increase its diameter, but Jada had made the dirt ring wide enough so they could do no damage.

"When I awoke I heard the three Silhouettes at the entrance point discussing the Lazuls at great length," the Chief said. "With my eyelids shut, they didn't know I had regained consciousness. Their suspicions are just now forming. I would even go as far to say they have something to be worried about. One of the three cited another Silhouette's observation of what they believed to be Lazul activity near the castle."

"What have they seen?" Jada asked when the Chief did not go into the details.

The Chief threw another log onto the fire. "When the rains started and the storms bombarded Candlewick's walls, black-cloaked individuals were spied rolling barrels near carts being loaded with them in the Western Yard. The driver took no notice of it, and was even talking to a soldier while the Lazuls carried out their plan."

Jada felt a crawling distress within her stomach, one that told her the barrels were not empty. "Barrels were shipped into the castle to collect rainwater flooding the corridors and gardens. Do you think it is possible they could have been shipping their own warriors inside?"

The Chief frowned and poked a stick into the fire. An orange flame latched onto the end and ate away at the bark to create the birth of a new fire. He pulled it out and stuck the end into the dirt, ending its new life. "We know that not all soldiers under the King's command have kept their obedience. I have an inclination the soldier diverted the driver while the new barrels were added to the supply. It's as clever a plan as any."

They said little else as the glow of the fire died. Jada couldn't force herself to sleep as she thought about Asial's involvement with the Silhouettes. She also toiled over her own involvement with them and how Rydor would even digest that information. Tears filled her eyes as she thought of how she could lose his love when the truth was revealed. His reaction could be harsh if she kept it a secret, and that was something she wasn't sure she was prepared for. But how could she tell him the leader of the Silhouettes was his very own mother? Was it better that he not know? Finally, not long before dawn, her grief took her into a sleep that was filled with those nagging thoughts.

By the time the first bird of the morning sang its melody, the Chief was already reorganizing the supplies in their wagon. He whistled the two white gandalay stallions over so he could hook them up. The gandalays whinnied enthusiastically after the restful night and full morning's meal. They trotted over, turned themselves into position and backed up to the cart to make it easy for him.

"Good boys," the Chief said. He fed them each a slice of sweet roi and then woke Jada.

She pulled a knife on him as she rose from her deep sleep and yelled, "You will not have him!"

The Chief jumped back and tripped over a rock to avoid the close shave. There was a gray storm in her eyes that told him she was fighting an opponent that had not released her from their dream duel. "Wake up, Jada," he said, kicking her in the shin.

She started blinking and then saw she held her dagger in her hand. Luckily, she thought, it didn't have any blood on it . . . as it did in her dream. It fell from her hand when she looked at the Chief sitting up a few feet away. "Where are we?" she asked.

"On our way to meet the ranger. Remember? You were having a nightmare."

"Oh, I . . . I didn't injure you, did I?"

"My reflexes still work well enough," he said, grinning. "You can eat on the way. Our time to find the mangler is at hand. Lumly moon will be rising tonight. Its red rays will cause the beast to rear its ugly head. The King will be attacked again if we don't find it first."

Jada nodded and found a yawn escaping her mouth. "Guts Gorge is less than a mile away. We will be there soon enough." She stood and stretched. Once she started to change her undergarments, the Chief let her be and took a brief walk around the perimeter of the camp.

While she got her things in order for the ride, he poured a gallon of water onto the smoldering fire and then buried it under a mound of dirt. Satisfied it had no chance of catching again with a strong wind, he locked the rear panel of the wagon and pulled himself up in the driver seat next to the Baron. With a snap of the reins they were on their way again. The gandalays bolted forward as if they had wings on their hooves, not slowing until they reached the edge of the gorge. They neighed the moment the cart cut through the grass of Snake's Weave to take them west.

"The Silhouettes didn't happen to mention what traps we were supposed to watch out for, did they?" the Chief asked, holding the gandalay's reins tightly so they didn't accidentally veer off onto the wrong slope.

The trail was hard to see, overgrown with several years of weeds. The only distinction the Chief could make out was the weeds on the path were a few inches shorter than the ones on the outside of it. He had no intention of looking toward the gorge's steep drop-off, for fear of his stomach losing breakfast.

"There was not enough time. The negotiations were short, but effective in most aspects. We'll have to figure them out ourselves."

"I don't plan to lose my leg to a karrik trap. That's one snare we can be sure there may be a few of."

Jada pointed to a bump coming up. The Chief pulled on the reins to slow the gandalays so they could take it without bucking their passengers out of their seats. After they cleared it, the path alternated back and forth as it wound left and right for the remainder of their way to the fork. They were both content with their progress when the gorge's end came in sight. As Asial had said, there was a sign warning all not to take the left road, stating a list of reasons why it was not in their best interest. A shady patch in a grove of firs provided the perfect spot to unhitch the gandalays and hide their provisions. They found a lengthy rope in the pile of equipment they had hauled along. Jada tied one end to a tree and then went to one after another until she had completed a circle around the horses.

"That's enough to keep them from roaming?" the Chief asked.

"The gandalays are trained to recognize many types of barriers, even ones as simple as a rope fence. They are also smart enough to know how to escape if danger finds them. We don't want them wandering into areas and grazing where it isn't safe."

They took two flasks of water, pouches of various dried fruit, one torch and several weapons with them. Happy to have his axe again, the Chief smiled as it filled his grip. The gandalays whinnied when Jada and the Chief ducked under the rope and said their for-now-farewells to the stallions.

"Wait a moment," the Chief said when they came back to the edge of the road. He picked up a stone almost as large as his hand and threw it into a thick patch of weeds. A net shot up from where the stone landed and lifted into an overhanging bow. The Chief turned and smiled. "Freed a few messengers from those at times. That's one way a ranger catches larger game. Their bait sometimes draws in messengers, however. Here I see none."

"Rangers don't actually eat the messengers, do they?"

"Dobbin meat is too tough, and against the law, of course. We have put up posters to tell the rangers the nets are illegal. To no one's surprise, they ignore them."

"I think it would be best if we stay to the edge of the woods. At least the ground cover is clear here."

Jada took another step and was slammed against a tree. Two stones were fired from another tree a dozen yards away with a rope between them. The stones flew around her and the tree, tying her to it.

The Chief laughed when she gave him a scornful look. "Hold still, Baron."

With a swing of his axe he cut it apart. The rope ends and stones fell to the ground harmlessly. "Rangers are not so dull-witted, Baron." The Chief bent over and picked up a fishing string that had snapped in half from Jada having walked through it. "Hard to see this line in the shadows of the forest."

Lifting her chin to show her pride wasn't wounded, she cut past him and forged a new trail by swinging her sword back and forth in front of her. The Chief followed and kept an eye on other movements in the trees dozens of yards away. He wasn't positive of their shapes, but was certain they weren't human.

Jada cut two more fishing lines like the one she had set off, but was able to elude the flying ropes with ease. They struck the trees next to her and tied themselves around their midsections.

They walked for two miles before they agreed to take a rest. There was little to talk about, for both of their minds were on what lay ahead. The Chief picked up another stone and tossed it at angle past Jada. She was about to yell at him when the sound of a karrik trap snapping closed behind her caught her words. He smiled and drank half his flask of water.

"We're almost there," she said when they heard the bark of a dog in the distance. The barking ceased a short time later.

"Let our wits be with us," the Chief said, holding the handle of his axe with both hands as they got up and walked further in.

A scent on the wind struck the Chief hard when they hiked another half a mile. "Smoke. Someone's just started a fire. They're using mince grass as a base."

"Cooking?"

"Yes. Fowl. Maybe a gragon steak. There's also sweet potatoes and fresh baked bread. Most likely mixing a stew."

Jada raised an eyebrow at the Chief, smiling. "Anything else?"

"No. That's it." His stomach growled.

"No need to ask why your nose is working so well."

"I can hold off hunger as long as any other man."

"But not a woman?" Jada replied. They pressed through wall after wall of branches.

"Do women eat?" he asked, chuckling.

"Now I smell it," she said after they entered a glen with a cabin standing squarely in the middle of four large trees. The sun was reflecting off a tub near the front door. Sitting in the tub was the dog they had heard, scratching at something irritating behind its right ear. Smoke was rising through the trees from the back of the cabin. The door creaked as it opened. They found themselves diving behind a bush for cover. The dog jumped from the tub and landed at the steps. A figure dressed in deer hide and a feather crown walked out and placed the entire kettle of stew in front of the dog so it could stuff itself full.

"Relic may even have women beat," Jada whispered to the Chief.

The Chief smiled. "A small dog for such a large appetite. Let's wait until it's finished before we make our acquaintance. It will be less determined to have us for dessert after that course."

Jada caught the Chief licking his lips several times as they waited. She shook her head and handed him a piece of jerky to suffice his hunger. By the time the Chief finished the small piece that would've been a full meal for her, the dog had lain down in a basket under a tree and had fallen asleep.

They crept from the bush and quietly strode down a narrow path leading to the front door. The trees hovering over the cabin were richer in color than any they had seen yet. Some leaves were even falling about them, creating a beautiful path to walk on. Jada kept eyeing the dog, nervous it would suddenly jump to life and run after them with snarling teeth. But it stayed where it was, dozing in the cool breeze for a long, late-morning nap.

One quick rap was all that was needed to bring the ranger to the door. It flung open wide with the ranger standing where light couldn't reach his face. "Baron Annalee," he said, recognizing her immediately. "Your presence here alerts me. Who is the flame fighter?"

"I'm glad you know who I am, Relic. I didn't know who you were until just two eves ago. This is Chief Braiy Decker."

"To not know the Barons would be a mistake," the ranger said as he stepped into the light to reveal a smile. Relic's eyes were a dark brown, his hair black and his face was tanned and filled with scars on every angle.

Jada felt herself shivering when she looked at him. "Why is that? I thought the rangers were very content to keep to themselves."

"One should be aware of their friends as well as their adversaries, don't you think?"

"And what adversaries do rangers have?" the Chief asked in a gruff voice.

The ranger chuckled and waved them inside. "Please, come in, otherwise Pharus might find you fit for a meal."

Jada took one last look at the dog and then entered behind the Chief. The cabin was smaller inside than it looked on the outside. There was hardly enough room for a bed and a table to eat at, much less the hearth.

"It is good you arrived now. I was about to put out the fire now that Pharus's food has been cooked and fed to him." Relic shut the door and said, "There are many seats you may choose from, none of which are too comfortable, though."

Every chair leg in the cabin had been chewed off, most likely by the dog, and then mended. They both decided to stand. The bed was neatly made and the table clear of any dishes, showing the ranger had not eaten a bite of the meal he had made. There were several weapons on the wall, including a blade that was not crafted by a Yawranan blacksmith.

"That sword belonged to a Lazul," she said, pointing to it. "By what chance did it come into your possession?"

"A sharp eye you have, Baron. I see why men find great worth in you." Relic crossed his arms and grinned as he studied her. "How comforting it is to know that you arrived at my door safely."

"The sword?" the Chief asked, slinging the axe over his shoulder, not liking the ranger much.

"I can see that you are no ordinary flame fighter, Chief Decker," Relic said, not intimidated by the Chief's bigger frame. "You brandish an impressive weapon yourself and I can guess that you have chopped down more than just trees in your day. I found the sword at Soul Lake, two miles west of here. You could find many more like it if you were willing to look for them." The ranger decided not to sit, remaining eye level with the Chief and Jada.

"What do you mean?" Jada asked.

"What do you want to hear?" Relic replied.

The Chief interrupted, "Is that where the secret Lazul Guild members have been hiding?"

"Some. They come and go at their leisure. Ahh, youths. There is nothing I care to do to stop them. Perhaps you should talk to Deardrop's army—"

"Have you seen any tracks of a mangler near the lake?" Jada asked impatiently. "We believe the Lazuls could be controlling it."

"I am very curious to know why the mangler would be here when it has only been seen in Dowhaven."

"There is more than one of the creatures upsetting the tranquility of the castle and neighboring towns," Jada said. "One captured the King, and was fought by Baron Ilos in Bramble Wood."

"How interesting." Relic thrummed his fingers on both arms. "That is very good to know. Then the manglers are breeding in the territories. Enlightening."

Finding the comment ridiculous, Jada replied, "The creature does not breed, Relic. Normal men are being changed into the beast when they become infected."

As if this was new information to the ranger, he paced the floor, refraining himself from acting on anything without hearing the rest. "And how do they become infected, Baron Annalee?"

"That knowledge has been as evasive as the manglers. General Fields should be returning from Dowhaven soon to give us more information on his encounter with it. I heard it wiped out an entire squad but he managed to kill it before it could escape."

"The General killed the Dowhaven mangler? He is a better warrior than I thought him to be." The ranger paused to contemplate the matter and then moved on. "I will take you to the lake if you wish to look for tracks. I know the fastest route from here. If all goes well, we can be there before three. I still have much to do before this day ends."

"We have traveled by horse," the Chief said. "We can be there faster than at a steady walk."

"You may leave your horses where they are. They cannot take the direct path that we will travel. There is too much of a grade and many holes that could break their legs. They will be tended to upon our return and could use more of the rest they are currently relishing. The path will also keep you safe from any Lazul ambushes."

The Chief grunted. "You believe there to be some along that trail?"

"I wouldn't have mentioned it if there weren't. Now, if you are ready, we should no longer waste any more time here. There is much to talk about on the way." The ranger grabbed a leather sack near the door. "This should do for a day's journey. It will be a rigorous hike, Chief Decker, I hope you are in proper shape for it."

The Chief said with pride, "A walk in the woods is no comparison to one through fire."

"You may be disagreeing with that belief before we are done."

"Don't you need your walking stick?" Jada asked.

"Yes, I suppose so," the ranger replied, taking it from her.

The ranger shut and locked the door as Jada and the Chief descended the steps. Pharus awoke and ran at them, barking wildly. Jada backed up when the dog charged her.

"No, Pharus!" Relic commanded. The dog stopped dead on the path and obeyed. Relic raised his hand as if he would strike the animal, but held his arm back. The dog turned, dropped its tail between its hind legs and whimpered as it waddled away with its full stomach.

Jada sighed, almost feeling sorry for the way the poor thing was forced to react. She detested animal abuse, and this dog clearly reacted to his raised fist. For the sake of the mission, she avoided the topic for now.

"He's got a mind of his own, but he's learned where his place is," Relic said, directing Jada and the Chief to the back of his cabin. "This way. This way. Let us be off."

The Chief was proven wrong when his feet, calves and thighs were put through the mill. His knees were holding up but his self-esteem was at an all-time low. Jada saw him lagging behind and decided to slow so he wouldn't become lost.

"Why are you dawdling now? We shall be there after we cross that ridge!" Relic shouted from ahead. The ranger pointed to a rocky formation along the horizon that was no closer than two miles away. Her estimation told her they had already gone four and had a great deal longer to travel than they were led to believe. Jada didn't know if the Chief could last the remaining distance, seeing him hobble from what could only be blisters forming on his feet.

Jada waved for Relic to stop but the ranger continued on at his own steady pace ahead, ignoring the repercussions of pushing the Chief's health to its limits. "Do you want to stop?" she asked him, even though she knew the Chief would resist.

"Baron Annalee, don't you know me better than to ask that question?" He strode by her and finally let his weight fall back onto his blisters. His breathing grew heavier as a result, showing her it was causing him intense pain.

"We can camp at the lake if need be," she said, easily catching up with him. "Relic doesn't have to set our agenda. Your health—"

"Is not a concern unless I say it is," he retorted. "The goal is more important than the grind of getting there. My body will heal and this jaunt will be put out of our minds before we reach the castle with our finds."

"We don't know if we'll learn anything from him that can aid us. Battered bodies and weary minds won't do us any good if we're to be of help to the King." Jada whistled loudly, but Relic did not return back over the ridge. "That fool! I know he heard me."

The Chief grumbled, "I can hold together the rest of the way. All we have to do is reach the ridge. We should be able to see the lake once we're on the other side."

Jada slackened her pace, but not to the point where it was noticeable to the Chief. She was letting him stay step for step with her. The ground rose dramatically when they started their ascent up the ridge's slope. The Chief fumbled for every tree branch, plant and rock along the path that would help him pull his way to the top. Jada did the same, but more out of respect to the Chief so he wouldn't feel embarrassed that she could do it without the help. He glanced at her every so often to see how she fared. She saw the relief in his reaction, which brought hope they would be at the lake before he died of a heart attack.

"The blue," the Chief said as they came over the top of the ridge.

"Gorgeous," Jada added.

Since the rains had started over the territories, they had seen few breaks from the wind or clouds. As if they had crossed a magical boundary, the clouds ended and the full sun and its glorious rays shone above them, inviting them into the serene valley below.

"Have you ever seen such a clear sky? There's not a cloud beyond this ridge."

The Chief smiled for the first time in the last few miles, feeling more energetic as the sun warmed him from his misery. "And there's the lake!" he cried.

Jada saw it through the trees, too, a body of water no wider than the distance they had to cross to reach it. "A good soak in the lake for these feet will do me wonders in this weather. I can't wait to take these boots off."

The Chief appeared rejuvenated after the sun lifted his spirits. They found it ironic since the name of the lake had the word "Soul" in it. When Jada brought up the coincidence, the Chief burst into laughter, his joy returning.

Blue sky was replaced by towering trees after they left the top of the ridge, but knowing they would see it in its broad scope again once they reached the lake, they practically raced each other to get there. The slope on this side of the ridge was also not so steep, making their descent a rapid one.

When the land rose slightly again after a short dip, the Chief said, "The eyes of Yawrana have fallen on us. The answers we seek will be made clear. I can feel it!"

Jada smiled and now found herself running for real to keep up with the Chief. The expanse of the crystal waters filled their vision when they came over the last hill and left the shelter of the forest. Jada turned her body sideways to stop her forward momentum. She had to prevent herself from plowing into the Chief when he suddenly stopped before her, kicking up dust where she slid to a halt. Her heart felt as if the ice-cold hands of winter had curled their fingers around it. Unable to contain her scream from the terror that had seized her, she let it echo across the valley.

"I couldn't have said it better myself, Baron Annalee," Relic said, standing a dozen feet away from them. The ranger was facing them, full of confidence. More than one thousand gray-skinned warriors were brought to their feet as a result of their enemy appearing before them. Swords and shields stood ready in their hands, and visors were pulled down to protect their eyes from the sun.

"Why?" was the only word Jada could articulate as her shock overtook any understanding she had of the world around her.

"Why, Baron? Because it was meant to be." Relic's voice shredded and stabbed at her logic like knives. She felt her body wilt like a flower in frost and her mind melt under the heat of the intense sun. The ranger laughed and said, "Your past is now your future," before he turned toward the assembling Lazul army and shouted, "We march to war! On to Candlewick!"

# CHAPTER FIFTEEN
## A Race Against Sundown

Four hissing, black baskals with riders slithered their way from the center of Soul Lake as Jada and Chief Decker ran east into the forests of Marshant. The Chief started to run on the path that had brought them to the lake until Jada screamed for him to take to the woods instead. The switch would soon prove to be an advantage over the giant serpents as they tried to cut through the dense underbrush. One of the four became caught between a pair of thick trees, throwing its rider into a patch of lethal poisonberry. It only took one scratch of a needle that injected a blue fluid into the warrior to end his life, quickly flooding his heart and stopping all blood flowing through it.

The Chief zigzagged back and forth through the trees to make it difficult for the warriors to follow. Jada didn't stray far from the Chief as they climbed to the top of the ridge resembling a dragul's back.

The cries of more than a thousand warriors rose above the treetops, scaring every animal in their path to run. Jada and the Chief wished they could do the same, but their only thought was to somehow get back to the gandalays more than seven miles away. Tears streamed down the Chief's face as he fought off the mounting pain in his legs. Jada spared much of her own energy to assist him.

"Don't let me hold you back," he yelled, awkwardly jumping a log that cut across his path. The closest serpent fifty yards away went around the obstruction with ease, which closed the gap between it and the Chief.

Jada didn't respond and continued to shout orders on how to utilize less energy while he ran. The Chief lowered his head and focused on the ground only a few feet in front of him to release some of the tension that had knotted in his back and legs. He also swung his arms less and held them tighter to his body. Both techniques worked to double his speed. But the lead serpent and rider were gaining on them with fewer obstacles to block their chase.

The moment they reached the top of the ridge, Jada pulled the Chief behind a boulder and picked up a stone from the ground. When the serpent and rider came into view, she lobbed it at the warrior's head. It cracked loudly against his skull, dismounting him. The blow sent the warrior rolling down the hillside, out of view. The serpent turned and went back to the rider as the Chief and Jada broke back into their run.

"The serpent has chosen to stay with its master rather than come after us?" the Chief said. "They're predators and it shouldn't make much difference to them if they have a rider or not."

"With us out of its sight, perhaps it didn't know which way to go," Jada said.

They were running downhill again, something the Chief was thankful for as he let his weight carry him to the bottom.

The march toward Candlewick had begun, the warriors' footsteps turning into a pounding rhythm that would trample everything along the forest floor. The Lazul scouts not only watched for the Yawranan enemy, but they also cut and cleared away anything that could bottleneck or break apart Herikech's straight lines.

Jada's hearing was better than the Chief's. She discerned a voice within the Lazul forces calling a command to slay all women and children in the castle. Her stomach felt upset, spurring her to run harder. The one thing she was determined to do was reach the gates of Candlewick before the Chief and she could be caught by the baskals.

With the ridge fading behind them, the two of them disappeared into the thick forest surrounding the gorge. The uncountable scratches the Chief had received to his face and hands were bleeding and running down onto his black outfit. He pulled off his orange armband and wiped away some blood that mixed with the sweat draining into his right eye.

In light of their situation, the Chief held up better than Jada hoped he would, and he did it carrying an axe and other provisions that would slow most travelers.

The sound of a hunt horn echoed at the top of the ridge, which told them their struggles were only beginning. "They may be sending more baskals after us," Jada said, now running with the Chief as if they were training partners.

"How are we going to throw them off our trail? These are skilled hunters."

"I don't know. First we have to find the gandalays. Without them, we won't make it out of this sector alive. The next four miles will be the hardest we'll have to run. My own legs are beginning to tire, but Candlewick's army must be forewarned to give them enough time to set up their warfront defenses."

"If I fall, don't wait for me, and this time I mean it," he said, glancing at her sideways.

"Fine," Jada said to appease the Chief. "For now, we must go north, find the edge of the gorge and take it to the forked road. It's the only way we'll locate the gandalays without getting lost or bypassing them."

"Didn't Relic say there were ambushes along that trail?" the Chief asked.

"You still believe him? He probably said that so we would take the long way to the lake to tire us. No, we must go back to the gorge. If there are ambushes, then we'll just have to cope with them when that time comes."

Talking became an inconvenience the further they ran. They fought for every ounce of energy they had left as they moved at a sharp angle northeast toward the gorge. Before long, Jada and the Chief came to the edge of it, a small victory they savored. They cut west but stayed in the shadows of the forest to prevent being picked off in the open by a Lazul archer.

The Chief was stumbling again, using trees to push himself along. "Can't we take a moment to rest?" he asked.

Jada shook her head and was gasping for air. "I think I saw the head of a serpent emerging from the brush at the base of the gorge not long ago. We can't afford to."

"Then this may be where we part." The Chief's face was red and dripping with sweat. He looked ready to pass out, accept death, or both.

Jada felt the frustration bubble up inside her and then it finally exploded. "We're nearly to the gandalays!"

"My body needs the rest, Baron. Maybe I can at least slow them and give you a better chance."

"I will not have bargained with the Silhouettes for your life for nothing!" she snapped.

A loud hiss sounded from the path to their left.

"Warn the King!" the Chief cried, falling back.

He lay on a pile of fir needles as he agonized over every sore his body was trying to repair. The Chief felt like a balloon swelling in the hot sun, about to pop. His feet were the worst, riddled with blisters and bruises after running what felt like a marathon to him. He looked at the clouds above and saw they were gray with blue lightning crackling through them.

A loud hiss brought him back when a large black form with a warrior upon its back came toward him.

"They are weak," the warrior rider said. The baskal's jaws opened as the mammoth snake moved forward to bite and swallow the Chief. "Prepare for the greatest pain you'll ever feel!"

A branch cracked above the warrior. The moment he looked up he found a sword impaling him at a downward angle through his shoulder. His chilling scream broke the baskal's attention long enough for the Chief to let a dagger fly. The blade struck the serpent perfectly between the eyes. Its body thrashed from the fatal wound, tossing Jada three trees over, breaking several branches along the way. She landed on her side and watched as the creature shook and let out a final hiss.

The Chief pushed himself up and asked, "Are you all right, Baron?"

"Couldn't be better." She sprinted back through the woods to him. Helping him up, she asked, "Can you go?"

"Yes. I think so. The gorge is widening," the Chief noted. "I think our luck may hold out long enough for us to sleep another night."

"Don't get ahead of yourself. When I was up in that tree I saw two more baskal riders coming up the path. It won't be long before they also catch us."

"I knew I blabbed too early," the Chief growled as they ran again.

The hiss of the baskals could be heard more clearly, increasing their prayers. The Chief was crying as he ran. Jada's heart sunk as she yanked him along by the elbow, not giving up trying to save him. And just when the Chief thought he would need to lie down again, a cold gust of air pressed against them. They looked up and saw the forked road ahead.

"There it is!" Jada cried. "Let the strongest winds try to stop us now."

When they rounded the corner, a long black tail with coarse scales lashed out of the tall weeds growing along the forest. They were batted backward, knocking the wind out of them. The warrior riding the snake waved to another coming up behind them.

"We're surrounded," Jada groaned, feeling the ribs on her right side. When she got to her feet, a bolt of pain shot through them. "Ahhh!" she cried. She helped the Chief up and wondered which of the baskals would strike them first, both less than a dozen feet away. Their hypnotizing golden eyes entranced Jada, her body becoming stiff from fright.

"Look there!" the Chief screamed, snapping Jada out of her locked stare with the one behind them. The Baron turned and saw the gandalay stallions emerging from the trees ahead. They ran near the lead baskal to entice it away from them.

"They're drawing it away!" the Chief exclaimed. The warrior waved to the one behind them and ordered, "You take those two. We'll go after the stallions. Herikech will want them."

When the baskal in front of them went after the gandalays, Jada and the Chief found themselves chasing it to get away from the one behind them. "If we stay close to the leader the other won't strike," Jada said. They were no further than five feet behind the slick tail, chasing it like a fish after bait being reeled in by a fisherman.

The gandalays galloped hard, running close to the edge of the gorge, outdistancing the serpent.

"Move over, you beast!" the Lazul rider commanded his baskal. Sand and rock started to give way from the heavy weight of the serpent, crumbling the section of the wall it was traveling dangerously close to. Jada and the Chief watched the rider and baskal suddenly drop into the gorge in front of them. They heard the scream of the warrior as he and his baskal plummeted five hundred feet to the bottom.

"Jump for that sapling!" Jada yelled. A solitary sequera no taller than seven feet stood only a foot from the edge of the gorge ahead. It was only thirty paces away if they could reach it.

"Are you mad?" the Chief asked. "You'll send us to our deaths!"

"It's not far behind us anyway!"

The Chief saw the gandalays were still running at a full gallop and would not circle back to them in time. The serpent was on their heels when Jada leaped for the sapling. Her hand, arm and body stretched as far as they could go, catching the two-inch diameter base of the sapling. Her body swung forward as she hung on. The Chief, only moments after her, shot out for her legs. Jada extended her right for him to catch when she swung back. At first it looked as if he would fall short. The Chief grasped the tip and heel of her boot as he cried for help. The Lazul warrior screamed for his baskal to turn but the serpent went the same path as its prey. The baskal's head fell a foot shy of the Chief's legs, shooting downward underneath him. Not one to succumb to death easily, the Lazul warrior jumped for the Chief from the baskal's basket seat and caught the Chief's leg.

Jada screamed from all the weight dragging her down. The sapling bent over in a severe arc as its roots started to tear loose from the ledge. Almost six hundred pounds were pulling on it as her hands slid down the branch to which she was clinging.

"Get off my leg, you brigand!" the Chief yelled at the Lazul.

The warrior bit into the Chief's leg in defiance and came up with blood in his teeth. The Chief emitted a scream and shouted, "Pull us up, Baron!"

Jada couldn't believe her ears. It wasn't as if she wanted them dangling over a five hundred foot drop and would have gladly done so if she didn't have over four hundred pounds hanging off her right leg. Her fingers were going numb and her hands continued to slide down the branch, ripping off leaves as they went. When she was near the end, tears fell from her eyes. At first she thought the white blur in them was caused by the tears, but then to her elation, the whiteness moved and whinnied. The gandalays had come back!

Risking losing everything, she let go with her left hand and held it up. The stallion lowered its front legs and head to use its mouth to pinch the Baron's sleeve in its teeth. The muscles in Jada's biceps were tearing. Tears were now soaking her face as she cried and shakily held on. They began to move upward as the gandalay backed up, digging its hooves into the sandy path. Inch by inch they neared the ledge until Jada's right elbow connected with it. She dug it in and used it to work her away from the drop-off.

"Let go!" she cried once the Chief appeared over the edge and could support himself with his own arms. He did and felt the Lazul warrior attempting to climb up his back.

The gandalay let go when Jada stood. She saw the Chief slipping back into the gorge. The warrior's hand appeared on the Chief's shoulder as she cried. She unleashed her sword and screamed, "Duck!"

The Chief threw his face into the dirt and listened to a lopping sound behind him. The weight on his back shed itself a moment later. The Baron knelt down and pulled the Chief up the rest of the way. He looked down into the gorge and saw the head and body of the warrior land separately at the bottom. Out of breath, he rolled onto his back and moaned.

Jada collapsed on the ground, clutching her right arm. "Uhhh," she said and rubbed her arm muscles to help make them feel better.

"We must ride now, Baron. Our wounds will have to wait until they can be properly tended to." The Chief was crawling toward the gandalay, which made Jada burst into laughter.

She got up and helped push him into his saddle. A cloud of dust rose a mile to the south as the sound of the Lazul army began to catch up with them. Jada quickly mounted. "Hurry!" she said. They rode through rain, hail, snow and wind until Snake's Weave was a best-forgotten memory.

The gandalays were a sight to behold as they carried the Chief and Jada safely through the forests of Marshant. But Jada's arms and the Chief's feet, legs and back had been punished to the point they couldn't do without some rest.

"Whoa, Oliver," Jada said. She pulled up on the stallion's reins to slow him. The gandalay whinnied a protest and walked underneath a bough, coming to a standstill.

The Chief fell from his saddle onto a wet, grassy knoll, his leg muscles cramping. Rain poured on him while he stretched them out in front of him.

"Are you holding together?" Jada asked, her arms hanging loosely at her sides.

"I look worse than I am . . . if that's possible." He opened his mouth to let rain fall in it and wash his tongue clean. The more water he drank, the better he felt. He touched the wound where the Lazul warrior had bitten him, feeling its tenderness beneath his pant leg. "Our stay here must be short. The army's rapid march to the castle will get them there by eight, just before sundown. We all know how much they like the dark. It will be to their advantage."

She pulled a long piece of cloth out of a medical kit in her saddle and made a sling out of it. Carefully placing her arm inside it, some of the pain vanished from the support. She turned her face upward to gaze at the dark cloud moving over them and toward Candlewick. "I've never seen weather act so strangely. This single cloud has produced rain, hail, sleet and snow in waves, the hail by far being the worst we ran into. My chest plate has taken a few sizeable dents and my face feels like it was pelted with pebbles."

"You had something to protect your head at least," the Chief grumbled. "The only roof I could find for mine was a medical book I dug out of my saddlebag. My fingers took a fairly good beating as I held it over my head." The Chief raised his hand to show the blood leaking from his knuckles.

Despite the rain, the Baron's and Chief's eyes wanted to close and lure them into slumber. The Chief caught himself when he felt his head falling to the side. He forced himself to sit up and wash water into his eyes. When he was able to see again, he said, "I heard the Lazul army was supposed to be in Emison. How is it they came to Marshant without being seen by a farmer, rancher or any town folk along the way here?"

"It tells me Herikech is domineering more than just King Deardrop's men. Several messengers sighted him in the woods during their race. Herikech is employing individuals other than soldiers and guards, Relic being one. For the first time since the grassland war of the Waungee, I fear we may fall to the Lazuls. Herikech has powers we don't know how to reckon with. He's having his way with the castle and the Yards, going wherever he wishes, showing his insolence for Noran and his laws."

The Chief couldn't help but reflect on his own situation. "I can't even say for certain that my own flame fighters aren't bowing to Herikech's command. Some of them have been ignoring some of their duties—the young and more inexperienced ones. I have given them strict warnings, but it has now become clear to me they have no intention of carrying out their chores, doing the minimum requirements to keep me from throwing them out of the waterhouse. I attributed their behavior to bad upbringing, but my tolerance of their ill manners has far exceeded my normal limit. They were waiting all along for the Lazul army to strike, and at the right moment rebel against me and the other men when we were distracted. How many other townspeople or even tower servants have fallen under Herikech's influence?"

Jada shook her head. "You raise a valid point. We'll only know when one side has prevailed. The hail is catching up with us. We better move on before we are bombarded again." They ran to the gandalays, who were nervously neighing as the hail pellets struck their haunches and necks. They sped away quickly after the Chief and Jada mounted them, running at an intense pace through the woods and toward a growing speck in the distance named Candlewick Castle.

The wind howled and blew fiercely at the Chief and Baron, pressing them back as if it didn't want them to succeed. Lightning stuck trees all around them, misdirecting the gandalays from the Western Gate of the castle less than a mile ahead. Jada and the Chief held their reins tightly, not letting the scared mounts wander too far off course. A tree fell before them but the gandalays hurdled it without losing their riders.

Jada was the first to enter the Western Yard and break her horse into a fast run. The castle's watchtowers rose up before her when she passed the dragul keep. When she could see figures in the watchtower windows, she raised her hand and hollered, "Open the gate! It is I, Baron Jada Annalee and Chief Braiy Decker! The Lazul army approaches from Marshant!"

The guard of the closest tower stood as if there was nothing to be panicked about. The man slowly turned away from the window and disappeared as she stopped her stallion. Jada waited for the guard to reappear or the gate to open as the Chief came up along side her. Her anxiety became substantial when the gate didn't invite them in. She kept looking toward the window, hoping she was wrong. And then he was there, bow and arrow in hand and ready to fire.

"Get down!" The Chief screamed as he jumped from his saddle and tackled Jada out of hers. They fell onto the soggy yard with a loud splash as the arrow struck Jada's saddle horn. The gandalays whinnied and put their bodies in front of their masters to shield them.

More arrows whizzed around them as they remounted and sprinted three hundred yards to the next tower. Jada looked up and saw several archers firing at them from the wall tops.

"Is there anyone left who can help us?" the Chief asked.

"I just hope Herikech hasn't harmed the King." They rode on. The guard wasn't visible in the window in the second tower. "On to the next," Jada cried.

After reaching each tower one at a time, they grew more and more nervous that they all had been taken. When they arrived at the last, the southwestern facing Gillwood Territory, their hope was gone. They rode out of the archers' range and aimed for the drgaul keep to find shelter from the new sweeping sheets of sleet.

"Where are the draguls?" the Chief asked once they had crossed over the fallen doors and were inside.

"In the Gaming Yard. They were recently attacked by the soldiers who guarded the keep."

The Chief couldn't help but curse. "They would've been a fine way to get inside the castle. They're the only flying mounts that can manage to get us over those walls."

"We can't stay here. The Lazuls will be here before sundown. They'll burn this building to the ground if they know we're in it."

A light suddenly came on in Jada's eyes that was promising. Words were always better than silence to the Chief, and Jada's were filled with promise when she said the exact ones he desired to hear: "I have an idea."

When Jada and the Chief reached the base of the sequeras, High Elder Elenoi was waiting for them near a cart that was regularly used to transport the Elders to the castle. Jada jumped down from her gandalay and embraced the High Elder with a warm hug.

"You knew of our coming?" Jada asked.

"From a reflection in my bath water," Elenoi said. "Sanda is getting prepared as we speak. She will be loaded into this cart. Please be very careful. Quargo sloths are not as enthusiastic about climbing stone walls as they are about trees."

Jada smiled. "We need whatever shields your guards have. We'll tie them to her sides. It will help protect her from the archers' arrows."

"It's already being done."

"Then you know the watchtowers have been overrun by traitors."

"I don't know what power Herikech holds over the King's men, but they are just as devoted as any other creature who follows him and will gladly go to their graves on his behalf before this war ends. The other Elders were denied entrance to the castle this afternoon. The King has no idea that no one has been able to enter since that time. I fear his death will be coming soon if someone doesn't warn him."

"It's a relief to know the King still lives," Jada said, "but Herikech's army is marching toward Candlewick from Marshant and will be here by sundown. We've already lost valuable time."

The Chief smiled at the High Elder when she looked his way and said, "Once again your skills have been used to help more than fighting flames, Chief Decker. Your aura is strong today and will serve you well. I can see Yawrana is with you."

Not knowing what to make of the comment, the Chief replied, "I would be better off fighting fires."

There was a loud bark that made Jada turn her head to the left. Sanda was being led to the cart next to the High Elder. A guard led the dark-eyed, brown beast up into it by a rope and closed her in. The guard gave the sloth a hand of carrus and scratched it behind one of its floppy ears.

The guard then hooked up two shayas to the cart when Jada intervened. "No. We shall use our gandalays. They are more cunning and will flee for shelter once we have unloaded the sloth." The guard saluted the Baron and then helped Jada and the Chief attach the stallions.

When they were finished, Jada turned to the High Elder and said, "Evacuate your trees before the army arrives. You'll be much safer in the woods to the north. Go to the Sweet Wine Tavern in Shaba. If we are victorious, we will send a messenger to inform you all is safe. If we're not, our fate should spread by word of mouth to the tavern. I don't believe there's enough time for local sector forces to rally to the castle's aid at this time, but if you want to organize the effort, you are more than welcome to do it."

The High Elder nodded and hugged the Baron one more time. "May the Circle of Life bring good of your sacrifices."

"And to you." Jada climbed back into the saddle of her gandalay and kicked her boot heels in to send them on their way. The sloth barked from the sudden movement of the cart and then nestled down onto the hay bedding the guards had laid down for it to rest on. The cart trundled toward the castle, the gandalays utilizing their mighty strength to pull the creature along. The north watchtower came into sight well before they even arrived at its imposing presence.

"Use a shield to help deflect the arrows when we start our ascent," Jada said, pointing to the one that had been strapped to the Chief's saddle. "I'll take the other side while Sanda takes us up. If she is injured in her climb, she could fall. Stones are no match for bark."

"It would help if we had some of our own archers."

"At this point, I'm not sure what kind of help we can expect once we get inside the castle."

The window in the northern watchtower was as black as midnight inside. If anyone was in the watcher's room, they were either ignoring their post or hiding. Jada steered the cart toward the center of the tower so no archer from the wall tops running east or west could take a clean shot at them. The Chief pulled on the rope around Sanda's neck. The sloth climbed out of the cart and sat by the base of the tower for instruction. Jada didn't have any carrus, something she forgot to ask for when she was at the sequeras. Instead, she offered up a juicy roi by cutting it in half with a hunting knife. She mashed it into her palm and held it beneath the sloth's nose. Sanda took a sniff and started licking her palm, finding the food satisfactory.

"Load," Jada commanded. The sloth went into a sitting position and stretched its muscular and lengthy limbs around the tower as far as they could go, not intimidated by the slippery task ahead. Jada opened the door to the reed basket on its back when it was vertical and stepped in after the Chief. She latched it shut and whispered in the sloth's ear, "Up!"

The first few feet would tell them how fast they would be able to go, if at all. The sloth scraped its huge claws down the wall until they caught a hold between two stones. Sanda pulled herself up, clinging to where she found her clawholds. They had already risen five feet. Then they had gone another five and another, providing promise they would reach the window. When they were almost halfway up, the archers reappeared at the wall tops and fired. Many of their arrows either bounced or skipped off the watchtower to land in the Northern Yard below.

"Watch out!" The sloth stopped when a stone plummeted toward its head. Jada extended her shield over Sanda's face to let the metal take the brunt of the blow. The stone bounced off and fell around them. "Up!" Jada cried again as an arrow thudded into the lip of the basket near her arm.

The sloth pulled up again, able to find crevice after crevice while using the strength in its powerful arms and legs. The Chief deflected two arrows on the left side that would have struck the sloth in the rear leg. The higher they climbed, the closer the archers came in line with them to take cleaner shots. A larger stone was thrown from the window, but it was slightly off, allowing Jada to knock it away before it hit Sanda's shoulder.

"Another!" shouted a voice above them.

The window was less than a dozen feet away. The Baron and Chief turned back and forth between the window and their sides to protect Sanda. But while Jada was shielding the sloth from another falling stone, an arrow struck the creature's upper arm. Sanda cried in pain and wanted to grab at the shaft.

Jada cried, "Up!" once more for the sloth to keep its focus on the window. With the arrow having struck the sloth in the elbow, Sanda found it hard to bend her arm. Jada and the Chief screamed when Sanda jumped the last dozen feet and caught hold of the window's ledge. The Chief immediately climbed over Sanda and punched the soldier who had been dropping stones on them. Jada worked at the arrow in Sanda's elbow and yanked it out. The sloth growled as Jada tossed the shaft away.

After Jada had climbed out and joined the Chief inside the tower, she looked at Sanda and ordered, "Down! Back to the Elders!"

Not having to depend on her arms for most of its decent, Sanda managed to work her way down the side of the watchtower without further harm now that the Baron and Chief became the center of attention.

A group of five soldiers and two archers entered the watcher's room. The Chief slashed the first soldier left and right. Jada beheaded another who tried to do the same to her first and then pushed an archer out of the room and over the staircase railing when she went out the door. The Chief killed the second archer as he let off his shot, the arrow striking a soldier coming up behind him. Jada cut down the last with a direct thrust to the man's midsection. They looked at each other as they took a deep breath of air before they hustled down the watchtower's staircase.

"Did the sloth survive?" the Chief asked when they reached the bottom, worried about the creature.

"Yes. And now, to the bell tower!" Jada cried, slapping him on the back.

The private meeting hall adjacent to Noran's old bedchamber was packed with many bodies of high-ranking officers in the army, the Barons, and their personal guards. Noran notified specific people he wanted to attend through Majestic Messenger mail. The dobbins were to travel in pairs when they delivered the messages throughout the castle and were to inform no one else about the meeting. The King sat at the head of a long oval table. When everyone saw him stand, a hush fell.

"Thank you for coming as quickly as you could, Barons, Generals and all other participants," Noran said, looking pale.

"Baron Annalee is not present," Fields said. "Should we not wait for her?"

"The Baron is on a special assignment at the moment. I don't know when she'll return, so we'll begin now. We're in grave danger of losing the castle to the Lazuls." A murmur ran through the room until Noran continued. "Our own men are turning against us and joining Herikech Illeon's ranks. Many of the corridors in the castle and the roads leading to Candlewick are under his control, allowing Herikech to go wherever he wishes to execute his plans."

Windal asked, "If that's true, then whom do we trust? There may be men in this very room who are no longer loyal."

"There is a way we have learned to distinguish friend from foe," Noran said. "Each one of you does not carry the scent of this." He held up a bottle of the honey Fields had brought from Dowhaven so all in the room could clearly see the yellowish liquid inside. "This is Gillwood honey, and none of you are wearing it. It throws a powerful odor when worn. We have sent a bottle to the maker's labs in the Southern Yard for testing. We'll know soon what ingredients it contains that are controlling men's minds. The court announcer, Ballan, has been found wearing it, as have several other soldiers near the treasure vaults and my old bedchamber. Ballan and those from the vaults were all being held for questioning in Candlewick's dungeons, as were three Lazul men from Dixon. I was to meet with them this morning until they were all discovered dead."

"How?" Oreus asked, not familiar with the layout of the dungeon's cells.

"'How' is the question I've been asking myself since I learned of the information, Baron Blake. We recently learned Thorn, Captain Winslow's personal bodyguard, was entering the cells through a stone in the floor. Once we learned tunnels from each of the cells existed, we had them filled, leaving no other way in. The ventilation shafts are barred and have all been verified to be firmly in place. It was then we found the honey covering the men that were being held."

"The Lazuls, too?" Windal asked.

"No," Noran said. "They hung themselves with their own bed sheets."

"Excuse me, Your Majesty," Rydor interrupted. "I must speak on behalf of Jada and bring up an event that is related. There have been disturbances in the Catacombs of Emison where the intruders have been found rummaging through the preservative supplies, which I believe contains honey. Nothing was taken and a few bodies were found moved in their graves. How this is related is uncertain, but perhaps we need to send someone to the catacombs to investigate the matter again."

"Thank you, General, for making us aware of that information. I think it also would be wise to do so."

Rydor smiled and nodded.

"I want every soldier and warrior in Candlewick to be examined for traces of the honey on their skin. If any man is found to be coated with it, I want him imprisoned. General Fields has also notified me the Lazuls are searching for natron and cooking oils. This also is possibly related to the mystery surrounding Emison's catacombs and the traitorous acts of Yawranans."

"What about the mangler?" Oreus asked. "I've heard now there is at least one more. How will we capture it?"

"Baron Annalee is trying to learn that now. The mangler is a normal man like us when either moon isn't red. We know a mirror's reflection of the red moonlight can kill it, but only if the beast comes into contact with the rays."

Noran continued, "Fortunately, the mangler didn't kill me when it thought I wouldn't give it a fight. Imagine its surprise when it found out otherwise." The men in the room laughed and saluted him.

"But you have been unable to recall any details of the incident," Master Hurran reminded Noran. "It is more likely you were saved by the guards in the bell tower room who sacrificed their lives to save you, than by your own hand."

The room was silent. Noran didn't appreciate the challenge when he was trying to raise the men's belief in his abilities. "Then how do you explain my escape, Master? I wouldn't be living now unless there was some kind of struggle on my part to get away from the beast after it killed Master Oyen and took me from the medical wing. I'm no longer the boy I used to be."

Hurran decided to hold his tongue, seeing his words were not well placed. He nodded and said, "Forgive me, Your Highness. You are correct."

"Your battle with it will become legendary in time," Rydor said, noticing the King was uncomfortable with the truth Hurran had stated.

The men banged their fists on the table until the King smiled again and raised a hand for them to stop. Just as Noran was about to mention the disappearance of the Lazul army in Emison, a tower bell rang out, calling every able body to arms.

Noran, Viktoran, Bruneau, Blaynor and Rydor raced down the corridor to the bell tower room toward a fight ensuing between Jada and a handful of soldiers. The Chief was further down the hall, battling others. When the soldiers fighting Jada and the Chief saw the King's approach, they fled.

"Bloody cowards," the Chief said, running after them with his axe held high. He cut down one man before he could get out of range.

"Baron," Noran said, surprised to find Jada was the one who set the sequence of chimes into motion.

"My Lord," she said out of breath, "the Lazul army marches from Marshant and will be here after sundown! Soldiers who are under Herikech's command patrol the watchtowers. The western and eastern towers that control the gates must be recaptured immediately before they are opened for Herikech's forces."

Rydor and Viktoran volunteered to take command at each post. Since Viktoran no longer had Heaven's Light in his possession, Noran no longer saw the advantage to keep the Baron at his side. He gave the order and released Rydor and Viktoran to their stations.

"What of the Silhouettes?" Noran asked Jada.

"They gave us the name of a ranger named Relic in Bane Sector who ended up betraying us. He took us into the enemy's camp at Soul Lake. The Chief and I luckily escaped and raced back here. I believe the Silhouettes had no knowledge the ranger was a traitor, though they were suspicious when three army Yawranan soldiers tried to enter their hideout, more of your men serving Herikech. The weather is picking up ahead of the Lazul army and is giving them a clear path to the castle. Prepare for ice and snow."

"The Elders—" Noran said, his thoughts reaching out for the prophets.

"The Chief and I already have sent them into hiding. They'll be safe for now."

Noran was relieved and put a hand on her shoulder. "You have done well, Baron. Take pride in what you have contributed. A simple thank you is not enough. I hope to repay you for your efforts better in the near future. However, I still need you for one other important matter."

"Anything, my Lord. What is it that you shall have me do?"

Oreus and Quinn met up with Rydor and Jime at the Western Gate. When the four met, they saw the draguls being fired upon by archers from the Gaming Arena's upper seats. Oreus took up his bow and fit an arrow to the string, aiming at one of the men at the bowl's rim. He fired and hit the man in the throat. The figure wavered from the impact and fell over the side when he couldn't keep his balance. His fall was seen by several guards at the entrance to the arena. They ran over to investigate the body.

"Those two men look innocent," Rydor said. "Take them and help free the draguls from their chains."

"What about you? Any plans for the Lazuls?" Oreus asked.

"Jime and I will make a visit to the western watchtowers. It has been seized by Herikech's men."

"Yawrana be with you," Oreus said, shaking Rydor's hand.

Rydor waved to Jime while Oreus ran with Quinn to their new destinations. All four men knew time was short before the Lazuls arrived at the gates to lay siege to the castle. Their victories or failures in preparation would determine which way the scales of favor would tip when the war began.

# CHAPTER SIXTEEN
## The Battle for Candlewick

At the opposite end of the castle, at the Eastern Gate, Viktoran was joined by Barons Windal Barrow and Edin DeHue to find a way into the watchtower, where the release levers to the portcullis and outer gates resided. They met at the doors of the tower and found it locked, as expected. When Viktoran ordered a nearby guard to fetch more men and bring back a battering ram, the guard punched the Baron. When the guard's fist hit Viktoran's face, the Baron could feel a sticky wetness on his cheek. He wiped it away when he recovered from the blow and smelled it. "Honey!" he grumbled. Windal and Edin saw Viktoran fall and ran after the guard, who was escaping back up a ramp into the castle.

"Let him go!" Viktoran yelled.

The Barons stopped, turned around and came back. "He'll bring more men to stop us," Edin said. "Let me get him. It's the least I can do after General Keys made me look like a buffoon by forging my name."

"The King knows the truth behind that matter. Come, we still have enough time to access the tower," Viktoran said. "Help me turn that tension catapult toward the door."

The three men went to the large contraption fifty yards away and each grabbed a section of rope attached to the circular turntable platform it sat on. Viktoran unlocked a pin that kept the platform from rotating while the catapult was fired so they could turn it. Slinging the rotation ropes over their shoulders, they walked away from the tower to spin the catapult's arm toward its door.

"That's good," Viktoran said as he let go of his rope. He relocked the pin and said, "Now for the proper angle." He put a pair of large wood blocks in front of the first two wheels and pulled at a lever on the right side of the catapult. The top tipped downward until it could go no further. Taking a look at the catapult's arm from the side, he predicted where the stone from the leather-lined basket would land. "Perfect," he said when it was ready.

Together, Windal and Edin lifted a hundred pound block and dropped it into the ammo bucket after Viktoran cranked back the arm. "Stand back," Windal said to Edin. The tension of the winch released as the arm pivoted forward. The stone shot from the bucket and slammed into the wall next to the watchtower door, collapsing both. The watchtower rumbled from the direct impact but didn't tip, but a sizeable three-foot by five-foot hole was punched out. Dust and debris settled quickly enough for them to find their way through and access the stairs inside.

A dozen soldiers greeted the three Barons before they took their first step upward. Viktoran drew his sword and gathered his courage. When the blade didn't light, he remembered he no longer had Heaven's Light. The feel of the new blade would take getting used to, but he fought with the same tenacity as he always did. With his first two swings he cut three men down and pushed them off the stairs.

Windal cut a soldier from the stomach up on the first swing. The Baron threw the soldier behind him and sent him tumbling down the stairs.

Edin was not as skilled a fighter as Viktoran or Windal and decided it would be best to attack opponents that had already been injured and fell his way. He swung at them until they died.

It wasn't long before Viktoran had cut through the wave of men to finish his ascent. Windal and Edin turned to see more soldiers coming up after them. The two Barons ran after Viktoran to fight them on the upper platform.

The door to the watchtower room was open. Trusting his instincts, Viktoran kicked it open and threw his body to the side. An arrow shot out, barely missing him. It clacked against the stone of the far wall of the tower. Viktoran rolled inside and whipped his sword at the archer. The blade went through the man, causing him to fall backward and drop his bow. As if he was still in shock, the archer pulled the blade slowly from his torso. Viktoran helped him and then swung the edge across the archer's throat.

Windal and Edin burst into the room and slammed the door behind them. Windal found the lock broken. He picked up the deceased archer's bow and used it as a door jam. Shoving an end underneath, he tried to open it himself from the inside. It held tight.

Viktoran opened another door that led them back down the tower and to a room filled with cranks and gears. As they reached the chamber, a guard came at them. Viktoran disposed of him with one swing.

"I'm glad I didn't fight you in the Tournament of Wills," Windal said after he witnessed Viktoran's clean and precise strokes at close range.

"I am, too," Viktoran smiled. "The watchtower guard has opened the gates. Release the portcullis and I will crank the gates to close again."

Windal nodded and went to a wall where a thick chain ran up it and through a hole in the ceiling fifty feet above him. Pressing down on the catch, the chain rattled as it unwound from a wheel a few feet to his left and disappeared back through the ceiling. "That should do it," he said to himself.

Viktoran was sweating by the time he heard the outer gates boom shut. Edin went to a beam running through a different hole in the wall and was joined by Windal as they grabbed the iron handles screwed into it. With a good push, the beam slid across the iron resting arms extending from the wall it sat in and slid out the hole. When they heard a thud, they knew the crossbeam had barred the entrance. Windal hooked the beam to multiple rings attached to the wall to prevent it from being slid back into the tower from the outside.

Above them they heard voices and the clinking of metal boots on stone.

"More company," Viktoran said, before they charged up the stairs to take the new adversaries head on.

Quinn couldn't match the strength and swiftness of Oreus's legs as they sprinted for the Gaming Arena. All the draguls were now screeching and writhing in their restraints. The chains rattled as they attempted to snap them and break free, but the links were too thick and heavy, even for a dragul.

The two guards who had inspected the body of the fallen archer stood and saluted Oreus when he and Quinn approached. "Baron Blake," they each said. "Did you see what caused this man to fall?" one of them asked.

"Yes. Me," Oreus replied.

The guards looked at each other and then back at Oreus.

"There are archers firing at the draguls. Do you not hear their cries?" Oreus asked.

"It's feeding time for the draguls, Baron," the taller of the two guards said. "We were just about to take care of it—"

Oreus cut him off and pointed to the dead archer. "This man was firing arrows at the draguls. They are in danger. Come with me."

The four men entered the arena through a side entrance and went down a long tunnel to reach a five-foot sand ring that circled around the entire arena. On the inside of the ring was a ten-foot high wooden fence. Oreus climbed the closest ladder and peered over the top of the wall to scan the grounds. His jaw dropped when he saw one of the draguls lying motionless. The other draguls were squawking and using their powerful limbs to crawl along the ground to try and rip up the stakes holding them in place.

"Illeon!" Oreus cried. He threw his bow down and jumped from the top of the wall, landing on his right knee and hands to absorb the impact of his fall.

"Baron, no!" Quinn cried and turned his head to scan the stands behind him. Three archers stood in a row by the King's arena seat, ready to fire at Oreus as he ran to save the draguls. Quinn pulled a dagger from his belt and threw it as hard as he could. He watched the blade spin end over end as it sped toward the three archers. His aim was true, striking the one the closest to him in the temple. The man was thrown sideways into the other two archers just as they let off their shots. Their arrows shot wide right, missing the tail of the closest dragul, Plunav, by ten feet.

Quinn ordered the two guards to follow him along the ring wall so they could get near enough to make a charge. If they entered the stands too soon, the archers would reload and kill them before they took a dozen steps. They heard an arrow whiz over their helmets as they hunched over and stayed low. One archer continued to fire arrows at Oreus, who was now being shielded by Plunav. The dragul lashed out with his tail to knock the arrows away.

Firewing screeched when she saw Oreus come to a halt at Ileon's head. Tears fell from Oreus's eyes as his mind tried to understand that his old friend would never fly again. The dragul had taken an arrow through its left eye, its soul no longer within. "NO!" he screamed, lowering his head to rest on the dragul's neck. Memories came like a flood upon him. A sharp pain filled his shoulder again like it had once before when Illeon had lifted Rydor and him to safety before they were assailed by pursuing baskals in the Waungee. The dragul had carried them for many miles throughout their journey to retrieve the snowtears and save Noran's mother. He suddenly felt the need to vomit. Not wanting to hold it back, he unleashed the wave of warmth from his stomach. When it had passed, he wiped his mouth and lowered his head once more on Illeon's neck. Firewing nudged him with her snout, sharing in his pain.

Oreus looked up at the giant golden-bellied female and saw a tear form and start to fall from her right eye. He found the sight captivating, for how often does one see a dragul cry? Jada had shown Oreus once how to make a dragul laugh, but his thoughts told him what he was witnessing was extraordinary. Oreus petted Firewing's snout to console her and let the teardrop fall into his hand. The tear washed his skin. She had taken great affection to Illeon, which made him adore her even more.

A few moments passed when Oreus realized something unusual was happening after the dragul's tear coated his hand. Instead of it dripping from his fingertips, the tear was starting to be absorbed by his skin. His hand was glowing and pulsing, feeling strangely vibrant. The pulse spread down his arm to his elbow, and then up to his shoulder. The sensation moved throughout his entire body until it had filled every part of it. Firewing watched the Baron become luminous and then smiled at him. Oreus felt a wind swirl around him as a thousand lives rush by him before they turned into a whirlwind that whipped against his face, blowing his hair back. An archer's arrow struck his chest but passed through him during the experience. The next thing he knew, he was gasping for air on the ground, searching for his next breath. When he had regained his awareness of his surroundings, he saw Firewing wrapping her giant wing over him. She was no longer weeping and the other draguls had turned their attention toward him. Firewing looked at him and opened her mouth. Expecting to hear a loud screech from her, Oreus was stunned when he realized she was . . . speaking.

"What?" Oreus mumbled, as if he was imagining it.

Firewing seemed to be equally stunned that they were verbally communicating. She repeated her words. "Free me."

Oreus fell backward. His tongue was tied and his mind reeling. "Did . . . did you say 'Free me?'"

"Yes, Oreus Blake. FREE ME!"

As another arrow missed Firewing's head, Oreus forced himself into action. He ran to where the chain was connected to the stake running deep into the ground. A lock connected the two. "I'll have to get the key."

"The archer has stolen it," Firewing said, using her wingtip to point at the fleeing man running along the stands. Oreus turned and saw him. Further away Quinn and one of the two other guards were still trying to apprehend the second archer near the King's throne. The second guard with Quinn had been slain, his body visible in the stands, draped over a carved stone bench with an arrow out of the side of his head.

Oreus was about to run after the archer with the keys when the Firewing yelled, "Baron, do not forget your bow!"

He stopped, almost losing his balance, and then turned around to pick it up. The archer was passing the middle section of the northern stands, taking time to stop and fire a random arrow at the draguls. Oreus became obsessed with killing the man. He lifted his bow, put an arrow to the string and lined the running archer up in his sights. Right before the archer reached a door, Oreus fired a shot. The arrow sped fifty yards and hit the man in the side, throwing him down. When the soldier started to crawl toward the door, Oreus ran and hit the arena's ring wall at full speed with a jump. He hooked his arm over the top and let himself down onto the sand on the other side. The archer took one final shot at him before he disappeared into the stairwell. The arrow failed to find its mark as it embedded itself in a wooden railing near

Oreus. Pumping his legs, he climbed up into the stands and toward the exit door.

Oreus ran hard before he exited the arena and picked up the man's muddy trail in the castle's gardens. The footprints curved back toward the gandalay stables. The archer appeared from behind a stone bench and fired. Oreus threw himself down into the mud and looked up in surprise to see an arrow sticking out the top of his left shoulder. He waited for the pain to come. When it didn't, he used his right hand to take an arrow from his quiver and took aim at the archer, who had foolishly come closer after seeing Oreus fall. Oreus judged his target and fired, pinning the man's hand to a tree as he was kneeling to assume a better position to take his final shot. The archer struggled to pull himself free but the feat was beyond him.

Taking his left hand, Oreus pulled the arrow in his shoulder straight up and out. To his amazement, there was no blood on the arrow's head, and if there were going to be pain he would have felt something—anything—by now. But somehow his body refused to yield to it, his shoulder feeling as strong as ever when he rotated his arm. He looked back toward the archer and saw the man pulling the shaft through his hand to free himself of it. Oreus fit another arrow to his string and this time aimed where its penetration would leave a lasting effect. The archer's head whipped backward violently and then his body slumped against the tree after Oreus released. The Baron exhaled a warm breath into the cold air around him, seeing a cloud form from it. He walked over to the archer and collected the keys as sleet rained down.

By the time he was back within the arena, Quinn and the guard he was with was waving from the King's throne. Only the bottom of the boots belonging to the last archer could be seen between them. Oreus waved back and held up the keys so they could see he was successful in the same respect.

"Well done, Baron," Plunav said when Oreus walked around the dragul and came to his lock.

"Ummm . . . thanks," he replied, finding it odd to be receiving a compliment from the great red beast. The lock fell away after he fiddled with a few keys before he found the right one to open it.

He went to Jallad next, who said in a deep voice, "You have harnessed the power of a dragul."

Oreus stopped and looked up at Jallad before he finished unlocking his chain and asked, "How can a teardrop give me that? And what have I actually gained?"

Jallad laughed and jingled his chain in front of Oreus's eyes. When Oreus went back to work on removing it, Jallad explained, "The teardrop of a female dragul is a wondrous thing. No male dragul has the ability to cry. Only the female holds such an honor . . . and she may only do it once in her lifetime."

"That's hard to believe," Oreus said, finally getting the clamp to unlock. "There you go."

"Thank you."

Firewing came over to him, stretching her link chain as far as it could go before it snapped and caught her. Oreus worked on her clamp next, choosing the biggest key on the ring first since there was no other that would be large enough to match the keyhole. "Oreus," she said, "you have done something no other human in your history has accomplished. Our tales go back to the beginning of time when draguls were first born, when the stars fell from the heavens like rain on a golden pond. My body is stronger now that I have shed my weakness, my tear, which has now become your strength"

The lock fell away from Firewing's leg. She lifted her claw up and moved her leg in a circle to make it feel better. Oreus pointed to a hole in the top of his armor and said, "An arrow struck me here, fired by the archer. But there was no pain or blood when it found its mark."

Firewing nodded in understanding. "Your skin has become hardened like the scales of the draguls. It is a curiosity that others will seek to see for themselves."

"I hope this doesn't mean I'll be breathing green fire fumes at anyone when I become angry," Oreus said.

Firewing laughed, making Oreus turn to see what only Jada had accomplished before. "Over time we will learn the traits you now possess, Baron. You have an advantage over any other man in battle. It will aid you well during this war."

Oreus walked over to Veragos and fumbled at the lock of the youngest dragul in service to the kingdom, but remained talking to Firewing over his shoulder. "But what is in the tear that has transferred your likeness to me?"

"Even the draguls have not learned such knowledge. Perhaps they work in the same fashion as the snowtear. They both are a gift created by the forces that surround us. In time I believe you will learn both answers, for they may be one in the same. To hold a dragul's teardrop in your hand is comparable to catching a falling star, an act not easily replicated, if ever achieved."

Veragos was free. Hollinfil was lying on his back and enjoying the cold sleet. Oreus realized it had been coming down harder and that he was enjoying it, too. "How old are you, Firewing?" Oreus asked.

Firewing smiled. "Eight hundred and eighty-eight of your human years. Only man has found a way to surpass the life expectancy of a dragul."

"You mean the Elders," Oreus concluded.

"Yes, Baron," Jallad said. "Creatures like us are not reproduced as fast as any other land animal. Our systems are complicated and require a lengthier period of time to create the next generation. A female dragul must be willing to sacrifice much of her own energy to birth a young one. Therefore, they must be in the right mood to mate, not an easy feat to accomplish if you are a male." Jallad rolled an eye toward Firewing, who ignored his comment, even though it was a fact. Jallad continued. "As far as the sea is concerned, the depths of it may contain many beasts even we have never seen, with uncountable life spans and terrifying features that would put us to shame."

"A dragul is enough to scare any human. I can't imagine encountering anything worse than your own kind," Oreus said, chuckling. "Firewing scared me to death before we brought her to the castle."

All the draguls around him laughed, which Oreus found contagious. Even Firewing found Oreus's humor whimsical. She watched him go to the last chained dragul, Garagor, and said, "Oreus, your wit has put life into these old bones. I shall be honored to have you ride me into battle."

"As would I," Hollinfil added.

"And I," said the other four males in agreement.

"I am lucky you are a brave warrior, Baron," Firewing said. "I have never failed at killing a human who has crossed my path. And now that I have spoken to one, I will find the task incomprehensible. I thought humans only to be loud and destructive creatures who didn't know how to keep to their own homes."

"A pest I called them. Almost as bothersome as snakes," Veragos said.

"And to think we believed your kind had crawled out of the sea after you magically appeared one day," Jallad joked.

"In a way I am part of the sea. I have traveled it enough to not disagree with that thought," Oreus replied. He was about to approach Illeon when he was reminded the dragul had met death.

Firewing noticed Oreus's grief had returned. "Your face tells me that humans do not deal with the loss of life in the same manner as the draguls. You will carry it until your own death?" she asked.

Oreus nodded. "I guess that's a trait you didn't transfer to me. I will miss Illeon. He was a good friend. I wish I could have said goodbye to him in the way I can speak to you now."

"I think he would have understood the old way just as well," Firewing said with a nod. "He has returned to the stars for now. Someday he will be ready for physical life again and will fall back to Elvana to start anew."

Once Oreus had freed Garagor, he turned to find Quinn and the other guard staring at him. "What?" he asked, knowing they had overheard part of his conversation with the draguls.

"You were making strange noises, like a wounded dog, and the draguls seemed to be responding to it," Quinn said. "It sounded like you were trying to talk to them."

Oreus didn't know how to explain it, nor did he have the time. He replied unconvincingly, "I was clearing my throat."

"You are an oddity, Baron," Quinn said with a smile.

"Ola would probably agree with you. I wish she was here so I could ask her to watch the sunset with me, if this weather ever would part." Oreus winked at Jallad. The corner of the dragul's mouth curled.

Disgruntled by the hanging cloud that had stopped over the open Western Gate, Rydor temporarily abandoned his efforts of getting inside the tower. The sleet was beginning to turn to snow, numbing his hands and face.

"Do you hear that, General?" Jime shouted through the howling winds.

Rydor had to stop what he was doing to listen to what Jime was referring to. As he focused, the pounding of a thousand footsteps rumbled in the distance. "Hurry! Help me with the beam!" Jime and several men he could trust pushed the two enormous panels until they closed. In the meantime, Rydor had another guard use an axe to chop the crossbeam in half that was locked into place from inside the tower. They slid the remaining end into place across both panels. It didn't completely cover the width of both doors, but it would hold long enough for Rydor to get his men organized before the Lazul army arrived.

"Get all the men lined up," Rydor ordered other guards. "I want them in rows five feet apart in the gardens."

The guards nodded and yelled for every soldier, guard and higher-ranking officer to respond. Rydor and Jime walked into the gardens and watched the men enter and fall into place where a sergeant directed them to stand. The footsteps of the Lazul army grew to a constant thunder as the Yawranans came together. A dragul with a rider on its back circled over them and landed at the opposite end of the gardens. Rydor and Jime strode over to them. It was Oreus on the back of Firewing.

Rydor waved to the Baron and said, "Get the draguls to the top of the western wall. We need them lined above the gate, ready to breathe their toxins as a deterrent."

Oreus replied, "The Lazul army is less than a mile from the gate. Whatever you are doing, I would do it quicker!" Oreus whispered in Firewing's ear, "He's one of the good ones."

"He's in love with Baron Jada. Any friend of hers is a friend of the draguls."

"I have assembled a group of qualified riders to make combat aerial maneuvers," Oreus said to Rydor.

"Watch out for Herikech's lightning strikes," Rydor said. "The draguls can't sit in one place too long or he may kill them."

Oreus waved and then commanded Firewing to the Western Gate. He asked her to call to the males in the Gaming Arena with her strong voice and have them come along.

Rydor and Jime returned back to the ranks. Less than two hundred men were in line and there didn't appear to be any more coming. "This is it?" Rydor gasped. "Are you sure there aren't others?"

"I am just as appalled as you are, General," the Sergeant said. "This isn't even half of the Western Gate's men."

Rydor rubbed his jaw to help him think. "We must send half of the draguls for reinforcements from the other towers. We'll have to hold off the Lazul army and those inside who have turned their backs on us." Having already sent Oreus away, he had Jime go inform Oreus so he could remain and talk to the men. Rydor told Jime he would prefer to have the three closest towers notified: Priswell, Gillwood and Serquist. And they were no closer than a six-day march. But they had no other choice. He also stated he would like the three best dragul fighters to stay at the Western Gate: Hollinfil, Firewing and Jallad being the preferred choices. When Jime left, Rydor turned toward his small army and went to the front row. The men saluted him and he returned it with a stern look.

He yelled, "Do not move unless I give you orders to do otherwise."

The men saluted Rydor again as he walked forward to stand before the middle of the front row. He was so close to one soldier that he was practically touching noses with him. The soldier didn't flinch as he held his breath. Rydor proceeded to every man on the soldier's left and then back to the soldier's right. Once the General had finished with the last man in the front row, he went to the next row and then to each after that, giving each soldier his fullest attention. When he reached the last row, he paused a long time in front of one particular man and said, "Whom do you owe your allegiance to, soldier?"

When the soldier hesitated, Rydor stepped his left leg behind the man's left and shoved his left elbow into the soldier's chest. The soldier went flat onto his back into the mud with Rydor on top of him. Rydor had his dagger out and pressed at the soldier's throat. "Traitors are not allowed in my ranks!"

The man didn't reply and muttered words he couldn't understand that sounded like another language.

"You dare speak Lazul code in front of me?"

He shut his mouth and went silent as the General held his dagger up, ready to drive it into the soldier's skull.

"Answer me, soldier!"

When the soldier's eyes glossed over, Rydor brought the dagger down at the man's chest, stopping with the point touching above the top of his chest plate. Rydor scraped the blade up toward the soldier's neck and scraped off some of the man's stubble. He lifted the dagger to smell the scent of honey. Rydor brought the dagger down again at the man's head, but the soldier caught Rydor's wrist and began twisting it. Rydor fought against the pain, but could only scream and was forced to his side into the mud.

"Your time is at its end, General," the soldier whispered into Rydor's ear before the soldier's head was lopped off by the Sergeant.

"General, are you all right?" the Sergeant asked, lending Rydor a hand to help him up.

Rydor nodded, scraped away some of the mud from his armor with his dagger and went back to the last rank, finishing the row. No other man held the honey scent the King had warned him about. Satisfied all the men before him were loyal, he went back to the front of the ranks and said, "Candlewick will soon be under attack by the Lazuls. They march toward the Western Gate with one purpose in mind. Their army is what is left of the grassland war and they seek revenge for our victory. They can't win this war by themselves and have enlisted the help of our own comrades inside the castle. You are the only men we can count upon to defend the castle until reinforcements arrive." Some of the soldiers looked at one another with skepticism and then returned their gaze back to Rydor as he paced back and forth in front of them. "Our forces will only be split into two. One shall go to the Eastern Wall and report to General Ilos while the rest of you will remain here under my command."

Rydor waved to the Sergeant, who stepped forward with a wooden box he was holding. Putting his hand inside, Rydor pulled out a black band. He held it above his head and said, "These have been brought up from the dungeons. Each of you shall wear one in place of your red band. Any member of the army you see without it is your enemy. You have my orders to kill them on site." Rydor removed his own red armband from his left bicep and slipped the black one on to replace it. Once each of the men had them on, he continued. "Last five rows fall out and report to General Fields at the inner wall of the Western Gate."

Three loud screeches circled above Rydor and his troops. They all looked up to see Veragos, Plunav and Garagor breaking off to fly in separate directions toward their intended destinations. He felt confident that their defenses were moving into position. The fifty men in front of him drew their swords and held them at an upward angle toward him as a salute, a custom of the Yawranan army before they went to war and laid down their lives for king and kingdom.

Rydor unsheathed his sword and cried, "From the fall of the moons to the wake of the morn, we will fight side by side, with the blessed grace of Yawrana, until victory is declared by the silence of battle horn. Defend the royal family and His Majesty Noran Deardrop, the life and land of Yawrana. To the Western Gaaaate!"

As Jada recounted most of her conversation with the Silhouettes for Noran, the King couldn't stop looking down upon the scrambling bodies near the Western Gate. His heart was beating fast as he felt the rush of combat filling his soul until, at some point, it would be too much to ignore. He was fighting the urge to hold Arc Glimmer in his hand and smite the first foe that tested his skills. It was his hope that it would be Henkech.

"Your Highness, did you hear what I just said?" Jada asked him.

"I'm . . . yes, Baron. Chief Decker is no longer hunted by the Silhouettes."

Jada smiled and said, "I said that awhile ago, my King." Repeating herself, she said, "I would like to ask you to pardon the Silhouettes for the death of Dami Ironwood."

Noran balked at the request and said, "Elder Elenoi would not take that well, Jada. When the war is over, I will have no choice but to allow General Fields to resume his search for the Silhouettes. Of course, I won't give him you as a resource. I will protect you whatever way I can until they have all been imprisoned."

"Please, my Lord. The High Elder doesn't need to know that you have their location. Over time she'll let go of her vengeance for Dami's death."

"Jada, what happened during your meeting with them? I get the feeling there is something you are withholding."

Jada was quiet and avoided the King's gaze. To her relief, Bruneau came out onto the balcony and said, "My Lord, sorry to intrude. General Regoria has just called all men to arms, and not all are responding to his call."

"Where are the others going?"

"Blaynor saw them heading for the Secret Halls."

Noran started to stand up when Jada grabbed his arm. "Wait, Your Majesty, what is it that you wanted me to do?"

"Ah. Yes. Thank you for reminding me. I want you to take the Salmus voyagers back to their ships in Drana Bay and send them on their way before the army gets here. Take any available men you can find and trust. The one called Thorn will not return with them, though, for he is still to stand trial by the Elders for his crime, which will be banishment to Arna."

Jada asked, "But what if the voyagers tell their people about Yawrana? Whatever arrangements you have had with them will no longer be adhered to on their end. They are a sordid lot that will send more of their kind to our shores. We someday could be at war with them."

"That's only if we survive this one first. I've toiled over this issue since the day they set foot ashore. I can't hold all of Winslow's men in Candlewick's dungeons, nor do they all deserve to be there. Not all men are as evil and underhanded as he is, even if they keep his company. If I hadn't met Oreus Blake, I would have agreed with you. I don't want them to become casualties if we are to lose, for this is not their fight. The world is expanding, whether we like it or not. The sooner we accept our neighbors, no mater how far apart they live from us, the better prepared we'll be when they decide to be more than acquaintances."

Jada resisted, "These men are bandits with court polish. They will not put us in a favorable light with their King."

"Then let their King come here and see us for himself."

"And if he refuses?"

"Then we shall be the ones who make the next visit," Noran said.

Jada stood and walked from the balcony with the King when the sleet started hitting the arm of her chair. "I would never question your decision, my Lord, but someday I feel this may become our nightmare."

"I've had my share of nightmares to deal with already, Baron. I'm getting good at it."

Jada smiled and saluted Noran as he left her. Noran met Bruneau, Blaynor and a dozen guards with black armbands in a corridor not far from the bell tower room.

"We're going to make this easy," Noran said to the men. "There's only one entrance into the Secret Halls. If they are planning in secrecy there, we will seal them in so we may join our friends at the Western Gate and give them any help we can. We can dig them out in a few sunsets and see if any are worth keeping. Captain Horitz," he said, addressing the only officer in the group, "fetch Candlewick blacksmith Boris Groffen. Have him bring a small keg of blast powder and meet the rest of these men at the final set of stairs leading down into the Halls. They will prevent the others from escaping until Boris can bring down the ceiling. Be sure the fuse is no shorter than a hundred feet."

The Captain nodded as the soldiers split and went their own ways, leaving Noran, Bruneau and Blaynor standing alone in the flickering torchlight.

"Your armor is ready in your old bed chamber, my Lord," Blaynor said.

"Excellent. I feel I'm the only one who isn't dressed for the occasion."

Noran was fitting on his leg plates when there was a loud blast, sending a tremble through the entire castle. He smiled to himself, proud of the fact that in one swift stroke they had just buried half of Herikech's forces deep in the underbelly of the castle.

Not long after the blast Bruneau threw open the door to his chamber. "A tornado approaches the Western Gate!"

"Damn it," Noran scowled. "I should have seen this coming. Herikech is getting even."

"The tornado will only blow down the outer wood gates. It shouldn't harm the portcullis."

"But the Lazul army will be one step closer to breaching the outer wall."

Bruneau shook his head. "There are new archers in place along the wall tops. Oreus led the draguls to a victorious fight in removing the men who tried to kill Jada and the Chief."

Noran finished dressing and strapped Arc Glimmer to his waist. As a tribute to the Kings of old, he had put on a suit that once belonged to a *Bethlen*, one of Herishen Illeon's own personal guards. He couldn't see a better time to seek the aid of his ancestor's spirits and wondered if the suit once belonged to Gerrith Dragul. The gold armor glistened even after four thousand years, having been polished regularly by the castle's servants. The highly decorative red dragul emblem on the chest stood out against the solid gold background color. Noran slid his helmet on and asked, "How do I look?"

Blaynor got down on one knee and lifted the King's hand, kissing his knuckles. "My Lord, you are the light that will shine through this darkness. I will follow you into the Underworld if it will bring victory and save our people."

Bruneau bowed and said, "For once Blaynor has taken the words out of my mouth."

"Rubbish," Blaynor said, smirking at Bruneau. "Say what your heart tells you to."

"Oh, all right. But I'll keep it simple. No storm can cast a shadow over the hearts of our men."

Blaynor thought about Bruneau's statement and then grumbled and rolled his eyes, knowing he was bested.

The bell tower chimes rang and the draguls screeched, indicating the storm was about to strike. The three men looked at one another and then hurried off to battle.

When the tornado's howls had died, Noran looked up from between his knees in his huddled form and saw the stained-glass windows of the Grand Hall had all been destroyed again by the two-hundred-and-twenty mile-an-hour winds. After they stood and left the hall, they saw what else the violent winds had left in their wake. The tornado had cut a wide path through the Gaming Arena and gardens, having punched holes in every wall and ripped up every tree. Part of the tunnel Noran, Bruneau and Blaynor walked down was collapsed with stone rubble lying along the length of the corridor. The sun had broken through the parting clouds and shone into the passage. It was setting, its rays quickly vanishing in surrender to the blanketing night.

Noran spotted two guards standing at the entrance to the gandalay stables. They were at attention, seeming to ignore the destruction around them. "You two, to the Western Gate."

Blaynor drew his sword, stepped in front the King and said, "Stand back, Your Majesty! They do not bear the black band."

Bruneau also unsheathed his sword and approached the two men, shouting, "Put down your weapons!"

"They haven't even drawn them," Blaynor said.

"Shut up!" Bruneau snapped. "They know what I mean."

When they were only a few feet away, Blaynor stopped and studied the guards' expressions. "It looks as if they are sleeping with their eyes open," he said, reaching for the closest guard's sword. The man suddenly sprang to life and grabbed Blaynor's wrist. Blaynor was ready, and thrust his sword through the man's chest. After he pulled it out, he expected the guard to drop where he was. But the man reached out with his hand and seized Blaynor's throat.

Bruneau saw Blaynor was unable to break away from the guard's grip as the guard pulled his own sword. With one swing, Bruneau cut the guard's hand off to free his friend.

Blaynor stumbled backward, choking and trying to get his breath back as he tossed away the disconnected appendage.

Bruneau was astounded when the guard continued to fight with his free hand. He was just as effective with his sword after having sustained a devastating injury.

Noran saw the second guard come to life. He unsheathed Arc Glimmer and wielded it with accuracy, beheading the guard before the man could cut Bruneau down from behind.

Blaynor tripped Bruneau's opponent to throw him off balance. The guard fell backward next to Blaynor, who was ready with stone in hand. He began pummeling the man in the face with it, breaking the guard's nose and eye sockets. The guard still struggled without a scream, as if he had no concept of pain.

Lifting a giant stone over his head, Bruneau yelled, "Get out of the way!" Blaynor rolled just in time as Bruneau threw it down, crushing the guard's skull inward. Finally, the guard showed he no longer had any fight.

All three of them were speechless, waiting for one another to come up with a good explanation. Noran was about to say something to wipe away their shocked looks when he heard the gandalays whinnying loudly inside the stables. Feeling his flesh crawl, Noran said, "There's an evil here that tells me these guards were protecting more than just the stallions." The King reached out and pulled on the door handle. It began to open and creaked on its hinges, increasing his desire to just shut it and move on.

Seeing the King's apprehension, Blaynor asked, "What do you fear, my Lord?"

"I don't know. I just . . . sense something is wrong." He raised Arc Glimmer and pulled the door wide open to stare into the darkness of the building. In the few closest stalls he could see the snow-white gandalays moving their heads back and forth, looking for a way out of their stalls. Further in, other gandalays were rearing and hitting their doors with their front hooves, trying to break them open.

"I have never seen the gandalays this uneasy," Blaynor said, stepping inside with his sword ready. He slowly walked forward and inspected the first stall. The gandalay neighed, calming from the sight of the familiar guard. He petted the horse's head and felt a strange electricity in the air. The hairs on his arms began to stand up from the charge.

Something rustled at the back of the stables in a black space between two empty stalls. Blaynor squinted at the shape. He could barely discern the outline of a standing figure. "Who's there?" he called out, finding his courage.

Bruneau was now entering the building, with Noran bringing up the rear.

"Show yourself," Blaynor demanded.

The figure in the black space began to glow. The form went from a dull light to an intense bright white while a crackling noise filled the air. A thick bolt of lightning shot from the individual and struck Blaynor directly in the chest. He was lifted into the air by the blinding white arm as his body went into convulsions.

"Blaynor!" Noran and Bruneau screamed in horror. The lightning vanished and dropped Blaynor hard onto the ground. They rushed forward to help him. A strong wind picked up inside the corridor and went outside the stables, slamming the door shut. Noran looked behind them to see who had closed it, but no one was there. As Bruneau tried to find Blaynor's pulse, a familiar cackle echoed throughout the stables.

"Where's the General? Has anyone seen General Regoria?" Jime asked, running from one soldier to the next. Everyone he encountered was shaking their head and moving past him in what felt like slow motion. Not seeing Rydor among the faces going around him and toward the Western Gate, he finally turned to see the Lazul army pouring in. The metal of the inner gate's portcullis had been twisted as if the hand of the Maker had reached down and crumpled it into a column. Not having any other choice but to fight, Jime ran with the last wave of men into the center of battle. The Lazuls were swimming across the moat while the tornado was still causing chaos as it moved northeast, away from Candlewick.

Jime killed two warriors with his first two swings. He stepped on their bodies to get to the next warrior, who carried a giant axe. He pivoted left and watched the blade fall past his body and into the back of one of the Lazuls he had cut down. With one high swing of his sword he took the warrior's head off while the Lazul tried to pull his axe out.

Behind him there were the cries of many voices. Jime spun to see General Fields's forces coming to their aid. The Lazuls were immediately pushed back by the onrush of new men. Fighters on both sides were having trouble finding their balance as they tripped over bodies and rubble from the tornado.

"Where is General Regoria?" Fields asked.

"I don't know. I couldn't find him after the storm blew through," Jime said.

"You search for him while we fight."

Jime nodded and fell back to take on more Lazuls. Thinking Rydor had been wounded and was under a pile of stone or wood somewhere, he inspected the biggest mounds he could find. He tossed aside wood and pulled stones away from each of them until his fingers bled from the tiresome work. A strong hand suddenly gripped his shoulder. He turned to see Rydor with blood smeared across the side of his face. "General!" Jime exclaimed, dropping the stone he was holding.

"Why are you not killing Lazuls?" Rydor asked with a grimace.

"I was searching for you. I thought you were—"

"I don't die that easily."

Jime smiled and saluted Rydor with a grin. He hugged him, happy he was alive

"Not now. Not here," Rydor said, pushing him away.

"Um . . . right. Sorry, General."

"Where is Oreus? I need him."

Jime looked toward the sky and saw no sign of the draguls anywhere. "I haven't seen the draguls since the tornado came through."

"Damn the Lazuls!"

Confused as to why Rydor wasn't more concerned with the Lazul army, he asked, "What is it?"

"Come. We have very little time."

Jime ran after Rydor through the castle, leaving the raging battle behind. "Where are we going?"

"To find our best blacksmith."

Rydor had heard the blast from inside the castle and was soon informed by a soldier what had caused it. The soldier also mentioned Boris was helped to the medical wing after a large stone fell on his leg.

"How badly injured is the barbarian?" Rydor asked one of Master Hurran's servants when they came into the waiting room of the maker's wing.

The servant stifled a laugh and said. "He's fine."

"But a stone fell on his leg—"

"Not his good one. The wooden one took all the damage."

"Oh," Rydor said, the thought not occurring to him.

"He's in that room over there, General. You may go in and see him." The servant pointed to a white wooden door. Rydor went to it and knocked. A voice asked for them to enter. Boris was sitting patiently in a chair as a maker tested the mechanics of the leg's ankle.

"General, what ya be doin' here?" Boris asked with a deep rumble in his voice.

"Is Baron Blake's ship functional?"

"What?"

"Can it fly?"

"Yes, but it still needs a bit o' work on the drag chute and some of the deck heaters."

"But the blower engines and propeller thrusts are fine?"

"Yes, why do you—"

"Can you walk?"

The maker who was testing Boris's ankle looked up at the General and shook his head. "It doesn't rotate properly. It'll take several days before it's fixed."

"Then tie it to a peg for now," Rydor ordered.

"What do you want with the ship?" Boris asked.

"I saw one of the Salmus ships flying toward the Eastern Gate when Fields's forces left to defend the western side. It was *The White Fin*—Winslow's ship."

"His crew took it onto land?"

Rydor nodded as the maker went and found two metal rods and some binding twine to stabilize the ankle.

"Comin' to his rescue, eh?"

"They do more than that. They are loading the ship with the treasure from the royal vaults."

"Impossible! We just blasted it shut!" Boris said.

"They must've dug their way out because the men you buried are helping them."

"What?" Boris yelled, his face turning red. "I bummed me leg fer nothin'?"

"If you hold still, I can tie faster," the maker said, dropping the rod he was trying to tie to the barbarian's leg when Boris sat up.

"Sorry," Boris said, sitting back. "Why don' ya use the draguls to stop 'em, General? They'll block Winslow's escape before we reach *Wind Gust*."

Rydor shook his head, growing impatient as his eyes focused on the maker and burned with a passion for him to finish repairing the leg. "Oreus and the draguls are missing and we can't spare any forces from the Western Gate. Every man there is needed to hold off the Lazul army. Our only chance of stopping Winslow and his men is Oreus's ship."

"Who cares 'bout the treasure. Isn't the castle more important?" Jime asked.

"Good point," Boris said as he fiddled with a golden bead in his beard.

"There's one treasure among the horde that is more important to me than any other. They have Jada with them," Rydor said.

"Why didn't ya say that in the firs' place!" Boris's voice boomed inside the small room.

Rydor blushed as he looked toward the window. "I wouldn't want anyone to think less of me if they learned I put my love for her before the welfare of the King and castle. Most now know of the relationship the Baron and I share."

"Love is the noblest of all causes to fight for, General, and you needn't be embarrassed 'bout it. The King would throw himself in shark-infested waters to save 'is son, wife or any of those dozen sisters he's got."

"There are four princesses, blacksmith" Jime said, correcting him.

Boris waved the comment off and said, "Besides, she is part of tha Court."

"But she's not the King and any one man or woman's personal quandary comes second in times of war, according to the laws of Yawrana. Many, due to the conditions the kingdom is facing, would consider her a casualty. If we lose the castle, we lose everything."

"Well, if we don' protect our friends, then who do we 'ave to depend upon? Let the King imprison me if he wants to. I'll tell 'im it was my idea. Fret no more about it, General. Good enough, Master," Boris said, dropping his pant leg before the maker could tie the last string. He quickly hobbled after Rydor as a loose end of twine from his ankle trailed behind him.

"Wait!" the maker said, as they left the room. "I wasn't done!"

"Where are those draguls?" Viktoran yelled at General Fields, having joined them after the Eastern Gate became resecured. The two men fought valiantly side-by-side, holding ground, but no longer were able to push the Lazuls back. Using his superior skills, Viktoran fought two Lazuls at once to help save a soldier who fell near him. The man was able to crawl to safety while the Baron became a whirlwind of blades with a sword in each hand. Two warriors perished when Viktoran slit one's throat and stabbed the other in the stomach. The Lazul doubled over and fell face-first onto the Western Gate's stone walkway.

Fields grimaced when a Lazul knife sliced the top of his hand. He kicked the opponent across the face and brought his sword down with one quick stroke to end the fight. "The tornado may have forced the draguls out from the castle. Let's hope the Baron is not wounded." The Lazul he had stabbed suddenly came back to life and cut Fields across the leg above his shin plate. The General screamed and beheaded the warrior. The Lazul's head rolled down the walkway and out of sight as Fields pulled his black armband off and slid it up his leg and over the wound to keep constant pressure applied to it. To his relief it was shallow enough that it wouldn't hamper his fighting.

Viktoran also found the two warriors he thought he had killed rising again for another round. Many of the bodies that had fallen along the walkway were now stirring in their piles, standing to look for the next opponent. "They have rejuvenation powers!" Viktoran shouted.

"I see that," Fields yelled back. "Decapitating them seems to be the only thing that is working right now."

"Good to know." Viktoran kept his strikes high and finally was able to remove their heads. "Where are the other Barons?"

"They're inside the castle, taking care of some of the ones that slipped by us."

The Lazuls in the tunnel moved aside as a rumble came up the walkway toward Viktoran and Fields.

"Karriks!" a soldier screamed, running from the ramp.

"Karriks?" Fields asked. "What are they doing in the castle?"

Viktoran shook his head. "Herikech. I was afraid this was going to happen. He's doing the same thing he did in Serquist, enlisting the help of animals and beasts to fight in his army."

Fields waited for the creatures to come charging toward them. The Lazuls were also starting to back up toward the wall to let the creatures through. "It would help if we could find out how Herikech has been getting animals to fight for him."

"If you find out, let me know!" Viktoran said, hearing one of the karriks roar. A large black body appeared with thick fur and a pair of green eyes above a short snout. A spiked tail whipped behind it and lashed out at two Yawranan soldiers who speared its side, knocking them from their feet.

Fields took a spear from a dead Lazul warrior and hurled it at the karrik's eyes. It struck dead on. The karrik dropped right where it had been impaled.

"Think I'll try that," Viktoran said, finding his own spear. Any Yawranan soldiers that were at the edge of the moat ran inside to serve as a backup to the General and Baron.

"How many are out there?" Fields asked one soldier.

"Ten," the soldier replied.

Fields shook his head when Viktoran raised an eyebrow. "Aim for their eyes," Fields commanded to the soldiers behind him.

What they didn't expect was a full-out charge from all ten karriks at the same time. Not having enough spears and swords to take them all down in the first launch of weapons, and with nowhere else to go, Fields, Viktoran and the soldiers were pushed back past the gandalay stables into the Gaming Arena. One soldier was trampled and another ripped in half when the jaws of the karrik bit down around his waist.

Fields was backed up against a wall. The karrik swiped at his head with one of its massive claws. The General ducked and heard them scrape against the wooden fence behind him. He raised his sword to defend against another attack. Part of the creature's paw was removed when it met with the edge of Fields's blade. The karrik put its severed paw back on the ground for support, but its bulky weight could no longer support its frame on the weakened limb. It fell over and struggled to get back up. Fields moved in quickly and hacked its head off.

The General had no time to celebrate the small victory when a larger karrik replaced the one he defeated. He ran along the wall inside the arena, enticing the creature to chase him. The karrik roared and trailed, snapping its tail as it went. Fields tripped over a ground stake and fell, losing his sword in the mud. He looked up to see the creature closing in on him. With no time to reach for his sword, he rolled when the karrik pounced. It landed over him, all four paws surrounding his body. Fields reached down into his boot and pulled out a dagger. He thrust it up into the bottom of the creature's jaw before it could lower its head and bite his head off. Hanging onto the handle tightly, he controlled the karrik's head as it tried to rip free from it. Using the strength in his wrists, he rotated the blade left to make the creature roll off of him. The pressure of the blade against its jaw was too great. It had no choice but to go where the blade dictated. As it fell it tried to roll through and get back into its stance, but it slipped at the edge of a massive bonfire pit. Its body disappeared into the black hole as it fell fifteen feet down and became trapped. A cloud of ash kicked up when it landed.

Viktoran and the other three soldiers took care of the last karrik, slaying it as it tried to crawl over a netted box. Its foot came entangled in the rope, putting it at a disadvantage. The karrik continued to swipe until Viktoran spun and brought down the edge of his sword on its neck.

Fields ran over to them and asked, "Is that all of them?"

As the General asked the question, the rest of the Lazul army flooded into the arena, followed by a swarm of fist-sized honeybees and a large cluster of other land-dwelling animals.

"What in all that is holy is that?" Viktoran asked, looking past every recognizable creature to the back of the masses.

"My god. It's the legendary deep-sea dredger," Fields said, as the twenty-foot-long white, spiked head of the serpent rose up above Herikech's forces to emit an eerie wail.

# CHAPTER SEVENTEEN
## The Beetle on the Window

Craning her neck into the whipping winds, Firewing held strong to the wall top of Candlewick's Western Gate. Her claws gripped the stones so tightly they cracked the edges and crumbled away parts of the old masonry. Both wings were extended behind her and stretched out to allow the air currents to flow over her with the least amount of resistance possible. "The draguls are no match for this wind, Baron!" Firewing screeched. "We must relocate or risk death! These are tornado winds!"

Oreus turned his head to glance at Hollinfil and Jallad. Both draguls were nodding, ready to let go. Quinn and Baron Bal Grady of Priswell Territory rode each and were shouting the same message.

"A black funnel cloud pokes from the sky!" Jallad roared.

"Which way should we fly?" Oreus asked.

"To the north!" she said, lifting her wings to let the wind currents pick her up above the castle. Hollinfil and Jallad followed, using their tremendous strength to avoid the tornado's rapid advance. They heard the Western Gate explode behind them and the scratching of metal against stone, which could mean only one thing.

"The gate falls!" Quinn cried as he saw wood fragments fly up in a spiral from where the tornado hit.

"Fly around behind the storm," Oreus shouted. "We'll attack the Lazul army from the rear."

Jallad screeched, saying, "They may have the sun slayers like they did in the grassland war, Baron. Remember Xada's death?"

"We'll have to take the chance," Oreus cried.

When they started to circle west, the tornado moved northeast, traveling to the end of the Royal House Territory's Yard before it sucked back up into the overhanging clouds. But Oreus and the others took no notice, set on carrying out their plan. Trees shook and fell as the army continued its stampede toward Candlewick. Battering rams were carved from the trees' long, sturdy bodies.

"They destroy our resting beds!" Hollinfil screeched.

A Lazul scout shouted below them and ran.

"They have seen us!" Quinn yelled. "Watch for flying arrows!"

From the patch of trees where the scout hid echoed the sound of a hunt horn. Four long notes squealed before the annoyance ended.

Oreus shuddered when four red bodies appeared on the horizon answering the horn's call. "Firewing, are those—"

"Yes, more draguls. Four wild males. I will call to them." Oreus's ears rang when she screeched a deafening pitch to hail them. "Hoh, brothers! Raise one wing for the land and another for the sea!"

When the four draguls didn't take the position Firewing asked for, Oreus asked, "What purpose does your request have?"

"It is an ancient call all draguls must respond to, no matter what quarrels divide us. When land or sea is threatened by invasion of a shared enemy, the draguls bury their blood feuds and unite."

Jallad called this time, but received the same lack of respect. The four draguls lifted their wings up and put their clawed feet out in front of them.

"Wing out!" Firewing screeched. She swerved left and Jallad and Hollinfil right. A wide cloud of green toxic gas shot from the four, spreading with the wind toward Oreus and Firewing.

"It's blowing toward us!" Oreus screamed, afraid of being melted by the deadly fumes.

"Hang on, Baron!" Firewing yelled, going into an all-out dive. The ground rushed up at Oreus as he squinted his watering eyes. His clothes flattened against his body and his lips quivered around his bared teeth. Oreus felt they were going to crash when Firewing adjusted her wings and changed direction at the last moment, grazing the tops of the trees with her belly. She flew underneath the four draguls and shouted, "We must split them up." Jallad heard the suggestion, confirmed his agreement with a low grunt and then notified Hollinfil. The tactic worked, but less in Oreus's favor when two of the four decided to chase them.

"What are you doiiieeeeahhh?" Oreus screamed as Firewing spun upside-down and raked her claws along the first dragul's stomach. Oreus fell out of his seat and hung onto his saddle horn for dear life, his legs kicking as they hit tree branches. "Firewiiiinnnggg!" Blood and guts rained briefly around him on both sides of Firewing's body until the wounded dragul above fell and crashed into a thick section of woods, flattening a hundred yards of forest.

Firewing rolled back to her stomach. Oreus's body slapped against the dragul's scaly hide. He could feel the heat coming from beneath her coarse scales as she exercised her muscles to their full use. Her heartbeat pounded in his ear until he pulled himself back up into the saddle to hang on tightly.

"Are you injured, Baron?" she asked, circling back to see if Jallad and Hollinfil had survived the maneuver.

"I don't know," Oreus said, too afraid to let his hands go to feel his legs.

Firewing screeched when Hollinfil took a claw across his back, the enemy dragul attempting to rake Quinn from his saddle. Hollinfil curved upward and headed for the clouds with Quinn clinging to his saddle. Jallad and the fourth dragul were fighting in midair, clawing out at each other like roosters in a ring fight.

Oreus looked around for the second dragul that had been chasing them, but saw that it had broken off its flight and was heading away from them, soaring over the battle occurring between Jallad and his attacker. "The other one heads back east," Oreus yelled. "Where's he going?"

Firewing stroked her wings. "I think I know," she said, diving beneath Jallad, who now had the head of his opponent down to take a bite out of the back of its neck. The dragul eventually gave in and fell onto a cabin below, Jallad screeching a victory cry.

"Two down!" Oreus exclaimed before he saw the dragul they were following was flying directly for an ancient ring of giant trees. The Baron lost his breath when it dawned on him what was about to happen. "Don't let him harm the sequeras! One broken branch could mean a serious injury or death to the Elder who is bound to it!"

"What about the Elders themselves? Have they been evacuated?" Firewing asked, gaining hundreds of feet on the male dragul with her wider wingspan.

"Yes. Baron Annalee has done the deed. But it matters not where the Elders are in Yawrana. Their spirits are bound to the sequeras wherever they roam until death."

"Not entirely true, Baron. The Elders can break their bond, but it's a dangerous task."

"How?"

"It has been done once, a tale for another time that includes a prophecy that carried the name of Oreus."

The prophecy Firewing spoke of was one of the first recorded in the history of Yawrana by Elder Harland Ghere, approximately four thousand years ago. Oreus heard many speak of it when he first arrived in Yawrana, but his refusal to believe the Elders' work was authentic turned many away, including Noran, from revealing the entire tale to him. This was the first time he had heard anyone mention this part of the story, which made him feel ashamed about how naive he was about the world. The Elders were fragile humans, but strong in spirit when it came to their duties. Oreus couldn't help but feel flushed that Firewing knew more details about the prophecy named after him than he did.

"I should be grateful if you would let me know the rest on a day when we have no troubles."

He lowered his head as Firewing continued to increase her speed to catch the other dragul. Insects were hitting him in the face and hands. He dared not open his mouth any more for fear of eating one. Gauging the remaining distance between the enemy dragul and the sequera, Oreus said, "I don't think we're going to catch him."

"Then you have never seen a female dragul in her finest form!" Firewing's body lurched forward as if she tapped into a reserve energy somewhere deep within her body. Oreus's hands were cold as they entered the sleet and snow of Herikech's storm. His fingers turned red and his lips became chapped from the extreme temperature change and wind. Only his legs were spared from the freezing air, snuggled up against Firewing's body as it exerted a soothing warmth. Wanting his face to feel the same comfort, Oreus leaned forward and laid his head down beyond the saddle's edge.

The pleasure lasted briefly when Firewing suddenly cried and her body shook. Oreus looked up to see she had caught the male by the tail and was dragging him down. Having no choice, the male dragul flew upwards to break free, but Firewing refused to release him as she regathered the energy in her wings to build her strength. The male whipped his snake-like tail back and forth, taking them for a ride Oreus would never forget. He clamped his legs down and wound his wrists in Firewing's reins so he could not be thrown as easily as he was the last time.

The higher they climbed, the tighter Firewing clung to the enemy. "You can take us to the stars and we shall go with you!" she screeched through clamped teeth.

"Please, no," Oreus mumbled, hoping Firewing didn't mean her words.

But something told him her threat was no lie. He looked down and saw shapes on the ground beginning to blend into one another. The castle was now only the size of his thumb and the sequeras were indistinguishable. The lack of oxygen to his lungs was making him light-headed. He felt himself start to faint when the male dragul broke off his climb and took a sharp angle to reverse their direction. Oreus's stomach lurched from the abrupt change and was emptied of everything he had eaten before the tornado struck Candlewick. The cold wind beating against his face made him feel better this time. But the ride wasn't over yet. They were spinning now as they fell. He closed his eyes to make the blurred images stop. When he reopened them, they were almost upon the trees.

"Firewing! Let go! He'll kill us all! Don't call his bluff!"

Sensing Oreus was right, Firewing relinquished her hold. The male swung his head up and made a clean glide above the treetops with Firewing closely pursuing.

"Rest will be coming soon, Baron! My strength is leaving me!"

A screech came from their right. Oreus lost his concentration on the dragul they were chasing to see Hollinfil and his opponent locked together in a freefall as they tumbled from the sky. The two streaking giant red forms hung onto each other, neither releasing as they plummeted. Quinn screamed as he huddled against Hollinfil. With a crack of his tail, Hollinfil smacked the enemy across the face, blinding it in one eye. Before they collided with the forest, both draguls rolled to their stomachs like a cat with four feet sprawled for the impact. They each flapped their wings to help cushion the landing, but leaves and branches flew out in every direction. There was a rustle and screeches where they had landed, but Firewing had flown far enough away from them that Oreus couldn't determine who the victor was, or if there would be one.

He turned his attention back to the male they had been hounding. Firewing had lost a hundred feet and didn't have any of the reserve energy left that she had drawn upon earlier. Oreus could hear her breathing had intensified, her lungs heaving to find air. "He heads back toward the Lazul army."

"Where we wanted to be to begin with," she yelled. "Perhaps now we can do some damage before we make another run for the sequeras." Firewing swooped in low and opened her jaws as she came up on an outer band of warriors that had broken off from the main group. The Lazuls' fear was recorded in Oreus's mind in the last few moments of their lives when they saw they had nowhere to go. The green toxic fumes caught them whole. Their mutating bodies floundered about in the mist.

"A dozen less the castle has to worry about," Oreus shouted.

The male dragul circled back around to judge Firewing's fatigue. He screeched his taunts, words that sounded more Lazul in nature than dragul.

"Alas, the male shows his dark self!" Firewing cried. "No dragul would show such disrespect in battle. We do not resort to ridiculing when the champion has not been declared. It could change the Creator's mind of who will live to see another day."

Oreus chuckled, which helped make his stomach feel better while it settled. "You are superstitious?"

Firewing was using her wings to coast more now as the male dragul took a long lead ahead. The sequeras would soon be in sight again, but this time Oreus's instincts told him one of the Elders would be affected. "We do not believe in such things. By nature we are not boastful creatures. Confidence must come only when it is called for or it will trick the mind. The voice of caution is the only thing we can rely upon to guide our thoughts."

"Could these draguls have been drugged to take commands from the Lazuls?" Oreus asked.

"I am too unfamiliar with the Lazuls and their history. The Yawranans are far more fit to solve that problem."

Oreus saw two red forms up ahead. One was thrashing about while the other lay still, holding its ground. When they flew over them, Oreus caught a glimpse of Hollinfil's tail tightening like a rope around the enemy dragul's neck. The dragul's bones crunched loud enough for Oreus to hear them as its body went limp. Oreus cringed from the awful noise, goose bumps forming all over his arms. Quinn waved to show he was well. A cheer rose up in Oreus as he shouted, "For Yawrana!" He didn't know if Quinn heard him or not, but it made him feel good to say it just the same.

The sight of the sequeras brought the sense of urgency back to him, and Oreus wondered if these male draguls were taking orders from the Lazuls. Why would Herikech waste time using them to destroy the trees when he could have had the tornado do the same work and get better results? Reasoning led him to the only answer there was; the sacred volumes of written text that were stored inside them, containing over four thousand years of ancient studies and practices. He remembered the Elders informing Noran, Rydor and him about the snowtears the first time he visited them. And from that conjecture he believed Herikech could be seeking more information about the ancient flowers. Did Herikech think that the Yawranans were hiding specific knowledge about the snowtears that he didn't already know?

The Baron's eyes grew wide when Firewing said, "The game is up!"

With Baron Bal Grady still on his back, Jallad flew out of the sequeras and intercepted the enemy just before he extended a claw to snap off a large branch. Jallad was like an arrow as he flew at the enemy, his head a battering ram. The three horns on the top of Jallad's head gored the enemy and drove him backward. When Jallad ripped them out, the enemy surprisingly decided there was enough left in him to charge again. The beast flew over Jallad and straight for the largest tree at the center of the ring, High Elder Elenoi's dwelling.

Firewing saw she had a slim chance of knocking the male off course. Lowering her head, she sped forward and cried, "Brace for impact, Baron!" Oreus threw his body flat against the top of his saddle, his shoulder pushing against the horn. He held his breath, closed his eyes and waited. The moment he thought they had missed, a jolt reverberated through Firewing's mass as they were sent spinning. Oreus saw many things flash past him while Firewing tried to stop their uncontrolled acceleration: a green blur, Jallad's flying form, several lightning strikes from a thunderhead and the broken tail of the male dragul. The treetops suddenly rose up and greeted them with a resounding crash. A dozen branches whapped against Oreus's body before they landed in a streambed. Water splashed up and soaked his clothes. A moment later everything stopped moving. He took a deep breath and gazed up toward Firewing's head to assess her injuries. To his surprise, she was laughing.

"What tickles your ribs?" Oreus asked, feeling blood drain from his face. "We have not succeeded." A loud crash echoed in the distance, followed by another pair of coinciding screeches.

"Forgive me, Baron, but humans tend to make me laugh, even in times of war."

"What are you talking about?"

"Two drift ships fly east toward the Racorn."

"What?"

"One is from Salmus and the other is yours."

Oreus became angry. Who would dare steal his ship? "Quickly! Rise up so I may see!"

Firewing tested both her wings and then pushed off the rocks along the streambed's shore. They were above the treetops and looking eastward. Oreus scanned the horizon and saw the two faint images Firewing was referring to. "Yes, that could only mean the people of Salmus have come back for Captain Winslow and the others."

"Your eyes are as good as a dragul's, Baron. No ordinary human can see that far."

Oreus realized Firewing was right. The ships were over five miles away, their engines flying them over the treetops. The two were racing from what he could tell, the second gaining on the first, until a blast of fire shot from the rear of the Salmus ship to send it rocketing away.

"The Salmus ship has the glint of gold aboard her decks."

He thought about Firewing's comment and what she meant before he said, "You think they have stolen treasure from Candlewick?"

"A dragul can smell riches from that distance," Firewing said, flying once more toward the sequeras. "Only humans would put metal before honor."

"Winslow has no honor. He's a thief! And in my opinion, doesn't qualify as a human." Oreus inhaled deeply and caught a strange scent. He pulled out his Lazul dagger and held the metal to his nose. The two smells were different, his dagger's blade being far less intoxicating. The smells of the two different metals emitted a sharp odor, like the inside of a wet wine goblet. The type of metal, he decided, was what made each have its own distinct quality. He guessed the better scent on the air to be the gold of Candlewick, coming from the Salmus ship.

"Our effort was not in vain. The High Elder's tree has sustained no damage, but the one to its left is to be uprooted!" Firewing screeched.

Oreus put his dagger away and laid his eyes upon three shapes shifting within the shadows of the giant trees. Hollinfil had now joined Jallad's fight. Both draguls were tugging at the enemy dragul's back to rip him away from the tree he had attached himself to. Bark was scraped away from the trunk as he held on with all four legs. Oreus didn't have to imagine very hard that Elder PaCant was screaming in pain somewhere many miles away, his skin being ripped away from his muscle, inch by inch. The tree's roots started to become exposed at the base when the enemy dropped his legs onto the ground and pushed them away from his upper body.

Firewing flew around the opposite side of the tree and flew into it at the top, pushing it back into its normal position. The tree groaned under the pressure being created at the middle of the sequera. Wood began to crack from within the tree. Oreus looked down and saw Jallad taking hold of one of the enemy's back legs and lifting it up. The male dragul let go of the sequera and struggled to flap its wings to right itself. Hollinfil punched a hole through one of the enemy's wings, and then clawed two long streaks in the other.

Oreus hung on as Firewing flew into the forest and searched for a small tree, one fifty-feet high. She put her body vertical to it and grabbed hold, pulling up to tear it from the ground. Dirt flew up when it became free. Her claws snapped at the branches to break and rake them off. Using her teeth, she bit off the entire top, leaving a jagged point at the end. She tucked it under one leg and flew back toward the sequeras with it out like a jousting pole. Jallad couldn't hang onto the enemy's foot much longer, but he scrounged for a few more moments when he saw Firewing speeding toward them.

"Back up!" Jallad cried at Hollinfil, which the dragul managed to do with no time to spare. Jallad swung the enemy left by the ankle and into the pole. It impaled the beast through the back and exited through its chest. Firewing let go to allow the enemy to plunge to the ground. The ground shuddered, shaking leaves from the sequeras' branches. The wounded dragul crawled several dozen feet, the end of the post through its stomach creating a ditch beneath its body. Finally, the resistance was too great. The dragul's wings lay down and its mouth exhaled a small wisp of green gas before it closed its eyes.

"And here it will be written that Cormoor found his end," Firewing said.

"You knew this dragul?" Oreus asked, shocked.

"Yes, Baron. If you were the rarest breed in the land, it wouldn't take you long to list all the names that belonged to your kind."

"How many draguls are in Yawrana?"

"To say a hundred would be an exaggeration, however, not far under it."

Oreus replied, "You would be considered an endangered species in Zonack."

"A hundred is not the most the dragul population has ever seen, nor is it the smallest. There was a time early in Yawrana's history, when it was first founded, that the draguls quarreled with another enemy, before humans were considered a nuisance."

Hollinfil walked over to Firewing. Quinn called to Oreus from the dragul's saddle. "Baron, now that the fight here is done, shall we head back to Candlewick?"

Oreus yelled, "If Hollinfil and Jallad are up for the flights. Firewing and I will rest here for a bit longer."

"Then we shall see you at Candlewick shortly?"

"No. There is another matter we must investigate before we return there. Jallad and Hollinfil should be enough to give the Lazul army their share of problems."

Quinn waved and kicked his boots against Hollinfil's side. The dragul flew up between two of the sequeras. Bal waved from the back of Jallad and took the same route to join Quinn. Oreus saluted Bal before he and Firewing were left alone.

"These creatures you fought, they were large land creatures like yourself, Firewing?" Oreus asked.

"Yes. They were only a myth to humans—until the grassland war of the Waungee."

A picture of the creatures Firewing was hinting at formed in Oreus's mind. Their large red eyes, crown of horns and golden-scaled hides were intimidating when encountered on foot. "The nefars."

"The draguls drove them far to the south, beyond Rock Rim Territory, to the Windy Hills surrounding Mount Grim. It was a great victory, so we thought, until Herishen Illeon and his people walked from the dunes like a nightmare. It was the first time we had come into contact with humans, and we studied you from afar until we could determine your strengths and weaknesses. For a creature so small, we were impressed with your prowess. And you multiplied like dobbins."

Oreus couldn't help but laugh.

"Eventually we considered you to be no harm and a good meal if you decided to step foot where you shouldn't."

"Then why didn't you unite to battle us when we began capturing your kind? Didn't you find that offensive?"

Firewing smiled. "Of course, we did, but we had to learn why. When the first dragul was captured and was given free food and shelter, his complaints were few. Others males became jealous and allowed themselves to be taken for the indulgence. For all you wanted was to use us to fly from one territory to the next. What complaint could they find in that when it is what draguls do anyhow?"

"Then why do not all draguls serve Yawrana?"

"Your questions are many, Baron, but I shall indulge you this time. Like humans, not all draguls have the same desires. Most of us wished to remain in the forests, especially the females. We are not as lazy as the males."

"Good thing Jallad and Hollinfil didn't hear you say that."

"They would not deny it. Their bodies require more food to keep their health. Hunting is viewed as a burden to many of the older males. It pleased them there was another alternative that allowed them to rest more. They knew what they were getting into when they ventured near the humans' traps."

"You did seem far too clever a creature to be caught so easily."

Firewing chuckled. "Yes. After the first male was captured four thousand years ago, word quickly spread about your methods."

"But here you are. If you knew about the traps, why did you come near the King and me that summer day in Marshant?"

"The heat was unbearable, even for a dragul. I was cooling in the shade when I caught the aroma of the meat you offered. It was too tantalizing to ignore, and I had not eaten for three days. I decided to tempt fate."

"Sorry," Oreus said, feeling he should apologize.

"Do not be, Baron. One important reward came from my mistake."

"Our friendship?"

Firewing roared with laughter. Oreus blushed, his face feeling as if it were burning from his embarrassment.

"There you have me. Perhaps now we can say two."

"Oh. Well, I'm glad a human can be considered a friend."

"My body swells . . . but it's not from pride."

Oreus smiled when he realized what she was saying. He pressed his ear against Firewing's back to see if his hearing had also improved. When he heard a second tiny beat buried within her, he asked, "You are with young?"

She nodded.

Suddenly it struck Oreus why Firewing had cried in front of him at Illeon's death. It was not just for the loss of a friend, or even for one of her kind. She had been in love with Illeon. His loss seemed magnified now that the hatchling would never know him. "The father would be proud."

Firewing replied, "Thank you, Baron. But there are enough males in the keep to honor his role. They will gladly vie for it." She looked to her right and fluttered her wing. "I think we are ready."

"I don't wish to put the life of your young in danger," Oreus said. "To ask this of you would be selfish, even for the King."

"Heh, heh, heh. Baron, do you now speak for my young?"

Oreus blushed again, hoping he had not insulted her. "I'm sorry if I—"

"Your heart is good, but what would I tell my little one if I allowed the Lazuls to wreak havoc upon our home? I couldn't allow my fledgling to fall into such circumstances. We will all go into battle together, though I am curious as to why we embark for the ships instead."

"There are few who could fly my ship, and from what I saw it was not acting as a guide for the Salmus vessel. Someone is trying to stop the voyagers from reaching the sea." Before Firewing could mention the treasure, Oreus continued. "Winslow must have taken some of our people prisoner, maybe even the King."

Firewing nodded and took to the air. "The draguls have granted you wisdom as well," she said.

"No, I'm just getting used to politics!"

Fields didn't know how to react as he watched a long silver tongue flicker out of the sea serpent's mouth. The beast was the size of three draguls put together, and its body crushed everything in its path. Even the Lazul warriors running toward them were not foolish enough to get in its way. Their luck had not completely disintegrated, though. The honeybees veered off and flew through a window of the castle to search for refugees. Their stingers would only be effective for one strike, and would cost them their lives if used.

Ten warriors ran toward them, raising their swords, spears and axes. Fields and Viktoran led their own charge to slow them down. The two bands melted into one, weapons striking in every direction. Fields beheaded the first two warriors leading the charge and then spun between their falling bodies to take on a third. Viktoran flanked the Lazul group, while other Yawranan soldiers attacked from the other side. The Lazuls' band was disrupted by the hard counter-attack.

"Take their heads!" Fields cried. "Spare none!"

Viktoran found it easier to wound his opponents before he took off their heads, instead of just aiming high on every single swing. His arms retained their strength longer if he changed the height of his blade periodically. He and Fields met at the back of the group, both coming upon the last Lazul at the same time. The warrior didn't know who to fight first, which cost him his head. Viktoran and Fields both swung, their swords scraping against each other as they passed through the warrior's neck.

The next wave of Lazuls decided to let the serpent do its work since they were being unsuccessful against Fields's group. They ran from the Gaming Arena and back into the castle's corridors to seek less-trained Yawranan soldiers.

"If only I had Heaven's Light," Viktoran said. "I would throw a stream of fire at the beast for it to feast on instead."

The serpent turned its head toward them once the Lazul warriors went inside the castle. Its milky-white eyes were nearly four feet in diameter. The beast's body cut off their escape by blocking the path the warriors had used.

"Into the stands!" Fields cried.

The men turned and fled for the wooden wall. The serpent wailed and used a claw to mash the last soldier who was climbing over.

"Spread out and make for the archery range," Viktoran ordered.

The serpent smashed part of the arena wall and climbed up into the stands after the men. Fields saw the hole in the arena wall where the creature had burst through. Its body still was not entirely inside as it stretched for over a hundred yards from one end of the arena to the other. A back of wavy white bumps cut through the air and eight pairs of legs crawled across the field, leaving behind great footprints two feet deep. Lobed fins sat above each set of legs, giant propellers that could help it swim through the salty depths of the ocean. Fields never thought a creature so large could've existed in the world. His awe was wiped away when the serpent closed its jaws around another one of his men. The man's scream was a hurtful reminder that now was not the time to show hesitation in his actions. The archers' range was fifty feet from where he was, with the bows resting in a rack to the right of a row of targets.

Two men were ahead of Fields before he made it to the rack. They were strapping on loaded quivers and choosing bows that suited them. The serpent crawled into the stands before its tail came through the wall in the arena. The tail was tall and thin, more like an eel's than a snake's. Two false, small iridescent green eyes decorated its side for luring in sea creatures.

The first soldier fired a shot off before the creature could claim another soldier. The arrow pierced its skin, just below one eye. It scratched the arrow out and then the beast went for Viktoran. The Baron was in trouble as he tried to draw the beast away from the archery range so as many men as possible could gain possession of a bow. He jumped just before the mouth clamped down on a stone bench, breaking a few of its teeth in the upper part of its jaw. The beast threw the bench to the side and wailed.

Four arrows flew into its side, and a fifth bounced off one of its bony knees. Viktoran took only a dozen steps before the creature snapped at him again. He sliced his sword upward to split its lower and upper lip. The row he ran down began to curve to the north and would end at a staircase. His only chance would be to reach it before being devoured or crushed. The serpent was enraged at Viktoran's elusiveness. It moved faster to snatch him up. Viktoran jumped down two rows but was hit in midair by the massive head. He was thrown ten feet and landed hard against a bench, knocking it over. The bench started a domino effect as one fell into the next toward the arena's bottom row.

The serpent's milky, wide eyes scanned right and left to see where Viktoran had gone. When its gaze fell upon his dazed form, it curled its body to the left, knocking down hundreds of other seats in the process. Viktoran screamed when he looked up to see the serpent's head coming at him. A rain of arrows struck the creature's face, but it continued its descent to gobble him up.

Two dark forms appeared behind the serpent's horns, each one flying toward an eye. A green cloud of gas spread from them and swirled in the air toward the pupils.

Viktoran pushed himself up and jumped his way down the rows to escape the struggle he expected to come. The serpent's wail and two loud screeches echoed throughout the stadium. Glancing back, he saw Jallad falling through the air. The dragul landed on its back in the stands. There was a man's scream upon impact. Another wail filled the air, one indicating the serpent wasn't in pain. Viktoran looked up at the beast and saw the green toxins from the draguls' lungs had not harmed it. He bent over as if someone had just punched him the gut.

Another rain of twelve arrows filled the air. Viktoran took the opportunity to investigate Jallad and his rider's injuries. He ran along the row and hopped over any overturned benches. The dragul had rolled to its side, exposing its stomach to him. A gaping wound had punctured through its scaled hide, letting a large amount of blood pour from Jallad. The dragul rested its head on a bench and whined when Viktoran approached. The Baron ran to the opposite side of Jallad and saw Baron Bal Grady's body broken in many places, with most of it lying beneath the dragul. Viktoran knew the worst for the Baron had already passed, and what would come now could only be liberating.

"Bal," he said taking the Baron's free hand and holding it tightly.

"Vik . . . toran." Blood leaked from his nose and his right eye. "Save . . . King." Bal's head rolled to the side as his hand unclenched Viktoran's. With his index and middle fingers, Viktoran closed the Baron's eyes.

Jallad also released his last breath before he traveled with Bal on to the next plane. The dragul's snout touched the ground and his lungs let out a long sigh as death won the creature over.

"May the Maker speed your journey, friends," Viktoran said, turning his attention back toward the sea serpent. Viktoran watched several more waves of arrows fire in rapid succession from Fields's men. They were accumulating at a fast rate on the serpent's face. When one struck its eye, the beast decided it had had enough. It wailed and lifted its head high into the air, pushing itself up with the legs at the middle of its body.

"Run!" Fields shouted, ordering his men across the arena. The serpent's head came down with enough force to crush the archery racks and send a tremor throughout the arena. Several of the archers lost their footing and fell onto the muddy field. In four steps the serpent caught up with them and took their lives before they could load more arrows. Fields felt the cold breath of the creature blast him from behind when it snorted.

As Viktoran watched the serpent's tail follow its body, a screech sounded above him. He moved out of the way to allow Hollinfil to land.

"Need a ride, Baron?" Quinn asked, extending down his hand.

Viktoran put his own out at first, but then withdrew it before Quinn could grasp it. "I should stay on the ground with the men."

"At least let me give you a lift to the other side of the field," he said, reoffering.

The Baron nodded, took Quinn's hand and put a foot in a stirrup. Once he was in the second saddle, Quinn hollered, "South, Hollinfil." The dragul pushed off from the stands and flew along the serpent's tail, staying well above its body to avoid being battered by the white beast's humped form.

"The dragul's breath had no effect on the serpent," Quinn said. "It didn't even give it a rash."

"That was my only hope to kill it," Viktoran said, disappointment in his voice. "This thing will destroy the entire castle if it leaves the arena. We must keep it here as long as we can."

"I think we have little hope of making it to do anything that it doesn't want to do." Quinn looked up and saw a large trail of black smoke rising south of the arena. "Fire consumes the gandalay stables!"

As if the idea was waiting to be plucked from a tree, Viktoran said, "That's it! Fire! We can burn the beast!"

"How? No flame will catch to its slick hide."

Ignoring his comment, Viktoran said, "Head for Fields."

Quinn nodded and shouted, "Down, Hollinfil."

The dragul dove and swooped beside the General as Fields sprinted for his life with a half dozen soldiers behind him. "General!" Viktoran cried. He shouted several times before Fields looked up. "Keep it in the arena! I have a plan!"

"And where am I to hide?" Fields yelled, appearing to not like the idea.

"We're going to burn it!" Viktoran said before he asked Quinn to have Hollinfil fly up before the serpent's head closed in on them. The jaws snapped at them in the air as they flew out of range. Fields was cursing as they pulled away and flew over the top of the arena's western wall. The two moons of Elvana were rising as dusk surrendered to the night. Lumly was bathed in red.

Checking Blaynor's neck once more, Bruneau felt tears begin to flow from his eyes when he could find no pulse. He shook his head when he looked at the King. "There's no sign of a heartbeat. He's dead, Your Majesty."

Noran's fists curled into balls. Anger was rising in him like the building pressure inside a volcano. His blue eyes darkened when he turned toward the figure emerging from between the two stalls at the back of the stables. The gandalays were whinnying loudly through the entire building. One older stallion continued to kick at its stall to escape. "How did you get into my castle?"

The dark figure cackled as he floated forward. The individual held up his palm. Crackling energy jumped from his fingertips and danced across his hand. The light from the electricity grew until the burned features of Herikech's face became highlighted by its glow. He stopped five feet from Noran and Bruneau when they each drew their swords. Herikech's laughter rang out as he held up a long object in his hand. "I no longer fear any blade now that I hold the only one that can harm me." The sword suddenly lit with flame. "It is a wondrous weapon that harnesses a lethal power I will soon learn to master." Herikech turned his eyes back toward the King and furrowed his brow. "Tell me, King Deardrop, how does it feel to be inferior?"

"You bastard!" Bruneau yelled, raising his sword to strike. A bolt of electricity shot from Herikech's hand, singeing the guard's wrist. He cried and dropped his weapon. It clanged on the polished stone floor of the stables.

"Do you wish to lie next to your comrade, guard?" Herikech asked, a smile forming on his lips. "Or would you rather fight by his side?" The Lazul king slipped his hand into the pocket of his robe and said, "Arise, my servant, and show Deardrop whom you now obey."

Blaynor's body suddenly was moving. His arms and legs bent to push himself up into a standing position.

"Blaynor!" Bruneau said. He embraced his friend and patted his back. When Blaynor didn't show any emotion in return, Bruneau looked into Blaynor's eyes and saw that the fire in them was gone forever. "What have you done to him?" he snapped, whirling on Herikech.

"He is what the Lazuls refer to as a hollow," Herikech said. "A soulless body. He will do whatever command I give, like many of the creatures that will tear this castle down block by block. Ask the King for a dance, will you, Blaynor?"

The guard approached Noran and bowed. "Would you care to dance, Your Majesty?" Blaynor's lips moved in unison with Herikech's as if they were both part of a ventriloquist act. When Blaynor reached for Noran's hand, the King recoiled and backed up to the door. A wave of screams ran outside the stables, making him jump. He spun to hear warriors fighting Yawranans until they were pushed back by the sound of many growls.

"Yes, do you hear it, Deardrop? Your castle, all your worshipers, and even your guard here, will soon be mine."

"Dance with me," Blaynor said again, trying to grab the King's hand.

"Get away from me," Noran yelled, pushing Blaynor down. Noran's heart was beating fast. His head was pounding as if a migraine were coming on. A tremor suddenly shook the castle as if something had made a large impact with it. A piercing wail followed, chilling Noran's nerves and bones. "What was that?"

Herikech grinned. "Have you ever heard of a deep-sea dredger?"

Noran replied in doubt, "Ancient Yawranan fishing vessels once spoke of them. But how "

Pulling his hand from the pocket of his robes, Herikech held up hundreds of tiny transparent threads that were writhing in his hands like snakes. "Do you know what these are?" When Noran didn't respond, Herikech finished, "Life strands. Each one of them once connected a spirit to their flesh shell."

"You're a liar!" Bruneau yelled. "No man can have such power . . . ."

Herikech replied, "What couldn't be conceived has now been proven. As the spirit passes through an elemental portal to leave its body, I seize the end still connected to its physical body before it vanishes. With only a thought they will do whatever I want, as if they were an extension of me."

"This is how you've been controlling my men?" Noran shouted.

"They are my ears and eyes. Everything you say in their presence passes on to me."

"You have raised an army of the dead? It is unholy!" Bruneau yelled.

Herikech laughed. "If your god truly did exist he would have stopped me."

Noran said, "Ballan. General Keys. Relic. They were all your puppets."

"And countless others. You will also be a face among them."

Bruneau replied, "But Keys committed suicide—"

Herikech cackled. "I only made it look that way. He was already dead. Like glass, the hollows are vulnerable. If they are broken the right way, they are useless, their strands evaporating like water."

"That's what the honey, the cooking oils and the natron was being used for," Noran said. "It was your men who broke into the Catacombs of Emison. You wanted the ingredients to disguise the putrefying smell of your army. I should have listened to Martell—"

"The Nax will fail. The prophecy his people have feared will turn for the worst, as will every vision the Yawranans have seen. Your waters will run red with your own blood." Herikech smiled.

Bruneau bent down to pick up his sword but was blasted backward by another bolt of energy that shot from Herikech's hand. His body hit the doors of the barn.

Noran rushed to the guard and helped him up. "Bruneau, are you all right?"

The guard's legs wouldn't work. Noran tried to help him but Bruneau couldn't find the strength in his body to stand up. He fell to the floor on his hands and knees and then vomited.

Herikech began to speak again when a loud buzzing noise suddenly flooded out the Lazul king's words. Noran put a finger in his ear and opened and closed his jaw to try to make it stop. When Herikech saw Noran was no longer paying attention to him, he looked on in curiosity, wondering what was distracting him from hearing his declaration. The buzzing became louder after Noran pulled his fingers from his ears. His eyes searched the stables for the source of the sound. They fell upon a large insect crawling up the window of the stables. He shook his head and said, "No. Not now." The large horned beetle beat its wings against the glass, creating the buzzing noise again.

"What is it that ails you?" Herikech demanded to know.

But Noran couldn't respond. Herikech became only part of the stable's darkness. A patch of long red moonlight shone into the stables through a hatch in the roof. The beetle's form was illuminated as Lumly rose in the distance. The light was so strong it was almost blinding, but it was warm and inviting as it drew Noran into it.

"Don't go near the moonlight, Your Highness!" Bruneau yelled when he lifted his head to examine the situation. "Remember what the High Elder said about the mangler!"

Noran knew the beast would attack him if he entered it, but he couldn't stop himself, no matter how much he resisted. His legs shuffled forward on their own, the magnificence of the light pulling him toward it. Herikech continued to watch, but said nothing, interested by what he was witnessing. The moment Noran's hand entered the red beam, the rest of his body fell completely into it. He looked up at its glorious invitation and felt a fierce growl come from his own mouth. Shock overtook him. His body suddenly was no longer comforted by the moonlight as it betrayed him and became his enemy. His blood was boiling and a tearing pain tore at skin. Every hair from every follicle on his body grew five inches long. When he looked at his fingernails, they stretched out and became pointed at the ends. His mind was reeling from the transformation his flesh was going through, and soon his thoughts became all encompassed by the red fire.

Bruneau was stunned by what he saw. Tears flooded his eyes as he found his strength returning with a headache. Herikech was silent while he watched Noran rip the armor and clothes from his body during the transformation. The gandalays were throwing themselves against the stable doors, fearful of the creature in their midst. Bruneau ran to the stable's main doors and threw them open. He then ran back inside and began opening the stall doors to free the stallions. Herikech shot a bolt of lightning from his hand to prevent the guard from opening any more. Bruneau ducked. The wood where his head had been caught fire and began to spread. He popped out another bolt and freed a third stallion. The horse galloped out of the stables and headed down the ramp toward the western forests.

When Noran's transformation was complete, he lifted his snout and howled, paying tribute to the red master hanging in the sky. Herikech turned back toward the mangler and shot a bolt of lightning at Noran, bringing him to his knees. "Bow to your new king!" Herikech commanded. "Obey me!" The lightning ceased flowing from his fingertips when the mangler whimpered. "Who would have believed the King of Yawrana to be the second mangler? Hah! Hard to fathom, even for me. I was to have the Dowhaven mangler kill your Generals and Barons, but it appears I will have you do the task instead, or maybe I will have you bite them and make an army of your kind to be at my command!"

Bruneau continued to free the gandalays. The guard moved dangerously close to the Lazul king, raising Herikech's awareness that he was there.

"And now to deal with you, meddlesome fool. Kill him!" Herikech yelled.

Bruneau turned to find Blaynor jumping toward him. He fell backward from the blow of Blaynor's sword. He picked up his own and fought against a carcass that once was his longtime friend. The two guards' swords met and sparked.

"Enjoy the dance!" Herikech said. The Lazul king threw a ball of ice on the fire that was spreading from the gandalays' stable and toward the ceiling. It sizzled as it went out, sending up several tendrils of smoke. When he turned back toward the mangler, it had already pounced. A bolt of lightning discharged from Herikech's hand, but the mangler had knocked it away, sending it wide right to strike the barn doors. A new fire started, which spread more rapidly than the first.

"You must obey me!" Herikech said, his hand like ice as it gripped the fur on the mangler's chest. The mangler's undercoat was thick, protecting Noran's body from harm. With a swipe of his claw, the mangler tore Herikech's hood from his face, revealing the scarred remains of a being that once held a human appearance. Now mostly bone was revealed in his face where Herikech's flesh had been burned away along his cheeks and forehead, leaving a grisly display.

Herikech raised Heaven's Light and let it burn brightly. The mangler released him as fire spread along the blade. The mangler jumped for the ceiling and swung around an angled post, catching Herikech across the face to send him sprawling. His hand lost his grip on the sword as it went spinning underneath a gandalay stable door. "No!" he screamed as he ran for it.

The mangler tackled him and picked him up over his head. The creature howled and threw Herikech through the door of another stall filled with pigs. They squealed and tried to get out of the way.

Bruneau and Blaynor struggled against each other in another corner of the stables, less than a dozen feet away from the mangler and Herikech's fight. Bruneau punched Blaynor twice in the chest with each of his fists and sent him flying backward. Blaynor landed in a trough filled with dry grain.

Bruneau could smell burning wood, a sign he and the King were in trouble if they remained in the barn for much longer. He blocked with his sword as Blaynor got to his feet and tried to stab him in the chest. In a decisive move, Bruneau spun away from the trough before he was trapped. A cloud of grain billowed up where Blaynor's sword struck.

A blast of ice hit the stall Bruneau was standing near. He looked to his left to see Herikech throwing ice balls at the mangler. Then the Lazul King switched back to zapping it with lightning bolts, which launched the beast into the air and out of his line of vision. Bruneau couldn't allow the King to die, not even while he fought against his old friend. Blaynor was always a better swordsman than Bruneau was, but now it was Herikech's fighting skills Bruneau was facing, not his comrade's.

This realization helped him find his pure form as he attacked from both sides to keep Blaynor off-balance. The guard fell against the same trough as before, giving Bruneau a glimmer of hope he could win. But being the dirty fighters the Lazuls were, Blaynor reached into the grain and threw a cloud into Bruneau's eyes. He staggered back as the pain stung his eyes. Tears ran down his face in streams when he tried to open them. His sword fell from his hand as he tripped over a bucket. As he scrambled to get up, the blurred form of Blaynor was running at him with his sword out to stick him. Bruneau felt behind him for any kind of weapon. His hand gripped the handle of a stable door, and he unlatched it only a moment before he was run through. The door swung out behind him to allow him inside the stable. Blaynor's momentum carried him forward, his sword impaling the wall next to a stallion.

The gandalay reared and kicked out, striking Blaynor at the temple. The guard fell face down onto the hay-covered floor. The gandalay trampled Blaynor to get free, forcing him back down. Bruneau pressed his body against the door so the mount could run by him and out of the building. Bruneau saw Blaynor was already rising from a blow that would have killed any living man. The guard drew a quick circle around his heart, pulled his friend's blade free from the wall and said, "Peace to you, brother." The sword caught Blaynor at the back of the neck to remove his head. The body turned on its side and tried to get up but fell when incapacity finally took over. For a brief moment, Bruneau saw the transparent, wispy life strand connected to Blaynor's stomach become visible and then vanish.

Smoke was filling the stables, making Bruneau choke. He took Blaynor's sword and strapped it around his waist to give him another weapon to fight with after he regained his own. As fast as he could, he unbolted the other stable doors to free the last of the gandalays and other animals trapped within. The fire had caught to the ceiling and was burning along its length. A torched board fell down in front of him. Dirt rained down from where it had broken away and fallen. Bruneau looked up at the hole and watched as a white petal floated downward in front of him. It fell onto the burning broken board from the ceiling and melted.

Certain what it was, he scanned for the nearest ladder leading up into the loft. Between the two stables where they first saw Herikech, he spotted one. Bruneau ran over to it and climbed upward. With his right hand he threw open the hatch and poked his head up by a rafter. Through the haze of smoke, a sweet but strong scent struck him. Going up one more step, his eyes fell upon thousands of delicate white flowers spreading from end to end across the loft. Reaching forward, Bruneau picked up a handful of the soil they were planted in and felt it was moist and fertile, the only kind that could grow something so pure. Two doors in the roof were open on each sloping side, letting cool air and light in to keep the flowers alive. Bruneau surmised they needed a certain amount of fresh air and sunlight to keep them from dying. It was the perfect hiding place. No one would have ever suspected they were here, right under Noran's nose, allowing Herikech to keep them close so his power would be at its full strength. He could see a red moon shining through the doors onto the ones closest to him.

"These can cure the King!" he exclaimed to himself. As he put his hand forward, the ladder beneath him suddenly collapsed. Bruneau's hand clawed for the closest snowtear but fell inches short, raking only a handful of dirt across the wooden board that held him up. Something grabbed hold of his legs and was extremely heavy. When he looked down, he saw the mangler climbing his body to avoid another ice blast by Herikech.

The beast growled when Bruneau could no longer hold on. The guard's fingers slipped from the edge of the loft's entrance and sent them both crashing onto the stable's floor. Bruneau landed on his side, his head slamming against stone. He was thankful he still had his helmet on. The mangler bounded up and forward, clawing Herikech across the face and sending him flying against a burning wall.

Herikech's black tweed cloak caught fire. He screamed as he tried to stop the flames with ice-filled hands. But the flame was beginning to singe his back, bringing back a rush of painful memories from Maramis. With one tug of his belt's end, it came undone. His garment swung wide open to allow him to thrust his fingers inside and pull out a handful of the snowtears. With his free hand he stripped his robe from his body before the mangler jumped on him. Herikech flung the burning cloak at the beast and ran for the door, but a massive burning form suddenly shot through the wall and barricaded his path. Herikech cursed, looked at the snarling mangler and leaped through the window where the beetle sat, shattering the glass and sending it flying outward. The mangler jumped out after him and howled.

"I will find more! This war is not over! I will come and take your children as you did mine!" Herikech screamed in the distance.

Bruneau ran to the window and stuck his head through, careful not to cut himself on any jagged shards that were still jutting out of the wooden frame. "Your Majesty, come back! We can cure y—" he cried, his voice catching on the last word. The guard turned to go back for the precious flowers but the burning loft and ceiling was collapsing. Dust and smoke filled the air. He covered his mouth and nose with his red armband as his eyes drained streams of tears at the corners. The haze only seemed to grow worse. He pressed forward into it anyway and knelt down onto the floor to take one last look. Sobs rose in his throat when he saw a snowtear shrivel before his eyes. He tried grabbing it but it burned his hand. He yelled and dropped the tiny ball of flame onto a mound of dirt. The heat was baking him as another section of the roof caved in and fell. Past the first snowtear, he couldn't make out anything else.

"Get out, Bruneau," a voice said in his ear.

He looked up to see a familiar face appear and disappear within a breath of wind mixed with smoke. "Blaynor!" he cried.

"Save yourself," the voice said before the face disappeared behind the next wave of smoke. He was gone.

Bruneau picked himself up off the stone floor and lifted the window up in its frame, jagged shards of glass rimming the area Herikech had jumped through. Once the shards were above him, Bruneau crawled out and let himself drop to the ground with a thud in the next room. He choked and coughed, and then passed out. The next thing he remembered was hands lifting him. Dark faces with features he couldn't identify looked down upon him and spoke, but the words sounded jumbled to him. The room began to spin until all shapes and colors went black.

*The teeth are the size of my entire body!* Fields thought as he got another close look at them before they scooped a soldier in its mouth. The General looked away as the man screamed and fell backward. He waved his men out into the corridor connected to the gandalay stables and ordered them back into the castle to find the honeybees and kill them. He shut the double doors to the Gaming Arena behind him and locked them. Being the only man left for the serpent to hunt, he ran back along the arena's western wall and followed it north as the beast finished chewing the last soldier it had caught.

Going into the stands had proven to be more of a hazard to his men as the beast tipped over benches and blocked their running paths between the rows of seats. He needed to stay in open ground, despite his slim chance of outrunning it. Every gaming ring within the arena was void of weapons, except the archery range, which now had been depleted of all its resources. Someone had reloaded the quiver racks and it wasn't by the order of a Yawranan officer. Fields guessed one of the wall-top archers had become a traitor.

The serpent wailed and was on the move again, having located Fields's figure running along a wall. The General spat, "I'm going to kill Viktoran if he doesn't get here soon."

His legs were tired and his joints ached. The playing field was slippery from the heavy rain, sleet and snow. He slid multiple times and even fell once when he hit an ice patch. After he fell, he changed his mind and jumped the wooden wall, staying on the sandy path between the stands and the wall. If the beast was going to take him, it was going to have to work for it by ripping down every board and post along the way. It didn't take long when the first ones began to splinter and fly. The beast tilted its head to use one of its horns to smash down the planks as it pulled its legs inside its body to slither instead of crawl. It coiled its body every fifty feet to spring forward and plow through long strips of the fence. Wood fragments rained all around Fields. He prayed under his breath and continued to run.

He had circled almost the entire arena when a screech came from above. Fields couldn't afford to stop running but glimpsed at the dragul flying overhead. His legs found more energy but there was only fifty feet of fence left before he would be in the open for the serpent to take him. Beneath Hollinfil was a large black cauldron. The General had seen them before, used on the wall tops of the gates. Hollinfil centered the cauldron over the serpent's head.

"Now!' Viktoran cried. Hollinfil released to let the cauldron fall. The serpent looked up when the cauldron hit one of its horns, spilling oil over its head and down its back. "Fire at will, Quinn!"

Quinn and Viktoran raised their bows. The tips of their arrows glowed brightly as they fired at the same time. One struck the serpent in the back of the head, and the other hit the middle of its back. The flames burst forth when they touched the oil, tearing out large chunks of flesh. The fire spread wherever the oil had covered and then began to eat the natural oil being secreted by the serpent as its body temperature rose. The dredger wailed while Fields ran for the gates of the arena. The entire head of the serpent was now engulfed in flame, but the creature still acted as if it could see Fields's movement. It slithered after him as he pushed open the bar locking the arena's door. It was heavy and didn't want to move easily, but it slid out when the beast was less than ten yards away. Fields pulled open the door and dove through. A moment after his boots disappeared, the serpent's head crashed through the gate.

Fields crawled up the corridor toward the castle. The serpent twisted its body awkwardly, not to be denied its meal. Seeing it was going to catch him, Fields drew his sword and spun to the side to stab the creature in its right milky-white eye. Black fluid oozed from the wound. The serpent pulled away, blinded and confused, not knowing which direction to go. Its head slammed through the gandalay stables' wall as it burned. With its head and body jammed between two walls, it became trapped and began to burn to death, struggling to the end.

Fields hacked his sword below its head to wound it further, but its hide was unbelievably thick. It took him several swings before it began to split open. Once he was through the outer skin, the rest of the creature cut like butter. He was halfway through the neck before it finally laid stone cold. The General raised his sword into the air and yelled, "The beast has fallen!" There was a crashing noise and a loud growl coming from inside the stables. Smoke and the stench of the serpent's burning flesh were now filling the corridor.

Viktoran and Quinn came into the passage and hugged the General, happy to see him still alive. "Come. We need your help," Viktoran said.

Fields followed the two men back inside the arena. A blizzard arrived and was blowing across the field, which made it hard to see more than a dozen feet in front of them. They stayed along the wall for some protection and walked toward a giant door that connected to a corridor leading to the Western Gate. But before they reached it, they turned into a smaller side door that was open and entered into a narrow hallway lit with torches.

"Where are we going?" Fields asked, glad to be out of the snow.

"The mangler is in here."

"You mean the one that kidnapped the King?"

"Yes. It chased a burned and screaming man from this hallway into the arena. We ordered Hollinfil between the beast and the fleeing victim to save his life. The mangler retreated back into this hallway to escape."

"Where did the victim go?"

"Don't know. By the time we chased off the beast, the wind and snow had picked up. We tried to follow him through the blizzard, but we lost him. There will have to be a search for him when the weather calms."

Fields shook his head. "You can't just kill the beast with ordinary weapons. You must use a mirror to reflect the moon's red rays at it."

"That's why I borrowed my mother's compact mirror, General," Quinn said. "I thought it would give Baron Blake a better chance of surviving if we encountered it."

"You are a devoted and prepared guard," Viktoran said, slapping Quinn on the back. "And for that you get to take the lead." Quinn grunted and stepped in front of the General and Baron, holding his sword out in front of him. They smelled burning wood when they came to the end of the burnt corridor and entered the next one on their left. Smoke was pouring out of a window with a body lying below it.

"Quickly," Viktoran said as they ran forward.

"It's one of the King's guards—Bruneau!" Quinn cried.

"Baron, take the guard from here," Fields said. "Quinn and I will look for the mangler and the King. Hopefully we find both."

Fields lifted Bruneau up so Viktoran could slip a hand under each armpit. Viktoran pulled Bruneau backward toward the arena door, the guard's boots dragging along the corridor.

Fields's and Quinn's eyes were watering from the heavy smoke. "Through that door!" Fields said, pushing Quinn toward the only one a few feet away. It was unlocked. They made their way in. This room was hot but clear of any smoke. It was a storage room filled with equipment for the gandalays. They rubbed the tears from their eyes and went to a door to their right. It was another corridor, and at the end was a different door that was connected to the arena. A growl sounded above them.

"Look out!" Fields cried. The General shoved Quinn out of the way as a dark brown shape jumped from a beam above them. Fields took most of the blow. He crashed into a table along the wall. It toppled over and destroyed an elegant display of trophies won by many of the stables' top stallions. The mangler landed on all four of its lanky limbs and howled at Quinn.

"Back away from him, you foul thing!" Quinn cried, putting himself between it and the General.

The mangler saw Quinn shaking and smelled his fear. It growled and lunged for him. Quinn fumbled for his mirror, raised it into the red moonlight, and reflected a beam from the open section of roof with no time to spare. The beast was hit in its upper right arm. It whined and fell back, bleeding heavily.

"Aim for its face," Fields said.

Quinn reflected the beam again, but he was too slow. In one swift move, the mangler jumped up against the wall, clawed Quinn across the side of his face and sprang for the door. Quinn fell to his back.

"It's getting away!" Fields cried, chasing after it.

The guard put a hand to his face and felt wetness. From what he could tell, there were three long scratches. He got to his feet and ran toward the blizzard. Snow and wind swept against his face, forcing him to squint. The General was hollering in the middle of the field, the mangler outdistancing him with each stride. Fields gave up, too exhausted to run any more. The beast jumped into the stands and exited into a staircase that led down to the gardens.

Quinn ran over to help. "I'm sorry, General. I let him get away."

"I'm more worried for the King than the beast. I fear he may have fallen in the fire."

Two figures entered the arena by climbing over the body of the slain serpent. Their arms were adorned with the green bands of royalty and their expressions were filled with content. Windal and Edin walked over to Fields, Quinn and Viktoran. Bruneau had now opened his eyes.

"Baron Ilos," said the first man as his face became clearer in the snow.

"Baron Barrow. Baron DeHue," Viktoran replied. "Have we lost the castle?"

The two Barons looked at each other and laughed. "I think not," Windal said with an arrogant tone in his voice that made Viktoran smile. "The Lazul army has been broken and driven out through the Eastern Gate."

Edin elbowed Windal in the side and gave him a glare.

Windal sighed and said, "Well, that's not entirely true."

"None of it is," Edin said, correcting him.

"Then what did happen?" Fields asked.

Edin shook his head and said, "It was a strange thing, General. Some of us were cornered in the Banquet Hall by the beasts and honeybees. They were about to strike when they all of a sudden—"

"What?"

"They just died," Windal finished. "Almost twenty animals and the swarm perished as if some strange force overtook them. When we saw them fall, we thought we were next. But nothing else happened."

"We then believed it to be the watchers, but we later learned they were still in the heart of the castle," Edin continued. "Our forces joined up with theirs once we were free. But our numbers were still not great enough to fight against eight hundred Lazul foes. The corridors were tight enough to keep us from losing too many men until two companies from Dowhaven arrived, not half of them soldiers. Several townspeople came together as well to help the army. Redstone, Dixon and Ashland to name a few. But the reinforcements were enough to take the Lazuls by surprise and even the odds. Fearing they were led into a trap, the Lazuls ran. Men are being posted around the entire castle until the gates are boarded up."

"This doesn't make sense," Fields said.

"What doesn't, General?" Edin asked.

"The draguls we sent to Dowhaven Tower weren't supposed to arrive there until tomorrow evening."

"These men weren't called from the tower by a dragul's messenger. They were all from Shaba Sector."

"Then who notified them the castle was under attack?"

"I did," said a voice behind Fields.

"High Elder!" the General cried.

Viktoran smiled, clapped his hands and asked, "Was it a vision that guided you to do so, Elenoi?"

"No," she said, shaking her head. "Just some good advice from a friend." She smiled and didn't tell them who.

The men couldn't help but laugh.

"The King!" Bruneau exclaimed when he revived.

# CHAPTER EIGHTEEN
## The End of the Storm

Once the clouds broke on the horizon, the two moons of Elvana revealed how choppy the waters of the Racorn could be. The wind was strong but Oreus was glad to see the ocean again. His heart swelled when three ships were still visible. But to his surprise, the one that remained in Drana Bay was not his own.

"The Misty Eyes has not raised her sails," Oreus cried. "Why didn't Captain Soar leave with the others?"

"Shall we pay them a visit?" Firewing asked.

Oreus wanted to find out why its crew had chosen to stay behind, but since they weren't going anywhere, conversation with them would have to wait. "No! Not while *Wind Gust* is on the sea without me at her helm!" Oreus felt he could have been asking too much from the dragul after the long distance they had already traveled. Guilt entered his conscious again about the egg Firewing carried. He didn't want overexertion to harm it or her for something that could be built again in time. He said, "But if your body has been strained, then I will ask no more from you. There are other options."

"Are you up for a swim, Baron?" Firewing said with a chuckle. "The gatha sharks would gladly welcome you as a meal. The storm stirs them in the waters like soup in a bowl. You would make a fine seasoning."

"I was thinking more along the lines of convincing Captain Soar if I could borrow his ship."

Firewing lowered her head and tried to determine what was happening on the ship's deck. Men were in rank while Soar spoke to them. "The Misty Eyes's engines may just be stalled. You could find yourself in a pack of rats if you set foot aboard her. Enough with your rambunctious ideas. And behold, *The Wave Shocker* sails off course! Whoever steers your ship is causing them delay." Firewing flapped her wings and went higher. Oreus was freezing from the cold, biting wind blowing across the Racorn.

A blast rang out from *The White Fin*. Oreus and Firewing saw a cannonball cut across the bow of *Wind Gust*, missing it by a few feet.

"That was a warning shot," Oreus said. "The next one will be in the center mast if they don't back off. I didn't know those ships had cannons."

The second Salmus ship, *The Wave Shocker,* was turning its bow toward *Wind Gust* to come up behind her. Firewing was still too far from helping the Baron's ship and had to glide the last hundred feet to catch her breath. Another cannonball shot out, this time from *The Wave Shocker,* striking the stern's railing. The ball bounced and then rolled across the length of the ship before it flew off the bow.

"The one who steers your ship is twice the size of any Yawranan," Firewing said, seeing a barbarian.

"Boris! He's the only one I could trust her with since he built her."

When they came within five hundred feet of the flying vessels, Oreus could hear the hum of blower engines and the whine of propeller thrusts.

"There's Rydor at the harpoon gun, starboard side," Oreus said.

The General cut the rope that attached the harpoon to an anchor and fired the weapon. It hit two men on board *The White Fin* and threw them overboard.

"And three others," Firewing said, seeing the individuals coming up from below deck. They each carried a small wooden crate by rope handles on its side. With a pry bar, they popped open the lids and took out bottles of alcohol. Two more cannonballs fired from *The White Fin.* One struck the prow and the second, a catena. When one of the men looked up at Oreus, he could see it was Jime. The guard saw their descent toward the ships with the red moon behind them. Jime waved. Oreus returned it as Firewing strove for the stern of *The Wave Shocker.*

Men aboard the ship also saw them diving. A handful of them went to another section of deck to wheel a cannon over and face it in Firewing's direction. "We have to get to them before they get that shot off!" Oreus yelled.

Firewing dug deep and flapped her wings with new determination. Oreus hung tightly to the reins as she dropped like a stone in the sky toward the craft. The cannon stopped rolling while the men turned it. Once they began lifting a cannonball, Oreus said, "Hurry!"

Firewing screeched to distract the men, but then it also made them move faster. With the wind at her back, she opened her mouth as the fuse was lit to the cannon. The dragul took in a deep breath and then exhaled a ten-foot wide cloud of green gas. She pulled up just as the cannon fired. Oreus screamed as Firewing spun, the ball missing her right wing. It sailed skyward until gravity pulled it back to sea.

The men on *The Wave Shocker* shrieked when the gas passed through the stern's railing and blew across the deck. Firewing swung back around to see the effects of her strike. All five individuals at the cannon fell down, gasping for breath as they tried to understand what was happening to their bodies. The green cloud spread out with the wind and killed dozens of more men by the time it had reached the center mast. Captain Rollins saw the fumes come toward him and began ordering men below deck. Those who were swift were spared while the rest were either consumed or jumped overboard to take their chances with the sharks. Firewing shrieked as the ship veered east to let Boris and his crew devote their efforts to *The White Fin.*

"Brilliant," Oreus said with a smile. They stayed on the tail of *The Wave Shocker* and watched as men reappeared from the lower decks. Firewing dove in, ripped the eel flag from the main mast and let it flutter into the sea. Less than ten men were scrambling to every section of the ship. Every cannon, harpoon and net thrower was being aimed at them.

"They are well organized," Firewing growled.

"These ships have seen many battles," Oreus said, pointing to mended patches along the side of the ship. "They will be hard to defeat with their experience."

"But have they ever provoked a pregnant dragul?"

Firewing screeched and shot along the ship to get a closer look and sent the men into a panic. Oreus's eyes met Captain Rollins's for a brief moment. Rollins shouted orders and went to a harpoon gun. He looked through the scope and searched the sky until the crosshairs were on Firewing's body. He was about to squeeze the trigger when a sail unhooked, billowed and blocked out the image. The sail distorted the silhouette of the dragul but Rollins remained patient and turned the harpoon back toward the black shape. He waited for Firewing to show her head on the other side of the sail but the silhouette suddenly grew large. His eyes widened when he realized what was about to happen.

Firewing tore through the sail and yanked it away from the yard. The sail covered men who were at a cannon a dozen feet from Rollins.

"Get down!" the Captain screamed as the dragul came directly at them. Rollins's body hit the deck and saw Firewing's claws miss him as she flew over the railing. When the Captain stood, he saw a net thrower had fired, sending a patchwork of criss-crossed rope flying his way. He and three other men were thrown backward into the railing.

Oreus and Firewing laughed and cheered as the man at the controls of the net thrower ran over to help cut Rollins and the others free. Rollins unsheathed his sword and slew the man when he began apologizing. He then ordered another sailor to take the man's place, shouting new orders. The ship steered back north in line with *Wind Gust* again. The propeller thrusts kicked in hard and sent the ship speeding like an arrow at Oreus's prize ship. The men on the *The Wave Shocker's* deck turned the cannons back toward Oreus.

"I want you to drop me onto the deck of the *Shocker*," Oreus said. "We'll cause more problems for them if we split up."

Getting no argument from Firewing, the dragul dove again for the stern. Rollins spun the harpoon gun in their direction and smiled after he looked through the scope.

"Watch out for the harpoon!" Oreus yelled.

"I see it," Firewing screeched and then rolled left as the weapon was fired. A blur flashed over them. Oreus felt his head spin until Firewing righted herself. The dragul grabbed hold of the harpoon gun's launcher and bent the barrel in a curve. Rollins's men rushed toward the dragul with bows and arrows but Firewing unleashed a cloud of gas on them. One arrow got off before the gas enveloped the last archer. The barbed head cut through her leathery wing. She looked at the tear and snorted.

The ship was dragging at the rear with her heavy weight pressing down. "Now is as good a time as any, Baron!" Firewing roared.

Oreus let go of the reins and unbuckled his boots from the seat. He swung a leg over and slid down her side. Firewing immediately flew upward and grasped a man from the mizzen topcastle. She took him out to sea and released him into the icy cold waters. Cannons fired at her as she took to the air, but all balls missed their target. The men reloaded as they kept track of her location in case she decided to come back within firing range.

Springing into action, Oreus saw Rollins waving men toward him, ordering them to kill. Oreus ran forward with his sword and Lazul dagger, tapping into his *Urra Dur* skills and putting them to full use. He pivoted and stabbed one man in the neck and then used his leg to trip a tall sailor. Using his sword hand, he killed the tall man and took a few steps closer to Rollins before another man brought the fight to him. In two swings Oreus had defeated him and made for the Captain, who decided it was best to run. Rollins ducked around a corner. Before Oreus rounded it, a giant body came from the opposite direction. Oreus collided with it and fell down, losing his sword.

He looked up and saw who had interfered. Windreed Sinker swung her club at his hand when he went for his sword. He moved it and saw the glass pommel ball at the base of the handle shatter underneath the brunt force. Slicing his Lazul dagger through the air on a back swing, he cut her across her leg. Windreed shrieked and threw her fist in retaliation, connecting with Oreus's shoulder as he tried to get up. A fire exploded from the punch as his shoulder was separated.

"Ahhh!" Oreus used his free hand to back up. He looked to his right and saw four more men running toward him. A large shadow fell over them when they left their cannons to follow Rollins's orders. The dragul picked each man up in one of her four claws and flew skyward.

Windreed tromped toward Oreus, readying her club for another attack. Oreus crawled behind a barrel, which took the next blow for him. Oil splattered out onto the deck, creating a slick that was hard to keep footing on. The barbarian fell onto her side and cracked several boards with her elbow. Oreus tipped the rest of the barrel over toward the stern to cover the entire area with oil around him. Men were slipping, including Rollins, who was about to throw a spear at him. Windreed used the length of her armspan to knock away another barrel and expose Oreus. He jumped over her swing as she tried to cut his legs out from under him.

Firewing screeched as she made another pass over the bow, bowling over a cannon and the voyagers who manned it. The bow dipped when she landed to rake them with her claws, sending *The Wave Shocker* straight into the water. The impact threw everyone forward. Oreus hung onto a railing spindle to stop his momentum. Windreed slid along the oiled deck and crashed into a pile of crates. They tipped and fell toward her. She put up her hands and caught one before it crushed her head. Firewing lifted from the deck to allow the blower engines to push the bow back up from the sea. Saltwater rushed down the deck to mix with the oil, spreading the slick farther across the ship.

Oreus slammed his shoulder into another barrel to pop it back into place. He cried and fell onto his knees. Tears ran from his eyes as he bit down on his lower lip. Using an *Urra Dur* technique to trick his mind, he pretended the pain was not his own. He ignored it and focused on getting to his feet.

With the deck being too slippery to walk on, he ran for the next cannon along the top of the railing and killed two more men, stabbing one through the back and pushing the second overboard after jabbing him several times. He threw his good shoulder into the cannon and bore down, spinning the barrel toward the stern. He centered it on the steering wheel when he stopped pushing. With a cannonball already in the barrel, compliments of the two men he just killed, he lit the fuse. The only thing Rollins could do was cry a short protest. Oreus cupped his hands over his ears and let the blast do its damage. The wheel and aftercastle behind it both burst into hundreds of pieces. Rollins's face was peppered with wooden projectiles before he could shield it with his cape. He screamed and scraped his fingernails against his skin to dislodge them.

Firewing continued her assault on the ship. She tore sails and breathed her fumes whenever a sailor let his guard down. One man dropped his torch when the cloud mutilated him. It fell onto the oil slick along the deck and set it ablaze. Total chaos erupted when the flames grew into an inferno. The dragul circled the ship as all men abandoned their weapons to dump water on the fire. She screeched, calling to Oreus that it was time to go.

When the Baron looked for Windreed, he saw she was no longer near the crates. He heard a loud thud behind him, prompting him to spin with his sword up. It was quickly batted from his hand by the barbarian's club. Windreed was enraged and punched Oreus in the chest. He was sent flying into the fire, becoming engulfed by the flames. She raised her club in triumph as she shouted her war cry.

Firewing screeched when she saw Oreus fall into the flames. "Baron!" But she could shed no tears for her rider. Out of revenge, she dove for the deck and picked up a cannonball from a pile. She circled back around and curled her tail around the ball while she hovered in the air. As if her tail were a slingshot, she spun in a circle and tossed the ball at the propeller thrusts at the back of the ship. The engines exploded as the ball mangled their blades and shafts. The ship slowed and coasted to a standstill above the sea.

Suddenly, a streak of fire shot from the inferno where Oreus had disappeared and connected with Windreed's chest. She was stunned when she looked down to find an arrow protruding from her. Another impaled next to the first, and then a third beside the second. Oreus emerged from the flames like a ghost, his skin white hot, but uncharred. His clothes were burning and all the metal on him glowed red from the heat. Windreed screamed and dropped her club as she fell backward in denial. Oreus's bow was on fire along its length but he continued to fire arrows into the barbarian. When she was struck with her sixth, it was the last. Her eyes closing and her breath stolen, she fell over onto a pile of netting. Oreus dunked his bow into a water barrel to save it before it turned to ash. He then removed what was left of his cape and doused it to pat out his clothes and wrap it around the peeled and cracked wood of his bow.

Firewing's claws slammed into the side of the ship, rocking it to one side. Oreus fell as he called to her, using her formal name, "I'm here, Immana! I'm here!" The dragul looked up for the familiar voice and saw the glowing Baron crawling his way across the width of the ship through the flames and smoke. Her eyes lit up in elation. She released the ship's side and turned parallel with it. Oreus picked himself up and went into a run. As he jumped for Firewing's saddle, a figure lunged at him from the dark.

"You have destroyed my ship!" Rollins yelled as they went crashing into the railing.

Oreus's bow landed beneath him, but due to its excellent flexibility it didn't break. He couldn't grab his dagger or sword before Rollins punched him. The strike had a better effect on Rollins than Oreus. The Captain shook his hand after hitting, what to him felt like, metal. Oreus threw a left hook and sent Rollins reeling. The fire caught hold of the Captain's cape as it touched the burning oil slick. He spun to try to put it out while Firewing held her position for Oreus to jump. Blood in his eyes, Rollins ran for the dragul with his flaming cape whipping in the wind behind him.

"Now!" Oreus said once he had found his seat on Firewing's back.

She pulled away as Rollins jumped over the railing for Oreus. It appeared the Captain was going to make it until his body began to fall. Oreus saw the fear in Rollins's eyes as he flailed in the air and plummeted into the sea. Waves pounded against his body and fins swarmed in as the Captain tried to stay above the surface, gasping for air. When he saw the first fin, he screamed and attempted to swim away from it. His body lurched dramatically to the side, freezing his face in shock before he was pulled under.

Oil barrels along the ship's starboard side exploded as the fire caught hold of them. Firewing flew higher and glided on currents. The blower engines of *The Wave Shocker* groaned and were now blowing fire and smoke instead of air below it. Any sharks and other sea creatures near the surface below the ship were scorched or boiled to death. The ship slowly sank in the air until its base met water. The engines then died completely, sending up one wave of bubbles along the sides.

As the bow dipped back into the sea, Oreus said, "Let's help our friends."

Firewing replied, "For having just walked through fire, you have much energy. How do you feel?"

"Never better!" Oreus said, laughing. "I have new respect for the draguls!"

Firewing grinned as they flew northward.

Boris turned the wheel left as far as it could go, taking them further out to sea to keep pace with *The White Fin.* Winslow had a greater advantage with more men aboard to help his ship run smoothly. Flying into the wind instead of against it gave Winslow an advantage as his crew dropped his ship's sails. Jime and the other two guards assisting him with the alcohol bottles had to change their priorities and help Boris tie down their own so the wind wouldn't slow them. Rydor feared the sails would become torn with the propellers and the wind working against each other.

Jime untied the topsails while Rydor worked on the fore. The other two guards split up to help Jime and Rydor. *The White Fin* was gaining distance, hammering Rydor's hope they could make it up. Winslow's ship was faster and had more weapons. Rydor didn't know what chance they would have in making up the lost ground, but he would pursue Winslow across the Racorn to save Jada. They had only half the sails tied down when a screech rang out alongside *Wind Gust*.

Oreus whistled from the back of Firewing.

Rydor dropped his sail and ran to greet the Baron. "Oreus!"

"Rydor," he replied with a salute and smile. "Sadly, I must report Captain Rollins and his crew won't be coming to dinner tonight."

Rydor shouted back, "You deliver a blessing for us. Can I encourage you to take a second helping for Jada?"

Oreus looked toward *The White Fin* and saw it was becoming smaller with each new wave crest. "The Baron's aboard the ship?"

Rydor nodded. "We can't harm the *Fin*. Just slow her down. I don't want Jada going down with Winslow's rats."

Oreus waved and asked, "Ready for a repeat, Firewing?"

The dragul screeched, "This one's for Illeon!"

His heart thumping, Rydor went to finish bringing down the sails. When he was done, he ran to the stern. "Boris."

The barbarian turned to see the General standing next to him. Boris pushed forward on the propeller thrusts to put them back into full speed and said. "I see someone's joined our adventure."

"Baron Blake."

Boris chuckled. "I should've known it was him when I saw tha gold belly scales of that beast."

"They should provide enough of a distraction so we can run *Wind Gust* up alongside the *Fin*. We'll use the grappling hooks to tie us together after we board. They'll be forced to tow us until this battle is done." Rydor kept his eyes focused on Firewing and Oreus, who were nearly at the *Fin's* stern. The General's nerves tightened when several explosions could be seen from the back of the ship. Firewing did a quick loop to avoid what was fired at her. He breathed a sigh of relief when the dragul stayed in the air and tore the tied mizzen course sail away from the mast. Rydor and Boris cheered when they saw it blow down and over the cannon crews at the stern.

"They can't see a bloody thing. Look at 'em frettin' like ants whose hill just got stepped on," Boris said before letting out a rumbled laugh.

"Yawrana!" Rydor said raising a triumphant fist into the air.

Winslow's crew recovered before Firewing and Oreus had gotten out of range. They turned the cannon and fired. Firewing heard the ball's whistle long before it could strike them, telling her which way to fly. After the first cannonball was fired, they all seemed to be coming at once now, which also forced Winslow to order the ship to be slowed so they could have more accurate shots. With every blast, the fatal shot came closer and closer to hitting Firewing and Oreus.

"Wait until they've spent a round before you bring her in," Rydor said, not wanting any of the cannons to suddenly turn back on them. Boris pulled back on the propeller thrusts to slow the engines. The moment Firewing and Oreus began their dive, the barbarian brought *Wind Gust* back up to full speed. The ship hurtled forward above the sea. Firewing sprayed a cloud of gas near the wheel, sending men running in all directions. The time couldn't have been more perfect for Boris. He turned the wheel a few degrees to the right, letting the starboard side scrape against the *Fin's* port side.

Rydor saw men running from the gas cloud, leaving their cannons behind. "Wait until the fumes are carried downwind. I hope Jada is nowhere on the deck."

"Oreus wouldn't let the dragul gas 'em unless he knew fer sure," Boris said. "It helps us out, though. Winslow's men are runnin' to tha other side o' the ship."

Once the bows were even with each other, Rydor waved his arm in the air. Boris locked the propeller thrusts to hold the speed. Jime and the other two guards threw dozens of grappling hooks over the railings of *The White Fin*. Some connected to the railing itself while others hooked onto masts, crates, shrouds and gun carriages. Rydor and Boris assisted Jime and the guards in tightening the slack to keep the ships locked together.

A sailor on *The White Fin* began hacking at the grappling hook lines without being burned.

"All gas traces have blown downwind," Rydor said as he threw down a plank to create a walkway between the two ships' railings. The General was only halfway across when the sailor who was cutting the lines ran over to break the bridge. Rydor jumped the rest of the way and punched the man before he pushed the board into the sea. The sailor fell back while Rydor crawled over the railing. He recentered the board and took on the sailor with one swing to end the duel.

Boris held the plank steady while Jime and the other two guards walked across. They returned the favor, but when the barbarian was midway across it, his weight bowed the board and made it crack.

"Keep coming!" Jime hollered. "Stand there long enough and you'll fall in!"

Boris took three giant strides and jumped down. "Here they come!"

Winslow's men put their blades into the air as if they would see the metal melt before their eyes. One sailor shoved one of his comrades forward to see what would happen if the gas was still present. The man turned around and argued, not tolerating the other sailor's brash move. The rest of the crew separated the two and pointed at the enemy who was ready for them.

"They'll bore me ta death before we start this fight," Boris complained.

The barbarian tipped a barrel over on its side and kicked it their way. Winslow's men stepped aside to let it roll to a stop against the railing. Boris ran forward, taking a wide swing in front of his friends. The club bashed four men, injuring them enough to the point they couldn't fight.

Boris repeated his swings, taking out dozens of sailors without working up a sweat. "Like swattin' flies," he said, waiting for them to take offense from his words.

Rydor took Boris's left side and Jime, his right. Then two guards, Trixel and Lwer, brought up the rear to guard the three men's backs. Over a hundred sailors swarmed around them, emptying the decks below as a figure near the bow stood and rang a bell. Rydor identified the man as the one who had caused the most trouble since his arrival in Yawrana.

"Thorn!" Boris cried, catching a glimpse of the nightwalker out of the corner of his eye.

Thorn put his hands on his hips and waited for any of the Yawranans to take a step toward him. Not to his surprise, Rydor filled the role. A sailor was about to attack Rydor from behind when Thorn put his hand up to stop him. The man nodded and fought Lwer instead.

Rydor tuned out all the screams behind him and scowled. The fishhook in Thorn's upper lip rose with his smile to aggravate the General. The nightwalker clenched his fists, cracking his knuckles, and stood straight with his arms out like the wings on a glider. He closed his eyes and turned his back to Rydor, enjoying the cold sea air against his shirtless, tanned upper body.

"Face me!" Rydor shouted.

Thorn didn't move, standing still while the ships drifted from west to east with no one at their wheels. Rydor charged and swung his sword at Thorn's waist. The nightwalker jumped up and backward in an arc over

Rydor, landing on two feet behind Trixel. Before Trixel could turn, Thorn broke his neck. The guard fell at Boris's feet, catching the attention of Lwer.

"No!" Rydor screamed, wanting the guard to leave him. But Lwer was already swinging when the General cried for him to back off. Thorn ducked and spun in a circle to sweep Lwer off of his feet. Lwer fell onto his back and had his windpipe crusheda moment later by Thorn's heel.

Rydor ran at Thorn and, in an unexpected move, jumped with his right knee out. The move caught the nightwalker by surprise, breaking Thorn's collarbone. Rydor rolled backward and cut down a sailor, shouting, "Boris, watch your back!" The barbarian glanced over his shoulder and shook his head as he went back to demolishing men.

The General saw Thorn look in Jime's direction. Rydor sprinted forward and threw a fist, catching Thorn in the jaw before he could lay a finger on the guard. The nightwalker stood back up, furious Rydor had beaten him twice on consecutive moves.

Firewing screeched overhead and slammed into the main mast, breaking it off at the main yard. The falling beam killed seven men. Others were distracted by the loud crash behind them and fell to Boris's and Jime's swings because of it. Cannons fired upward. The crew's aim became worse when rain clouds darkened the night sky and blanketed the twin moons.

Boris and Jime were far outnumbered, but their skills were superior to any man that took their turn in line to fight them. More dared to fight Jime than the barbarian, but they had to get around the barbarian's club first. Jime ended up slaying more men who were moaning in piles along the deck than those who were looking for a fight. Boris had pushed the sailors back between two stacks of crates, forcing Jime behind him. The guard grunted and looked upward to see an archer in the fore topcastle fitting an arrow to his bowstring. He searched the bodies along the deck for a dagger, but couldn't find one. The archer was now pulling back his string and taking aim at Boris's back. Jime knew he had only a few moments left before the arrow would hit its home. Not knowing what else to do, he ran at the barbarian and tackled him. The arrow hit a man in the chest who had avoided three of Boris's swings. He screamed and fell backward. Jime leaped over Boris to attack, seeing the barbarian was now vulnerable.

"Archer at your back!" Jime cried. "Fore topcastle!"

As Boris got up, he turned and saw the archer getting ready to fire another arrow. Depending upon his strength for what any normal man would deem as impossible, Boris picked up a cannonball and heaved it at the archer like a shotput. The man screamed when the ball smashed through the side of the topcastle and fractured his leg. He fell forward, losing his bow over the side of the ship. Boris turned back toward the fight and grabbed Jime by his collar. He yanked the guard backward behind him to resume his position.

Jime saw the man struggling in pain as the cannonball fell back through the hole it had created. It smashed through the floor of the upper deck. "Impossible," he mumbled.

"Here's one for ya," Boris said to appease Jime as he tossed a sailor over his head to land near him.

With one stab the man was dead. Jime frowned until he saw Firewing take out the entire foremast. The wounded archer in the topcastle screamed as the giant red claws of the dragul knocked him over the side of the ship.

Firewing flew low enough to let Oreus off onto *The White Fin's* deck and then took off to the sky to glide on the winds for a much-needed rest. The dragul screeched when rain began to fall upon the ships below.

"Not again," Jime said, feeling the droplets hit his arms as he approached Jime. The guard spun, hoping to fight an opponent, but grimaced when his wish wasn't granted.

"That happy to see me, eh?" Oreus asked.

"Nothing against you, Baron. Boris is having all the fun," Jime replied.

Oreus looked past the guard and saw the crew of *The White Fin* had been dwindled to almost nothing. "That's what happens when a barbarian has been cooped up for too long in a blacksmith shop. Killing is in their blood, whether it be for animal or man. They have to answer the urge when the opportunity arises."

Jime nodded. "I've heard Boris speak of his blood wraths. I never imagined it could wipe out almost an entire crew of sea rats."

"Winslow's men are not well trained. There is little to brag about in defeating men of such low caliber. Come. Let's go below deck and see what lurks there." Oreus smiled and slapped Jime on the back as they found the nearest stairwell and descended into the ship's bowels.

His lower lip bleeding heavily, Rydor fell back until the two Thorns before him melded back into one. "That's more like it," he sneered. "I thought you saved the best for those who didn't deserve death."

Rydor's comments spurred Thorn to kick him again in the face and gut. The General fell backward against the mizzenmast. He ducked when Thorn attempted a spinning kick under his chin when he was getting to his feet. The miss made the nightwalker land awkwardly on an ankle and twist it. "Errrhhh!"

"I really don't like your style," Rydor said, swinging his sword. Thorn rolled backward to let the General's blade bounce off the deck. He advanced and swung again, this time cutting a long gash across Thorn's chest two feet long. The nightwalker appeared unfazed but quite impressed with Rydor's speed. The General watched the wound quickly scar over. "What the hell are you?"

"When you drink the blood of the dead, many things become less complicated." Thorn did a cartwheel when Rydor swung vertically. The sword and Thorn's body missed by inches in the air as they passed by each other. The General felt a sharp blow to his shoulder and was thrown ten feet toward the stern of the ship. His sword lay a few feet away near a pile of anchoring rope. Thorn vaulted himself into the air off a barrel and pounced on it. Rydor watched his weapon get launched like a javelin over the side of the ship.

"You fought admirably with it," Thorn said. "Now let's see how good you really are." He allowed Rydor to take his *Mellano* stance, right knee bent forward, shoulders angled and hands up in front of him.

Rydor replied, "It will be just as satisfying to kill you with my bare hands."

Thorn ran forward and jumped to kick out with his foot at Rydor's face. The General caught Thorn's leg and whirled him around in a circle, letting go at the end to send him flying into a fallen yard. Rydor ran forward while his opponent was dazed and punched him behind his right ear, putting him back down. Using his knee in the middle of Thorn's back to keep him pinned, he assaulted the nightwalker with hit after hit. The more Rydor struck the man, the quicker Thorn responded, and then finally flipped his body up to throw Rydor forward into a cannon. He cried when his hip hit the hard metal of a wheel's edge. Pain shot through his leg when he got up.

Thorn ran forward and did a simple maneuver, which caught Rydor unaware. The General was expecting another kick, but instead took a fist to his mouth. He was knocked over the cannon's barrel and fell onto the floor with blood dripping from his mouth and chin.

The nightwalker jumped on the cannon's barrel and smiled. He was about to deliver his deathblow to the back of Rydor's neck when the two ships suddenly lurched, their speed slowing. He fell forward onto Rydor. The General bucked him off and threw an uppercut when Thorn looked up at him. Rydor then rolled and kicked out, his foot connecting with Thorn's face. He couldn't help but smile when he saw Thorn was wearing down. Rydor picked up a mallet near the cannon and slammed it into Thorn's forehead. The nightwalker's head snapped backward. He slowly toppled over onto the deck. The surge of power Rydor was feeling lasted only a few moments, however. Incredibly, Thorn bounced back from the blow, pushing himself up one limb at a time. Rydor hit him harder and looked to his right at the pile of anchoring rope.

The General ran to it, picked up several loops and dragged them over to Thorn. He wrapped the rope around Thorn's neck and struck him again with the mallet when he saw him reviving. Rydor quickly ran to the rope's loose ends, tying both to the cannon's carriage. He then slung the nightwalker over his shoulders and staggered to the stern's railing. Thorn grabbed Rydor's chin and pulled up to prevent the General from lowering his head and dumping him over the side. Rydor clenched his jaw shut and lifted his arms straight above his head. The wind worked to his advantage as it caught Thorn's body when he threw him. The rope pulled taut from the cannon carriage due to the weight of Thorn's body. He couldn't remove the tight loop around his neck fast enough before it ripped his head from his body. Rydor watched both parts of the nightwalker vanish into the dark ocean, leaving only the dangling middle section of the rope trailing behind in the wind and rain.

Rydor slumped onto the deck and felt every wound he had incurred come back to haunt him. When his head had cleared, he realized the fighting and screaming had silenced at the center of the ship. The propeller thrusts also had slowed considerably on both ships until they finally shut off altogether, letting them cool, and leaving only the blower engines to hum him into a short rest. Boris came hobbling toward him on his broken leg from the steering wheel. The barbarian threw his club on the deck by Rydor and wiped the blood from his hands on his sea coat.

"Where's Jime?" Rydor asked.

"Don' know. I didn't see 'im on the deck anywheres—dead or alive. Probably went below for some fun with Oreus."

"What 'appened to the fish?" Boris asked.

Rydor chuckled. "I threw him back." The General stood up as Boris sat down.

Boris rumbled a laugh. "Ha! Ha! He woulda been a fun one ta grapple with."

"I think you were plenty busy. A hundred foe?"

"Ya think I did that all that meself? When Firewing saw me back was open, she decided she wanted to help and cleared out the rest. Me arms are tired, General. I feel like I felled a thousand trees, but at least we're no longer heading any further out ta sea. The propeller thrusts are off."

"So it's you I have to thank. Well done." The General stood and stretched his limbs, taking a deep breath.

"Best o' luck," Boris said as he watched Rydor salute and leave to search for Jada.

The rain turned into a downpour, drenching the barbarian where he sat. He looked at the sky in exasperation, but couldn't find the ambition to move. "Buggers! Would it hurt ya to spare me a ray?"

The bottom of the staircase led to a long and gloomy corridor lit by lanterns hanging from both walls. Each time they were about to enter a new room, Oreus's mind flashed back to the day he asked Captain Lanu to use *The Star Gazer* to transport fifteen hundred Lazul children into Yawrana. The Captain's stern face mocked him as he tried to convince Oreus to return to Zonack with him. Oreus's mind jumped ahead in the memory to the corridor he walked down to reach Lanu's cabin door. It was all too familiar and made him feel sick that he was retracing his historic footsteps.

"Something wrong, Baron?" Jime asked him. "You look ill."

Oreus shook his head and tightened his grip on his sword. He left his bow back at his saddle with Firewing, deciding swords and knives were more effective in tight spaces like these. He could still see his Lazul dagger protruding from Captain Lanu's chest as he died, warning with his last breath that more ships like this would follow *The Star Gazer* to Yawrana. His words had played to be true, giving Oreus that nagging feeling again that maybe he should have returned to Zonack. But then he remembered how long it had been since he had seen Ola since she had gone into hiding with the royal family. Her smile warmed him inside and replaced the Captain's cold, uncompromising image.

"Baron." Jime shook Oreus's shoulder, breaking him out of his trance. The Baron looked at the guard, who tilted his head to the side. Oreus turned around and saw Rydor coming up behind them.

"General," Jime said, saluting him.

"Baron," Rydor said, saluting Oreus.

"I need someone to salute me," Jime said. "Where's Boris?"

"Catching his breath. He's done for the year," Rydor said. "He wouldn't like walking down here anyway. Ceiling's not tall enough. Any sign of Jada?"

Jime and Oreus shook their heads. "We've searched every room connected to this passage . . . except that one," Jime said, pointing to the last door a dozen feet away.

"It's in the same location as Lanu's was on *The Star Gazer,*" Oreus said. "I have a feeling if she is still on this ship, it would be in there." Oreus didn't have to explain what he meant by "on this ship" with sharks swimming in the sea for hapless men who had fallen into the water.

"I brought us here. I'll go first," Rydor said, walking between Oreus and Jime.

"And none of us blame you for it," Jime said.

"Love is love," Oreus added.

"Stop already," Rydor grumbled.

The General put his hand on the polished brass knob and slowly turned it so he wouldn't make any noise that could spoil their surprise. But it stopped before it rotated halfway, forming a scowl on his face. "Locked! So much for being quiet." He backed up to the other side of the corridor and ran forward, throwing his shoulder into the center of the door. It held, making Rydor grunt.

Oreus winced from the sound of the impact. He thought of his own swelled shoulder. He rubbed it and rotated it in its socket to make sure it worked. The pain still throbbed and he knew that once he got a full night's rest it would be unbearably sore and stiff in the morning.

Rydor backed up again and looked at the door. "Did you see where the door buckled, Jime?"

The guard nodded and said, "The bottom appears the strongest. You hit it too low. Something must be bracing it from the inside. Maybe an arm bar."

"We'll have to cut it apart," Rydor said. He took a hack at it with his sword. The door held, only chipping slightly from the strike. "This wood has been hardened almost to the point of metal. My blade should have cut through it with no trouble. Not even sequeran wood is this strong."

"Stand back," Oreus said. Rydor stepped aside as Oreus pulled out his Lazul dagger and pressed the flat side of the blade near the handle. Thinking of how Lanu had betrayed him, he felt himself become angry and wished he could confront the Captain again. The blade of the Lazul dagger caught flame and started to burn the door. As the Baron's hatred grew, the blade became hotter. It glowed a dull red, shooting long flames along its sharp edge. When the door caught fire, he backed up.

Rydor removed his cape and smothered the flames above and below the handle to keep it from spreading. Jime took off his cape and helped when

Rydor's caught fire. The General dropped his and stomped it out. The knob grew hot as the remaining flames burned their way through the door.

"Put it out," Oreus said.

Jime covered all the flames and patted them down. Smoke had filled the corridor. An oval burn a foot high had weakened the wood around handle enough that Oreus could kick it through. It fell and clanged on the floor inside. He tried pushing the door open but it held. He reached through where the handle had been, going in up to his elbow. Feeling around the inside of the door, he found a sliding bolt and pushed it away from the door. With another push the door held yet again. Oreus shook his head and put his arm back through. His fingertips touched a horizontal piece of wood running across the door. He pushed his arm in up to his shoulder and grabbed hold of it. It wouldn't slide, so he lifted and felt it come free. When he pulled his arm out, the door creaked ajar on its own.

Rydor kicked it wide open and ran inside, taking a defensive stance. He lowered his weapon when he saw the room was filled with books, maps, a desk, and large stacks of missing gold from Candlewick's vaults. A porthole was on one wall and one door was visible at the back of the room. When the General opened it, he found a washroom inside lit with candles, a spotless washbasin and towels. The room connected to the corridor outside through another door. The General stepped inside and saw the door blended in with the wall's paneling that ran from floor to ceiling. He guessed the Captain had used the towel bar as a handle since it was screwed into the backside of the door.

Oreus stuck his head inside the washroom and said, "This we've already seen."

Rydor hung his head and grumbled, "For someone who was so bent on protecting the cabin, Winslow could have at least been in it."

"Not this Captain," Oreus said, going to the wall behind the desk. "Remember Lanu's cabin had an entrance that opened to a secret room. The cabin's outer door wouldn't have been locked if there truly was no one in here."

"He could've left through the washroom when the fighting started and may be hiding somewhere else on the ship," Rydor said. "However, let it be noted that I hope I'm wrong, Baron."

Oreus searched the bookcase behind the desk, looking for a hidden handle tucked within, but found none. He went to the map wall and took each off by removing the pins that held them on a board made of wine corks. Nothing presented itself. He took the corkboard down and saw a blank wall behind it. Oreus kicked the desk chair, tipping it over. "Nothing." He looked through the drawers of the desk, pulling each one out completely to dump them on the floor and shift through the contents to find a key of any kind. When he got to the bottom drawer, he saw the floor underneath the desk had tracks built into it. Crawling underneath, he found a foot pedal that he pressed down. Something clicked. He came out, got to his feet and pushed. The desk rolled away from the wall to reveal a trap door in the floor.

"Look here!" Oreus exclaimed.

Jime and Rydor came over to see the door. Rydor pulled up on the handle and flung back the lid. A ladder led to a bright light in a room five feet down.

The General jumped into the hole and fell to the floor with his weapon ready. Two men rushed him with axes. He slashed diagonally and took out the first. The man screamed and fell. The second axe flew over Rydor's head when he ducked. He jabbed upward and caught the sailor in the gut. He twisted the blade and yanked it free. The man kept looking at his wound as if he couldn't believe he was going to die. Rydor waited until he finally accepted it and fell over.

"Have no doubts about what I am prepared to do, General," Winslow said, holding a knife to Jada's neck in a corner of the cramped quarters.

Oreus and Jime climbed down into the room and saw Rydor's predicament. They didn't budge and waited for the General to make the next move.

"You have no one left to help you, Winslow," Rydor said. "Even Thorn has taken a swim. It takes more than one man to run a ship. You will not reach Salmus by yourself."

Winslow's face showed no concern for his men. "Congratulations. But you are wrong. This ship can be sailed by one individual if it stays out of water for most of the journey. These are not the same engines Lanu's crew introduced you to." The Captain ran his hand up Jada's side and smelled her neck. "She is quite a good catch."

Jada turned her head away from him in disgust. "You'll have to slit my throat before you'll have your way with me!"

"Bold words for someone who should be trying to do anything she can to save her own life."

"I would gladly die knowing General Regoria will rip you apart in my honor," she spat.

"Up the ladder, General," Winslow snapped. "It is time we set sail."

Oreus nodded to Jime, who climbed toward the desk. The Baron followed on his heels and waited for Rydor to come up, but the General did not follow. "Come, Rydor," Oreus said. "Do not try the patience of a desperate man."

Winslow laughed. "The man of Uthan Mire doesn't even know me. Desperate? I think not. Just a different hand to play."

"The treasure is what you really want. Give me the Baron and I will let you have it all," Rydor said.

"A trade? I don't believe you."

"Think of it as a bet. If you want the gold you'll have to give up the Baron. It will take a leap on your part to trust us."

Winslow held the blade closer to Jada's neck, making her feel its cold, sharp edge. Jada's face grimaced. "Hmmm. I never thought you to be a gambler, General. But your offer is too hard to ignore. I will agree on one condition."

"Yes?"

"That Baron Blake return with me. If you pursue us, I will kill him."

Oreus heard Winslow's offer and looked at Jime in confusion.

Rydor responded, "Baron Blake? He is of no use to you—"

"Zonack's court has made him worth a large sum of money. He is, of course, worth more to me alive than dead, but I would be more than willing to take either amount to hire a new crew and make repairs to my ship."

"Take it!" Oreus called.

Rydor tried to think of another way, but Winslow said, "The deal is growing cold, General, and is about to be pulled off the table."

"Done! If you harm her before we board—"

"You will have her back, as she is now."

Rydor backed away and went up the ladder, keeping his eye on Winslow as the Captain and Jada shuffled forward. "Back out of the cabin." Winslow called up the hole. Rydor, Oreus and Jime did as he asked while he dropped his knife and exchanged it for a crossbow.

"Up we go, Baron." Jada climbed up and through with Winslow having the arrow at her back until they reached the top. He pulled her close again and tied her wrists behind her back before they entered the corridor outside the cabin.

"All three of you where I can see you," Winslow said sharply when he didn't see Jime in the door's frame. The guard appeared to the right of Oreus. "Now up to the deck." Winslow kept his left hand on Jada's shoulder with the arrowhead snuggled against her spine and his finger resting on the trigger.

Boris rushed over to them when he saw his three friends come out of the stairwell. "Did ya find tha Baron?"

"Get *Wind Gust* ready for sailing, Boris," Rydor said.

"You're not gonna—"

"Now!" Rydor yelled.

Boris's face turned red when he sensed something was wrong. He turned and made his way across the plank. With a dagger, he cut half the grappling hook lines and went to the wheel to check the temperature of the engines. All looked to be in order. He turned his head toward Firewing in the sky and whistled for her to fly upward. He watched the great red beast disappear into the clouds above. "Stay out of sight," he whispered in hope. He cried, "Ready, General!"

Winslow and Jada appeared from the stairwell. "Tie up the Baron," the Captain ordered as he looked toward Oreus. "Hands to feet."

Oreus got down on the deck and put his wrists behind him. Jime found some rope and handed it to the General. Rydor bound the Baron's wrists and ankles securely and then attached them to one another with another short length.

"Gag him," Winslow said. "I don't want to hear his complaints all the way back to Zonack."

Rydor pulled off Oreus's green armband, pulled it over the Baron's head and down to his mouth.

"Now, get off my ship!"

Rydor leaned over to Oreus and said, "Our prayers are with you, Baron. I hope one day we shall reunite."

Oreus nodded while Rydor slapped his back. The General and Jime made their way across the deck and to the plank. They looked at Oreus one last time before crossing over.

As soon as they had jumped down onto *Wind Gust's* deck, Winslow prodded Jada up onto the plank without removing the rope tied around her wrists. Rydor and Jime leaned forward across the railing on each side of the plank and put out a hand as she neared. Boris was about to whistle for Firewing to attack when Winslow kicked the plank off the railing and sent Jada plunging into the water below.

"No!" Rydor and Jime cried, unable to grab her before she fell.

Winslow quickly cut the remaining four grappling hook lines and shouted, "Better hurry, General! The sharks won't pass up a tender morsel like the Baron!" He laughed, ran toward the stern and the wheel. He pushed the propeller thrusts all the way forward. *The White Fin* rocketed away.

Boris looked up and whistled as hard as he could. There was nothing at first, but then a large shadow appeared in the dark sky. Firewing dove from the clouds like an anchor falling toward the water. A large fin was moving in on Jada as she kicked hard to keep her head above the water. Firewing extended her claws and grabbed onto the shark's dorsal fin as it opened its jaws to bite Jada. The dragul threw the fish up toward her mouth and crunched down. The shark wiggled only for a few moments before the struggle was over. It fell into the water beside Jada, making her scream as its bloody form floated toward her. Jada felt something grasp her shoulder from behind and raise her out of the sea. Her legs kicked until she realized it wasn't a shark attacking her. Firewing screeched and lifted Jada to *Wind Gust's* deck, setting her down gently.

Rydor breathed a sigh of relief and kissed Jada before he unbound her wrists. She laughed and cried in the same moment and then yelled, "Go after Winslow. He'll kill Oreus!"

"He will kill him if he sees us coming," Rydor said.

"Then send Firewing!"

Rydor looked at the dragul who hovered over them, flapping her wings. "Fetch Oreus," he shouted. The dragul screeched and flew upward into the clouds.

"I hope she's not going back to Yawrana," Jime said.

"She's too fond of Oreus," Jada said, smiling. "Winslow doesn't know what he's in for."

Rydor shook his head and replied, "It's only fitting for one who cheats at his own games."

Oreus wormed his way along the deck, trying to find a hiding place, until Winslow's boots came into view.

"Baron Blake, it appears I have gotten the best end of this deal. Lanu should've done the same as me. He might still have been alive and a very wealthy man by now. But, like a fool, he had sympathy for you. Not good for business." Winslow laughed and kicked Oreus across the face. The pain shot through Oreus's skull. His eye watered and fluid drained from his nose. His thoughts were fuzzy as he laid his head down on the deck.

Winslow began dumping bodies over the side of the ship to take weight off the blower engines so they would last longer. Some men weren't dead when he disposed of them, their screams echoing through the night air as they splashed into the Racorn. He turned around to grab another arm of a dead sailor when he heard a thud behind him. Turning around, he saw the body of a man he had just dumped overboard. The Captain leaned his head over the side of the ship and saw his reflection in a pair of large golden eyes. He screamed when Firewing screeched, her breath blowing back his hair. He stumbled backward, tripping over the body she had thrown back up.

Firewing flew higher, extended her teeth and bit down on his foot, lifting him upside-down in the air. Winslow screamed as she climbed into the sky. In the last few moments of his life, he saw how beautiful the twin moons were as the storm began to break over the sea, one red, one white. Their combined orbs shone brightly and cast warm rays upon his body as he felt himself falling.

"I fold," he mumbled before the broken top of *The White Fin's* mizzenmast impaled him through his back.

Firewing set down onto the deck and used her claw to scrape away the Baron's armband from his mouth. "Oreus," she said, her image appearing blurry to him.

He laughed, making Firewing smile. "Take me to the wheel," he replied. "I miss Ola."

Using one claw, Firewing gently curled it around Oreus's body and flew him to the stern. She sliced the rope connecting his wrists and feet so he could put his feet through his arms, bringing his hands to the front of his body. She extended the same claw toward him. He sawed the rope that bound his wrists on it and then pulled out his Lazul dagger to separate his legs. Firewing flew back to the clouds and the cold night air above. Her screech echoed across the waves as Oreus slowed the propeller thrusts and spun the wheel left to make a soft turn toward home.

# CHAPTER NINETEEN
## Captain Soar's Confession

*Wind Gust, The Misty Eyes* and the heavily damaged *White Fin* were in a row in Drana Bay along Emison Territory's coast as a party of men sat on the beach just beyond their shadows. A large campfire threw off a pleasurable heat for the ring of leaders that surrounded it. Food was brought to the shore from both ships to feed the starved individuals, which included Oreus, Rydor, Jada and Captain Eason Soar. Beyond them another ring of warriors silently listened in on the budding conversation: Boris, Jime and Captain Soar's three personal bodyguards, Gen, Her and Trus. Rydor felt the talks would go smoother with a full stomach and some rest. There was no longer any need to rush since word had arrived to them by a dragul messenger that the Lazuls had been defeated once again and were on the run from the Yawranan army. Captain Soar agreed and had plates, utensils and goblets brought from his ship to make the meeting more civilized. Once the last plate had been collected from Oreus, the Captain cleared his throat to request everyone's attention.

"General Regoria. Baron Blake. Baron Annalee. I personally would like to thank you for not rushing to conclusions about all representatives of King Roule's Royal Court. I am embarrassed for the others' crews and my country by what has transpired. We are in debt to you for the kindness you have shown us, which, to this point, Captain Winslow and Rollins have taken advantage of." Soar took a sip of wine and shook his head. "You see, we did not find Yawrana by our own doing. We were cast astray by a violent storm that threw off our instruments. Our compasses did us no service, as our ships were literally blown westward by a squall that never seemed to end. But as suddenly as it blew up, it died, and a mysterious figure came aboard *The White Fin*. There was a call for Captain Rollins and me to board Winslow's ship and meet this . . . person, if that's what you could call him."

"Herikech," Oreus said, when no one else wanted to say his name.

Soar nodded with a frown and continued. "The most powerful man I have ever encountered, including Thorn."

Rydor couldn't help but say, "At least one of those two we no longer have to worry about."

"You are very fortunate, General Regoria, but you are wrong. You have not killed Thorn. Somewhere, he is alive, and may one day return here. Removing his head was not enough. He may only be killed by the demon that gave him the life he now possesses. The nightwalkers are a feared cult in Salmus, and now Zonack, and have given the Courts their share of worries. Their reign has spread through many divisions and they select the most rugged cutthroats they can find to undergo their transformation rituals."

"Has anyone managed to kill a nightwalker?" Oreus asked.

"Yes. None other than the man who is after your head, Baron Blake."

"Malcolm Hayward? How did he do it?"

"It was the reason he was promoted to knighthood and is now the champion of Majesty Rimshaw's Court. No one knows. If I were you, I would never return to Zonack. Ever. Hayward never forgets those who have crossed him."

Oreus didn't answer and couldn't help but think of his brother, whom he would one day like to see again. His friends were few there, but those that were would invite him in for a drink if he passed them on the streets of Beggar's Square. However, those who knew him may now be hiding from the Court to protect themselves, especially his brother. The Court was known for imprisoning innocent relatives of an outlaw until the guilty came forward to take their place.

"The Baron has found his worth here," Rydor answered for Oreus. "How is it someone as powerful as Thorn ended up reporting to a man like Winslow?"

"Another one of Winslow's gambles," Soar said. "One I can't give too much detail on." He moved past the uncomfortable subject and said, "Herikech assured us that we wouldn't survive the storm if we didn't do as he commanded. And to prove his words, he called up a creature called a deep-sea dredger as a warning. All he had to do was snap his fingers and we would've been strewn across the Racorn by it. We were forced to comply and listened to his directives, which led us to your shores. We were to be a distraction to the Yawranans and draw the King away from the castle while Herikech carried out his plans to capture it. In the end, Winslow struck a bargain with Herikech, which would allow us to have a portion of the castle's riches to carry back to Salmus."

"And that sat well with Herikech?" Rydor asked, sounding skeptical.

"At first, no, until Winslow agreed to help Herikech overthrow Salmus's Court when the day came where his power extended beyond the sea. Since Rollins and Winslow were good friends, that left me in an awkward position, as you can imagine. Not only did I have to stand by and stomach Yawrana's fall, but now had to contend with men who were ready to hand their own countrymen over to a madman."

Jada smiled. "Captain Soar, at times we are most effective when we do nothing. Solutions do not always present themselves when a problem first becomes known. You had your men to protect, and for that I do not blame you for your inactions. However, for now we must ask you to live up to Winslow's agreement of never mentioning Yawrana or its people to your king. Our kingdom is one built on preservation of the environment in which we live. The impact your society could have upon ours could destroy the fragile balance we have maintained for thousands of years. The Lazuls have taught us invaluable lessons about living harmoniously with the land and to not take more than what is required."

"But Herikech one day could have your army under his rule," Soar said. "Would your people not be better off having Salmus's aid when it is needed?"

"An alliance could be formed if circumstance dictated it. Until we are forced into that decision, our principles remain unchanged," Jada said.

Rydor added, "Your proposal is generous, Captain, and will not be forgotten. And if Salmus ever finds itself in need of help, it may call upon us."

Jada looked at Rydor. "This is an offer that is not yours to make."

Rydor played upon Jada's weakness. "Oppression will not exist in Elvana. No child will grow up a victim when I have the opportunity to prevent it." Rydor could sense that Jada's thoughts immediately turned to Gailey and Haley, knowing she had been away from them too long. She then smiled at Rydor and nodded.

"Noble words, General," Soar said, raising his goblet. "One worthy of a toast."

All those around the campfire raised their goblets and took another drink.

"What about *Tha White Fin*?" Boris asked from the outer ring.

"Keep it," Soar said. "It can be repaired and made your own. Consider it a parting gift and one that asks for forgiveness of the troubles we have caused you."

"Your crew is welcome to stay as long as you like," Rydor said. "Your return journey is not a short one."

Soar shook his head. "I think my men have sat too long already and we have plenty of provisions to get us home now. We cannot ask any more from you than we already have. Gen," Soar said, turning to his guard.

"Captain," the guard responded.

"Tell the crew to prepare for departure. We'll raise sail at dawn. I have a feeling the weather will cooperate now," Soar said with a grin.

Gen bowed and walked off into the dark whistling a tune that Oreus recognized from his adventures with Lanu aboard *The Star Gazer*. It was only sung when a sailor was to return to his homeland, called *Taking the High Crest*. A memory sprang forward in his mind of his first outing on the gallant ship, which made him gaze toward *Wind Gust* with a longing to take her back out to sea.

"Out of curiosity, Captain, did Herikech contact you while you were in Candlewick?" Rydor asked.

"Yes. Many times. As you know, General, he and Thorn were traveling between the walls of the castle to reach our room. He was rather pleased Winslow had baited King Deardrop into hosting the tournament and messenger race to be a distraction. It allowed Herikech to smuggle supplies and the snowtears into the castle inside water barrels."

"Water barrels?" Rydor said, glancing at Jada and Oreus.

"Do you think maybe the snowtears are still inside the castle now?" Oreus asked Rydor. "Herikech is more powerful when they are with him. It would explain the reason for the endless storms he brought upon the castle."

"What are snowtears?" Soar asked.

"How—" Rydor started to explain before Jada cut him off.

She cleared her throat and shook her head. "Those are matters not to be discussed without our King's permission. Sorry, Captain."

"Right," Rydor said.

Soar raised his eyebrows and shrugged his shoulders. "Very well, Baron Annalee. It is time I rest and leave this fire for the warmth of my cabin."

"And we need to be getting back to the castle," Jada said as she stood up.

"Yes," Oreus seconded. "Firewing is in need of a proper meal and attention." The Baron looked at the dragul on the beach and winked. Her golden eyes glowed at the center of her giant dark outline. She smiled to show two bright white rows of teeth that glistened in the moonlight.

Jada looked at Oreus in amazement. "Baron! Do you realize what you have just done?"

"I can also make them laugh," he replied with a smile.

She laughed and said, "We must talk of this more when we have spare time."

"That won't be far off, Baron." Oreus turned to Soar to shake his hand. "Captain, if I am ever in Salmus, I shall make it a point to pay a visit."

"Then I look forward to it if that day comes," Soar replied.

Oreus walked toward Firewing and made her laugh again. Jada heard the dragul's reaction and spun around, appearing jealous Oreus was able to make it happen on a whim just to tease her.

"He's reviving. Verona, please bring a basin of washing water, a towel, vapor cream and something to drink for His Majesty."

The House servant bowed to Master Hurran and left the room. Bruneau put a hand on Noran's shoulder to prevent him from sitting up. "Rest easy, my Lord. You've had a long night." The King looked to a bright ray of golden light coming in through the open window of the medicine maker's room. He had to cover his eyes with his right hand, for it was blinding him. "Close the drapes," Bruneau asked Viktoran. "I think he's not ready for the afternoon sun."

Viktoran began to shut them when Noran said, "No. No. Please . . . keep them open, Baron. The fresh air will help clear out this stuffy feeling I have in my head." Noran looked at the other faces near the foot of his bed and saw General Fields, Windal, Edin, his four sisters and someone he had missed very much, a lady with flaming red hair and a baby in her arms.

"Willow!" he exclaimed. "My son! Bring Varen here!"

Fields stepped aside to let the Queen by. "He's still sleeping," she said, handing him Varen. Willow kissed Noran deeply and blushed. "We have missed you, love. When we heard Bruneau's tale, we came immediately."

"Oh, Noran," Dea, his eldest sister said, breaking down into tears. "I'm so sorry this has happened."

Suddenly a rush of memories came back to him, making him feel ill. "Please take Varen, my head pounds."

Willow gently picked up their son and rocked him back and forth in her arms. "Blaynor?" he said, not seeing the face of his guard located anywhere in the room. He turned to Bruneau on his left, who shook his head and hung it in respect.

"He will be honored in the coming days in the catacombs," Ola said, wiping tears from her eyes.

"It was how he would have wanted to die, Your Majesty," Bruneau said, choked up. "There is no greater honor than dying by protecting the King. It is better than what will probably happen to me. I will be cursed to rot away in my house on the hill until my body rebels against me."

Noran laughed and then felt tears pouring down his cheeks for his friend. His four sisters ran forward and hugged him, doing what they could to restore the King's comfort.

"Careful, Princesses. Careful," Master Hurran said, not wanting Noran to become smothered.

They were all weeping now until Anyiar said, "Look at us. We're all sappy. What would Mother think?"

The King and his sisters couldn't help but laugh again.

"Where is Mother?" Noran asked, not seeing Mia in the room.

"She's in the Grand Hall, of course," Dea said. "Someone has to run the kingdom until you feel better. There is word that *Wind Gust* and another ship docked at the Western Gate not long ago."

"What other and why is *Wind Gust* not in the shipyard?"

Fields explained, "Jada was taken prisoner by Captains Winslow and Rollins aboard *The White Fin*. She is safe," he quickly added when Noran was about to ask. "General Regoria, Boris Groffen and Baron Blake managed to bring her back without a scratch and the treasure Winslow tried to steal from the secret vaults."

Noran shook his head. "I knew it. I knew he was a thief!"

"*The Wave Shocker* is at the bottom of the Racorn and *The Misty Eyes* has set sail for Salmus. I will let General Regoria tell of those details when you are well."

Confusion crossed Noran's face. He looked toward Bruneau and asked, "I must have suffered a concussion. I remember we encountered Herikech in the gandalay stables, and Blaynor's suffering, but there is a black void as to what occurred next."

Bruneau looked at everyone in the room. Their expressions were of gloom until he turned to Master Hurran, who was nodding. The guard took a deep breath and said, "You . . . you are . . . are the other mangler."

Noran started to laugh until he realized Bruneau wasn't joking. "Me? But I . . . I don't understand how—"

"Arna," Bruneau interrupted. "You were bitten by a strange maddon when we were in Arna. The animal must have carried the disease and, at the time, was traveling with the pack of maddons we met before we found the Ice Shadow Caves. Your sword hand."

Noran lifted his right hand up to examine it closely and saw the faint scars from the sharp teeth that had punctured his skin. He curled his hand into a fist and replied, "Then it is I who killed Master Oyen."

"No it wasn't. It was the disease," Ola said, reassuring him. "Do not think for a moment you are responsible for his death—"

"I've killed others! The bell tower guard, the men in my old bedchamber, farmers—" Noran said, his voice angry.

The room was silent until Master Hurran saved everyone the difficulty of confronting the King. "The mood swings, your sleepless nights, how fast you have been healing and your sporadic eating habits—they are all symptoms of what ails you. The High Elder has been informed and they didn't know of your . . . condition. No one could have saved the lives that have been taken. But now—"

"It's still too late," Noran groaned, his stomach feeling upset.

"Many innocent lives have been taken by the war," Fields said so he wouldn't feel guilty. "Ballan, General Keys and nearly three quarters of the castle's army members."

"Why can't I remember changing into the mangler? I was speaking to Herikech about the life strands when . . . all went black."

"It's the disease's way of protecting itself so the stricken individual doesn't choose to take his or her own life," Fields said. "But as you know, the mangler may be killed either by reflection of the moon's red rays, or possibly old age. No other method is known to take the creature's life. Even though you now know what you are in human form, it won't prevent the blackouts when you transform."

"That's enough, General," Roma, Noran's second youngest sister, said.

Fields nodded and apologized, "Sorry, Your Majesty."

"But I found a nail that came from the mangler when it took over you," Viktoran said. "Master Hurran will study its properties and see if there is anything that has an effect on it besides a red moon ray. There was also the drape you covered yourself with in the bell tower room when you hid in the gear chamber. But Thorn stole it and Herikech may still have it in his possession."

Noran looked at the band of transparent colors stretching through the bright blue sky outside his window. "The rain clouds have moved on. Have we defeated Herikech?"

"No, my Lord," Bruneau responded. "When you were the mangler, you battled him and forced him to flee. His cloak burned, which destroyed all the life strands he had collected within it, forcing the remaining hollows under his command to be freed. You chased him from the building as it burned to the ground. Luckily, there was enough time for me to save all the stallions."

"Where do we believe Herikech to be now?" Noran asked. "Is he back in the castle again?"

"We don't believe so, my Lord," Bruneau went on. "We learned from General Regoria that Herikech smuggled the snowtears into the castle through the barrels that were used to collect the rainwater. He had stored the snowtears in the loft of the stables. My guess is he spent most of his time there to gather enough power to conjure up all the storms we've been having."

Noran's eyes suddenly lit up. He sputtered, "T-then you have saved some of the snowtears. They can cure me."

Bruneau hung his head again and grumbled. "The fire that consumed the stables also destroyed the snowtears. I . . . failed to retrieve one for you."

An anger rose within Noran that he unleashed on the guard, taking everyone in the room by surprise. He was yelling at the top of his voice as he sat up and shook his fist at Bruneau as if he wanted to punch him. *"You couldn't save one snowtear? How could you be so incompetent? Now what am I to do? I will be cursed with this plague until someone else ends my misery!"*

"Noran," Willow said softly, seeing the tears in Bruneau's eyes. "He tried to save them. You . . . the mangler prevented him from doing so."

The King's face went red as Noran felt ashamed for having lost his temper in front of everyone. He wanted to speak but the words weren't there. Unable to bring himself to look at Bruneau, he covered his face with his hands and wept.

"I'm sorry, my Lord," Bruneau said. "I believe you may be right, that I am no longer competent to be your personal guard. A better man under the same circumstances would have been able to succeed where I let you down."

Hearing the guard's genuine sincerity forced Noran to turn his gaze back upon him and dry his eyes. "No, my friend. Your time serving me is not yet through. We both will have more chances to redeem ourselves. Forgive me for my thoughtlessness."

"It is the disease speaking for you, Your Majesty," Fields said to ease the tension in the room. "You would never say such things if the beast was not within you. The longer it remains a part of you, the more it will destroy the man that you are. One day you will not be able to turn back from its form when the red moon goes to rest. Roma and I have been speaking at great length with Ean Maxhaw's daughter, Etna, about the effects the disease had on her father before I took his life. Near his end he and his family were abandoned for the violence he craved and the isolation he sought."

"How long do I have?" Noran asked, looking at his wife and son. Willow had a hand across her nose and mouth to stifle her crying. Tears were running between her fingers. She left the room with Dea and Anyiar following to comfort her.

Fields frowned and said, "According to Etna, you can only change if you come into contact with the ray of a red moon. So as long as we keep you under supervision and in the dark during those times, it will prolong the process. The disease was dormant in you for some time, thanks to the Elders, who kept you hidden during many of the previous red moons, for fear of the mangler attacking you. Ironic that it was you all along. The High Elder believes you completed your first transformation when the livestock killings began in the farming communities surrounding the castle. And you have transformed three times since the first. Ean Maxhaw had only two red moons left before his transformation was permanent, which would bring the total required for the process to be completed to twenty-four. That's one transformation for each moon during the span of one year."

Noran actually felt relieved when he heard this information. He lay his head back down to relax. "Then there's hope."

"Now that the snowtears in the stables have been destroyed, we believe Herikech will search for others to replenish his strength," Viktoran said. "He has been weakened."

Noran turned toward the Baron and saw Heaven's Light hanging at his side. "You have found your sword."

"Claimed from the ashes of the stables. The fire did not harm it."

"It once belonged to a General in the Lazul army. Murka was his name, if I remember it correctly," Noran said.

"After the swamps of Serquist?" Viktoran asked.

"Yes. It would be safe to assume the General survived the journey across the Dunes of Pydora to bring it here. Herishen's will spoke of a dagger that held the same quality as your sword. Both were bonded to fire, courtesy of our ancestors, before some of them were captured and became slaves to the Lazuls. That dagger is now in Oreus's possession."

"How was the ritual performed?"

"I don't know exactly. The passage I read does not entirely explain it. But what knowledge it would be to gain if we were to learn it." Noran smiled as he thought of the possibilities they could do with more weapons like Heaven's Light to protect Yawrana from future invasions.

Fields interrupted Noran's thought. "The Lazul army is on the move again, but we just haven't located their position yet. Nearly eighty percent of them survived the battle and fled into the forests. Most likely, Herikech has rejoined them and needs their help now that he has been weakened from his battle with you and the destruction of the snowtears in the stables. We should be getting a scouting report in soon. The Eastern and Western Gates are under construction by every available blacksmith and carpenter we could find and should be repaired within days. Boris is overseeing the projects and will make sure they are stronger than before."

"Where did you find me once I changed back into the mangler?" Noran asked, not yet ready to talk about the Lazuls.

"A farmer found you in his pigpen. Apparently the beast likes bacon, too. Something odd did happen when we found you," Bruneau said.

"What?"

"As we were carrying you from the farmer's barn, the horses reared in their stalls when you came near, as if they were afraid of you. I think they sense the predator within you. It could be why your gandalay threw you the last time you attempted to ride him. The stallion lives still, which means it wasn't under Herikech's control, thus proving my theory. The only way to be sure is to study the horse's behavior when you try to ride him again."

"I don't think I will be doing any riding any time soon," Noran said, putting a hand to his arm. He saw a thick white bandage wrapped around his shoulder. "This wound hurts terribly."

"Ummm . . . yes. Quinn Rainsmoke apologizes for hurting you," Fields said.

"Quinn?"

"He and I encountered you in a corridor near the stables. At the time we had no idea you were the creature. Quinn was carrying a mirror with him when he injured you. I am now thankful he didn't have a better aim."

Noran couldn't help but laugh. "Perhaps he should've. It would save me all the grief I will have to endure. I suppose that sounds selfish of me, considering all the families that are now grieving for the loss of their loved ones. Herikech was killing my men and stealing their corpses to take the castle. I never imagined such a thing could happen."

"And can still happen," Bruneau said. "To raise an army of the dead, beast and man side-by-side, can give him the power to control the world. This war is no longer just about Yawrana."

Noran nodded. "If the world depends upon us to save it, then we shall die trying if we must."

"Oh," Fields said. "This is for you," The General handed Noran a deck of cards with a circle of fins swimming in the ocean printed on them. "Oreus asked me to give them to you."

"This is Winslow's deck."

"Yes. Pick up the top two cards," Fields said.

Noran did and saw they were both jesters. "Snake! I should've flipped the last card over! I would have lost with either one I picked!"

"What puzzles me is why he left the Zonack voyagers behind," Fields said.

"He did what?"

"Winslow didn't bring Stoffer, Crag or Gunner aboard *The White Fin*. He killed Gunner when he tried to jump on the deck of his ship. The other two are back in their cells."

Noran nodded. "Well, he only did need them to find the treasure vaults. Once he got what he wanted, there would be no use in bringing along the extra baggage. Winslow and Lanu weren't exactly the best of friends. Luckily, this time it was us who won the whole pot." The King added the jester cards back to the deck and held the stack up between his thumb and index finger. He sprayed the deck into the air by applying pressure to the back of it with his middle finger. "The mangler beats the shark."

# CHAPTER TWENTY
## The Expedition List

His vision bleary from his first full day in the Grand Hall since the Salmus voyagers first arrived in Marshant, Noran struggled to find the energy to even put on his night robes as he dressed near his open window. Herikech and his army were nowhere to be found in the Royal House Territory. The last traces of their escape were found at the edge of Murka Swamp in Serquist Territory. From there, the noon hunters picked up the Lazul army's trail, but even they couldn't catch Herikech or his people. The Lazuls had reached the shores of the Sarapin, and disappeared into the waters without being seen from since.

The white crescent moons shone into his old bedchambers, reopening the wounds in his soul. Every death the mangler was responsible for gnawed at his insides like the teeth of his alter being. He tried to recount the details of his victims' last moments in life, but not a single one surfaced. Closing the stained-glass windows with the emblem of a dragul and drawing the drapes gave him instant relief. It felt calming to be in his old room again.

Herishen's Will and Testament was back on his desk, waiting for him to finish its final page. Somehow, he already knew what it would say, but yet he felt obligated to give Herishen the respect of reading it. Thinking ahead of what needed to be accomplished, he would be limited in finding any reading time in his latest schedule. The new court announcer and second in command, Martell Fedrow, had quickly taken a liking to the power he was given. Noran could see no better position for the Nax that would keep him near and safe. Martell's arm had healed nicely due to the maker's immediate response in closing the gash.

Since Blaynor's death, Bruneau had been moping around as much as Noran was for the loss of their friend. He tried to speak to Bruneau about the incident, but the guard wasn't ready, asking him to put it behind them so Blaynor's spirit could have time to move on and find peace in the afterworld. "There will be a better day to remember him," Bruneau had said. Noran could accept that answer for now, but he knew the loss was eating him up inside.

Law required at least two first rank guards to be available to the King at all times. Noran felt two was no longer enough and Bruneau was getting old, whether either of them wanted to admit it or not. Three young men, no more than thirty-five each, had now replaced Blaynor. It took only one day before Bruneau had them all informed of the King's habits and daily routines.

Noran felt it wise to make all three report to Bruneau, even though they were equal in rank. Charlton, Synne and Gile had no complaints and had many of the same mannerisms and morals Blaynor once possessed. Bruneau had purposely chosen three individuals like his old friend to keep him sharp. After all, what fun would service be if he had no one to banter with? Noran smiled, recalling many of the arguments Blaynor and Bruneau had found themselves caught up in, one always trying to outdo the other. Most of their challenges ended in a drink and a joke, showing the true depth of their relationship.

After Noran rubbed his eyes and drank a glass of water, he decided to read the last passage to remove the worry from his mind. He pulled the heavily padded desk chair out and settled himself in, finding the bookmark at the end. The binding crackled as he spread open the book before him to display its last desperate entry, which began with the image of a crescent moon pierced through the center by an arrow.

*It is with great haste that I, Dirm Evermann, servant and seer to the King, write these last words into Herishen Illeon's journal as he, Queen Immana, most of his army, his other prophets, the stranded Methalisians and three Shonitaurs enter the Uratan's overflow channel to escape. Gerrith Dragul's plan worked almost without flaw and the other Shonitaurs and some Methalisians have remained behind to aid us in hindering Heritoch's guards from pursuit. I was to be with them, but became separated. Entrusted with this journal, it must remain hidden from King Herishen's brothers until it can one day be returned to Herishen or one of his rightful heirs in the new kingdom.*

*Yarba Scraw, main prophet and advisor to Herishen, will ensure the Secret Society of the Arrow Moon will continue its traditions even in the new lands. The King can never be accountable for all activities and plots working against him and the Royal Court, which is why the Arrow Moon must deal with the darker matters that threaten the existence of the kingdom. Our members are cunning and brave to undertake such adversaries so that the balance of the land can remain intact. Sacrifices have labeled the Arrow Moon's members as mercenaries. However, death is sometimes required for the best outcome. Each Silhouette and Shade has been carefully selected and assigned for specific tasks that will influence the Royal Court for every new generation. I hope the future King will someday come to understand our purpose if all is ever revealed.*

*The battle draws closer. The Shonitaurs have informed me that Heritoch's men have broken into the weapon-shaping rooms and will be here before the ink in my bottle runs dry. It will be far too late before Heritoch discovers Herishen's trail in the Uratan overflow channel. I cannot escape to the surface yet, for Herikech's warriors are patrolling the grass blades in their hunting lines, combing them for the refugees that they believe will be hiding in their protection. I must not chance walking the land until the sun has risen. It will help blind them as I seek to rejoin my King. Dawn will be here very soon. If there is only one true god, then I pray that the breath of Yawrana will guide me and this Will and Testament to its rightful owner.*

*Heritoch's men have now reached the water-cleansing caves. It is here time shall stand still.*

Noran felt he was beginning to understand the complexity of the Silhouettes and their more unfamiliar and rare male counterparts, the Shades. He had toiled over sending Jada into their den for many days, knowing she could have been murdered for even making an offer. Shaking his head, he decided he couldn't afford to compromise her life like that again. The prying limbs of the Society of the Arrow Moon were too strong to be easily trimmed away. They would forever be watching the Baron from the shadows, wanting to know everything he told her in confidence. Noran couldn't compromise the kingdom any longer by including her in on discussions pertaining to the safety of the Royal Court and family. And yet, the other Barons would question as to why she wouldn't be present at such meetings, a complicated obstacle to overcome. Lying to the Barons was not a habit he wished to become regular. But his feeling was that the Society knew too much already, leaving him with no other choice.

There was a knock at the door, startling Noran from his concentration. "Enter," he said, sitting up and closing the cover of the will. His smile wiped away his concerns when Willow walked through the door. "My love!" he said, rushing to embrace her.

Willow hugged him tightly and did not wish to let go. "Varen is sound asleep."

"He doesn't get that from me," Noran said with a smile. They stood bound together by each other's arms, feeling each breath they took together. Noran held onto her until she was ready to release him. Finally, she sniffled and pulled away.

"I'm happy you're here," Noran said, taking her hands in his.

"I had to talk to you. With us having been in hiding for so long and now—"

"That time will come when it is ready," he said, not wanting the moment to be spoiled by future obligations.

She sat down on the edge of his bed and said, "I can't bear to be apart from you that long again." A single tear ran from her eye that he wiped away with his thumb.

"I can't remain here and put our family in danger while this disease has its chains on me. My mood swings are erratic and I wish not to display that emotion in front of you or my son. You are deserving of better and I vow to find a way to end this curse so we may live a normal life again one day."

She wiped away more of her tears before he could and then stood. "I would take you as you are if that is all I can have. Life would not be normal without you in it."

Noran felt himself blush. He smiled and looked at her flowing red hair and blue eyes as if they were a million miles away. His mind froze the image so he would always remember her this way, when loneliness was his bedmate. Her white gown flowed over her elegant form, calling his hands to her. They kissed. How soft her lips were, he had forgotten. He slid his hand up over her shoulder and then pulled the strap of her gown away from it. Their passion began to take over, when she suddenly stopped and had to push him away.

"What?" he asked.

"I don't know if I can do this." She put a hand over her mouth as if she had done something taboo. "Our love can only be shared through a kiss. The mangler—"

Noran nodded and said, "I understand. I am sorry if I led you on."

"A husband has a right to love his wife. You have not offended me."

"Until we know the nature of what plagues me, your kiss is all I need to sustain me."

She threw her arms around him and cried. Noran felt his own tears come forth. They wept for a long time, and kissed longer.

Bags began to form under Noran's eyes, exhaustion overcoming him. "If I don't return—"

Willow put her hand over his mouth. "You will. There will not be a day that goes by that I do not pray for it. Varen will not grow up without his father, nor will I be left to wander the cold corridors of this castle as a widow."

"When you think of me, look upon the star of the Maker's eye. It shall be the last light I see before I go to sleep each night, and I will know we will be together in here," he said as he put his hand over her heart. She walked with him to the window and he pulled open the drapes. They looked up at the star he mentioned, which was centered in a ring of five. They kissed one last time, wondering if what they had promised could only be a dream.

If there were an ounce of air left in Oreus's lungs after Boris quit hugging him, he would have been surprised. A tuft of hair was stuck to his tongue as he pulled away from the barbarian's fur coat. He scraped it off before he gagged. The fall had grown cold, demanding warmer wear. Boris preferred to be adorned in his clan clothing, giving him a rougher appearance, which all barbarians desired in order to intimidate one another.

Boris laughed and said, "Sorry 'bout that, Baron, but I had to show me appreciation for puttin' Windreed in 'er grave. Me brother would give ya ten hugs like mine and I speak for him when I say yer now a member of the Shale Buck Clan."

"That really isn't necess—"

"No use arguin' with me! Ya jus' need a name that'll fit ya now. Let's see . . . Edge is already taken by General Regoria. You two are almost one an' the same, only he's a bit older than ya, of course."

"Boris—"

"Pillar! You're like a tower o' strength!"

"Ummm," Oreus mumbled, shrugging as if it didn't matter. When the barbarian looked offended, he said, "It's perfect."

"Perfect? Well, then that's what it'll be." Boris slapped Oreus on the back and went to his seat.

Oreus shook his head and sat next to Baron Bal Grady's pushed in, empty chair. Only the Barons sat at this particular table, four on each side. On his left were Edin DeHue of Dowhaven Territory and Priswell's Baron Bal Grady's empty chair. On his right was another empty chair for the yet unanointed new Baron of Gillwood. Facing them on the right side of the table were Viktoran Ilos of Serquist, the recently anointed Baron of Rock Rim, Trafford Gresham, Jada Annalee of Emison and Windal Barrow of Overbay. And at the head of this table in the Banquet Hall was Martell Fedrow, Royal Court Counselor, though most believed him to be just a guest.

Sitting one table over, where it was much noisier, were the Generals: Rydor Regoria of Dowhaven, Lenn Trippett of Priswell, Sim Hatcher of Marshant, Mendel Ghosney of Gillwood, the newly appointed Rizzel Corsay of Serquist, Irvin Yeats of Rock Rim, Rojer Meel of Emison and Lyon Rammel III of Overbay. General Fields, four-sun General and commander of the Yawranan army, who was always stationed at Candlewick, sat at the head of this group with a grim look upon his face as he listened to the eight territory Generals arguing.

And finally, the third and last table was filled with dinner settings for the Elders, respected prophets and visionaries of the kingdom: Kreg Garan, Dibrell Relegard, Res Mercer, Counce Moriana, Lani Lenee, newly anointed Tonjia May, and in the head chair, High Elder Elenoi Ironwood. Elder Dillon PaCant was absent due to the injuries he had sustained when the dragul Cormoor attacked his sequera. The seven Elders present were in a meditative trance, fixated to the water bowls placed on their plates until the King entered the room. Tonjia kept glancing up from her water, curious as to what the other Elders were seeing.

Elder Garan caught her attention drifting and said, "You're losing your focus, Tonjia. Concentrate and relax, it will help the visions come sooner."

"Sorry," she said, her face becoming red. She turned back to her bowl, but nothing came during the period of time it took for the House Servants to fill their wine goblets and bring food to their table. She grumbled when only her own reflection stared back up at her.

Behind each of the Barons', Generals' and Elders' chairs stood their personal guards, some new faces and some old. Some whispered to each other of what the King was arranging now that the castle was nearly restored, secured and restocked. The only ones that really knew anything were the King, Queen and High Elder. Others talked of the King's disease and how he would address it tonight, if at all.

In the northern section of the room was the royal family's table, running perpendicular to the three occupied by the Barons, Generals and Elders. All chairs were lining the opposite side to face everyone. At its center were Noran's and Willow's chairs, with the King's mother and sisters to his right and Willow's mother, one brother, Melvine, and three guests on her left. Noran also invited three guests for their contributions in the war. Boris sat next to Melvine as he stroked his beard while Master Hurran and General Hithel of the Majestic Messengers talked to each other at the end of the head table.

Everyone in the room immediately rose when trumpets blared to announce the King and Queen's arrival. Noran and Willow entered through the entrance connected to the Grand Hall, with eight guards surrounding them, two on each side and four behind. Noran's crown glistened with dozens of rare jewels and his cape was long enough to hang just above the ground. The heavy material was lined with white silk and decorated with leaf and vine patterns sewn into the fabric. Each person in the hall bowed until he had passed him or her.

Willow was dressed in green as well, with white undertones and the sleeves bunched at the shoulders and elbows. House servants carried the end of her gown three feet behind her to keep it from touching the floor. An arced crown sat upon her head, shimmering with white pearl beads and hundreds of diamonds.

Once they were seated, everyone else resumed their conversations while the meal was served. Most cared little for what the servants had to dish out due to the growing tension in the hall. They instead drank more than they ate while Boris, General Hithel and only a handful of others asked for several helpings of the sweet roasted goose, peapods soaked in a vinaigrette dressing and baked rois covered with a caramel glaze.

As Oreus took the last bite of his roi, Noran rose from his chair and spoke into a large shell echoer placed on his table before him so all could hear. "Good evening to you, my family, Barons, Generals, Elders and my special guests."

"Good evening, Your Majesty," everyone replied, mostly in unison.

"It is good to see all of you in one place again. Not since my union of soul with that of the Queen have we all been called together for an important announcement." Noran smiled at Willow. She smiled back and he continued, "Herikech Ileon's army has once again been denied victory as a result of the valor and heroism in this hall." The Generals and Barons applauded while the Elders stood and bowed to them. "Yes, it is a grand celebration that we should share this last meal before we depart for the island of Methalis."

Many murmurs began before General Fields rose from his chair and bowed to the King, saying, "Permission to speak, Your Majesty?"

Noran nodded while everyone turned their eyes toward Fields.

"Since the Yawranan army hasn't captured Herikech or any of the army that managed to flee Yawrana, should we not hold here longer to ensure they will not try to retake Candlewick again?"

"Please sit, General. I will explain."

Fields bowed and quickly did as Noran asked, looking apologetic he had interrupted too soon.

"Herikech Illeon does not have the strength to take the castle without the snowtears, which he needs near him to draw on their powers. I have read Herishen Illeon's Will and Testament and believe he will make for Methalis, home of the sacred flower and our original ancestors."

More murmurs ran through each table, including the royal family's. Mia was pale while his four sisters bickered with one another of what should be the correct course of action. Noran put up his hands to make everyone silent. Whoever was in conversation hushed and listened.

"Thank you," he said, putting his hands down. "All snowtears must be destroyed. Herikech no longer threatens just the safety of Yawrana. He will seek to find others to conquer in time. We believe he is heading to Methalis for that sole purpose. The entire world will fall to pain and suffering if he is allowed to slip through our fingers. Believe me when I say that I have seen firsthand how Herikech has the ability to raise the dead. Between the castle's army and the people in the surrounding territories, he managed to control two thousand of our deceased family and friends. This number does not include the animals and beasts he also has done the same with during Candlewick's and Serquist Tower's battles."

There wasn't a soul in the room that had not heard of Herikech's amazing accomplishment. They all remained silent as Noran took a sip of wine and continued, "I have been speaking with Higher Elder Elenoi almost the entire day and there is only one conclusion as to where our responsibilities lie." Noran looked behind his chair and put out his hand, taking a scroll from Bruneau. The guard bowed and disappeared from candlelight. Noran raised it and said, "In my hand I hold an expedition list. On its parchment contains the names of the individuals who shall accompany me on my journey across the Sarapin. I will spare the announcement of the names until sunrise in the Grand Hall, for tonight I only wish there to be peace in our hearts and minds as we enjoy one another's company. The Elders compiled this list from wisdom sessions and visions dating back to the end of the grassland war. They are the only ones who know of the names on this scroll. Not even I will review it until the new day dawns. We shall all hear the names together, tomorrow.

"Thanks to the Royal House blacksmith, Boris Groffen, all repairs have been made to the drift ship *The White Fin,* which has been renamed to *Mourning's Light,* for the grief we carry for those we have lost to this war. But their sacrifices will not be in vain and have given us something in return: a chance for survival. Both Baron Blake's ship, *Wind Gust,* and *Mourning's Light* have been heavily supplied. We will set sail at the rooster's crow three sunsets from tomorrow." A few guards and servants whispered to one another until Noran raised his voice. "For those new passengers who will be called upon, I wish I could grant you more time to say farewell to your loved ones, but it is imperative we find the snowtears before Herikech does or we will fall to an evil that has no boundaries and knows no mercy." Noran took a drink from his wine goblet and wiped his brow with a moist towel from a shallow, golden bowl resting on the table.

Viktoran rose from the Barons' table this time and asked for permission to speak. Noran replied, "Please, Baron Ilos."

"My Lord, how will those who are chosen find the island of Methalis? Does Herishen's journal speak of directions?"

"I wish the answer was, 'Yes.' However, as far as I know, Herikech has no advantage over us in this matter. We will use whatever maps and writings we can from the Historical Record Keep to aid us. I think we can all assume Boris Groffen's and Baron Blake's knowledge of the ships and sea will be essential to guide us through danger-riddled waters." Noran looked to the High Elder, who nodded.

Ola suddenly found herself tearing up and had to excuse herself from the table. Oreus rose and bowed to Noran. The King dismissed the Baron with a wave of his hand, knowing his sister would need comforting only Oreus could provide.

Boris, on the other hand, was smiling, eager to be off and making preparations as soon as the meal ended.

General Hithel gave the barbarian a toothy grin and shook his hand. "Best to you on your quest, Mr. Groffen."

"Maybe you're comin' with me," Boris said, making the dobbin's smile instantly vanish.

Hithel replied, "What would I be needed for on this type of task? Who would I deliver messages to?"

"That's up for fate ta decide," Boris said with a wink.

The dobbin scoffed, "Preposterous! I think fate would be better off leaving me in the mail room where I belong!"

"If there is anyone missing from the expedition list," Noran continued, "whom we may have overlooked, they will be immediately informed. I would not doubt that last moment adjustments will be made before the ships leave their docks. What we do now could influence the outcome of our journey. The Elders are still receiving visions, which could alter this list. I know there could be some individuals who are not in this room tonight who will be joining us. Each one of them is as vital to the success of the mission as any of us here now. We will stand shoulder to shoulder upon the decks and face the winds together!"

Everyone stood and applauded Noran's speech. "To the end!" Fields cried from across the room.

"For Blaynor!" Bruneau shouted from behind Noran's chair. Noran met the guard's eyes and smiled when he looked back at him with a nod. Tears of pride filled Bruneau's eyes.

"For Bal!" Edin shouted next.

"And General Keys!" Hithel said out of respect for his fellow dobbin.

The applause and whistles grew to a deafening pitch as each name of a fallen friend was called out to honor his or her family. There were many. All who were mistakenly forgotten would later be recognized at their wakes in the catacombs, where their bands would be retired forever.

Noran looked to Willow, smiled and embraced her as the applause and cheers carried on. Over her shoulder, in a window high upon the wall, he could see a white crescent moon rising in the distance.

The following is an excerpt from
Scot R. Stone's upcoming novel

The Mirrors of Methalis

due out in December 2008

Tears were still forming in Ola's eyes as she sat in a rare hand-carved sequeran chair near the throne. Her brother, King Noran Deardrop, paid her no attention. His eyes were fixated on the Elders congregating near the seven stained-glass windows on the western wall of the Grand Hall. He and Ola's three sisters, Dea, Roma and Anyiar were sitting still, each watching the most influential and skilled people in the kingdom pour into the lavishly decorated hall for the announcement of the names of the anticipated Expedition List. Food was plentiful for all guests, but no one was eating. Noran figured they were too excited to hear the names of those who had been chosen for the journey to the mysterious island of Methalis.

Ola wasn't one to draw sympathy from her siblings or friends, and therefore, sat as still as a statue with a gray storm brewing in her eyes. If anyone would notice something was wrong with her, it would be from the two people who knew her best. The first was her mother Mia, who was currently not present because of an untimely flu spreading throughout the castle.

The second person close to Ola who would realize she was distressed was Oreus, who was actually the one responsible for her melancholy condition to begin with. Oreus could feel the guilt catch in his throat again as he tried to repeat the apologetic words that he mumbled to her this morning. He wanted to tell her he would stay behind with her instead, but he knew what the consequences to kingdom, and others, could be if he didn't assist the expedition party. An entire race of people could be in danger if the Yawranans didn't arrive at Methalis before Herikech Illeon and his Lazul army did. As it was, they already had a good head start. Ola requested Noran to block Oreus from leaving, but her brother overrode her pleading, deciding Oreus was far too valuable to the expedition to leave behind.

Oreus wanted to go to Ola again when he saw her briefly wipe away a tear from her blue eyes. But he didn't react quickly enough. His small window passed after she took her seat among the other Royal Court members. Her green gown lay against her beautiful form, and a golden tiara sat upon her black flowing hair, shimmering in the presence of the hundreds of candles positioned throughout the Grand Hall. She would no longer look at him before he left, her anger evident in her emotionless features. Their love was fading with each new moment. As a last attempt to keep him here, Ola warned him she would not invest emotions in a love that could easily be lost in the waves of the Sarapin Sea. Oreus didn't believe her at first, until this morning, when she wouldn't join him for what would be one of their final meals together.

Elenoi Ironwood, the High Elder prophet, broke away from the other Elders to approach the King. She held a long tube in her right hand that was capped with a bone dragul head at each end. It swung at her side, swishing her robe against her hip. Without a doubt, its contents contained the final expedition names.

The High Elder appeared ruffled as she approached the King. The Elders were arguing over details regarding the mission and its related documents. Most believed they were making the final adjustments of unshared but important information before the ships set sail. Elder Tonjia May, the newest of the Order, strode away with a furrowed brow after the High Elder scolded her in front of her peers. No one could hear what the High Elder had said to Tonjia, but it was now clearly understood a rift existed between them. Tonjia's reaction had been severe. She stated her opinion about the decision by throwing her hands up and scoffing. Her face was red and soaked as she left the hall in a hurry. Local townspeople and farmers moved aside to let her through. Elders Garan and PaCant were shaking their heads in disappointment as they helplessly watched her go.

Noran sat up and accepted the tube from the High Elder. She leaned over and whispered something into the King's ear, which elicited a nod from him. Noran popped off one of the bone caps to slide out the golden parchments hidden inside. They fell into his hand and easily unfurled.

Oreus glanced around the rest of the hall to see if anyone else had noticed the exchange between the High Elder and the King. To his surprise, nearly everyone was leaning forward with prying eyes as Noran unrolled the lists. The last few voices that could be heard silenced as Noran slowly read and reread the writings to himself. The High Elder stood close to him—waiting.

"Is this correct?" Oreus heard Noran say to the High Elder. The King pointed to something at the middle of the parchment. Moving in to hear the rest of the conversation, Oreus slipped between a pair of guards and stopped next to Baron Windal Barrow of Overbay Territory. Windal smiled at Oreus, then turned back toward the throne, also hearing the stress in Noran's voice.

"Yes, Your Majesty" the High Elder said. "Everything on the list is correct, and is specified why it is there—except for that."

Noran frowned as if he didn't understand, shaking his head. Looking at the list again, he pointed to something else, which the High Elder confirmed by nodding. The King grimaced more and more with each new question until finally the High Elder leaned over and whispered once more in his ear for a lengthier period of time. Whatever she had said made the flushed color in his face slowly return to normal. He nodded and waved to a male servant to ask for a glass of water. Once he had finished a third of it, he waved for the services of his second in command, Court Advisor Martell Fedrow.

Noran's crown glistened from the hundreds of jewels embedded in its golden wavy ring. He clipped a one-inch seashell echoer onto his green robes and spoke in a tone that was surprisingly soft. "Good morning, friends. This announcement should not be viewed upon with regret, but with hope."

Noran glanced toward Ola. She didn't flinch, acting as if she couldn't hear what was being said. He turned and gazed back at the hundreds of faces burning with desire to hear what they had come for.

"Those who are chosen to ride the seas with me, I thank you for the sacrifices will, and the ones your families will make in your absence. We are … obligated to succeed, for the sake of the world. Many of you are asking why this responsibility should lie with us. The answer is simple: because we are most familiar with the problem. If we do nothing, King Herikech Illeon and his Lazul army will certainly return and destroy us all. Pretending he does not exist is not an option." The crowd remained quiet until Noran asked, "Are there any questions before we read the names?"

A Royal House Territory farmer stepped forward. "Your Majesty, who will oversee the kingdom in your place?"

Noran expected this and replied, "That will not be determined until the names are read. I will base my decision on many qualities, experience in leadership not being the only factor. This decision will not be declared until the day we depart."

"Will it be your mother?" another pressing voice asked, Noran unable to locate its origin.

Noran's face turned red again. "No," he said sternly. "Queen Mother Mia Yorokoh will no longer carry those duties. She will live the remainder of her days in peace. Her health has been weakened by the Binge Flu and she will need all the rest she can attain to overcome it. Again, the decision has not yet been made whom I will choose." He recomposed himself and asked, "Any other questions besides that issue?"

"What about Queen Willow?"

Noran's temper flared suddenly, "No! Damn it, people!" The person who asked the question hid from the King's view so he could not be seen. "I said the decision hasn't been made!" Noran yelled. "Your queen is taking care of our future king, Varen, who needs all of his mother's attention."

"What if you don't return?" said a fisherman with a dark tan and thinning gray hair. A cane made from a tree root held him up and a pair of thin-rimmed spectacles encircled his eyes. A broad-rimmed straw hat sat upon his head, chewed away in places by weather and insects.

"You expect your king to fail?" Baron Viktoran Ilos of Serquist Territory asked the man, breaking away from the other barons positioned along the eastern wall. He crossed his arms and glowered, tired of hearing doubt from those who had no faith in the mission.

"Well … it's possible," the man responded, being honest while holding his ground.

Viktoran began to counter but Noran put up his hand. The King was calm again, glad the topic had changed. "It is a valid viewpoint, Baron Ilos." Now speaking to the crowd, Noran said, "You all have the right to believe we may not achieve our goals. My infant son will one day take my place. I wish it to only be when the hairs on my head are as gray as the wall mouse I caught eating crumbs in my bedchamber last evening."

Everyone laughed, including Viktoran and the fisherman.

Noran continued, "I ask all of you not to not think ill thoughts of our adventure before we have even set out. Prayers, however, are welcome in abundance."

Everyone laughed harder, some whistling and applauding. Noran waited for others to raise their hands. Few shot up. Those who did ask questions received glares from their friends for delaying the announcement of the two crew lists.

When the hall was quiet, Noran let out a sigh of relief and pointed at Martell, who stepped forward and pulled the bottom of the Elders' scroll toward him, separating the two ends. There were three sheets in all that Martell looked through. The first two were filled with names down the center. The last had special instructions for the Royal Court which were not be stated aloud. What they were in regards to, no one could guess. Not a single person was breathing when Martell began reading.